RULER

OF

THE SKY

RULER OF THE SKY

A Novel of Genghis Khan

PAMELA SARGENT

Crown Publishers, Inc., New York

For Joseph Elder

Copyright © 1993 by Pamela Sargent
All rights reserved. No part of this book may be reproduced or transmitted
in any form or by any means, electronic or mechanical, including photocopying,
recording, or by any information storage and retrieval system,
without permission in writing from the publisher.
Published by Crown Publishers, Inc., 201 East 50th Street, New York,
New York 10022. Member of the Crown Publishing Group.
Originally published in Great Britain by Chatto & Windus in 1993.
CROWN is a trademark of Crown Publishers, Inc.
Manufactured in the United States of America
Library of Congress Cataloging-in-Publication Data
Sargent, Pamela.
Ruler of the sky / Pamela Sargent. — 1st American ed.
p.   cm.
"Originally published in Great Britain by Chatto & Windus in
1993"—T.p. verso.
1. Genghis Khan, 1162–1227—Fiction. 2. Mongols—History—
Fiction, I. Title.
PS3569.A6887R8 1993
813'.54—dc20   92–1687
CIP
ISBN 0-517-57364-4
10 9 8 7 6 5 4 3 2 1
First American Edition

CONTENTS

Part One   1

Part Two   43

Part Three   111

Part Four   183

Part Five   253

Part Six   335

Part Seven   509

Part Eight   641

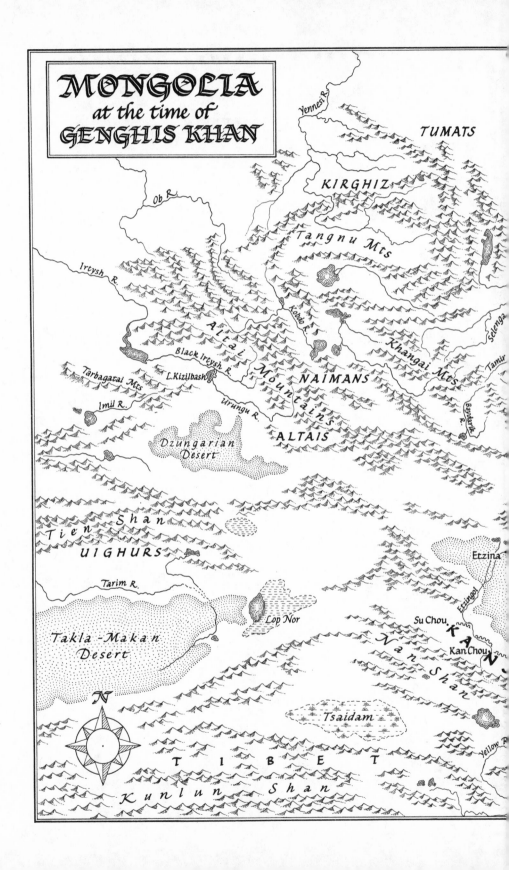

MONGOLIA
at the time of
GENGHIS KHAN

TUMATS

KIRGHIZ

Yenesei R.

Ob R.

Tangnu Mts

Irtysh R.

Altai

Kobdo R.

Khangai Mts

Selenga

Tamir

Black Irtysh R.

Tarbagatai Mts

L.Kizilbash

NAIMANS

Imil R.

Urungu R.

Mountains

Baykarik R.

Dzungarian
Desert

ALTAIS

Tien   Shan

UIGHURS

Etzina

Tarim R.

Etzingol

Su Chou

KAN

Lop Nor

Kan Chou

Nan Shan

Takla-Makan
Desert

N

Tsaidam

Yellow R.

T   I   B   E   T

Kunlun   Shan

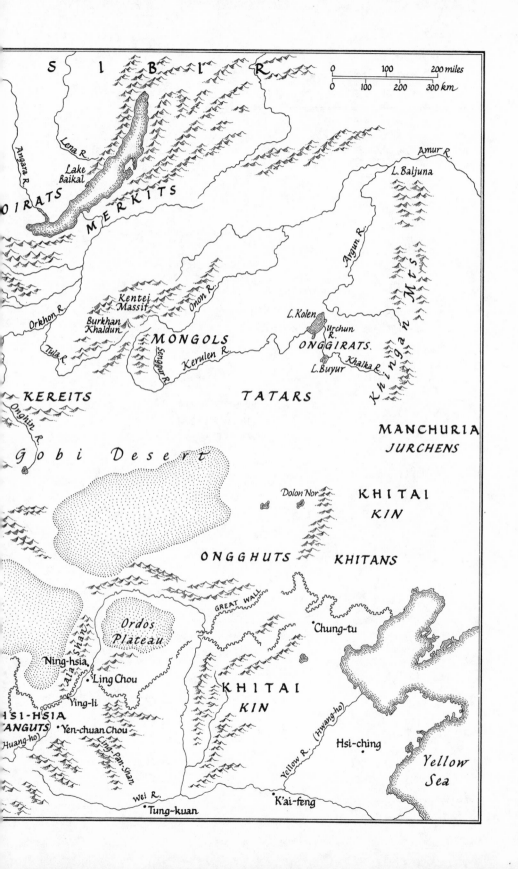

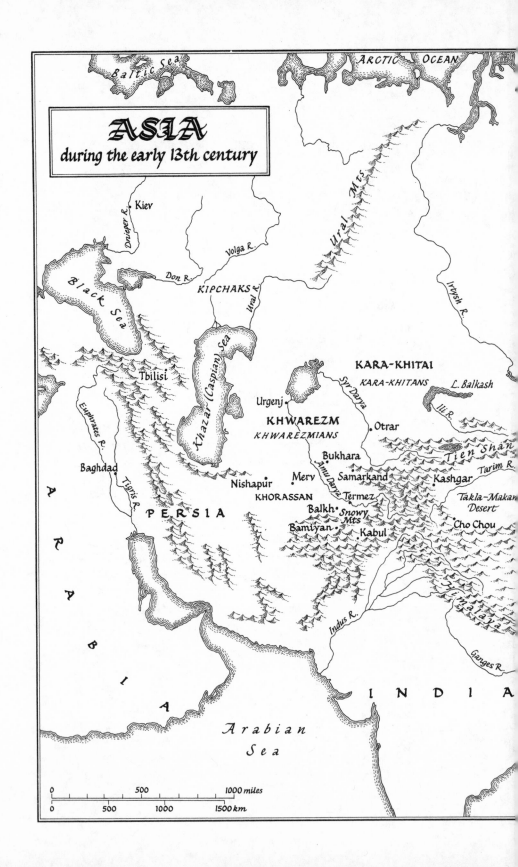

ASIA
during the early 13th century

Baltic Sea

ARCTIC OCEAN

Dnieper R. • Kiev

Volga R.

Don R.

Ural Mts.

Irtysh R.

KIPCHAKS

Ural R.

Black Sea

Khazar (Caspian) Sea

Syr Darya

KARA-KHITAI
KARA-KHITANS

L. Balkash

Ili R.

Tbilisi •

Urgenj •

KHWAREZM
KHWAREZMIANS

Otrar •

Tien Shan

Euphrates R.

Baghdad •

Tigris R.

Bukhara •

Amu Darya

Merv • Samarkand

Kashgar •

Tarim R.

Nishapur •

KHORASSAN

Termez •

Takla-Makan Desert

P E R S I A

Balkh •
Snowy Mts.

Cho Chou •

Bamiyan •

Kabul •

Indus R.

Himalaya

A
R
A
B
I
A

Ganges R.

I N D I A

*Arabian
Sea*

| 0 | | 500 | | 1000 miles |
| 0 | 500 | 1000 | | 1500 km |

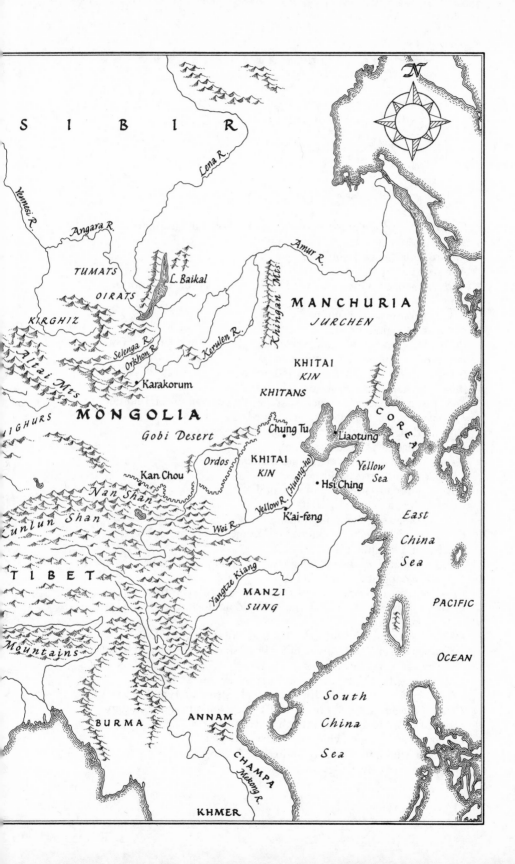

LIST OF CHARACTERS

Aguchu Bahadur, son of the Taychiut chief Targhutai Kiriltugh
A-la-chien, a Tangut follower of Temujin
Alakha, daughter of Temujin and Jeren
Altan, surviving son of Khutula Khan
Anchar, son of the Onggirat chief Dei Sechen and brother of Bortai
Arigh Boke, a son of Tolui
Arkhai, a follower of Temujin
Artai, an Onggirat girl
Bai Bukha, a son of the Naiman ruler Inancha Bilge and father of Guchlug
Bekter, older son of Yesugei and Sochigil
Belgutei, younger son of Yesugei and Sochigil
Biliktu, a young girl and slave to Hoelun
Borchu, son of the Arulat chief Nakhu Bayan; a comrade of Temujin
Boroghul, a Jurkin and the fourth adopted son of Hoelun
Bortai, a daughter of the Onggirat chief Dei Sechen
Bughu, a shaman in Yesugei's camp
Buyrugh, a son of the Naiman ruler Inancha Bilge
Chagadai, second son of Bortai
Chakha, a Tangut princess and wife of Temujin
Chakhurkhan, a follower of Temujin
Ch'ang-ch'un, a Taoist monk and sage
Charakha, a Khongkhotat follower of Yesugei and father of Munglik
Checheg, an Onggirat girl
Cheren, a Tatar chief and father of Yisui and Yisugen; also called *Yeke Cheren*
Ch'i-kuo, a daughter of the Kin Emperor Chang-tsung
Chilagun, a son of the Suldus chief Sorkhan-shira and brother of Khadagan
Chiledu, a Merkit warrior and first husband of Hoelun; also called
    Yeke Chiledu
Chilger-boko, a Merkit warrior and younger brother of Chiledu
Chimbai, a son of the Suldus chief Sorkhan-shira and brother of Khadagan
Chinkai, a follower of Temujin
Chirkoadai, a Taychiut; later named *Jebe* by Temujin
Chohos-chaghan, chief of the Khorolas and husband of Temulun
Daritai Odchigin, youngest brother of Yesugei and uncle of Temujin
Dayir Usun, a Merkit chief and father of Khulan
Dei Sechen, an Onggirat chief and father of Bortai
Doghon, a Merkit woman and mother of Khojin
Doregene, chief wife of Ogedei

Gorbeljin, a Tangut queen
Guchlug, son of Bai Bukha and grandson of the Naiman ruler Inancha Bilge
Guchu, a Merkit and the first adopted son of Hoelun
Gurbesu, a Naiman queen and wife of Inancha Bilge
Gurin Bahadur, a Kereit general
Hoelun, an Olkhunugud and mother of Temujin
Hulegu, a son of Tolui
Ibakha Beki, a daughter of Jakha Gambu and niece of Toghril Khan
Inancha Bilge, Tayang of the Naimans
Jakha Gambu, a brother of Toghril Khan; father of Ibakha and Sorkhatani
Jamukha, a Jajirat
Jebe: see *Chirkoadai*
Jelme, an Uriangkhai and comrade of Temujin; older brother of Subotai
Jeren, a Taychiut girl and mother of Alakha
Jochi, first son of Bortai
Jurchedei, chief of the Urugud clan
Kerulu, a servant in Bortai's camp
Keuken Ghoa, a wife of Jakha Gambu and mother of Sorkhatani
    and Ibakha
Khachigun, a brother of Temujin
Khadagan, daughter of the Suldus chief Sorkhan-shira
Khagatai Darmala, a Merkit chief
Khasar, a brother of Temujin
Khojin, daughter of Temujin and Doghon
Khokakhchin, a servant of Hoelun
Khorchi, a Bagarin chief and shaman
Khori Subechi, a Naiman general
Khubilai, a son of Tolui
Khuchar, son of Nekun-taisi and first cousin of Temujin
Khudu, son of the Merkit chief Toghtoga Beki
Khudukha Beki, an Oirat chief and shaman
Khulan, daughter of the Merkit chief Dayir Usun
Khuyhildar, chief of the Manggud clan
Kokochu, a shaman and son of Munglik; also known as *Teb-Tenggeri*
Koksegu Sabrak, a Naiman general
Kukuchu, a Taychiut and second adopted son of Hoelun
Kulgan, son of Khulan
Lien, a Han concubine
Liu Wen, a Khitan follower of Temujin
Mahmoud Yalavach, a Khwarezmian follower of Temujin
Mongke, a son of Tolui
Mukhali, a Jurkin and comrade of Temujin
Munglik, a Khongkhotat and son of Charakha
Mu-tan, a slave of Ch'i-kuo
Nayaga, a Bagarin warrior and follower of Temujin
Nekun-taisi, older brother of Yesugei and father of Khuchar

Nilkha, son of Toghril Khan; also known as the *Senggum*
Nomalan, chief wife of Jamukha
Ogedei, third son of Bortai
Ogin, a follower of Jamukha
Orbey, a Taychiut Khatun and widow of Ambaghai Khan;
    grandmother of Targhutai and Todogen
Samukha, a follower of Temujin
Seche Beki, a Jurkin chief and kinsman of Temujin
Shigi Khutukhu, a Tatar and third adopted son of Hoelun
Shotan, wife of Dei Sechen and mother of Bortai
Sochigil, a wife of Yesugei; mother of Bekter and Belgutei
Sokhatai, a Taychiut Khatun and widow of Ambaghai Khan
Sorkhan-shira, a Suldus chief and follower of Targhutai; father of Chimbai,
    Chilagun, and Khadagan
Sorkhatani Beki, a daughter of Jakha Gambu and niece of Toghril Khan
Subotai, younger brother of Jelme; a follower of Temujin
Sukegei, a follower of Temujin
Tabudai, a Tatar warrior and husband of Yisui
Taichu, a Jurkin chief and kinsman of Temujin
Targhutai Kiriltugh, a Taychiut chief and brother of Todogen
Ta-ta-tonga, an Uighur scribe and adviser to Inancha Bilge
Taychar, a cousin of Jamukha
Teb-Tenggeri: see *Kokochu*
Temuge Odchigin, a brother of Temujin
Temujin, son and heir of Yesugei; later, *Genghis Khan*
Temulun, sister of Temujin
Todogen Girte, a Taychiut chief and brother of Targhutai
Toghan, a Taychiut warrior and husband of Khadagan
Toghril, Khan of the Kereits; later known by the title *Ong-Khan*
Toghtoga Beki, a Merkit chief
Tolui, fourth son of Bortai
Tolun Cherbi, a follower of Temujin
Tugai, a Merkit woman and a wife of Temujin
Yeke Cheren: see *Cheren*
Yeke Chiledu: see *Chiledu*
Ye-lu Ch'u-ts'ai, a Khitan nobleman and scholar
Yesugei Bahadur, a Borjigin chief and head of the Kiyat subclan
Yisugen, a daughter of the Tatar chief Yeke Cheren
Yisui, a daughter of the Tatar chief Yeke Cheren
Zulaika, a young girl of Bukhara

Table of Important Mongol Clans

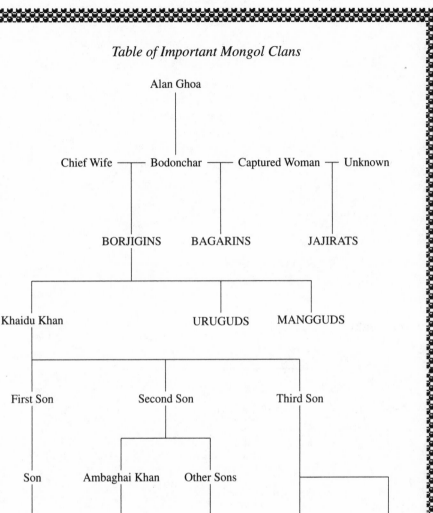

Alan Ghoa

Chief Wife —— Bodonchar —— Captured Woman —— Unknown

BORJIGINS   BAGARINS   JAJIRATS

Khaidu Khan   URUGUDS   MANGGUDS

First Son   Second Son   Third Son

Son   Ambaghai Khan   Other Sons

Khabul Khan   TAYCHIUTS   KHONGKHOTATS   ARULATS

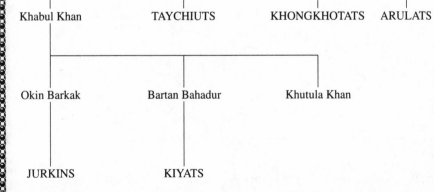

Okin Barkak   Bartan Bahadur   Khutula Khan

JURKINS   KIYATS

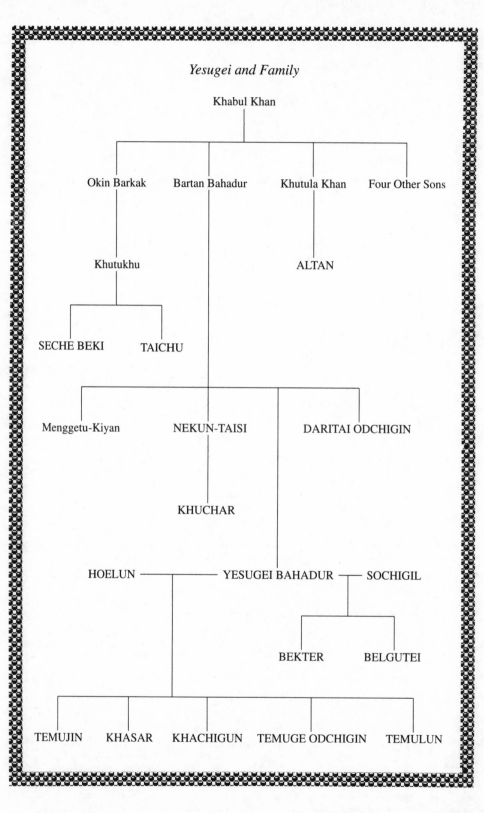

Yesugei and Family

Genghis Khan and His Heirs

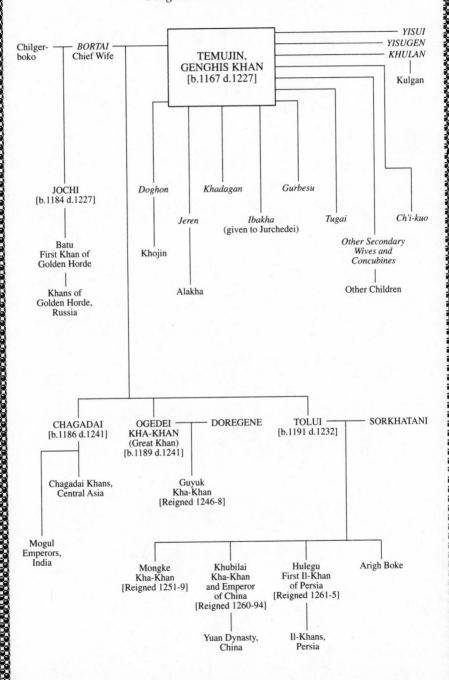

PART ONE

Hoelun said, "He rides into the wind, fleeing for his life. I call out his name, but he cannot hear me."

1

ON THE NORTHERN bank of the Onon River, a grove of willows and birches rippled in the heat. Hoelun gripped the reins of the horse that pulled her covered cart. The gently rolling green land, bright with wild flowers, would soon grow parched and brown. Spring and early summer were no more than a brief respite between the icy winds of winter and the scorching midsummer heat.

Hoelun's robe and leather trousers lay next to her, under the square, feathered birch head-dress she had worn at her wedding. A short woollen shift covered her; she had shed her other garments earlier that morning. Her home was under the curved covering of her two-wheeled wooden cart – the frame and felt panels of the yurt she would erect in her husband's camp, the trunks that held her pots, clothes, hearth, jewellery, and rugs, the bed where they would lie.

Yeke Chiledu rode at her side, his back straight under his quiver of arrows. His bow was inside the lacquered case hanging from his belt; his short, trousered legs hugged the flanks of his chestnut horse.

At fourteen, Hoelun had known that she would be married before long, yet her wedding had been upon her as swiftly as a summer storm. A month ago, Chiledu had come among the Olkhunuguds to find a wife, and had seen Hoelun outside her mother's yurt. By that evening, he was speaking to her father of the gifts he would offer for her; before the moon had grown full once more, she was Chiledu's bride.

Chiledu turned his head, and the faint lines around his small black eyes deepened as he smiled. His teeth were white against his brown skin; his face was broad, his cheekbones flat. He was eighteen, his moustache only a light sprinkling of hairs above his mouth; two coiled black braids hung down from under the wide brim of his hat.

"You should cover yourself," he said, accenting his words as his Merkit people did.

"It's too warm."

Chiledu scowled. She would put on her clothes if he ordered it. The young man suddenly laughed. "You are beautiful, Hoelun."

She flushed, wishing he would say more, remembering all the words he had used to praise her golden-brown eyes, her small flat nose, her thick, braided hair and pale brown skin. She had closed her eyes during their first night together, unable to stop thinking about her father's mares and the way his stallion mounted them. Chiledu's quick thrusting inside her had brought her pain; he had moaned, shuddered, and withdrawn, to fall asleep at her side a few moments later. The next night had been much the same; she had hoped for more.

Chiledu turned and scanned the horizon. On open land, any danger could be seen from afar, but here, with patches of wooded land by the river, they would have to be more cautious.

They rode slowly towards the Onon's narrow stream. The river was shallow here, barely more than a small creek; they would be able to cross it easily. A small flock of ducks were feeding upriver. Chiledu trotted towards them. Further up the bank, he dismounted, took out his bow, and crept towards the distant flock.

Hoelun pulled at her reins; the cart rolled to a halt. She untied the spare horse from the back of the cart and led the animal to the water. Long fingers of willows and birch trees came nearly to the edge of the opposite bank; in the distance, a massif abruptly jutted from the land. Tengri, Heaven, was a vast yurt under which parts of Etugen, the Earth, thrust upwards, reaching towards its roof. The mountains, with pines and larches that hummed and sighed whenever the wind stirred them, were places of spirits, of voices that might whisper to

2

shamans, of ghosts that might enter the bodies of animals to protect a man or lead him to his death. The slender stream of the Onon trickled as it flowed over the rocks; running water also harboured spirits.

Upriver, Chiledu was intent on his game, his bow raised. A shadow moved under the trees across from Hoelun; a twig cracked. She turned towards the sound and saw a man with a falcon on his wrist. The stranger leaned forward on his horse, his shoulders broad under his long, open coat, his eyes tilted, but also long and oddly pale, unlike any eyes she had seen. She tried to cry out; her voice caught in her throat. The man suddenly vanished among the trees.

The spell of those strange eyes was broken. "Chiledu!" she shouted as she tugged at the horse. "Husband!" Chiledu had not even sensed the stranger's presence; she wondered how long the hunter had been watching them. "Come quickly!"

He ran towards his horse, his game forgotten. She glimpsed the stranger riding around a small hill before trees hid him once more.

"What is it?" Chiledu called out as he reached her.

"I saw a man there, under the trees." She pointed. "He rode away. You had better go after him and see – "

"And leave you unprotected?"

"He was alone," she said.

"He might want me to follow him. He could have friends nearby. Water the horses, and then we'll go on."

They crossed the Onon and moved north-west. Chiledu rode ahead of the cart. Hoelun touched the flank of her horse lightly with her whip. Here, the land sloped into hills, slowing her pace.

The cart rattled as she rounded one grassy slope. The stranger had not greeted them, or held out his hands to show that he meant no harm, but maybe he had not wanted to provoke Chiledu by gazing openly at his unclad wife.

Such thoughts were not keeping her fears at bay. Clans of Mongols roamed the lands to the south, and she knew that they were enemies of the Merkits; Chiledu had told her about their raids. Resentment clogged her throat. She would not be worrying about the unknown hunter now if Chiledu had kept his men with him instead of sending them ahead to his camp after the wedding. He should have been more alert, and not so certain that he could protect his bride alone. He had been thinking only of how he could enjoy his new wife during the journey, instead of waiting until she raised her tent in his lands.

"You should have gone after him," she muttered, "and put an arrow into his back." Chiledu was silent. The sun hung overhead; she thought of the cool shade under the distant willows where they might have rested.

She urged her horse on, then heard the distant thunder of hooves. She looked back. Three riders were moving towards them from the south. A small hill hid the men for a moment, before they reappeared.

Chiledu rose in his stirrups, then galloped towards a nearby hill, trying to lead the men away from her. She lashed at her horse and the cart bounced and swayed as the animal broke into a trot. The three men raced past her after Chiledu; she recognized the stranger. He grinned at her, his greenish-brown eyes filled with a wild joy.

The men soon disappeared behind a distant hill on which an obo stood. The shrine was a small pile of stones with a spear jutting from the mound; she whispered a prayer to whatever local spirits the obo honoured.

Chiledu could not have carried her on his horse; that extra burden would have ensured his capture. His only chance was to outrun his pursuers. She trembled with rage at her helplessness. Her husband had failed her. Maybe that meant he deserved to lose her.

Chiledu burst out from behind a hill; he was riding back to her. She tensed, then stood up as he galloped towards the cart.

"What are you doing?" she shouted, as his chestnut gelding skidded to a halt. "I saw their faces when they passed – they mean to kill you."

The young man panted for breath. "I can't leave you here."

"You'll die if you don't. Go – you can always find another wife." Her words were more bitter than she intended. "You may call her Hoelun in memory of me, but save your own life now!"

4

He hesitated. The three strangers rounded the hill. "Listen to me." How could she convince him to save himself? She clutched at her shift, then pulled it over her head and threw it at him. "Take this as a keepsake, to remember my scent. Go to your people, and come back for me with your men later."

Chiledu pressed the garment to his cheek. "I will come for you, Hoelun – I promise you that."

"Go now!"

He lashed at his horse, then galloped away. His looped braids beat against his back, then were tossed forward as he glanced back at her one last time. The three strangers neared her; they whooped and circled the cart. For a moment, she thought they would let Chiledu escape, but then they rode after him. She stared after them until she could see only four small clouds of dust on the horizon.

Hoelun sank to the seat of the cart. Despite Chiledu's brave promise to come after her, it was not likely his people would trouble themselves over one stolen bride. The Merkits would wait before they sought vengeance for this wrong. By then, Chiledu would have another wife to console him.

She was still naked, except for her oxhide boots. She reached for her robe, pulled it on, and tied the strings at her waist. Even if she fled on the spare horse, she did not know where she could find safety. Her bow lay behind her, but she made no move to fetch it; forcing the strangers to kill her would gain her nothing. The pale eyes of the hunter had told her that he wanted her alive.

2

THE THREE STRANGERS rode back along the river-bank, following the stream towards Hoelun's cart. Chiledu had evaded them. They would have taken his horse and weapons, and perhaps his head as a trophy, if he were dead.

The three trotted up to her. Unable to control herself, Hoelun began to cry; the pale-eyed man burst into laughter. His smile enraged her. As he leaped from his horse, she lashed at him with her whip. He grabbed it from her, nearly pulling her to the ground, then climbed into the cart.

"Cry all you like," he said. "Tears won't help you." He pushed her down to the seat and jerked the reins from her hands.

"Be grateful," one of the other men said. "Being a Borjigin's woman is better than being a Merkit's." He reached for the reins of the pale-eyed man's horse. Their speech was much like her people's, easier to grasp than Chiledu's northern dialect had been at first.

"He'll come back for me," Hoelun gasped between sobs.

"I might, if I had lost such a wife," the man next to her said. "That Merkit won't." He urged her horse forward. One of his companions rode ahead to lead the way; the third trotted at their side.

"You made my husband leave me. He rides into the wind, fleeing for his life," Hoelun wailed. "I call out his name, but he can't hear me." Her grief tore at her, yet she was dimly aware that her captors expected such lamentations; they would not think much of a woman who forgot her loyalties too quickly. "You drove him away, you – "

"Be quiet." The man riding next to the cart had spoken, in a voice that sounded like a boy's.

Hoelun shrieked; the pale-eyed man winced. "My master Yeke Chiledu – "

"Be quiet!" the younger man said again. "He can't hear you now."

"You're finished with him," the man next to her muttered. "I won't have all that wailing under my tent." She hated him even more then.

"So you mean to keep her," the younger man said.

"Of course," the man with Hoelun replied.

"You have one wife already."

"Do you expect me to give her to you? I saw her first. Go find your own woman, Daritai."

"Very well, brother," the younger man said. "I should have known you wouldn't – "

6

"Stop this talk!" The man riding ahead of them turned in his saddle. "You two fight enough without having a woman come between you."

So her captor had a wife. She would be the second, with a lesser place; she regretted the loss of Chiledu more than ever.

"We had so little time, Chiledu and I." Hoelun dabbed at her eyes with a sleeve. "We were wed only a few days ago."

"Good," the pale-eyed man replied. "That will make it easier to forget him."

She covered her face, then peered through her fingers at the stranger. He was taller than Chiledu, and broader in the chest. Long moustaches drooped on either side of his mouth, but now that she was closer to him, she saw that he was not much older than her husband.

"What's your name?" he asked. She refused to answer. "Do I have to beat it out of you? What are you called?"

"Hoelun."

"These two are my brothers." He gestured at the man leading the way. "Nekun-taisi is the eldest." The rider grinned back at them with a smile as broad as his brother's. "Daritai Odchigin rides at our side. When I rode back to tell them of the beauty I'd seen, they were on their horses in an instant. I am Yesugei."

"Yesugei Bahadur," the one called Daritai added. Bahadur – the Brave. Hoelun wondered what the man had done to merit such a title.

"Bartan Bahadur was our father," Yesugei said. "Khabul Khan was our grandfather, and Khutula Khan our uncle."

"The voice of Khutula Khan," Daritai said, "could fill a valley and reach to the ears of Tengri. He could eat a whole sheep and still hunger. He could lie by a burning forest and brush away the flames as if they were cinders. Once, he and his men were attacked while out hunting, and he fell from his horse. Everyone believed he was lost, and our people gathered for his funeral feast, but no sooner had his wife shouted that she didn't believe he was dead than he rode into camp, alive and with a herd of wild horses he had captured on the way."

Empty boasts, Hoelun thought, the proud words of those whose pride was greater than their possessions. She knew something of the Borjigin Mongols. Their clan had been powerful once, but the Tatars, aided by an army of the Kin, had crushed them. Khutula, the Khan who sounded so invincible in Daritai's words, was dead, along with his brothers.

"And who is Khan now?" Hoelun asked boldly. Yesugei scowled. "You have no Khan – that's what I have heard." She wanted to anger this man, to pay him back somehow. "You lost two Khans – the one your brother brags about and the one who led you before him. Isn't that so?"

"Be quiet," Daritai muttered.

"The Tatars killed your uncle," she continued, "and the Kin killed the one before him."

Yesugei's jaw worked; for a moment, she thought he would strike her. "Ambaghai Khan was going to the Tatars to make peace," he said, "when the Tatars seized him and sold him to the Kin. They impaled him on a wooden donkey in front of their Golden King, and the Kin mocked him as he died, but in his last message to us, Ambaghai Khan told our people not to rest until he was avenged. The cursed Tatars will suffer for that."

"So of course you have to fight," Hoelun said. "The Kin will help the Tatars to keep you from growing stronger, but if the Tatars grow too powerful, the Kin may turn to you. It keeps Khitai safer, having such battles outside their Great Wall."

"What would you know about such things?"

"Only that wars here serve the Golden King of Khitai more than they serve us."

Yesugei gripped her arm hard, then let go. "You've said enough, woman."

She rubbed at where he had bruised her. "I think you had enough enemies without stealing me."

"You may be worth a few more."

Hoelun closed her eyes for a moment, afraid she might start crying again. A sudden gust swayed the trees. She thought of Chiledu, riding on alone with the hot wind burning his face.

South of the grove where Hoelun had first seen Yesugei, the land was flatter and empty of trees. A small herd of horses grazed in the distance.

"Ours," Daritai said as he waved a hand towards the horses and the men guarding them.

Hoelun was silent. "My brother Yesugei," the young man continued, "is the anda of Toghril, the Kereit Khan, who lives in a tent of golden cloth." So Yesugei and the Kereit Khan had sworn an oath of brotherhood. Daritai shifted in his saddle. He had already told her that Yesugei was chief in his camp and head of his subclan of Kiyat Borjigins, with followers from other subclans. "They swore their oath after Yesugei fought against Toghril Khan's enemies and restored him to his throne. An uncle of Toghril's claimed the Kereit Khanate for himself, but our forces defeated him, and Toghril was so grateful that he offered my brother a sacred anda bond. The Kereits are rich, and Toghril Khan a strong ally."

"So your brother has some friends," Hoelun said. "I thought his only skill might be stealing brides from their husbands."

Daritai shrugged. "Men of the Taychiut clan live in our camp, and Khongkhotats, and many more of Bodonchar's descendants follow us in war."

She soon glimpsed Yesugei's camp on the horizon. Circles of yurts, looking like large black mushrooms, stood on the lower grassland near the river; plumes of smoke floated up from the smoke-holes in the roofs. Carts sat at the sides of each dwelling. She guessed that about three hundred people lived in this camp, but after Daritai's bragging, she had expected more.

"Stop the cart," she said. "I want to be suitably clothed."

Yesugei lifted his brows. "You weren't so modest by the river." The cart rolled to a stop; she grabbed her trousers and climbed under the covering, then rolled down the flap over the opening. She found another shift in one of her trunks, pulled on her trousers, adjusted her silk robe, and tied a blue sash around her waist.

Yesugei was fidgeting when she sat down next to him. The cart rolled forward as she picked up her bocca; the hollow head-dress, decorated with a few mallard feathers, was almost a foot tall. She secured the bocca on her head, pushed her braids under its hood, and tied the ends under her chin.

The pale-eyed man snickered. "Now you look respectable."

Nekun-taisi's horse broke into a trot. In the camp, the work

9

of the evening was under way. Amid the cattle at the edge of the camp, women squatted to milk the cows; other women and children were tending the sheep. Foals were tethered to a long rope stretched between two stakes while men milked the mares. Outside a large tent, other men churned mare's milk in large leather sacks; their arms rose and fell as they pushed at the heavy sticks. Hoelun thought of her father's camp, where her family would be going about the same tasks, and felt a pang.

Several young men rode out to them, calling greetings to Yesugei. "The Bahadur's made his capture," one man shouted; another laughed. Hoelun looked down, hating the way they stared at her.

"We'll celebrate tonight," Yesugei said. Hoelun tensed at his words.

Yesugei's camping circle was in the north end of the camp. His standard, a long pole adorned with nine horse-tails, jutted from the ground near the northernmost yurt. Yesugei lifted Hoelun down from the cart, led her between the two fires outside the circle to purify her, then unsaddled his mount. A boy hurried to the brothers to lead their horses away.

"I see why the Bahadur went riding out of here," a woman's voice said. A group of women had gathered by the cart to stare at Hoelun. Outside a camping circle to the west of Yesugei's, two old women in tall head-dresses were watching her; with such boccas, they had to be important.

Yesugei's brothers returned, and Daritai unhitched the horse in front of Hoelun's cart, while Nekun-taisi moved off with one of the women, who seemed to be his wife. Yesugei waved his arms at the others. "Get to your work," he said. "We'll feast later."

"I must put up my yurt," Hoelun said.

"Tomorrow," Yesugei said in a low voice. "You'll stay under my tent tonight." His fingers dug into her arm.

A young woman stepped through the doorway of Yesugei's tent; a baby was tied to her back. She came towards them, gazed steadily at Hoelun with her large, dark eyes, then bowed from the waist. "Welcome, husband," she said softly.

He smiled. "She's called Hoelun." He pushed Hoelun forward. "This is my wife, Sochigil."

Hoelun bowed. Some women did not like it when their husbands took another wife, but Sochigil's face was calm. "My son." Yesugei waved at the infant on the woman's back. "His name is Bekter."

So the pretty young woman had already given him a son. Her place as his first wife was assured; she had little to fear from Hoelun.

Two large black dogs bounded up and snarled; Yesugei scratched one behind the ears. "Leave us," he said to Sochigil. His wife lowered her eyes and moved towards the yurt to the east of his.

The door flap had been rolled above the entrance. Yesugei entered from the left, to avoid bad luck; Hoelun stepped carefully over the threshold out of respect for the household spirit that it harboured. A small couch was just inside the door; the dirt floor was covered with dried grass and felt rugs. This dwelling was larger than her own. Two felt dolls, images of household spirits, hung from the wooden framework at the back of the tent with an ongghon, a carved mare's udder; she averted her eyes from the wooden bed with felt cushions and blanket beneath them.

An older man was hanging a joint of meat on the western side of the tent. He rushed towards Yesugei and embraced him. "That was quick work," the man said.

"This is Charakha," Yesugei said to Hoelun. "He's been with me since I was a boy."

The older man grinned and said, "You'll want to be alone," then left them.

Hoelun looked around uneasily. The hearth, a circle of curved iron bands, stood on six metal legs in the centre of the tent; a pale stream of smoke drifted up from the fire towards a hole in the roof.

Yesugei reached for her; she stepped back. "I saw two old women outside," she said hastily, wanting to distract him with talk. "They were standing in the circle to the west of yours."

"They are Orbey and Sokhatai, the widows of Ambaghai Khan." He scowled. "Orbey Khatun thinks a Taychiut should lead us, but her grandsons Targhutai and Todogen chose to follow me." He came at her and pawed roughly at her clothes. She slapped his hands away.

"Do you want me to wait?" He squeezed her arm, hurting her. "Maybe you do. Maybe you want to dream of what it will be like." He let go. "Make yourself ready. I want you looking your best."

3

HOELUN SAT ON Yesugei's left; Nekun-taisi and Daritai were on his right. People had ridden to Yesugei's circle from other parts of the camp, to sit by the fires outside his tents and to peer at his new woman. They had little for a real feast, this early in the season; the animals had to fatten and their young grow larger before more meat was butchered and stored. But they had curds, some dried meat, a few birds, and jugs of kumiss to drink. They would enjoy what they had, and be grateful for an occasion to celebrate.

Daritai was entertaining the crowd with the tale of Hoelun's capture. "She wailed so loudly," he said, "that her voice rippled the Onon's waters. Her cries made the trees sway and swept over the grass in the valleys as she wept."

Hoelun felt the stares of the two old Khatuns. The women near her were already drunk. Nekun-taisi's wife passed a ram's horn of kumiss to Sochigil. A few of the men stood up and danced, lifting their short legs as they stomped on the ground, their voices bellowing a song.

Yesugei thrust an oxhide jug at her. "I'm not thirsty," Hoelun whispered.

"Drink it, or I'll pour it down your throat."

She took the jug and drank; the tart, fermented mare's milk eased the tightness in her throat. Two men leaped up to wrestle. One of the Taychiuts leered at her. It would soon be too dark to see; she wanted to hide in the shadows.

12

Yesugei grabbed the jug from her, then pulled her to her feet. Daritai held out a piece of meat; Yesugei took the food from the end of his brother's knife. "I'll finish feasting inside my yurt," he shouted.

The men laughed. The fingers around Hoelun's arm were as hard as talons. Yesugei was silent until they reached his dwelling. He pulled her inside, then pushed her towards the hearth. "You didn't eat," he said.

"I wasn't hungry."

"It's wrong to waste food."

She sat down by the fire as he seated himself. He pulled his knife from under his sash, cut a piece from the meat, and speared it with his blade; she took it. He gulped kumiss from his jug, then wiped the ends of his moustache.

"I should have killed that Merkit," he said, "but I didn't want to run more flesh off my horse chasing him."

"Killing my husband wouldn't have warmed my feelings for you."

"It would have settled things, having him dead."

"You couldn't even face him alone," she said. "You had to fetch your brothers."

"I wanted to be sure of success."

The shaved bald spot on the top of his head gleamed in the light of the fire; his eyes narrowed as he watched her. She took off her head-dress and set it down. "I hate you," she said softly.

"That's too bad." He wiped his hands on his tunic. "He was a fool for letting me see you, for not making you cover yourself. He didn't deserve to keep you." He paused. "I saw you give him your shift before he rode away."

She took a breath. "I wanted him to have a keepsake. He didn't want to leave me, but you would have killed him if he had stayed. I told him he had to go, that he – " Her voice broke.

"And now he can dry his tears on your garment," Yesugei said mockingly. "But maybe you didn't give him your shift just to console him. Perhaps you wanted to inspire me as I rode past by showing me everything I would get."

She said, "No."

"Are you going to weep over him again? You made your

13

little show of loyalty before — don't go on pretending that you're sorry." He rose swiftly to his feet, then pulled her up and dragged her towards him. Hoelun yanked her arms free. He shoved her towards the bed and fumbled at his belt. "Take off your clothes."

"Take them off yourself, if you can."

"I'll beat them off you if I must." He sounded as though he meant it. She took off her boots and trousers. "The robe, too."

Her hand darted towards his face. He struck her arm away and knocked her to the bed. Her head swam. He came at her, grabbed her wrists, then pinned her down.

"Hold still," he muttered. She tried to kick, but he gripped her wrists with one hand and forced her legs apart with the other. His knee dug into her left thigh; his fingers were inside her cleft. Her wrists felt bruised, but the hand probing her was strangely gentle.

He thrust inside her. Hoelun closed her eyes; her jaws were clenched, her body rigid. It would be over soon. She remembered how it was with Chiledu, how quickly it passed for him.

He pushed her right leg up until her knee was against her chest; he was moving more slowly now. She twisted under him, wondering how long he would go on, hating the slapping sound his belly made against her body.

His thrusts became more rapid, and then he groaned as he fell across her. His outer garment was open, and the rough wool of his shift chafed against her cheek. He withdrew, got up from the bed, and fumbled at his trousers.

"You enjoyed it," he said as she sat up.

"You disgust me. Chiledu gave me more pleasure than I'll ever feel with you."

"I think not." He moved towards the hearth; his odd, green-ish-brown eyes glittered in the fire's light. "His only use was to make you ready for me." He tied his belt, picked up his knife, and went outside.

She heard the sound of voices raised in song; some of his people were still celebrating. Hoelun's face burned with fury. She imagined him out there, taking a piss, laughing with his friends about his new woman. The songs of his people seemed to mock her; she covered herself and wept.

14

He wrenched her out of her sleep when he returned and took her again, then fell into the deep, untroubled sleep of a man content with the work of the day.

Hoelun tossed at his side as she listened to his even, steady breathing. Yesugei lay on his stomach, his bowed, muscled legs bare below the edge of his shift; he smelled of sweat and leather and kumiss. She thought of reaching for his knife and plunging it into his back.

At last she got up and crept from the yurt, then walked quickly until she was near a shrub. The camp was silent, the night sky above her clear. Hoelun looked up, noting the positions of the stars, the smoke-holes of Tengri; it would soon be morning.

She squatted behind the shrub and relieved herself. I have to live with him now, she thought. I have to be a good wife and help him however I can, because that's the only way I can protect myself and any children he gives me.

She walked back to the camp. Yesugei was stirring as she stepped inside; he sat up and beckoned to her. She came towards him and seated herself on the bed, as far away from him as she could get.

"You are my wife, Hoelun Ujin." He was addressing her respectfully now, but his mouth formed a half-smile, as though the formality amused him. "You see what I have, but I mean to get more." He tilted his head. "You will have your share of my herds, and a third of whatever I take in any raid, when you have children. What you brought with you is yours to do with as you like. You'll manage what we own and make any decisions about it when I am away."

Chiledu's words had been phrased more poetically, but had amounted to much the same thing. "So now you have a second wife," she said bitterly.

Yesugei pulled at his moustache. "When you give me a son, you will be my first wife."

"Sochigil Ujin may have something to say about that," she objected. "She's already given you a son."

"She'll say nothing. Your sons will be first and hers second." He rested one arm against his raised knee. "I know her – I wanted her, but I also see how she is." His face was solemn.

"I have to lead these people, Hoelun, and I have rivals among the Taychiuts who sometimes question that. If I fly to Heaven before my sons are men, my chief wife will have to hold these clans together until a son of mine can take my place. Sochigil wouldn't be able to do it."

Hoelun recalled the young woman's placid gaze, how calmly Sochigil had accepted her presence. "Oh, she pleases me well enough in some ways," Yesugei went on, "but as soon as we were wed, it was always, 'Yesugei, what do you think? My master, what should I do? Husband, I don't know what to tell you – you decide.' A man needs better counsel from a wife."

"Some men say so," she replied, "and then don't listen."

His mouth twitched. "You'll say what you think. You may even tell me how much you hate me, as long as you say so only when we're alone."

"You're quick to trust a woman you hardly know."

"I have to see these things, know who will help me right away. If you don't offer good advice, you'll be very sorry – I won't have two weak-willed women clinging to me."

Hoelun was silent.

"But I don't think you're weak," he continued. "It was Heaven's will that I have you – I knew that when I first saw you." He glanced up at the smoke-hole; it was still dark outside. "We have some time." He reached for her again.

4

HOELUN ROSE EARLY. By the time Yesugei was awake, meat broth was simmering in the kettle hanging from the tripod over the hearth, and she had set out some kumiss. Her husband watched her from the bed she and Chiledu should have shared, inside the yurt she had expected to raise in a Merkit camp.

Yesugei groaned, got up, and pulled on his clothes before she brought him his food. He picked up the jug, sprinkled a few drops of kumiss as an offering to the spirits, then drank.

"I spoke to Sochigil yesterday," he said. "She knows you'll be my chief wife when you have a son."

"You might have waited to tell her that." Perhaps that was why Sochigil avoided her. "I could be pregnant now." His eyes narrowed. "You would always have to wonder if it's yours if I have a baby nine months from now."

"He wasn't enough of a man to give you a child so soon." Yesugei showed his teeth. "If I have doubts, you may not be first wife."

She lifted her head. Her ongghon, a carving of a sheep's udder, hung over her bed next to one of his. Several women had helped her raise the yurt, working together to secure the wooden framework before tying felt panels to the wood. She had given the women the soft woollen scarves intended as gifts for Chiledu's family.

Apart from Yesugei's brothers, he had no family to welcome her here. His father Bartan had died three years ago when Yesugei was sixteen, stricken by an evil spirit that had robbed him of the power of speech and movement. Yesugei's mother had followed her husband two years later.

Yesugei was now head of his Kiyat clan. Nekun-taisi was older, but his mother had been a second wife; he had yielded to Yesugei when an older brother was killed in a raid. Daritai was the Odchigin, the Keeper of the Hearth as the younger brother, but he veered between devotion to Yesugei and resentment against him.

"The days are too long," her husband said. "I get impatient for your bed. I see how you are when we join."

"You flatter yourself." She gestured at the place between her legs. "I could give myself more pleasure alone."

His face darkened; his scowl pleased her. She was waiting to see how angry he would get when Daritai called out from beyond the entrance.

"Enter," Yesugei shouted. Daritai entered, followed by Targhutai Kiriltugh.

"Greetings, brother." Daritai leered at Hoelun. "Targhutai says he's tired of herding – he's been eating dust for days. We could go hunting."

"You'll herd," Yesugei replied. Targhutai's boyish face congealed into a pout. The Taychiut stayed with Yesugei because many of his people were content to follow the Kiyat; Hoelun's husband had told her that. But Targhutai dreamed of being a chief himself, an ambition which she supposed was fed by his grandmother Orbey.

Yesugei stood up. Hoelun handed him a skin of kumiss; he would not return before the evening meal.

When the three men had left the yurt, Hoelun smoothed down the felt blanket and hides on the bed. The basket near the doorway was nearly empty; she would have to gather more argal as fuel. She picked up the basket and went outside.

The air was already hot and dry; even this early in the day, she might find dung dry enough to use. The eastern horizon was red, the sky growing lighter. She turned west. Dark, rolling land stretched beyond the few trees bordering the river; in the distance, an escarpment jutted towards the sky.

Koko Mongke Tengri was everywhere. No place existed where a man could hide from the Eternal Blue Sky above. Tengri burned His people with the heat of the sun, sent storms against them, lashed them with winds, and chilled them with the ice of winter. Tengri forged them in heat and then plunged them into the cold, shaping them as smiths crafted the swords they made with ore scraped from open veins on mountainsides.

Cattle moved towards the open land near the camp. The legs of the beasts were hidden by clouds of dirt; their bodies seemed to float forward on the dust. Men on horseback guided the camp's horses towards the plain, while women and girls, aided by dogs, herded sheep. The air was filled with lowing and the trampling of hooves.

Hoelun searched for dry dung. Sochigil, with her baby tied to her back, was also out looking for fuel. The dark-eyed young woman walked towards her, then abruptly turned away.

A voice said, "Greetings, Hoelun Ujin." Orbey Khatun stepped from behind a wagon next to her tent.

Hoelun bowed. "I greet you, Honoured Lady."

"There will be a storm soon," Orbey said. "I feel it in my bones." The Khatun's small black eyes narrowed. "You have not visited my tent, young Ujin."

"I have been here only a little while," Hoelun said.

"You will come to me tomorrow, when we gather to honour the spirits," she commanded. "The new wife of the Bahadur should be with us. Sochigil Ujin is also welcome, of course."

"I am honoured," Hoelun said. She bowed, murmured a farewell, then hurried towards her own camping circle. The old dowager's prediction had been sound; the sky was darkening in the north.

Between two poles near Hoelun's dwelling, long strips of meat were drying; an old cow had died the night before. She took down the meat, carried it inside, then tied down the flap over the opening.

She dreaded the storm. Once, lightning had struck a yurt in her father's camp. Everyone had wondered what the family inside had done to summon the bolt. They had been forced to purify themselves by walking between two fires while two shamans chanted, and had been forbidden to enter the camp for a year.

Thunder was rolling by the time Hoelun slipped a little dry dung under the cauldron hanging over the hearth. She pulled at the rope dangling from the smoke-hole to close the opening, then dropped to the ground, stretched out, and drew a piece of felt around herself.

Storms terrified her. She heard the screams of young children and the cries of women as they ran for their dwellings. The men out on the plain would be lying on the ground, wrapped in whatever was handy as they prayed that no lightning would strike near them.

Hoelun trembled under the felt as the wind raged and rain pelted the yurt. Storms were always a reminder that Tengri could not be appeased, only appealed to for mercy or thanked if one were spared Heaven's wrath. "Etugen," she whispered, praying that Earth would protect her even as Earth Herself was lashed by the wind.

The storm passed almost as quickly as it had come. She lay under her covering until the wind died, then got up to open the smoke-hole.

Her quiver and the case holding her bow hung on the eastern side of the doorway. She had only a bow that a boy might use, not one of the heavier ones for a man that took years to make, but her younger brother had told her she could shoot almost as well as he. She longed to go down to the river and hunt birds, as she had when she was a child.

Hoelun sighed; she had other obligations now. Sochigil was probably still inside her yurt. She checked her cauldron; the cow's milk could simmer a little longer. It was time she spoke to Yesugei's other wife alone.

"Welcome." Sochigil stepped back, her baby in her arms. The infant was tied to the wooden board with rounded ends that was its cradle.

Hoelun followed the other woman inside and sat down near the hearth, her back to the doorway. Sochigil closed her robe, set her son on the floor, tied her sash, then seated herself on a cushion.

Hoelun held out the pelt she had brought. "This is for your son Bekter."

Sochigil ran her hands over the fur. "I must give you something. I have a necklace with an amber stone. It would look well on you — the stone almost matches your eyes."

"You need not fetch it now," Hoelun said.

"Later, then." The young woman poured kumiss into a ram's horn, flicked a few drops towards the images of household spirits hanging over her bed, then handed it to her; Hoelun drank. "I wanted to speak to you before," Sochigil continued, "but then Orbey Khatun greeted you. I'm afraid of her."

"I'm not," Hoelun said.

The dark-eyed woman made a sign to avert misfortune. "Some say she knows magic."

Hoelun shrugged. "Some old ones in my camp wanted us to think they knew more than they did, so we would work harder to keep them alive. The Khatun wants us with her tomorrow, when the ladies gather in her tent."

Sochigil shivered. "Then we must go." She rocked the cradle, crooning to her son.

"The Bahadur told me," Hoelun said carefully, "that he wants to make me his first wife when I bear a son. I didn't ask him for that. I was content to leave that place to you. I'm

20

surprised he would make such a promise so soon after finding me."

"He decides everything quickly," Sochigil murmured. "He doesn't wait to act."

"So I have seen."

"It's my fault," Sochigil said. "Somehow, I've failed him. I try to be a good wife. I've always done what he wanted."

"He may like it better when you don't," Hoelun said. That was certainly true in bed. Yesugei seemed more aroused when she fought him, more fervent when he had to overpower her.

"More men are with him now," Sochigil went on, "than when we were wed last summer, and he's bound to win more followers. Being his second wife may be better than being the chief wife of another man."

Hoelun studied Sochigil's pretty, accepting face. "He is fortunate to have a wife who cares so much for him."

"I never gave him cause to doubt me." Sochigil sighed. "I thought, when Bekter was born, he would come to love me more."

"I will always honour and respect you, Sochigil Ujin," Hoelun said. The other wife's passivity would make her own life easier.

5

A LAMB BOILED in the pot over Orbey's hearth. The women had finished making their images, stuffing the felt with dry grass and sewing the ends together before praying over the dolls. These images of household spirits would hang inside their yurts to protect them, keeping evil at bay. A shamaness chanted near the fire as two other women put pieces of the sacrificed lamb on wooden platters.

Hoelun glanced at the Khatuns. Orbey had seated her next to Sokhatai. Hoelun forced herself to smile as Sokhatai offered her meat.

"May the spirits protect us," Orbey said, "and watch over the new wife of Yesugei Bahadur." Nekun-taisi's wife was here, along with the young wife of Targhutai and several other women, and Hoelun had seen that all of them were wary of the old dowagers.

Orbey looked towards Hoelun; the old woman's black eyes glittered. "Yesugei's brother, the Hearth Prince, tells the story of your capture well."

"Daritai Odchigin seems to have a way with stories," Hoelun responded.

"He speaks so movingly of how you wept," Sokhatai said. "I wonder. Sometimes a story-teller hides the truth for the sake of lovely words or a phrase's rhythm. Maybe you didn't weep so much at your plight."

Sochigil drew in her breath. In the silence, Hoelun heard Bekter whimper faintly; Nekun-taisi's wife was suddenly fussing over the cradle that held her son Khuchar.

"You are mistaken, Honoured Khatun," Hoelun said. "I was with my first husband for only a few days, and wept greatly at losing him."

Orbey leaned forward. "But now," she said, "you belong to a man who is the grandson of a Khan and nephew of another. The Odchigin says that his brother had to have you when he saw you by the Onon, displaying yourself in no more than an undergarment. I find that strange. There you were, a new bride, not keeping yourself decently covered while riding through strange territory. Maybe you had already tired of your husband. Perhaps you summoned spirits from the river to lure Yesugei to your side."

Hoelun stiffened. They would not dare to insult her husband openly, but might strike at him through her.

"The weather was warm," she said evenly. "My husband expected no enemies to cross our path. He was mistaken, but I cannot dwell on what is past. I'm not the first woman who has had to dry her tears and make peace with her ravisher."

Orbey's lip curled. Hoelun supposed that she should pity the Khatuns, with their husband so cruelly killed and their sons dead in battle, but she despised them. These people had enough

22

enemies, and had to remain united; the two were thinking only of their own failed hopes.

Orbey said, "You're a proud one."

Perhaps they were testing her. "By serving my husband," Hoelun said, "I serve you as well. The Bahadur will seek my advice, and I shall ask for counsel from older and wiser people. But we should be thinking of the spirits we have gathered to honour, Wise Ladies, not these other matters."

The other women were staring at her now. Orbey held out a horn of kumiss. Hoelun had won, at least for the moment.

The yurt in which Hoelun sat, where Yesugei had first taken her, had been his mother's. No mistress ruled it now, but he had promised to give it to her when she had a son. In the meantime, she and Sochigil tended to it, and their husband often met there with his men, as though his mother were still alive to serve them. Yesugei held court there as if he were a Khan.

Hoelun and Sochigil sat at their husband's left. Bekter, swaddled and tied to his cradle, lay between them. Yesugei was sitting on a cushion in front of the bed, his men at his right. A few small boys had been allowed to join the men, and Charakha was telling a tale.

He spoke of a woman called Alan Ghoa, an ancestor of the Borjigin clans. The men, most of whom were already drunk, seemed content to listen to the story again.

Yesugei's eyes darted restlessly, then narrowed as he gazed at Daritai, who sat next to Targhutai Kiriltugh. The two brothers had been arguing again earlier. Charakha's son Munglik was staring intently at Hoelun. She shook her head, for the boy should have been listening to his father; this tale was one he would have to learn.

"Alan the Fair seated her sons before her," Charakha continued, "and handed each an arrow. Each brother took his arrow and – " He paused. "Munglik."

The boy started, then blushed.

"You're not listening," Charakha said. "We'll see what you remember. Each of Alan Ghoa's sons held his arrow. What happened after that?"

23

Munglik's cheeks grew redder. "Each broke his shaft easily."

"And then?"

Munglik bit his lip. "Alan Ghoa tied five arrow shafts together, and gave the bundle to each son in turn, but they were unable to break it."

Charakha nodded, then said, "Alan the Fair told her first two sons, 'You've doubted me. You've said that, even though your own father is dead, I have given birth to three more sons who have no father and no clan. You mutter of how a servant has lived in my tent, and say that he must be their father. But I tell you that your three brothers are the sons of Koko Mongke Tengri, the Eternal Blue Heaven above. At night, a man as yellow as the sun came into my tent through the smoke-hole on a beam of light, and he is the father of your brothers.' "

The boys nodded solemnly. Hoelun wondered how these men would react to such a tale from their own mothers, but everyone knew that signs from Heaven were more numerous long ago. Alan the Fair had promised her sons they would be rulers, and descendants of hers had been Khans, which seemed to prove the truth of the tale.

Charakha turned to an older boy. "And what did Alan Ghoa say to her sons then?"

The boy cleared his throat. "She said, 'All of you were born from my womb, and I am the mother of all of you. If you separate yourselves from one another, each can be broken as easily as those single shafts. If you are bound together as tightly as the bundle you could not break, united in one purpose, no one can break you.' "

Charakha peered at Daritai, then at Yesugei. The Bahadur glared back at Charakha, then suddenly grinned.

"A man can't stand on one leg!" Daritai shouted, and gestured with his horn. Hoelun got up to pour more kumiss. The men muttered of a raid they would make later in the season when their horses had put on more weight. Targhutai's brother Todogen Girte stumbled outside to relieve himself. Two men leaned over a third, forcing his lips open as they poured kumiss into his mouth. One man began to sing and others quickly joined in, the raid forgotten.

Bekter wailed; Sochigil leaned over the cradle. Yesugei waved a hand at his wives. "Leave us."

Hoelun wanted to refuse, but Sochigil rose and picked up her son. Yesugei's face darkened as Hoelun gazed up at him. "I told you to leave," he said. "Go to your tents."

Hoelun waited as long as she dared. Yesugei raised his arm, and she got up and followed Sochigil outside.

Hoelun woke. The raucous sounds of the men were fainter, but Yesugei had not come to her tent. Maybe he was with Sochigil. She stretched against the cushions. I'll tell him, she thought, that I still think of Chiledu when he's with me. It was not true, but it was a way of getting to him. I'll tell him that I only pretend to feel pleasure with him, and then he'll never be sure if I have.

She was suddenly aware of the dampness between her legs. Her monthly bleeding had started. There would be no child of Chiledu's, no link to her lost husband.

Someone was retching outside. She was about to get up to put on a loincloth of skins when Yesugei entered, weaving as he stumbled towards the bed.

"Get out," she said, "or a shaman will have to purify you."

He swayed unsteadily. "We'll hunt tomorrow, you and I."

"I can't handle weapons now," she said. He sat down heavily and grabbed at her. "Don't touch me. You can't stay here – you shouldn't even be inside. You'll have to go to Sochigil. My monthly bleeding has begun."

He stared at her, then laughed. "Good," he muttered as he got to his feet.

"I wanted his child," she said.

"I don't believe you, Hoelun. You want your place as my first wife now."

"I won't ever love you."

"I don't really care."

He turned and left her yurt. With a pang of regret, she realized that she could not call up a clear image of Chiledu's face. She remembered only a distant rider, fleeing from her as his braids beat against his back.

6

HOELUN WORKED AT a hide. From the higher ground where her yurt stood, she could see to the southern end of the camp. Yesugei's people had moved near the end of summer, stopping on the eastern side of the Onon, under the high cliffs bordering the Khorkhonagh Valley. White clouds of sheep, mottled with the grey and black of goats, grazed near camping circles; cattle roamed the flatter land near the river that snaked through the valley.

The women near Hoelun chattered. Sochigil was making a rope of twined horsehair and wool; those women not watching the sheep sewed or worked at hides. Autumn was approaching, the season for war, and the camp was filled with talk of battle. Yesugei wanted to strike at the Tatars before his enemies attacked him. The loot of a Tatar camp would include goods from Khitai.

Yesugei despised the rulers of Khitai, and not only because the Kin had made allies of the Tatars. Once, the Kin had roamed the wooded lands north of Khitai, but had let themselves be softened by the settled ways of townsfolk. Before that, Khitans who had roamed the steppes had ruled there, but they had grown weaker in the new realm that was still called by their name. The Kin had found the Khitans and their subjects easy prey. Some of the Khitans had fled to the west, to claim a new kingdom they called Kara-Khitai; those remaining inside the Great Wall now served the Kin.

Two pairs of booted feet stopped near her. Hoelun looked up at Daritai's broad face. Todogen Girte was with him; his sullen face was much like his brother Targhutai's. Daritai's eyes lingered on her. He smiled at her too often; it was time he found a wife of his own.

Daritai waved an arm at the giant tree beyond the camp. The tree's wide, leafy boughs cast a shadow over the ground underneath. "There it is," Daritai said, "the tree where my uncle Khutula was proclaimed Khan. When the kuriltai chose him, the men danced until the dust reached their knees, and their feet beat a ditch into the ground." The Odchigin should

26

not have been reminding Todogen that the Taychiut's father had been passed over by that assembly of chiefs and nobles for Khutula.

"They couldn't have made a deep ditch," Hoelun said, "since I saw no sign of it."

Todogen laughed; the two men walked away. Hoelun scraped the hide with her bone tool. Two women whispered to each other. One of them glanced at Hoelun, then covered her mouth. Sochigil leaned forward, anxious to overhear.

Hoelun knew what the women were saying. Sochigil had carried the gossip to her, while insisting that no one believed it. Such doubts did not keep others from murmuring that Daritai was too friendly to his brother's new wife, and that Hoelun encouraged him.

She scraped at her hide. Targhutai and Todogen were often with Daritai; they would speak carelessly to their grandmother Orbey without thinking of what they said. The old woman would have spread such stories.

She would have to confront Orbey before the men left to fight.

Leaders of other clans were summoned to Yesugei's camp for a war kuriltai. Among these Noyans were his Jurkin cousins and Altan, the last son of Khutula. The number of horses tethered in the space beyond Yesugei's tent grew, and Hoelun admitted to herself that she might have misjudged her husband. Some of these men might have claimed the right to lead, but were willing to follow Yesugei.

Yesugei sent out his scouts. The shaman Bughu studied the stars, then brought three clavicles from dead sheep to the chiefs. When the bones were burned, all three cracked in straight lines down the middle: the omen was clear. Yesugei took off his belt, hung it around his shoulders, and offered his prayers as a sheep was sacrificed. They would ride out in three days.

The men now spent most of their time lacquering their leather breastplates, honing and oiling their knives and hooked lances, practising with their bows, and grazing the horses they would ride. The rest of the work had fallen to the women, the old, and the boys still too young to go to war.

Hoelun walked past a flock of sheep grazing near her camping circle; her turn at herding would come tomorrow. The women outside the tents chattered as they spread out wool, knelt by their long hand-looms, and hung out strips of meat. Preparing for battle always lifted people's spirits. Men had to fight, instead of waiting for war to find them. They could hope someday to carry war far from these grazing grounds to the east, where the Kin and those they ruled hid inside their dwellings, to the oases south of the Gobi, and to the west, at the ends of the trails the caravans followed. Yet Hoelun could still dream of a land where no one had to search the horizon for signs of an enemy.

A vision suddenly seized her. She saw other plains and pastures, and vast camps forced to bow to one Khan. Tengri had a purpose in forging His people into a weapon: to hurl them at those who were weaker. Her vision faded as she neared another circle of wagons and tents. It was useless to think of this now, when she did not know what the next day would bring.

Orbey and Sokhatai sat outside a tent, mending garments. Near them, three women beat at a mass of wool with long sticks, softening it so that the fibres would mesh.

Hoelun bowed from the waist. "Greetings, Honoured Ladies. I wish to speak with you, if you will allow it."

"Greetings, young Ujin." The wrinkles around Orbey's narrow eyes deepened as she peered up at Hoelun. "And have you finished the work of the day so soon?"

"I have beaten wool all morning. It's drying now, and my other tasks can wait. I wanted to pay my respects to you, and also to speak of a matter that concerns me."

Orbey glanced at the other Khatun, then waved a hand. "Please be seated."

Hoelun inclined her head. "Perhaps we may speak inside," she said softly. The other women looked up from their wool.

"Very well." Orbey stood up slowly, still holding her sewing, then helped Sokhatai to her feet. Hoelun followed them into Orbey's yurt. The old women sat down at the back, just beyond the beam of light shining through the smoke-hole; Hoelun knelt in front of them and sat back on her heels.

Sokhatai's dark eyes were as hard as the black stones hanging around her neck. Orbey reached for a jug, sprinkled a blessing towards her ongghon, then handed the kumiss to Hoelun.

"What brings you to us?" Orbey asked.

"I seek your counsel," Hoelun replied. "I am young. I have been a wife for only a season, and lack the wisdom of others." She was silent for a moment. "I know that you helped to guide your people after your husband was so shamefully betrayed. I fear that my husband is forgetting what is owed to you, but please believe that his only wish is that his followers remain united against their enemies."

Orbey gestured with one callused hand. "My son could have brought us victory. He might have been Khan now, but the Noyans had to choose Khutula, and your husband's father was one of those who brought the men to that choice. Bartan Bahadur wasn't thinking of who would be the better leader, only of seeing his brother as Khan." She set down her sewing. "Men so often believe that one who has large appetites and who brags of his prowess will make a leader. They had to choose Khutula, and because of him, the Tatars and the Kin crushed us, and my son was one who died at their hands."

"I grieve for you, Khatun," Hoelun said. "Yet I've been told that your husband himself, in his last message, asked his men to choose between Khutula and your son."

"Even Ambaghai Khan could be deceived, and see Khutula as more than he was. My son might have been Khan."

"My husband can bring you victory," Hoelun said.

"I doubt that very much."

"He might benefit from your advice."

Orbey showed her teeth; despite her age, she still had them all. "He does not seek my counsel."

"I can seek it," Hoelun said, "and offer it to him. When he praises my wisdom, I can tell him that you guided me. I can see that he grants you every honour you are owed."

The two dowagers were silent.

"Our bonds must be strong," she continued, "if you are to have your revenge against those who robbed you of your husband and son. I only want to do what I can to strengthen those bonds."

29

Orbey glanced at Sokhatai, then turned to Hoelun. "I want my husband avenged," she said in a low voice. "I want to see the heads of his enemies struck from their bodies and their blood staining the ground. I want to hear their children weep when they become our slaves. If Yesugei Bahadur gives me what I want, I can put my doubts aside."

"He will succeed."

"And if the Bahadur wins more glory for himself," Sokhatai muttered, "then you won't have to hope another man will claim you."

Hoelun lifted her head. "Honourable Khatun, that isn't talk to be spread. It will only anger my husband." She stared into Sokhatai's glassy eyes until the other woman turned away.

"Perhaps we misjudged you," Orbey said.

"I beg to depart now." Hoelun stood up and bowed. Orbey Khatun waved a hand, dismissing her.

She left the yurt. The two widows had reminded her again of how fragile the ties between the Taychiuts and their Kiyat kinsmen were.

Yesugei was still. Hoelun thought he was asleep, and then he stirred and moved closer to her. "You spoke to Ambaghai's widows today," he muttered. "You haven't told me what was said."

"I would have, in time."

His fingers dug into her arm. "I'll decide what I have to know and when. Orbey Khatun wanted to rule through her son. I won't let her use you against me."

"The Khatuns want their husband avenged," Hoelun said. "I told them you could bring that about."

"Orbey wants one of her grandsons in my place – Targhutai or Todogen might listen to her. I won't."

"Let the Khatuns think that you might. When you've won your victories, you'll be strong enough to keep the loyalty of the Taychiuts. Until then, you don't want those women as enemies."

"They are my enemies now," he said. "I know what they've said about you."

She tensed, suddenly afraid, and whispered, "I thought you didn't care about women's idle talk."

"A man was foolish enough to tell the story in my hearing. Luckily for him, he also said he didn't believe it, so I forgave him, and told him only that I would kill him if I ever heard it again."

"And you said nothing to me?"

Yesugei sat up. "There was no need. I'm certain I can trust you." His pale eyes glittered in the dim light of the fire. "If I ever found you with another man, I'd kill him, whether he's a brother of mine or not."

"Of course you would."

"I'd kill you, too."

"I know." Hoelun closed her eyes for a moment, thankful for his trust. "You won't hear such stories again. The Khatuns know that they misjudged me."

"Don't misjudge them, Hoelun."

The men rode out at dawn and moved east, towards the flatter land beyond the valley. The boys and men left behind to guard the camp galloped after them, shouting farewells; children on horseback shrieked and waved at the departing soldiers.

Hoelun's feet pushed against her stirrups as she urged her horse on. A cool wind slapped her face and burned her cheeks. Yesugei had been impatient to be gone, his greenish-brown eyes aglow with the prospect of war.

She galloped ahead of a group of boys. Sunlight glittered from the metal ornaments on the men's helmets and breastplates; strings of horses led by soldiers whinnied as she passed. They were an army now, following Yesugei's standard, a weapon aimed at the Tatars. On the horizon, a mountain thrust towards Heaven, its pines green spears.

Nekun-taisi held Yesugei's standard aloft; the tugh's nine tails were stiffened by the wind. Men shook their leather shields at Hoelun. A wing of the army was fanning out to the south.

"Yesugei!" she cried as she spotted her husband's bay gelding. Yesugei's helmeted head turned in her direction. She suddenly wanted to be riding with him. His men would bring him victory. For this brief moment, she could imagine that she loved him.

7

"THE SHEEP," HOELUN said to Munglik. Three lambs were straying from the others; the boy moved towards them on his short, bowed legs. Charakha's son often found reasons to be near her. The child stared at her dreamily and beamed whenever she praised him for his help.

The sheep had been led further from the camp to graze, having nibbled the land by the tents nearly bare. The camp would have to be moved again soon.

"Look there," a woman called out. Hoelun lifted her head. Against the eastern sky, the tiny black forms of riders flickered. Munglik ran to her side. The sheep milled and bleated as women pushed their way through the flock.

Hoelun squinted, then spotted the nine-tailed standard of Yesugei. Behind the riders, a dark mass of men on horseback was moving towards her from the east. Yesugei had sent no messengers ahead to tell them of the battle. Hoelun had thought the bulges on the backs of several horses were sacks of loot; now, even at this distance, she saw that they were the bodies of men.

Daritai, galloping ahead of the others, was the first to reach them. He reined in his horse; his face was sallow and drawn with fatigue.

"Yesugei," Hoelun said; the women near her were silent.

"He's alive," Daritai said; his brown eyes stared past her. A few women and children were running towards the approaching men. The dead would have to be buried; they could not be carried into the camp.

"What happened?" Hoelun whispered.

Daritai slumped forward in his saddle. "They met us at Lake

Buyur. When our advance force attacked, they retreated, and then more struck at us from the rear. We had to retreat then, with little cover and Tatars hitting us from both sides. Their scouts are better than I thought, or ours are worse. We didn't expect to meet so many there."

Hoelun's hands fluttered. "I must speak to my husband."

"Don't." The Odchigin gazed at her sternly, then rode towards the camp.

The dead were laid to rest on the side of a mountain that jutted to the east of the camp. Carts carrying small yurts in which the fallen men would be buried were driven between two fires to be purified. Two shamans, their faces hidden by wooden masks, swayed and chanted as the graves were dug.

Hoelun stood with the women. One young widow swayed at the edge of her husband's grave before another woman caught her. Weapons and offerings of food and drink were placed beside each body; the air stank of the blood of sacrificed horses.

Yesugei did not speak, and kept his eyes lowered as the small yurts were set over the graves. In time, the dwellings marking the graves would vanish. New trees would spring up on this spot; there would be nothing to mark the place.

Hoelun had seen death before. These men had died fighting, and their bodies had found rest here instead of falling into the hands of enemies; it was a better death than some. Bones would be burned for them, and another horse sacrificed to feed the spirits and the mourners. The widows would become part of other households, wives of their husband's surviving brothers or charges of grown sons.

Her own husband lived, yet his spirit seemed as far from his people as those of the dead. She knew what some were thinking. Heaven had turned against Yesugei; their young leader had failed them.

A cold autumn wind rose, lashing the people as they moved down the slope. Hoelun lifted her head and saw the dark, accusing glance of Orbey Khatun.

8

HOELUN WAS FEEDING the fire of her hearth when Yesugei entered. He had left the camp three days ago, alone with his falcon; even his brothers had not dared to follow him. He hung up his weapons, grabbed a jug of kumiss, then sat down by the bed.

She let him drink in silence for a while, then moved towards him. "You might have sent someone to tell me you were back," she said. "Did you find any game?" He did not reply. She knelt next to him and sat back on her heels. "Winter will come soon. You have to lead the hunt and take us to new grazing grounds."

"Will you be silent?"

"You've lost one battle, Yesugei. There will be others."

He reached for another jug. His moustaches dripped with kumiss. "You should speak to the men tomorrow," Hoelun said. "You're a Bahadur – act like one."

He backhanded her to the ground. "I told you to be quiet," he muttered.

She struggled to sit up. "You're not mourning your comrades," she whispered. "You're sorrowing for yourself. Learn from your mistakes, or these people will turn to another leader. Is that what you want? Will you give up now, and leave your sons with nothing?"

He jumped up, reached under her scarf, and grabbed her by one loose braid, jerking her painfully to her feet. "Do you carry my child now?" he asked. "You should know if you are – we were gone for nearly a month. Are you carrying a son?"

She already regretted her words. She wanted to tell him that she was pregnant, but could not be certain. Her monthly bleeding had been late before.

"I don't know," she replied.

He pulled her hair, hurting her. "What do you mean, you don't know?"

"I'm not sure."

"Useless woman." He struck her hard in the face; she cried out and covered her head with her arms. "You're worthless, you and your brave words." His fists hit her in the chest, jolting

34

her. The toe of one thick-soled boot caught her under a knee; she toppled forward.

Her mouth was filled with blood. She kept her eyes on his feet, afraid he would kick her again.

He stepped back. "I'm going to Sochigil," he said at last.

She did not move until he was gone, then crawled towards the hearth. Her mouth was raw, but he had not loosened any teeth; her bruises were deep, but she felt no broken bones. He had not beaten her so badly after all. She lay by the hearth and let the fire warm her face.

Sochigil gathered fuel for Hoelun and sat with her while she sewed. "The first time he beat me," the other wife said, "I couldn't move from my bed all morning."

Hoelun said, "I didn't deserve this."

Sochigil sighed. "Maybe you said something that angered him."

"I spoke the truth. He beat me because he didn't want to hear it."

Yesugei went to Sochigil again that night. Hoelun slept uneasily as the wind howled through the camp. Her husband had spoken to the other men; they would break camp tomorrow. He had taken her advice, however angry he still was. She let her rage fill her, then waited for it to subside. He would have beaten her sooner or later. It was part of a woman's life, and for some it came more often.

Hoelun rose before dawn, and was about to sip some meat broth when a wave of dizziness caught her, then passed. She would say nothing, not until she was certain. She placed one hand on her belly, hoping.

By mid-morning, the women had taken down their yurts and piled the felt panels in the wagons that held their household goods. Yesugei led most of the men in search of game; the women followed in rows of carts lashed to oxen, trailed by the men and boys with the herds. The sound of barking rose above the creaks of wooden wheels as dogs circled the flocks of bleating sheep and goats.

They stopped at sunset. The abandoned camp-site was still

barely visible on the northern horizon, a wide patch of barren land marked by the black spots of ashes and flattened places where tents had stood. The women made fires, milked the sheep and cattle, boiled the milk, then climbed into the covered wagons to sleep. The men slept outside with their horses.

Hoelun woke during the night and crawled to the back of her wagon. The Golden Stake, the star that always pointed north, flickered among Heaven's camp-fires in a sky blacker than felt. To the south, shadows crouched near patches of flame; the men were awake.

The hunters would be on the move before dawn. They would fan out in two wide wings to encircle their prey, then close in around the game, trapping the animals inside a circle. Milling deer and panicked gazelles, surrounded by hunters, would fall under a shower of arrows. The hunt would hearten her husband. Yesugei would track and encircle his enemies another season; the fire would burn inside him once more. Hoelun's safety and that of her children lay in the warmth of that fire.

Sixteen days after the hunt began, the women came to a flat, frost-covered steppe littered with the bodies of deer and smaller game. The hunters were still butchering carcasses; women left the herds with the older children and went to the men to help.

Hoelun was kneeling by one small deer, her knife out, when a wave of nausea caught her; she leaned over to retch. A hand suddenly gripped her arm. "It will pass," she heard Sochigil murmur. "Let me do this."

Yesugei trotted towards them. "What is it?" he called out as he reined in his horse.

"Can't you see?" Sochigil sounded strong for once. "Her sickness is upon her now." Yesugei's eyes widened; he leaned forward in his saddle. "Hoelun's with child," Sochigil continued. "I suspected it days ago."

Their husband smiled. "Get back to your work," he muttered before he rode away.

They made camp where the animals had fallen. The herds would graze here until they moved to their winter grounds. The wooden lattices of tents amid circles of wagons sprang up to the south of Yesugei's camping circle and were cloaked in dark panels of felt.

Yesugei came to Hoelun's yurt after it was raised, ate his evening meal in silence, then took her to the bed. He was gentle with her, rousing her with his hands before entering her; perhaps that was as close as he would get to an apology.

He was silent for a while after he finished, then said, "How long have you known?"

"Since we broke camp."

"You should have told me then, before the hunt."

"I had to be certain. I didn't want to be beaten again if I were wrong."

He raised himself on one elbow. "It will be a son — I feel it."

She closed her eyes. He would make her the first wife then. She drifted into sleep, content.

9

THE SUN WAS a red shield. Spearpoints of light glittered in the Onon's waters. The plain, its tall grass burned brown, stretched to the east beyond the hill called Deligun. Hoelun glimpsed a distant shape that shimmered in the heat.

That rider might have news of her husband. This time, Yesugei had decided to strike in summer, when his enemies would not expect it. A successful raid would hearten his men and wound the Tatars; he could build on that small victory.

The women gathering plants along the river-bank straightened as the rider came nearer. Hoelun moved heavily, barely able to see past her large belly to find roots. She no longer recalled what it was like to move easily, to leap on to a horse or stoop quickly to pick up a bucket. The burden of the child she carried made the heat seem even more oppressive. She poked at the ground with her juniper stick; her hand tightened around the wood as her abdomen cramped.

The pains were coming more frequently. It would be over

soon. She would know if the child who had beaten against her insides during the past months was a son.

Sochigil passed her, shooing a stray lamb towards the camp. Hoelun gasped; the other woman looked towards her. "Is it time?" Sochigil asked.

"Soon," Hoelun said, suddenly frightened. Her grandmother had died in childbirth, but she had been old then, with other children who were grown.

Sochigil rested her hand against her own swollen belly; the dark-eyed woman was expecting her second child in the autumn. The rider moving towards them shouted at the boys standing guard out on the plain, and Hoelun recognized Todogen. The Taychiut swerved to avoid the cattle grazing downriver and galloped towards the women.

For a moment, Hoelun pitied the Tatars. Children would weep with terror as their fathers and brothers lay dead and their mothers and sisters were taken by Yesugei's men. But the Tatars would have done the same in this camp. Her pain worsened; the struggle of her own child to enter life wrenched her away from thoughts of others.

Todogen slowed to a trot. "Victory!" he shouted. "We surprised an enemy camp – only a few had time to escape."

"My husband," Hoelun said.

"Yesugei has a Tatar chief for a prisoner," Todogen said, "and other captives to bring to us – he's already sending one to you. When I left him, he was embracing one of the women. She missed him with an arrow, then tried to get him with her knife. He saved her for last."

Hoelun was no longer listening. She leaned against Sochigil as the other woman led her away from the river.

Sochigil helped Hoelun out of her clothes, held her up as she circled the hearth, and rubbed her back. The pains came more quickly, until she had only a few moments between one pain and the next.

"This is your first," Sochigil said. "Maybe you should have an idughan."

Hoelun shook her head. The spells of such a shamaness might help her, but she wanted no one's hands poking inside her.

38

Outside her tent, people were laughing and shouting to the men who had returned. She crawled towards the bed as someone called out beyond the doorway.

"My brother told us to bring her here," Nekun-taisi's voice said. Hoelun grabbed a cushion and buried her face against the felt. Sochigil was speaking, but she could not make out her words. Let it be a son, Hoelun thought; let it be over.

"Ujin," a strange voice said, "your husband said you would have need of me soon. I see he was right."

Hoelun looked up. A middle-aged woman with heavy-lidded brown eyes was leaning over her.

"Have no fear, Ujin," the woman said. "I'm called Khokakh-chin. The Tatars killed my husband and made me a slave long before your men rode against them. When I told your chief I knew much about birthing, he had me brought to you, and said he would reward me for my aid."

Hoelun tried to speak.

"You can trust me," the woman continued. "The one called Yesugei Bahadur also said he would kill me if harm came to you or the child."

It seemed that Yesugei had decided quickly about this woman. Hoelun ground her teeth as she sank back against the bed.

Her body fought itself. The child pushed to get out; Hoelun's body resisted, and the pain subsided, only to return with more fury, its claws ripping at her insides.

In the midst of her struggle, she dimly noticed that the sky above the smoke-hole was growing light. Had this child been contending with her for a day and a night? It had to be a son; everyone knew a boy entered life more violently than a girl.

Her labour continued. Khokakhchin chanted; Hoelun could not make out her words. The band of pain held her in its vise. She no longer cared what she brought into the world; she only wanted the struggle to be past.

Something flowed from her body; her thighs felt wet. She lay on her side, panting, her knees pulled up towards her chest. Khokakhchin's hands were warm as they rubbed her back and legs.

39

"The child's coming," the older woman said. Hoelun bit down on a piece of leather and knelt, pressing her hands against the felt carpet. Her belly heaved as her body expelled what was inside her.

Hoelun fell against the cushions. Khokakhchin lifted a small, bloody form and held it up by its feet, one hand under its shoulders. The baby shrieked. Hands thrust the newborn at her; she held it tightly, afraid it might slip from her grasp.

"A boy," the woman muttered, "and an omen – your son clutches a clot of blood in his hand. It's a sign of power – a son marked for greatness." Hoelun looked down. Her son's tiny fingers gripped a mass of red as bright as a ruby.

Her body contracted; more wetness flowed from her. A knife glittered as Khokakhchin cut the cord. The child wailed; the older woman picked him up and wiped him with a piece of wool. "He's a fine boy, Lady. The Bahadur will be pleased, and I will live. Look at your son."

He was small. It was hard to believe that one so small could have caused her such pain. Khokakhchin picked up a jug, poured a few drops of kumiss into the baby's mouth, then began to smooth fat over him. Hoelun closed her eyes.

Hoelun remained inside her yurt for seven days, as all new mothers had to do. The shamans entered only to bless the new baby and to tell her that his stars were favourable.

Khokakhchin brought her food and fuel. No one else, not even Yesugei, could come inside the tent until the next full moon. She had peace, with no work except caring for her son. At night, she lay with him and listened to the voices of Yesugei and his comrades as they sang.

Her son's eyes were as pale as his father's. Yesugei would name him, but Khokakhchin had already told her what the name was to be – Temujin, He Who Forged Metal. The Tatar chief Yesugei had captured was called Temujin-uge; the name of his son would commemorate that event. The death of the Tatar chieftain would clear a place in the world for Yesugei's son.

Temujin, small as he was, showed strength. He sucked her nipples until they were sore, and struggled against the strips of cloth that tied him to his cradle. His pale eyes held the light of heated metal and the fire of a forge. She swelled with pride whenever she looked at him; she crooned to him while rocking him to sleep. But when he was silent and still, looking up at her from his cradle with his cat's eyes, she felt a chill, as if a piece of cold iron had touched her.

On the eighth day after Temujin's birth, Hoelun secured him in his cradle, picked him up, and left her yurt, walking between the two fires that burned outside the entrance. A bow and a quiver of arrows hung by the doorway, a sign that the newborn was a boy.

Women and girls hurried towards her to admire the baby. She walked to the edge of her camping circle, trailed by Sochigil and the other women. Munglik was gathering dry dung with some other children; he peered into Temujin's scowling face, then laughed.

"Someday," the boy said, "he and I will fight together."

"Yes," Hoelun said. Her husband and several other men were practising their archery near the camp, aiming at a distant target of leather stretched over wood to which a Tatar girl was bound. Several arrows jutted from the leather at her sides. Yesugei stepped up to take his turn. His arrow flew from his bow and stabbed into the target just above the girl's head.

Yesugei laughed; no one was likely to better his aim. "Cut her loose," he shouted. "She deserves some reward for not screaming." He turned towards Hoelun, then strode to her side.

Yesugei grunted at the other women; they scattered. "I chose a good name for him," he said.

"Khokakhchin told me."

"We'll have the naming ceremony as soon as the shamans allow." He waved his bow at the infant and chuckled as Temujin wailed. "He could be a son of Heaven."

"Perhaps he is," Hoelun said. "Maybe a beam of Tengri's light quickened my womb while you were sleeping." She paused. "And am I your first wife now?"

"I promised you would be."

The other men drifted over to admire their chieftain's new son. Hoelun glanced to one side. A woman stood near one wagon, her arm around a small boy; she stared past Hoelun with empty eyes as the boy hid his face against her coat. Two Tatars, Hoelun thought, two more who would now be slaves labouring for Yesugei's people. Her husband reached for his son and lifted the cradle above his head. Temujin's wail rose above the cheers of the men.

PART TWO

Hoelun said, "Who is left to fight with us now? Only our own shadows. What whips do our horses have? Only their own tails."

10

YESUGEI AND MUNGLIK dismounted by the two fires at the western edge of the camp; a few men rose to greet them. Hoelun wondered what news her husband had brought from the Kereit Khan.

Patches of snow still dotted the valley by the Onon; blades of grass had begun to sprout. The old ones claimed that the grass had been thicker and the winters shorter years ago. Yesugei and his people had been forced to move camp more often during the past seasons.

Circles of tents and wagons sat to the west of the river. Yesugei had won more followers, here and in other camps. Yet there had also been sorrows during that time – Nekun-taisi lost in one battle, friends and kinsmen falling to the Tatars.

Hoelun walked around her wagons and entered her yurt. Temuge, her youngest son, was pushing a knuckle-bone across the felt-covered floor. Her daughter Temulun whimpered in her cradle as Biliktu rocked it.

Old Khokakhchin did more work than Biliktu. Hoelun frowned as she gazed at the girl. "Bring me my daughter," Hoelun said. Biliktu picked up the cradle to which Temulun was bound. "Then work on that hide you've neglected. Temuge, go outside and tell me when you see your father coming."

The little boy picked up his bone and scurried through the doorway. Hoelun smiled as she suckled her daughter. Yesugei had given her five children. He had not neglected Sochigil, but there had been no more children for his other wife after the birth of her second son Belgutei.

Biliktu was dressing the hide with salted milk when Temuge ran back inside. "Mother! Temujin's fighting with Bekter!" Hoelun set the cradle down, then hurried through the entrance.

The two boys rolled in the dirt near Sochigil's wagons. Bekter grabbed one of Temujin's dark reddish braids and yanked it; Temujin clawed at the other boy's face.

"Stop!" Hoelun shouted. She ran to them, grabbed her son by his collar, and pulled him to his feet.

Bekter stood up. "Temujin started it."

Temujin's greenish-brown eyes narrowed. "That's a lie." He stepped to the dead hare lying at Bekter's feet. "My arrow found that hare, not yours. It's mine."

Hoelun turned to Sochigil's son. "Is that true?" she asked. Bekter's dark eyes glared back at her.

"I saw it first," Temujin said softly, "and I shot it."

"You wait." Bekter shook his fist. "You'll be sorry. I'll send the dogs after you."

Temujin paled; he hated dogs. Bekter showed his teeth. Temujin's fist shot towards his brother; Hoelun seized him by the wrist.

"Enough!" she said. "Bekter, go to your mother's tent and skin that hare — then I'll decide what to do with it. Any more fighting, and your father will hear of it from me."

Both boys tensed. The last time Yesugei had beaten them for fighting, Temujin had been unable to lie on his back for three nights. Bekter glowered at Hoelun, then picked up the hare and went inside his mother's yurt.

She would have to speak to Sochigil again. The other woman doted on Bekter, and often pleaded with Yesugei not to punish him, but never disciplined her son herself. Lately Belgutei, who behaved well enough in Bekter's absence, was following his older brother's lead.

Temujin lifted his head. In the sunlight, his dark hair was more coppery than black — his grandfather's hair, Yesugei had told her. "I see Father," Temujin murmured.

Hoelun turned. Yesugei and Munglik were walking towards her tent, trailed by her sons Khasar and Khachigun with their father's saddle. Temujin ran to them; Yesugei's arms closed around him.

Hoelun waited until her husband set his whip outside the doorway, then stepped forward. "I've missed you," she said.

He smiled, but his eyes were solemn. "We'll talk after I've eaten."

Munglik lingered near the yurt as Yesugei and the boys went inside. "Spring," he said, "always brings a light to your face, Ujin." He still seemed like the boy who had once found excuses to be near her.

"I would ask you inside," she said, "but your wife must be impatient to greet you." His face fell; he bowed, murmured a farewell, then walked away.

She went inside. Yesugei sat in front of the bed, his sons around him. Biliktu had set a few curds on a platter. The girl brought a jug of kumiss to Yesugei, then backed away, sat down near the hearth, and plucked at one long black braid. Preening herself, Hoelun thought as she settled at her husband's left; Biliktu was so obvious. Yesugei ate in silence, wiped his mouth on his sleeve, and pushed the platter aside.

"The camp of Toghril Khan is larger," Yesugei said at last, "and his people prosper. His priests said prayers for us."

Hoelun shrugged. Toghril Khan and many of his Kereits worshipped the Christian god, but the Khan consulted shamans as well. Heaven could be called by many names.

"And was the Khan pleased to see you?" Temujin asked.

"Of course. We went hawking together, and he feasted me in his ordu. Many came there to his circle of great tents to greet me."

"Then he'll fight with you this autumn," Temujin said.

"We'll see," Yesugei muttered. "I told him my young son already shows a warrior's spirit." His eyes were grim. Hoelun knew then that Yesugei had failed to win any promise from the Khan.

"Temuge can sit a horse by himself more easily now," she said quickly. "Khachigun's better with the spear." Her five-year-old son brightened at this praise. "Charakha says that Temujin and Khasar have become the best archers among the boys."

"I shoot well enough," Temujin said, "but Khasar's better, even if he is only seven." It was like Temujin, Hoelun thought, to say such things; her oldest child was quick to give others their due.

Yesugei's eyes narrowed. "And are you getting along with Bekter?" Temujin looked away. "Remember the story of your ancestor Alan Ghoa's sons. A shaft of arrows bound tightly together cannot – "

"He's the one who wants to fight," Temujin burst out. "He steals and lies about it, he's always – "

"Enough!" Yesugei raised a hand. "How do you expect to lead if you can't get along with your own brother?"

Temujin lifted his head. "You used to fight with Uncle Daritai when he was in your camp. You sent him – "

Yesugei slapped him. Temujin's cheek flamed; his eyes glistened with tears. "Daritai's the Odchigin," Yesugei said. "It's only fitting that he dwell closer to our father's old grazing lands. He and his men fight beside me when I need them, and that's all that matters. You must learn how to handle Bekter."

Hoelun averted her eyes. Temujin should not have mentioned Daritai. As long as the Odchigin was chief in his own camp, he would grudgingly follow his brother; Yesugei had not kept his own shafts tightly bound.

"It's time I spoke with your father alone," she murmured. "Temujin, you and Khasar may take Temuge riding, but make certain one of you is on his horse with him. Khachigun, my hearth needs more argal. Biliktu." The girl looked up. "Gather fuel with Khachigun."

The boys scrambled to their feet, and Temujin led them outside. Biliktu stood up, glanced at Yesugei from the sides of her long dark eyes, then slowly walked towards the doorway.

"The girl's growing up," Yesugei said when she was gone.

"She'll soon be fifteen."

"It may be time I took another wife, and Biliktu – "

"She would make a poor wife," Hoelun said. Biliktu was lazy, always quick to remind others that she was a Noyan's daughter, that only her father's death and her capture in a raid had made her a slave here.

Yesugei stroked his moustaches. "Why, I almost believe

you're jealous of the girl. You needn't be. You're still much as you were when I found you."

It was kind of him to say so, but her children had left their mark; her waist was thicker, and her breasts and belly sagged a little. She kept her face veiled when fierce winds raged and oiled her skin with animal fat, but felt the tiny traces of lines around her eyes when she lifted her hands to her face. She was nearly twenty-five, her youth almost gone.

"I must get more," Yesugei continued, "to support another wife, and I'm not likely to increase my wealth soon."

Hoelun let out her breath. "Toghril won't ride with you."

"Oh, he was happy to see me. He wished me well."

"He's your anda. If he stood with you now – "

"Toghril stands with me," Yesugei said, "but he won't ride with me – not this time. It serves him to wait and to see who gets stronger – my followers or my enemies."

"He wouldn't be Khan if it weren't for you. He'd still be wandering among the Merkits begging for help and getting none while his uncle ruled the Kereits."

"That's true, Hoelun, and it doesn't matter. He also wouldn't be Khan if he hadn't put his older brothers under the ground. Toghril isn't a man to let his bonds get in the way of his interests." Yesugei lifted his jug and drank. "We may do well this autumn, and if we win enough, a kuriltai might proclaim me as Khan. Toghril would ride with me then."

But there would be no kuriltai as long as the Taychiuts clung to their own hopes. They were content to follow Yesugei as a general, or during the hunt, but they would never make him Khan – not while Toghril offered only words of friendship, and not while the old Taychiut Khatuns lived.

"Well, then." Hoelun rested one arm on her upraised knee. "There's something else I want to talk about. I've been thinking we should find a wife for Temujin."

"He's only nine."

"Old enough to be betrothed. He would have time to know the girl and to serve her family before he's wed, as my father did before he married my mother. Better for Temujin to win his wife peacefully instead of making more enemies by stealing her."

"Some women are worth that risk." He touched her hand. "And where shall we look for Temujin's betrothed?"

"Among my Olkhunugud people, perhaps, or others of the Onggirat clans. You could use an alliance with one of their chiefs, since their lands lie close to those of the Tatars."

"They're not much at fighting, but their women are beauties." He patted her hand. "I'll think about this."

Hoelun stood up. "Sochigil will be anxious to greet you, and your comrades will want to hear about the Kereit Khan. Tell them that he trusts his anda to lead them. Let them think he wouldn't remain such a close ally of another chief."

Yesugei slept at her side. Hoelun had felt no urgency in his embrace, even though he had been gone for nearly a month. He took her in the way he satisfied his hunger with food and drink – quickly, with little thought of her after his need was met. His passion flared up only a little, as a fire's embers might before the flames died, and no flint remained in her to ignite new sparks. Even his rage at his enemies was a flame that burned less often; she sensed that he was weary of battle.

Fear rose inside her at that thought. Men had to fight until every enemy had surrendered or lay under the ground. Hate was the fire in which their swords were forged. If it burned too fiercely, it would soften the metal too much; if it cooled, the weapons would not be strong enough. People had to tend their hatreds as they tended their fires; hate kept them alive. Maybe Yesugei no longer hated enough.

Hoelun slipped from the bed and knelt by Temulun's cradle, then untied the straps around the baby and lifted her to her breast. Her sons slept on in their small beds of cushions on the tent's western side. Perhaps Temulun would be the last of her children. She had other joys to anticipate now – seeing her sons wed, becoming a grandmother – yet she shivered, as she did when cold winds warned of autumn's approach.

Hoelun's arms tightened around her daughter. Her loves and her hatreds were bound up with her children – love for those she had brought into the world, hate for any who threatened them. She would not let that love and that hatred burn low, not until she was ready to die.

11

BORTAI STOOD ALONE on a vast, grassy steppe under a starless black sky. A ghostly, winged shape, illuminated by the bright light it carried, flew towards her. She covered her face, then peered through her fingers at the white falcon. Its left claw held a sphere of flame; its right clutched a large white pearl.

Bortai held out her arms, no longer afraid. She marvelled at the fiery light and the dimmer, softer glow that shone from under the bird's talons. The falcon circled her and released its catch; she caught the lights in her hands as the white bird alighted on her wrist.

"I have brought you the sun and the moon," the bird said. She looked into its eyes and saw flecks of green and gold. The spheres she was holding suddenly blazed into a blinding white light.

Bortai cried out and awoke. Her soul had returned to her. Only the light of the hearth fire remained, where the shadow of her mother bent over the kettle.

"What is it, Bortai?" her mother asked.

"A dream," Bortai replied as she sat up in her bed.

"This seems to be a night for dreams," her father's deep voice said from the back of the yurt. He sat on his bed, pulling on a boot. "Put on your clothes, child, and then tell me about your dream."

Bortai scrambled out of bed, straightened her shift, then reached for her trousers. Her brother Anchar sat up in his bed and yawned. "More dreams?" the boy asked.

"This was the strangest one," she said.

"You said that about the last one, when a wild white horse came to you and let you ride it."

Bortai frowned. Anchar was eight, two years younger than she was, but lately he teased her more. She dressed in her knee-length tunic, went to her father, and sat down on the carpet by his bed.

"Don't mock your sister," he said to Anchar. "Dreams can tell us much. The spirits send them as warnings, or to show us what might happen. Now, daughter, tell us about your dream."

"I was standing alone outside," Bortai said, "and I saw a light. Then a white falcon flew towards me with a flaming light in one claw and a paler light in the other. It dropped the lights into my hand, landed on my arm, and told me they were the sun and the moon."

Her father plucked at the thin greying beard under his chin. "Are you sure of this?"

She nodded. "And I saw the bird's eyes when it spoke – they were brown and green and gold. Then the lights got very bright, and then I woke up." Bortai tilted her head. "What does it mean, Father?"

"I can't say, but it must be an omen of some importance, because I think my dream was much like it."

"Is that so, Dei?" Bortai's mother said from the hearth. "It's hardly unknown for a family to have dreams that are much alike. How many times have I told you one of mine, only to have you dream it next?"

"But on the same night?" Dei shook his head. "And this dream is most unusual. I've dreamed of the sun and moon before, but they always remained in the sky."

"Did you see a gyrfalcon, too?" Bortai asked. "Did you hold the sun and moon in your hands?"

"I recall a white bird," her father said. "It might have been a gyrfalcon. Something was carried to me, so I suppose the bird must have brought it. I think you saw this omen more clearly than I." Dei stretched his legs, then beckoned to his wife. "Shotan, where's my breakfast?"

The round-faced woman reached for a bowl. "Sometimes I wonder why people call you Dei the Wise. You might better be named Dei the Thief of Others' Dreams. This isn't the first time you've heard of a dream and convinced yourself you dreamed it, too."

"No, Shotan." Dei twirled one end of his long moustache. "I believe Bortai and I shared this one – it's only that mine wasn't as clear. I had a piece of her dream, and she's shown me what I didn't see as well in mine."

Shotan gazed at him affectionately with her warm dark eyes. "Perhaps you should have been a shaman, Dei."

"The call wasn't strong enough in me, but perhaps our daughter has the soul of a shamaness."

"That's all very well, but she'll have to be married someday, and some men don't like it when their wives make magic or send their souls travelling outside their bodies."

"It isn't a bad omen, is it?" Bortai asked.

"The bird was white," Dei responded, "and that's a colour of good omen."

"Pray that we aren't given the moon and sun," Shotan said. "If they were in this camp, there would be darkness everywhere else under Heaven." She ladled broth from the kettle for their meal; Bortai got up and went to the hearth to help.

12

THE SHEEP BLEATED; lambs huddled close to the ewes. At the edges of the camping circles, other clumps of sheep and goats grazed on the short grass sprouting amid small patches of melting snow.

Bortai wandered away from her mother and settled herself on a small rise to the north-west of her father's flock. Usually she gossiped with her cousins and the other girls watching the sheep, but she wanted to be alone now, to ponder her dream.

The yurts of the Onggirats who followed her father stood to the west of the Urchun River. Dei was chief of a small camp, with fewer than two hundred people. Other Onggirat clans joined them in the autumn, when they moved south towards Lake Buyur to hold their great hunt before travelling on to winter grounds.

Like many Onggirat warriors, Dei had not been to war for some time. As a young man, before she was born, he had gone on raids, but the Onggirats, unless they were threatened, preferred to avoid battles. Trade with the merchants who sometimes sent caravans through the neighbouring Tatar lands could bring them as much as they might take in a raid.

The Onggirats also bragged to every visitor about the beauty of their girls. There was no reason to war with Tatars when a truce could be had by marrying an Onggirat woman to a Tatar chief, no purpose in fighting Merkits or Mongols if other Onggirat daughters dwelled in their tents.

The Onggirats had bought some safety in this way, surely wiser than swearing oaths to one chief or another and thus making those people's enemies their own. In return, others knew that Onggirats were not likely to be among those they met in battle. Her people fought when honour demanded it – if horses or women were stolen, or a promise was broken – but were content to live peacefully at other times.

Bortai's father had done his share to ensure some peace for his camp. Maybe that was why they called him Dei Sechen – Dei the Wise. Her older sisters, young women she could barely remember, were the wives of Noyans and chiefs in distant camps; the bride-prices had increased the herds her brother Anchar would inherit. Dei's first son had died five years ago; Anchar was likely to remain his only surviving son unless Dei took a second wife, which he did not seem inclined to do.

Bortai's peaceful life here would end when she married. During the past winter, she had overheard her parents whispering about possible mates for their youngest daughter. Her woman's bleeding would be upon her in three or four years, and Dei would not wait too long after that to have her safely wed.

South of the camp, a few men were riding out with their birds. One of the men loosed a hawk; the bird spread its wings and soared. Bortai smiled, feeling pleasure at the sight of the hawk's beauty and strength. She remembered the falcon in her dream and imagined it was flying to her once more.

"Look," a girl called out. "Strangers."

Bortai straightened up and clung to her bark pail. Sheep milled around her; most of the ewes had been milked and freed from the long rope to which they had been tethered, and were now being herded towards the tents.

She looked west. Two riders were moving towards the camp, with a string of four horses behind them. Visitors came among them from time to time – hunters who stopped for a meal, traders from south of the Gobi with goods to offer for furs, hides, and wool, young men taking their brides to a distant camp, a wandering shaman who might tell stories or summon spirits in a trance. The sun was low in the west, the riders small black shapes against the red orb. Bortai thought of the fiery ball the gyrfalcon had given to her.

"Come along!" her mother called out.

She followed Shotan to their yurt. By the time the milk was simmering on the hearth, Bortai was bursting with impatience. Dei would bring the strangers to his tent; she was already curious about them. While her mother skimmed the milk, Bortai set out a duck she had plucked to cook, then moved restlessly around the yurt, straightening the bed coverings and poking at the carpets under her feet.

The dogs barked outside. Anchar entered and hung up his bow and quiver. "Two visitors," he announced, "a Mongol and his son. I heard them talking to some of the men while Okin went to get Father. They're Kiyats, a bone of the Borjigin clan. The man says he's a chief and the grandson of a Khan."

"Well!" Shotan was clearly impressed. "I'll serve them the rest of the boiled lamb – guests must be honoured, especially such noble ones." Bortai fidgeted; her mother glanced at her. "Bortai, if you can't be useful, sit down and keep out of my way."

"I'll get more argal." Bortai grabbed a basket and hurried outside.

Dei's circle was north of the rest of the camp. Bortai moved away from the tent, then stooped to pick up some dung. One uncle and a cousin were churning mare's milk outside their yurt, but most of the people were already inside. The visitors would be near the roped enclosure where horses were kept.

A wagon with a large wooden trunk stood between a yurt and the enclosure. Just beyond the back of the wagon, Dei was talking to the strangers, who had dismounted. Bortai crept forward, grateful no sheep were by this wagon, then shrank back against its side.

The man was tall and broadly built, but his hat hid part of

his face. " – so you're riding to the Olkhunuguds, friend Yesu-gei," Dei was saying.

"We're going among your brothers to find Temujin a wife," the strange man replied.

"And a fine boy he is. I see fire in his eyes and a light in his face."

Bortai could not see the boy's face, but he had the height of a boy of twelve. "His mother is my chief wife," the man named Yesugei said, "and she's given me three other sons and a daughter." Bortai strained to hear their words over the murmur of voices inside the nearby yurt. These formalities might go on for some time.

"I have a young son," Dei said. "My daughters are grown and married – all but one." Bortai tensed.

"Your camp seems prosperous," another voice said; that had to be the boy. "I've rarely seen such beautiful horses as you have here." His voice was high, but there was a confidence in it that she had seldom heard in a boy.

"They are hardly a match for your own fine horses." Dei paused. "Friend Yesugei, I had a dream last night, and I've been wondering what it means. A white falcon carrying the sun and moon in its talons brought them to me and alighted on my hand. And at the moment I dreamed this, you and your son, of a Khan's noble line, were riding to my camp. The falcon must be a spirit that watches over you, and I see the light of its eyes in yours and your son's." He was silent for a moment. "You have a son of nine, and I have a daughter close to his age." Bortai's hands tightened around her basket. "Our daughters are our shields, friend Yesugei – their beauty protects us. Instead of fighting with others, we put our beautiful girls in their carts and lead them to the tents of chiefs and Noyans."

"I know of their beauty, Dei Sechen," Yesugei said. "My son's mother belongs to your Olkhunugud clan."

"Unsaddle your horses," Bortai's father said. "Come to my humble tent, eat your fill of our poor food, and see my daughter for yourself."

Bortai crept away, then ran for her dwelling. She stopped by the door only long enough to subdue the snarling dogs with a glare, then hurried inside.

"You didn't find much fuel," Shotan said.

"They'll be here soon." Bortai thrust the basket at her mother, wiped at her face, then smoothed down her thick black braids.

"Really, child. Come and sit down, and try to act as you should."

She followed her mother to the back of the yurt, where they sat down to the left of the bed; Anchar settled on the right. She curved one leg under herself, rested her hands on an upraised knee, and struggled to compose herself.

Her father clearly believed that her dream had something to do with these visitors. The stranger wanted to betroth his son, and Dei must have seen some good in the boy, but she knew nothing about him except that he had a noble lineage and was tall for a boy of nine.

Their dogs barked. "Call off your dogs!" Yesugei shouted.

"Come inside," Dei replied. Bortai lowered her eyes quickly as the visitors came through the doorway. "I bring guests," her father continued, "who rode here from under that part of Heaven to the west. This Noyan is Yesugei Bahadur, chief of Kiyats and Taychiuts and leader of Borjigins in hunting and war, grandson of their Khan Khabul and nephew of Khutula Khan. His son's name is Temujin."

She was afraid to look up. "This is my wife, Shotan," Dei went on, "and my son Anchar, and here you see my daughter Bortai."

She lifted her head. The stranger named Yesugei stared at her with large pale eyes, then smiled. "You spoke the truth, brother Dei. The girl is beautiful. I see light in her eyes and fire in her face."

"A noble man has praised our daughter," Dei said. Bortai's gaze shifted towards the boy, who was still hidden in the shadows beyond the hearth. He stepped to his father's side as the light caught his face.

She nearly cried out. He has the falcon's eyes, she thought wildly. They were as pale as his father's, green and gold mixed with brown, but his seemed colder and steadier than Yesugei's warmer ones. His eyes held her, and she seemed to feel the falcon clutching her wrist.

Yesugei offered a small scarf to his host; Dei responded with a jug of kumiss. The two were soon seated in front of Dei's bed while Temujin and Anchar showed each other their knives and bows.

Bortai sprinkled blessings over the images of their household spirits. Her mother set out boiled lamb, duck garnished with wild onion, a few dried curds, and some airagh, the stronger kumiss Dei usually saved for special feasts and occasions. They sat down on the carpet to the left of the men, while the boys sat to the right.

"You have a fine-looking son, Yesugei Bahadur," Shotan said. Their guest grunted; like most men, he was not likely to say much until he had finished eating. "My own son may be small, but he wrestles well, and is a match for any boy here." She clearly intended to fill the silence with praise for her children.

Dei speared a sliver of meat with his knife and offered it to Yesugei. "My daughter is also small for her age," Shotan went on, "but no illness has ever troubled her. She rides like the wind, and I've never seen any animal that can frighten her."

Bortai felt fearful now. Her mother was bragging too much. Were they so certain this Bahadur would want her for his son? She sneaked a glance at Temujin. He was staring at her across the platter of meat slivers; she blushed and took a piece of food.

Temujin seemed unlike the other boys she knew. His forehead was pleasingly wide, his dark hair had a reddish sheen, and the well-formed cheekbones of his broad face showed that he would be as handsome as his father someday. She had also seen how he acted towards Anchar. Temujin had spoken warmly, but almost as a man might speak to a boy, even though he was not much older than her brother. There were also his eyes, as wary and observant as a cat's, pale eyes unlike any she had ever seen.

Yesugei gulped down the last piece of duck and let out a belch. "Bortai brought down that duck," Shotan said, "so I hope it pleased you. Her aim with the bow's quite remarkable, and her cooking will soon be as good as her aim. In some, beauty isn't a guise that hides flaws, but only one of many fine qualities."

"I see what your daughter is, Ujin," Yesugei muttered, sounding a bit drunk. "You've fed us well, Dei Sechen. You deserve to be called the Wise for choosing such a wife."

"He chose me," Shotan said, "but it was I who begged my father to accept him. Dei had to ask three times before my father would agree. I myself have never felt that delay in such matters serves any purpose."

She motioned to her daughter. Bortai picked up the platter and went outside to throw some bones to the dogs. They may leave tomorrow, she thought. Yesugei and his son might stay only long enough to exchange tales with her uncles and the other men before riding on.

She came back through the doorway, rinsed the platter with a little broth, poured the liquid back into the kettle, then fed the fire. Anchar and Temujin were playing with antelope bones on the other side of the hearth. Temujin aimed one of his bones, flipped it, and hit one of Anchar's.

"You're good at this game," Anchar said.

Temujin shrugged, then looked up at Bortai. "Sit with us," he said.

She sat down. He grinned at her, then aimed another bone. Her parents and Yesugei were deep in conversation over another jug of airagh.

" . . . farmers had just brought in their wheat," Dei was saying, "so we had enough fodder for our horses and the animals we stole. There was a woman — " Dei sighed. "She was so slender my hands could encircle her waist easily. But she tried to run away, and one of my men had to shoot her." He sighed again. "Just as well. She might not have survived the journey across the desert."

"I remember a raid two autumns ago." Yesugei's voice was slurred. "We took a Tatar camp. I ate in the chief's tent that night. His back was a cushion for my feet while his daughter's tears salted my food."

Bortai pressed her lips together. The two men might get so involved in their happy reminiscences that she would be forgotten.

Temujin leaned forward. "Your father told us about a dream

57

he had," he said, "where a gyrfalcon brought him the sun and the moon."

"Bortai had the same dream," Anchar said. Temujin raised his brows. Bortai heard one clink and then another as her brother's bone struck others. "There, Temujin – I won."

"You're good at this game, too, but I'll win next time." Temujin paused. "You dreamed your father's dream?"

"He dreamed mine," she said.

"I had one last night," Temujin said. "I've had it before, but this time it was different. I stood on a mountain, so high that I could see all the world. Before, whenever I dreamed it, I couldn't see what was below, but this time, I could see everything."

"What did you see?" Bortai asked.

"I saw the steppe, and thousands of yurts, and valleys near mountains, and so many herds of horses I couldn't count them all, and hundreds of hunters chasing deer and wild asses. There were other animals, too, and a caravan with camels, and hawks and falcons soaring above all of it."

"Did you see any villages?" she asked. Temujin shook his head. "Then it couldn't have been the whole world."

"It was the world," Temujin said, "and we were the only people under Heaven. In the dream, I took off my hat, put my belt around my shoulders, and offered mare's milk to Koko Mongke Tengri in thanks for showing it to me."

"What does it mean?" Bortai asked.

"Maybe it means the world will belong to us. My father says we're the best fighters in it, that God made us that way. Why shouldn't we have it all? And why shouldn't one Khan rule everyone?"

Bortai frowned. "Everyone?"

"There's one sun in Heaven. Why shouldn't there be one Khan on Earth?"

Bortai rested her hands on her knee. "You sound as if you mean to be that Khan."

"I'll be a chief someday," Temujin said, "but maybe the spirits will favour another. If he's brave and strong enough, I'd follow him."

"I wonder if you could follow anyone, Temujin." She would

have laughed at any other boy talking this way, but his soft voice did not sound like a bragging boy's.

"Temujin!" Yesugei bellowed from the back of the yurt. "Show our host how well you can recite the tale of the ancestors, the Tawny Doe and the Blue-Grey Wolf."

Bortai straightened. Her own name meant blue-grey, and Temujin's eyes were as tawny and golden as the hide of the ancestral doe must have been; maybe Yesugei meant to turn the discussion to her.

Bortai lay in her bed, unable to sleep. After several stories and songs, everyone had gone to bed with no talk of a marriage.

She peered over her blanket. The guests were asleep, stretched out against cushions near the hearth. A shadowy form crept towards the doorway; she waited until her father had gone outside, then got up and pulled on her boots.

The dogs growled softly as she stepped outside. She found her father outside the camping circle, his back to her as he urinated. She hung back until he had fastened his trousers, then hurried to him.

"Father," she whispered. Dei grunted. "Father, the eyes of the falcon in my dream – they were Temujin's eyes. It meant he was coming here for me – I'm sure of it."

"You made up your mind fast enough."

"It's true, it has to be true."

"We've done what we can, girl. The Bahadur would offer enough for you, but we don't want him to think we're too anxious. We must wait."

13

Bortai was awake before the others. She tugged at the clothes in which she had slept, pulled on her boots, and crept to the hearth to check the fire.

His father will ask, she told herself; he has to ask. But

59

perhaps this Bahadur was more ambitious for his son; he might look elsewhere instead of asking for a minor chief's daughter.

She heard a yawn. Temujin sat up and looked at her; she tried to smile. "Good morning, Bortai," he said softly.

"Good morning, Temujin."

Yesugei stirred and shook himself as he rose unsteadily to his feet. He mumbled a greeting, then went outside with his son.

Bortai stared at the hearth until her family was awake. Shotan frowned at her as she peered into the kettle; Dei and Anchar left the tent to relieve themselves.

The broth was simmering when the men and boys returned. Maybe Yesugei had already spoken to her father. Bortai searched Dei's face, but his eyes were slits and the lines around his mouth deepened as he scowled; he usually looked that way after drinking too much. He said nothing as he sat down, and Yesugei did not seem in the mood for talk.

Bortai forced herself to sip some broth. Temujin and Anchar whispered to each other, but she could not hear what they were saying. She was suddenly angry with her father for telling Yesugei about the dream, and at Shotan for speaking of Bortai the night before as though her daughter were a horse she hoped to trade.

"You've treated me well, Dei Sechen," Yesugei said at last. His skin was ruddier and less sallow, now that he had drunk some kumiss with his broth.

"But you deserve a feast," Dei replied; he also looked a bit more alert. "My brothers will want to talk with you, and your horses can rest while they graze with ours."

"That sounds most pleasant," Yesugei murmured, "but I've been away from my own camp too long already – first among my Kereit allies, and now here."

Bortai peered at Temujin from under her long lashes. He caught her eye, then looked up at Yesugei. "A few more days won't matter," the boy said.

"They will if we have a journey to the Olkhunuguds ahead of us."

Temujin's eyes narrowed; he pressed his lips together. Bortai's heart fluttered.

"I could leave," Yesugei continued, "and come back another time, but that would serve no purpose. Maybe we've circled this ground enough." He shifted on his cushion. "You have a daughter, and I have a son. She's as beautiful a girl as I've seen, and the fire in her eyes matches that in the eyes of my son. I've seen enough of her to know she would make Temujin a good wife, and he seems to have a liking for her. Brother Dei, will you consent to their marriage?"

Bortai's cheeks burned; her heart leaped. Temujin was watching her father, his eyes wide, his body tense.

Dei stroked his thin beard. "I could wait for you to ask again," he said, "but I wouldn't be praised for delaying, and no one would think badly of me for agreeing now. It isn't a girl's fate, especially one with my daughter's beauty, to grow old in her father's tent. I'll gladly give my daughter to your son."

Bortai swallowed hard. Her heart was beating so loudly that she was certain the others must hear it.

"But they are still children," Dei went on. "Brother Yesugei, will you leave your son with us? Bortai and Temujin can grow closer before they wed, and my son would benefit from having a companion who would be like a brother."

Yesugei looked down at Temujin. "I wanted to ask you that myself, since I meant all along to leave my son with his betrothed and her family. Much as I'll miss him, I will look forward to the day he and your daughter are wed."

"I'm glad you asked for Bortai, Father," Temujin said. "If you hadn't, I would have asked for her myself."

Yesugei laughed. "I know." He clapped Dei on the shoulder. "I should warn you of one thing – keep back your dogs while Temujin's with you. My son's fearless with anything else, but he's afraid of dogs."

Temujin reddened. Bortai would not have believed anything could frighten him. Anchar snickered. "Afraid of dogs?"

"You were scared enough yourself when one bit you," Bortai said quickly. "Don't worry, Temujin. I'll show you how to make them afraid of you."

He lifted his chin. "I won't let them frighten me."

"Shotan, you'll kill a sheep today," Dei said, "and this camp will have a betrothal feast." Bortai trembled as her father thrust her hand into the boy's warm palm.

14

THE MOUNTAIN CALLED Chegcher loomed to the north, its eastern slope darkening as the sun dropped lower in the west. Below the mountain, twenty yurts sat in a circle; plumes of pale smoke climbed from the roofs towards the sky.

Yesugei slowed to a trot; his spare horse whinnied softly. The people had gathered near a pit where meat was roasting. Many of them wore the bright red silk sashes he had seen in Tatar camps.

He could ride on, but they might wonder why he had not stopped, and it was unlikely that any of them would recognize him. These Tatars would not expect Yesugei the Brave to stop there and claim the hospitality all owed to any stranger. He could rest for a little while before moving on across the yellow steppe towards his own lands.

The hide that was Dei's parting gift lay across the back of his spare horse; Yesugei had given the other horses to the Onggirat chief as a token. He was pleased that Temujin's betrothal was settled, and the bride-price agreed upon. Hoelun, he thought, must have been much like Bortai as a child. Beauty was desirable in a wife, but he had also noted the strength in the girl's small frame, the health that lent a peach-coloured glow to her high golden-skinned cheeks, the liveliness and intelligence in her large, almond-shaped brown eyes, and the calluses on her hands that marked a willingness to work. He had read what was in Temujin's heart the moment his son first saw the girl, and Dei Sechen's dream was an omen he could not ignore.

He was satisfied, although he would miss Temujin. He loved his son's bravery and quickness, even his stubbornness and pride. Temujin had been six when he made his first kill; Yesugei still recalled the intense pleasure he had felt when anointing his son's bowstring finger with fat and blood from the fallen oryx. A few years would pass before the boy was wed, but Temujin would not have to dwell with the Onggirats all that time. He would return to fetch the boy next spring, and Temujin could pay another long visit to Dei before the wedding.

Hoelun would be happy to hear his news. His spirits rose; arranging for their son's marriage had reawakened his old feelings for her. It would have surprised her to know how much he longed for her at this moment. Being inside her, feeling the warmth and tightness of her sheath, was still the most comforting sensation he knew. Yet lately it passed too quickly for him, and, he was sure, for her. He promised himself to greet her more warmly when he returned, to rediscover the body that had given him so much joy and to share that pleasure with her again. The coming campaign would take him away from her soon enough.

He felt a pang; the joys of battle no longer seemed so enticing. He almost wished that the battles were past and that he could grow old at Hoelun's side.

His mouth twisted; he felt shame at allowing himself to indulge in such thoughts. Dei the Wise and the Onggirat chieftains might buy some peace with their daughters, but Yesugei and his sons would have to win it in other ways.

He was closer to the Tatar camp. The dogs chained near the yurts bayed at him. He smelled the odours of roast lamb. The Tatars around the cooking pit gazed up at him with the curious but distant look of people preparing to greet a stranger.

He would have a brief respite at least. Yesugei reined in his horse. "Are you at peace?" he called out.

"We are at peace," a man replied. "And you?"

"I am, and my ride has made me thirsty." Yesugei dismounted, held out his hands to show that he came in peace, then led his horses towards their fires.

63

15

"FATHER'S BACK," KHASAR called out.

Hoelun looked up. "You didn't have to ride back here to tell me – "

"He's ill." Khasar gulped air. "The men grazing the horses sent me. Dobon's riding back with him."

Hoelun stood up. "Biliktu!" The girl peered out from the entrance to Hoelun's yurt. "Get jars and put this away." Hoelun gestured at the curds she had set out on rocks to dry.

Biliktu glanced at the boys gathering near one wagon. "Ujin, what – "

"Just do as I say." Hoelun hastened after her son towards the edge of the camp. Two riders were approaching from the east. Yesugei was slumped forward, his head against his horse's mane. Dobon sat behind him, leading another horse by the reins.

Hoelun drew Khasar to her. "Fetch Bughu," she said. The boy hurried away. People were gathering outside the nearest camping circles. I mustn't fear, she told herself. Yesugei was strong; Bughu would drive the evil spirit from him.

Two men rushed to Yesugei's side and helped him from his horse. His face was sallow; he clutched at his stomach as the two men held him up. The people around Hoelun backed away as Dobon and the men holding Yesugei followed her towards her dwelling. "What happened to my husband?" she asked.

The men were silent as they walked between the fires outside her tent. "Poison," Yesugei muttered. Hoelun shivered and made a sign against evil, then followed the men inside.

They dragged Yesugei to the back of the dwelling, lowered him to the bed, then pulled off his boots. Dobon moved towards her and said, "Yesugei spoke of poison while we were riding here. That's all I know."

The two men by the bed stood up. "You've done enough," Hoelun said. "Khasar's gone to get a shaman. I'll tend to my husband myself."

The three left the yurt quickly. They think he's going to die, she thought; no one would willingly stay near a dying man.

She bent over Yesugei; he groaned as she took off his sheepskin coat.

"Poison," he whispered. "After I left Temujin – "

She had nearly forgotten her oldest son. "Where did you leave him? What's this about poison?"

"He's in an Onggirat camp by the Urchun River. I betrothed him to the daughter of their chief." He moaned as she slipped a pillow under his head. "On the way back, I stopped at a Tatar camp. They gave me drink and food before I rode on. I didn't think they would know me, but someone there must have – "

Fool, she thought, did you forget how many Tatars you've killed? She steadied herself. He had stopped there only to claim the hospitality owed to travellers; such treachery against a lone stranger was not common. The Tatars must have expected Yesugei to die before reaching his camp, so that no one would ever learn of their evil deed.

Sochigil entered, followed by Biliktu. "What is it?" the other wife asked. "Biliktu says our husband has been stricken – "

"The evil spirit will be driven away," Hoelun said firmly. "Sochigil, look after my sons. Biliktu, take my daughter to Khokakhchin. I'll stay with my husband."

Biliktu set down her jars of curds, then picked up the cradle holding Temulun. "It can't be," the girl said.

"Leave me!"

The two departed. Hoelun touched Yesugei's forehead; his skin felt hot. She did not want her children near whatever evil spirit had taken possession of their father, or inside the tent where he might die.

Khasar entered with the shaman. Hoelun lifted her head. "Khasar, you'll stay in Sochigil-eke's tent with your brothers. Go, so that Bughu can tend to your father."

"Mother – he'll be all right, won't he?"

"We must see what the spirits will for him."

Her son walked slowly towards the doorway. When he was gone, the shaman leaned over the bed. "How long has this illness been with you?" Bughu asked.

"I felt the pain here, two days after leaving a Tatar camp." Yesugei motioned at his belly. "By the third day, I knew I'd

65

been poisoned. Those Tatars did this to me. I stopped there to rest, and they gave me food and drink. Someone must have added poison to it."

The shaman peered into Yesugei's eyes, then lifted his shift to feel his abdomen; Yesugei groaned. Bughu moved his hands over the ailing man's body and prodded him until he moaned at the shaman's touch.

"What can you do?" Hoelun said at last.

Bughu stood up and led her away from the bed. "If I had been with the Bahadur when he first felt this," he whispered, "I could have given him a potion to purge him. Vomiting then might have saved him if it was poison that brought this about."

"What do you mean? My husband said – "

"That he was poisoned. The Tatars have reason to hate him, and I know of slow-acting poisons that can bring this about. But I don't think your husband was poisoned. I've seen people in this state when poisoning was unlikely – even when they vomit right away, they aren't free of pain, as they would be if poison were the cause. They worsen, and one feels the viscera swelling on the belly's right side. That is what I felt now in the Bahadur."

"And what can be done?" she said softly.

"Nothing, Ujin, except pray that the evil spirit leaves him. Otherwise, his pain will increase and his entrails rot." Bughu spread his hands. "I've seen such evil spirits come upon the strong and the young. Sometimes there is no reason for it, but Yesugei stopped at a Tatar camp, and maybe one of his enemies was powerful enough to curse him in this way. Whether this is the result of poison or a curse, we can assume his enemies brought his suffering upon him."

The sound of the shaman's high, soft voice repelled her. Bughu was only another carrion-eater, stalking an ailing man to see what morsels he might take for himself. The meaning of his words was clear. If Yesugei's followers believed him poisoned, desire for revenge on the Tatars might hold them together. But if an evil spirit was afflicting him, some might see it as a loss of Heaven's favour. People understood poisoning and curses, while the ways of spirits were harder to grasp. Her own position would be weaker if people doubted that Yesugei's illness was the work of Tatars.

"Thank you for what you have told me," she murmured. "You'll be rewarded – that is, if you're silent about it."

"I shall summon the other shamans, Ujin, but you must prepare for his passing. You should move him from this tent before – "

"Leave me."

The shaman left. Hoelun stared helplessly at the bed where her husband lay. The camp seemed oddly silent. At last she went to the entrance and looked outside, knowing what she would see.

Someone, perhaps Bughu, had stuck a spear into the ground just beyond the doorway; a piece of black felt dangled from the shaft. Everyone would know that this dwelling was to be shunned and that a dying man lay inside. She bowed her head and rolled down the flap.

Hoelun sat at Yesugei's side. Despite the spear, many of the men had come to the yurt to gaze at their ailing leader, but now they were alone. Bughu and two other shamans had come there in their wooden wolf masks, shaken their bags of bones, beaten their drums, and murmured their chants. She could hear them outside, still pleading with the evil spirit to free her husband.

Yesugei's moans were fainter; his skin burned when she touched him. He opened his eyes, but did not seem to see her. "I told you once that I would never love you," she said. "I never thought I would say this to you, Yesugei, but I love you now. I want you to hear this, so that your spirit will stay here with me."

"Ah." She bent closer to him, but he said no more. A sweet sickly smell came from him, unlike the odours of sweat and leather that had become so familiar. His death had to be near, and if she was with him when he died, she would have to stay outside the camp until three full moons had come and gone.

A shadowy form entered the tent and crept past the hearth. "You shouldn't be here," Hoelun said as the light flickered over Khokakhchin's lined brown face.

"So the shamans warned me," her old servant replied, "but you may need me. Biliktu is watching the baby. If your husband rallies, he'll need nursing." Khokakhchin made a sign. "If he doesn't, and you're put under a ban for staying with him, you'll need someone to look after you. I'll risk sharing the curse."

Hoelun was moved. "You do more than you should, old woman."

"You've been kind to me, Ujin. I might have grown old in a Tatar camp, lashed by my former mistress's tongue and my master's stick. Rest — I'll tend the Bahadur."

Hoelun slept at the side of the bed, her head against a pillow. She woke to the sound of shouts over the steady drone of the shamans. Dawn would come soon. A familiar voice called out to her as a hand lifted the flap at the doorway; she sat up and adjusted her head-dress.

Munglik stepped inside. Hoelun said, "You mustn't stay."

"I've always served the Bahadur. I can't fail him now." Munglik came to the bed. "Yesugei, I'm here to do whatever I can for you." The young man stared past Khokakhchin at Hoelun; his dark eyes filled with tears.

"Who's there?" Yesugei asked faintly.

"Munglik," Hoelun answered.

"Faithful Munglik." Yesugei sighed. "Come closer." Munglik knelt by the bed. "I'm dying, friend."

"Yesugei — "

"Listen." Yesugei's voice was so low that Hoelun had to strain to hear him. "I left Temujin with his betrothed, in her father's tent. He's called Dei Sechen, and his Onggirats are camped north of Lake Buyur, by the Urchun between the mountains Chegcher and Chikhurkhu." He gasped for breath. "My sons will have to avenge me. Never let them forget the evil done to their father. Take care of my wives as though they were your sisters, and care for my sons as if they were your brothers. This is my last command, friend Munglik. Go to Dei Sechen's camp quickly and bring Temujin back safely. He must prepare to take his place here."

Munglik stood up. "Before the sun rises, I'll be riding to him." The young man's voice broke; tears streamed down his face. "Farewell, Bahadur."

Hoelun followed Munglik to the entrance and caught his arm. "We know little of this Dei Sechen," she said. "If he finds out that Temujin is without a father's protection, he may consider his agreement at an end and keep my son there as a slave."

"I understand. I'll tell Temujin the truth only when we're safely away." He took her hands. "Hoelun – "

"Go. May the spirits protect you."

She went back to her husband's bed. Khokakhchin settled the blanket around him; Yesugei's eyes were barely open. "Who's there?" he whispered.

"Hoelun."

"Leave me, wife. This is my last command to you – I won't have you here when I fly to Heaven. Take my place and hold these people together. You'll need every day to strengthen your position, and that will be harder if you're forced to stay outside the camp."

She hesitated.

"Farewell, Hoelun. My life will be over before the sun's high. Go from here now."

She knelt to kiss his forehead one last time, then let Khokakhchin lead her from the yurt. Sochigil, Biliktu, and the children were already seated outside the camping circle. Hoelun sat down and rocked her daughter until Temulun's cries subsided.

"Hoelun-eke – " Bekter began.

"Hush." Hoelun glanced from him and Belgutei to her own sons. They were all so young, and now they would have to become men. People stood by wagons and yurts, watching the family from a distance; the shamans continued to chant.

Hoelun did not move or speak until the sun was climbing the sky. From the corner of her eye, she saw the shamans enter her yurt. When they came outside, she knew her husband's spirit had fled.

She stood up. "My husband's love for life is completed." She felt dimly surprised at how steady her voice was. "His spirit has flown to Tengri." She must not speak his name aloud so soon after his death, and refused even to say it to herself silently.

Sochigil shrieked and tore at her clothes. "My husband's left us too soon!" the dark-eyed woman screamed. "What will become of us now?" Khokakhchin clutched Khachigun to her chest; Khasar was trying to comfort Belgutei. Sochigil clawed at her arms and face; Biliktu huddled on the ground and smeared her face with dirt.

Hoelun was numb. Everyone would expect her to show her own grief. She ripped beads from her head-dress, but her tears still refused to come. In a moment, her husband would come outside and laugh at them for believing him dead, as his uncle Khutula had done when his people were holding his funeral feast.

The shamans walked towards her. She heard the rattling of the bones they carried.

16

THE BODY BEING carried to its grave was not her husband. The man Hoelun had known would live among the spirits.

The procession neared the mountainside. The Bahadur's closest companions rode on either side of the ox-drawn cart carrying the body and the possessions to be buried with him. His favourite horse, harnessed and saddled, was led by one of the shamans.

Hoelun rode in a cart behind the men. Sochigil sat at her side, still weeping. Biliktu and Khokakhchin were behind them, under the covering with the children; the girl had been crying nearly as much as Sochigil. Shed your tears, Biliktu, Hoelun thought; your sorrow will end soon.

She wished that she could cry as easily as the others. Her chest seemed encased in iron bands. She had endured the past days numbly, feeling that her own spirit had already flown to her husband's. She barely remembered taking down the yurt in which he had died and gathering all he had owned so that the possessions could be purified. She and her family had carried their belongings between two fires, then under a rope strung with strips of leather and connected to two tall poles as the

70

shamans chanted. Her hands and body had done the work, with no will to direct them.

A large pit yawned in a clearing on the slope; men had gone ahead of the procession to dig the grave. Others had been buried on this mountainside; small birches now grew over those graves. Hoelun saw a grassy spot where the tattered remnants of a horsehide fluttered on poles, a mound of snow near the lattice of a yurt. Her husband would be put into the ground and horses would trample down the grave. After a few seasons, nothing would mark the spot where he would rest forever.

The men dismounted and walked towards the pit. The chestnut horse snorted as one man mounted it; the animal would be ridden into exhaustion before it was sacrificed. Another horse had already been slaughtered for the funeral feast; men worked at the carcass with their knives. Birds circled overhead, the shadows cast by their wings dappling the ground.

Hoelun reined in the ox drawing her cart, then climbed down with Sochigil. The other woman whimpered as she looked towards the pit. She would join him in the grave if she could, Hoelun thought, as wives of chieftains had done long ago.

A few men carried the dead man to the grave. He would be buried with all that he might need in his next life – his favourite horse, a mare and colt to increase his herd, his lance, breastplate, arrows, and bow, kumiss and some meat from the sacrificed horse. The mourners would share their funeral feast with him before the earth covered him.

The shamans stood by the grave, sprinkling drops of kumiss over the ground as Bughu chanted. "Where have you gone, brave leader? Why have you abandoned us now? Who will lead us in the hunt and in war?"

Other women left their horses and carts to gather near the two widows. Hoelun remembered the times she had comforted those who had lost husbands, how she had circled graves with them and sat at funeral feasts as they burned bones for their dead. She had pitied the bereaved, never quite believing that she would become a widow herself.

Her children huddled near her. Khasar had one hand on Temuge's shoulder; his little brother peered up at the people around him. Bekter and Belgutei caught their weeping mother

71

by the elbows. Someone jostled Hoelun's arm; Biliktu handed Temulun to her.

She watched as the body was lowered into the grave, its limbs and torso bent, so that the dead man could sit at the table that would hold his provisions. Hoelun suddenly longed for Temujin, the son most like his father.

Her inner voice echoed in her mind, drowning out the chants of the shamans. I have to hold these clans together until Temujin is old enough to lead them. The Tatars will think my husband's death has weakened us; we must strike at them again and show them that they still have much to fear.

A man was carrying her husband's bow to the grave. He still lacked one thing in death, something he had certainly valued in life. Hoelun cradled her daughter in one arm and moved closer to Biliktu.

"Child," Hoelun said, "I see how you grieve for the one we have lost." Bughu fell silent. She had spoken to him earlier, although not to the girl. She had seen his eyes glow in anticipation, as though her request were yet another reward for his discretion. The shaman reached inside his coat and pulled out a long silken cord.

Biliktu's eyes widened. Show some courage now, Hoelun thought; don't plead with me for mercy. The girl was her chattel; she had the right. She could not leave her husband alone in his grave.

"My master will have many to serve him in the next world," Hoelun said, "his beloved steed, cows for his herd, the spirits of the enemies he's killed. He will have his food and drink, and a yurt in which to rest, and his bed shall not be empty."

Another shaman seized Biliktu by the arm and pulled her forward; Bughu looped the cord around her neck. "I shall pay you the great honour," Hoelun said softly, "of allowing you to join the master you loved."

Biliktu screamed and clawed at the air with her hands. You should be pleased, Hoelun thought; you were anxious enough to be his bedfellow before. The shaman holding Biliktu grabbed her wrists. Hoelun caught one last glimpse of the girl's frightened eyes before Bughu tightened the cord around her neck.

17

BORTAI FLICKED HER whip against her horse's flank as Temu-jin's brown horse bounded ahead of hers. She rose in her stirrups; her bay was soon at his side. Temujin turned to grin at her and his dark reddish braids danced in the wind.

Bortai howled with delight. Birds flew up from a patch of grass in front of her. She looked back; Anchar was several paces behind them.

Her horse pulled ahead of Temujin's. She tightened her reins slightly; her bay horse slowed, just enough for Temujin to catch up. His horse edged hers by a head as they passed a small tree.

They slowed to a trot and circled back to meet Anchar. "Temujin won," her brother shouted.

"No," Temujin replied. "Bortai let me win." He scowled; his gelding trotted closer to hers. "I saw you pull up. I could have won without that. Don't ever do it again."

She looked away, embarrassed. Other boys and girls were out riding over the bare land, but they were keeping away from the tree, maybe because they assumed Bortai wanted some time alone with Temujin.

During the nine days Temujin had been here, she had not seen much of him except in the evening, when the family told stories before going to sleep. While she helped her mother, the boys practised archery, sat with Arasen the bowmaker to learn some of his craft, went out herding or hunting with her father, and played endless games with their antelope bones.

Temujin gestured at the tree. "We'll rest here for a while." He turned towards Anchar. "Ride back to the others if you want."

"Aren't you coming?" Anchar asked.

"We'll join you later," Temujin replied. The other boy shrugged, made a face at Bortai, then galloped away.

Bortai and Temujin dismounted and tied their reins to a low-hanging limb. She was about to slip the bowcase from her belt when Temujin lifted his hand. "Don't leave that. My father says you should always keep your weapons close, especially when you're away from camp."

She followed him to the tree, set her bowcase and quiver next to his, then sat down. "We're safe enough, Temujin. We'd see anyone coming from a long way off."

He stared out at the flat open ground. "I know, but why lose even a little time running for your bow?"

"I am sorry." She felt awkward, uncertain about what to say to him now that she had him to herself. "I mean, about letting you win. But you would have won anyway."

"Then you didn't have to do it. If I'm good enough, I'll win by myself. If I'm not, I'd better find that out."

Bortai drew up her legs. "I haven't seen you fail at anything yet."

He laughed. "Anchar's won a few of my bones." He rested his back against the tree trunk. "When we're men, maybe he'll be one of my generals."

"How many do you plan to have?"

"As many as I need."

Bortai searched for more to say. "You have brothers," she said. "Do you get along with them as well as you do with Anchar?"

"All except one. My father's second wife gave him a son before I was born. Bekter picks any excuse for a fight. He doesn't like knowing that I'll be Father's heir."

Bortai shook her head. "But if his mother's a second wife, he can't expect – "

"She was father's wife before he found my mother."

"And he made your mother his first wife?"

"He knew Mother was a stronger woman. He often talks of how he knew she'd have to be his as soon as he saw her." Temujin grinned. "She was a bride, travelling with her new husband. My father and uncles chased him off and brought Mother to their camp."

Bortai was appalled, but also thrilled. "She must have been very angry."

"Father says she wept and cried, but that passed. She's been a good wife to him, so maybe she didn't really mind that much. What if your father had promised you to someone else before you met me? You might have wanted me to steal you."

"Well, it's silly to talk about it – we're betrothed."

"I know," he said. "I knew we had to ask for you right away. Father doesn't wait to get what he wants – why should I?"

Bortai plucked at one of her braids. "When we talked that first night," Temujin continued, "I was thinking of how my parents talk sometimes. You'll have to tell me when I might be making a mistake – my father says some of his men tell him only what they think he wants to hear. Mother's more honest with him. If she weren't, he'd beat her as often as he beats his other wife."

"I won't let you beat me!" She struck his arm; he grabbed her wrists and pinned her to the ground. She laughed as she tried to free herself. "If I think you're going to beat me, you'll never get past my dogs."

His grip tightened. "Don't say that." His face reddened; his hands were bruising her wrists.

"You're hurting me."

He let go and pushed her away. She sat up and rubbed at her wrists. "You're brave to pretend the dogs don't scare you any more," she said at last. "Just keep acting as if you're not afraid until you believe it. Then, when you have them cowed, give them a piece of meat or a bone. You have to make them too fearful of you to harm you, but let them know they'll get a reward if they obey."

The boy was silent.

"Did something happen to make you afraid?" Bortai asked.

"When I was little, Bekter was supposed to be watching me – that's what mother says. I don't remember it myself. Mother found me with a dog on top of me, trying to chew my arm, and Bekter just stood there and laughed. She says Father beat him raw for that." He leaned towards her. "You'd better not tell Anchar I'm still afraid."

"Of course not – I promise." She gazed out at the steppe. More green patches of grass were sprouting; in a month, the land would be alive with blue and white flowers. Her father's horses grazed near one small rise. A man was riding towards the herd from the river; the other children galloped after him, their voices a dim murmur on the cold wind.

75

Anchar left the others and rode towards them. Bortai and Temujin got up and went to their horses.

"A man's here," Anchar shouted as he neared the tree, "from Temujin's camp. Arasen rode out to get Father." He reined in his horse and trotted closer to Temujin. "The man wants to see you."

"Did he say why he's here?" Bortai asked.

"Arasen says his name is Munglik, and that Temujin's father sent him."

Temujin frowned; his greenish eyes were solemn. "He's a Khongkhotat," he said, "one of the men Father trusts most. I'll ride back with your father." He mounted his horse and left them by the tree.

18

TEMUJIN WAS WAITING for Bortai and her brother outside their father's yurt. "Munglik's inside," he murmured. "He hasn't yet said why he came."

Bortai and Anchar left their whips by the doorway and followed Temujin inside. Dei and his guest sat in the back of the tent; her father looked up as Shotan sat down next to him. The children hung up their bowcases and quivers, then walked towards them.

"Our visitor is called Munglik." Dei gestured with his jug of kumiss. "He tells me that his father Charakha has served Yesugei faithfully since the Bahadur was a boy." He turned towards the stranger. "My daughter Bortai and her brother Anchar."

The man nodded at Bortai; his dark eyes were mournful. "My brother the Bahadur chose well. Your daughter will be a beauty, Dei Sechen."

The children settled themselves on the carpet in front of the bed. Munglik took a long drink. His fingers tightened around the leather jug; his knuckles were white.

"Bortai and Temujin are becoming close companions,"

Shotan went on, "although no closer than they should be before they are wed. Anchar's a brother to the boy, but you'll see that for yourself while you stay with us."

"I cannot stay long, Ujin," Munglik replied. His pleasantly broad face was solemn; he had not smiled at all since Bortai had come inside. "I must tell you now why I am here. The Bahadur longs to see his son once more – his heart's ached ever since he left the boy. He misses him so much that he asked me to ride here and bring Temujin back to him."

Bortai shot a glance at Temujin, who seemed as surprised as she. "Friend Munglik," Dei said, "the boy hasn't even been with us for a season. We would all grieve to part with him so soon."

"Then you'll understand how the Bahadur feels at being parted from a son he loves so much. Yesugei remains your khuda, bound to you by the promise of the children's marriage. He asks you only to allow Temujin to return to him for a time."

Temujin's pale eyes were wary as he gazed at Munglik. Something was wrong; Bortai could feel it. Munglik was as tense as a man sensing danger, his face as stiff as a mask.

Dei stroked his thin beard. "If my khuda Yesugei wants his son so much," he said, "then of course I must let him go." Bortai opened her mouth to protest; her voice caught in her throat.

"I don't want to leave," Temujin said in an oddly toneless voice, "but if my father wants me, then I must go to him."

"But the boy will come back," Dei said. "After he's seen his father, Yesugei can be at peace about him. I ask you to let him return as soon as possible."

"Yes," Munglik replied. "As soon as possible."

Bortai did not believe it. Why wouldn't the man say when? Ten days, a month, a year? Soon could mean any of those.

"I'll miss you," Anchar said to the other boy.

"So will I," Bortai said softly. Temujin did not reply.

"Well," Shotan said, "at least we can feed you and give you a place to sleep before you leave."

"I'm grateful," Munglik said, "but I promised the Bahadur that I would leave as soon as I saw his son and spoke to you.

It's still light outside, and we can cover some ground before we sleep."

Bortai's heart sank. She would not even have one last night in Temujin's company.

Dei motioned to her betrothed. "Better collect your things, boy."

"I'll be back," Temujin said as he stood up. "Father will send me here again when I tell him of the kindness you've shown me." He went to the bed where he and Anchar slept, put his few belongings into his pack, then reached for his bowcase and quiver.

Bortai watched numbly as her mother gave Munglik a small pouch of curds, a skin of kumiss, and a piece of meat. "Take this," Shotan said. "If the boy's father misses him so much, then you shouldn't delay."

The men stood up. Temujin went to Anchar and embraced him. "I'm leaving my bones with you," he said. "I'll win them back when I return." Bortai rose unsteadily to her feet as Temujin took her hands. "I'll come back," he said, searching her face, as though worried that she might not believe him. "Promise you'll wait."

She nodded, not trusting herself to speak. He knows something's wrong, she thought; he knows there's more to this than his father missing him.

Temujin turned away. Dei led Munglik and the boy to the doorway and murmured a few words to them before giving Temujin a last embrace. Munglik lifted the flap, and then the two were gone.

I won't cry, Bortai told herself.

Dei paced by the doorway. "Odd," her father murmured at last, "that Yesugei would send for him so soon. I wouldn't have thought he was one who gave in to such feelings so easily, and his comrade Munglik seemed very unhappy about making his request."

"Maybe it's his mother who aches for him," Shotan said, "but when she hears about Bortai, and how well we've treated the boy, she'll rest easier."

"Something's wrong," Bortai burst out. "I just know it, and Temujin did, too — I saw it."

"That may be," Dei said. "I had the same feeling myself, but there's nothing we can do about it. Have some faith in your dream, daughter – some faith in your betrothed."

Bortai bolted towards the door and ran from the yurt.

Bortai found her saddle and reins inside the small tent near the enclosure where Dei's horses were kept. Some children were there, watching the horses. "Temujin's going home," one of the girls called out. "Maybe he doesn't want to marry Bortai now."

"Shut up, Ghoa," Bortai muttered.

"He didn't stay long," Ghoa said. "Maybe – "

Bortai shoved past the children, nearly knocking Ghoa to the ground. The men had finished milking the mares. Bortai whistled for her bay gelding; a man led the horse to her.

She saddled her bay, tightened the girths, then mounted. Temujin and Munglik were already two small figures on the plain, riding at a gallop. The men with the horses grinned at her. "Is this some new kind of courtship," one man said, "a girl riding out to seize her betrothed and drag him back?" The others laughed.

She dug in her heels and set off after Temujin. The wind was picking up; it blew towards her, slowing her pace. She urged the horse on. The distance closed between her and the two riders. Munglik was leaning towards the boy as their horses slowed to a walk and then halted. Temujin suddenly slumped forward in his saddle; the man's hand gripped the boy's shoulder.

Bortai slowed to a trot. "Temujin!" she cried when she was closer to them. The boy looked towards her; she was startled to see tears on his face.

"What are you doing out here, girl?" Munglik shouted. Pale streaks marked his dirty brown face; the man had been crying, too.

"I wanted to say farewell." She reined in her horse.

"Then say it quickly. We have a long ride ahead of us."

Temujin sat up straight and wiped the tears from his face. "I don't want to leave," he said, "but I have to. I felt it even back in your father's tent, that I had to go with Munglik."

"I know." She glanced from him to the man. "You wouldn't be crying just because the Bahadur misses his son."

Munglik said, "I can tell you nothing."

"I knew something was wrong when I saw you. My father did, too. You lied to us."

"He didn't lie," Temujin said. "My father did ask for me."

Munglik motioned with one hand. "Say farewell, Temujin. We must ride on."

"I'll keep on your trail," Bortai said, "until you tell me the truth, so you'd better say it now."

"I'll tell you." Temujin leaned towards her. "But you can't tell anyone else. Your father will learn the truth later, and you have to pretend you don't know it until then. Can you do this?"

"I can for you," she replied.

"Swear it."

"My promise lives here." She put her hand over her heart. "May I be cursed if I forget it."

"Temujin – " Munglik began.

"I have to trust Bortai," the boy said. "If I can't trust her now, what kind of wife will she be later?" He clutched at her wrist. "Munglik came here because my father is dying. Tatars poisoned his food when he stopped at one of their camps – that's what Munglik says. A spear was in front of his tent when Munglik left to fetch me. You see why he couldn't say this to your father."

She swallowed. "You would be safer here. Father would never harm you."

"I can't think of safety now. My mother needs me. I must prepare to lead my people."

Yesugei was dying. She could hardly imagine it when she recalled how alive the man had been, how his songs and laughter had filled her father's dwelling. Temujin might already be the head of his clan.

"You see what this means," Temujin continued. "I don't know when I can return. You may have to wait a long time."

"I promise to wait. I couldn't forget you now, Temujin. I rode here because I wanted you to know that."

"I'll come for you, Bortai — I swear it to you, and if you've been given to someone else, I'll steal you back."

Her eyes stung. "I'll pray for you," she said, "and make an offering to your father's spirit."

"Do it in secret until your father knows about mine. Farewell, Bortai."

"Farewell."

She stared after them as they rode away, then turned back towards her camp. Her parents would expect her to be sad at parting from him, but she would pretend that it was not for long. She would act as if she expected his return soon, and when her father finally learned the truth, she would have to feign surprise. Her only solace was knowing that Temujin trusted her with this burden, and his promise that he would reclaim her.

There was enough distance to the camp left, she realized, for her to weep.

19

HOELUN STUDIED THE shadowed faces of the men sitting in her tent. There was old Baghaji, who had fought with her husband for the Kereit Khan. Charakha was next to Dobon; Targhutai Kiriltugh and Todogen Girte sat to the right of Temujin. She gazed past them at the others, old men who had followed her husband's father and younger ones who had sworn oaths to Yesugei.

"We mourn for your father, young Noyan," Targhutai murmured to her son.

Todogen nodded. "The cursed Tatars wounded us deeply with the evil they did to the Bahadur."

Temujin watched them coldly. Hoelun lifted her head. The two Taychiut brothers were speaking for the others; that worried her.

"The Tatars will regret what they did," Temujin said softly. "You will soon have a chance to avenge my father."

Todogen shifted on his cushion. "We long to do so, but that will be hard without a leader."

"You have one now," Temujin said. "My father often listened to my mother's words. She will lead us until I'm a man, and I'll have the same wise counsel she gave my father."

"Forgive me, Temujin Noyan," Targhutai said, "but a woman and a boy cannot lead us in battle."

"My uncle Daritai can lead his men," the boy said, "and you may command my Taychiut cousins. I'll ride with you to war and learn from you what my father would have taught me."

Todogen glanced at his companions. "It may not be wise to ride against the Tatars this autumn. We're not used to being without your father's leadership, and that gives our enemies an advantage."

"But we would have the advantage of surprise," Temujin said. "They won't expect an army to face them so soon after his passing."

"You'd have all our allies fight them?" Todogen asked.

"This will be war," Temujin answered, "not just a raid."

Hoelun gazed at her son, feeling pride in his steady and commanding tone. He reminded her of his father, yet he had a coldness and calm that her husband had rarely possessed.

"My father will haunt us," the boy continued, "if those who took his life remain unpunished."

"They will be punished, Temujin," Targhutai said, "but surely we're more likely to have our revenge when this wound is not so fresh."

They won't fight, Hoelun thought. She saw what the two Taychiuts were thinking. A victory soon would hearten her husband's followers and make them more willing to accept her leadership. But if they did not fight this year, their doubts about her would grow. Targhutai and Todogen were thinking of their own ambitions.

"My wounds are healing," Hoelun said, "but leaving my husband unavenged will open them again. I won't have his enemies think that they robbed us of all courage, even if I must ride into battle bearing his standard myself."

"Listen to the Bahadur's widow," Charakha said. "Surely we can show as much courage. Will you allow this woman to shame you?" Hoelun turned towards him gratefully; Charakha was still loyal.

Targhutai's eyes narrowed. "Forgive me, Ujin," he said, "but sometimes there's wisdom in caution."

"The Ujin shows more faith in us than we show in ourselves," Charakha shouted. "She sees victory, while you talk of defeat."

A familiar voice suddenly called out from beyond the entrance. "Daritai Odchigin wishes to enter the dwelling of his sister Hoelun."

"You may enter," she said. Her husband's brother and several of his men had arrived last night, but the Odchigin had not yet spoken to her.

Daritai came through the doorway, greeted the other men, then went to her. "I'm filled with sorrow," he said. "The river that once flowed in me is dry. You should have sent for me at once."

Temujin stood up; his uncle embraced him. "My brother's spirit still lives in you," Daritai continued. "I would have entered this camp last night, but didn't want to disturb your sleep, since I was told you had only just returned here yourself."

Hoelun narrowed her eyes. She had not slept well since the funeral. She had been outside to see Todogen and Targhutai ride out to where Daritai was camped with his men, and wondered what the Taychiuts had told him.

Temujin let go of his uncle. "I'm pleased that you're here. We'll need your help in planning our campaign, and I want you at my side tonight when we meet with more of my father's comrades."

"Since the Odchigin is here," Targhutai said, "perhaps you and your son wish to talk with him, Ujin." He stared at Daritai, then looked away.

"You may leave us." Hoelun waved a hand. "Please consider what's been said here until we meet later." The men got up, backed towards the doorway, and went outside.

"I am betrothed now, uncle," Temujin said.

"So I was told." Daritai sat down next to his nephew. "I'm

sorry your happiness was marred by such grief. We must see that you aren't parted from the girl for too long."

"She promised to wait," Temujin said. "I'll claim her when I take my father's place." His voice was steady, betraying no doubt. Hoelun wondered if he realized how uncertain their future was. He was still a child after all, with a child's certainty and faith in those around him.

"Temujin," Hoelun said, "I have much to say to your uncle. Tell Khokakhchin to prepare lamb for the Odchigin."

The boy got up, bowed to Daritai, then left them. "A pity about the betrothal," Daritai said. "I hope he hasn't grown too attached to the girl. Her father may feel that, with my brother gone, he's no longer bound by that promise."

"Temujin hasn't told me much about her, but insists she'll still be his wife."

Daritai shrugged. "How clear and simple things look when one is a boy."

"My son can't be a boy any longer." She rose, took a horn and jug from the wall, handed them to him, and settled herself next to Temulun's cradle.

"I can't believe he's gone." Daritai flicked a few drops of mare's milk from his fingers, whispered a blessing, then drank. "No matter how far I camped from him, or how we argued, or how much time passed between our visits, I always felt his presence." He sighed and bowed his head.

Temulun whimpered; Hoelun rocked the cradle. "My nephew spoke of a campaign." The Odchigin gulped more kumiss. "Surely you know we can't fight one now."

She had expected him to say that, while hoping he would not. "My husband's spirit will guide you."

"We know how he fought, what commands he would give, but we're not used to fighting without him. We'd be at a disadvantage. We'll be able to win a decisive victory later."

Todogen's words, and Targhutai's – so he had already come to an agreement with them. Daritai preferred to plot with the Taychiuts now while hoping for more later. Deeply as he sorrowed over his brother, one obstacle to his own ambitions was gone.

"You're wrong," she said. "If the Tatars suspect we're

84

weaker, they'll attack. Do you want a war carried to our grazing grounds?"

"Retreat is sometimes necessary, Hoelun. Wise as you are, you're still a woman, and you know little about fighting. My brother often made use of retreat to lure the enemy on until another wing of his force could flank them."

"What would you have us do?" Hoelun asked.

"We might move our camps further west. If the Tatars attack, we'd be prepared to meet them, but I suspect they'd see our flight as a sign that we're uncertain. We're better off letting them think that for now. Our scouts can keep track of their movements, but they're likely to decide there's no need to waste men on us, and we'd have a chance to grow stronger before we meet them again. Let them be lulled into thinking they won a victory when they murdered my brother."

"They may just think they can have an easy victory over us now. I can rally the men if you'll help me. We – "

"At the moment, I have enough to do fending off the Merkits north of my lands." Daritai wiped at his moustache. "A war would cost us much, and the Tatars aren't our only enemies. The Merkits also have reasons to wish us ill."

"There's something I haven't said to the men yet." Hoelun paused. "Toghril Khan might ride with us. My husband was his anda – I can send a message to the Kereit Khan and demand that he avenge the death of the man who helped him win back his throne."

Daritai frowned. "No, Hoelun."

"He owes something to me and to his anda's son."

"Oh, he'll mourn, and have his shamans and his Christian priests say prayers for my brother. Gifts from him may wend their way to you. But he wouldn't fight with us when my brother was alive, and now he'll be waiting to see what he can gain. Don't force the issue. Our people will only see you as even more powerless when he refuses you."

No one would stand with her. Daritai had been her last hope. The men might have fought if he had stood with her; Toghril Khan might have listened to a plea from Daritai.

"You disappoint me," she said. "I thought you had your brother's spirit, but you care nothing for us."

"I came here to show my concern for you." He set the horn down. "You're right about one thing. Our people need a battle now. A few well-planned raids against Merkit camps would keep us honed. We should see that those wretches suffer a few wounds before we ride against the Tatars. Temujin must gain more experience in raids before he rides into war."

"I see." Perhaps he had also discussed this with Targhutai and Todogen.

He leaned closer to her; she smelled the sour odour of kumiss on his breath. "My brother," he said, "would expect me to look after you now. I have two wives, but can easily take another. Become my wife, Hoelun."

Her hand tightened on the cradle. She remembered how Daritai had wept over Nekun-taisi's death, and how quickly he had spoken to Yesugei of their obligation to their older brother's widow. Now he wanted to make another brother's wife his own.

"I'm not asking only out of duty," he continued. "You're still much as you were when we found you. It would be a pity to leave you with an empty bed. Your children would have a father, and I could forget a little of my grief if I found some happiness with you."

He would not only be claiming his brother's widow, but also Temujin's legacy. Such a marriage would make it easier for the Odchigin to claim leadership; he could secure his own position while pretending that he was acting for Temujin.

"Sochigil," he went on, "was only his second wife. Taking her under my protection would be enough, and leave me free to devote more of my attention to you."

"No."

His hand fell on her shoulder. "Perhaps I asked too soon, but there's no gain in waiting. I know you still mourn, but – "

Hoelun shook off his hand and slowly got to her feet. There was no sorrow in his dark eyes now, only anticipation of what might be his. His broad, crafty face repelled her; how little there was in him of the man she had lost.

She said, "I won't marry you, Daritai."

"Life can be hard without a man."

"Munglik promised to look after me, and I have my sons. I

need no husband. I couldn't look at you without thinking of your brother." She knew she should fall silent, let him think that only love for Yesugei kept her from accepting him, but was unable to hold back her words. "I couldn't live with you knowing you'll never be the man he was. You want to pretend you are, but it seems all the courage and strength of your father went to my husband and sons, and none to you."

Daritai was very still; a muscle near his mouth twitched. Be wise, Hoelun's inner voice whispered. You may need this man's help sometime; you've already gone too far.

"You should have agreed to stand with me," she said, "and I could have respected you. But I won't tie myself to a man who thinks only of claiming what his brother had."

He jumped to his feet and seized her by the arms, then shook her so hard that her head-dress wobbled. "You'll be sorry, Hoelun."

"Sorry? You've shown me what you are. I've lost nothing."

He pushed her away. She staggered, then righted herself. "You need allies," he said. "You're making a mistake if you think you can lead until Temujin is grown."

"I have no doubts."

He moved towards her; she braced herself for a blow, but his arm fell. "I must try to keep you from harming your own interests," he said. "I owe that much to my brother's widow and his children. When you're past your grief, you'll see who your true friends are."

He gazed at her in silence, then left. Temulun's whimpers rose to a wail. Hoelun knelt by the cradle, loosened the baby's straps, and lifted her to her breast.

She felt her loss keenly as she sat down on the bed to suckle her daughter. Her body shook as she wept. Yesugei would never again stride into this yurt demanding food and drink while his sons clustered around him. He would never look at her with doubtful yet respectful eyes as she offered her advice. He would never pull her down to this bed and move his body against hers.

She looked up as the door flap was lifted; Temujin came inside. Hoelun wiped her face with one arm.

"My uncle shouldn't have spoken that way to you," he muttered.

She closed her garments and laid Temulun on the bed. "It's not right to listen in secret, Temujin."

"A dog was poking at the back of your tent. I chased him away before he could damage the felt. I can't help what I happen to overhear."

"You were never so quick to bother with the dogs before."

"Bortai was teaching me not to fear them." He came to her and sat down, resting his arm against the bed. "You'd like her, Mother. I didn't tell you before, but she rode after Munglik and me, and wouldn't leave us until I told her why I had to go. She swore not to speak of it, and I knew I could trust her promise. She'll be as good a wife to me as you were to Father."

"I was foolish just now, my son. I gave your uncle reasons not to help us."

The boy shook his head. "You spoke the truth about him. Don't be afraid. When I lead, Daritai will follow me, as he followed Father."

His words heartened her, even if they were only those of a trusting child. "Your uncle might be right about one thing," she said. "We may not be ready for a campaign against the Tatars."

"No, Mother. If we fought and lost, you and I would be no worse off, and if we won, there wouldn't be talk of other leaders. It would have been worth the risk for us."

She touched his hand lightly; he did not sound like a child now. "You may get a chance at some fighting against the Merkits."

"And if I went with our men, I'd have to watch my back. Putting me out of the way in the middle of a battle would decide things." He paused. "We can trust few now. Munglik told me about Father's last words, how he said that my brothers and I would have to avenge him." Temujin lifted his head and gazed at her with his father's eyes. "I won't forget those who failed us."

She pulled him to her, wishing that she could restore the childhood he had lost so soon.

20

Hoelun lay in her bed, unable to move. Temulun's wails rose to a shriek.

"Mother." A hand touched her face. Temujin leaned over her, then moved away from the bed. "Khasar," he said, "watch the others. I'll be back soon."

Hoelun closed her eyes. An evil spirit pressed in around her, closing her off from everything outside. She no longer had the strength to fight it. The spirit had hovered near her during the meeting with the men. Now it was inside her, numbing all feeling.

The spirit had spoken to her with Daritai's voice, and Targhutai's. Listen to us, it whispered. Your husband is gone: the beautiful gem lies in shards, the herd is without its stallion and needs another to lead it.

Only Munglik and Charakha had spoken for her before the others silenced them. The men would swear no oath to her and her son. She could not stand against them. Easier to let Daritai seize the leadership of his clan and allow Targhutai and Todogen to lead the Taychiuts. Daritai had left this camp, but it was not too late for her to follow him.

Temulun was screaming. "You see how Mother is," Hoelun heard Temujin say.

"Take your brothers outside and watch the sheep." That was Khokakhchin's voice.

Hoelun lay still. Temulun's cries soon subsided. "Are you awake?" Khokakhchin asked.

She opened her eyes. Khokakhchin held her daughter, feeding her with a skin of sheep's milk. "Temujin came for me," the old woman said, "but perhaps I should have brought a shaman."

"No," Hoelun managed to say.

"Then your affliction isn't so great." Khokakhchin tied Temulun to the cradle, then pulled the covering from Hoelun. "Poor child." The servant held her up and began to dress her in her shirt and long tunic. "How tired you look." She secured Hoelun's braids under her birch head-dress, then bent to help her on with her boots. "The camp will buzz with talk if you keep to yourself. They'll say that Hoelun Ujin shows herself to be as weak as they feared, but that will relieve you of some burdens."

"No," Hoelun said. "I can't shrug off my burdens so easily." The dark fog inside her was lifting; the evil spirit was not so powerful after all.

"I've served you all these years," Khokakhchin said, "and was grateful for a kind mistress. I've never needed to say much to you, but wish to be frank with you now. You've been so concerned with your appeals to the men that you have neglected their wives. What have you shown them since your husband left us? Only a widow lost in grief and thinking of revenge, a woman who might bring them what they fear most — the deaths of husbands and sons in a futile battle, and captivity or worse for them."

Hoelun said, "We could have won that war."

"The men don't think so, and women believe men about such things." The servant paused. "Draw some strength from Etugen, the Earth that renews Herself after Tengri's storms have passed. You have to appeal to the women now, and show them that there's more to fear if we don't stand with you and your son. They must see that you're able to lead, but also that you share their concerns. Women fear the uncertainty that comes when men are without a leader. If they believe you can prevent that, they'll plead your cause to their husbands."

Hoelun lowered her eyes. "You're wiser than I knew."

The old woman shook herself. "Wise? If she lives long enough, even a foolish woman can learn some wisdom. You want power, Hoelun Ujin, yet fail to make use of the power women hold. You didn't have to when your husband was alive, but you must now. I've seen other chiefs die and their followers fight among themselves, I've seen sons of chiefs flee from those who once served their fathers. You must act soon."

The women would need to see determination, but also a mother concerned for all their children. She could not slight their husbands' courage, but had to make them believe she was able to lead the men.

The spring sacrifice to the spirits of the ancestors was approaching. That occasion might be useful to her. When the women gathered for the feast, she could remind them of their obligations to her.

Hoelun took Khokakhchin's hands. "Everything you've said, old woman, I should have seen for myself."

"You're still young, Ujin," Khokakhchin replied. "Young women think of serving their men and then of caring for their sons. They think men will always be their shields."

"Thank you for telling me this, Khokakhchin-eke."

"Ujin, you don't have to call me – "

"Yes. You are Mother Khokakhchin to me now." Another ally, she thought. She had so few.

The two Taychiut Khatuns sat in the back of Orbey's yurt, with cushions propped around them. Sokhatai's face was thinner and her yellow skin sagged below the hollows in her cheeks; weak as she looked, she still clung to life. Orbey's face was pinched and small under her bocca, but her black eyes were alert.

Hoelun bowed. "I greet you, Honoured Ladies."

"Greetings, Hoelun Ujin," Orbey replied. "We're always honoured to have a visit from you – there are so few."

Hoelun sat down in front of the bed and the old woman handed her a horn of kumiss. "Only my grief kept me from seeking your company earlier." She drew up one knee, careful to maintain her polite posture. "I come to you now to speak of our spring sacrifice."

"Perhaps," Orbey Khatun murmured, "you mean to preside over the sacrifice yourself."

"I won't deprive you of that honour. You may ask the shamans to set the day and time, and invite those women who must take part. I wish only to aid you in conducting the rite."

Orbey's mouth worked. "I see. If we make the offering together, the other women would see that we support you."

"Surely you see," Hoelun said, "that since I must lead until my son can take his place, that I must also take precedence among the women. We will chant the prayers together, and serve the meat of the offering to the ancestors together." Be grateful I offer you that much, she thought.

Sokhatai sank back against the cushions; Orbey was silent. "I must lead," Hoelun continued, "if we're ever to punish those

91

who so treacherously betrayed both our husbands. I must have your support if I'm to guide the people here. I wish no evil to come to these mothers and children, as it will if we fall out now."

Orbey leaned forward. "I can't see what we would gain by following you and waiting for Temujin to become a man."

"He'll prove he's worthy to lead – I promise you that. I know what he is."

"Every mother has praise for her sons. I admired mine as much, and now they're gone. Pray that you don't have too long a life, Ujin, or live to lose your sons."

Hoelun got to her feet. "We will make the sacrifice together. I shall await your invitation." She bowed from the waist.

Orbey lowered her head. "The sacrifice will be performed."

Hoelun leaned towards the hearth. Throughout the day, ever since leaving Orbey's yurt, she had sensed a change in the camp. The other women were avoiding her, perhaps wondering what the Khatuns had told her and if the two old dowagers would support her now.

Munglik stretched his hands towards the fire. Except for Temujin, who sat with them, the other children were asleep; Khokakhchin lay under a blanket at the side of Hoelun's bed. The old woman had asked to stay in this tent, and Hoelun felt safer with her there.

"Shall I get you more to drink?" Hoelun asked.

Munglik shook his head. "Keep what you have." He paused. "I'll ride out to hunt tomorrow. I may be gone for several days, and the game I track may take me near Tatar lands."

Hoelun glanced at him sharply. "So you intend to hunt there."

"Not for men – only for their trails. We should find out if they're moving closer to our territory. My father will look out for you while I'm away."

"Will others ride with you?" she asked.

"I'll go alone. Someone has to do some scouting. Others are too ready to forget our enemies now." He chewed on the ends of his moustache. "Hoelun, I promised to watch over you. Maybe you should appeal to Targhutai to lead now."

She sighed. "So even you have been listening to him."

"I'm thinking of you. The men would swear an oath to him. Let him have what he wants, with the understanding that Temujin will lead us later."

"They won't let me live long enough to lead," Temujin said.

"My son is right," Hoelun said. "If I give in now, Targhutai will see weakness. My only chance is to win others to my side, and force him to stand with them."

"I must support you, whatever you do." The young man stood up. "And now I must go, before my wife grows impatient with me."

Temujin stared at the doorway after the Khongkhotat was gone. "Munglik calls himself our friend," he said, "but I wonder how long he'll remain one."

"He loved your father."

"I know, but Father's gone, and Munglik must think of his people. Maybe he thinks his clan would be better off with a Taychiut chief."

"Please," she whispered. "Let's not doubt one of the few friends we have left."

"Maybe Father should have done more to secure the loyalty of his men. I must see that I don't make the same mistake."

Hoelun stood up and began to feed the fire. Munglik might find that the Tatars had moved closer to their lands. That danger would serve her at the moment; Targhutai and Todogen would have more to worry about than their petty ambitions. She almost hoped for war.

21

HOELUN SAID, "YOU can't go on this way." Sochigil sat by the hearth. Belgutei had come to Hoelun's yurt in the middle of the night, worried about his mother, muttering about bringing a shaman to lift the spell. Hoelun had told the other widow of her own fears, the despair she had felt and conquered, but Sochigil refused to respond.

"You aren't eating," Hoelun continued. "You're growing too thin."

"No food can fill the emptiness inside me." Sochigil covered her face. "No one can comfort me."

"Mother hasn't been sleeping well, either," Belgutei murmured from his side of the tent. Sochigil's sons sat on their beds, arms wrapped around their legs. "I thought it would pass, but – "

"The others avoid my tent as if I were dying," Sochigil said. "I almost wish I could."

"Stop it." Hoelun reached for Sochigil's hand. "You'll summon death if you talk that way."

"People avoid you, too, Hoelun-eke," Bekter said. "They whisper about you and keep secrets from you."

Hoelun frowned at him. Bekter had his mother's dark eyes and his father's strong-boned face, but his usual sly, resentful expression distorted his features.

"Listen to me," Hoelun said. "These people are uncertain. We have to show them that – " She heard a bark; the camp's dogs were howling more than usual. It was still dark outside, but it seemed that others were also awake. Horses neighed; the camp was as noisy as it usually was at dawn.

Suddenly afraid, she got up and hurried to the doorway, then ran outside. Beyond the back of Sochigil's tent, a procession of women, some in carts and others on horseback, moved across the moonlit plain.

Hoelun sagged against a wagon. The sacrifice, she thought. The Khatuns must have hidden this from her and anyone who was likely to tell her; the old women and the shamans had allied themselves against her.

She circled the yurt slowly. They would expect her to back down, perhaps to turn to Daritai, and he would swear an oath to Targhutai before he offered one to Hoelun's son.

Sochigil looked up as Hoelun went inside. "They've gone to make the sacrifice without us," Hoelun said.

The other woman gaped at her. Bekter jumped to his feet.

"What now, Hoelun-eke?" he asked. "This is what you get for not listening to them."

Hoelun slapped him hard; the boy stumbled back. "They'll regret this," she whispered.

"What can we do?" Sochigil wailed.

"Stay inside with your sons today. I'll settle this." Hoelun spun around and hurried through the entrance.

The sun was up by the time Hoelun went to the horses. The men there ignored her as she saddled one of her husband's grey geldings. She knew what the men were thinking; she had been marked as an outcast. She had warned her children not to leave her camping circle, to be on guard.

She rode west, following the women's trail. Amid the grass, the blue and white flowers of spring bloomed. She trembled with rage. Did Orbey and Sokhatai think they could exclude her from her rightful place? She thought of how they must have whispered to the other women, warning them to keep silent about the plans for this ceremony.

She lashed at her horse as it sped into a gallop. The women had gone only a short distance from the camp. On the horizon, to the south of a hill where an obo stood, a thin stream of smoke rose from a large yurt. An empty black pit scarred the ground near the tent; small bowls of food sat on the hillside near the obo's piles of stones. The sheep had already been sacrificed, then; the women would be feasting inside.

Hoelun tethered her horse near one of the carts. They had raised the tent and chanted their prayers without her. She walked swiftly to the entrance and threw back the flap.

The women inside fell silent. They sat in a circle; the two Khatuns were at the back, facing the entrance. The wives of the most important men were present, and Targhutai's wife sat at Orbey's left. Blackened bones lay in front of the Khatuns; a cracked shoulder-bone burned in the hearth.

Orbey Khatun lifted her head. "Your presence is not required, Hoelun Ujin," the old woman said. "The sacrifice was made at dawn, as the shamans told us it must be. Tengri and Etugen have heard our prayers. The bones have been burned, and the ancestors have had their offering."

Hoelun circled the group until she was near Orbey. The platters were nearly empty, and the shreds of meat on the nearest platter were bloody; they had begun the ceremonial meal when the food was barely cooked.

"I see what you're saying," Hoelun muttered. "My husband's dead and my sons are still boys, so you can bar me from my place. You think you can divide the meat and leave nothing for me." She sat down, elbowed Targhutai's wife aside, and grabbed a piece of meat.

Sokhatai's eyes were slits; Orbey leaned forward. "Hoelun Ujin doesn't wait to be offered our food," Orbey said. "She just takes it for herself. That's her custom – to come uninvited and to take whatever she likes."

"I'll take what's mine," Hoelun responded.

"Nothing here is yours. We made the sacrifice – we invite whom we choose. You think, because our husband Ambaghai Khan is dead, that you can insult his widows and grab what you want."

Hoelun chewed her meat and forced herself to swallow. She could not bring herself to look at the other women, knowing what she would see – indifference, fear of the Khatuns, resentment of the young widow who sought to lead these clans. The two old women had probably filled their ears with talk of how she would only bring disaster upon them if they supported her.

"I've had a share of the sacrifice in spite of you," Hoelun said slowly. "I say this now – I shall make the next sacrifice. You, Honoured Khatuns, will get only what scraps I choose to give you."

"Be silent!" Orbey shook a fist. "Yesugei the Brave is dead!" Hoelun caught her breath, shocked at hearing his name spoken aloud so soon after his death. "Did he destroy our enemies while he was alive?" Orbey continued. "Why does his widow believe she can lead, with only a boy who isn't yet a man?" The Khatun settled back on her cushion. "The men swore only to follow Yesugei, and he is gone. You have no place now, Hoelun. The spirits have abandoned you. You are only a widow who claims what doesn't belong to her."

"And you are only an old woman who will soon lie in her grave." Hoelun smiled as Orbey recoiled. "You've never thought of your people, only of what you lost and what you might have again through your grandsons. My husband might have been Khan but for you and your poisonous words against him. My son will be a Khan when you lie under the ground."

"Tell her!" Sokhatai whispered to the other Khatun. Orbey looked around at the circle of women, then turned back to Hoelun.

"I will say this now," Orbey said. "I summoned the shamans, and they set the time for this sacrifice. But I had another question to ask them. They burned the bones and read the cracks, and Bughu gave us the answer. The spirits have turned from you – that's what the bones told him. The spirits led Yesugei to his death, and you would only lead us to where he dwells now."

Hoelun shook with rage. The shaman had betrayed her. Bughu had seen how uncertain her place was, and how little he could gain from supporting her.

Orbey showed her teeth. "You should have surrendered your place for a humbler one while you still had the chance," the old woman went on. "You'll have nothing now." She gestured with one clawed hand. "Get this woman out of my sight."

Hands grabbed at Hoelun and pulled her to her feet. Women surrounded her, kicking her legs and clawing at her head-dress. She struck at them as she stumbled towards the doorway. Someone shoved her outside; she toppled forward and clutched at the grass.

A foot caught her in the side. She gritted her teeth, then got to her knees. Eyes watched her from the entrance as she stood up and walked towards her horse.

22

HOELUN KEPT TO her yurt. Temujin and Khasar settled their sheep, then came inside. There was just enough fuel to keep her fire going, but Hoelun refused to let Khokakhchin collect more.

When they finally went to their beds, she was unable to sleep. Rage and fear made her shake uncontrollably; her face grew hot, while her hands were like ice. Who would speak for her now? The men would know about the sacrifice, her exclusion, and what the bones had said.

Hoelun dozed, then woke to the sound of voices. The sky was still dark above the smoke-hole. She listened to the sounds of voices, barking dogs, and running feet.

She got up quickly and pulled on her clothes. Temujin slipped from his bed and went to the entrance, followed by Khasar. Khachigun sat on his bed with an arm around Temuge; Khokakhchin stirred at the foot of Hoelun's bed.

The voices outside were louder. Targhutai and another man suddenly burst through the entrance, shoved Hoelun aside, went to her bed, and dragged Khokakhchin to her feet.

"Leave me be!" the old woman cried. The other man forced her towards the doorway.

Hoelun stepped in front of them. "What do you want with this woman?"

"We're breaking camp," the man replied, "and leaving you behind. You'll have to get along without her."

Khokakhchin tried to pull away. "I won't leave the Ujin!"

"Then you'll die here."

"No!" Hoelun caught the man's arm. "You must go," she said to the old woman. "Look after yourself now, Eke, and stay alive until we meet again."

Khokakhchin covered her face; the man pushed her through the doorway. "You can't do this," Hoelun said to Targhutai. "Is this how you repay the family of the man who led you?"

"Your husband is dead." The Taychiut's lip curled. "I'll lead these people now."

"Orbey Khatun urged you to this," Hoelun muttered. "You won't follow a woman and a boy, yet you allow your spiteful old grandmother to tell you what to do."

His fist caught her on the side of the head; she fell, and when Temujin hurled himself at Targhutai, the man knocked him aside. "Don't leave this yurt," the chieftain said. "I won't stain my hands with your blood, but can't answer for what others might do." He went outside.

Hoelun's head throbbed. Temujin sat with her, holding her in his arms. At last she climbed to her feet and let him lead her to her bed.

She sat down and took off her head-dress. The sound of creaking wagon wheels and bellowing oxen filled the camp; the ground shook from the movement of animals and carts. Dust drifted under the door flap. The women would have their yurts down and their possessions loaded into the wagons before the sun was high.

A small hand touched her sleeve. "What will happen to us?" Khasar asked.

"I don't know."

"We'll stay alive," Temujin said softly.

Temulun was crying; Hoelun untied the baby's bonds, lifted her from the cradle, suckled her, then rocked her in her arms. Khasar sat with his two younger brothers while Temujin paced by the hearth.

Perhaps she would not have been able to lead. Old Khokakh-chin had offered her advice too late; Hoelun should have been following it years ago. She had trusted in the oaths sworn to her husband, forgetting how tenuous the bonds among these people were.

Temujin sat down by the doorway. She saw no fear in him, no despair over what might become of them. Then Temulun stirred in her arms and she thought of her daughter's helplessness, of all that lay ahead.

They waited in silence for a long time until the more muted sounds outside told Hoelun that the camp was nearly empty. Sochigil might have been forced to leave with the others; she would be no threat to Targhutai's ambitions.

Temujin said, "I think they're gone."

"Don't go out." Hoelun tied her daughter to the cradle, then stood up; her head still hurt where Targhutai had struck her. "Some may have stayed with us. I'll see."

She covered her head with a scarf, moved to the entrance, and lifted the flap. Someone had pulled her husband's standard out of the ground; the tugh lay in front of the doorway. The ground was scarred by the ruts of wheels and the flat, bare spaces where the other tents had been. To the south, where some of the Khongkhotats had camped near her husband's circle, one lone yurt still stood.

She crept outside and looked around. Rows of carts, lashed together, were moving north-west away from the river, following the herds and the riders leading the animals. Nine grey geldings grazed near the Onon, and a few sheep huddled near a wagon. The Taychiut chiefs could tell themselves that they had not entirely forgotten their duty, that the almost inevitable deaths of this family were no concern of theirs; they had left a few animals behind. They could always say that Hoelun had refused to follow them.

Sochigil's yurt still stood near her own. A black dog by the entrance slinked away as Hoelun approached. Belgutei suddenly poked his head outside.

"Is your mother here?" she asked him.

Belgutei nodded. Hoelun entered the dwelling. The hearth fire had gone out; Sochigil sat in the shadows just beyond the beam of light shining through the smoke-hole.

"Sochigil." Hoelun touched the other woman's shoulder; Sochigil did not move.

Bekter crept towards them. "We're lost," he said.

Hoelun said, "We're still alive."

He stepped closer to her. "This is your fault, yours and Temujin's."

She slapped him. The boy stumbled back, covering his reddened cheek with one hand. "I won't hear such talk from you, Bekter." He glared at her, his eyes wild with hatred. "Remember the tale of Alan Ghoa and her sons — the only chance we have is to remain together." Bekter looked away. "We'll survive, and you and Temujin will have your revenge on those who abandoned us — save your hatred for them."

She motioned to Belgutei. "A few sheep were left," she said to the younger boy. "Keep them from straying." He scurried from the tent. "Bekter, get your weapons and follow me." She led him outside. "Guard the horses, and warn me if you see anyone riding here."

Bekter hurried towards the horses. Temujin had left her tent; he bent to pick up his father's standard. "Come with me," she called out to him.

Temujin stuck the standard into the ground, then followed her towards the Khongkhotat yurt. No wagons were by the tent. Hoelun made her way past ruts and clumps of drying dung.

"It's Charakha's tent," Temujin said when they were closer.

"Yes." As they neared the yurt, she heard a moan. She hurried around the dwelling, Temujin at her side.

A man lay face down by the doorway, his back covered with blood. "Charakha," she whispered, and knelt; the old man was still breathing. "Help me carry him." Temujin grabbed Charakha's legs as she lifted him under his arms.

They carried him inside; the tent had been looted. The old man groaned as they laid him on his bed. "Who did this?" Temujin asked.

"Todogen." Charakha gasped for breath. "When he was forcing our people to leave, I went to him to protest. He said I had no right to stop him. When I turned away, he drove his spear into my back."

Hoelun's nails bit into her palms. Temujin knelt by the bed; his shoulders shook as tears rolled down his cheeks. "You were always faithful," the boy murmured.

"I don't forget my duty." The old man's voice was feeble. "Munglik's wife and my grandson are gone. She didn't protest, but doing so wouldn't have helped her. My son – " He clenched his hands. "At least he didn't have to witness this."

Temujin said, "I'll stay with you."

"You mustn't, boy. I'm dying."

"I'll stay with you as long as I can. I'm your chief now – I must." Temujin threw his arms over Charakha and buried his face in the man's coat.

Hoelun stumbled outside. The tails of her husband's standard fluttered in the distance. She ran towards the tugh, knowing what she had to do.

The grey gelding's hooves pounded beneath her. Dust stung Hoelun's eyes and made her gasp for breath. Through clouds of dirt, she glimpsed the rows of carts following the dark mass of cattle and the paler one of the sheep. She tightened her legs around the horse, holding the reins with one hand as she hoisted her husband's standard with the other.

She was soon abreast of the slow-moving procession. Several women stood up in their wagons; a few of the men riding alongside the carts twisted towards her in their saddles.

"How quickly you forget your oaths!" Hoelun shouted. "You swore to serve my husband, and now you desert his widows and sons!" She held the standard high. "Turn back! Abandon those who have betrayed me!" She swept past the lumbering cattle and caught up with the horse herd, then looked back. One line of wagons had halted; her hopes rose.

She galloped on until she was near the men leading the procession. Lances dipped towards her, and the tails of the Taychiut standards danced in the wind. A small hill lay ahead of her; the wind, blowing to the south, would carry her words to these people. She rode up the hill and reined in her mount.

"Stop!" she cried. "Will you leave mothers and children to die? Will you forget the oaths you swore to my husband?" She rose in her stirrups, holding the tugh high. "Is this how you reward him for the victories he won? Can you turn away from the spirit that lives in this tugh? Will you forget the son who could bring you more victories?"

A line of carts was moving out from the others. Hoelun saw Targhutai then, riding next to the man who held the Taychiut chief's standard. Targhutai looked back at the carts, then signalled with one arm. The men around him fanned out and rode back along either side of the procession.

"Heed my words!" Hoelun shouted. "This is the tugh you swore to follow!" Targhutai's men were surrounding the carts, lashing at the people in them and forcing them back. Two riders tried to break away; more Taychiuts blocked them. Some wanted to stay with her, but they would not be allowed to remain behind.

Hoelun shook her standard as the people moved on. "Remember me when your chieftains lead you to ruin!" she cried hoarsely. "Remember me when those you love lie dead at the hands of your enemies! Remember me when my sons punish you for what you've done today! It was my husband who brought you together and my son who would have kept you united! You betrayed me today – you'll betray one another tomorrow!"

The procession continued past her; the people, wagons, cattle, sheep, and horses were soon indistinct shadows in the drifting dust. She waited on the hill until they were only a distant cloud on the horizon.

23

HOELUN AND HER two oldest sons buried Charakha next to his yurt, digging his grave with long sticks and sharp stones. Belgutei joined them as they laid the old man in the small pit; Hoelun whispered a farewell.

"Cover the grave." She turned to Sochigil's son. "Is your mother still in her tent?"

Belgutei nodded. "I looked after I asked Khachigun to watch the sheep. She hasn't moved, and she won't speak."

Hoelun left the grave, walked between the two fires she had set beyond it earlier, and went back to her own dwelling. Temulun was shrieking the piercing cry that meant she was hungry; Temuge sat next to the cradle, poking listlessly at a piece of felt. Hoelun picked up her daughter, opened her garments, and thrust a nipple into the child's mouth.

Khachigun came through the doorway as she finished suckling his sister. "Will we be all right?" he asked.

"Yes. Your father didn't sire cowards. You're both brave boys, and I know you won't disappoint me." She set Temulun's cradle down. "Temuge, watch your sister. Khachigun, get back to the sheep." She picked up her head-dress, secured it on her head, then went to Sochigil's tent.

The woman was sitting by her hearth. "Look at you," Hoelun said, "letting your fire go out and giving no comfort to your sons."

Sochigil swayed. "They should have killed us," she said. "That would have been kinder than this."

"If you don't find more spirit than that," Hoelun said, "I'll drive you from this camp myself. If you're so willing to die, I can make it easier for you to do so." She paused. "You've grieved enough. We must think of our children now."

"We can't live alone."

"We have a few sheep and our horses. The Onon will give us water and fish. We'll live on rats if we must, but we will live." She hauled the other woman to her feet; Sochigil gazed at her passively. "You're going to gather all the dry dung you can find before dark, while I go down to the river to search the bushes for berries. We're lucky they deserted us in this season – we'll have time to prepare for winter."

If they could survive the summer, if no raiders came to steal what little they had left, they might find enough game by the autumn to live through the harsh winter. If they grew desperate, their animals could provide meat, although she did not want to resort to that, since they would be more useful alive. Ducks were returning to the river, and she could dig for roots. There was even a chance that some of the deserters would slip away to join her, but she would not hope too much for that. If would be easier for them to forget her, and to assume eventually that death had claimed her children.

She would not think too far ahead, but only of each day. She handed Sochigil a basket, then led her outside.

Temujin took the long stick from Hoelun. A thread made of tendons, with a bent sliver of bone tied to the end, dangled from the makeshift fishing rod.

"Catch what fish you can," Hoelun said. "Even the small ones will feed us." Bekter moved closer to the bank with the rod she had made for him. "We'll share the catch equally," she continued. "There will be no arguments about who caught more fish and deserves more to eat."

Bekter gazed at her sullenly. She picked up her juniper stick and walked along the bank towards a small grove of slender willows. Clumps of green sprouted next to the roots of the trees. Hoelun glanced towards the grassy spot where Belgutei and

Khasar were grazing the horses. Sochigil was sitting outside her yurt with the smaller children. Khachigun spent much of his time watching their few sheep; even young Temuge, who had the task of tending the fires, was more useful than Sochigil, who did little except rock Temulun's cradle and croon to her.

The morning sun had burned off the pale mists near the river. The Onon was narrow and shallow here, widening as it flowed on to where Temujin and Bekter were fishing. Hoelun looked up at the cloudless sky. The day would grow warm, but she did not think a storm would come. She recalled another warm day and the place further up the river where she had first seen Yesugei.

She was about to dig up a root when she saw a rider far to the east. She backed slowly towards the trees, set her stick down, pulled her bow from its case, then glanced down the river. The man might pass them by, but Temujin and Bekter were crouched behind a shrub, their arrows ready.

She waited until the man was closer, then drew out an arrow and took aim. The rider's horse broke into a gallop. Before he came within range, she had seen who he was, and lowered her bow.

"Munglik," she called out, then ran down to the bank. He rode through the shallow water, leaped from his horse, and caught her in his arms.

"Hoelun," he murmured. She rested her head against his chest, unable to speak. "What happened here?"

"They abandoned us," she managed to say. "They left us a few days ago." She drew away from him. "Orbey Khatun offered the spring sacrifice without inviting me. We didn't have long to wait. All of them broke camp the next day." She swallowed. "Prepare yourself, Munglik. Your father tried to stop them. Todogen Girte rewarded him for that by putting a spear in his back. We buried him five days ago."

She sank to the ground. Munglik was silent for a long time. "Todogen will pay for that." He sat down next to her and took her hand. "My wife and son – "

"They left with the others. They had no choice. Even Khokakhchin was dragged from my tent."

"Listen." He gripped her hand more tightly. "I can go to Toghril Khan."

She shook her head; she had already dismissed that possibility. "The Kereit Khan has nothing to gain by aiding helpless widows and children. He may think it wiser to keep the Taychiut chiefs as allies – my husband always said Toghril Khan was a practical man." She slipped her hand from Munglik's. "Even if he took us in, my sons would be hostages. He'd offer them to Targhutai if he had something to gain."

"But there's little hope for you if you have no one to protect you."

Hoelun turned towards him. "I refuse to believe that. Targhutai and Todogen might have killed us outright, but Tengri stayed their hands. They must still fear my husband's spirit."

"But your sons – "

" – will have to be even braver than their father." She drew up her legs and rested her hands on her knees. "I know Temujin," she said softly. "He wouldn't last long either as a hostage of the Kereit Khan or among his father's old followers. My son would demand his rightful place, and then they'd have to kill him. If he dies abandoned, his death won't come any sooner than it would have among them. But I intend to keep him alive."

"You're a stubborn woman, Hoelun. I would have expected despair."

"Sochigil does enough weeping for both of us."

"When Daritai hears of this – "

"He'll do nothing for us." Perhaps she would have spoken more kindly to the Odchigin if she had known what was to come. "We were left alive, so he doesn't have to avenge us. Targhutai must have considered that when he showed us mercy. Daritai will think of himself now."

Munglik took her hand again. "I can't leave you here. I promised the Bahadur to look after you."

"I won't ask you to keep that promise," she said. "You must think of your own son and the child on the way." She glanced at him briefly before lowering her eyes. His face was still filled with sympathy and concern, but she had seen relief as well. Munglik had made the offer that honour demanded and could hardly blame himself for leaving when she had told him to go.

Munglik cleared his throat. "I must go to my wife, of course. Other Khongkhotats may choose to travel to our old grazing grounds, and Targhutai would be willing to let us leave if he knows we'll remain allies."

Hoelun lifted her head. "You'd swear an oath to the brother of your father's murderer?"

"Todogen will be punished for that, but this isn't the time. I can't serve you or my own people if I make my wife a widow. I'll find a way to strike at Todogen Girte later."

How practical Munglik was. Hoelun released his hand and stood up, leaning against her stick. "I'll always remember," she said, "that your father gave his life for us."

She moved towards the trees. Munglik was suddenly at her side. "I haven't said all I wanted to say," he whispered. "Marry me, Hoelun. I've always cared for you. Wait here, and I'll come back for you when I know my wife's safe. You can live among my people if I take you as my wife."

How soothing he sounded. The Taychiuts would be relieved to know that Munglik sought no vengeance for his father's death. They would be even more pleased to see her reduced to being the second wife of her husband's old retainer, and Temujin would not be safe among the Khongkhotats unless he gave up his claims.

"No, Munglik," she said. "Perhaps I could be content with you, but my husband's memory is still too fresh."

He took her by the arms. "He wouldn't want you to struggle on alone, living this way."

"Were our lives ever easy?"

"When I come back for you – maybe then – "

"I won't change my mind."

His breath was warm on her face. She remembered how Yesugei had held her, how his strong hands could grow gentle. Munglik's arm slipped around her waist. She could pretend she was in her husband's arms once more and forget her duty to his heir.

"I love you," Munglik said. "I always have."

But not enough, she thought, then freed herself from his grip. "I will come back," he continued.

She would have to leave this place before he returned, and find shelter near the mountains to the west, where they could hide from their enemies. If the Taychiut chiefs believed them dead, they would be safe.

"You never told me," she said, "what you found out."

"The Tatars are keeping to their usual trails. We needn't worry about them this season." He bowed his head. "I must visit my father's grave."

"Temujin will show it to you."

"I'll hunt some game for you before I go. Khasar may come with me – his aim was always good. I'll come back as soon as I can."

He went to his horse and led it towards the place where Temujin and Bekter were fishing. Hoelun stared at the ground, spied some leaves, and dug for the root underneath.

24

BORTAI SHOUTED A farewell to the Olkhunugud girls, then raced past a row of wagons. Fifty Olkhunuguds had arrived at her father's camp; they would feast tonight before they all broke camp and moved south to join other clans for the autumn hunt.

She hastened towards her father's yurt. Maybe Temujin would return after the hunt. Whenever her people were on the move, she imagined looking out from the wagon to see him following their trail.

Her parents did not yet know the truth about her betrothed's sudden departure. She had kept her secret while praying for a miracle – that Temujin might have gone home to find his father alive and healing. Her wish now seemed more real to her than Temujin's sad parting words and the mournful, resigned face of his companion Munglik.

The odours of burning fires and roasting mutton made her smile. She was suddenly ashamed of feeling happy in the absence of any news about Temujin. Surely he would come back before winter; she would tell him that she had kept his secret, and he would tell her that his father was well. They would both laugh together at the tears they had shed.

Her father's dogs bounded towards her. She made a face at them, then entered his yurt. Her parents were sitting on their bed; Shotan's head rested on her husband's shoulder. Bortai was surprised to see Dei here instead of out drinking and talking with the other men.

Dei looked up; his face was solemn. "Come here, Bortai," he said. "I have unhappy tidings."

Shotan stood up, patted Bortai's cheek, then went to the hearth. Bortai sat down at her father's feet. "What is it?" she asked.

"An Olkhunugud told me the tale," Dei replied. "He married a daughter to a Taychiut Mongol not long ago." He pulled at his thin beard. "He told me that my khuda — that the father of your betrothed no longer lives."

Tears rose to her eyes and trickled down her cheeks; she would not have to feign surprise or grief after all.

"They say he was poisoned by Tatars on his way home," Dei continued. "I'm surprised we didn't have word of this before, given that our lands lie so close to those of the Tatars, but perhaps they didn't want to brag about such an evil act. The Bahadur was buried this past spring."

Bortai could not speak.

"How his wife must have wept," Shotan muttered, "to lose her husband so soon." She wiped at her eyes. "How cruel for the children he left behind — what will become of them now?"

Bortai tugged at her father's sleeve. "Temujin," she said. "What about Temujin?" She peered into Dei's sad brown eyes. "His mother will lead his people now, won't she?"

"I see now why his father's friend came here," Dei said, "and why he didn't tell me the truth, but he only took the lad back to great hardship. It seems Temujin's mother insisted on her place, even after the men refused to swear an oath to her son. The Bahadur's followers abandoned his family. No one knows what's become of them."

Bortai tensed; it could not be true. "They must be alive," she insisted. "Temujin wouldn't give up. He told me his mother was strong — she wouldn't give up, either."

"Even the bravest woman would find it hard to struggle on alone, with no protector and with sons so young. Face it, child — he may already have joined his father."

"No!" she cried, and held on to her father's coat. "Someone will help him." She took a breath. "We can help his family. You could bring them here. We're betrothed — you have a duty to him."

"I have a duty to my people." He shook off her small hands, then grabbed her by the shoulders. "Listen to me, Bortai. We might spend a season searching for them, and consider this — they have enemies who left them to die. Do you want those who abandoned them riding to our camp to finish the job?"

"I don't care!"

He released her. "Be sensible, daughter. Temujin might not be any safer here than wherever he is now, and I must think of what's best for us, however much it pains me. If he survives, I'll rejoice, but you mustn't raise your hopes too high."

"You're young," Shotan said from the hearth. "A girl can think her sorrows will never pass, but they do. I was sorry Temujin had to leave us so soon, but maybe it's a mercy you didn't have more time to form an attachment to him."

"Dry your eyes and help your mother," Dei said. "We'll pray for the Bahadur's soul and for those he left behind, but we must go on with our other obligations."

Bortai stood up slowly. "I won't forget." Her voice was steady. "I made a promise, and I'll keep it."

"The man to whom we made that promise is dead."

"I made a promise of my own, to Temujin." Her dream had foretold his arrival; how could she forget that? She thought of the hard look in his eyes when he promised he would find her again; there had been no doubt in his face. She could not bear the thought of disappointing him. If she ever failed him —

Bortai shivered, and realized then that she, who had never been afraid of anything, feared the boy she loved.

"I won't forget him, ever," she went on. "No matter what you say, I know he'll come back." Dei drew away from her. For a moment, she felt as hard and unrelenting as Temujin would expect her to be, then threw herself against her father and sobbed.

PART THREE

Temujin said, "I shall never forgive those who abandoned us, or forget those who helped us. That promise lives in my heart."

25

THE YOUNG SHAMAN sat by the hearth, staring into the glow of the fire. For a moment, Jamukha thought that the holy man was in a trance, his soul wandering elsewhere.

"You slept late, boy," the shaman said. "Were the efforts of the night too much for you?"

Jamukha sat up on the hide and said, "I drank too much. Perhaps you used a spell."

"You aren't new to such joinings." The young man leered as he looked at Jamukha. "I needed no spell."

Jamukha got up and dressed, suddenly wanting to get as far from this man as possible. The shaman saw too easily into his soul; he had probably sensed what Jamukha wanted the moment he had asked the man for shelter from the snowstorm. He had not been that drunk when the shaman began to fondle him, and had heard no chanting of spells before finding himself between the two hides. The wind had howled outside the tiny tent, drowning out Jamukha's cries as the pain he felt became the pleasure he sought.

The shaman did not know his name and Jamukha knew nothing about him. He might have left his camp to test himself in solitude or to send his soul wandering with spirits. Except for a bag of herbs and some provisions, the young man had little with him, and Jamukha had not examined his weapons to see if they bore the marks of any clans he knew.

"Stay if you like," the shaman said.

111

Jamukha picked up his bowcase and quiver, then went outside. The tent stood among birches on a southern slope, sheltered from the north wind; the shaman's white horses, their legs hobbled to stakes, sniffed at the snow.

Jamukha's own brown gelding was tied to a tree. He mounted his horse and rode down the slope into the valley below, wincing as he settled into his saddle. He had not bled too much this time, but remembered the man's hot breath on his ear and the bruising, almost painful caresses of his callused hands.

Jamukha welcomed that violence, the pain of the joining, the whirlpool of anger, rage, and desire that swallowed him. He felt purged afterwards, his fears and needs washed away by the dark flood. It had not always been that way, not the first time with another man out on the steppe, when the tearing of his flesh, his helplessness, and the man's power over him had made him feel violated. The pleasure had come later.

Now, he allowed this to happen, in spite of what he had said to the shaman. He endured the pain for the sake of the pleasure, taking pride in the strength that allowed him to bear it. When he became a man, he would no longer submit; he would inflict the pain himself and take only the pleasure.

Jamukha pulled his hat lower over his eyes and squinted at the whiteness of the new snow. The world was cloaked in white, the colour of purity and of luck. He sniffed at the clear air. The clean, pure feeling was already fading; the urges of his body would return before long. He thought of a boy back in his camp who often trailed after him, one he might use as the shaman had used him, one who might restore the feeling of purity and strength.

Jamukha rode south-west, towards the headwaters of the Onon. The valley lay between two ridges of mountains; high above him, the bare boughs of larches and the green limbs of pines were bowed under heaps of snow. More larches and a few pale birches covered the foothills; he kept near the trees. Occasionally, the wind rose and hid the landscape behind a veil of swirling flakes, forcing him to wait before he rode on.

He soon came to flatter ground. The Kentei range lay to the south; the massif was a distant dark ridge jutting up from the pale land. The shaman had mentioned seeing horse tracks and signs of people near the frozen river.

A gust of icy flakes blinded him for a moment. When the wind died, he saw two riders galloping east on grey horses across the flat land near the Onon. One figure lifted his bow; an arrow streaked towards a small long-eared shape darting across the snow.

Jamukha rode on slowly until he had a better view of the two hunters; they were only boys. The boy who had made the kill swung a leg over his saddle and slid to the ground. The other boy suddenly rode towards the one on foot, swung his spear at his head, knocked his companion to the ground, then leaned down from his saddle to grab the carcass. The boy who had fallen got to his feet; the other struck him again with the spear.

Jamukha urged his horse into a gallop. The mounted boy circled the other, stabbing at him with his spear. The boy on foot grabbed the shaft and yanked the rider from his horse. The two grappled for the weapon as they rolled in the snow.

"Stop!" Jamukha shouted as he approached. "Let him have his kill!" Both boys were still; then the taller boy seized his spear and ran for his horse. The other struggled to stand; his hat had fallen from his head, and there was a bloody spot near his temple.

"Are you hurt?" Jamukha called out.

The boy shook his head, then fell to his knees. His companion was riding hard towards the woods near the Kentei foothills. Jamukha trotted towards the remaining grey horse, reached for its reins, and led the gelding back to its owner.

"I can still catch him," Jamukha said, "and steal back your game."

The boy stumbled to his feet. "Don't bother. I'll get even with him another time." He lifted his head; his eyes were large and pale, greenish-brown with flecks of gold. "He's a coward and a bully," the boy continued as Jamukha handed him his reins. "That's the way he is — sneaking up from behind and stealing. This isn't the first time he's done it."

"It's good I was riding this way, then. He seemed ready to kill you. Well, you're rid of him now."

The pale-eyed boy picked up some snow, wiped the blood from his face, then leaned against his horse. "But Bekter won't leave me alone," he said, "and I'll have to put up with him. He's my brother — my half-brother. He'll go too far someday." The boy picked up his cap, donned it, then mounted his horse. "I'm grateful you came past."

"But I see you really didn't need my help. You would have got the better of him if I hadn't come along." Jamukha paused. "My name is Jamukha, and I am the son of the Jajirat chief Kara Khadahan."

"Then you are descended from the son of the woman captured by my ancestor Bodonchar." The boy fell silent; his eyes were suddenly wary.

"If Bodonchar was your ancestor, your line is more noble than my own. I can't claim descent from him myself, since the mother of my people was pregnant when he found her." Jamukha studied the boy. His clothes were worn and patched, his felt boots shabby; in spite of his proud bearing, he looked poor. "And what is your clan?"

The boy surveyed him coolly; Jamukha had the feeling he was being judged. "You rode to my aid," the stranger said, "so perhaps I can trust you. Only my family is here, my mother and brothers and sister — and Bekter's mother and brother. Will you swear an oath not to tell others you saw me?"

Jamukha slapped his chest. "My promise lives here. I swear before Heaven that I'll be silent." He had reasons enough not to tell others everything about his journey. "Trust me."

"I trust no one more than I have to. All you have to know is that if I ever find out you broke your promise, you'll suffer for it." He spoke softly, but his threat did not seem an empty one. "My name is Temujin," he continued. "I am the son of Yesugei Bahadur, who was the son of Bartan the Brave, nephew of Khutula Khan, and grandson of Khabul Khan. My father's followers abandoned us in the spring before last."

Jamukha gaped at him, impressed by his lineage and moved by his plight. "I know about your family," he said. "Some say you must be dead, and others claim you live, but your enemies have probably forgotten you by now."

"Our kinsfolk and friends have forgotten us, too," Temujin said.

"Fools. You don't deserve – "

"Let them believe what they like. If they forget us, I'll be safe until I'm strong enough to have my own way."

Temujin flicked his grey horse lightly with his reins and trotted towards the river; Jamukha kept at his side. "We have different burdens, Temujin. You have a family and no tribe, while I have a tribe and no family. My parents died when I was young, before I knew them, and I have no brothers."

"I'm sorry to hear it," Temujin said.

"Don't pity me. I'll take my place as a chief someday, and already sit at councils with the men, but I've grown used to being alone. I often go hunting or scouting by myself. Loneliness has its uses – it teaches you not to rely too much on others."

"I've learned that lesson," the other boy said.

They came to the bank of the river. The wind gusted, and a veil of snow rose from the Onon, revealing the ice below. The bank was higher on Jamukha's right; the boys guided their horses nearer to the frozen river, where the bank could shield them from the wind.

"How old are you?" Temujin asked.

"I'll be thirteen this spring."

"Then you'll be a man before long. I was eleven this past summer."

Jamukha glanced at him. Temujin was tall for a boy of his age, and the shoulders under his worn sheepskin coat were broad. "Why does your brother fight with you?" he asked. "Your lives must be hard enough without that."

"My father made my mother his first wife, even though his other wife had already borne Bekter. He hates knowing that I'm Father's heir." Temujin shook his head. "Little as we have, he wants to claim it all for himself. My half-brother Belgutei isn't so bad when he's not around Bekter, and my mother has three other sons."

"Then you have the beginnings of a new bone of your clan," Jamukha said. "When you and your brothers have wives, you can sire many warriors."

Temujin adjusted the collar of his coat. "I was betrothed to an Onggirat girl before my father's passing. We had only a little time together before I had to leave her."

"Will she wait?"

Temujin's pale eyes narrowed. "She promised that she would."

"Well, if she forgets, you can find another wife. It doesn't matter who the woman is as long as she tends to you and gives you sons."

"You wouldn't say that if you'd seen Bortai."

Jamukha felt a twinge of resentment. Yet Temujin, abandoned as he was, had little enough to sustain him; he would cling to the hope that at least one person, even a distant Onggirat girl, still thought of him.

Jamukha did not want to dwell on that girl. A man's bond with a woman could never be as strong as those with other men, who were comrades in battle and companions during the hunt. He shifted in his saddle. He never thought of love when he allowed men to take their pleasure and give pleasure to him; the act was one intense moment apart from such feelings. Yet he now felt that he had been seeking more without knowing what it was he wanted. Perhaps there could be love with a companion like himself, someone with whom he could both give and take, someone who would honour that love above all others.

"I should ride back," Temujin said. "My mother will worry when Bekter returns without me." He was silent for a while. "She kept us alive, after the few sheep we had with us died. We would have starved without the sorb apples and plants she gathered when we didn't have game."

Temujin smoothed down his coat collar. Jamukha noticed the hollowness under his wide cheekbones, then quickly reached under his saddle for some dried meat. "Take this," he said.

Temujin grabbed the meat and tore at it with his teeth. "Thank you," he mumbled, his mouth full, then gulped down the rest.

"We might hunt together," Jamukha said. "I needn't ride on right away, and together we'd have a better chance."

Temujin grinned, looking more like the young boy he was. "As long as you promise not to steal the kill for yourself."

26

B<small>Y THE TIME</small> the sun dropped towards the west, Jamukha
and Temujin had tracked a young deer and brought it down.
The animal was thin and weak, but Temujin was delighted with
their kill.

"We'll eat well tonight," he said as they lifted the carcass to
his horse. "You must come with me, Jamukha. My mother will
welcome you when she sees what we've brought. You don't
want to ride on yet, do you?"

"No," Jamukha admitted.

"Then come on."

They rode towards the foothills bordering the Kentei massif.
Soon Jamukha noticed a small stream of smoke rising from
near the edge of the forest, but they were amid the trees before
he saw two yurts. A rider passing this way might assume a
shaman had travelled here to be closer to the mountain spirits.
Mount Tergune towered beyond the hills, Burkhan Khaldun
lay to the south-east, and there were other places where a
powerful shaman might fly up to Tengri. A cart without a
covering stood behind one yurt; another cart holding a trunk
was next to the smaller tent. This family would have little to
steal.

"We have a barricade deeper in the forest," Temujin said,
"where we can hide. Sochigil-eke, my father's second wife, ran
there this autumn, when a band of men came to hunt by the
river, but my mother took out her bow and stayed with the
rest of us."

"What happened then?" Jamukha asked.

"Mother told us to wait until they were close, fire one volley
as a warning, and then retreat to the barricade. She said she'd
cover us while we ran, but luckily the men rode away without
troubling us."

His mother was obviously brave. Jamukha imagined a fierce
old creature with a heavy body and a strong, ugly face under
her high square head-dress.

Temujin called out his own name, then slid down from his
horse as a boy lifted the tent flap and came outside. "I've

brought meat," Temujin said, "and a new friend who needs shelter for the night – his name is Jamukha." He pulled the carcass from his mount.

The younger boy smiled. "Bekter came back a while ago, shouting about you and a stranger trying to steal his game."

"It's a lie. He took my kill for himself – Jamukha was trying to help me."

"You should have been here, Temujin. Mother was cursing Bekter for riding off and leaving you. Then she hit him so hard with her stick that it broke on his back."

Temujin chuckled, then turned to Jamukha. "This is my brother Khachigun."

Jamukha nodded at the child, then dismounted. Someone else peered out from behind the tent flap. "My mother," Temujin murmured. "Her name is Hoelun."

The woman's face surprised him. He had expected a woman aged by struggle and hardship, but Temujin's mother had smooth, pale brown skin, her lips were full, and her eyes a light golden brown. Two thick black braids were looped behind her ears under the fur hat that was her only head-covering. Beauty in women left him unmoved, but he saw something of Temujin in her steady gaze.

"Greetings," she said. "I was told you encountered a stranger."

"This is my new friend Jamukha," Temujin replied. "He's a Jajirat, the son of a chief, and you see that he brought me luck." He poked at the dead deer with one foot.

"I greet you, Ujin," Jamukha said as he bowed. "Your son has told me why you camp here. I've promised him not to speak of our meeting to others."

"I'm grateful for that, and also that you brought no harm to him." The woman stepped outside; she was small, and her long coat was as shabby as her son's. "Not many would help out-casts, and others who pass this way shun us. It's well that you mean to keep silent about who we are. It wouldn't do you much good to have our enemies think you've befriended my son."

"I wasn't thinking of myself when I made that promise."

Hoelun Ujin waved a hand at Temujin. "Take your horse

and our guest's to where we keep the others." Temujin led the horses away; Jamukha was about to follow when the woman beckoned to him. "Please stay, Jamukha. We're not going to steal your horse. Khachigun, you'll help me butcher and hang this meat." She knelt, slipped her bowcase from her belt, and pulled out a knife.

'I'll help you, Ujin," Jamukha said. "I'm partly to blame for bringing you this extra work."

Hoelun's grim expression softened. "You deserve praise and thanks for bringing it."

By the time the meat was butchered and hung to dry, Jamukha had met some of the others. Temuge, at five the youngest boy, had eyes like his mother's, as did Khachigun; only Temulun, a little girl of two, had eyes with the same greenish tinge as her oldest brother's. Belgutei emerged long enough to mutter a greeting before his brother Bekter, with an angry glare at Jamukha, pulled him inside. Their mother, Sochigil, was a dark-eyed woman with a sad face who fluttered aimlessly about while Jamukha helped Hoelun hang the strips of meat. Apparently the entire family shared this yurt; they would need only one fire and be warmer if they kept together. He supposed that they kept some of their meagre belongings in the other.

Night had come when Hoelun Ujin led him inside. "Temujin said you have three sons besides him," Jamukha said, "but I've only met two."

"Khasar's watching the horses," Khachigun said as he entered with an armful of deer bones. Hoelun shot him a glance. Jamukha was about to ask how many horses they had, then thought better of it.

The yurt was warm; smoke rose from the hearth. Jamukha and Khachigun picked over the bones while Sochigil cleaned the hide with a stone and Hoelun prepared a meal. She had taken off her coat; her long plain tunic was one a man might wear, without the pleats and tucks common to women's garb. The silence was broken only by an occasional gurgle from Temulun as she watched Temuge clean his knife. Bekter glared at Jamukha and swatted Belgutei whenever the younger boy seemed about to speak.

"Perhaps I should tell you more about myself," Jamukha said at last.

"Please do," Hoelun said from the hearth.

"My father was our chief. My mother died giving birth to me, and my father not long afterwards. It's said that a boy who loses his father knows one of the greatest sorrows life can bring, and I share that sorrow with your sons. But it's also said that one who loses his mother suffers an even greater loss." He glanced around at the other boys. "When I see how your mothers here care for you, I know the truth of that saying."

Temujin came through the doorway. "I told Khasar all about you," he said to Jamukha. "You'll meet him in a while."

"Isn't he going to share the meal?" Jamukha asked.

"He'll eat later. Someone has to keep watch." Temujin sat down as the others gathered near the hearth; Bekter winced as he seated himself. Temujin grinned at his half-brother. "I hear that my mother's stick danced on your back today."

"You and this stray." Bekter's lip curled. "Why did you bring him here?"

"Silence!" Hoelun said sharply. "Eat your food."

They ate quickly. Hoelun suckled Temulun, then put her daughter to bed before sitting down to eat herself. She had cooked a small piece of the fresh meat, but there were only a few shreds for each of them; the rest of the meal was a liquid that tasted of bark. Jamukha finished his food still hungry, although the others seemed satisfied; their pinched faces showed they were used to less. A bit of meat remained, but that was probably Khasar's portion.

"I am sorry for our poor hospitality," Hoelun murmured as she gestured at the platter.

"I enjoyed this supper," Jamukha said, "and you prepared it well, Ujin. I've never tasted fresh game as good."

Hoelun's eyes were still wary, but a smile played around her lips. "Someone has brought you up well, orphan that you are."

"My uncle cares for me." He wondered if his uncle would have so willingly assumed that obligation if he had sons of his own.

Hoelun got to her feet. "It's time you children were asleep."

"You may have my bed, Jamukha." Temujin gestured at one

of the hide-covered cushions, then stood up. "It's my turn to guard the horses."

"I'll come with you if you like," Jamukha said. "That way, I can watch for part of the night while you sleep."

Hoelun turned towards him. "You needn't."

"I don't mind, Ujin. I'd be sleeping on my horse under a tree if your son hadn't brought me here."

"Then come along," Temujin said. Jamukha picked up his weapons and followed the other boy outside.

They walked a short distance through the dark wood to a clearing dimly illuminated by the half-moon in the winter sky. Nine grey horses stood with his own brown gelding inside an enclosure of rope, where another boy was guarding them; a banked fire glowed on a bare spot of ground.

"You aren't quite as poor as I thought," Jamukha murmured to Temujin.

"Oh, they left us our geldings, but without a stallion and mares, we can't increase our herd. They must have thought someone would steal them by now and kill us while they were at it."

"And you didn't have to eat any of them?"

"Mother said we'd dine on rats and bark first, and we have, often."

The other boy came towards them. "You must be Khasar," Jamukha said.

"My brother told me how you met." Khasar clasped Jamukha's hands. "A pity you didn't put an arrow into Bekter." He laughed; except for his darker eyes and his readiness to smile, his face resembled his older brother's. "Maybe we can hunt together tomorrow."

"I'll have to ride on then," Jamukha said, already feeling some regret.

Khasar left them. Temujin circled the makeshift enclosure, reaching out occasionally to pat one of the horses. "I'm glad you came with me," he said. "I'm nearly falling asleep."

"Rest, then. I'll wake you later."

Temujin stretched out by the fire. The flames would ward off other animals, and Jamukha had heard no wolves, but would take no chances. Unlike the steppe, where danger could

121

be seen at a distance, the forest was a dark place that concealed much. He climbed into a tree, where he would have a better view of the clearing and be hidden from sight.

The wind whistled overhead, then faded; the half-moon rode above pale streams of clouds. Tengri's smoke-holes were bright against the black sky; the Seven Old Men twinkled near the Golden Stake.

Something rustled; it might have been the wind, but Jamukha tensed, sure that he was being watched. He scanned the area around him and saw nothing, but he had learned to trust his instincts. He drew an arrow from his quiver and readied his bow.

He remained on guard, stiff with tension, marking time by the passage of the moon and the turning of the stars. Even after nearly half the night had passed, he was afraid to leave the tree. This forest might be alive with spirits his weapons could not touch.

Temujin stirred, opened his eyes, and stood up. "Jamukha?"

"I'm up here." Temujin moved closer to the tree. "I think someone's watching us," Jamukha whispered.

"I suspect someone is." The other boy did not seem worried.. "Climb down – I'll cover you." Jamukha hung from the limb and dropped to the ground. "Get some sleep – I'll take my turn now." Temujin lifted his head and gazed past him. "Go to bed, Mother. You can see I'll be safe."

Jamukha wheeled around. A shadow moved out from behind a tree and disappeared in the darkness. He thought of the woman hiding there in the cold, watching him, ready to let an arrow fly. "But why – "

"You might have cut my throat while I slept and taken our horses. Mother was making sure that you didn't, as I expected she would."

"I wouldn't have harmed you."

"You've shown that. I never doubted you myself, but I'm happy you passed the test. Sleep soundly, Jamukha – you have nothing to fear now. I give you my oath on that."

The morning meal was a thin broth made with a bone. Jamukha

drained his small bark bowl, then leaned towards Hoelun. "Thank you," he said, "for welcoming me under your tent."

She smiled. "You must take some of the meat with you on your journey."

He accepted a piece from her. Belgutei had gone out to guard the horses. The rest of the family said farewell; Bekter looked relieved that Jamukha was going.

Temujin caught up with Jamukha on the way to the horses. "I'll ride out with you," the boy said. Jamukha grinned, pleased at having some more time with his new friend.

They rode out from the forest towards the Onon. The sun peeped out from the grey clouds, making the wide plain of snow a piercing white. They were silent as they rode, not speaking until they reached the river.

"Do you ever play knuckle-bone dice?" Temujin asked.

"Sometimes," Jamukha said. "I have my bones with me." They dismounted, tied their reins to the gnarled limbs of a shrub, then scrambled down to the ice. Jamukha took out two knuckle-bones and rubbed them in his gloved hands. "I'll throw first – east." He threw one bone across the ice; it slid to a stop and pointed north.

"One point for me," Temujin said triumphantly. "West." He tossed a piece of brass shaped like a knuckle-bone. "Two points for me!"

"I'll score more points, never fear. South." Jamukha threw his second bone and crowed as it pointed south.

They went on playing, adding up points, marking their scores along the snowbank with their knives when they began to lose count. Temujin seemed intent on the game; he had probably had little chance for such aimless pursuits.

They had each scored twenty points when Temujin signalled to him. "You're matching me point for point, Jamukha. Maybe it's a sign good fortune's with both of us."

"One more throw each," Jamukha said. "We'll let that decide the game." He threw and took another point; Temujin matched him.

"That proves it." Temujin picked up his brass bones, then flung one arm around Jamukha's shoulders. "We should play

123

together against my brothers sometime — nobody could beat us both."

They walked towards the bank and sat down. Jamukha wanted to prolong the moment. "It'll be clear," he said at last, "a good day for riding. I'd rather not leave, but the longer I stay, the more questions my uncle will have." He turned towards Temujin. "I'll come this way again, by spring at the latest."

Temujin's face grew solemn. "I think, apart from my full brothers, you're the first true friend I've found."

"You must have had friends among your people."

"Some of the boys looked up to me." Temujin shrugged. "But I was the son of their chief then, and when he was gone — " He sighed. "Bortai's a friend — I felt she'd stand with me, whatever happened." His mouth twisted. "But she's a girl, so it isn't the same."

Jamukha's face burned with jealousy. Any love that girl might feel would quickly vanish when she learned how precarious Temujin's life was. His own feelings were nobler. Seeing Temujin's plight only made him more determined to help his new friend claim his rightful place.

"I've known you for only one day," Temujin continued, "and yet I feel you're my comrade. I thought at first that my guard was down, that I longed for a friend too much, but — " He shook himself. "You'd be better off with a friend who has more."

"You have courage, Temujin. You said yourself that you won't be an outcast forever." Jamukha took a breath, knowing what else he wanted to say. "I've also wanted a true friend, but I mean to be even more than that to you. I'll be a brother who will never desert you. I would even pledge the bond of an anda to you."

Temujin's eyes brightened. "You honour me, Jamukha. That's the most sacred vow two friends can make."

"I'd swear such an oath to you, even with no one else here to witness it. Our two lives will be one. I'll always defend you, and will never raise my hand to you — I swear it now." Jamukha struck his chest with one fist. "May my promise live in my heart. You must become my anda, Temujin. Your life will be as dear to me as mine."

"Then I promise you the same. You are my anda, brother Jamukha. When we ride together, no one will come between us. I'll cherish you and love your sons as my own. Our bond will last for all our lives."

Jamukha took out his knife, pulled up his sleeve, and made a small cut along his wrist; Temujin did the same. He pressed his arm against the other boy's. "The same blood flows in us now," he murmured. "I'll never shed yours, nor you mine. We are brothers." He gripped Temujin's hand tightly. The solemnity of the promise and the joy welling up inside him nearly overwhelmed him. This was love, not that weaker feeling some men claimed to have for women, but a better love, one that added to one's strength.

"I should give you something to mark our pledge." Jamukha rummaged in the pouch hanging from his belt and pulled out one of his knuckle-bones. "This is only a small gift, but maybe it's fitting, since luck was with us both during the game."

"It always will be, now that you're my anda." Temujin put one of his brass dice into Jamukha's palm.

They sat in silence for a while, until the cold made Jamukha shiver. He got to his feet reluctantly; Temujin rose and brushed the snow from Jamukha's coat.

"I'll come back," Jamukha said, "by spring."

They embraced. Jamukha let go first, afraid his feelings might overpower him. He could wait. He would allow this love to grow, and wait for a time when their joining would express that love, when Temujin would see what had to exist between them.

Jamukha mounted his horse. "Farewell, my brother," Temujin said.

27

Khasar hunkered down behind a tree. In the grass just beyond the woods, Temujin and Jamukha were practising their archery. The Jajirat boy took aim at a lone tree in the distance; his arrow whistled as it flew, then embedded itself in the trunk. Temujin's arrow struck the tree just above his friend's.

His brother and Jamukha were both fine archers, but he was a better one. Khasar was certain that he could split Jamukha's arrow with his own. Temujin would often point at difficult targets – a tree limb barely within range, or a small bird on the wing – and dare Khasar to hit them. He rarely missed.

Jamukha's favourite horse grazed at the edge of the forest with his spare mount. The two boys slipped their bows into their cases, then jogged towards the tree. The high spring grass rippled as a cold wind blew. Jamukha retrieved his arrows, moved closer to Temujin, pressed something into his hand, and held him by the elbows for a moment. Temujin pulled an arrow from his quiver and offered it to the other boy.

Khasar felt a twinge of jealousy. Jamukha had arrived four days ago, with woollen scarves for gifts and several ducks he had killed along the way, and had rarely left Temujin's side since then. They hunted together, watched the horses together when Temujin's turn came to guard them, practised with their bows and spears together, and slept under the same hide. Temujin had admitted that he and the Jajirat had pledged an anda bond that winter. With a friendship so quick to flower, and with such a sacred tie, it was not surprising that the two were so close.

Temujin had always been closer to Khasar than to their other brothers, perhaps because they were only two years apart in age, but he had grown more distant during Jamukha's visit. Even when Khasar was with them both, he somehow felt excluded, as if the others had forgotten he was there.

He thought of the night before last, when he had awakened to hear Jamukha whispering to his brother. There had been the sound of muffled laughter, and then a strange gasping sigh that had startled him, and then silence.

He had not asked Temujin about that. If he had, Temujin might have questions about things Khasar did in the night, and he had never been able to lie to his older brother. His cheeks flamed as he thought of how he touched himself, how he had discovered the fierce pleasure he could give to himself with his hand.

Maybe Temujin had guessed. Perhaps he and Jamukha had been laughing at him. He was no better than someone who put it into a sheep; that was what they would say. A man had to save himself for women and use his seed to sire sons. If he kept this up, he might lose his strength and be unable to service a wife later; judging by the sounds he had heard from his parents' bed long ago, such acts required a lot of effort. Maybe Temujin and Jamukha had been laughing about what he did.

His brother could not know. Even if he did, he might poke fun at Khasar himself, but would never allow anyone else, even his anda, to laugh at him. He had enough to feel ashamed of, and had no right to resent Jamukha.

The two boys walked back to Jamukha's horses and sat down, their backs to him. Maybe he could sneak up on his brother and catch him unaware. Temujin would be annoyed at his lapse, for not knowing what was around him all the time, but he would not get upset with Khasar. Temujin was like that. Whenever he was careless, which did not happen often, he seemed angrier with himself than with anyone else, unlike Bekter, who was quick to blame others for his own mistakes.

Khasar was about to drop on all fours when Temujin turned his head. "Khasar," he called out, "you can come out now. Jamukha's leaving soon."

His brother had known he was there all along. Khasar sighed as he got to his feet and hurried towards them. Jamukha's black eyes narrowed as he looked up, and then a smile crossed his handsome face.

"I didn't even see you," Jamukha said. "But you didn't fool your brother."

"Nothing much fools him."

127

"I know." Jamukha and Temujin gazed intently at each other; Khasar felt excluded again.

"Look." Temujin held out his hand as Khasar sat down. "Jamukha gave this to me."

Khasar peered at the arrowhead in his brother's palm; two pieces of horn had been glued together and a hole bored through the middle. "A whistling arrowhead." He touched it, admiring the work.

"Jamukha made it himself," Temujin said.

"I'll show you how to make them sometime," the Jajirat boy said. "An archer with your skill should have such arrows — the sound of whistling arrows terrifies enemies." Khasar nodded, feeling ashamed again of his jealousy. "Your brother gave me this." He held out one of Temujin's cypress-tipped arrows.

They sat in silence. At last Khasar said, "We should go and watch the horses — it was our turn." Bekter would be getting impatient.

"I don't want you to go," Temujin said as they all got to their feet.

"I wish I could stay." Jamukha embraced Temujin. "I'll come back in autumn, when my people move south again. Farewell, my anda."

"Safe journey, Jamukha," Temujin said.

Jamukha walked towards his horses, mounted, then waved at them as he rode away. Temujin gazed after him, his face solemn.

"You think a lot of Jamukha," Khasar murmured.

"Of course — he's my anda."

"He seems closer to you than anyone else is."

Temujin put a hand on Khasar's shoulder. "What is it? You like him, don't you? He thinks a lot of you." Temujin peered into his eyes. "You're my brother."

"He's your anda," Khasar said. "Some would say that's even more than a brother."

"It's different — not more." Temujin led him towards the trees. "When he asked me to swear that oath, I knew he'd be a true friend. He has nothing to gain by joining himself to an outcast. I'm the one who gains — he'll be chief of his clan someday."

128

"Is that the only reason you became his anda?"

"No. I would have taken that oath even if he'd been an outcast himself." He laughed. "Still, it doesn't hurt that he'll be a Jajirat chieftain."

They fell silent as they entered the woods. Temujin glanced from side to side. Khasar did not like the forest, or having to hide among the trees. He longed for space, for flat land completely open to the sky. When he was a man, he would stay on the steppe, away from darkness and the nightly whispering of the spirits that dwelled here.

Temujin stopped, then slowly lifted his hand. A lark sang overhead. Khasar smiled, taking pleasure in its song, then glimpsed the small bird on a limb, barely visible among the leaves.

He took out his bow and aimed. His arrow struck, cutting off the bird in mid-song. A small feathery form fluttered down and fell at his feet.

"Good shot," Temujin murmured.

Khasar picked up the dead bird and drew his arrow out. "It's a fat one, enough for both of us."

They walked on until they came to the clearing where the horses were kept. Belgutei had joined his brother; he lowered his bow as Bekter got to his feet. "About time you got here," Bekter said.

"We'll take them out on the plain to graze," Temujin responded, "and you won't have to water them, either. I promised I'd take your turn tonight, too. You gained from the bargain."

"A pity your friend had to leave so soon," Bekter said. "Why, he hardly left you alone the whole time he was here."

Temujin said nothing. Khasar glared at Bekter, knowing he would try to start another fight, now that Jamukha was not around to take Temujin's side.

"Poor Temujin." Bekter's lip curled. "Maybe you'll never see him again."

"Be quiet," Temujin said.

"He'll be back," Khasar said. "You're just sorry you don't have a friend – not that anyone would want to be friends with you."

"I don't need that sort of friend."

"Don't worry." Khasar gritted his teeth. "You'll never have one."

Bekter stepped in front of them. Belgutei moved to his side and watched his brother warily. "You've been careless, Temujin," Bekter muttered. "I know what went on when you thought the rest of us were asleep. Hoelun-eke must be sleeping more soundly, or she would have found out. She'd be angry if she knew what you did."

Temujin's face was white. "Don't say any more, Bekter."

"No wonder you like him so much," Bekter said. "I saw you two moving around under your hide. Did you let him touch you? Maybe he did more than that."

Temujin flew at Bekter. The other boy's foot caught Temujin in the groin. Arrows spilled from Temujin's quiver as he toppled forward; Bekter kicked him again.

Khasar dropped the lark and swung at Belgutei, hitting him in the chest, then threw down his weapons and wrestled his half-brother to the ground. Blood pounded in his ears. He thought of Bekter lying awake, listening; maybe he knew about his own secret deeds. He pressed a knee against Belgutei's chest, wishing the other boy were Bekter and he could squeeze the breath from him. His hands were around Belgutei's neck when something hard struck the side of his head.

He lay on his stomach. Bright sparks danced before his closed eyes; he heard a groan. Khasar opened his eyes to see Temujin on his knees, retching; then a booted foot kicked him in the small of the back. The ground spun, and he squeezed his eyes shut, afraid he might be sick, too.

"That'll teach you," Bekter said.

"Khasar's not moving." That was Belgutei's voice. "You shouldn't have hit him with that rock."

"He'll recover."

"But what if he's really hurt?"

Khasar heard the sound of a slap. "Don't worry about him. Take that lark."

Khasar was still until he knew the two were gone, then opened his eyes. Temujin wiped his mouth and crawled towards him. "Khasar."

"I'm all right." Khasar rolled over on to his back; the ground under him was spinning again. He swallowed hard and sat up, then felt at his head. His cap was still on; apparently that had given him some protection.

Temujin grimaced as he sat back on his heels. "This has to end."

"We'll go to Mother," Khasar said. "When she finds out what they did this time – "

His brother's hand closed around his wrist. "We're not going to her."

"We can't just let it pass." His head was clearing. "What did Bekter mean about you and Jamukha – "

"It's a lie." Temujin tightened his grip. "You won't speak of that again."

Khasar was sorry he had spoken of it at all. He thought of his own secret, and vowed silently that he would never touch himself again.

"I promise you this," Temujin said. "Today is the last time Bekter will ever do anything like this to us." He rose unsteadily and helped Khasar up. "We'll graze the horses now."

28

KHASAR AND TEMUJIN returned to the forest with the horses in the morning. Their two younger brothers were waiting in the clearing.

"Bekter shot a lark yesterday," Khachigun said as Temujin led the horses inside the roped-off patch. "We had the last duck, though, and Mother wouldn't give him any of that – she said the lark could feed him."

"That was my lark," Khasar said. "I shot it."

Temuge squatted near the horses, gripping the small bow Khasar had used when he was younger. The five-year-old boy already had a hard and wary look. "I hate Bekter," Temuge muttered.

"So do I," Khasar said.

He followed Temujin back to the yurts, wondering what his brother would do now. As they entered their dwelling, he saw that his mother and Sochigil were alone with Temulun. Hoelun greeted them, then set out a few shreds of dried duck and bark broth.

"Where are Sochigil-eke's sons?" Khasar asked, hoping they were far from the tent.

"They went to the river to fish with the net."

"I think I'll go hunting, then."

"We might have more luck fishing," Temujin said. "The Onon should be filled with fish now." Khasar glanced at his brother, surprised.

"You may do as you like," Hoelun said, "as long as you bring back food. We have little enough, especially now that your sister needs more than my milk. Sochigil and I are going to look for roots. If you catch no fish, bring fruit from the bushes along the bank."

Khasar bit his lip. Gathering berries and plants was hardly fit labour for a man, and fishing was not much better. He might have to do such things to live, but despised such lowly work.

Sochigil left the yurt. Khasar took off his cap and sipped his bark beverage. His mother reached down and touched his cheek. He gazed into her face, surprised; she did not hug them as much as she used to, or sing to them. Her beautiful eyes were gentle as she smoothed back his hair; her fingers brushed against the bump above his ear.

He winced. She said, "You've hurt yourself."

"He fell," Temujin said quickly.

"Be more careful." Hoelun patted Temujin on the shoulder, then hoisted Temulun to her hip as she picked up her basket.

"I don't want to fish," Khasar said when she was gone. "When I'm a man, I'll hunt, and herd horses and cattle, and go to war, but I'll never fish or gather plants again."

"We'll fish today," Temujin said. "It's easier work than hunting."

"I don't want to be anywhere near Bekter and Belgutei."

Temujin finished his food and stood up. His eyes had a distant look, as if his mind were elsewhere. "I told you Bekter wouldn't trouble us again. Get your hook, Khasar – we'll see what we can catch."

Sochigil's sons sat on the river-bank; several gutted fish were drying on the rocks next to them. Belgutei was cleaning another fish while Bekter examined the horsehair net; the older boy looked up as Temujin and Khasar approached.

"We need bait," Temujin said.

"Take what you want," Belgutei replied. Bekter scowled at his brother. "Well, we don't need it with the net."

Khasar scooped up some of the offal from the catch, then followed Temujin upriver. They had brought one of their mother's buckets with them, made from bark and sealed with clay, to hold their catch.

Khasar sat down, baited his hook, and tossed his line into the river. "Bekter isn't happy with Belgutei for giving us bait." He slipped his line around his fingers as Temujin dropped his own into the water. "I don't know why we're here. Mother will see we get a share of what they caught, and we don't want to take too many from one spot."

Temujin shrugged. Maybe he was still hurting from Bekter's assault, and did not feel up to hunting, although he would be too proud to admit it.

Sunlight danced on the water as it flowed towards the open land. The net would trap more fish, but Khasar did not mind using a hook instead. Either he or Temujin would have had to wade across the river to hold the net from the other side, then wade back to secure their catch, and the Onon was deeper in spring. Khasar hated being in water; getting drenched if he tripped was even worse.

His line suddenly jumped. He gripped it tightly as he stood up. A large silvery fish struggled on the hook. Temujin took the line from him; Khasar grabbed the bucket, filled it with water, then reached for his line. The fish's gills fluttered as he removed the hook and dropped his catch into the bucket.

"You did well," Temujin said.

"It's a beauty. Bekter didn't catch any this big." Khasar peered down the river. The other two boys were staring at them; they had not yet put the net back into the water. Bekter stood up, motioned to Belgutei, then started towards them. "We may have trouble," Khasar added.

"Ignore them."

Khasar was baiting his hook when a shadow fell across him. "I see you caught something," Bekter said.

"Just one fish so far."

"That fish belongs to us."

Khasar let his line fall. "You didn't catch it."

"The bait was ours, and we'd have caught it with the net if you hadn't been here."

Khasar got up slowly. Temujin hooked his hands around his belt. "You'll catch enough with the net," Temujin said. "Our hooks won't rob you of that many."

"But I want that one. What are you going to do – go whining to your mother about it?"

Khasar could bear no more. He lunged at Bekter. A fist struck him on the still-tender spot above his ear; another punch caught him in the abdomen. He doubled over, his head swimming.

"Let them have the fish," Belgutei said.

"Shut your mouth. I want it, and they're going to learn to give me what I want."

Khasar swayed dizzily, wondering why Temujin had not defended him. "Listen to me, Bekter," Temujin said in his soft voice. "This is the last time I'll warn you. You'd better swear to stop stealing and sneaking around and fighting me. If you take that fish, Tengri alone knows what will happen to you."

Khasar shivered at the cold tone in Temujin's voice. Belgutei touched Bekter's sleeve, looking fearful himself; his brother pushed him away. "Temujin fights with words now," Bekter said mockingly. "Take the bucket, Belgutei."

The younger boy hesitated, then picked up the bucket. Khasar raised his fists, ready to fight them by himself. Temujin grabbed him by the arm, holding him back.

"I see you're learning," Bekter said. "I'll take what I please and you'll do as I say, or you'll get another beating like the one I gave you before."

Khasar struggled to free himself from his brother's iron grip. Belgutei retreated with the bucket. Bekter turned to follow the other boy, then looked back. "Woman," he muttered. "Cata-mite."

Khasar knew the word was a deadly insult. Temujin was pale, his cat's eyes filled with rage and hatred.

Khasar shook himself loose. "Don't go after them," Temujin said in a low voice.

"Are you going to take that?" Khasar gripped the knife under his belt. "He deserves to die for what he said."

"I told you. This will end – I promise it."

"Words and threats won't stop him."

Temujin lifted his head. "I said this would end." His voice, oddly gentle as it was, chilled Khasar; his brother's greenish-brown eyes were as hard as gemstones. "You'll help me put a stop to it."

His brother's eyes terrified him; a demon in a nightmare might have such eyes. He knew then that he would have to obey, whatever he was asked to do. If Temujin ever turned against me, Khasar thought, Heaven couldn't protect me.

"Get your line," Temujin said, "and come with me."

They waited inside the yurt until the women returned. Hoelun set down her basket of roots, stared into Temujin's grim face without speaking, then sent Sochigil outside with Temulun.

She sat down in front of them. "You two have something to tell me."

"We caught a fine fish," Temujin said. "Bekter and Belgutei took it away from us."

"So instead of catching another," Hoelun said, "you come back empty-handed."

"Yesterday, it was a lark Khasar brought down, and today it was a fish. Mother, this must end."

"Yes, it must." She leaned forward. "Don't I have enough worries? Who's left to fight with us now? Only our own shadows. What whips do our horses have? Only their own tails. How can you ever face our enemies if you can't make an ally of your brother? Must I keep telling you what Alan Ghoa told her sons when they fought?"

"If they'd had a brother like Bekter," Khasar said, "they'd never have stopped fighting."

"I won't listen to this," Hoelun said. "Temujin, you were able to make a friend of a stranger. Surely you can find a way to make peace with Bekter."

"There can be no peace with him," Temujin said.

"If you can't deal with him, you'll never be a chieftain." Hoelun reached for a root and scraped at it with her knife. "Never forget that your father's brother abandoned us. He might not have done so if your father had done more to ensure his loyalty, and the Taychiut chiefs might have given in to Daritai if he had vowed to support you." She finished cleaning the root and took out another. "Your father was a fine man, and I'll never stop mourning for him, yet he failed to keep a strong bond with the Odchigin. It isn't surprising that others would desert us when they saw that your father's own brother wouldn't defend us."

Temujin said, "Then you'll do nothing."

"What do you expect me to do? Beat him every time you complain about him? He's getting too strong to take that from me. I've done what I can – I can't control him any more – and his own mother's useless for that. You have to find a way to live with him."

"There's no living with him!" Khasar burst out.

"He's your brother! Let him have his way for now. He'll grow bored if you don't fight back, and maybe then he'll leave you alone."

"You're wrong, Mother," Temujin responded. "He'll think I'm weak and unable to stand up to him."

"A man, so I've been told, knows when fighting can gain nothing and it's time to retreat. Behave like a man now."

"Then I must settle this matter myself."

"Yes." Hoelun worked at her root. Temujin stared at her for a long time, then got up and left. Khasar scrambled to his feet and followed. Temujin strode past Sochigil and disappeared among the trees; Khasar hurried after him.

He caught up with his brother as they neared the edge of the forest. "What are you going to do now?" Khasar asked.

Temujin leaned against a tree, then turned to him; his eyes glittered. Without thinking, Khasar made a sign against evil.

"You've said what must be done yourself," Temujin whispered. "Just now, inside our tent, you said there's no living with him. Before that, by the river, you told me he deserved to die."

Khasar shuddered, his heart racing with fear. He suddenly wanted to call back those words.

"You have to help me," Temujin said. "He's your enemy as much as mine. I can't risk doing it alone."

Khasar could not speak.

"I gave him one last chance," Temujin said. "Mother's left the matter in my hands. It has to be this way, Khasar – it won't stop as long as both of us are alive."

Khasar struggled against the thought. It would be over; he had to think of it that way. There would be no more stealing, no bullying, no evil insults thrown at his brother, no fear that Bekter might shame him by discovering his secret.

He listened as Temujin began to speak of what they would do, knowing he would have to agree to it.

29

KHASAR SQUATTED NEAR a tree; Temujin peered out from behind a shrub. Bekter sat on a small knoll amid the grass, watching the horses, his bowcase at his side. He glanced over his left shoulder at the woods; Khasar kept still.

They had waited for three days to catch Bekter alone. Belgutei had gone off to hunt birds that morning, taking Temuge with him. Temujin had been smiling when the two boys left the yurt.

Temujin hunkered down. Gripping his bow and two arrows, he began to creep towards the knoll; he would approach Bekter from the back. Khasar's task was more difficult; he had to sneak up from the front, and Bekter might spot him from the tiny hill. Temujin could still take the boy from behind, but Bekter might have time to shoot at Khasar.

He would have to make sure he was not seen. Temujin would

not have given him the riskier part of this task unless he had faith in his skill.

Khasar left his quiver and bowcase by the tree; he would take just one arrow. If his first shot failed, he was not likely to get a second. But it would not fail; he had hit harder targets than this. Stalking Bekter was much like hunting anything else.

He crawled slowly into the high grass. A breeze stirred the blades, making it less likely that his movements would be seen. Temujin had been patient awaiting his chance, while Khasar had been anxious for the deed to be done. The strain of waiting, once they had made their plans, had been almost too much for him, but his older brother had remained calm. Temujin had lulled Bekter into thinking he was finally cowed, refusing to rise to his taunts.

The waiting would soon be over. Bekter was only game after all, to be tracked, caught unaware, and then taken.

Sweat trickled down his neck and into his eyes; he blinked it away. His muscles tensed as he crept nearer to the knoll. Bekter was gazing to his right, scanning the horizon. Khasar's hand tightened around his bow as he readied his arrow. Temujin was probably in position, but he waited a few more moments to be sure.

"He won't stop," Temujin had said while they were laying their plans. "He thinks I'm beaten, but that isn't enough for him – he'll put me out of the way if I give him the chance."

Khasar took a breath, surprised at how calm he was. He could trust his aim; this would not be so hard.

He jumped to his feet and drew his bow; the string was taut in his fingers as he aimed. Bekter lunged towards his bowcase.

"Don't touch your weapon," Temujin called out, "or you'll die now." Bekter looked behind himself; Temujin stood up in the grass with his bow. "I want to hear your last words."

Bekter got up slowly, keeping his arms out; if he was afraid, he did not show it. "What's this?" Bekter said, keeping his eyes on Khasar. "What do you think you're doing?"

"Ridding myself of a cinder in my eye," Temujin answered. "Spitting out a splinter of bone that makes me choke."

"Haven't you got enough enemies? Being free of me won't help you against them."

"It will rid me of one stone on my trail."

Bekter's hands shook. "Whatever you do to me," he shouted, "don't kill my brother Belgutei, too."

Khasar lowered his bow, suddenly uncertain. He had not expected Bekter to plead for his brother.

"But you won't shoot," Bekter continued. "How foolish of me to be frightened by you two." He sat down and crossed his legs; Khasar could see the contempt on his face. "Temujin's just a snake who steals up on his prey from behind. And you, Khasar – you're only the dog that does his bidding. I know what he is, what he does, and maybe you're the same. Do you think you can hide the truth?"

Khasar shook with rage. Bekter's hand darted towards his own weapon. Khasar aimed and felt the sudden release of tension in his bow as his arrow sped towards his target. The shaft jutted from Bekter's chest as Temujin's arrow flew towards his back. Bekter's mouth opened; a look of surprise crossed his face. A dark liquid spurted from his lips as he slowly toppled to one side.

Khasar's feet seemed rooted to the ground. Then he was running towards the small hill, his heart pounding. He kept expecting Bekter to move, to sit up and pluck the arrows from himself.

Temujin climbed up and stood by the body. Khasar looked down. Bekter's dark eyes were still open, staring up at him. The horses lifted their heads, scenting death. Khasar trembled, terrified of what he had done.

"You did well, Khasar." Temujin's fingers dug into his shoulder. "We killed our first enemy together." He released Khasar, knelt, and pulled the arrows from the corpse, then smeared some blood on Khasar's hand. "Never forget what we did today."

They stripped the body, left it on the hill, and herded the horses back to the forest. Temujin was silent. Khasar could not tell if his brother was rejoicing over his deed or already regretted it.

Bekter was dead. A wild feeling that might be either triumph or terror swept over him. Bekter would never steal, taunt, or beat anyone again; Khasar no longer had to fear him. His arrow and his brother's had put an end to their tormentor. How simple it all was after all.

When the horses were inside the enclosure, Temujin picked up the clothes and weapons they had taken from the body. Khasar followed his brother towards their tents, his mouth dry. Somehow, he had assumed that Temujin would find a way to hide their deed. Mother will know, he thought wildly; she'll know what we did as soon as she sees us.

Khachigun was outside, sharpening his spear. Temujin motioned to him. "Go to the clearing," he said, "and guard the horses. I'll relieve you in a little while."

"But – "

"Go."

Khachigun's eyes widened as he gazed into Temujin's face; he jumped to his feet and hurried away.

They went inside. Sochigil sat on her bed, mending a shirt; Hoelun was picking lice from Temulun's braided hair. "Did you find game so soon?" she asked without looking up.

"We hunted other game today," Temujin said, "and brought it down. We came back with the horses – Khachigun's watching them." He threw the bundle to the ground.

He had admitted it. Khasar held his breath. Hoelun stared at both of them, then jumped to her feet. "I see what you've done!" She made a sign. "What evil spirit brought you to this?"

"This had to be settled," Temujin said. "I put an end to it."

"Murderers!" Hoelun shouted. "Murderers, both of you!" Sochigil dropped her sewing, looking bewildered. "How could you do it? How could my womb give birth to such sons? How much evil have you done today? Did you strike only at Bekter, or have you robbed poor Sochigil of both her sons?"

Sochigil screamed, tore at her scarf, then flung herself across the bed, clawing at the cushions. Temulun covered her face with her hands. "I curse you!" Hoelun shrieked.

"I did only what I had to do," Temujin said in his quiet voice. "I'm rid of my tormentor, and Sochigil-eke has one son left."

Hoelun struck Temujin on the side of his head. "Murderer! You came from my womb with a clot of blood in your hand, and now you've darkened the earth with your brother's blood!"

She hit him again; he staggered under her blows, but continued to stare at her with his icy gaze.

"And you!" She came at Khasar and slapped him hard across the face; he stumbled back. "You're like the savage Khasar dogs that gave you your name! You're animals, both of you, seizing prey without thinking, snapping at your own shadows – you're no better than a bird that eats its own chicks, or a jackal that fights any creature who comes near! May I be cursed for giving birth to you!"

Her fists drummed against Khasar's head until his ears rang. He struggled towards the doorway, wanting only to escape her. She grabbed him by the collar, threw him to the ground, kicked him in the ribs, then rounded on Temujin. "You led your brother into this evil – I know you! You made him your accomplice! Murderer!" She raised her arm; Temujin caught her by the wrist.

"No, Mother," he said. "You won't beat me any more."

Hoelun's eyes widened. Khasar waited for her to start shouting again, but she was silent; she even seemed afraid. Temulun's wail rose above Sochigil's hoarse sobs.

Temujin let go of their mother's arm; she watched him without moving. "It's over," Temujin said, then turned and went outside. Khasar fled after him.

They sent Khachigun back to the dwelling. Temujin paced, circling the clearing before he sat down next to Khasar. The horses milled around, nipping at one another until the forest began to darken.

Khasar put some fuel on the fire, then rested his back against a tree. He had done what Temujin said they must do. Once he had started to crawl through the grass, it had been too late to turn back.

He had not thought of what would happen after the boy's death. Sochigil-eke would weep and wail, but they had little to fear from her. Belgutei would mourn, but would also fear Temujin more from now on; he might even be secretly relieved at being free of the brother who had bullied him, too. Temuge and Khachigun had no fondness for the dead boy, and Temulun was too young to care. But he did not know what his mother would do.

She might drive them away. Even Temujin might shrink from confronting her if she barred the tent to them. They could go to Jamukha's camp, but maybe his Jajirats would not be so willing to take in two outcast boys.

Khasar knew then why his brother had been compelled to take Bekter's life. He had wanted to end the stealing and fighting, but might have found other ways to stop it. Bekter had been Temujin's rival, but that could have been settled when they were men.

Bekter's death might serve Temujin's aims, but that was not the only reason he was dead. His taunts about Jamukha and the evil word he flung at Temujin by the Onon had called his death to him. Maybe it was true. Khasar shuddered as he recalled the laughter and the odd sound he had heard in the night.

He would not dwell on such thoughts. Bekter had lied; he had told enough lies in the past. His death was a matter of honour; Temujin had silenced the lies directed against him and his anda.

It was nearly night when Khasar heard the sound of footsteps under the trees. His bow was in his hands when Hoelun stepped into the clearing, carrying a basket. She moved around the enclosure, stooping to pick up the drier dung outside it, then sat down in front of them.

"I've been doing what I can to comfort Sochigil," she said. "She refuses to eat and sits staring at the hearth, but she's stopped crying. I had to tell Temuge and Khachigun that it isn't right to show joy at a brother's death." Her face was hidden in the darkness beyond the fire; Khasar was relieved that he could not see her eyes. "I don't suppose you stopped to dig a grave."

Temujin did not reply.

"I thought not. We'll say no more about it." She rested a hand against her basket. "Belgutei's with his mother. He's showing some wisdom in spite of this. He's said nothing about avenging his brother, only that he must do what he can to ease

Sochigil-eke's grief. I think he sees that this fighting has to end if we're to go on.''

"Then there's no reason to kill him," Temujin said. "Without his brother, he won't trouble us. I'll do what I can to be more of a brother to him."

"So one murder is enough for you." Hoelun cleared her throat. "I'm partly to blame for this. I left it to you to settle things and didn't see where that might lead you. But I understand now, bitter as it is to accept it, that your evil deed has solved a problem." She glanced at Temujin. "You're rid of your rival, and I won't have to step between you and him."

"As you say," Temujin murmured, "a problem has been solved. I feel no regret."

She let out her breath. "And now I must be as wise and practical as you." She stood up, then picked up her basket. "Whatever you've done, you are my sons, and I have to live with that."

She left them. Khasar sighed; he would not have to worry about what she might do. He turned towards his brother. The firelight flickered on Temujin's face; Khasar saw his brother's smile.

30

"I WANT TO hunt," Temulun said as Hoelun came outside. Hoelun frowned at her daughter. "You and Temuge will find dry wood for our fire."

Temuge was sitting near the yurt, testing the spring in his small bow. "She can hunt with me," he said.

"Neither of you will hunt," Hoelun replied.

Temulun let out her breath. "Khasar and Khachigun won't take me with them, and now you won't let me – "

"Enough," Hoelun said.

Sochigil looked up from the bird she was plucking. "Listen

to your mother," she murmured. "You should be helping her, not running around after your brothers."

Temulun scowled. With her brown face, piercing pale eyes, and disorderly braids, she looked as wild as her brothers.

"Collect the wood," Hoelun said to the children. "If you happen to find small game while you're at it, take it, but you'll bring back fuel, and you're not to wander far."

Temuge thrust his bow into his case and moved towards the trees; Temulun hurried after him. The two roamed the forest like a pair of wild animals. In spite of her warnings to stay near the camp, she suspected they had been exploring the foothills.

"Hunting," Sochigil muttered. "Wrestling with Temuge and challenging him to horse races – that's all the girl thinks about."

Hoelun studied the other woman. Sochigil had aged in the two years since her son's death; her face was thin and worn, her dark eyes listless. Even Bekter's death had roused no fire in her spirit. She had accepted Temujin's hints that he had acted in self-defence, and Hoelun did not contradict her son.

Once, the other widow's passivity had exasperated her, but it served them both now. Hoelun saw to their needs, and Sochigil did as she was told, a companion when Hoelun told stories and reminisced about happier times, a sister for whom Hoelun could even feel some sympathy; Sochigil had never stopped mourning for what she had lost.

"It's true," Hoelun said, "that Temulun should learn more about a woman's duties. You might help instruct her in such skills."

"If you wish – not that I've done so well at certain tasks myself. I might have been a better mother to my poor lost son."

Hoelun did not protest those words. To have Sochigil shoulder part of the blame for Bekter's fate was preferable to having her turn against Temujin.

Hoelun moved towards the river with her basket. Some berries might have ripened on the bushes, even so early in spring. She remembered the last feast they had enjoyed, when Temujin and Khasar had gone off on their horses and returned with a stolen lamb. Her mouth watered; she thought longingly of curds and milk and boiled mutton.

Birds sang in the branches overhead. She had grown used to the woods. The few travellers who passed by usually avoided the region below the mountains where she had moved her camp, but some hunters on horseback had chased her and Khachigun into the forest last winter before retreating from Khasar's shower of arrows. One of the men had shouted to her in a voice much like Yesugei's.

A cool breeze chilled her face. In the mountains beyond the river, the snow would be melting on the higher slopes. They would have to move again by summer, when bands of hunters would follow the deer and gazelles up the mountainsides. She wondered if Jamukha would return soon. They had not seen Temujin's anda since autumn. She remembered the taste of the kumiss he had brought them, and sighed.

The boy's devotion to her son was apparent. He became Temujin's shadow while with him; she sometimes worried that he clung to her son too closely. But the Jajirat boy was a faithful friend, unlike Toghril, his clan's Kereit ally. Jamukha had talked of finding a way to speak to the Khan of their plight, but Hoelun had discouraged him. Pleas on behalf of outcasts were unlikely to move the Kereit Khan.

She glimpsed the Onon through the trees. Temujin and Belgutei would be near the river with the horses. "Come no closer," her son suddenly called out in the distance, "and keep your hands raised."

Hoelun set down her basket and took out her bow, then crept forward. Several paces downriver, near the herd, Temujin and Belgutei had their arrows trained on a rider. The stranger's arms were up; the way he sat in his saddle stirred a memory. She moved closer, her fingers tight around her bow, until she saw him clearly.

"Munglik," she whispered.

"Peace," the man shouted. "Don't you know your old friend? I searched this region for days, following old tracks, hoping they were yours." Temujin kept his bow aimed. "I know you, Temujin – your father's eyes look out at me from your face."

Hoelun hurried along the bank towards them. "And you, Ujin," Munglik continued, "I'd know you even after all this time. Call off these boys – I mean you no harm."

She circled the horses and came towards him as he dismounted. He walked towards her and caught her in his arms, then released her. His face was browner, and his moustaches had grown to his chin, but otherwise he was much the same.

"I prayed I'd find you safe," he said. "I feared I might not find you at all." Temujin lowered his bow, then shrank back as Munglik embraced him. "You've grown, boy." He reached for Belgutei and threw an arm over his shoulders. "And you must be Belgutei – your face is much as it was."

Belgutei shook off his arm. The boys gazed at the Khongkhotat in silence, their eyes filled with suspicion. "I've been looking," Munglik went on, "hoping the tales I've heard didn't mislead me."

"What tales?" Hoelun said.

"Of a tent near here, of boys who run from strangers. I couldn't believe you were still alive, but I had to search. The spirits guided me to your side." He clasped Hoelun's elbows. "Four years in hiding, yet you're still the beauty I remember."

She withdrew from him and adjusted her scarf, suddenly conscious of her ragged tunic and worn coat. "You flatter me, Munglik."

"Your son's nearly a man – he'll soon be as tall as his father."

"I'm pleased to see you, old friend," Temujin said in his soft voice, not sounding pleased at all. "So you've heard stories. Have our enemies also been told these tales?"

"Targhutai Kiriltugh has."

Temujin's eyes narrowed.

"When I was last in his camp," Munglik said, "he spoke of how your mother's brood might have moulted by now, of how her fledgelings could be old enough to fly against him. I was in a Dorben camp a few days ago, and there I heard that the Taychiuts mean to search for you after their mares drop their foals."

Hoelun tensed. "I knew we couldn't stay hidden forever," her son said. "What will you do for us now, old friend?"

Munglik hooked his fingers around his belt. "What can I do? I took a risk in looking for you. If I brought you to my camp, the Taychiuts would soon learn of it. Targhutai has his camp

146

north-east of you, five days' hard riding away. You have some time – find refuge somewhere else."

Temujin studied Munglik with calm, cold eyes. Hoelun guessed what her son was thinking. Munglik had taken this chance; maybe he still thought guiltily of the oath he had sworn to her husband. But he would not stand against his Taychiut allies openly.

"I'm grateful to you," Temujin said. "Targhutai wouldn't be pleased if he found out you warned us, so you've risked something for us." He glanced at Hoelun. "But Targhutai won't find us here. There are friends who will shelter us."

Munglik might believe that. Did Temujin plan to flee to Jamukha's camp? She did not know where else they could run.

"I can't stay long," Munglik said. "The comrades who rode with me are camped a day's ride away, and they'll be wondering what became of me." He took his horse's reins and walked towards the river, away from the boys.

Hoelun followed Munglik. "Don't go far," she said as his horse drank. "My son will want us in view."

"And within range of his arrows."

"He has reason to be wary even of an old friend."

"You have nothing to fear from me. I could never bring harm to you, Hoelun. It pains me to know how little I can do for you."

How useless his words were. She sat down; he settled on the ground next to her. "I expected to find a faded flower," he murmured, "but you've blossomed even more." She sighed; more useless words. "Temujin's grown quite handsome, and Belgutei has fire in his face. And the others?"

"My children are strong, no thanks to those who abandoned us. Sochigil's older son met his end two years ago."

"I grieve to hear it."

"Belgutei mourned, but Temujin's tried to take his older brother's place. The boy looks up to my son now."

He took her hand. "I remain your friend, Hoelun. I'd still have you as my wife if that were possible."

His gentle words did not console her. Munglik could resign himself to their capture, and then hope to persuade the Taychiut chief to give her to him. He could still feel he had honoured

147

his promise to Yesugei by warning them, but would not fight for her and her children.

"I hope the wife you have is well," she said.

"Indeed she is. She's just given me a fourth son, Kokochu, and it may not be long until a fifth's inside her."

Poor woman, Hoelun thought. Giving birth to sons was one of life's greatest joys, but having so many in such a short time was not something she would have welcomed.

"I'd stay with you," Munglik said, "but I must go."

She drew her hand from his and stood up. "Don't fear for us, Munglik. Living as we do has hardened us, and we have ways of escaping the Taychiuts." She wanted to believe her own words. "Orbey Khatun won't get another chance to gloat over me."

"True," Munglik murmured. "She followed Ambaghai's other widow to the grave last spring." Hoelun smiled at that.

They walked back to the boys. Munglik said his farewells quickly, then mounted. "Safe journey, friend," Temujin said to him. "I'll remember that you thought of us. I won't forgive the ones who abandoned us, but I also won't forget those who helped us. That promise lives in my heart."

"May Heaven protect you all."

Temujin moved closer to Hoelun as Munglik rode away. "Where can we go?" she asked. "Even your anda may not be able to protect us."

Temujin said, "We're not leaving."

"But we have a chance to escape," Belgutei said.

"Jamukha would fight for us, but his men might not. It won't help us if we come between him and his men." Temujin drew his brows together. "We know this land better than the Taychiuts do. Targhutai's men won't want to pay too great a price to rid their chieftain of one family. We have a chance if our courage doesn't fail us."

Hoelun could not let her son see her fears. "What would you have us do?" she asked.

"Hide in a place we can defend. One of us will keep watch at the edge of the forest. If Targhutai doesn't find us, he may think we've gone somewhere else. Otherwise, we'll fight." He paused. "Are you with me?"

"Yes," Belgutei said. Hoelun bowed her head.

31

HOELUN PEERED THROUGH the trees as Khasar rode up the hill; his horse was lathered with sweat. "I saw them," he said, dismounting. "They'll reach the woods before the sun's high."

Temujin was awake in an instant. "How many?" he asked his brother.

"Thirty."

"Then we have a chance."

Khasar led his mount to the other horses. The animals, six of them saddled, were enclosed by a wall of tree limbs. The family had built a makeshift barricade under the trees on this hill. Belgutei had done much of the work, pulling down boughs and stacking them on top of dead logs, but the others had helped him. From here, through the spaces between the trees, they had a view of the river below.

As they waited, Hoelun's heart skipped; she steadied herself. The Taychiuts would find nothing at their old camp-site. She and Sochigil had taken down the tents and hidden the panels and wagons deeper in the woods; the children had covered the tracks leading there and to their hiding place. Targhutai might think they had moved elsewhere. Perhaps he would search along the river and not approach the hill. She had set her husband's tugh inside the wall of wood; she looked up at the nine-tailed standard and prayed that its guardian spirit would protect them.

"Hide the children," Temujin commanded.

Hoelun took Temulun's hand; Sochigil reached for Temuge. Their eyes shone, as if their plight were only another adventure.

Khachigun led the way up the hill. The trees were thick here, their limbs hiding the sky.

They came to a rocky cliff shielded by trees. A narrow crevice, so small that it could barely be seen until one was near the rocky face, was at the base of the cliff. Temulun and Temuge had found the tiny opening some time ago. The two should not have wandered here alone, but Hoelun was grateful now that they had disobeyed her.

Temulun crept inside, followed by Temuge. Khachigun, taller and broader, barely squeezed through the narrow opening; Sochigil had to remove her coat before Hoelun could push her inside. Hoelun passed the garment to the other woman, then peered into the crevice. The Taychiuts might pass and never suspect that anyone was hidden there.

"There's just enough room for you," Sochigil said; her voice was surprisingly calm.

Hoelun said, "I'm going back. Eat and drink as little of what you've brought as you can. Don't make a sound, and don't come out until one of us comes for you." She hurried away before Sochigil could protest.

She descended the hill. Belgutei was with the horses, calming and steadying them. Temujin moved towards her as she crept behind the barricade. "I told you to hide," he said.

"You may need me if we have to fight." Hoelun took out her knife, wiped the blade, then thrust it under her belt. Khasar gazed over the pile of wood, watching the land below; Temujin plucked at his bowstring.

They waited in silence. The sun rose above the trees and glinted on the river. The Taychiuts might have found the campsite by now. At last she heard a man's voice in the forested land beyond the Onon.

Hoelun sipped from a skin of water; her mouth was dry, her muscles stiff from waiting. Another voice called out below, closer this time. A man rode out from the trees towards the river-bank; another man followed.

The boys readied their bows. The men murmured to each other, then started across the river, clinging to their horses as the water rose to their knees. Three other men followed them; other Taychiuts emerged from the forest.

The five forded the narrow river, then leaned down from their saddles to study the ground. Hoelun held her breath. One man glanced up at the hillside. His horse whinnied; she tensed as one of her geldings neighed.

"Now," Temujin muttered. Arrows flew from his bow and Khasar's; their hands flashed towards their quivers for more arrows. A flock of birds rose screeching from the trees as the next volley fell towards the Taychiuts. One arrow struck a man in the shoulder; another embedded itself in a leg. The five riders plunged into the Onon as other men fired back. Hoelun ducked as arrows soared past the barricade.

The Taychiuts retreated into the wood along the far bank. Hoelun cursed under her breath. Now that they knew someone was here, they might decide to wait them out instead of attacking.

Several men darted from the trees, then ducked down as the boys' arrows arched towards them. The Taychiuts behind the trees answered with another volley; Hoelun shrank against the barricade as arrows struck the ground behind her. The Taychiuts retreated again.

"They may storm the hill," Khasar said softly.

Temujin shook his head. "That would cost them. I think they'll cross downriver and attack us from the side unless – "

"Hoelun!"

She started, recognizing Targhutai's voice. "Hoelun!" Khasar aimed in the direction of the voice; Temujin pulled his brother's bow down. "I see the markings on your arrows! I know it's you and your fledgelings who are hiding from us!"

"Mother," Temujin whispered, "go and hide yourself now."

"Hoelun!" Targhutai cried. "We aren't here to fight with you! Send out Temujin – he's the one we want. Surrender the boy, and the rest of you may go free!"

So he would settle for her oldest son. Having Yesugei's heir would be enough of a triumph for him.

"Send out the boy!" Targhutai shouted. "I don't need the rest of your wretched brood – I only want the one who thought he could take his father's place! I swear by Koko Mongke Tengri that the rest of you will be safe when he's in my hands!"

Belgutei crept towards her. "He may not honour that oath, Hoelun-eke," he said.

"We can't let him take Temujin." Khasar aimed his bow. "Shall we lure them out and then give them our answer?"

"No." Hoelun clutched at Temujin's arm. "If he's speaking the truth, you have to get away."

"And abandon you?"

"The rest of us are no use to him without you. You're Yesugei's oldest son – you must survive to avenge your father."

Temujin stared at her without speaking. "Listen to Hoelun-eke," Belgutei said. "We can hold them off while you escape."

"Farewell, Mother." Temujin took her in his arms. "I promise – "

She pushed him away. "Go!"

He crept towards the horses, mounted a gelding, then touched his hat briefly before he rode away. The trees would conceal him; he might escape to Jamukha's camp. If he reached the Kereit lands, perhaps Toghril Khan would finally be moved to protect him.

"Temujin!" Targhutai called out. "Do you want your mother and brothers to suffer because of you? Give yourself up!"

Hoelun said, "Answer him." Khasar loosed his arrow; it arched over the river and struck the ground above the bank.

"Don't be a fool!" Targhutai cried. "Surrender yourself, and the others will go unharmed. Resist, and all of you will be ashes scattered in the wind!"

"Mother, you must hide," Khasar whispered. "Belgutei and I can try to lead them away from you. They may cross the river elsewhere, then surround us. You have to think of the others. If you can keep them safe until one of us returns, or Jamukha can find you – "

She touched his cheek. "Very well." She picked up some dried game and skins of water, then tucked them under her coat.

Belgutei was creeping towards the horses, Khasar at his heels, when a shout came from below. "He's getting away!" a man called out. "Look there, up on the mountainside!"

Khasar spun around, his face pale, then hurried back to her side. Other Taychiuts shouted to one another. They had spotted

Temujin, or he had deliberately shown himself to save the rest of them. Hoelun listened to the sound of hooves as the Taychiuts, hidden by the trees, rode up river after her son.

They stayed by the barricade. Khasar crept down the slope and returned to tell Hoelun and Belgutei that their enemies had left no guard behind. The air turned colder that night; Hoelun slept against one of the horses while the two boys took turns on watch.

In the morning, she made her way up to the cliff. "Temujin's ridden away," she said as the children crawled through the crevice. "Our enemies have gone after him – they claim he's the only one they want." She reached for Sochigil and pulled her through the opening. "But we're not safe yet. When they fail to catch him, they may come back for us."

Temulun rubbed her eyes. Khachigun stamped his feet and shook out his arms. "What'll we do?" he asked.

"Stay at the barricade by day and sleep here at night, and you're all to run here at the first sign of their approach."

The three children hurried down the hill. Sochigil took Hoelun by the arm. "We should try to get away," she said, "before they come back."

Hoelun said, "We must stay together now."

Sochigil's grip tightened around her wrist. "Your youngest children would be safer away from here."

"I can't leave," Hoelun said. "If they return for us, at least I'll know Temujin escaped."

"Then stay, and I'll take the youngest ones with me." The other woman's voice was unusually firm.

"You'd do that?" Hoelun asked.

"If Belgutei comes with us." Sochigil halted; then faced her. "You did what you could for your son. Let me save the only child I have left."

Hoelun pulled away and moved on; Sochigil walked behind her in silence. Hoelun did not speak until they reached the barricade, then went to Khasar and Belgutei. "Listen to me," she said. "Sochigil-eke will leave with Temuge and Temulun. Belgutei, you'll ride with them. Go to where the Kimurgha River meets the Onon, and wait for us there. When you feel you've waited long enough, seek out Jamukha and ask for refuge."

Belgutei frowned. "What if the Taychiuts come back? You can't hold them off without my help."

"It's unlikely we could hold them off with you, but we can keep them from following you." She glanced at Khachigun. "I'd send you with them, but we may need you here. I know you'll be as brave as Khasar."

Khachigun drew himself up. "You can count on me, Mother."

Hoelun picked up Temulun, wondering if she would ever see her daughter again, then carried her to the horses.

After Sochigil and Belgutei left with the children, Khasar led the four remaining horses to the river to drink while Khachigun collected the fallen arrows. When night came, they ate a few birds' eggs Khasar had climbed a tree to fetch. Hoelun wanted to save what food they had for as long as possible.

Her sons took turns climbing into a tree to keep watch by day. At night, she took a turn on guard. They rarely spoke. The boys honed their knives, sharpened their spearpoints, and tested their bows while she dug for roots. She hoped their enemies had not found the wagons and tent panels, but did not dare to leave the refuge to find out.

Every day that passed meant that Temujin was further from them, with the Taychiuts on his trail. Her hopes would rise, then fall when she thought of the perils her son faced. He had gone up the slope, towards the higher reaches of Mount Tergune, perhaps meaning to hide in the thick, upper forest until he could make a break.

At night, when a breeze rustled the horse-tails of Yesugei's tugh, Hoelun sometimes heard the whisper of the sulde that lived in the standard, and that spirit's murmured promise to protect them. The sulde was the guardian of her husband's clan, as Temujin was now the clan's heart; the voice promised her that she would live to press the tugh into her oldest son's hands. But during the day, the sulde was silent, and the voices of the forest spirits sighed mournfully amid the stirring trees.

154

By the eleventh day inside the barricade, their food was nearly gone. Khachigun was watching from a tree when Khasar came to Hoelun and sat down.

"We can't stay here, Mother," he said. "We could have escaped during the time we've waited. Targhutai might have given up the chase and gone back to his camp."

"And if we leave now, we might meet our enemies. They might even be waiting for us to follow Sochigil, or to ride after your brother. Temujin would come here for us once he's certain they're gone."

Khasar shook his head. "I think — "

Khachigun suddenly dropped from the tree and hastened to them. "They're coming," he said, "along the river. I saw Temujin's horse."

Khasar jumped to his feet and took out his bow. "I hope they stay in the open," he muttered. "They'll pay for whatever they did to him."

Hoelun rose; her legs shook. "Stay near the horses," she said to the younger boy, "and keep them quiet." She reached for her own bow.

Targhutai's men were soon within sight. They rode along the bank below the slope; one of them led Temujin's grey gelding. She drew back her bowstring and aimed at Targhutai's heart, then saw her son. They had bound his arms and legs and slung him across another horse; she saw him twist, as if trying to free himself.

Khasar took aim. "No," she whispered. "If we shoot, they'll kill him."

"They may anyway."

"We won't risk it."

Khasar glared at her, but she grabbed his wrist and held on until the men had ridden past. As long as Temujin was alive, he had a chance. Targhutai lifted his head. The chieftain had captured her son, but had not taken his life; she could still hope.

She watched until the men disappeared around a bend in the river. Khasar jerked back his arm and pushed her away. "I could have drawn some blood."

"They would have had all our lives then." She got up, went

to the tugh, and knelt. "Protect my son," she whispered, then clutched the standard to her.

32

KHADAGAN NUDGED A lamb closer to the flock, then saw the captive boy. He was pulling a wagon; the wide flat collar of a kang, a wooden yoke, rested on his broad shoulders. His arms, bent at the elbows, were bound by the wrists to the wings of the yoke, where his hands drooped above two holes in the collar. Someone had lashed him to the wagon's long poles. He strained as the wagon rolled slowly forward.

Chaghan moved to Khadagan's side and giggled. Khadagan glared at her cousin. "Don't laugh at him," she said.

Chaghan rolled her eyes. One of the women with the flock beckoned to the girls.

The boy had been with them for over a month, ever since Targhutai Kiriltugh had captured him. Khadagan had watched from a distance while men thrust spears between the captive's legs to make him trip or gave him heavy sacks to haul. Killing him might have been more merciful than yoking him and moving him from tent to tent, where he was often beaten and deprived of food. But some whispered that Targhutai feared taking his life, even that a shaman had warned him not to shed the boy's blood.

Several small boys ran towards the prisoner and danced around him as they pelted him with dirt clods and dung. The sight enraged Khadagan; she halted, then strode towards the boys.

One boy grabbed another by the arm. "Leave him alone!" he shouted.

The other boy pulled away from him. "What do you care, Chirkoadai?" Two boys grabbed Chirkoadai and wrestled him to the ground; a third threw a pat of dung at the prisoner.

"Stop it!" Khadagan cried. She knocked one boy aside, then

pulled another off Chirkoadai. A boy shoved her away; she slapped him. A fist caught her in the stomach, and she fell near the captive's feet.

As she stood up, the yoked boy lifted his head and shook back his long unbraided hair. The cold look in his pale eyes made her shiver; she could almost imagine him bursting from his yoke to strike back. His expression warmed as he suddenly smiled at her.

A boy came at Khadagan, but Chirkoadai pushed him away. The others were gathering around the prisoner. "Leave him alone!" Chirkoadai screamed.

"What's he to you?" one boy asked.

Chirkoadai glared at him. "Another boy."

One of the boys picked up a stone, but Khadagan grabbed his arm before he could throw it. "Stop it," she said. "You wouldn't treat a dog this way." She raised her fists, ready to fight them all. "Bullies."

A Taychiut man bore down on them; the boys scattered. "Get going," the man said as he climbed into the wagon.

Khadagan hurried back to the sheep. "Brave Khadagan," Chaghan murmured; a few of the girls giggled.

"Come along," Chaghan's mother shouted to them. Khadagan kept her eyes down as she followed the flock.

When the ewes were milked, Khadagan picked up her buckets and carried them towards her father's yurt. The sheep, including those that belonged to her father, would rest by her uncle's yurt that night.

Her father's tent stood near a bank overlooking the Onon. Wide spaces separated it from a circle of yurts to the south and the edge of the Taychiut camp to the north. Horses were tethered to a long rope behind the yurt, where several men were churning large leather sacks of mare's milk into kumiss. The rhythmic drumming of the churns grew louder as she approached; the men hummed as they pushed the long sticks inside the sacks.

Her father, Sorkhan-shira, had led his small band to the Taychiuts last autumn. Targhutai Kiriltugh claimed tribute from her father's clan, the Suldus, and some said he might grow as powerful as his grandfather Ambaghai Khan. Khadagan supposed that they were better off here, but she had seen Sorkhan-shira frown sometimes when he spoke of Targhutai, as if he had doubts about the man he had joined.

Her brother Chimbai was outside, pouring butter from a sack of churned milk into a jug. Chilagun, her other brother, dragged a sack towards a wagon. A cart heaped with newly shorn wool stood next to the yurt's entrance; the doorway was open, its flap rolled up. Khadagan carried the buckets inside.

Khaghar was sitting by the hearth, poking listlessly at the burning fuel. The old woman, the widow of one of Sorkhan-shira's kinsmen, was the only servant they had left.

"We need more fuel," Khaghar said as she looked up.

"Then you'll gather some." Khadagan set down her buckets and handed the old woman a basket. Khaghar got to her feet slowly, mumbled under her breath, and left the tent.

Khadagan was used to the work. Once, her father had two servants for his household, but one had been carried off by the same fever that had taken the life of Khadagan's mother. Perhaps her father would find another woman soon. She wanted to see the sorrow banished from his face by a new wife, who would also relieve Khadagan of some of her chores. Chimbai was sixteen, old enough to be wed, and Chilagun was almost fourteen. When her brothers had their own tents and wives, she might win a few moments for herself before she began serving her own husband.

She went to the hearth. Perhaps she should be grateful for her extra burdens. Other girls of twelve were still learning some of the skills she had already mastered. Her proficiency at such tasks would have to draw a suitor, since her mother had failed to pass on her beauty to Khadagan. She rarely looked into the polished piece of metal her mother had owned; she saw herself every time she looked at her brothers' plain faces, small dark eyes, and thin mouths.

The milk was simmering in the kettle when she heard her father's voice. Khadagan crossed to the entrance and peered outside. Two Taychiuts were speaking to Sorkhan-shira; the captive boy stood between them.

"What am I to do with him?" her father asked.

"Guard him," one of the Taychiuts replied. "Keep him in that kang – he's a tricky one. Took three men to subdue him when he was caught, and he's tried to escape, kang and all."

"Targhutai Kiriltugh is taking a lot of trouble over this boy," Sorkhan-shira said.

The Taychiut shrugged. "Don't waste any pity on him. Targhutai won't spill his blood himself, but he won't mourn if he dies on your watch."

"He might have given the boy an honourable death – had him strangled, stamped to death under a carpet, or tied in a sack and thrown to the river spirits." Khadagan heard a slight tone of mockery in her father's voice. "He wouldn't have had to shed his blood." He sighed. "Wait here while I fetch my sons." As Sorkhan-shira walked away, the boy lifted his head. His gold-flecked, greenish-brown eyes widened as he gazed at Khadagan. She turned away and went back to the hearth.

She was skimming the milk when her brothers entered with the yoked prisoner. "Father says we have to guard him," Chimbai said. "He's called Temujin."

"I know his name." Khadagan glanced at the boy as he sat down awkwardly. A dark bruise marred his broad forehead. His trousers were torn at the knees, and his tattered shirt hung loosely on his tall frame. "He looks hungry."

"I'd welcome some kumiss," Temujin said.

"Then you'll have it," Khadagan said.

Chilagun shrugged. "You see what our sister's like," he said. "Inside our tent, she even tells our father what he should do sometimes."

"Your sister's kind," Temujin said. "I haven't had much kindness shown me here."

Their kumiss sat in sacks and jugs against one wall. Khadagan picked up a jug and carried it to him. Chilagun took it from her, scattered a few drops, then held it to the boy's lips while he drank. "Do they ever let you out of that kang?" Chilagun asked.

"No."

"Even when you sleep?"

"No. Targhutai may cripple me if he keeps me yoked – that is, if beatings don't kill me first."

"It'd be easier for him to do away with you," Chimbai said.

"He'd rather leave that to others. In the meantime, he can show his clan how helpless I am."

"Helpless!" Chimbai chuckled as he sat down. "That's not what I heard. The son of one warrior told me about the trouble they had catching you. He said your family held them off from behind a barricade while you got away. They weren't expecting women and children to put up much of a battle."

Temujin's face was solemn. "At least my mother and brothers may be safe now." He paused. "I was told you're Suldus."

Chimbai nodded. "Father moved us to Targhutai's camp after our mother's passing – he's Sorkhan-shira, leader of our clan. I am Chimbai, and this is my brother Chilagun. Our sister's name is Khadagan."

"It's cruel," Khadagan said, "putting you in a kang and treating you this way."

"Our sister isn't always as hard as the rock for which she was named," Chimbai said. "The weakest lambs never lack her care. But she's right – you're badly treated for a boy." He leaned forward. "You could save yourself, Temujin. Swear to serve Targhutai. Give up your claim. You'd have your life, and a chance for more later – even a slave can rise. You won't last long this way."

"Targhutai claimed my place. My mother didn't keep me alive so I could bow to him." Temujin moved his fingers. A look of pain crossed his face; the yoke must be hurting him. Chilagun gave him more kumiss. Khadagan poured her whey into a large jug, leaving the curds in the kettle; she would set them out to dry later.

"You're a stubborn one, Temujin," Chimbai said, "and brave, for all the good it does you."

Khadagan moved towards them. "Can't we take off the kang?" she asked. "You can guard him without it."

"For once, I won't listen to you." Chimbai turned towards Temujin. "I'd let you out if it were up to me, but Father would beat me raw for disobeying Targhutai's orders."

"Targhutai tried to storm your hiding place, didn't he?" Chilagun said. "I know two men were wounded."

"They tried," Temujin replied. "Then they fell back, and

Targhutai shouted that he wanted only me, and swore to let the others go."

"Sounds like him." Chimbai fingered his faint moustache. "Father and I hunted with him not long ago, and we might have had even more game if he hadn't held the men back. He's like that, settling for what he can get without too much effort. Caution can be a virtue, but – "

Khadagan touched Chimbai's arm. "Let him tell his story," she said. Temujin smiled at her. Other boys had never looked at her that way, as if happy to be near her. She lowered her eyes. He was only grateful for the kumiss and a few kind words.

"My mother and brothers urged me to escape," the captive said. "I saw I might lead our enemies away, since they wanted only me. They didn't spy me until I was further up the slope. I rode for the forests near the top of Mount Tergune. The trees are too thick there for horses to pass easily, and the Taychiuts would have had to cut a path to pursue me. I hoped to circle back afterwards and escape."

Temujin was silent for a moment. "I hid for three days, hoping to wait them out. Then I decided to scout and look for an escape, but when I led my horse down the hillside, I heard something fall, and looked around to see that my saddle had slipped off my horse's back."

"You didn't buckle it properly," Chilagun said, "or else the cinch was loose."

"No, it wasn't that. It couldn't have happened, yet the saddle was on the ground. The spirits were warning me to stay there, not to ride away – that was all I could think. I waited three more days, then went down again. I didn't see any men, but suddenly a boulder as large as a yurt rolled in front of me to block my path."

"Another sign?" Chilagun asked with a smile.

"It had to be. Up there, so near to Heaven, I felt the presence of Tengri. When the wind moved through the pines, a voice whispered to me to go back. Weak and hungry as I was, I couldn't ignore it. After three more nights, my only drink was a lick of melted snow, and my only food a few small berries. I went back to the boulder and cut a path around it, praying that my enemies had given up the hunt." Temujin took a breath.

"They were waiting. They'd set men all around the woods to watch for me."

"It seems," Chimbai said, "that you misread those signs."

"I expected to die then, but I think Targhutai knew the spirits were guarding me. Several times, he came towards me, after his men had beaten and bound me, and each time he let me be. The men spoke of my courage in holding out for so long and mockingly said I deserved some reward for that. They told Targhutai he had nothing to fear from a boy." Temujin bowed his head, resting his chin on the yoke. "Targhutai says now that the spirits of Mount Tergune stayed his hand, but the words of his men also held him back."

"He was your father's comrade once," Chimbai said. "He might have been thinking of that, too."

"There's also my uncle Daritai to consider. He'll do nothing when he finds out I'm a prisoner, but my death might have forced him to break with Targhutai. This way, whatever happens to me, the Taychiut can tell my uncle that he spared me, that I brought whatever fate I suffer upon myself with my stubbornness." Temujin glanced from one brother to the other. "Tengri has spared me. I used to dream of standing on a high mountain, and on Mount Tergune, I saw the signs of Heaven. Targhutai held my life in his hands and failed to take it."

Khadagan heard no doubt in his voice. A light shone in his eyes, undimmed by his captivity, but it might be only the glow of madness. A starving boy on a mountaintop, harried by enemies, could imagine anything; a beaten prisoner might cling to the smallest hope.

Sorkhan-shira came through the doorway. "What's this?" he shouted. "I expected to find my meal ready."

Khadagan stood up. "I'll get it, Father."

"My daughter isn't usually so idle." Sorkhan-shira folded his arms as he looked down at Temujin. "A prisoner you may be, but it seems we're to be your servants. You can't feed yourself in a kang, or even lower your own trousers. What shall we do when you have to relieve yourself?"

"Assist me," Temujin said.

Sorkhan-shira laughed. "They don't free your arms even for that?"

"No. I don't ask until I must, and then I'm beaten for causing my guards more trouble."

"Well, I'll only beat you if you don't ask – you won't piss inside my tent." His foot moved against the empty jar. "I see my sons have given you drink. Chimbai, take him outside and help him with what must be done."

Chimbai and Chilagun helped Temujin up; the older boy led him from the yurt. "Fetch the food, girl," Sorkhan-shira muttered as he walked towards his bed and sat down on a cushion.

Chilagun seated himself near Sorkhan-shira. Khadagan set out some dried meat and curds, then handed her father a jug. "Targhutai should have killed that boy," Sorkhan-shira said. "He'd like to break the lad. If the boy doesn't give in soon, he won't live long." He sprinkled a blessing, then drank deeply from his jug. "A brave spirit – he might have become quite a man."

Khadagan said, "Remove the kang."

Sorkhan-shira lifted his heavy brows. "What?"

"Let him out. Chimbai and Chilagun can still watch him. You said yourself we'd have to feed him otherwise, so it would be less trouble for us."

"We'll have a great deal more trouble if he tries to escape."

"Please!"

"Silence, child." Her father's eyes narrowed; his drooping moustache twitched. "His plight may touch your heart, and you're at an age when a girl dreams of suitors, but an enslaved boy, however noble and good-looking, is hardly a fitting match."

"It isn't that," she said hastily. "I'd pity anyone treated that way, and if he somehow lives to challenge Targhutai someday, it might help to have him as our friend."

"Be careful, Khadagan," Sorkhan-shira said. "Targhutai has my oath. Would you have me dishonour it?"

"How can you break it by showing that boy a bit of mercy? He's Targhutai's prisoner – our clan has no quarrel with him." Her father would not be moved by those words alone. "And if we're kind," she continued, "that may weaken Temujin's will. Beating him and treating him badly hasn't broken him, so

163

maybe kindness will. Targhutai might be grateful to you for that."

Her father's small dark eyes grew more contemplative; he scratched at the band of cloth around his shaven head. She had reached him; he could see mercy as both a kindness to the boy and a service to his chieftain.

"Maybe you should listen to her," Chilagun said. "We'll keep an eye on him. We wanted to take off his kang before, but we couldn't disobey you."

"As if you haven't disobeyed, when you thought you could get away with it." Sorkhan-shira pulled at his moustache. "You're easily swayed by your sister. I hope you show more manliness with your own wife, but then she may not be as clever as Khadagan — even I often fail to cut a path through her thickets of words."

Khaghar entered and set down her basket. Sorkhan-shira waved an arm; the old woman brought him another jug before sitting down next to Khadagan. Chimbai and Temujin came back inside; Sorkhan-shira studied the captive in silence as the boys approached him.

"Temujin," he said at last, "you tried to get away once. You must spend a lot of time thinking of ways to escape."

"I won't deny it." Temujin's hands twitched above the yoke's wings. "But I wouldn't get far this way."

"Which is why you wear that kang. My daughter, however, is a stubborn girl, and tender-hearted. She'll be after me to free you from it until I either give in to silence her or beat her."

"We could unyoke him," Chimbai said. "He can feed himself then, and I'll watch him. I give you my word — "

"Are all my children begging for him now?" Sorkhan-shira scowled. "Very well. You're all likely to disobey me as soon as I set foot outside, so release him now."

Chilagun grinned. Chimbai began to untie the leather thongs around Temujin's wrists. "Listen to me, Temujin," their father continued. "If you make one move to escape, you'll be yoked again, and get the worst beating of your life."

Chimbai loosened the yoke, separated the pieces, and lifted it from Temujin's shoulders. Temujin's face was taut with pain

164

as he lowered his arms; his wrists were raw where the thongs had bitten into them.

Chilagun eased the boy to a cushion. "My arms." Temujin moved his shoulders. "Needles are stabbing them." Khadagan pushed the plate of curds towards him, and his fingers grabbed at the food. "I'll remember that you did this for me."

"Your next guards won't be as soft-hearted as my children," Sorkhan-shira said, "so this small taste of freedom may only make captivity more burdensome later." He paused. "Targhutai Kiriltugh might treat you better if you gave up your claims."

"I cannot."

Sorkhan-shira rubbed his chin; Khadagan saw a glint of admiration in his eyes.

They finished the meal in silence. "I'm sorry there's no more," Khadagan said.

"We'll eat heartily tomorrow," Chilagun said, "at the feast." Khadagan shook her head at her brother, wishing he had not mentioned that. The Taychiuts were not likely to share the feast marking the first full moon of summer with their captive. Perhaps Temujin would be left in her father's care; if so, she would find a way to bring some food to him.

Sorkhan-shira drained his jug and stood up. "I must see to the churning. Chimbai, you and your brother will take turns guarding him, and he may sleep without the kang, but put it on him if you have to take him outside."

Sorkhan-shira left. Khaghar picked up the platters and empty jugs and went to the hearth. Temujin stood up, stretched, then said, "Thank you, Khadagan."

"There's nothing to thank me for."

"Your words moved your father to free me."

She crossed to the entrance and went outside. The men sang as they churned. She went behind a wagon several paces from the tent and crouched to relieve herself.

Maybe Temujin would escape – not while her brothers were guarding him, but another time. If he survived, he would surely win followers and return one day to challenge Targhutai. He might remember her kindness then, and even come to court her.

She pulled up her trousers and walked back to the yurt.

Temujin, if he ever became a chieftain, would have his choice of women; he would hardly settle for someone like her. She lingered by the doorway. They would never let him escape.

Chimbai was talking inside the tent; she strained to hear him over the drumming of the churns behind the dwelling. "That noise may disturb your sleep," he said.

"I'll sleep well without the kang." Temujin murmured something she did not catch, then said, "You're almost a man, aren't you?"

Chimbai grunted. "Sixteen this spring. Father says we'll find a wife for me after the summer feast. He knows a Khongkhotat Noyan with daughters ready to be wed. I met them as children, and don't remember much about them, but Father claims they're quite beautiful now."

"He should find a wife for himself," Chilagun said.

"Maybe he will," Chimbai responded. "The man has three daughters, and Father smiles at the young women more lately. We may both come back with brides, and you could court the sister who's left. Then Father could see to getting Khadagan betrothed."

"Khadagan will have suitors," Temujin said. "She already does a woman's work, and there's beauty in her face."

A dog slinked towards Khadagan and whined. "Our sister's a good girl," Chimbai said. "She's clever and does her chores without complaining, but even I wouldn't call her a beauty. She'll have to hope for a man who can overlook that and value her for other things."

She winced. Her brother had always been honest, which was better than being a liar and a flatterer, but she wished he had tempered his honesty.

"Perhaps you haven't truly seen your sister," Temujin said. "When some boys were tormenting me, she spoke up for me, and I saw beauty in her."

The dog howled; the boys would know someone was outside now. Khadagan went inside to find her brothers chuckling. "You have an admirer, Khadagan," Chimbai said. "Temujin's captivity has scrambled his wits. He was just speaking prettily about you."

"I don't want to hear it." She stomped past the hearth, where

Khaghar was feeding the fire. Temujin knew she had been listening. That was why he had spoken kindly of her. He was desperate enough to try anything in the hope of escaping; he only wanted to find a way to use her. "Chimbai, you should be guarding the doorway." She turned towards Chilagun. "And you should be sleeping."

"You have a suitor at last," Chilagun said. "Too bad he's a captive."

"Maybe I shouldn't have spoken," Temujin said. "I didn't think that those who've treated me well would use my words to wound their sister."

Her brothers hung their heads, having the grace to look ashamed. "I was telling him," Chimbai said, "that Father and I will leave after the festival to find me a wife."

"If he forgets, I hope you'll find one by yourself. Things would be simpler for me and Khaghar if you had your own tent and a wife to do your work."

Chimbai grinned up at her. "You scold me like an old grandmother."

"My father and I rode out to find a wife for me," Temujin said, "before his passing. My betrothed is an Onggirat, and I knew she was meant to be my wife the moment I saw her. Father left me with her family, but we had only a few days together before one of my father's men came to tell me he was dying. I had to leave. She promised she'd wait for me."

Khadagan moved away, touched by the longing in his voice even as jealousy gnawed at her. She began to straighten the blankets on the beds. Everyone knew how beautiful Onggirats were, and his betrothed was probably like the rest.

"How old would she be now?" Chilagun asked.

"Fourteen."

Chimbai grunted. "Then she may already be warming another man's bed."

Khadagan looked towards them. She saw the pain in Temujin's eyes before he lowered his head, and was suddenly angry with Chimbai. Temujin had little to hope for; her brother might have left him the consolation of dreaming about the girl.

"I'm sure she'll keep her promise." She smoothed down her short tunic. "Let Temujin rest now."

Chimbai got to his feet. "Use my bed, Temujin. I'll be watching by the doorway, so don't try to run away. Chilagun, I'll wake you when I get tired."

Temujin stumbled to Chimbai's bed and fell across it. By the time the others were in their beds, the captive was breathing deeply and evenly.

She would not pity him too much, would not allow herself to fall prey to fanciful thoughts about him. He meant nothing to her. She had offered him only the kindness an abused dog or an old horse deserved.

33

TWO MEN CAME for Temujin before dawn. Sorkhan-shira met them outside while Chimbai and Chilagun hastily yoked the prisoner. Temujin smiled briefly at Khadagan before the men led him away.

The feast celebrating the sixteenth day of the summer's first moon was upon them. Sorkhan-shira and his sons rode off with the other men to make the sacrifice. Khadagan followed Khaghar to the empty space along the river-bank to help the women and girls prepare food. By late morning, fat lambs were roasting in pits, and the men had returned for the feast.

A pavilion of felt resting on poles was set up for Targhutai; the chief sat under it with his three wives, his children, his brother Todogen Girte, and several of his men. Khadagan searched the crowd, but did not see Temujin. Her father knelt before Targhutai, held out a scarf for the chief to touch, then led her brothers and a few comrades towards one of the pits.

Sorkhan-shira and his men were soon exchanging tales of past exploits. The women and girls gossiped as they ate and drank. Sorkhan-shira spread his arms wide while speaking of a past battle; Chilagun flirted with a passing Taychiut girl.

Two Taychiut boys made their way towards them, paid their respects to the Suldus men, and sat down across from Khadagan and Chaghan. The men sang songs and got up to dance, whirling and stamping their feet before dropping heavily to the ground. Several children ran along the bank; three boys were pushed into the Onon, to emerge drenched and cursing. The older women murmured that they had never enjoyed such a fine feast.

Khadagan ate as much as she could and drank airagh until her head spun. The sun beat down on the crowd. Men stumbled towards a small grove of trees above the bank to vomit or piss; a few rode off to relieve those on guard around the camp.

"The prisoner must be unhappy," one Taychiut boy said, "not being able to join the feast." He laughed.

Chaghan batted her eyes. "Khadagan feels sorry for him."

"I don't," Khadagan said. "Targhutai's soldiers should have killed him. I don't know why they didn't." He's better than all of you, she thought savagely, then glared at the boys. "You ought to be eating with your own families."

"How rude," Chaghan murmured, "after your father said they could stay."

Khadagan stood up and climbed towards the grove; the airagh made her bladder ache. Targhutai clapped and sang as one of his men plucked a one-stringed fiddle; some of the younger men were wrestling. She found a cool, dark spot under the trees, then slipped down her trousers. The others cared nothing for the boy who would be listening to the sounds of merriment he could not share. She thought of sneaking away with some food for him, but Temujin's guard would only take whatever she brought for himself.

Khadagan left the trees, stepped over a man who had passed out, and went back to where her father sat. Worrying about Temujin had only ruined the feast for her. She seated herself near her aunt, promising herself she would not think of the boy.

When the sun dropped towards the west, Khadagan knew the feast would soon end. More of the men, and some women, were vomiting by the trees; others were being carried to yurts by friends. Those who had tents at the far ends of the camp stumbled to the rope where the horses were tied. At last

Sorkhan-shira wiped his hands on his coat, got up, and beckoned to his children.

Her brothers held their father up by the elbows as they staggered towards their yurt. Khadagan and Khaghar followed them along the bank; the old woman, supporting herself with a stick, seemed about to collapse herself. A few people had passed out by the river; others dragged them up by the arms and flung them over horses.

The grounds around their yurt, except for the tethered horses, were empty and quiet, but men would come there to churn milk before dawn. Sorkhan-shira went inside, groaned as he stumbled to his bed, sat down with a grunt, then looked up at Chimbai.

"Son," he said, "it's time we visited my Khongkhotat friend and paid court to his daughters. We'll leave in a few days, and get you betrothed before the obo festival. In fact, it's time we both found wives, and maybe some young man will ride back with us to court your sister."

Khadagan moved towards Khaghar's bed. The old woman lay on her stomach, apparently dead to the world; Khadagan gently took off the servant's boots.

"Come here, girl." Sorkhan-shira beckoned to her; she crossed to his bed. "You should be betrothed, and I've neglected that."

"There's still time," she said. "I'm young. Maybe a Taychiut will ask for me – then I could stay near you."

Her father tilted his head. "I'll confess that I didn't expect this, but you show signs of becoming quite pretty."

Chilagun snorted as he pulled off Sorkhan-shira's boots. "Father," Khadagan said, "you're drunk."

"A man can see even when he's drunk. At the moment, I see that your nose is too long, and your eyes too small, and your mouth too thin and a bit crooked, yet your face is pleasant to gaze at in spite of that. Strange that I never saw this before, but maybe your mother's beauty blinded me. I'd see her face and think only that yours would never be like hers, but – "

Sorkhan-shira stretched out. Khadagan checked the fire and set a jug near her father's bed, knowing he would wake up later with a throbbing head and parched throat; he would need more kumiss then.

"Khadagan Ghoa," Chilagun whispered as she passed his bed. "Khadagan the Fair."

"Sleep it off, Chilagun," Chimbai said as he fell across his bed. "Let our beautiful sister rest."

Khadagan crawled into her own bed. The sky was light above the smoke-hole; the first full moon of summer brightened the heavens. Her father had praised her before, but only for her cooking or weaving, never for her looks. Temujin had said she had some beauty. Foolish talk, the words of a drunken man and a desperate boy.

She drifted into sleep. "Sorkhan-shira!" a man was shouting. Khadagan tensed against the cushions of her bed, then sat up. "Sorkhan-shira!" Other voices were calling out in the distance. She got up and ran to the doorway, then pushed the flap aside.

A Taychiut stood there; other men were gathering along the bank. "What is it?" she asked.

"Get your father up. Yesugei's son has escaped."

Her heart raced. "What happened?"

"Hit his guard with the end of his kang and knocked him cold. The boy's gone. Don't stand there, girl – get your father."

Khadagan waited by the hearth. Sorkhan-shira, shocked into sobriety by the news, had gone out to join the search. Her brothers had murmured about Temujin's daring before returning to their beds. She could not sleep, and was afraid to look outside, where the men would be fanning out to search the wooded land near the camp. The full moon would make it easy to spot the boy in the open, so they would expect him to run for the trees.

She sat up until she heard footsteps outside. Her father suddenly came through the entrance. "You should be asleep," he muttered as he passed her.

"Did they find him?"

"No."

Her heart skipped a beat. She followed him to his bed. "But he isn't safe yet," Sorkhan-shira continued. "We'll look again, when it's daylight." He heaved a sigh as he sat down, looking distressed. "Let's pray he's making his way to wherever his family's hiding now."

"Yoked, and without a horse?"

"It's out of our hands."

"But when he's found – "

"Quiet," he said softly. "You'll wake the others."

"What'll they do to him?" Her throat was so tight that she could hardly speak. "They mustn't – "

"Calm yourself, Khadagan." He put an arm around her and drew her to him. "I'm cursed with pity for him myself." His voice was very low. "He was clever enough to hide in the river instead of making for the trees – must have known the men would search the woods first. I saw him hiding in the Onon."

Khadagan stifled her joy.

"A face, barely above the water," Sorkhan-shira whispered, "and he was using the kang as a float. I told him to wait there. No one else saw him. I joined the others, then went back and told him to lie low until we'd gone back to our tents. At last I convinced Targhutai the boy couldn't go far and that we'd have better luck with a daytime search." His fingers dug into her. "And I'm only telling you this to console you. You know what will happen to me if anyone else finds out what I've done."

He grabbed for the jug by the bed, whispered a prayer, than drank. "Foolish of me, to risk so much for him. I told him not to speak of me if he's caught – I hope he's brave enough to hold his tongue. I did what I could, but we may all come to regret it."

"You're a good man, Father. I would have hated you if you'd surrendered him."

"Perhaps that's also why I didn't." He cocked his head, listening to the drumming of the churns outside. "There will be little sleep for me tonight. I must see to the churning, and then – "

The boys stirred in their beds. Chimbai sat up. "Was he caught?" he asked.

Khadagan shook her head, then heard a sound by the doorway. Chimbai jumped to his feet; Sorkhan-shira lifted his head.

A shadowy form pushed through the entrance. Temujin stood there, barely visible in the glow of the hearth fire, his yoke still around his neck. His wet clothes clung to his body; his hair was plastered against his head.

"The beating of the churns guided me to your tent," Temujin said. "It's dark now – no one saw me enter."

Sorkhan-shira got up and went over to the boy. "What are you doing here?"

"I can't get far this way. I beg you – you were kind to me before. Please help me now."

"This is how you repay me." Sorkhan-shira pulled him towards the hearth. "Don't you know what will happen to us if you're found here? I should take you to Targhutai now."

Khadagan ran to her father and grabbed his sleeve. "No!"

Sorkhan-shira let go of the captive. Khaghar was awake now, watching from her bed. Chimbai suddenly thrust himself between his father and Temujin. "You can't give him up," Chimbai protested as his brother hurried to his side. "If a bird flies from its cage and hides in a bush, does the bush surrender the bird?"

Sorkhan-shira struck his chest. "This bush may have its limbs torn from it for the sake of this bird."

"He came to us, he trusts us. How can we give him up?"

Sorkhan-shira glared at them. "Has this boy put a spell on all of you?" He looked towards Khaghar, as if hoping she might support him, but the old woman was silent.

Khadagan tugged at her father's sleeve. "Let me speak to you." She turned and walked to the back of the tent. Her brothers were already removing Temujin's yoke. Her father's hands tightened into fists as he strode to her.

"What is it?" he asked.

"You can't give him up," she said very softly. "We risk much if we help him, but you'll also be taking a chance if you give him up. Targhutai Kiriltugh may want to know why he came here, and a beating could loosen his tongue. He might speak of the kindness you showed him, and that you found him without giving him away."

Her father grunted. "How clever my daughter is."

They went back to the hearth. Temujin flexed his arms; Chimbai was holding the yoke. "We have to burn this," the older boy said.

"I can try to get away now." Temujin glanced at Sorkhan-shira. "I might have a chance."

"You're certain to be seen." Sorkhan-shira shook his head. "Burn the kang, then hide him. I'll go out and keep the men away from this tent."

Chimbai and Chilagun broke the kang into small pieces and Khadagan fed them to the fire. The wood was damp; she blew on the fire to keep it going. When the yoke was reduced to blackened bits of wood, Khaghar hung a kettle over the hearth.

Chimbai blocked the door while Temujin quickly gulped down some broth. Khadagan could not bear thinking about what might happen to them all if he were discovered. Her father would die for his treachery, and perhaps her brothers as well. Targhutai might be more merciful to her. He might settle for giving her to one of his men as a slave instead of throwing her to his soldiers.

Temujin said, "I have to hide."

"The cart outside the doorway," Chilagun murmured. "You could hide there."

Khadagan looked up. "He'll smother under all that wool."

"Exactly why nobody would look there."

"I'll chance it," Temujin said. "If they find me, I might convince them I crawled there by myself."

Khadagan took his empty bowl. "They'll wonder how you lost your kang. They'll know someone helped you, so you can't protect us if you're caught."

He gazed at her steadily. The boy was willing to endanger them to save himself. He must have thought hard about his chances, about the man who had protected him, the boys who had wanted his yoke removed, and the girl who had blushed at his compliments. He had known what they would do.

"I'll reward you someday," Temujin said. "I swear it."

Chimbai peered through the doorway, then motioned to Temujin. Khadagan followed him to the entrance. Dawn was near. Temujin crept through the darkness towards the cart.

"You'll have to watch him, Khadagan," Chimbai said. "Don't let anyone near the cart, and make sure he doesn't come out until everyone's asleep."

174

She stomped back to the hearth, cursing under her breath. A few words from her would have persuaded her father and brothers that hiding him was too risky. She had not even thought of them, only of how grieved she would be to see Temujin a prisoner again.

He knew how to bend people to his will even when powerless. Perhaps Tengri had touched him on Mount Tergune. Their fate was in His hands now. It was easier to believe that the spirits had made a tool of her than to admit that her weakness had led her family into danger.

34

KHADAGAN SET CURDS on rocks to dry, then knelt next to Khaghar in front of the long ground-loom. A yurt panel needed a new wool binding, and Chimbai could use a new shirt when he went looking for a wife. The tasks had given her an excuse to stay near Temujin's hiding place. Her aunt had praised her diligence before going off with the other women to tend the sheep.

Khadagan straightened a strand of wool, pulled on the hand-loom's shuttle, then looked up to see Chaghan riding towards her along the bank.

Her cousin reined in her brown gelding. "Some of us are going to look for that boy," Chaghan said, dismounting. "I told the others to wait until I fetched you."

"I have to work."

"Oh, Khadagan. You can tell your father you were helping us search. Everyone who isn't needed here is out looking."

"I can't leave everything to Khaghar-eke." The heat, even this early in the day, was making her flush; she wondered how Temujin was faring under the wool.

"He'll really get beaten if he's caught." Chaghan giggled. "Maybe he'll get away."

"He won't get far on foot and bound to a kang. Perhaps

he'll give himself up and take his chances with Targhutai. After all, he wasn't put to death before."

"Come with us," Chaghan said. "If we find him, we'll chase him like a hare!"

Khadagan pushed the shuttle. It was all a game to Chaghan. "He may already be dead," she said. "A cat might have brought him down and dragged him to its lair."

"No one's seen a cat near here, and there would be blood and some sign of a struggle." Chaghan led her horse closer to the cart. Khadagan's hand froze on the shuttle. A dog bounded towards the cart and sniffed at the wheels. "Well? Are you coming or not?"

Khadagan was afraid to speak. The dog howled. Chaghan stared at the cart, frowning. "I told you before," Khadagan said at last. "I can't go."

Chaghan mounted. "We probably won't find him." She paused. "Some of the others wouldn't care if he gets away, but if we see him, we'll have to tell the men."

Chaghan rode away. The other children might not mind if Temujin escaped, but none of them would take the risk of helping him. Even the Taychiut boys and girls, some of whom must have known him years ago, would not waste any pity on him.

"Foolish girl," Khaghar said. Khadagan wondered which of them the old woman meant.

Sorkhan-shira did not return until evening. "Your brothers won't be back tonight," he said. "They'll keep looking with the younger men."

Khadagan handed him a jug as he sat down on his bed. "How long will they search?"

"For tomorrow, at least. I have to join your uncle after I eat to look downriver. Targhutai thinks the boy must be hiding along the bank, since he'd be safer there than in the open, but he means to cover as much ground searching as he can."

"Then Temujin can't leave yet."

Her father shuddered. "No."

"May the spirits protect us," Khaghar muttered from the hearth.

Sorkhan-shira ate his food without speaking, then stood up. "My brother will want to share a drink with me in his tent after we've searched. Can you look after the boy?"

Khadagan nodded. He patted her shoulder, then left. She rinsed the platter with broth, set it down, and went outside.

Except for the sound of singing in a distant yurt, the camp was quiet; a cloud drifted across the bright moon. Khadagan crept to the cart. "Can you hear me?" she said softly, and was answered by a muffled grunt. "There's a jug of kumiss inside, by the hearth. Go in and drink it – I'll wait out here."

Temujin slipped out from under the wool; bits of fleece clung to his face and hands. He disappeared inside the tent. Khadagan sat down by the cart. No one was likely to come by, but she was ready to warn him if anyone appeared.

He came back out in a few moments, moved around the side of the yurt to piss, then hurried towards her. "I can't hide under that wool much longer," he whispered.

"You must. They'll still be searching tomorrow."

He knelt and put a hand on her shoulder; she pulled away. "Khadagan," he said, "your father, kind as he's been, might have given me up except for your words."

"He may regret that he didn't."

"You and your brothers have been my friends. I swear to you that one day you'll see them honoured, and that you will sit at my side."

The heat had affected him. Here he was, in grave danger, speaking of impossible triumphs. "Yes," she whispered, "if you don't bring us all to ruin first."

"I won't forget. If you're ever without protection, turn to me, and I'll hold out my hand to you."

"Don't soothe me with your talk," she said. "It's too late for us to give you up, anyway. Now hide yourself."

Khadagan kept near the yurt the next day, and did not see her father and brothers until after sunset. They all wore troubled expressions as they sat down to eat.

"Targhutai has to give up this hunt soon," Chimbai said. "His men are telling him that the boy would have surrendered by now if he were still alive."

"Until we're sure," Sorkhan-shira muttered, "the lad will have to sweat in his bed of wool." Khadagan got up and fetched another jug. "You're drinking more, child."

"It isn't for me, Father. I'll give it to Temujin when it's safe for him to come out."

Her father scowled. "We've done enough for him. He can go without food for one night."

She did not feel like arguing with him. The hunt would soon be over. The boy would escape, and they would be safe.

Khadagan slept soundly that night, not waking until she heard the familiar sound of the churning outside. Her father's bed was empty. She closed her eyes again and was dozing when the beating noise outside abruptly ceased.

Sorkhan-shira suddenly came through the entrance. "Get up," he said; Khadagan's brothers sat up in their beds. "We've been told to wait outside. Targhutai's ordered a search of the camp."

Khadagan stood outside the yurt with her brothers. The Taychiuts had been searching for some time, moving steadily towards her father's camping circle. She should have guessed that Targhutai would search the dwellings when the boy was not found, that he would suspect someone had hidden him.

In the distance, several men dismounted by her uncle's tent. Two rummaged through the trunks in his wagons as the others went inside. The searchers had started at the edges of the camp, moving steadily towards its centre.

They'll find him, Khadagan thought. Her father would be killed for hiding him, and perhaps her brothers as well. She had led them to this with her pleas, had allowed herself to be swayed by the captive's plight and his gentle words.

Five Taychiuts rode towards their dwelling. Khaghar's hand clutched Khadagan's shoulder. Sorkhan-shira sat by the cart, calmly sharpening a spearpoint. Khadagan's hands shook; she forced herself to be still.

Her father got to his feet and leaned his spear against the cart as the Taychiuts dismounted. "We'll look here now," one of the men said.

"Useless task," Sorkhan-shira replied, "but Targhutai's ordered it, so we must obey."

"Useless it may be," the Taychiut said, "and I'm weary of hearing the women curse at us for disturbing their things."

"Come inside, friend." Sorkhan-shira led the men into the yurt. Khadagan was afraid to move or to look into her brothers' faces. The men would never believe that Temujin had crawled into the cart without their knowledge.

She heard a thump, as though something had been overturned. " – must be dead," her father was saying. "He'd be easy prey with that kang."

"We'd have found the body by now," a man responded.

"He might have been dragged off," Sorkhan-shira said. "He may be lying at the bottom of Onon-eke, trapped and drowned by the reeds, or the current might have swept the body elsewhere."

Khadagan heard another thump, then the creak of a trunk being opened. "Still," another man murmured, "he'd have to get rid of the kang to have any chance in the open. Targhutai wonders if someone here might have taken pity on him."

Sorkhan-shira laughed; Khadagan was surprised at how natural his laughter sounded. "That's a good one," he said. "Anyone who did would deserve to die simply for being a fool."

"I pitied him a little myself," a Taychiut said. "There's something of Yesugei in him, and the Bahadur was a good man before he so carelessly allowed his enemies to poison him." Khadagan heard a clang as something struck the hearth.

"I'll admit I felt sorry for him," Sorkhan-shira said. "Natural enough, given the state he was in – he didn't have much strength left by the time I got him."

"He had enough to knock out his guard."

Sorkhan-shira laughed again. "A boy half his size could have taken on that weak fellow, even bound to a kang. Set down those cushions and rest here a while – you deserve a drink for your trouble."

"We'll come back for that drink another time," a deep-voiced man said. "Targhutai will rest easier when he knows the camp's been searched. We can stop hunting that accursed boy then."

Two men came out to search the wagon behind the yurt. Khadagan kept her eyes down as her father emerged with the other three. Their booted feet moved towards the cart. "We'd better look here," the man with the deep voice said.

Khadagan's throat tightened. Khaghar gripped her more tightly.

"Save yourself some effort," her father said. His hand grasped his spear; he thrust the weapon into the wool, then pulled it out.

The three Taychiuts grinned. "We have our orders," one said. They pulled wool from the cart, throwing it to the ground. Sorkhan-shira leaned against a wheel and fingered his drooping moustache as the pile of wool near his feet grew. Khadagan felt a hand on her other shoulder and looked up at Chimbai's tense, sallow face.

One man sighed, straightened, and wiped his brow. "Hot work," Sorkhan-shira murmured, "on a day like this." The man nodded. "And wasted effort, if you ask me. How could anyone live through this heat buried under so much wool?" Another mass of wool was thrown out; the cart would soon be empty.

"He's right," the man said as the other two Taychiuts came around the dwelling. "We're through here."

"My tent's in disarray," Sorkhan-shira said, "and now you leave my wool dumped on the ground."

The deep-voiced man shrugged. "Can't help you, friend. We want to be finished before dark."

The five men walked towards their horses. Khadagan reached for her father's hand and squeezed it. "We have work to do," he whispered. "Khadagan, this wool and our belongings must be put back in their proper places, and then you and old Khaghar will boil a lamb. Sons, come with me. It's time we sent our charge on his way."

It was night when Sorkhan-shira returned and sent Chimbai out to fetch Temujin. "Targhutai's angry," he said, "but he's been convinced that the bird that escaped is gravely wounded or dead. He also has the consolation of believing that none of his followers sheltered the fledgeling."

180

They would be safe, Khadagan thought, once the boy was gone. Temujin would be free. She did not believe that she would see him again; the life he faced now would not be easy. Temujin might vanish, to become only another nameless outcast swallowed by the steppe, his bones never to be found.

Temujin came inside, followed by Chimbai. The boy's face was flushed and he moved stiffly; it was a wonder the heat had not completely overcome him.

"It's clouding up outside," Chimbai said.

Sorkhan-shira nodded. "That will make it easier for our charge to sneak away." He put a hand on Temujin's shoulder. "You nearly got us all killed. We might have been scattered like the ashes of a fire. I felt death reaching out for me today."

Chilagun handed Temujin two small leather jugs of kumiss; the boy secured them under his worn belt as Khadagan handed him a large sack. "There's boiled lamb in the sack," Sorkhan-shira went on. "Get to the bank and head downriver. You'll find an unsaddled yellow mare in the copse of trees just beyond the second bend. My men will think she slipped her traces and wandered off, and since she's old and fallow, no one will look for her." He held out two arrows and a bow. "You'll have food, so you needn't hunt. Now find your family and leave us free of you."

He had given Temujin no flints for a fire, and no saddle. A bow with two arrows would not be much of a defence, but Khadagan did not protest. The danger was nearly past.

Temujin hefted the sack, then touched Sorkhan-shira's hand. "You'll be rewarded for what you've done someday."

"Having you away from here will be reward enough."

Chimbai and Chilagun embraced Temujin in turn. The pale-eyed boy bowed to Khaghar. "I'm also grateful to you, old woman." He glanced at Khadagan. "Remember my promise."

She lowered her eyes. When she looked up, Temujin had vanished.

PART FOUR

Temujin said, "I was no more than an insect scurrying for cover, and this mountain gave me shelter. I was no more than a bug crawling on the ground, and the spirit who dwells here gave me my life."

35

DEI SECHEN SAID, "You're growing older, daughter."
Bortai tensed, knowing what would come next.

"You're growing old inside my tent." Her father was drunk, glowering at her from his bed. "Some say I can't even break my own daughter to the bit. You're seventeen, Bortai – how much longer will you wait?"

She glanced at her brother. Anchar hunched over the arrows he was fletching. Shotan was silent as she moved towards the hearth.

Bortai said, "I'll wait until my betrothed comes for me."

"And when will that be?" Dei sighed. "I've been patient. I let you talk me into turning away suitors with many herds because I couldn't bear your tears."

"I made a promise," she said, "and so did you. Temujin is waiting until he has more to offer me."

"You deceive yourself, girl. He's dead, or he's forgotten you."

"You could have had a husband by now," Shotan murmured. "You won't have your beauty forever."

Bortai lifted her head, dismayed; her mother had always taken her side before. Even Anchar, who usually stood up for her, said nothing. She could feel her father stoking his rage.

"I'm still young," Bortai said. "Many are unwed at my age."

183

"The longer we wait," Dei said, "the less of a bride-price I'll get."

She knew that she was being obstinate. If any of the men who had asked for her had possessed the light she had seen in Temujin's eyes, maybe she would have given her consent.

Why did she cling to her hopes? Temujin was no longer the boy who had made that promise; she was not the child who had sworn to wait. All she could recall of Temujin was his eyes. She might be no more than a faint memory to him; he probably supposed she had been wed to another.

But she had sworn an oath, and the spirits had sent her a dream. If he were dead, she would know it somehow.

"Your mother's sewn your wedding robe," Dei said. "She waits, hoping for the day when she can embroider your coat for you." He paused. "I was fond of the boy. I'd give you to him if he were here, but I won't wait any longer."

Bortai forced herself to look into his eyes. "I made a promise."

His hand caught her on the cheek. "You'll give this up!" he shouted. "You'll marry the first man I find suitable. I swear it – if I must beat you and drag you to your own wedding, I will. You'll be settled by summer, one way or another."

"I'll wed Temujin."

Dei grabbed one of her braids, then struck her again. She suffered the blows, refusing to protect herself. He'll come for me, she thought despairingly; he must.

36

THE HIGH-PITCHED whistles of marmots pierced the air. Khasar stood up in his stirrups as Temujin loosed his hawk to soar, then dive swiftly towards a fleeing marmot.

Borchu laughed; the young Arulat had trained the bird himself before giving it to Temujin. The hawk's wings fluttered, and its beak stabbed at the prey.

Temujin and Borchu rode towards the bird. A cold wind rushed down from the snow-covered cliffs to the west, making Khasar sway in his saddle. Bits of green dotted the land before him; to the north, he could see the distant massif of Burkhan Khaldun in the Kentei range that marked the boundary between forest and steppe. The forest where Khasar had once hidden always grew darker in spring, when leaves sprouted from tree limbs and hid the sun, but in this valley, the spring brought light.

The hawk flew to Temujin's wrist, and he fed it a bit of meat while Borchu hung the dead marmot on his saddle. Temujin hooded the hawk, then looped the tether around his wrist. Borchu stepped to his own horse and swung into the saddle. The young man spent more time in Temujin's camp than he did in his father's. Khasar preferred the Arulat to Jamukha, although he would not have said so to his brother.

They had not seen Jamukha for nearly a year, largely because Temujin's anda had to lead his clan now. Jamukha had talked of joining their camps, but Temujin wanted to gather more followers first. Jamukha had been careless once, addressing Temujin as "younger brother", as though Temujin were his vassal.

Borchu was different. His oath of friendship seemed as binding as an anda bond, his wealth only a source of gifts for his comrade.

Khasar rode slowly towards the others. He could still marvel at how Temujin seized the worst misfortunes and turned them to his benefit. He thought of how his brother had laughed at their mother's tears when he had found the family again after his escape from Targhutai's camp.

Even Borchu's friendship had been wrenched from disaster. Shortly after the family had moved to the Senggur River valley, thieves had swooped down on them and stolen their eight remaining geldings. The thieves had missed taking the yellow mare Temujin had brought from the Taychiut camp only because Belgutei was away hunting on her.

Temujin had insisted on riding after the thieves alone. He had met Borchu along the way; the Arulat had seen men pass with eight silver-grey geldings. Borchu had immediately pledged to help Temujin steal the horses back.

Khasar had told the story often to those who had joined his brother since then. The two boys had crept up on the thieves, wounded two of them, chased the others off, and captured the horses. Borchu had even refused to accept part of Temujin's tiny herd in return for his help.

Having Borchu as an ally was welcome, and not just because he had been a brave and steadfast friend of Temujin's from the start. His father was Nakhu the Rich, chief of the Arulats. Nakhu Bayan had many herds, and Borchu was his only son.

"I'd like to keep this hawk," Temujin was saying as Khasar approached, "but I may make a gift of her to Bortai's father."

"You're going to claim her?" Borchu asked.

"I've waited long enough."

Khasar frowned; he had hoped his brother might have forgotten Bortai. That Onggirat girl would not have waited this long, with no word from him.

Khasar felt a familiar twinge in his groin. He could use a wife himself.

He lifted his head. Five riders, followed by six carts and other men on horseback herding a flock of sheep, were moving towards their camp from the north-east. More people had decided to join his brother, then. Their camp was still small, but over twenty yurts stood in the camping circles to the south of Temujin's own tents. The men with Temujin followed him south into the Gobi to raid unwary travellers at watering holes. Temujin always gave most of the loot to the others.

Temujin motioned to Borchu. "We must greet those people," he said. Khasar trotted after his brother and his friend. The sheep the newcomers were bringing would increase their herds; they would not have to steal more for a while. Perhaps the travellers were more young men who sought a new leader, who had heard that the young chief camped by the Senggur welcomed any who came as friends and was generous with his followers.

"Mother!" Temujin was shouting to her. "Mother!" Hoelun set down the garment she was mending as her son came around the wagon; an old woman was with him. "Look here – our old servant has returned to us."

Khokakhchin's face was even more wrinkled, but Hoelun recognized her small dark eyes. She jumped to her feet and embraced the old woman.

"I never thought I'd see you again." Hoelun trembled as she wept; Khokakhchin's brown cheeks were streaked with tears.

"She came here with some Khongkhotats," Temujin said. "A few from one of their camps wish to join me."

Hoelun glanced at him. "Is Munglik – "

"The men left his camp in the night. Khokakhchin-eke came with their women."

"I was given to a kinsman of Munglik's two years ago," Khokakhchin murmured. "Munglik let me go. He won't join you himself, but didn't stop us."

How like him, Hoelun thought. He would make this small gesture, in case Temujin grew stronger, but would not risk offending his Taychiut allies.

"You have a place with us," she said as she released Khokakhchin. "You always will, old friend."

"You come at a happy time," Temujin said. "I plan to fetch my betrothed soon, so you'll see me wed. I must go to the men now." He hugged the old woman, then walked away.

Hoelun led Khokakhchin inside her tent and settled her on a cushion. "Temujin's grown tall and handsome," the old woman said. "Khasar, too. Even young Khachigun seems like a man."

"They've had to become men quickly." Hoelun was suddenly overcome; she leaned against Khokakhchin. "What brought you and the others here?"

"Stories of the young chief who welcomes followers from all the clans, keeps his promises to them, and gives them most of what he wins, even when there's little."

"Then our enemies must have heard such tales," Hoelun said.

"They've also heard that a Jajirat chief allied with Toghril Khan is your son's ally. I don't think you have to fear them yet."

Hoelun spoke briefly of what had passed, all the seasons hiding in forests and foothills. Khokakhchin was silent, her dark eyes solemn. "That's quite a tale," the old woman said when she was finished.

"And now he wishes to claim his betrothed," Hoelun said. "If she's been married, I suspect he'd risk his life and those of his men to steal her."

"Does he still care for the girl so much?"

"I don't know," Hoelun replied. "She was promised to him – I think that's what matters to my son. Temujin will never surrender anything he considers his."

"Then tell him – "

"What? That he's still a minor chief whose dreams are greater than what he has? That he may throw away what he's won so far for the sake of a girl who's probably forgotten him? I can't stop him if he's determined to go to her." Hoelun sighed. "He's survived all his hardships so far. I think he believes that nothing can defeat him."

37

BORTAI WAS CARRYING milk back to her mother's tent when she saw the two riders. They trotted along the river-bank on grey horses, with two spare greys behind them. A hooded hawk clutched the wrist of one rider; the spare horses carried packs.

One of her suitors might have returned for her. If her father approved of him, Bortai would have to accept him.

They neared the horses drinking at the river. Dei rode towards the strangers, followed by Anchar and two other men. The travellers halted. The one with the hawk handed the bird to his companion, then dismounted, holding out his arms. He was broad-shouldered and taller than her father; she did not think he had been here before. Anchar suddenly leaped from his saddle and ran towards the stranger; they embraced. Her brother threw back his head, and seemed to be laughing, as Dei strode towards them and caught the tall man in his arms.

Bortai was afraid to hope. Her father had dislodged the traveller's hat; she caught a glimpse of his dark reddish braids before he reached up to tug at the flaps.

"Temujin," she whispered, and wanted to run to him, but whirled and ran towards the yurt.

She entered and set down her bucket, nearly spilling the milk. Shotan looked up from the hearth. "Child, what is it?"

"Temujin," Bortai said.

Her mother got up, hurried to the doorway, and went outside. Bortai tugged at her coat, smoothed down her hair, then went to the back of the yurt and sat down, clutching at her clothing with trembling hands.

"I saw them," Shotan said as she came back inside. "Your father seems overjoyed." She frowned. "What's wrong with you, girl? You've prayed for nothing else, and now you look as frightened as a lamb."

Bortai could not explain. What if Temujin had changed? What would he think when he saw her? Maybe she would not seem so beautiful to him now. What sort of man had he become? He had to be coming here to claim her. She would have to go with him and honour the old promise.

"I can't bear it," Bortai said.

Shotan came to her side and sat down. "Stop your foolishness, Bortai. Your father will bring him here, then settle with the young man before you're wed. It's what you wanted, isn't it?"

She was no longer sure. I won't look at him, she thought. I won't look up until I've heard his voice, and when I see his eyes, I'll know.

Shotan went to the hearth and poured the milk into a kettle. Bortai waited, her face growing hot, until she heard Dei's voice. " – feared your enemies had made an end of you," her father was saying. "I never expected to see you again. Set the bird on that perch there." Bortai heard them enter; she continued to stare at the felt floor. "Shotan, get drink for our guests, and rejoice with us. Temujin has returned with his brother Belgutei. Our daughter's shown herself wiser than I am. I thought her betrothed lost, but her faithfulness to him has been rewarded."

189

"How you've grown," Shotan said. Bortai refused to look up.

"Temujin is chief in his own camp now," Anchar said.

"A very small camp," another said then. That had to be Temujin; his voice was deeper, but still had his forthright tone. "Only a few men have joined me, but others will follow them." That also sounded like Temujin. "I wish I had more to offer a wife, but I promise you I'll win more than I have now."

Anchar chuckled. "You've lasted this long, even with all your hardships. I think you can provide for my sister."

Bortai lifted her head. He held his hat in one hand, to shake off the dust; a tuft of hair hung over his broad forehead, while the top of his head had been shaved and his braids were coiled behind his ears. Inside the dwelling, he seemed even taller. His pale eyes glittered in his handsome face, reminding her of the falcon's eyes she had seen in her dream so long ago. This man was a stranger, studying her coldly, perhaps disappointed in what he saw.

"Bortai," he said. His eyes grew warmer; his brown face reddened a little. "I promised I would return for you, and you kept your promise to me. I believed you would, but now that I see you, I wonder that no man claimed you."

"Many have tried," Anchar said. "My sister's beauty has some fame."

"I swear that she'll never regret her bond with me," Temujin said. "That is, if your father wishes to honour his pledge."

Dei Sechen waved an arm. "Is there any doubt of that? The girl's been in my tent long enough, and I can think of no man who's more worthy of her." He smiled. "Of course, we must see what kind of bargain we can reach."

Bortai bowed her head. The years of waiting were past. She would no longer endure the mockery of her cousins and friends and the pleas of her parents. She would have her husband, and not allow herself any regrets.

190

38

BORTAI WAITED INSIDE a yurt with her uncles' wives and her female cousins. The days before the wedding had seemed endless; now she felt that they had passed too quickly. Temujin and his brother Belgutei, as was proper, had remained outside the camp during the preparations. A day had passed in talk with Dei and one of Bortai's uncles before Temujin offered his gifts.

Her father had acquired silks and pots for Shotan taken from a caravan, and the hawk for himself, along with promises of many horses and other animals from Temujin's herds later on, when the young man had more to give him. Many would have called it a bad bargain, but Dei clearly believed Temujin would win enough to honour the pledge. To hear her father talk now, it was hard for Bortai to remember that he had once despaired of ever seeing Yesugei's son again.

A shaman had pondered the birth-dates of the bride and groom, the positions of the stars, and other omens before setting the date of the wedding. A week had passed while Bortai and her mother made a new sheepskin coat for Temujin and embroidered her own wedding coat. The camp smelled of roast lamb; the women had feasted with her last night and would feast again today. Bortai had been too busy to think of what lay ahead, and now her wedding day was upon her.

Outside, among the Onggirats, Temujin's dark-eyed brother would be chanting his wishes for the couple's happiness. Dei would reply in a similar vein, enlivening his speech with as many poetically phrased sentiments as possible. Her father was proud of his ability at such speeches, which was why, in defiance of custom, he was making this one himself instead of leaving it to one of his brothers. She had heard Dei at other weddings, and knew that he would shift metre unexpectedly, heightening his own words while making it difficult for Belgutei to frame an equally eloquent reply.

The women chattered, impatient for the groom to fetch his bride. Bortai's bark bocca felt heavy on her head; she clutched at the beads around her neck. Temujin had to be searching the camp for her by now. Did other brides feel this way, longing to run from their own celebrations? Perhaps their smiles and blushes only masked their fears.

"Bortai!" He was calling to her. The women quickly huddled around her, giggling. "I wish to claim my bride! Is she here?" He came inside, pushed his way through the group, and grabbed her by the arms. Bortai shrank back, knowing she should struggle, but then pushed against Temujin's chest and felt his grip tighten. "I have found the one I came here to find!"

His strong arms swept her up. The women rushed after them as he carried her outside. Bortai sagged against him, suddenly too faint to make even a token struggle. He lifted her to his horse, then mounted behind her; they trotted towards the river. Her aunts and cousins shouted as they followed, calling on the spirits to protect the bride and groom.

Most of the camp was waiting by the river. Lambs roasted in pits; men passed jugs to one another. Dei and Shotan stood on a small rise apart from the crowd.

"Bortai," Temujin whispered, "are you happy?"

She forced herself to nod. He dismounted by the rise, helped her down and led her forward. They bowed to her parents, then knelt as Shotan draped a cloak over Bortai's shoulders. Bortai barely heard the words of Dei's blessing as he presented the sheepskin coat and a quiver of arrows to Temujin; she hardly tasted the kumiss in the cup offered to her. I am his wife, she thought, and her spirit seemed to rise from her, fleeing from the cheers of the gathering.

The Onggirats feasted and drank, accompanied by the deep-throated songs of the men, the throbbing of fiddles, and the wails of pipes as the sun rode towards the western sky. People came to Bortai, bowed, and murmured good wishes and farewells.

At last Temujin rose and led her to his horse. Shotan climbed into the ox-drawn cart that held Bortai's belongings, along with the wicker frame and felt panels of a tent. She would ride with Bortai to Temujin's camp, and seemed as happy as a bride herself. Temujin helped Bortai on to his horse; she adjusted her long robe and coat as he mounted behind her. Pellets of dung rained around her, thrown by well-wishers.

They rode slowly west along the river-bank. Dei trotted near Shotan with a few of his men; Bortai heard her father and brother laugh as they joked with Belgutei. Temujin's horse trotted ahead of the rest of the party, then slowed. He was silent, his chest pressing against her back as he handled the horse's reins.

"It's good that you came when you did," Bortai said at last. "Happy as Father was to see you, he would have given me to someone else before long."

"I couldn't wait any more. Your father would have heard of me before long and wondered why I hadn't come for you." He paused. "I rejoice that you were given to me with such ceremony, but it would have pleased me just as much to ride here, offer my gifts, reach a bargain, and leave with you as soon as he gave his consent."

She twisted around. His skin was coppery in the evening light, his eyes shadowed by the flaps of his hat. He was aglow with hope for the years ahead, and she knew suddenly that she would never see him in quite this way again.

"But I wouldn't have had you miss your wedding feast," he continued. "Women set store by such things."

"I wouldn't have minded missing it," she said. "I waited for so long that I only wanted it to be over." Perhaps she should not have said that; he might misunderstand. She turned away.

"I knew you would wait," he said. "Anchar told me how you refused even to consider other suitors, ones with more to offer, and how you suffered for it, and I cursed myself for not being able to claim you before. Then, when I saw how beautiful you'd become, I worried that you might not think me worthy. I thought you might wed me only because you'd look foolish after waiting for so long if you didn't."

She swallowed. "I thought you might not want me, that you came only because of an old promise."

"How could you think that?" His arms tightened around her. "You've shown your loyalty by waiting – that's enough to make me know I chose well. But to see your beauty – " He sighed. "I'll win more than I have now for you – I promise you that."

She should have welcomed his words, and was moved by his admission of his own fears, yet sensed a colder tone in his soft voice. She thought of how he had looked at her in her father's yurt, as if judging her, before allowing himself a warmer gaze.

She could not fail her husband, nor would he allow her to do so; that much was clear. His fingers gripped her wrist for a moment, tight as talons; she closed her eyes.

The party stopped for the night. Bortai remained in the cart with her mother; Temujin would not come to her until they reached his camp.

Shotan slept deeply. Bortai lay next to her, restless, thinking of what her mother had told her before the wedding. There had been little for Shotan to say; Bortai had seen the stallions led to the mares and had heard her parents in their bed. Shotan claimed that the pain passed after the first joining and that one could learn to take pleasure in it, but Bortai knew that some women never did.

Dei left them on the second day. Bortai stared after her father from the cart until he and his men were only black specks riding towards the sun. Anchar and two of his comrades continued on with them while Belgutei rode ahead to tell Temujin's people that their chief was returning with his bride.

Belgutei met them two days later at the fork where the Kerulen River flowed into the Senggur. Another brother was with him, a sharp-eyed boy named Khasar. Anchar and his men shared some kumiss with the brothers, then came to the cart to say their farewells.

"You have a fine husband, sister," Anchar said. "There aren't many who could start with nothing and become chiefs at sixteen." He laughed. "Temujin won my last antelope bone this morning."

"I'll miss you," Bortai murmured.

Her brother leaned towards her in his saddle, touched her cheek, then galloped away with his companions.

The party rode north along the Senggur. The valley was growing green; tiny white buds poked through the grass.

Bortai's husband turned in his saddle to grin at her, his teeth white against the brown skin of his face, his eyes filled with the light she had first seen in them.

The sun was rising when Bortai first saw her husband's camp. The yurts and wagons were grouped in circles near the river, where a few cattle were drinking, and a small flock of sheep grazed. Khasar had ridden ahead to announce their arrival, and people had gathered outside the tents to greet their chief.

Shotan's eyes narrowed as they neared the modest encampment. "He has brothers," she said softly to Bortai, "and he's won followers. He should be able to provide more for you in time."

Temujin led them to the northernmost circle; people called out to him as he passed their tents. Three women stood outside one yurt. The oldest had a wrinkled, leathery face; another gazed up at Bortai with dark eyes, then quickly lowered her head. The third was a small woman, a little shorter than Bortai, her perfect face marred only by tiny lines around her large golden eyes. She held herself as proudly as a Khatun, and Bortai knew that she had to be Temujin's mother.

Shotan and Bortai climbed down from their cart; Temujin led them forward to make their bows. His mother's name was Hoelun. Bortai glanced at her shyly as Hoelun Ujin and Shotan exchanged formal greetings.

"May my daughter be a worthy wife to your son," Shotan said.

"A beautiful girl," Temujin's mother replied. "I see why my son didn't forget her." She lifted her head and gazed at Temujin; Bortai saw the fierce light in her eyes. This woman had kept her brood alive when they were abandoned by all.

I must never come between them, Bortai thought; I can never fail either of them.

"Welcome, daughter," Hoelun Ujin said. She smiled, but the smile did not reach her eyes.

Temujin's followers feasted until dark, sitting out in the open spaces between the yurts. Bortai had blessed Hoelun-eke's household spirits with drops of kumiss, and Shotan had presented the sable coat she had brought as a gift for Temujin's mother. The women of the camp had helped Bortai raise her yurt, doing the work slowly, murmuring blessings for the bride as each panel was tied to the frame. Hoelun-eke's old servant Khokakhchin had blessed the hearth and lit the fire.

The others were still feasting when Temujin stood up, helped Bortai to her feet, and bowed to her mother and his own. The two women had spoken easily to each other during the feast. Whatever Temujin's mother thought of Bortai, she clearly had a liking for Shotan.

A few men called out advice to Temujin as he led Bortai towards her yurt. At another fire, Belgutei was reciting some of the verses he had sung to Dei; she thought of her old camp with a pang of homesickness.

A soft light glowed from the entrance to her dwelling. Bortai followed her husband inside, knelt by the doorway, and anointed it with a small bit of fat. Temujin murmured a blessing, then went to the hearth, warming himself by the fire as Bortai rolled down the flap.

"My mother feared for me," he said, "when I went to claim you. I told her you would wait, and now she sees I was right. She'll grow to love you."

She moved slowly towards the bed at the back of the yurt. Her ongghon, a carved image of a cow's udder, hung over the bed from a horn set into the wicker frame. She lifted off her head-dress, then removed her coat as Temujin began to undress; she hastily looked away. It would be over soon; she would know if her mother had told her the truth.

When she was clothed only in her shift, she pulled back the blanket and sat down on the bed. "No," Temujin said, "the shift, too."

"I'll be cold."

"No, you won't. I want to see you."

She pulled off the shift and stretched out. He came towards her, still wearing his shift; she could not see his eyes in the shadows.

"Bortai." He was suddenly upon her, pushing her legs apart with his knees, and she felt his breath on her ear. "Bortai." He fumbled at her roughly, something firm and hard pressed against her thigh, then abruptly he thrust inside her and she gritted her teeth at the pain. His fingers dug into her hips as the weight of him drove the breath from her lungs. He gasped as he moved inside her, groaned, and shuddered as he sighed.

He rolled off her and lay at her side. She reached for the blanket, glimpsed the traces of blood on her inner thighs, then covered herself. So that was all there was to it. She had not felt too much pain, but wondered how any woman could welcome this act. Maybe Temujin was also disappointed. She would have to please him even if she felt no joy herself, and take her pleasure in thoughts of the children she would give him. She squeezed her eyes shut; she had hoped for too much while waiting for him.

"Bortai," he said at last. "I didn't think it would rush from me so quickly." She opened her eyes as his arm encircled her waist; his nose touched hers lightly. "I thought there would be more pleasure for you."

"There wasn't time for me to feel anything."

"Others tell me that a man must seize his woman, that otherwise she'll think he's a weakling and mock him in secret, and when I saw you, I couldn't hold myself back. But I – " His throat moved as he swallowed. "I wanted it to be more."

She touched his cheek. "If I please you," she said, "that's what matters. It'll be easier for me next time."

"That isn't enough. I want you to love me and welcome this. I want you to long for me, I want to know I can give you joy. I can't have a wife who shrinks from me and does only what she feels she must."

"Some men don't mind that."

"I'm not like other men. I'll bring you to love me." He made it sound like a battle; perhaps it was. "Are you sorry you waited for me?"

"No. I could never regret that." She meant it this time; her fears were gone.

He took her hand and pressed her fingers around his member as it swelled and grew hard against her palm; then he touched her awkwardly, smoothing the flat hairs between her legs and probing her cleft. She shivered, and knew at last that she would welcome him. He entered her more gently this time, resting his

197

weight against his arms. She burned as she felt herself tighten around him; he gripped her by the hair, forcing her to look at him. His pupils were enlarged in the dim light, making his eyes darker.

She felt a quiver deep inside her that grew into a throbbing; her body arched suddenly. She moved under him as a spasm of pleasure swept over her, and saw his fierce, triumphant smile.

39

TOGHRIL WAS DRUNK. Khasar glanced to his left; the Kereit Khan lolled in his wooden throne, still stroking the sable coat Temujin had brought to him. The Khan's ruddy face gleamed with sweat as his fingers clutched greedily at the fur.

Belgutei, sitting at Khasar's right, lifted a cup and drank. Temujin sat next to Toghril Khan, in the place of honour. Toghril had sent slaves to fetch his guests' horses, yet seemed reluctant to let his visitors depart.

Khasar's belly ached with food; the Kereits had been feasting them for two days. He and his brothers had planned to leave at dawn, but Toghril had urged them to share a last drink with him, and now the large tent was crowded with the generals, soldiers, and traders the Khan had summoned.

The Khan rose; the sable coat fell to his feet. Temujin stood up, leaned down to pick up the coat, and draped it over the throne. Toghril embraced him as Khasar and Belgutei rose from their bench.

"I am pleased," Toghril said in his resonant voice; the feasters fell silent. "You've brought me the finest of gifts, you who are the son of my anda. I do not speak only of this coat, as fine as it is, but also of the pledge you've given to me."

"You honour me," Temujin said, "by accepting it, and for saying that you'll always be a father to me. I swear to you again that nothing will come between us."

"My promise lives here." Toghril struck his chest with a fist.

"I'll gather those of your people who have scattered and return them to you. All will know that the son of Yesugei is my son." He had made this pledge before, offering sacrifices to seal the oath, but had repeated it often, as if to remind himself and everyone present that he had made it. Winning the Kereit Khan to his side had been easier for Temujin than Khasar had expected. Toghril had welcomed them warmly, and had shared his memories of Yesugei, who had restored Toghril's Khanate to him.

Khasar glanced around the large tent. Toghril had reason to be grateful to Yesugei. The Khan had served them kumiss in cups of gold and given them garments made with the hair of his camels. His herds were so numerous that he might mount a different steed every day and still not have ridden all his horses by year's end. His warriors numbered in the thousands; his ten wives, sitting at his left, were adorned in silk-lined coats and head-dresses gleaming with gold and shining stones. Caravans from east and west stopped in his camp to trade and offer tribute for safe passage through his lands.

Perhaps the sight of his anda's son had reminded the Khan of the source of his good fortune. Toghril would never have won back his throne without Yesugei's help.

People lifted cups, saluting the Khan and his new ally. Only Toghril's son Nilkha, the Senggum, who was seated near his father, seemed unmoved by the gathering's high spirits. The young man's eyes were hard as he stared at Temujin; the Senggum had avoided the Khan's guests during their stay.

Toghril's bulky body swayed. Temujin caught the Khan in his arms, then released him. "I would remain with you," Temujin said, "but my men await my return." He bowed as Khasar and Belgutei backed towards the doorway. "I shall serve you faithfully, my father."

"Go in peace, my son," Toghril said. Nilkha's eyes narrowed. Temujin retreated, still bowing to the Khan; Toghril sank back on his throne and fingered his grey moustaches. One of his Christian priests made signs and chanted a blessing as another swung a golden vessel from a chain.

A wide ladder of steps rested against the large wheeled platform that held the yurt. Khasar took a deep breath of cool air, relieved to be away from the oppressive heat inside, then descended quickly. Two boys were waiting with their four horses, all of them burdened with the sacks that held Toghril's gifts.

They mounted. The Kereit camp sprawled to the south along the Tula River, its circles of yurts and carts stretching as far as Khasar's sharp eyes could see. Dark masses of cattle grazed in the open land bordering the forest to the west. Envy clawed at Khasar; all this belonged to Toghril, who had done nothing for his anda's sons before. But the Khan was now their protector, and his power would serve Temujin's ends. He looked back at the Khan's ordu as they rode away; the great tent's limed yellow panels were golden in the noonday light.

The brothers rode east along the Tula, then turned north. Beyond the barren patches where the Kereit herds had grazed, white flowers bloomed amid the grass of the plain. A distant dark ridge marked the mountains to the north. Temujin seemed deep in thought. He did not speak until the camp was far behind them and they had stopped to water their horses.

"What do my brothers think," Temujin said, "of our father's anda?"

Belgutei swatted at a fly. "He was quick to accept you as a vassal," he murmured. "Hoelun-eke will be glad that the coat your wife's mother gave her was of some use. She must have been sorry to part with it."

Khasar glanced at his half-brother. Belgutei rarely answered Temujin's questions directly, but instead circled them the way hunters surrounded game, then closed in on an answer Temujin might welcome.

"I'll give Mother one of the Khan's gold cups," Temujin said, "and promise her another coat." He dismounted, then looked up at Khasar. "And your thoughts?"

"Toghril Khan wouldn't be grateful just for a coat," Khasar replied, "even one as fine as that. I suspect his old bond with Father wasn't much on his mind before our arrival. He lost his Khanate before, and must sit uneasily on his throne now, with an exiled brother who could still threaten him." One of Toghril's brothers had taken refuge among the powerful Naiman tribes in the west; the Naiman ruler might take up his cause and move against the Kereit Khan if Toghril seemed vulnerable. "As long as you serve his ends, he'll be your friend. It's good his men mentioned the wisdom of this alliance, but it makes me wonder what he would have decided if no one had spoken for you. I don't think his son Nilkha wanted this bond."

Temujin nodded; he had clearly been thinking the same thing. "He needs me to throw against his enemies," he said, "and I need his support. We both have what we want, which makes for the best of alliances." He rested his hand on Khasar's saddle. "I'm anxious to be home, as you must be, but I want you to postpone your return for a few more days."

Khasar leaned forward. "What do you wish me to do?"

"Ride to Jamukha's camp. I'd do so myself, but I grow impatient for my wife."

Khasar grinned. "I understand, but why do you want me to go there?"

"Jamukha is also Toghril-echige's vassal, and when he learns of my oath to him, he may wonder about my intentions."

"Why would he worry about that?" Belgutei asked. "You're his anda – he has no reason to doubt you."

"Indeed he doesn't." Temujin's mouth twisted. "It would be wise to remind him of that. Toghril's support will bring more men to me, and I don't want Jamukha to think that this makes me his rival. If Toghril Khan thinks either of us may grow too strong, he's capable of using us against each other. My anda must be reassured that I'll never forsake our bond."

"Surely he knows that," Belgutei said. "Do you doubt him?"

Temujin scowled. "I have no doubts," he said very softly. "Jamukha was our comrade when we had no friends – do you think I can ever forget that? But he's used to seeing me as someone less powerful than he is, and that will soon change. He must be told that this won't alter things between us."

"I'll go," Khasar said, although he did not welcome the journey. Temujin might not have doubts, but he did.

"Give him one of the Khan's golden cups," Temujin said, "and tell him that he lives in my heart."

Khasar found a small Jajirat encampment along the Onon. The men there told him that Jamukha Bahadur's main camp was just below the Khorkhonagh Valley, and sent a rider ahead to tell the Jajirat chief that Khasar was on his way to see him.

Khasar slept in the small camp that night and rode on in the morning. Jamukha was waiting for him outside his camping circle with a few men. He embraced Khasar warmly, then quickly led him between the fires to his tent. After dismissing his men, the Jajirat ushered him inside.

A young woman standing by the hearth bowed; an older woman with her knelt. "My wife, Nomalan," Jamukha said.

Khasar bowed to the women. "I rejoice for you. I didn't know you had taken a bride."

"We were married in early spring." Jamukha waved one arm. "Leave us." The young woman hurried towards the entrance, her head down; the servant followed her. "A man must have a wife," Jamukha continued, "but it's a pity such creatures can't be kept with the brood mares much of the time."

Khasar grunted, trying to imagine his brother saying that about Bortai. Jamukha led him to the bed and seated him in front of it, then handed him a jug.

"I'll summon those closest to me later," Jamukha said as he sat down, "but now you must tell me of my anda."

Khasar told him about the journey to the Kereit camp. The young man smiled and nodded, seemingly pleased at the news. His handsome face brightened as Khasar gave him the golden cup and then recited the oaths his brother and Toghril had sworn.

"I am happy to hear this," Jamukha said. "Men will flock to join your brother now, and other chiefs will see him as their equal."

"I thought – forgive me if I'm wrong – that you once hoped Temujin would follow you."

Jamukha laughed. "That he would ride at my side. Do you think I could ever consider my anda less than myself? I thought only of lending my strength to his." He shifted on his cushion. "I'm pleased you told me this, Khasar. I sorrow only that my anda didn't ride here himself to tell me. I've missed him greatly."

"As he's missed you. His friend Borchu, Nakhu Bayan's son, dwells in our camp now, and has sworn never to leave Temujin's side, but even he can't take your place in my brother's heart, beloved though he is."

Jamukha's dark eyes flickered. "I recall him with some fondness. Perhaps he and your brother are even closer than they were."

The slightly colder tone in Jamukha's voice made Khasar uneasy. "They are fast friends. Of course it isn't the same as an anda bond. Temujin will never forget that you were his friend when he had no other." He swallowed some kumiss. "He longed to come here, but he has duties in our camp and a new wife who awaits him. You can understand why he's impatient to be with her, after waiting so long to claim her."

"His wife?" Jamukha said softly.

"Bortai, the Onggirat girl he was betrothed to as a child. She's as beautiful as he said she would be. During his first days with her, he didn't leave his tent until the sun was two hands' breadth above the horizon, and he often carries her inside before the sun sets, the two of them laughing – "

"Men often act foolish when they're first wed." Jamukha's face was taut, his eyes slits. "It passes."

Khasar cleared his throat, thinking that Jamukha should have been pleased to hear of his anda's happiness. "She's only a woman," he said, "but when you see her beauty, you'll understand why he loves her – and she's a good wife to him."

"A woman's a good wife if she does her work and bears strong sons – the rest matters little." Jamukha got up and went to the doorway. "I'll summon my men."

40

TEMUJIN SAID, "I'LL race you to the trees."
Bortai glanced back at Borchu and Jelme. "You wouldn't want me to beat you in front of your comrades."

Temujin lifted his brows. "We'll see if you do."

Jelme rode towards them, followed by Borchu with a hawk

riding on his wrist; dead hares and cranes hung from each young man's saddle. Temujin handed his falcon to Jelme. "I've challenged my wife to a race," he said. "She thinks she'll win this time."

Borchu chuckled. "Maybe she will."

Bortai struck her horse lightly with her whip. The mount bolted, moving into a gallop; Temujin raced after her and closed the gap quickly. She leaned forward, tightening her legs around the animal. A rodent darted through the high brown grass, narrowly evading the gelding's hooves.

The grove of trees stood just above the river. Bortai's steed inched ahead of Temujin's. She bore down on a small patch of marsh, thought of swerving to her right to avoid it, then changed her mind. Rising in her stirrups, she jumped her horse over the marshy ground; the ducks feeding in the reeds quacked loudly and scattered.

She neared the trees and drew on her reins. The grey gelding slowed as she passed the first tree, then skidded to a halt. Temujin reined in his horse and trotted to her side. The horses were slick with sweat; Bortai rubbed hers along its neck.

"You won, but not by much," her husband said.

"I still won." The horse danced under her. She circled the small grove at a walk, letting the gelding cool; Temujin kept near her. Beyond the trees, north of their camp, more horses grazed, guarded by men.

She thought of how small the camp had been when she arrived nearly three months ago; but the Kereit Khan had kept his vow, and news of Temujin's new alliance had travelled quickly. The camp had grown since their move to the Kerulen River, filling with members of Borchu's Arulat clan and sons of warriors who had ridden with Temujin's father; Temujin welcomed them all. He refused to claim a portion of their belongings as tribute; he had even given a coat to one man whose garment was in tatters, and arrows to another so that he could hunt. Word of his generosity had brought more followers. The land west of the camp had been grazed nearly bare by the increased herds of horses, cattle, and sheep; the camp would have to be moved again soon.

Bortai kept near the trees; it was cooler in the shade, away from the hot summer sun. Temujin leaped from his horse, pulled her from her saddle, and wrestled her to the ground.

"Stop," she said, giggling. "What will Jelme and Borchu think?"

"Only that I can't wait for night."

She struggled. He knelt over her, his knees on either side of her, pressing against her hips. She wondered if the trees hid them from view, and suddenly did not care. Her hands slipped around his neck, under the knotted cloth of his head-band; he lowered his head and rubbed his cheek against hers. She closed her eyes, thinking of how he had moved inside her last night while she sat astride him, riding him.

"Bortai," he whispered. Her arms tightened around him. He removed her hands from himself and sat up, his mouth curving into a smile. He had the small victory he wanted, of knowing that she would welcome him at any time, even out here, within sight of the horseherders and his two friends.

She sat up slowly and adjusted the scarf that covered her braided hair. "We should show more dignity, Temujin. Your men will wonder."

"They'll know I love my wife." He tilted his head. "But maybe I should be more of a man. When we ride back, I must look very stern, and order you to clean and skin the game. Then I'll shout for my supper and threaten to beat you if you're not quick about it."

Bortai wrinkled her nose, then frowned. "I should have been beating wool today instead of hunting with you. Your mother will think I'm a foolish, lazy girl."

"She'll never think that. She can hardly praise you enough."

That was, she supposed, her victory. She had worried that his mother, who had endured so much, might never warm to her, that she would see any woman as less than herself. When Hoelun-eke had taken her aside a month ago, she had expected a scolding. Temujin's mother had studied her for a long moment before saying, "My son has a great love for you. I didn't believe you could be what he said you were. Even after you came here, and I saw what a good woman your mother is, I had my doubts about you, and feared your beauty might have blinded my son to your faults. Now I'm sorry that you have no unmarried sisters for my other sons."

With those words, the last traces of Bortai's longing for her father's camp were banished. She could speak easily to Hoelun now, and they often agreed in their judgements. Hoelun-eke sensed which men might serve her son best, and who might lead him astray with bad advice. She knew which women were wise, and how to speak carefully to those who might be jealous or envious.

Bortai remembered what Hoelun had told her yesterday, when they had been weaving cloth with old Khokakhchin. "Men come here," Hoelun had said, "to follow a chieftain who has the protection of the Kereit Khan. They also think Temujin will help them win much for themselves. But it won't be their oaths to him that hold them, or even the victories he might bring them. He must have their loyalty, their obedience, and their love, so that they will never think of abandoning him even if thousands are marshalled against him. It means he must have our loyalty and love, too, especially yours."

"He'll always have that," Bortai said.

"You're a woman to trust." Hoelun's words had made her swell with pride. "Another wife might have wailed at him, and said, 'Where is my servant? Why don't I have more hides and carpets? Why don't you claim a larger share of game, and give me what I should have?' And my son would have listened, and his men would soon be saying that he was no better than any other chief."

"We will win more in time."

"You're a good wife, Bortai, but there's more to that than being steadfast and obedient. You must also see your husband clearly, with a falcon's eyes, and know when he might be mistaken. You may have to say things to him no one else would dare to mention, things even I might fear to say. He was alone for so long, with no one but me and his brothers and sister. He has learned to trust others, but his joy at having comrades at last may blind him to their faults. You must be able to see what they are and warn him if necessary." Bortai had been surprised that Temujin's mother saw any flaws in him.

She leaned against her husband, her cheek against his coat.

Borchu and Jelme trotted towards them. Borchu was quick to smile, to laugh, and to follow Temujin on risky forays without question, while Jelme's dark eyes were always cautious and watchful. She had no worries about those two; their devotion was evident. Borchu had bound himself to Temujin; with one command, he would have given everything he owned to his friend. Jelme, an Uriangkhai, had come out of the northern forests with his father, a blacksmith named Jarchiudai, who had long ago promised Yesugei that his son would serve the Bahadur's; he was always near, often anticipating Temujin's wishes before they were spoken.

The two young men grinned as Temujin helped Bortai to her feet. Her husband motioned to them with one hand. Borchu nodded and rode on; Jelme dismounted and led his horse down to the river to drink. The Uriangkhai would stay near, ready to ride to them if he was needed.

Temujin lifted her to her horse. "You've brought me luck, Bortai. Everything's changing for me."

She laughed softly. "Your alliance with the Kereits has something to do with that."

He mounted his own horse. "After we move camp," he said, "I'll join my anda before autumn. It's time we renewed our bond."

Bortai was silent. Hoelun-eke had told her about Jamukha, praising him for his devotion to her son, but her eyes had grown colder when she mentioned him.

"We always said we would ride together when we were men," Temujin continued. "We should join our forces permanently. He asked me to do so before."

"And which of you would command?"

"We're brothers — we'd both command."

She said nothing to that; it seemed as unlikely as wild stallions refusing to challenge each other for a herd of mares. She would not think of Jamukha now; autumn seemed far away.

They rode towards the camp, circling the herd of horses; Jelme trailed them at a distance. To the south, a dark circle of yurts and carts rippled in the hot air. Summer stretched before her, with its long days that were endless, yet endurable, because she could go about her tasks anticipating the night. In her bed,

207

time always stopped; there was only Temujin when her spirit soared to meet his, when no world existed outside their bodies and souls. There would always be Temujin. The days ahead were landmarks on a trail that through the years to come would wind from night to night, unchanging.

41

HOELUN AWOKE, THEN sat up. Her three youngest children were asleep in their beds, but Khokakhchin had left the yurt. She listened, but heard only silence; the wind that had followed the evening storm had died at last.

Khokakhchin entered the tent. "Ujin," the old woman whispered, "get dressed and come with me."

Hoelun pulled on her clothes, covered her hair with a scarf, then followed her servant outside. "What is it?"

"I felt the ground tremble before, and thought another storm was coming, but the sky's clear." Khokakhchin dropped to the ground. "I put my ear to the earth and heard rumbling." She rested her head against the dirt. "I hear it still. It sounds as if an army's coming this way."

The old woman had a weasel's ears; she often heard sounds others could not. Hoelun knelt and pressed her ear to the ground. She heard it now, the low, barely audible sound of distant hooves.

The Taychiuts, she thought; they're finally going to make an end of us. She looked up; the sky was dark, but growing greyer. Their enemies might reach the camp before sunrise.

She jumped to her feet. "Wake Temujin! Sound the alert!" Khokakhchin hastened away, calling out as she moved towards Temujin's yurt. Hoelun ran back inside and shook Khachigun awake. "We must flee," she said. "You children will take only your weapons and any provisions you can carry — we must get to the horses and escape."

Her son bolted from the bed and woke the other two children as Hoelun gathered what she could.

The shouts outside woke Bortai. Temujin rolled from the bed, pulling on his shift and trousers. Khokakhchin's voice rose above the others. "An attack is coming! Make your escape!" Bortai grabbed her clothes as Temujin bounded towards the entrance and lifted the flap.

Khokakhchin panted as she came inside. "Taychiuts are after us," the old woman gasped. "The ground shakes with the sound of their steeds."

Temujin shouldered his bowcase and quiver. Bortai tightened the sash around her waist, handed her husband his spear and two skins of kumiss, then reached for her weapons.

They hurried outside. Two men were riding towards the yurts south of Temujin's circle. In the distance, Bortai heard screams and the terrified shrieks of children, and glimpsed Hoelun-eke running towards the rope where Temujin's horses were tied.

Borchu and Jelme rode towards them, each on one of Temujin's geldings, leading a third by the reins. "Come," Jelme shouted as his horse skidded to a halt. "We can't find Sochigil Ujin, but your mother and the children will come with us. Khasar and Belgutei are with them."

Bortai's heart strained against her chest. The men could not make a stand here; their only hope was to get away and strike back later.

Temujin looked up at his two friends, hesitating. "We have my nine horses," he murmured. "Mother and Temulun will ride on one." He reached for Bortai; she pulled away.

"Go," she said. "You'll need one horse as a spare, when the others tire." She pushed him towards Borchu. "Go! You're the one they want – if they get you, we're all lost. Searching for captives will delay them. I'll find my way to you later."

"Your wife speaks wisely." Jelme leaned down and grabbed Temujin's collar. "Come!"

Temujin glanced at her one last time, then mounted his horse. "Guard her, Khokakhchin-eke," he said. "Get her to a safe place." He pulled his standard from the ground, threw it to Borchu, then rode away.

Bortai leaned against the old woman, watching riders stream across the plain. The Arulats had been grazing their horses away from the camp; she would find no mount nearby on which to escape. Cattle roamed over the grass; bleating sheep milled around in the wide spaces between the tents. A few people were riding towards the Burgi cliff to the east while others galloped after Temujin's standard.

"We'll fight," Bortai whispered. "If we can hold them off for even a little while – "

"A few women and children can't fight an army," Khokakhchin muttered. "Trust me, young Ujin – I'll see that you're safe."

Khokakhchin found an old speckled ox and hastily hitched the animal to a covered cart. A few women were fleeing on foot along the river-bank; Bortai ran towards Sochigil's yurt, calling her name.

"We can't look for her now," Khokakhchin shouted after her. "Hurry!" Bortai raced back to the cart. Temujin had been too generous with his followers; there would have been horses for her and Khokakhchin if he had kept more for himself.

"Get in," the old woman said. Bortai climbed into the cart; newly sheared wool lay under its arched leather covering. Khokakhchin settled herself on the seat in front. "Cover yourself, Ujin, and lie still – don't make a sound, whatever happens."

Bortai slipped off her quiver and bowcase, covered them, then burrowed under the wool. The cart rattled and shook as the ox pulled it forward. "I'm going to make for the Tungelig River," Khokakhchin continued. "If we can get to the woods, we'll hide there."

The cart creaked and its boards bounced under Bortai. Temujin had told her of how he had hidden in a wagon of wool before slipping away from the Taychiuts. She prayed that he would be safe.

They went on until she could hear only the creaking of the cart. Through a gap in the wool, she saw a gleam of light at the back of the cart; the sun was rising. Then she heard a low, rolling sound that might have been thunder or horses' hooves. Her mouth was dry; she waited, expecting to hear the drumbeat of a naccara, but no war-drum sounded. The enemy had meant to swoop down on the camp and surprise Temujin.

The sound of the horses grew louder; soldiers were riding towards them. She burrowed deeper. The wool covered her ears, muffling the shouts of the men.

"Stop!" a man called out. Bortai lay very still as the cart creaked to a halt. "Where are you going?" She had heard the accents of his dialect before, from the mouths of those who belonged to northern tribes.

"I've just come from the yurt of the chief Temujin," Khokakhchin replied. "I beg you to let me go on my way."

"And what were you doing there?"

"Shearing his sheep. I'm one of his servants, and now I'm going to my yurt with the wool to make felt. Please let me pass – surely you can leave an old woman her bit of wool."

"Is his yurt far from here?" another man asked.

"Just go that way. It isn't far. I didn't see the young Bahadur myself, so I don't know if he's there now, but you'll reach his camp soon. I was shearing the sheep, you see, so I couldn't tell – "

"Leave her," one man said angrily. Bortai kept still, certain the men were peering past Khokakhchin at the wool. The wool made her face itch; she clenched her teeth.

"On your way," a man said. The cart began to roll; the rumbling of horses' hooves faded. Bortai waited until she was sure the enemy was gone, then crawled forward and rested her hands on the seat.

"It was a small party," Khokakhchin murmured, "about thirty men. The other wings rode on towards the camp. There must be nearly three hundred of them." She paused. "They aren't Taychiuts. Merkits are after your husband."

Bortai tensed. Yesugei's old enemies must have decided to strike at his son before Temujin's strength grew. The Taychiuts had spared her husband before; she had held a faint hope that they might let him live if they caught him. The Merkits had no reason to show mercy.

"Get back," the old servant said. "We're not safe yet."

Bortai lay down. The cart bounced over a bump with a loud creak; the vehicle groaned under her, jostling her against the boards over and over until her body seemed a mass of bruises. They must be nearing the woods that bordered the small river. The cart rocked, pitching her to one side; she heard a sharp crack. The wagon shook and shuddered to a stop.

The axle, she thought, terrified. Khokakhchin cursed and lashed at the ox, then leaned towards her. "Don't move, child," the old woman said. "Some are riding back to us."

Bortai threw herself down and waited. The ground shook as the riders came closer. "Old woman!" a man shouted. A horse whinnied; she could hear them crowding around the cart. "There's no one in the camp but a few women and children — where are the rest?"

"I don't know," Khokakhchin said. "When I left, everything was quiet. I – "

"You know more than you told us." The man's voice was much louder now. "Someone warned them — we saw trails leading away from the camp. You aren't taking wool to your yurt — you're running away."

"I know nothing about this. All I have is the wool I sheared. Let me go."

"She can't carry it far with a broken axle," another voice said from the back of the cart. "There may be more than wool in this cart."

"There's nothing," Khokakhchin cried.

"I'll see for myself," the second man said. Bortai huddled under the wool. The cart shook as someone crawled inside. Hands slapped at the wool; fingers suddenly grabbed her around the calf. She kicked, then was dragged from the back of the cart by her legs. A pair of small dark eyes peered at her; Bortai's hand darted towards the man's broad face. He knocked her arm aside and dumped her on the ground.

"So this is what the old woman was hiding," the man said. He was large, with wide shoulders and a wrestler's massive build, but his moustache was the thin faint one of a young man. Bortai scrambled to her feet. Their horses were all around her; a few men leaned forward for a better look. "Now there's a prize," the young man went on. "The old bitch was hiding a beauty."

Bortai swayed dizzily. Khokakhchin struggled as another

man dragged her around the cart. On two of the horses, captives lay on their stomachs across saddles; thick braids hung down from under one woman's scarf. The captive woman turned her head; Bortai gazed into Sochigil's dark, fearful eyes.

Khokakhchin freed herself and stumbled to Bortai's side. "She's just a foolish girl," the servant said. "Pretty she may be, but she's a lazy child, and feeble-minded. She came to shear wool with me, and even then left most of the work to me – you don't need the burden of her."

"You talk too much." A man prodded Khokakhchin with his spear. "You lied before, and you're lying now."

"Does she speak the truth?" The man who had Sochigil slung across his horse was speaking. "Do you know who that woman is?" He took out his knife and pressed it against Sochigil's throat. "Speak!"

Sochigil yelped as the knife pricked her. "She's Bortai – Temujin's wife. Old Woman Khokakhchin serves his mother. It's the truth – don't hurt me."

Bortai threw her arms around the old servant. They were lost; Temujin would expect her to do what she could to stay alive. "She speaks the truth," she said. "I am Bortai Ujin." She shot a baleful glance at the other woman. "She would know – she was Yesugei Bahadur's second wife."

The young man who had dragged her from the cart roared with laughter. "Temujin's wife!" he shouted, slapping his thigh. "I've found his wife! We have our revenge on that Mongol bastard already!" Bortai drew herself up; the longer he stood here gloating, the more distance her husband would put between himself and these creatures. "My brother will dance with joy when he learns what we've found!" His big hand fell on her shoulder. "Do you know who I am, woman?"

Bortai opened her mouth; her voice was locked in her throat. "How could I know?" she managed to say at last. "You're a stranger to me. Are you so famous that even I should know who you are?"

A few men chuckled. The young man scowled and raised an arm; she shrank back. "My name is Chilger," he bellowed, "and my comrades call me Boko, the Athlete." He flexed his arms. "My older brother is Yeke Chiledu. Do you know what

213

your husband's father did to my brother?" He showed his teeth. "He stole his bride, only a few days after she and Chiledu were wed. He chased my brother from her side and took her away from him."

Bortai sagged against Khokakhchin. Hoelun-eke had never talked of her first husband. The men were laughing again; she buried her face in Khokakhchin's coat.

"She'll ride with me," the man called Chilger-boko said. "I have more right than any to claim her."

"Take her with you," an older man said. "The chiefs will decide whether you keep her. We've delayed long enough."

The young man dragged her away from Khokakhchin, lashed her wrists together, and forced her on to his horse.

42

"I'M HUNGRY," TEMULUN said.

"Hush." Hoelun patted her daughter's hand. Below them, on the thickly forested slope, the men rested against their horses, exhausted by the climb.

Fewer than twenty of Temujin's men had followed him to Mount Burkhan Khaldun; the others had scattered. Hoelun wondered how many of the people left behind had escaped; those who made for the cliff or the wooded regions might have a chance. Hoelun doubted that the Taychiuts would search for them; they would be too impatient to track her son.

Temujin moved among his men, trying to rally them. He had led them through the marsh and thickets surrounding the mountain and along a deer trail through the thick, nearly impassable forest. They had been forced to lead their horses through the marsh on foot, mud sucking at their boots as they moved over the shifting, treacherous ground, mosquitoes swarming around them; Borchu had nearly lost his horse in a mire. Going up the eastern slope had been nearly as hard, and they had to hack their way through the underbrush to make a path for the horses.

But her son's choice of a refuge was sound. The dank, muddy ground of the marsh had flowed over their tracks. Even if their pursuers made it to the foot of Burkhan Khaldun, trees would block their way. Temujin had sent three men below on foot to cover part of the trail they had used.

"Mother," Temulun whispered, "how long will we stay here?"

"I don't know."

Temujin climbed towards them, trailed by Temuge and Khachigun. Hoelun's sons settled on the ground around her. Temujin would be thinking of Bortai, but he had needed the spare horse when his mount flagged, in order to ride ahead and find a way through the marsh.

A shadowy shape moved up the slope towards them. "The trail's covered." Hoelun recognized Jelme's voice. "Saw fires beyond the marsh, and climbed into a tree to take a look." Jelme caught his breath. "The enemy's camped below."

"How many men?" Temujin asked.

"Nearly three hundred, and they aren't Taychiuts. I've seen the standards before, when my father and I camped in the north. They belong to the Merkit chiefs Dayir Usun, Khagatai Darmala, and Toghtoga Beki. It's Merkits who are after our heads."

Hoelun covered her face. Yesugei had brought this upon his son.

"We must move higher," she heard Temujin say, "before it gets any darker. They'll try to reach us in the morning, and we have to be ready for them." Leaves rustled under his feet as he descended to his men.

The captives, freed from their bonds, sat together surrounded by guards as other soldiers lit fires. Bortai leaned against Kho-kakhchin as Sochigil-eke wept. The Merkits sent ahead of the men bringing the captives had ridden hard along Temujin's trail, but had not overtaken him. They had followed his trail to the marsh, but had found no tracks through the thickets.

Her husband must be on the mountain, but attacking him

would be perilous. Temujin would be on higher ground, and many Merkits might fall before he was captured. Perhaps they would give up and settle for the prisoners they had.

Twenty women and several children sat with Bortai and her two companions. She ached from the ride. It was strange to feel that this was all a dream, that she would wake soon and find herself in her tent, Temujin at her side.

"My son abandoned me," Sochigil said, wiping her face. "Temujin must have forced him to that – he wouldn't have left me if – "

"As long as the men escape," Bortai said, "we can hope for rescue later."

Sochigil shook her head. "Don't hope for that, child. Years may pass before Temujin grows strong enough to take revenge, and it'll be too late for us by then." The dark-eyed woman adjusted the scarf that covered her hair. "You see how long it took these Merkits to punish us for what my husband did. They know I'm Yesugei's other widow. They were pleased to hear it, almost as happy as they were when you fell into their hands." She plucked at her coat. "Given who we are, they're unlikely to offer us to common herdsmen."

Bortai glared at her. The fool took pride in being a captive of some importance. Her jaw tightened. These men might have an ancient grudge against Yesugei, but that alone would not have brought this attack. There had been no reason to strike at Temujin before, but now he was a rising young chieftain and a possible threat to them.

Temujin would want to fight for her, but he needed an army to ride against the Merkits, and striking at them too soon could end in disaster. It would take time for him to marshal his forces, and by then she would be a Merkit's woman. Even Hoelun-eke would have advised her to make the best of her lot, as she had when Yesugei captured her.

Three men came towards them; one was Chilger-boko. A bitter taste filled her mouth. He had strutted among the other men after they stopped to make camp, pointing at her from a distance as if she were already his.

Three pairs of booted feet stopped in front of her. "This is the one." She recognized Chilger's voice. "Temujin's woman."

Bortai looked up. One of the three Merkit chiefs, a squat man called Toghtoga Beki, was with him. The third man was smaller and less massive than Chilger-boko, but his small dark eyes and wide mouth resembled the young man's. She knew who he was before he spoke.

"She should go to my brother," he said. "Temujin's father took my first wife from me, and Chilger has no wife."

"We'll decide that," Toghtoga said, "after we capture her husband. Many here would like to take her into their tents. But you have some right to decide this woman's fate. I think Dayir will agree, and Khagatai has enough wives already."

Chiledu stared at Bortai for a bit, then walked away with his brother and Toghtoga. These Merkits obeyed their chiefs readily. Toghtoga and the two other leaders had ordered them to stop their raping of the women in the camp and the pillaging of the yurts in order to pursue Temujin. The soldiers had restrained themselves since then, but Chilger-boko might not be willing to wait much longer. The thought of being his woman filled her with disgust.

She glanced at the other prisoners. One young woman was weeping; Bortai had seen her lying outside a yurt, trousers around her ankles, her long robe pushed up to her waist, the body of a small boy with an arrow in his chest at her side. A little girl nestled against her mother. Two captive boys sat among the guards, looking up at them uneasily as the men told stories.

Bortai's eyes stung; she reached for Khokakhchin's hand. "Stay with me, Khokakhchin-eke," she whispered. "I couldn't bear it if we were parted."

"Poor child." Khokakhchin draped an arm over her shoulders. Bortai gazed up at the dark wall of Burkhan Khaldun, praying that the mountain's spirit would protect her husband, then remembered the story Temujin had told her long ago, of how he had dreamed of standing on a mountain from where he could see the world. She wondered what he saw from this mountain.

Dreams, she thought despairingly. A dream had promised Temujin to her, but had not shown her that their time together would be so short.

The Merkits stayed by the mountain for three days. Each morning, men rode off to look for a safe path through the thickets and marsh; each evening, they returned without having found a trail. The Merkits muttered about the perils of the land, the mires that had trapped a few horses, the thickets that did not allow them to pass. Even if they found a way through, wooded slopes lay ahead, with places from which they could be ambushed.

On the fourth day, no one rode out. The faces of the men were sullen as they gathered to hear what their leaders would say. Bortai watched from where she sat with the captives, realizing that the Merkits might give up the search.

The chief called Khagatai Darmala stepped forward. "It's useless to search here," he said. "The cursed son of Yesugei has escaped us." A few men murmured to one another. "Yet we've wounded him – his tents are empty, his people scattered, and his own woman is our captive. We've had revenge on him – he'll shed bitter tears over what he's lost, and trouble us no more. We'll ride out of here today, and take any of his people we find along our trail. In his camp, the frame of his yurt will be broken, and the entrance that harbours his household spirit will be trampled under our feet. Be at peace, brothers – we have a victory."

The men bowed their heads; only a few cheered. "Hear my words, Temujin!" Khagatai shouted at the mountain. "Heaven has abandoned you! Your camp lies empty, its hearth fires have died! Your followers will curse the leader who could not protect them! Your women will weep when they lie in our arms!"

This speech brought a few more cheers. The chiefs strode towards the prisoners; Bortai huddled against Khokakhchin. One woman was pulled to her feet and handed to a Merkit, who dragged her away as she screamed. Sochigil shot a last desperate look at Bortai before she was thrust at the man who had captured her. A girl was dragged from her mother's arms and thrown to a warrior; one bewildered boy was led away by another man as his mother cried out after him. The chiefs were quick about this business, pointing at captives and parcelling them out until only Bortai, old Khokakhchin, and four other women were left.

"This is Temujin's woman," Khagatai Darmala said, "and Yeke Chiledu's bride was taken from him by our enemy's father. Our comrade is avenged. Chiledu might have claimed this woman for himself, but has asked that she be given to his younger brother, who was among those who found her. I say there's justice in that."

Chilger-boko stepped forward; his eyes gleamed. Bortai's gorge rose. "I won't be parted from my servant." Her voice was weak; the men near her laughed, mocking her plea. "I must have her with me." Her throat locked.

"What's an old woman?" Toghtoga Beki said. "Let Chilger keep the old one as a slave."

Chilger lunged at Bortai and hauled her up by the arms. She pulled a hand free and clawed at his face; his fist struck her on the side of the head and she fell, stunned by the blow.

"As for these others," she heard Khagatai say, "do as you like when we're finished with them, and those left alive will serve as slaves."

The women screamed as Chilger dragged Bortai away. She glanced back; Khagatai lowered himself on one woman as the men around him cheered. Khokakhchin stumbled after Bortai and reached for Chilger's sleeve. He knocked the old woman aside with one powerful arm, and she lay in the dirt, her body still. Chilger threw Bortai to the ground.

She twisted under him as he tore at her clothes. He slapped her hard, then pinned her to the ground, his weight crushing her chest. A forest of legs surrounded her, and voices shouted encouragement as Chilger thrust inside her.

She clenched her teeth, holding herself rigid, and squeezed her eyes shut. Screams soared above the shouting; the wailing rose, then broke, shattering into shards against the roars of the men.

43

HOELUN CREPT OUTSIDE her shelter of tree branches. Temulun and Temuge were outside, testing the spring of their bows. The two children spent the days following deer and elk trails while hunting birds and small game. She studied their small, fearless faces, then pulled her daughter to her.

"Mother." Temulun squirmed out of her arms.

"I must speak to Temujin," Hoelun said. "Stay here until I return." She turned away and began to climb the slope, digging at roots with a stick as she went, then slipping them under her belt.

Temujin's makeshift hut was above, in a small clearing. Khasar sat outside, shaping a long piece of wood into a spear shaft. As she approached, he put away his knife and got to his feet.

"Is your brother still asleep?" Hoelun asked.

"He's awake." Khasar led her away from the hut. Temujin had not left his shelter since sending Jelme, Borchu, and Belgutei down from the mountain. The three were trailing the Merkits, making sure the enemy was not planning to ambush them when they left their refuge. For days now, her oldest son had brooded, eating almost nothing of the game his men found or the plants she brought to him.

"His scouts will be back soon," she said. "He'll have to speak to the others then and tell them what to do."

"I know." Khasar folded his arms. "He's thinking of Bortai. I hope she was able to escape."

"I pray for that, too, but I've learned not to hope for too much." She recalled the words she had shouted after Chiledu so long ago. "There will be others to choose from, and another wife to sit in his cart."

"You must fear for her," he said.

"Of course I do. I know what it is to be torn from a husband. I can hope that whoever may have her now treats her kindly. But I also know that any sons she gives that man will be our enemies. She'll think of her children, not my son."

Khasar was about to reply when she heard a shout below.

220

Jelme hastened up the slope on foot, followed by Borchu and Belgutei. Their faces were grim; Hoelun knew then that Bortai and Khokakhchin had not been found.

Hoelun went to Temujin's shelter, called out his name, and crept inside. She could barely see him in the darkness; he did not move as she knelt next to him.

"Temujin," she said, "you must come outside. Belgutei and your comrades have returned."

"And Bortai? But I don't have to ask, do I? Their shouts of joy would have filled this forest if she were with them."

"Come – your men need you." She got up. At first she thought he might not leave, but he rose and followed her outside.

Borchu hurried to Temujin and clasped his arms, then stepped back as Jelme embraced him. Hoelun sat down, waiting to hear what the young men would tell him.

"We're safe for now," Borchu said. "The enemy's left these lands. We followed their trail to our camp, then scouted north of it, far enough to know they're not waiting for us. They tore down the yurts and broke the frames. Everything they could carry is gone, but some of our people who hid on Burgi cliff came back when the Merkits rode away. They'll gather what they can and bury the dead, and then they'll search along the river for stray cattle and sheep before riding here. The enemy took the animals near our camp."

Temujin said nothing. Borchu glanced uneasily at Jelme. "I thought it might be worse," Borchu continued. "If some were able to hide, we may find others."

Temujin said, "You have more to tell me. You know what news I seek."

Borchu took a breath. "Near the Tungelig, we found a cart with a broken axle. The land still bore the marks of many horses, so some Merkits must have found the cart." The Arulat paused. "Under the wool in the cart, I found a bowcase, quiver and bow. They were – " He fell silent.

"Say it," Temujin said hoarsely.

"I knew the design. They were Bortai Ujin's weapons."

Hoelun swallowed. The young woman would have taken her bow with her had she been able to escape on foot. She peered up at her son; his face was impassive. Khasar rested a hand on his brother's shoulder. Temujin shook him off, then beckoned to Belgutei. "And Sochigil-eke?"

Belgutei tensed. "There's no sign of her."

"I am sorry, brother."

"I should have looked for her and put her on my horse."

"No, Belgutei. I sorrow with you for what we've both lost, but that we're safe here shows that we acted correctly. Even a moment's delay might have meant your capture, and I need every man I have now. I promise you our enemies will pay for taking your mother and my wife."

Her son, Hoelun thought, sounded like himself again, resigned to his losses but ready to face whatever came. "We'll gather more men," Borchu was saying, "and my clan will aid you." It was not such a defeat after all; they had more than they had possessed when they were hiding from the Taychiuts.

"I owe my life to old Khokakhchin-eke," Temujin said. "Except for her sharp ears, the Merkits might have been upon us before we could run. I owe my life to the spirit of this mountain, the spirit that guided me to the deer trails and kept me safe under the branches of its trees. I must give thanks to Burkhan Khaldun and to Koko Mongke Tengri for protecting me and being my shield."

The sun was above the tree-tops. Temujin lifted his face to the light, took off his hat, then loosened his belt and hung it around his neck as he bowed towards the sun. Hoelun got on her knees as the others knelt around him; Borchu handed her son a skin of kumiss. Temujin struck his chest with his free hand and knelt nine times, pressing his forehead to the ground and sprinkling the mare's milk after each genuflection.

"Burkhan Khaldun shielded me," he said softly. "I was no more than an insect scurrying for cover, and this mountain gave me shelter. I was no more than a bug crawling on the ground, and this mountain kept my enemies from crushing me. I'll sacrifice to this mountain every day, and my children and their children will remember that the spirit who dwells here gave me my life."

He scattered more droplets, sat back on his heels, and looked around at the others, his pale eyes cold. "We'll come down

222

from this mountain. I'll speak to my men after that. I must pray some more and listen to what the spirits say to me, and then you'll hear what Tengri wills for me. Leave me, and tell the men I'm ready to lead them once more."

The young men stood up. "They'll rejoice to hear it," Khasar said.

"We'll follow you," Jelme added, "whatever you decide."

The four descended the slope. When the trees hid them, Hoelun said, "I want to know what you plan to do."

"You'll know when I speak to my men. Leave me, Mother – I wish to pray alone."

"I think you've already decided what to do."

His eyes narrowed. "You won't make me turn from my path."

"I'll say nothing in front of the men," she said, "but I'll tell you here what I think of your intentions."

Temujin's face was drawn. "Toghril Khan and I have sworn an oath. Jamukha is my anda. They have to aid me now. Together, we'll ride against the Merkits before another year passes – I swear it to you."

"You have no power to swear such an oath," she said. "They may not want to rush into a war with the Merkits."

"Do you think I'll leave my wife in their hands?"

"You risk too much for her," Hoelun said. "I loved her, too, but she's gone, and you have to strengthen your forces before you can fight. You must think of your followers now."

"I am thinking of them. Others here have lost their women. Our enemies must learn that those who take what is mine will suffer for it."

"You'll have your revenge in time," she said, "but you have to grow stronger first. Toghril Khan and your anda may regret their oaths if you push them into this war too quickly. You're not prepared for this – you should wait – "

"That's what my enemies expect," he muttered, "that I'll nurse my wounds. You know nothing of these matters, Mother." He stood up and paced. "The Kereit Khan has reason to hate the Merkits, but was content to leave them to their lands as long as he was safe on his throne. I must show him that, by striking at me, they threaten him, now that we're allies.

Jamukha will welcome this campaign if he knows the Kereits will fight with us. The Merkits won't enjoy what they've stolen for long."

"We want the same thing." Hoelun lifted her head, forcing herself to gaze into his angry eyes. "I've prayed for Bortai, and for Sochigil and faithful old Khokakhchin, too, but I can't watch you rush into a battle you cannot win."

"Be silent!" He crouched down and grabbed her wrist, twisting it hard. "I should have put Bortai on your horse and left you behind." His fingers tightened before he released her. "No woman will tell me when to fight, not even you. I have the right to demand that Toghril and Jamukha honour their pledges to me, and this battle will strengthen the bonds among us. I know what I have to do, and if you speak openly of your doubts, I'll drive you from my camp myself."

She rose unsteadily to her feet, knowing he meant it. "I've told you what I think, Temujin. I won't speak of it again – Tengri will decide our fate." She rubbed her wrist; his fingers had left marks.

"I'll speak to my men," he said. "After we move camp, I shall ride to Toghril Khan."

She bowed. Whatever he did, she would follow him, even if he was riding to his death. "May the spirits give you what you want," she said without conviction, then left him.

44

WIND GUSTED ALONG the ribbon of ice that was the Uda River, lifting the snow into pale swirls. Bortai pulled at her hat and adjusted the woollen veil that covered the lower part of her face. The women in this part of Toghtoga's camp had herded their sheep together; a few dogs circled the flock, nipping at strays.

Further down the valley, other women, children, and young men tended part of the cattle herd. To the north, high mountains sheltered the camp from the fiercest northern winds, but the cold was numbing.

Bortai bent over and swept away snow with her tree branch. The sheep, like the cattle, could not paw through the snow to uncover food for themselves, and one of Chilger's sheep had already died; she had fed the animal by hand, only to lose it in the end, and Chilger had beaten her for that. The dark, distant mass of the horse herd grazed on land further from the camp. Chilger was away, out hunting with some of the men.

One of the younger sheep bleated. Bortai pulled out a tuft of thin dead grass and fed it to the lamb. A Merkit woman hummed, her voice barely audible above the wind. The women had told Bortai of Chilger-boko's triumphs at wrestling; they had considered her fortunate to have such a strapping young man as her husband. They rarely spoke to her about him now; they knew how often he beat her.

Bortai's head throbbed; a wave of dizziness caught her, then passed. She had hoped she was recovering from the last beating, when Chilger had been too drunk to hit her that hard. The wind howled; white veils of flakes whirled around her, blinding her. She huddled against the sheep, welcoming its warmth. Ice floes had clogged the Uda when Toghtoga Beki left the other two Merkit chiefs to lead his men back to this camp. By the time they had moved closer to the mountains, nearly a month ago, the river was frozen and the larches in the foothills had dropped most of their needles; winter came even more quickly to these northern lands.

The wind subsided. Bortai stood up and cleared away more snow. She could not recall much about the ride from Burkhan Khaldun. Perhaps Chilger's beatings had driven the memories from her. She knew that she had resisted him, and dimly recalled a blow to her head that had blinded her for a moment; pinpricks of light had danced in the darkness before her vision returned. She had learned not to fight him, afraid to be hurt yet again, but sometimes angered him without knowing why. He punched her with his fists or hit her with a stick, and lashed out at Khokakhchin whenever the old woman tried to protect her.

One of her ribs ached. Khokakhchin had bound her torso

with a wide sash after Chilger had broken the rib. She had been his prisoner for nearly three months.

His captive – that was how she viewed herself, not as his wife. Whatever happened to a woman during her life, her soul would join that of her first true husband in death; she would escape Chilger-boko then. During the early days of his assaults, she had thought this escape might come soon, but her body was not so willing to free her spirit.

Bortai swayed, then doubled over, thinking she might be sick. An arm caught her; she gazed into the heavy-lidded eyes above Khokakhchin's woollen veil.

"I'm all right." Bortai swallowed and leaned against the old servant. Two women near them whispered to each other as they peered at Bortai. Another woman waded through the snow, chasing a stray lamb that had somehow evaded the dogs. Bortai freed herself, made her way to the animal, and grasped it by its thick wool.

The woman, bulky and awkward in her heavy coat, stumbled to her side; a familiar pair of dark eyes stared out from the slit between her scarf and hat. Bortai had known Sochigil was in this camp, but had not spoken to her during their captivity.

"Greetings, Sochigil-eke," she said.

"Bortai – it is you." Sochigil knelt by the bleating lamb and patted its head. "I've wanted to talk to you, but – " She paused. "I heard that your Merkit husband's a hard man. I didn't want to make trouble for you."

"Chilger-boko – " Bortai's throat tightened, as it always did whenever she said his name. "He doesn't like to see me talking to anyone, even the women." She looked around instinctively, almost expecting him to appear near her suddenly. "And his mother often carries false tales about me to him." The old woman would be gossiping with Chiledu's wife inside a warm tent while Bortai and Khokakhchin watched the sheep. "How have you fared, Sochigil-eke?"

"My master's first wife is forever scolding me, and his children are shrieking brats, but he's kind enough. Unlike some men, his anger cools when he's drunk, and he can sometimes be moved by my tears." The other woman's voice was calm. Most would call her wise for accepting her fate.

226

Rage and longing burned inside Bortai, then flickered out. Better to be numb, to thrust aside any thought of Temujin. He had no army great enough to ride against these people; hundreds of men would defend this camp, and thousands more could come to their defence. Years would pass before Temujin could take his revenge. Even if he found her then, he would hardly honour her again as his wife.

"Then your life isn't so bad," Bortai said.

"It's bearable," Sochigil replied. "Wretched as this Merkit is, he's often kinder than my first husband." The older woman adjusted the collar of her shabby sheepskin coat. "It's an easier life than the one I had when the Taychiuts abandoned us." Sochigil shook herself. "I must go." She stumbled away, clutching the lamb.

Bortai returned to her flock. The women sang and chattered as they cleared away snow, working steadily until the sky grew darker and the wind rose. Bortai prayed silently for another storm and more snow, even though that would only make feeding the animals harder tomorrow. A storm might keep the hunters from returning; she would have another night without Chilger.

Towards evening, Bortai and Khokakhchin separated their sheep from the others, then drove them back to Chilger's camping circle. His black dog raced around the flock, keeping them together. His tent, which sat with those of his family at the eastern end of the camp, was one of the smaller dwellings, its felt panels part of the loot Bortai had been forced to bring from Temujin's camp. Khokakhchin settled the animals in a space between the dwelling and the cart as Bortai took the two smallest sheep inside.

The lambs huddled by the entrance. The fire was burning low; Bortai stood by the hearth, warming herself before removing her thick fur coat. The two animals bleated weakly; she might have to feed them some of her stored wild millet to strengthen them. Chilger would surely beat her if they died, but might also punish her for wasting the grain. The pain in her head suddenly sharpened, and nausea made her gorge rise.

"Bortai!" Khokakhchin stepped through the entrance and

lowered the flap behind her. "I see your sickness is upon you again." She took Bortai's arm and led her to the bed at the back of the tent. "Sit – I'll tend to the fire."

Bortai put her hand on her belly, waiting for the dizziness to pass. "My head rings, and the ground moves under me. It must be the beatings." She had thought she would be used to them by now.

"Don't be foolish, child." Khokakhchin put some argal on the fire, then came back to her. "You know what this sickness is – I saw it some time ago. A child's inside you – don't keep denying it." The old woman sat down near the bed. "Perhaps part of Temujin lives in you."

"Now you're being foolish, Khokakhchin-eke. This child cannot be his." Khokakhchin was only trying to console her. She had not bled since her capture, but that meant little; the horror of her first days among the Merkits might have dried up her womb's blood. If this child were Temujin's, the sickness would have come to her sooner, and her breasts would have swelled earlier; the old woman had to know that.

"One thing's true," Khokakhchin murmured. "It will be your child. You'll grow to love it, and your Merkit husband would only make your life harder if you gave him no sons." Khokakhchin patted her arm. "Maybe he'll be gentler with you now."

Bortai rested on the bed until she heard the voices of men above the wind, then got up and moved towards the entrance. Chilger would expect her to greet him.

His big body, made broader by his two heavy coats, filled the doorway. He hung up his weapons, shook the snow from his hat, then motioned to her. "We took an elk two days ago," he muttered. "My share's outside – fetch it."

"I'll get it," Khokakhchin said.

"Is my wife unable to work?"

"She has a spell of the sickness that comes to women when they're with child." Chilger's small eyes widened. "It cannot be such a surprise, Master," the old woman continued. "I'll fetch the meat before your dog feasts on it."

Khokakhchin crept through the doorway. Chilger took off his outer coat; the one under it was turned skin-side out, so

228

that the fur could rest against him. He warmed his hands, then shed the second coat, handing the garments to Bortai.

She laid the coats on a chest, then brought him a horn of kumiss. Chilger sat on his bed, ignoring Khokakhchin as she dragged the skinned haunch inside and knelt to cut it up. Bortai seated herself at Chilger's feet.

"It's true?" he said at last. "You're going to have a child?"

"Yes." She stared at his felt boots. "I wanted to be sure before I told you."

He waved a few drops of kumiss from his fingers, then said, "Is it mine?"

She lifted her head and gazed into his eyes. "It is," she answered, certain this was true and knowing he would see that in her face. He always knew when she was hiding her thoughts from him; she had learned not to look directly at him unless she was being honest with him. "Women know these things. The child is yours."

His faint moustache twitched as he smiled. "Things will be better between us. You'll give me my first son."

She kept her face still as she looked down. "I hope it is a son," she said, whispering the words so that he would not hear the bitterness in her voice.

"I wanted you," he said, "as soon as I pulled you from that cart. After I took you, after I beat you for trying to refuse me, I thought you'd learn how matters must be between us, but I feel you resisting me still."

She averted her eyes, not wanting him to see how much she despised him. Obedience was not enough for him; he wanted something she could never give to him. He sounded like a boy demanding his due, a boy pretending to be a man. She had heard such words from him before, always offered in the same regretful, pleading tone, and had thought him a fool for saying them, but he was not as foolish as he seemed. He knew how much Temujin still haunted her thoughts.

"I wouldn't beat you so often," he said, "if I knew you were truly mine." He had also said that many times. She might have set aside what he had done to her at the foot of Burkhan Khaldun; that was part of war, the victor claiming his prize. No place existed under Heaven where men, even the kindest,

229

did not surrender to the spirits of war. She might have endured him if he had demanded less of her.

"I'm yours," she said. "I carry your child. What can bring us closer than that?"

He gulped down more drink. "You think I don't deserve you." He wiped his mouth. "You belonged to a chief, and now you scorn the little I can give you."

These words were unexpected; she wondered how to reply. Surely he knew that Temujin's wealth had not been great. "I am grateful for what we have," she said, "and you're certain to win more in battle. You're young yet, not much older than my husband – "

She saw her mistake immediately, just before his boot caught her in the ribs. She cried out and rolled away, clawing at the felt.

"I am your husband!" Chilger roared, then hauled her to her feet. "You're my woman now, not his!" He seized one of her braids, forcing her head back. Khokakhchin lunged towards him; he knocked her aside, then threw Bortai to the floor.

"Stop!" the old woman shouted. "Think of your child! Do you want her to lose it?"

Chilger stepped back. Bortai sat up; Khokakhchin shielded her with her body. "You force me to this," Chilger muttered. "You bring it on yourself with your words." Bortai leaned against the old woman, afraid she would retch; he would beat her anyway, in spite of the child. "Get me my supper."

She got up and staggered towards the hearth. This was only a respite, until unguarded words or the wrong expression roused him once more. Maybe the beatings would stop after the child was born. Temujin had joked with her that summer, saying he should pretend to beat her so that his brothers and comrades would know he was a man; she buried the memory quickly. Chilger grew most enraged when he guessed she was thinking of the past, and it was becoming easier to push her former life aside. One day she would have trouble remembering it at all.

45

THE DARK FOREST was thick with the scent of pine. Jamukha could barely hear the breathing of the riders near him as they slowly advanced towards the Merkit camp. His legs hugged the barrel of his favourite horse, a charger with a black stripe along its back. He inhaled the cold, piny air. This was what he lived for, the preparations for battle, the anticipation of victory. He had known, when Khasar and Belgutei came to him to plead for his help, that he would have to fight.

The last of the torches used to signal to his men flickered out. A full moon shone above the trees, casting pale beams through the branches along the trail. Toghril Khan and his Kereits would be approaching from the east, while Temujin's followers moved up the centre; Jamukha's army was the left wing of their force. Temujin, to his surprise, had gathered nearly a thousand men. With the two thousand commanded by Toghril and the Kereit Khan's brother Jakha Gambu, and Jamukha's three thousand, they had more than enough soldiers to wound the Merkits deeply.

He swayed as his horse stepped over a thick root. In spite of the cold, rhododendrons were flowering on shrubs, and the ground was already thick with the budding orchids of spring. The Merkits would not expect an attack during this season, which was why Jamukha had decided to ride against them now. His men had objected that the horses would be too lean; he had replied that they would have grazing along the way. Temujin wanted to fight now, so Khasar had claimed; he had sworn to rescue his Bortai before the year passed.

But this war was not for a woman's sake. The theft of his wife had given Temujin a reason to reach for more than he had, to demand that Toghril and Jamukha honour the pledges they had made to him. Khasar had spoken movingly about the wound to his brother's heart, but Temujin's pride bore the injury. Bortai's name might be useful in rallying the men, but the woman herself did not matter.

The rider ahead of him slowed; Jamukha's hands tightened on his reins. His anda had ridden to Toghril first, securing his promise of aid before sending Khasar and Belgutei to Jamukha's camp. It was clever of Temujin to get a promise from his stronger but less reliable ally first, and Toghril had promised to fight only if Jamukha joined them and agreed to lead the armies. Temujin must have had difficulty persuading the Khan, but Toghril would have shown weakness by refusing to honour his oath. He could, however, have backed away from his promise if Jamukha refused to act, while Jamukha would bear most of the blame if the campaign ended in failure.

He had known all this, but had told Khasar he would summon other chiefs and come to Temujin's aid. His friend's misfortune was regrettable, but also gave Jamukha more power over his anda. A victory would strengthen their bond, and earn Temujin's gratitude.

The trees were thinning. The advance scouts had learned that Toghtoga Beki's camp was now on the Uda's south bank. Khagatai's camp lay to the west, while Dayir Usun was in the south-west, where the Selenga and Orkhon Rivers met. They would strike at Toghtoga's camp first, then sweep towards the others, cutting them off from a retreat north to the lake of Baikal.

Jamukha was happy, his senses alert. While planning the campaign, he had seen these soldiers and their movements as if looking at them from above; now he was a falcon prepared to swoop down on his prey.

Only one delay had marred his plans. He had waited at the head of the Onon, where the Kereits and Temujin's forces were to meet his, for three days past the appointed time. His first sight of Temujin's men had shown him the cause. They were little more than young herdsmen who had joined a new leader in the hope of winning more wealth; Jamukha doubted they had fought many battles. But seeing his anda once more had cooled his wrath, and whatever Temujin's men were, they obeyed him readily. They had crossed the Kumirs, undaunted by a late snowstorm, before separating into smaller groups to cross the Kilga River on makeshift rafts of thick reeds. A few had fallen along the way, but not one had deserted; Temujin had forged his men into an army.

Someone whispered up ahead. The man riding in front of

Jamukha turned towards him. "Bahadur," the warrior said quickly, "the enemy's been warned. The Merkits are fleeing their camp."

Jamukha cursed. "Let me pass." He rode past the man to the edge of the wood, followed by his drummer. Above him, the full moon hung in the sky, and bright coloured bands of light flickered, spirits dancing at the Gate of Heaven. Tiny figures raced from the dark humps of yurts; a band of riders was fleeing west along the Uda. Jamukha ground his teeth. His men had chased down and killed the few fishers and trappers they had seen, but others must have ridden here to warn the enemy.

Temujin and the Kereits were awaiting his signal. He had planned to come upon the Merkits while they slept, and surround the camp before they could flee or mount a defence; Temujin did not want his wife harmed if she was here.

It was too late to worry about the woman. Jamukha lifted his lance; the drummer near him beat on his naccara. Another war-drum echoed the sound, as Jamukha howled and lashed at his horse. Riders burst from the trees. The drumbeats were swallowed by the steady, rolling sound of hooves and the shrieks of warriors.

Chilger lifted Bortai into the cart as Khokakhchin secured the ox. People ran past them towards the horses; others were making their way to the river on foot. Out on the plain, Bortai saw the standards of Toghtoga Beki and Dayir Usun bobbing above one band of riders; the two chiefs were abandoning the camp. Dayir Usun had ridden there with some of his men only that morning; he would have to warn his own camp now.

"Go west, towards the birches," Chilger shouted. "Cross the river there and make for Baikal – I'll find you later."

His solicitude was for his child, not for her. Bortai felt a kick inside her and covered her belly with one hand.

Khokakhchin scrambled into the cart. Chilger's mother was screaming near one wagon. Chilger turned, elbowed two women aside, and ran towards the horses. "Run for your lives!" his brother Chiledu shouted, although all the camp had to be awake by now.

Old Khokakhchin lashed at the ox. The cart creaked forward, following others towards the river. A woman on foot stumbled past them, then looked up; the moonlight caught Sochigil's face.

"Sochigil-eke!" Bortai cried. The sound of thunder could now be heard above the shouts of frightened Merkits. "Sochigil-eke! Come with us!" The other woman darted away and was soon lost in the crowd.

Bortai clutched at her swollen belly and shivered in the cold. Her long tunic was tight across her abdomen; there had been time to grab only a cloak after Khokakhchin helped her on with her boots. She was suddenly terrified for herself, afraid of what might happen if her child came too soon.

The cart bounced over a rut; she groaned. The thunder was louder; war-cries rose above the noise of the crowd. The spirits of light leaped overhead; to the south, bright flames streaked towards the camp.

Jamukha rode past a burning yurt. Merkits shrieked as men on horseback herded them to one side; other soldiers were looting the tents. A woman screamed as a Jajirat threw her to the ground, then fell across her. The dead lay on the ground, still clutching bows and knives.

His horse reared as an arrow whistled past and struck a man behind him. A shadowy form lowered a bow and ducked inside a yurt. Jamukha motioned to a warrior near him, threw him his reins, then leaped from his horse and ran towards the yurt.

He had his sword out as he came through the entrance. "Spare us," a voice said. A girl stood near the hearth, her hand around a bow, an empty quiver hanging from her belt. A boy was next to her, his eyes slits; he held a knife.

Jamukha smiled. "Spare me and my brother," the girl said. He smelled her fear; his heart was beating as hard as a war-drum. "I beg you for mercy."

Something throbbed deep inside him, seeking release. "Throw down your weapons," he said softly, still smiling. The girl let go of her bow; the boy hesitated, then threw his knife down. Jamukha's grip tightened on his hilt. The girl stepped back and clutched at her coat; he knew what she expected.

He swung with his sword, severing the girl's neck with one sweep. Blood poured from the headless torso as it toppled forward. The boy scrambled for the knife; Jamukha grabbed him, threw him face down, pulled down his trousers and thrust inside him.

The boy squirmed under him, fighting the assault. Jamukha's spasm passed quickly; he withdrew, then buried his knife in the boy's back. When the small body was still, Jamukha closed his trousers, wiped his knife and sword on the dead boy's coat, then moved towards the hearth.

He was calm, his mind clear, his body subdued. A glance around the tent told him that he would find little here. He knocked the metal hearth to the ground, then left as the flames spread across the felt.

A line of carts rattled along the river-bank. Bortai could no longer see the Merkits who had fled on horseback. A cart suddenly stopped in front of hers, its right wheel trapped in a rut.

Khokakhchin whipped the ox; Bortai looked south. Several yurts were engulfed in flames, silhouetting the riders who circled the camp. Other soldiers galloped towards the river. A few women leaped from their carts and raced upriver on foot.

Bortai knew that she could not outrun the enemy. The horsemen shrieked as they fanned out around the fugitives; more carts shuddered to a halt. Warriors galloped after those on foot. A few arrows flew from the carts; Merkits screamed as the horsemen responded with a volley.

"Bortai!" The voice calling her name was hoarse, as though the man had been shouting for some time. "Bortai!"

"Surrender!" another man cried. "Give up now, and we will spare you! Resist, and all of you will die!"

The attackers pressed in around the carts. "Bortai!" Her head shot up; she knew the voice now, ravaged as it was. "Bortai, are you here? Bortai!"

"Temujin!" She rose in the cart, then spotted his grey horse; its flanks were white in the moonlight. "Temujin!"

He rode towards her, heedless of the riders around him. Khokakhchin climbed out quickly, then helped Bortai down.

They stumbled towards him and grabbed at the reins of his horse.

"Temujin," Bortai whispered. He dismounted and caught her; she buried her face against his bloodstained coat. "Temujin. I didn't know — I thought — "

"I swore I'd find you," he gasped.

"But how — "

"I have an army now. Jamukha and Toghril Khan rode here with me. I told them I wouldn't rest until I found you."

She reached up and felt his face with trembling hands, assuring herself he was really there. "Temujin." He pressed her to him; she was suddenly aware of her swollen belly. As he glanced down, the glow in his eyes faded. Around them, she heard the despairing cries of women and children as Temujin's men pulled them from the carts.

"Jelme!" he shouted. The Uriangkhai trotted towards them. "I've found what I came here to find," Temujin continued. "There's no need to go further tonight. We'll camp here, secure the prisoners, and rest."

"But others will escape," Jelme said.

"We can capture them later. Give the order."

Jelme disappeared into the throng. Bortai swayed as a cramp seized her, and gasped. "What is it?" she heard Temujin ask. "Is your time upon you?"

"It can't be," Khokakhchin replied, "not yet." They lifted her to the cart. "She has to rest."

Temujin had gathered an army to rescue her. His arm tightened across her belly as he settled her in the cart, and she wondered dimly if he would regret finding her.

46

BORTAI AWOKE. THE pain was gone, the child still inside her. The grey light of dawn was visible beyond the opening in

236

the back of the covered cart. The soldiers would be sorting out their loot and deciding which captives would live.

The cart shook as someone climbed into it. "Khokakhchin-eke," Temujin murmured.

"Speak softly," the old woman said. "The Ujin is still asleep." Bortai did not move as Khokakhchin crept forward. "Poor child. She endured much after you were so cruelly parted – but that's past."

"Yes." Voices keened in the distance, mourning the dead and dying. "You will tell me what's happened to my wife."

Khokakhchin was silent for some time, then said, "They gave her to a man called Chilger-boko."

"That I was told." His voice was toneless.

"He treated his horses and sheep more kindly than he did the Ujin. He beat her often. There were times I was afraid he might kill her and the child."

"May he be cursed," Temujin said.

"He was a buzzard, thinking he could feed on crane instead of rats, but he's lost his crane now."

"He'll suffer a slow death when I find him," Temujin said. "Anyone who shelters him will die, and I'll see that all his kindred pay for what he did."

"They deserve to suffer," the old woman said, "and I rejoice at seeing you and the Ujin reunited. You've won her back in time to have your first child born under your tent. We learned she was with child soon after we were captured. I think that made her able to endure that cruel man."

Would Temujin believe that? Bortai wondered. Would he be joyous enough at winning her back to accept it? Tears welled up under her lids.

"I have much to be thankful for," Temujin said. "It's good that you were with her, Khokakhchin-eke." He sounded strangely unmoved. "When my wife wakes, you'll tell her that those who mistreated her will never trouble her again. Now that Heaven has restored my Bortai to me, we'll speak no more of this." His words had the sound of a command.

Bortai was afraid to call out to him, to look into his face and see what truly lay in his heart. She kept her eyes closed until she knew he was gone.

When the sun was higher in the east, Temujin rode to Bortai's cart with a few of his men; the soldiers guarding the two women cheered him. Temujin's anda, a handsome man with sharp cheekbones and dark, piercing eyes, was with him. Jamukha smiled and spoke of his joy at finding his comrade's wife safe, but his words sounded false.

Temujin gave her a head-dress heavy with stones and beads of gold, draped her in a sable coat, then led the cart towards the ravaged camp. Bodies lay in the grass as black birds circled overhead; their fluttering shadows made Bortai think of curved swords. Prisoners, their arms bound, sat in groups, many still weeping for those they had lost. Soldiers shouted her name and Temujin's as they passed, and held up the heads they had taken; she did not see Chilger's among them.

Temujin left her with her guards, then rode off with his anda to meet with Toghril. The army would search for those who had escaped from Toghtoga's camp before striking at Khagatai's people. Captive Merkits, most of them women and children, were already being forced to take down tents while horsemen rounded up the herds. Bortai and the captured people and herds would soon begin the trek south with part of the army while the rest of the force launched its attack on Khagatai. She would return to Temujin's camp with Merkit slaves to serve her.

The men sang of their victory. Bortai sat with Khokakhchin in the cart, grateful that the heavy fur coat hid her belly. Her husband had gathered this army for the sake of a tainted prize, a wife carrying an enemy's child. Yet this victory would also give him more power and make him feared; perhaps that was why he had fought.

"My sister!" Belgutei rode towards her; Bortai longed to crawl into the cart and rest. He panted and his horse gleamed with sweat. "I've searched for my mother," he said, "and can't find her. I was told she was in this camp. Can you tell me what's become of her?"

Bortai glanced at Khokakhchin; the old woman was silent. She was suddenly certain that Belgutei would never see Sochigil-eke again, and wondered what to say.

"I haven't slept," Belgutei continued. "I've searched everywhere."

He would not want to hear the truth. Bortai recalled the foolish, accepting look in Sochigil's eyes when the woman had spoken of her Merkit captor. Sochigil had been content in her captivity.

"Your mother's a proud woman," Bortai said. "She was ashamed to face you after being forced to lie with a Merkit. She preferred to flee rather than have you see her in her dishonour."

Khokakhchin peered at her. Belgutei shook his fist. "Those who took her will die. The blood of every Merkit who attacked our camp will be shed."

"So be it," Bortai murmured.

Belgutei left them. Bortai leaned towards the old servant. "I give his mother more honour with my words," she whispered, "than I have myself."

"Ujin! No dishonour stains you. Your husband's revenge shows how much he honours you."

Women were screaming in the camp as the soldiers celebrated their victory and Bortai wanted to muffle her ears in the sable coat. Her abdomen knotted; her belly had dropped a little. The child might be expelled too soon, and be too weak to survive. Perhaps Temujin would be grateful if it died.

It was her child; he would have to accept it. She covered her abdomen with one hand, willing the child to live.

Bortai's labour began after they had left the Kumir range behind, skirting the mountains on the journey south. By the time Temujin's camp below the massif of Burkhan Khaldun was in sight, her water had broken, wetting her thighs. The pains were coming quickly when Khokakhchin and a few other women had finished raising a tent for her.

Khokakhchin stayed with her. The child was born in the night. "A son," she heard Khokakhchin whisper. A shaman was chanting outside, marking the position of the stars.

Bortai did not look at her son when the old woman brought him to her, knowing that she would see nothing of Temujin in him. The baby wailed lustily; the small body she held was strong, even though the child had entered life too soon. The

239

camp would soon be alive with the news of Temujin's first-born, another cause for rejoicing.

She clutched her son to her breast and he began to suck. He would always remind her of her captivity; she wondered if she could truly love him but knew that she must do so. The boy would need her even more if Temujin's heart did not warm to him.

47

HOELUN SEARCHED THE forest of lances moving towards her. A man on foot, a yoke around his neck, had been bound to a long row of roped captives, who were being driven ahead of the mass of mounted men. Messengers had ridden to the camp a few days earlier with news of her son's latest victory. Merkits were dead, captured, or scattered, their tent frames broken, their tughs desecrated. The yoked man was the Merkit chief Khagatai Darmala, who had been forced to lead the triumphant army back to the lands near Burkhan Khaldun.

At last she spotted Temujin; his uncle Daritai rode at his side. Daritai had brought his men to fight with his nephew when Jamukha had summoned him. Yesugei's brother had only seen a chance to gain something for himself, but Temujin would tell her there was nothing to be won by holding a grudge against Daritai.

Several children, Temulun and Temuge among them, rode towards the returning men, shrieking a welcome. Hoelun turned away, moved past the women preparing the feast, and entered her yurt. Temujin would wait before he visited her, to remind her that she had been wrong to doubt him. He might allow her to offer him counsel again, but she did not think he would heed her advice. Her joy at her son's achievement would always be dampened by knowing that he no longer needed her.

*

Khasar and Belgutei came to Hoelun's tent with a few of their comrades to share her feast. The young men settled on cushions as Hoelun's three Merkit slaves set out lamb and kumiss.

Khasar lifted his horn. "I drink to my brother's first son!" The others held up their horns and jugs. "I was told he was born a month ago, as soon as my sister Bortai was safely among you."

Hoelun nodded. She had counted the months in her head; the boy might be Temujin's.

"Temujin is preparing to thank the spirits of the great mountain for his victory," Khasar continued. "Toghtoga and Dayir may have escaped us, but Khagatai will suffer for their deeds. Temujin means to sacrifice him on the mountain. He may show him respect by letting the horses trample him instead of taking his head." The other men chuckled. "Toghril Khan is leading his men back to their lands, and Jamukha will camp near us. Temujin doesn't want to be separated from him, and we'll be stronger if we stay together."

"Indeed," Hoelun said, wondering which of the two would be the stronger leader. Her son's victory would bind him even more closely to his anda; he would ignore her doubts.

Belgutei stared morosely into his horn. Hoelun leaned towards him. "I'm sorry," she murmured, "that you didn't find your mother."

"The Merkits have answered for that." Belgutei took a breath. "We did find most of the men who attacked us last summer. I saw that each of them died, along with their sons, but we kept the fairest of their women for ourselves. Khasar and I will have wives now, Hoelun-eke." He smiled briefly, then frowned again. "I only wish we'd found the wretch who claimed Temujin's wife, but he'll die soon enough, wandering the forests with no one to help him. We found his brother, a coward who called himself Yeke Chiledu. I shot an arrow into his chest myself, after his two sons died before his eyes."

Hoelun started, then sighed. "One of those who raided our camp had asked for mercy if he pointed out his comrades," Belgutei continued. "He told me that this Chiledu had an old grudge, that he was one of the first to urge the enemy to attack us. I let the informer think he would live, then killed him after the others were dead. That cursed Chiledu begged for the lives of his sons, but I – "

Khasar was motioning at his half-brother. Belgutei looked away and gulped his kumiss. Hoelun's hand tightened around her golden goblet. She had never spoken the name of her first husband to her sons, but Khasar must have discovered who he had been.

It was just, she told herself. Temujin was a better man than Chiledu; her son had won back his stolen wife. She should not mourn the man who had lost her, for that part of her life had ended long ago. Chiledu had brought his death on himself; better if he had forgotten her. Yet she still grieved for the man she had once loved.

Two men came through the entrance with a small boy. "I almost forgot," Khasar said quickly. "This boy is a present for you – his name is Guchu."

Hoelun studied the Merkit boy. His hat and coat were sable, and he wore doeskin boots. He could be no older than five, but he held himself erect and gazed steadily at her.

"We found him in Toghtoga's camp," Khasar went on. "You can see by his clothing that he's a Noyan's son. The men wanted to make a gift of him to you, and Temujin agreed."

She beckoned to the boy. He walked towards her and peered boldly into her face. "I am Temujin's mother," she said.

"I know, Lady, but you don't look it. You seem so young."

The men laughed. "The boy knows what to say," one man muttered.

"He was alone," Khasar said. "We didn't find any of his family."

"They ran away," Guchu said softly. "Mother had me by the hand, and then she fell, and I hid behind a cart, and then – " He blinked and wiped at his eyes. "A man came at her. She ran into a yurt, and then it was burning, and I heard her scream, but she didn't come out."

Hoelun took his hand, thinking of how much he had lost. This campaign was over; wounds had to heal. "You'll stay with me, Guchu." She saw the boy struggling to hold back his tears. "I have four sons. You shall be the fifth. Think of me as your mother now."

"I'm not to be your slave?" Guchu asked.

"You'll be my son. This battle's over for you. I'll care for you in place of the mother you lost, and my other sons will be your brothers."

The boy pressed her hand to his cheek. Let it end, she thought fiercely, knowing such a prayer was futile, that more wars would inevitably be fought.

Temujin came to Bortai's tent three days after his return. His eyes did not meet hers as he gazed at the cradle that held her son. The men with him laughed and praised the sturdy boy as the infant wailed.

"Your son should be named," Jamukha said. His glance fell on Bortai. She disliked the way he looked at her, as if she were only a slave.

"I have a name for him," Temujin said. A thin moustache like Jamukha's had begun to grow above his mouth; his face was taut with fatigue, his eyes the colour of flames. "His name will be Jochi." He draped one arm over his anda's shoulders. "We'll drink to my son together."

Jochi, she thought – the Visitor, the Stranger, the Guest. The men seated themselves as the three Merkit women she had been given brought jugs to them. Bortai rocked the cradle, soothing the baby when he cried, saying nothing as the men drank and talked of the Merkits they had killed, the captives and herds they had won.

After a while, Temujin dismissed them; Jamukha was the last to leave. The two embraced by the entrance and Jamukha whispered to Temujin before releasing him.

One of the Merkits lowered the flap. Temujin gestured at her. "Go to Khokakhchin-eke's tent," he said, "and come here again at dawn. I wish to be alone with my wife."

The women scurried from the yurt. Bortai opened her garment and suckled Jochi. Temujin came towards her and looked down at the child. His eyes were cold; she was suddenly certain that he knew the boy was not his. He would not repudiate her, not after fighting a war for her, but he might choose to make another his chief wife, as his father had done when he found Hoelun-eke.

243

"You've won much," she managed to say.

"Yes."

"You must have claimed a great share of what was captured."

"I was offered my choice of the fairest prisoners, but commanded that they be parcelled out among my followers. I told my men that I have my beautiful Bortai now, and need no other."

Her arms tightened around her son. "A stallion can sire many foals on many mares."

"So the men said, but there will be other battles, and a chance to claim my due then. I wanted to reward all those who rode with me in my first campaign. I'll win more followers when others hear how generous I am to my men."

She secured Jochi in the cradle and set it down. Temujin stared at the child, then said, "I'll ask this only once, and then we will never speak of it again. I must know if he's my son. Khokakhchin-eke says that he is, and perhaps it's so, but I want the truth from you."

She could not speak.

"If you don't know," he continued, "if you have no way to be sure, say so. I've acknowledged him as my son, and no one will say otherwise. What you tell me will be between us."

He would believe what she told him. The boy might grow as tall as Chilger, but Temujin was also tall; Jochi's dark eyes were much like her father Dei's. She wanted to tell him the baby was his, but could not say the words. The lie would always be between them.

"I'll tell you the truth." Bortai lifted her head. "I knew he couldn't be yours when I first realized I was with child. I wanted to believe he was, and then it was easier to know that he wasn't when I thought I'd never see you again."

"You shouldn't have doubted me, Bortai."

"Hope was too hard to bear." She took a breath. "Khokakhchin-eke will never speak of this, and it's been only nine months since I was taken. He was born too soon, but he's so vigorous already that no one will suspect that – they can believe he was inside me before we were parted."

Temujin said, "They will believe it because I say it's so." His

244

eyes were darker in the shadows; she could not see his thoughts in his face.

"I know you won't shame me," Bortai said, "but I'll understand if you take a new wife and set her above me."

"No one will take your place, Bortai." He turned away from the cradle. "If you hadn't urged me to abandon you, my enemies would have had my life. My people will not whisper that I fought a war for my wife, only to have her deliver a Merkit's bastard to me."

"You're as generous to me," she whispered, "as you are to your men."

"I told you," he said, "that I always wanted you to welcome me, that no shadow would fall between us. My enemies have suffered for what they did, and you'll forget your time among them. This boy is my first son. There will be others, but Jochi is the first, and I'll care for him no less than for his brothers."

"Jochi," she said. "The Stranger."

"A stranger because he grew inside his mother while she was a captive, and a guest I now welcome under my tent. That's all it means."

He shrugged out of his coat. She rose, took off her headdress, trousers and boots, and went to the bed, covering herself quickly with the blanket. Temujin stripped to his shift, then got in next to her.

His arms slipped around her. He would expect her to hold him, to rouse him as she had before, but she could not will herself to reach out to him. Her body tensed as Temujin entered her; she closed her eyes, enduring him, wanting to forget. Chilger lay between them, and perhaps he always would.

He shuddered, making no sound, then withdrew and touched her face lightly. "It isn't the same," he said.

"No."

"This will pass. Things will be as they were."

He would have to believe that, having gone to such lengths to win her back. He stretched out at her side. She lay there, awake, listening to his deep, even breathing until Jochi began to cry for her.

48

HOELUN GAZED AT the camp from the hill. Yurts dotted the Khorkhonagh Valley; bright sparks danced in the streams that rose from hundreds of smoke-holes. The pale smoke, carried by the hot summer wind, drifted towards the wall of cliffs to the west. The air was thick with the odour of burning meat.

Temujin's tent stood to the north of the camp, at the edge of one camping circle; Jamukha's was in the place of honour at the north of the circle nearest her son's. She could not even see the southernmost tents. All of this belonged to her son — and to Jamukha, she reminded herself.

The two young chiefs had ridden here together, and had treated each other as equals ever since returning from their campaign. Hoelun had expected Jamukha to take precedence, to show in some way that he considered himself the greater leader. He had commanded the armies and had more followers; he had reason to claim a higher place. Temujin might believe that he and his anda could rule together, but she could not accept it.

She glanced to her right, where Jamukha's wife Nomalan sat with Bortai. Nomalan Ujin's head was bowed; she seemed as fearful of her husband as his men were said to be. Her face was small under her square head-dress, and her body, in spite of the child she carried, was thin under her coat.

That girl, Hoelun thought, has a weak spirit. The women whispered that Jamukha had rarely gone to his wife's bed even before learning of her pregnancy. Bortai murmured to Nomalan as she rocked Jochi's cradle. Temujin had accepted the boy as his own; Hoelun would refuse to believe otherwise.

Men had gathered by the hill, and others were streaming from the camp on horseback. Those standing in the front leaned against their lances; those in the rear sat on their steeds, waiting to hear what their chiefs would say before the feast.

Temulun fidgeted at Hoelun's side. "How much longer?" the little girl whispered.

"Hush," Hoelun replied. A kinsman of Jamukha's was lead-

246

ing a tan horse taken from the Merkits to the hill; Khasar followed him with a black-maned yellow mare.

"Khachigun said that Temujin told him he could go with him on his next raid," Temulun murmured. "I can shoot as well as he can. Why can't I go when I'm older?"

"Don't be silly," old Khokakhchin whispered. "You'll be betrothed by the time you're Khachigun's age – you'll be getting ready for your wedding."

Above the women, Temujin and Jamukha sat under the great tree. Four shamans stood behind them, rattling their bags of bones gently as they swayed. Hoelun's neck prickled; she wondered what the spirits had told the shamans before they set the time for this feast, and what her son and his anda would say to their men now.

The two chiefs got to their feet and the mass of men crowding the land between the hill and the camp grew silent. Temujin raised his arm; Jamukha did the same.

"The old men tell us," Temujin shouted, "that when two men swear an anda oath, their lives become one."

"My anda and I have fought together," Jamukha added. "It is time we renewed the oath we made as boys. We shall make our pledge once more, in this place before all of you."

The men roared their approval. "We are brothers," Temujin said. "Nothing will part us."

"We are brothers," Jamukha called out, "who will never desert each other. The same blood flows in us both." A shaman offered Temujin a cup of kumiss. Temujin pricked his finger with a knife, let the blood drip into the kumiss, then handed the cup to Jamukha, who did the same. Jamukha drank from the cup and gave it back to his anda; Temujin lifted it to his lips. The men below shook their weapons as they cheered.

Hoelun shivered in spite of the heat. She could feel the spirits the shamans were summoning to the wide shadows under the great tree's branches. Temujin beckoned to his brother. Khasar moved towards him with the yellow horse, then handed Temujin a belt thick with plates of gold.

Temujin hefted the belt. "I renew my pledge with this gift to my anda, a belt I took from the tent of Toghtoga Beki." He slipped the belt around Jamukha's waist. "I also give him this

247

horse, which that Merkit will never ride again. May she increase the herds of Jamukha.''

Jamukha motioned to his kinsman; the man went to him with the tan horse and another golden belt. "I renew my bond with my anda," the Jajirat said, "by offering him this belt from the spoils of Dayir Usun's camp." He put the belt around Temujin. "And may this mare I took from our enemies increase the herds of my brother."

Sunlight glinted from hundreds of upraised lances and swords, blinding Hoelun for a moment; the roar of the men slapped against her ears. The two young men mounted their horses and circled the hill as their men shouted and stamped their feet.

"Never shall we be parted!" Jamukha cried. "Those who follow me follow Temujin! Those who follow him are my comrades as well!"

"We are one people!" Temujin shouted. "As my anda and I are one!"

They dismounted, linked arms, and climbed the small hill. The shamans chanted and beat their drums. Voices swelled in a guttural song as Temujin and Jamukha danced together under the wide limbs of the great tree.

Do you know what this means? a voice whispered inside Hoelun. *Once I dreamed of dancing under this tree, as my uncle did with his men.* Yesugei's spirit was speaking to her. Khutula had danced under this tree when a kuriltai proclaimed him Khan, and her son was doing the same, but with Jamukha, as if they both claimed Khutula's place. She glimpsed Daritai among the men, still and silent as those around him cheered and pounded the ground with their feet.

Jamukha and Temujin lifted their knees as they danced. They could not both be Khan. One sun shone down from Heaven; a people could have only one Khan. Hoelun felt that spirits were dancing with the two men under the tree, that Khutula himself was there, repeating his old dance. One Khan would have to rule in time. The spirits of Temujin's ancestors would surely favour him; she would burn fat in her fire during the feast to feed those spirits. Hoelun bowed her head and prayed that her son would rule.

Jamukha sat under the tree, gazing south at the moonlit camp. Except for the guards, the horsemen watching the herds on the plain below the Khuldaghar cliffs, and a few feasters riding towards their yurts, the rest of the people were asleep.

Temujin stirred next to him, caught in the restless sleep of drunkenness. The grass around them was flattened by their dancing; the men had beaten patches of ground bare with their boots. The two mares they had given to each other grazed below, guarded by Jelme.

They were united now; their feast had marked that, as had their dance. They had gone among their men to share in the feast, staying at each other's side, sitting together in the place of honour.

His head was clearing. Beyond the great tree that sheltered them, the camp-fires of Heaven flickered. Temujin's uncle Daritai had sung of Khutula Khan as they danced, but had added a new verse to the song. "In Heaven," he had chanted, "there is a sun and a moon." He had honoured them both with those words. They would rule together, first among the chiefs.

Temujin grunted, then pushed away the blanket Jamukha had laid over him. "My throat burns," Temujin said. Jamukha handed him a jug. "When did we ride back here?"

"Towards sunset," Jamukha replied.

"I must have drunk more than I thought."

Temujin sat up and draped an arm over his knees. Jelme turned his head towards them. Jamukha did not want to go to the yurt where his wife Nomalan would scurry after his attentions like a dog hoping for scraps.

"Jelme awaits your command," Jamukha muttered. Temujin had not lain with Bortai for some days, and might feel he should go to her now. Some still whispered that Jochi was not Temujin's son; they would probably die for it if they ever said such words in Temujin's presence. His anda had been thinking of Bortai in refusing his pick of the most beautiful Merkits. It was enough that he had rescued her, yet he seemed compelled to prove that she had not lost his esteem. No woman had ever been so honoured.

The drink in him was making him sullen. He had accepted his share of the captive maidens only because his men might have wondered if he refused them. A few might turn to boys or young men while away from their wives, and others took boys after raids to instil fear and mark their triumph, but all would despise a man who preferred that to lying with a woman. He wished now that he had given his Merkit girls to his generals; he could have made it seem an act of generosity, as Temujin had.

His anda gestured with the jug. Jamukha shook his head. "Jelme," he said, "will sit there all night if you don't send him away."

Temujin got to his feet, moved down the hill on unsteady legs, then turned back to him. "I want to sleep here, under the tree where we swore our oath today."

Jamukha's darker mood vanished. "So do I."

Temujin shouted an order to Jelme. The Uriangkhai caught the reins of the mares and rode towards the camp. "You might have sent him back earlier," Temujin said as he sat down again. "You are also his chief now. He must be longing for the woman I gave him from my share of the spoils."

"Many wondered why you didn't take that one for yourself."

"I'll win other women later, and my men were grateful for the ones I refused."

"Men serve a leader best when they fear him."

"His enemies should fear him," Temujin responded. "His men should fear him only if they betray him, or fail in their duty. One must swoop down on such men as the falcon does upon a bird in flight, but men should also know that the faithful among them will be rewarded."

Temujin sipped from the jug. They would be safe enough here for the night, this close to the camp. Jamukha had seen no sign of predators, and felt that the spirits they had called here were still protecting them.

He thought of what lay before them. More clans and tribes were likely to seek an alliance with them; those who did not would have to be subdued. The scattered Merkits were likely to regroup, and another campaign against them might be necessary. The Tatars might attack if they grew fearful of the Mongol clans. Temujin and he had spoken of all this before.

Temujin finished the kumiss, then stretched out under the

blanket, leaving half of the covering for Jamukha. "I knew you were my friend when we first met, when you rode to my defence." Temujin's voice was slightly slurred by drink. "I never doubted that you'd aid me against my enemies, because I remembered the boy who swore his oath to me when my family was alone and friendless."

Jamukha lay down next to him and covered himself. They had slept this way as boys, in one bed, one covering over them both. A fierce longing filled him as he recalled those nights. Temujin had accepted his touch then, welcoming the way they could give pleasure to each other with their hands, but perhaps he saw that only as boys' play, something to be put aside when one was grown.

He circled Temujin's waist with one arm. His anda sighed, but did not push him away. They had a sacred bond; whatever they did now, in this place where they had proclaimed their brotherhood, could only strengthen it. He would have the purer love he sought, and bind Temujin closer to him.

He lowered his hand. Temujin was already hard against his palm; Jamukha rejoiced. His brother's fingers slipped under his trousers, his brother's strong, callused hand grasped his member firmly. Temujin had not forgotten.

Jamukha's seed spurted from him after only a few strokes and he moaned as his hand tightened around Temujin's shaft. His anda gasped as his seed came and trickled over Jamukha's hand. He needed no more now; they could share themselves in this way for a time, until the Noyans raised Jamukha to Khutula's place. They would have to turn to him, but his anda would remain at his side. Temujin would be his completely then, swearing his oath and later surrendering himself.

He held his friend until he knew that Temujin was asleep, then slipped his hand from under his anda's clothing. Nothing could separate them, now that they had made this offering to each other. They were one.

PART FIVE

Jamukha said, "If we camp by the mountains, those who tend the horses and cattle will have food. If we camp by the river, those who herd the sheep will feed their flocks."

49

JAMUKHA MOUNTED HIS horse as two men led the Khongkho-tat messenger towards the camp. He had circled the grazing cattle when his cousin Taychar caught up with him.

"When will you give me what I want?" Taychar shouted.

Jamukha slowed to a trot. "When my anda and I come to a decision."

Taychar's mouth twitched below his faint moustache. "Perhaps I should speak to Temujin and not you," he said, "since you do nothing without his consent."

Jamukha lashed out with one arm and caught his cousin in the chest. Taychar gasped, but stayed in his saddle. "Be careful what you say," Jamukha said. "Temujin does nothing without my consent, and you need me to speak for you."

Taychar glared at him. "Very well," he muttered before he rode away.

On the open land ahead, several boys were practising their archery, aiming their arrows at a lone tree. Khasar stood with the line of boys; Temujin leaned forward on his horse as Temuge stepped up and took aim. The arrow soared, then fell just short of the target.

Jamukha reined in his horse. Borchu shouted a greeting; Jelme nodded at him. Lately, Temujin spent more time with his two close comrades. Jamukha wondered if his anda spoke to the Arulat and Uriangkhai of their disagreements.

No, he told himself. Temujin's anger flared readily whenever anyone spoke against Jamukha. Temujin argued with him only when they were alone, and their disagreements never lasted for long.

But this winter, Temujin's patience and steadiness had begun to irritate him. His anda's judgement always seemed to prevail. Temujin chose their camp-sites, led the hunts, and decided which men should have more authority, while making sure he had Jamukha's consent. Taychar had said only what others thought.

The summer wind rose, lifting dust, as Jelme's younger brother Subotai stepped up to take his turn. The wind and the dust would make the shot more difficult, but Subotai, at the age of ten, showed Khasar's skill with the bow. Subotai aimed; his arrow sped towards the tree and pierced the trunk.

"Ha!" Jelme shouted. Khasar slapped the boy on the back. Jamukha motioned to Temujin; his anda trotted towards him, trailed by Jelme and Borchu.

"A Khongkhotat messenger is here," Jamukha said, "sent by your old friend Munglik." Temujin's eyes narrowed. "I think Munglik means to join his camp to ours."

Temujin nodded. The Khongkhotat chieftain, in spite of his old ties to Temujin's family and his alliance with Jamukha, had been careful not to do anything that might anger the Taychiuts; Munglik was a cautious man. Now he might join them openly, a sign he was aware of their growing strength.

Borchu frowned. "Munglik did little for you before."

"He did what he could," Temujin said, "and if he binds himself to us, I'll welcome him."

Temujin, Jamukha thought, was always so reasonable. He would never allow an old grudge to deprive him of an ally.

"We'll have to speak to the Khongkhotat together," Jamukha said. "He'll have passed between the fires by now – perhaps Borchu and Jelme can ride ahead to tell him we're on our way."

Temujin motioned to his comrades. The two galloped towards the camp; Jamukha and Temujin followed at a trot. Jamukha glanced at his anda. Hearing of a message from Munglik had clearly put Temujin in a better mood; maybe he would listen to Jamukha's request.

"My kinsman Taychar has spoken to me." Jamukha swatted

at the large black flies that buzzed around his head. "He feels he should have command of a mingghan."

"I know," Temujin replied. "He complains often enough about it."

"I wish to grant his request, or at least promise him a thousand men later."

"He commands one hundred now."

"He wants a mingghan," Jamukha said. "You gave such commands to Borchu and Jelme, and promised them to Khasar and Belgutei. You told them they would each command a tuman when you had the ten thousand men to give them. I agreed, and now I want my cousin to be their equal. He proved himself against our Merkit foes."

Temujin scowled. "He's too rash. He rushes into raids and loses more men than he should. Let him show he can command his hundred before he's promised a thousand."

Jamukha's face flamed. "You raise two who aren't your kinsmen, then refuse – "

"Why do you say that?" Temujin's voice was low. "Can I refuse anything to one who's my anda and my equal?" Their horses slowed to a walk. "If you want to honour Taychar, I can't stop you. I was only saying that he may not be ready for such a command."

Jamukha struggled to control himself. Temujin would let him do as he liked, but everyone would know that his anda had doubts about Taychar. How clever Temujin was, and how steadfast, so anxious to show that their bond was unbreakable, so quick to turn aside any complaints about Jamukha. He knew there were such complaints, that others spoke to Temujin of his temper and unpredictability before Temujin silenced them. They did not understand that fear of a leader was useful, that uncertainty about exactly what his chief might do could keep a man obedient. How just Temujin was, and how ready to let others believe that their successes were his, while their failures were Jamukha's.

"I can't fault Taychar's courage," Temujin continued, "and a man should look out for his kin. But you won't serve him well if you raise him before he's ready."

Whatever he said, however kindly he meant it, Temujin could

255

make him feel he was in the wrong. Temujin would go along with him, then remind him of his error if Taychar failed as a Mingghan-u Noyan and general.

"I'll tell my cousin," Jamukha said, "that we haven't refused him outright. Perhaps later – "

"You might also tell him that a man should trust his leader's judgement about such things. Taychar is impatient. Jelme and Borchu didn't plead for commands."

His hands tightened around his reins. Temujin had both insulted his cousin and implied that his own judgement was sounder than Jamukha's.

His anda smiled suddenly, looking like a boy for a moment. "You're like a brave stallion," Temujin murmured, "with so much spirit that it sometimes gets the better of you. You lend me some of that spirit, and I temper yours with my caution. Without each other, we would both be less."

These words nearly roused his anger once more. A stallion was curbed by the man who trained him; Temujin was calling himself Jamukha's tamer. He swallowed hard, then forced himself to smile back.

The Khongkhotat made a speech vowing friendship, then presented gifts of scarves and furs. When the men Temujin and Jamukha had summoned arrived, the envoy delivered his message. Munglik wanted to bring his people to their camp, and hoped to join them for the great hunt that autumn. Jamukha ordered that a bone be burned, then passed it to Khorchi, who nodded; the Bagarin chief was a shaman.

Temujin made a speech welcoming the Khongkhotats; Jamukha followed it with a few phrases of his own. His wife Nomalan and her serving women set out jugs of kumiss and slivers of lamb with salt water.

The men were soon drunk. Nearly thirty were crowded into Jamukha's yurt; the women brought them more jugs, then sat on their side of the dwelling to eat. Nomalan was silent as the other five women gossiped; one of Jamukha's Merkit women was with them. Useless creatures, he thought, who could not give him one son between them. Still, he preferred gathering with his men here, even if it meant enduring Nomalan's presence, rather than going to Temujin's yurt, where Bortai and that old woman Khokakhchin would listen to every word.

Temujin murmured to the Khongkhotat, who already looked too drunk to sit up. "Charakha, the father of your chief, was always faithful," Temujin said. "He was my father's shadow. He stood by us, and paid for his loyalty with his life."

Jamukha glanced at Daritai, who had not been so faithful to his nephew. "I've regretted Charakha's death all these years," Temujin went on. "I'll always honour his courage, but perhaps he would have done better to shepherd his people so he could return to me now." Daritai's tense face relaxed; his nephew had forgiven him long before.

"Maybe," Khasar muttered to his brother, "that dream you had last night foretold this. You saw a great camp, and now ours will grow greater."

"What dream is this?" Belgutei shouted. Khorchi lifted his brows; two men stumbling towards the entrance looked back. "Tell us your dream, my brother."

Temujin drank, then rested an arm on his knee. "I was flying above the earth," he began. "Below, I saw a camp with many circles, so many that they covered the earth as far as I could see. I spread my wings, and the wind carried me north. I flew over so many yurts that I couldn't count them, and came to the last, the greatest dwelling of all. Its panels were of gold, and a hundred oxen would have been needed to pull the platform on which it sat. I hovered over the smoke-hole and smelled the fat of roasting meat, then alighted by the doorway. The men guarding the dwelling bowed low before me, and it came to me that this was my tent and that those inside were waiting for me to join their feast."

"And what did you find inside?" Daritai asked.

Temujin said, "I awoke before I could enter."

Jamukha clenched his jaw so tightly that it hurt. Temujin's eyes met his. "But surely," Temujin continued, "my anda was inside, awaiting me."

"Yet you didn't see him there," Belgutei said.

"As I told you, my spirit returned to me before I went inside, but how could it be otherwise?"

He means to lead alone, Jamukha thought; he dreams of

being Khan. This dream was a challenge, as all the men would see. No one spoke; even Khorchi, who was usually so quick to interpret any dream, said nothing.

"Whatever else this dream means," Belgutei muttered, "it foretells great things for you." Jamukha gulped more kumiss; Temujin's dull-witted half-brother could be counted on to speak when a wiser man would have kept silent.

"I would have nothing without Jamukha," Temujin said. "Whatever I have is his." His hand touched Jamukha's shoulder lightly. "Would the spirits have to show me what I already know to be true?"

The knot in Jamukha's chest loosened. Whatever Temujin thought his dream foretold, he was saying that he was not yet ready to challenge him.

The men went on drinking. Daritai recited the tale of his ancestor Bodonchar and the woman he had captured, the woman from whom Jamukha was descended. Men left the yurt to urinate, then returned. When the Khongkhotat passed out, Daritai and Khorchi dragged him to one side and covered him with a blanket. Jamukha passed another jug to his anda; perhaps Temujin would get drunk enough to stay in his tent tonight. Nomalan might suspect that they sometimes shared more than sleep, but was too cowed to speak of that.

He thought of their first night together under the great tree. Temujin had given no sign afterwards that anything had changed, and at last Jamukha had realized that drink had drowned his anda's memories. So little had passed between them since that night nearly a year and a half ago; how carefully his anda guarded himself, refusing to admit the true nature of their bond. He shared so little, and then only when he was too drunk to care what was happening. Jamukha had never spoken of his deeper and more violent longings to him.

"You're silent, brother Jamukha." Temujin shifted on his cushion. "Munglik will soon know that he's welcome here. The Taychiuts will hear of it by summer's end, and wonder about our intentions."

Jamukha shrugged. "Perhaps we should send a message to them. They may decide it's in their interest to ally themselves with us."

"Targhutai and Todogen forgot their oath to my father," Temujin said softly. "How can I trust any promise they might make?"

"You'll welcome Munglik." Jamukha glanced towards the Khongkhotat; the envoy slept on, snoring loudly.

"Munglik didn't yoke me and have me beaten."

"And Targhutai didn't kill you outright when he might have." Jamukha nudged Temujin in the ribs. "Things have changed. Your Taychiut cousins aren't foolish men — what can they gain by standing against us?"

"It might be well to strike at them before they can."

"Munglik is their ally," Jamukha said. "He may not be so willing to turn against them. Why fight men we may win over without a battle? I think we can bring them to swear an oath to us."

"They might swear it, then try to set us against each other. I have no faith in any promises they might make."

A few men whispered to one another. First Temujin had spoken of his dream, and now he was disagreeing with Jamukha openly. His anda wanted war, and the bitterness he had expressed was unlike him. Temujin had many reasons to hate the Taychiuts, but had always put his grudges aside when he could gain from forgetting them.

He doesn't want the Taychiuts with us, Jamukha thought, because he knows they'll be my allies and not his, that they would rather have me as leader here than him.

The Khongkhotat snorted, started up, then lay down again. A few men got up, bowed to Jamukha and Temujin, then left. The others soon followed them from the yurt; Jelme was the last to leave.

"Stay a little," Jamukha said to his anda. "We'll share another jug."

Temujin shook his head. "I've drunk enough."

Jamukha waved at his Merkit woman, dismissing her; she hurried from the tent with the servants. He gazed bitterly at his wife as she got up to dump scraps into the kettle. Nomalan had given him only a stillborn girl; his seed had not grown inside her since. Bortai was pregnant, and Temujin could be certain he was the father this time. He had also promised a

Merkit he had recently claimed as a bedfellow that she would be his second wife when she gave him a child. With a wife able to give him children, it was easy for Temujin to be kind to his Merkit, who rewarded him with her mindless devotion.

Jamukha drank; a plan was forming in his mind. Temujin had disagreed with him openly and if he did nothing, his men would see him as weak. The others did not want war with the Taychiuts; of that he was sure. Even Temujin's close comrades would have doubts about a battle that did not have to be fought.

Taychar would be angry at being denied the command he wanted. He was impulsive enough to strike at Temujin himself if Jamukha encouraged him. Jamukha would have to see that his anda was not harmed, only subdued.

"We must move on soon," Jamukha said at last. "This land is nearly grazed bare."

"So we must, and celebrate midsummer elsewhere." Temujin rose; Jamukha followed him to the entrance. They waited outside as a boy led Temujin's mount to him.

"Go in peace," Jamukha said, then caught Temujin's arm. "When we move on, if we camp by the mountains, those who tend the horses and cattle will have food. If we camp by the river, those who herd the sheep will feed their flocks." He waited for his anda's answer. Tell me what I want to hear now, he thought, and I will forget what's happened today. Tell me you wish to camp by the river, and let me send my message to the Taychiut chiefs.

"You confuse me, Jamukha." Temujin shook off his hand, then embraced him. "We'll talk of where to camp another time." He swung himself into his saddle. "I leave in peace, my brother."

Jamukha watched him ride away. If Temujin chose war, his own men would know he did not. The fire of Taychar's anger had to be stoked. The others would support Jamukha if he brought them an alliance with Todogen and Targhutai. A pain caught him around the heart; he suddenly wished that he and Temujin were only boys again.

50

JOCHI CLUNG TO the sheep as his legs hugged the animal. "Hang on," Bortai shouted to her son. Temulun kept near, ready to catch the little boy.

At last Hoelun lifted Jochi from the sheep. Temujin was dismounting near the wagons. He strode towards Bortai, alone for once; even Jelme was not with him. Jochi ran to him, and he grinned and hugged the child. He was no longer as cool to Jochi as he had been, and Bortai knew why. He was certain the child she now carried was his own.

Her husband came to her and put his hand on her belly; Jochi clutched at Temujin's coat. Guchu, aided by two dogs, herded more sheep towards the tents. "Greetings, Older Brother," the boy called out. "We should break camp soon — we have to go further every day to graze the sheep."

"You tell me what I know," Temujin replied. "We'll take down our yurts in two days." He motioned to his mother; his smile faded. "I want to speak to you and to my wife."

Bortai knew by his tone that he wished to talk to them alone. "Temulun," she said, "watch Jochi." She beckoned to Hoelun's foster son. "Guchu, gather some fuel."

She followed her husband into her tent. Two women laid the blankets they had beaten clean over her bed; Bortai sent them out to milk the sheep. Khokakhchin was about to follow them when Temujin held up a hand. "You may stay, Khokakhchin-eke."

The old woman fetched a jug as Temujin sat down in front of the bed. Hoelun eased Bortai to a cushion, then settled at her son's left. Khokakhchin sprinkled kumiss over the ongghons hanging by the bed before handing Temujin the jug. The servant's eyes were as watchful as ever, her ears still sharp, but her bent body moved slowly, as if her bones ached. She retreated to the hearth and sat down; even in summer, Khokakhchin craved the fire's heat.

Bortai picked up two pieces of leather, threaded her needle with a strand of sinew, and drew it through one of the holes she had made with her awl. Jochi was growing, and needed a new shirt. "Say what you wish to tell us, son," Hoelun said. "We have the milking to do before we can eat."

"I gave you slaves for your work, Mother."

"They can't do it all, and a lazy mistress is a bad example."

Temujin sighed and drew his brows together. "Both of you have always been honest with me," he said. "I'm bound to Jamukha, yet some of those closest to me say he can't be trusted. Once no one dared to tell me this, but Borchu and Jelme now repeat such things to my face. They say that some who have given me their oaths are unhappy and may leave our camp."

Bortai had heard such talk; his words did not surprise her. That he was speaking of this to her and Hoelun-eke did. Temujin had sought no advice from them since pledging himself to Jamukha. Now she heard doubt and uncertainty in his voice.

"Your anda must be aware of these complaints," Hoelun murmured. "Maybe you should talk to him. You've always said you have no secrets from him."

Bortai pulled her needle through another hole. Her husband would not listen to evil words about his anda. Bortai had told him only once that Jamukha's sudden rages disturbed her, that without Temujin to restrain him, he would make an inconstant leader. He had struck her before she could say more; the blow had thrown her back into Chilger's tent, surrounding her with the terror she thought she had escaped. She had guarded her tongue after that.

"What do your closest comrades advise?" Bortai asked.

"I don't have to ask them," he said. "I know what they'll say."

He would not have come to them unless his own doubts about Jamukha had deepened. The two had disagreed in front of their men; Jamukha's servants had spread that news. Temujin might want only reassurance, comforting words that would restore his trust in his friend, but she could not utter them. Yet she might only drive him further from her if she spoke against Jamukha.

Bortai set down her sewing. "I have heard," she said, "that you spoke of a dream you had to your men. In your dream,

262

you flew over a great camp, then came to the tent of the Khan who ruled it all, and saw that this great tent was your own."

"So you know of that." Temujin tugged at the scarf tied around his head. "Some see omens in that dream that aren't there."

"Are you so sure? You told me long ago of a dream where you stood on a great mountain and saw all the world. When we were children, you asked me why there shouldn't be one Khan on the earth. Your dreams are showing you what must be, and yet you refuse to see it. Do you ever see two Khans ruling in the same camp when your soul wanders with the spirits? Your feelings for your anda may blind you to the truth."

"When a kuriltai is held to choose one of us, the Noyans will choose me." A muscle twitched near his jaw. "I can wait until then. Jamukha's my anda — he'd give me his oath."

"He'll never agree," she said. "He'll never assent to seeing you raised above him. The longer you stay with him, the weaker you'll become. The Noyans will never turn to you then."

"I thought you were wiser than that, Bortai. If I parted with him now, I'd be weaker — I'd lose half of what we rule together."

"Are you so certain? Your men follow you willingly, while Jamukha's follow him because they fear him. You might win more men to your side if they can follow you alone. Even some of his own men might join you. Why do you think he lets you share his place when he could have claimed more honour for himself? He wants to lull you, to use you, to bind you to him until — "

"Be silent!" His face was pale; Bortai shrank back.

"You asked us what we thought," Hoelun said. "Bortai has told you. Why come to us if you don't want to hear it?"

'And you, Khokakhchin-eke." Temujin got up and walked towards the hearth. "What do you say?"

"It isn't my place to say anything, Bahadur. I've seen enemies join, and brothers become enemies, and it will all go on happening long after I'm gone."

He paced around the tent. Bortai expected him to leave and go to Doghon, his Merkit woman, but he sat down near her once more.

"Tell me the rest, Temujin," she said. "I sense there's much you haven't said."

"I expected Jamukha to grow angry when I told him of my dream, but he said nothing. I grew bolder, and disagreed with him in front of the others, but even that didn't rouse him." His pale eyes glistened. "Always before, I could see his thoughts, but I can't now." He paused. "When I left his tent that night, Jamukha said something that still puzzles me. He said that if we make camp by the mountains, those who tend the horses and cattle will have food. Then he went on to say that if we make camp by a stream, the shepherds will be fed. He said no more than that, and I couldn't think of how to reply."

Jamukha, Bortai saw, had asked him a question, although she wondered why he had asked it in that veiled way instead of outright. If they favoured the sheep in their new grazing grounds, they would have more wool for clothing and more felt for their tents; favouring the horses meant preparing for war. Temujin had counselled war against the Taychiuts, and Jamukha had disagreed; that rumour had also spread through the camp. Jamukha knew what her husband wanted, so what was the purpose in his question?

"He's challenging you." The words left her before she could find a way to soften them. "You should have seen it yourself. You want to fight and he doesn't. If we camp by a river, the men will know Jamukha has won. If you answer that we'll camp by the mountains, he can't agree without showing his own weakness. Whatever you say, he'll use it against you."

"No," he whispered.

"You brought this into the open," Bortai persisted. "Maybe you should have waited, but it's done. You knew this day would come, but told yourself Jamukha would step aside for you. His words show you that he won't. You say you know him, but he knows you, too. Once you were alone, and now you've won the devotion of many. You can't bear to think that you might be deserted again, or that anyone close to you might wish you harm. Jamukha remembers the boy you were — it's his weapon against you."

Temujin's body was rigid, his hands fisted tight.

"I speak the truth," she said. "You gave him no answer, so

he'll ask the question again, when others can hear his words. If you say we must favour the horses, the men will see you still want war, and that will give Jamukha an excuse to move against you. His words hide a plot."

"We swore an oath." His voice was faint.

"He could keep his while letting others act for him. You must listen to me, Temujin."

"And what would you have me do?"

"Don't give him an answer. Let him think you're unwilling to confront him. Then we must leave him before he can stop us, before he knows we're gone."

"You know what this means," Temujin said. "If I break with him, he won't forgive me, and the break will weaken us."

"It will reveal your true strength," she replied, "when you see who stays with him and who follows you. Anyway, you're better off alone than staying with a man you can no longer trust."

She saw him still resisting her words. "And there's this," she went on. "If he truly means you no harm, he'll send a message to you affirming his friendship, and you'll lose little."

"He came to me when I had nothing. I can't forget that, whatever happens now." He let out his breath. "But you are correct, wife. That's something I must put aside." He bowed his head; when he looked up, his face was impassive. "I'll say nothing of this until we've broken camp. Our carts and herds will keep in the rear, and I'll ride in the lead with Jamukha, as I always do. When we stop to graze our animals, I'll tell him that I must see to you, that your time may be nearly upon you. He'll believe that – he knows some still whisper that Jochi was born too soon."

Bortai flinched. She had hoped those tales had finally died.

"Jelme and Borchu will be told of my plans then," her husband continued in a toneless voice, "and they will tell those we can trust to drop behind, but we'll keep in sight, so that Jamukha thinks we are still with him. When night falls, we'll turn from his trail and press on. He won't know we've abandoned him until dawn."

Bortai took a breath. "Heaven will favour you, Temujin."

"Heaven's favour can feel like the kang I once wore." He

got to his feet; his broad shoulders sagged with weariness. "You've given me wise counsel, Bortai. I'll go to Doghon's yurt now. It would be best not to startle the child you carry with my attentions."

She gazed after him as he left the yurt. He would respect her advice, yet feel bitterness towards her for giving it. His Merkit woman would console him and allow him to forget the burdens he carried, as she could not.

51

THE BLUE SKY was cloudless on the day they broke camp. Temujin and Jamukha led the procession, followed by their closest comrades. Carts filled with women and children trailed them, Jajirats near the front, other clans grouped behind them. Bortai saw that her own servants took down her tent slowly before her carts were lashed to Hoelun-eke's and Doghon's. She wanted to keep back, just ahead of the riders bringing their herds.

Their progress was slow, as always. Carts creaked as they rolled across the flat plain; the cattle, horses, and sheep were kept to a walk, so that they would not lose too much of their fat. Bortai sat between Hoelun and Khokakhchin and gripped the reins of their ox; Temulun was behind them, under the covering.

It was nearly noon when Temujin rode back to them. By then, the convoy had slowed to a crawl; through the dust raised by the carts, Bortai saw the riders far ahead of them disappear over a rise. A small river glistened in the distance. The women at the head of the rows of carts were climbing down to unlash their wagons from the ones behind before crossing the stream.

Temujin halted by Bortai's cart and motioned to her to stop. "When you reach the river," he said, "wait before you cross, until the Jajirat herds are on the other side."

"What did Jamukha say to you?" she asked.

266

"He asked his question again. I said he would have my answer later."

Jochi stirred on Hoelun's lap; Bortai reached for her son's hand. "I had three bones brought to me this morning," Temujin said; she could barely hear him above the lowing of the oxen. "They were burned. With only Borchu and Jelme to hear me, I asked if I must do what I now mean to do. The bones all cracked down the middle."

He had been hoping for another omen, then, a reason to stay with Jamukha. "The spirits are with you, my husband."

"Yes." His voice caught on the word.

The sun was in the west by the time their animals had been watered and the last of the carts were across the stream. Borchu's Arulats had remained with them, along with the Uriang-khais and some from other clans. The rest of the convoy was a dark line moving west, trailed by the mottled mass of Jamukha's herds. When the sun set, and only clouds of dust could be seen in the west, Temujin led his people north.

Old Khokakhchin nodded in her seat; Hoelun soothed Jochi while Bortai held the reins. The night air was cold on her face. Jamukha would have stopped by now to make camp. He would believe that Bortai's time had come, that his anda would join him after the child was born.

When the half-moon was above the horizon, the men leading the way fanned out and galloped ahead. Hoelun handed Jochi to Temulun, then reached for her bowcase and quiver. The men riding with Temujin were soon out of sight.

The moon was high above them when Bortai glimpsed the specks of distant, dying fires and heard faint shouts and screams above the creaking of the carts. Temujin's men had come upon another camp. A few wagons stood in a circle, but she saw no yurts; those people had also been on the move. Men circled on horseback, laughing as they threw jugs to one another; others climbed into the wagons to loot them. A strangled cry reached her before the laughter drowned it out.

Khasar rode towards her. "Taychiuts," he shouted to Bortai. "Most of them ran before we got here, and following them would only take us closer to Jamukha. We'll have to settle for what's left." He galloped away.

Hoelun gripped Bortai's wrist. "Wait here, until they're done." Bortai shook off her hand. Two small dark shapes writhed on the ground near one fire; a man was taking a captive. A group of men near them cheered and stamped their feet. She thought of how the Merkits had laughed at her cries that night below Burkhan Khaldun. The man by the fire got to his feet; Bortai recognized Temujin's tall, broad form against the light of the flames. He fumbled at his belt as a comrade caught him around the shoulders.

Bortai lashed at her ox. Men were throwing dirt over the dying fires; riders streamed from the looted camp. Temujin leaned over the dark form huddled on the ground, then walked towards his horse.

The small encampment was nearly empty when Bortai reached it. A few of Temujin's men were lashing the wagons together. A girl lay near one dead fire, her trousers around her ankles, black streaks of blood on her thighs. Belgutei trotted to Bortai's side. A small boy lay across his saddle; he dumped the child beside the cart.

"Take him," Belgutei muttered, then gestured at the girl. "Bring her along, too – Temujin wants her."

That explained why these men had left her alone. Hoelun climbed down and knelt over the boy. Bortai waited until Belgutei had ridden back to his comrades, then got down and went to the girl.

"Can you walk?" Bortai asked. The girl shivered, plucking at her garments as if wanting to tear them from herself. Bortai helped her adjust her clothing, then pulled her to her feet.

The Taychiut leaned against her, still trembling. "Steady," Bortai murmured; the girl made a choked sound. "I've suffered the same. It will pass. I'll look after you." She repressed the curses rising to her lips. "What's your name?"

"Jeren." The girl's voice was hoarse.

Wagons rolled past Bortai's cart and the vehicles lashed to hers. She led Jeren to Doghon's cart; the Merkit woman was silent as she held out a hand to the girl.

Hoelun was waiting with the Taychiut boy. Bortai climbed

268

awkwardly into the seat beside them, then flicked at the ox lightly with her whip. Old Khokakhchin glanced at her, but kept silent; Temulun and Jochi were still asleep under the covering.

Hoelun-eke draped an arm over the boy, then said, "What are you called?"

"Kukuchu," he whispered.

"Is that girl your sister?"

The boy shook his head. "I was asleep," he said. "Then everybody was shouting, and I fell and hit my head. Then a man was grabbing my hair, and they threw me to each other, and one of them said he'd take my head and use it for a target if I cried." He gulped air. "My mother – I don't know where – "

"She'd want us to look after you," Hoelun said. "Listen – there's another boy in one of the carts behind ours. He isn't much older than you. Our men found him in another camp, among our enemies, and I told him I'd be his mother. That's what I'm telling you now, Kukuchu. You'll be my son."

"Why? Don't you have sons of your own?"

"I have four sons I bore myself, and a fifth – Guchu – who was found in a Merkit camp. You shall be the sixth. You see, I have no husband, so I can bear no more brothers for my sons. But I can find them elsewhere, and bring them up. A man is stronger when he has many brothers." Hoelun took a breath. "Men have to fight, or be killed themselves. I know you understand that, Kukuchu. Your people failed to protect you, but my sons will not. Women and children can only pray that the men guarding them are stronger than their enemies."

Bortai wondered if the child knew what Hoelun-eke meant, but then the older woman's words were probably meant for her. Letting herself feel pity would only make her forget that her own safety lay with her husband's mercilessness towards enemies. The boy dabbed at his eyes, then nestled closer to Hoelun.

They stopped when the eastern sky was grey. Wagons and herds dappled the plain; some of the men and older boys went off to clear watering holes for the animals while the women milked sheep, then made fires to boil the milk.

Temujin sat under a lone tree beyond his camping circle. Bortai had watched as men rode to him, dismounted, and bowed. He would be asking for their oaths; they would all know by now that he meant to leave Jamukha. Bortai settled on two cushions and rested her back against a wheel as her servants set curds on flat rocks to dry. She would finish the shirt for Jochi before the light grew too dim.

The sun was low in the west when people began to settle themselves for the night. Women fed their families and put children in the wagons to sleep; other people stretched out under shelters of hides and sticks. Men sat by watch-fires at the edges of the circles of wagons, keeping guard while others rode out to relieve those with the grazing herds.

Bortai, squinting to see in the dusk, made her last stitch, then bit off the thread. Temujin was coming in her direction, trailed by Borchu's kinsman Ogele Cherbi and several other men. Subotai trotted at her husband's left, trying to keep up with the men; Temujin was fond of the boy, and often allowed him to sit with the men when they talked. They stopped by the rope where their horses were tied. Subotai was the first to mount, leaping into his saddle the way the men did.

She bowed her head and smoothed the shirt over her knees. A shadow blocked the light; she looked up.

Her husband was alone. "More followed than I expected," he said. "There are some from nearly all of the clans. I told them what I mean to do, and not one asked to return to Jamukha."

"He's lost supporters, then."

"He still has many." He looked around. "Where's that girl?"

"Asleep in Doghon's cart." Her hands tightened around the shirt. "Leave her alone, Temujin. She'll scream if you come near her."

He shrugged. "There's some pleasure even in that."

He said only what all men thought. Bortai would surprise him if she told him that dreams of Chilger still occasionally woke her and made her tremble. Temujin would never understand her hatred of this part of him.

She gave him some curds and ate a few herself; her women scooped the rest into small pouches. Several men rode towards them, skirting the circles of carts; Borchu was with them. Temujin whistled, then got to his feet. "Khorchi," he whispered. "I didn't think he'd come to me."

The riders halted. Borchu and Khorchi dismounted and walked between the two fires beyond the wagons. "I welcome you," Temujin called out as the men approached. "Do you bring a message from Jamukha?"

"I bring myself," Khorchi replied.

"I am honoured. A shaman-chief with your skill is always needed."

Khorchi bowed. "I have little enough skill," he said, "but enough to know I had to join you. I suspected what you were planning before we stopped. A dream brought me here, waking me in the middle of the night – we left before dawn." The Bagarin gestured with one hand. "My people followed willingly."

"It must have been quite a dream," Temujin said, "to take you away from Jamukha."

"Jamukha has a brave spirit," Khorchi said. "If this dream hadn't come to me, I would have stayed with him. The same womb gave birth to Jamukha's ancestor and to my own, but I can't turn from such an omen."

"I would hear of this dream." Temujin sat next to Bortai. Borchu and Khorchi settled in front of them; the other Bagarins gathered behind them to listen.

"I was standing in our camp," the shaman began. "A great cow appeared, with horns nearly as long as a man's bow and as thick as a tent pole. She lowered her head and charged at Jamukha's yurt, and then at Jamukha himself. One of her horns broke against him, and she cried out, calling to him to bring her the horn she had lost. As she cried to him, I saw a great ox pull up the stake holding the yurt and harness himself to a cart. I followed that cart, Temujin, and the ox led me to you. He bowed low and shouted to all that the spirits had decreed you should rule, and that Etugen and Tengri agreed that all the clans will bow to you." He was silent for a moment. "How can I deny a dream that speaks so clearly?"

"You cannot," Temujin responded. "Neither can I."

"The will of the spirits grows clear." Khorchi smiled. "I'll speak of this dream to others. When more hear of it, more men will rally to you. And what will you give me for bringing you such a omen?"

"The command of a tuman," Temujin said, "when I have ten thousand men to give to you."

"Can you doubt that you will?" Khorchi shook his head. "But if you're going to make me a Tuman-u Noyan, will you also allow me to choose thirty wives from among the most beautiful women we capture? They would give me more happiness than ten thousand men, and I can hope that they match the beauty of your own good wife."

Temujin laughed. "You'll have both the army and the women. I know better than to deny a powerful shaman his due."

"You were always generous." The Bagarin bowed his head. "Now I must leave you, and see to the wives I have."

"Go in peace," Temujin said.

Khorchi left with his men. Borchu stood up and grasped Temujin's hands, then went to his horse.

Bortai handed Jochi's garment to a servant. Temujin was silent as the women went to the carts. "If you had stayed with Jamukha," she said at last, "your spear would have been shattered, as the cow's horn was."

"I don't need you to explain dreams to me, Bortai."

"I think you're still sorry you left him."

"You're wrong." He stood up; she could not read his face in the shadows. "The spirits spoke in my dreams, and in Khorchi's, and through you. Jamukha and I are no longer boys playing at dice by the Onon, and can never be those boys again. I knew only one of us could lead when we danced under the great tree." She should have been relieved that he had no regrets, but his words were a barrier between them.

Temujin lifted his head and sniffed at the air. "The clouds hide the stars," he said. "A storm will come tonight."

"I know." She held out one arm. "Help me to my feet."

He pulled her up. On the dark plain, fires flickered, looking like the stars that were now hidden. Inside the nearby enclosure, mares whinnied and nudged their foals, skittish about the storm soon to come.

Temujin picked up the cushions and followed her to the back of the cart. He lifted her into it, then climbed in after her. Khokakhchin, lying at the other end next to the chests, slept on with Jochi. Bortai wriggled out of her coat and long tunic, then covered herself with a blanket; Temujin pulled off his coat and boots and stretched out at her side. His arm tightened around her, then relaxed. She touched his face gently; he was already asleep.

Wind slapped against the cart's leather covering; a child wailed in a nearby wagon. Temujin was her only shelter against the storms men created when they fought. She pressed closer to him. He would rule; she would be safe.

52

THE SLAVES SETTLED the lambs inside the tent. Jeren stirred the broth in the kettle on the hearth as Bortai suckled Chagadai. She had laboured for a day and a night giving birth to him last summer. Chagadai's brown eyes had the gold flecks of his father's; Temujin had noticed that.

Someone shouted outside. Temujin entered; one girl soothed the startled lambs while another secured the flap behind him. He stamped the snow from his boots, then hung up his weapons.

"Lazy old woman," Temujin said to Khokakhchin, who looked up from where she was playing knuckle-bone dice with Jochi. "I spend the day hunting in the cold while you and my son sit here gaming."

"And did you bring us anything?" Khokakhchin asked.

"Would I be standing here empty-handed if I had?" He took off his hat and shook the snow over Jochi, making him squeal. "We found a tiger's tracks near here. It's scaring off the game. We'll have to set out a poisoned carcass for the beast before it starts feeding on our herds."

"Then Jochi's done more than you have today," Khokakh-chin said. "He won two bones from me."

Temujin laughed. "Lazy old woman." He had whispered to Bortai only that morning not to send Khokakhchin out with the sheep, to let her rest.

Jeren glanced at Temujin, then scurried away from the fire towards Bortai. The Taychiut girl was still skittish around him; having her own small yurt and knowing she would be his wife when she gave him a child did nothing to ease her. She kept near Bortai, as if for protection, unlike Doghon, who resented having to share him with anyone. Temujin took what he wanted from Jeren and left her alone the rest of the time. Bortai supposed that made him a better man than Chilger-boko.

Temujin slipped off his two heavy coats, handed them to a slave, then crossed to the back of the yurt. "Daritai's outside," he said to Bortai. "He came here with Altan and my cousin Khuchar, and my two Jurkin kinsmen are with them. They rode in just after I did – they'll come here when their horses are settled."

Bortai nodded, tied Chagadai to his cradle, then got up. The slaves had set out bowls of broth and a few shreds of venison on a platter when the visitors entered. Temujin murmured a greeting and embraced them all. The five men sat on cushions at his right and asked about his hunting.

"A cat's prowling nearby," Temujin said. "I told those watching our herds to be alert."

Bortai settled the four slaves on her side of the tent, near Khokakhchin and Jochi, then sat by Chagadai's cradle, close enough to hear the men. Jeren sat next to her, refusing to look at Temujin.

Daritai and the men with him would not be here merely to pass the time and tell stories. Daritai and Khuchar had joined them after they moved camp to the Kimurgha River; Seche Beki and Taichu, the two Jurkin chiefs, had come to them that autumn, and Altan soon after that. Jamukha had surely been weakened by their loss.

"Spring approaches," Altan said. He dipped a bit of meat into his broth, chewed it, and licked the fat from his fingers.

"It will be good to taste kumiss again, and all the more welcome if we have something to celebrate."

"Indeed it will," Temujin replied.

"Decisions must be made," Daritai said; he gulped down some broth. "It will soon be time to hold a kuriltai."

Bortai's hand tensed on the cradle. "Yes," Temujin said softly. "We should prepare to take up arms against the Taychiuts, and my father's spirit still cries for the punishment of the Tatars who took his life."

"I want vengeance for Yesugei," Altan said. "I well remember how I once fought with your father. But to fight a war, we must have a leader. To be strong, we must be an ulus, a nation, as we once were under my father Khutula Khan. It's time we had a Khan again."

The tent was silent except for the slight crackling of the fire. "You speak the truth," Temujin said at last. "Others would see that we're more than men who have come together for only a while."

"Every man here has a claim to the Khanate," Daritai said, "Altan, because he's the son of Khutula, and Khuchar, because he's the son of my brother Nekun-taisi. Then there are Seche and Taichu here, who are grandsons of my father's brother Okin Barkak." He paused.

"You have forgotten yourself," Temujin murmured. "As the nephew of Khutula Khan, you also have a claim."

Bortai glanced up. Daritai leaned forward on his cushion; she lowered her head. "And you, of course, my nephew – your claim is as great as ours."

"And shall we each rally supporters," Temujin said, "and present our claims at the kuriltai?"

"The Noyans," Altan replied, "could spend days debating our claims instead of choosing the one they want right away. We've come together too recently to risk arguments that might make unity harder to come by later."

"And whom do you think the Noyans favour?" Temujin asked.

Taichu laughed. "Isn't it obvious?" Seche Beki said. "Who took it upon himself to leave Jamukha, and saw we could further our ends without him? Who is the man Khorchi's dream told him to follow?"

"You must be Khan, Temujin," Daritai said. "We left your anda, and came to you. You'll lead us in battle, and we'll offer you the most beautiful of the women we capture, and the strongest geldings and mares. When we hunt, we'll surround the game until the animals are as close together as trees in a forest, and drive them to you."

Temujin said, "The kuriltai must decide who will be Khan."

"But we know what they will decide," Altan said, "if we support your claim. If we give up our own claims, the Noyans must turn to you."

"You honour me," Temujin said. "I cannot turn away from what is asked of me. If the Noyans choose me, you'll all be rewarded."

"Then all that remains," Khuchar muttered, "is the formality, my Khan and cousin."

Bortai rose, motioned to a girl, and had more broth brought to the men and herself, then sat with them as they told stories of old victories. The five must have argued heatedly before coming here; none of them could be supporting Temujin so willingly.

Temujin pressed his guests to stay for the night, but they remained only long enough to finish their broth. They made their farewells quickly, clearly anxious to put distance between their horses and the tiger that might be prowling nearby. "Good hunting," Daritai said from the doorway. "It might be wise to have a shaman cast a spell – that tiger could be a ghost." He made a sign against evil with his hand, then ducked through the entrance; a woman lowered the flap.

"What do you think of this?" Temujin murmured to Bortai.

She leaned closer to him. "I'm surprised that they want to set a master over themselves so soon. The Noyans will choose you – that's certain, now that your rivals have given up their claims. They know they can't push you aside now, but I wonder how loyal they'll be if they see a chance to do so later. Every one of them would rather be Khan himself."

"I know." Temujin rubbed his chin. "They want a Khan only for a while, until they're stronger and can press their own claims. I'll let them have their leader. Once chosen, I won't be so easy to push aside." He stood up. "Jeren, bring me my coats. I'll sleep in your yurt tonight."

The girl's brown eyes widened; her pretty face went pale. She fetched his coats and put on her own, keeping her eyes from him, her small body trembling under her bowed shoulders. Bortai rocked her son's cradle. It would have been easier not to know that Temujin took as much enjoyment in Jeren's aversion as he did in Bortai's assent.

53

JAMUKHA STUDIED THE young horses inside the enclosure. A roan horse snorted, then snapped at the hindquarters of another. The roan had spirit; he might make a stallion.

He gazed past them at the horses grazing on the steppe. Ten men rode towards the herd; Taychar was with them. A few men guarding the herd trotted towards the new arrivals; the small forms rippled in the summer heat.

Jamukha had been up here for half a month with some of his men, two days' ride south of Munglik's camp, breaking horses and deciding which of the two-year-olds would be gelded. He welcomed the work; anything was better than going to his women, labouring to produce a son. Nomalan had whelped too soon a second time, and the others were as useless. He thought of giving them away and starting again with fresh stock.

Two men entered the enclosure; one held a long stick with a loop of rope at its end, and as he slipped the noose over the head of one grey horse, the other approached with a bridle. The grey horse whinnied and tossed its head. Temujin had always favoured grey or white horses. Jamukha's mouth twisted. His anda had not only abandoned him, but had also won over several of Jamukha's allies.

Taychar was riding towards him. Jamukha circled the

enclosure; his cousin slowed, then reined in his horse. "Messengers," Taychar said. "Arkhai and Chakhurkhan rode to our camp from Temujin's." The young man scowled as he spoke the name of Jamukha's anda. "We've been riding hard all morning. I asked them for their message, but they said their words were for you."

Jamukha swallowed hard. Maybe his anda regretted his actions. "Bring them to my yurt," he said, "after they've passed between the fires. We'll speak to them alone."

He stomped towards the small yurt, wondering what Temujin wanted. His scouts had told him of movements near his anda's camp by the Senggur, of chiefs riding there nearly a month ago for a kuriltai. A war kuriltai, perhaps; Temujin would still be anxious to fight the Taychiuts. That would not be so easy now. By taking in a small band of Taychiuts who had been attacked by Temujin last summer, Jamukha had opened the way to an alliance with them.

He went inside. His tent was filled with saddles, bridles, and weapons; he sat down on the bed and waited until he heard the men outside.

Taychar entered, followed by the two envoys. Jamukha rose and rattled off a few words of greeting as his cousin fetched skins of kumiss.

"We come in peace," Chakhurkhan said. The short, broad young man presented a scarf, then seated himself on a cushion.

"Is that so?" Jamukha asked as Arkhai and Taychar sat down. "I heard that you held a kuriltai not long ago. I thought my anda might be planning war."

Arkhai smiled. "He wishes only to send you greetings – his thoughts often turn to his anda. We held our kuriltai not to make war, but to choose a Khan. This is the message I bring – we have chosen a Khan, after only a day of deliberation. Temujin has been raised on the felt and given the name of Genghis Khan."

Jamukha ground his teeth, too stunned to speak. Taychar choked on his kumiss. "What's this?" his cousin burst out. "Who gave him such a name? How can he call himself – "

"The kuriltai proclaimed him Khan," Chakhurkhan replied. "The shamans chose his name."

Genghis Khan, Jamukha thought. The Universal Khan, the Strongest, the All-Powerful; the name held great power. How had he dared to accept that name? It was a challenge to anyone who heard it.

"I'm sure Temujin had something to do with the choice of a name," Taychar muttered. "How could this happen? Didn't his cousin Khuchar object? Didn't Altan have more right to be Khan, if you were to choose one?"

"Altan spoke for Temujin at the kuriltai," Arkhai said, "as did Khuchar and Daritai Odchigin. Seche Beki and Taichu made no objection."

Jamukha thought of sending Arkhai and Chakhurkhan back to their new Khan with their braids lopped off, perhaps even their heads. He steadied himself. Altan was behind this, along with Khuchar and Daritai. They would not have given up their own ambitions unless they were sure they could dispense with Temujin later. He had raged when they had gone over to his anda, but perhaps they would be more useful to him there.

Taychar cursed. Jamukha held up his hand. "Silence, cousin," he said. "Let us enjoy our time with these old friends. Clearly Temujin thought only of sharing the news of this great honour with me."

"True," Arkhai said. "His bond with you endures, as does our Khan's friendship with the Kereits. Toghril Khan received our envoys not long ago, and claims to be delighted that the Mongols are no longer without a Khan."

The foolish old man was thinking only of having a strong ally at his back, to shield him from Merkits and Naimans; he could not see that Temujin might pose a threat to him. But perhaps Toghril suspected this unity would not last long.

"Temujin spoke well after he was raised on the felt," Chakhurkhan said. "He made Borchu's cousin Ogele Cherbi his chief archer, and Khasar his chief swordsman. Soyiketu Cherbi's in charge of his cooks, while Degei is now chief shepherd and Mulkhalku will tend the cattle. Belgutei will look out for the horse herds, and Borchu and Jelme have been raised over all the other chiefs." Chakhurkhan drank, then belched. "We ourselves – Arkhai and I, and our comrades Taghai and Sukegei, he calls his arrows, which he'll aim near and far."

Jamukha plucked at his moustache. "Then many have been honoured." He wondered how Altan and the others who had given up their claims had felt at seeing such honours go to Temujin's close associates.

Taychar reached for another jug. "I must ask you this," Jamukha said. "If you wanted a Khan, couldn't you have chosen one while Temujin and I still camped together? Why did you choose one now?"

"You sound displeased," Arkhai replied. "I assure you that our Khan still has the greatest regard for you. He knew when he left you that you could no longer lead together, that his men chafed at following you while yours resisted him as a leader. He thought it wiser to let the men choose which of you to follow. He saw that many would stay with you, that you would still be strong without him. He never intended to harden his heart towards his brother. He was anxious for us to assure you of his love."

Oh yes, he thought. Remain my friend, but bow to me as Khan; that was what his anda wanted. Temujin had waited until he sat on a throne to send a message.

"You have made your choice," Jamukha said. "You must abide by it." Taychar glowered at him. "You will tell your Khan his message pleases me. The Noyans have chosen their Khan – you must tell them all to serve him loyally. You must tell Altan and Khuchar in particular not to forget their promises to him."

Chakhurkhan grinned. "We'll carry any messages you give us, friend."

Jamukha stood up. "You may rest here – I have to break another horse to the bit. We'll drink later while you tell me all about the kuriltai and Temujin's enthronement. I will expect you to recite all the speeches."

"All that we can recall." Arkhai let out a braying laugh. "We were quite drunk by the time many of them were given."

"Then we must see you drink enough to restore your memories." Jamukha strode outside, Taychar at his heels. His cousin caught him by the arm as they neared the horses.

"Genghis Khan," Taychar muttered. "Temujin planned it all along. That cursed Altan – "

"May already be regretting his choice," Jamukha said. "Temujin has his throne. We'll see if he keeps it."

54

A DREAM CAME to Hoelun. Yesugei rode towards her, a falcon on his wrist, his face as youthful as on the day she had first seen him over twenty years ago. He lifted her to his saddle; she leaned back against him.

"You have done well," Yesugei said. "My sons couldn't have become men without your courage, Hoelun. The spirits favour only the strong. God sweeps away the weak."

She woke. Her husband's spirit was watching over their son. Yesugei would have been pleased to hear the men swearing their oaths, and Altan's speech had been more eloquent than she expected. If we ever disobey you in war, Khutula's son had said, take away all that we have and strike our heads from us. If we disobey you in peacetime, take away our wives, our children, and our herds, and abandon us in the Gobi.

Temujin had taken command quickly, appointing his closest comrades to different posts. Altan and the Jurkin chiefs must have been dismayed at this sign that Temujin meant to be more than just a war chief and leader of the hunt.

Her son might have been a Khan all his life instead of for only a month. She had watched him ride off to an Arulat camp that morning, his men a wall around him, to claim his tribute as Khan. His demands would not be great; her son knew how to be generous. She thought of how he had danced with the men under his pavilion after they had carried him to his throne, and the old ones said he danced as fiercely as Khutula himself.

You should have been a Khan, Yesugei. Her husband was still near, his spirit hovering over her bed.

She heard voices at the doorway, and then Temulun was standing at the foot of her bed. "Mother," the girl whispered.

"One of Bortai's servants is here, and asks that you come to her tent at once."

Hoelun got up quickly and dressed. A boy led a horse to her as she went outside. She mounted and rode the short distance to Bortai's circle, where servants sat outside the yurt. A slave emerged, carrying Chagadai outside in his cradle, and Jochi clung to the hand of one woman. A shaman sat near two fires; behind him, a spear was embedded in the ground.

"Don't go inside," the shaman said. Hoelun dismounted, walked between the fires, and hastened into the tent.

Bortai knelt by Khokakhchin's bed, her face streaked with tears. Hoelun went to her and dropped to the carpet. The left side of old Khokakhchin's face was stiff; she blinked with one eye as Hoelun took her hand.

"You shouldn't be here, Khatun." The old woman's words were so slurred that Hoelun barely understood them. "I tell the young Khatun to leave me – instead, she summons you." Her throat rasped as she struggled for breath. "I'll be gone before sunrise."

"I can't let you die alone," Bortai whispered.

"What foolishness." The old servant sighed. "This tent will have to be purified. You should put me outside the camp. What trouble for an old woman."

"I don't care." Bortai wiped at her eyes. "I will get a shaman to lift the ban – I'll pay whatever he asks."

"The wealth of the world couldn't lift that ban." Khokakhchin gasped; Hoelun smelled death. "I lived to see you become a Khatun, child. I lived to see Temujin a Khan. I am ready to leave you now."

"My husband came to me tonight in a dream," Hoelun said. "Now I think he was coming for you, Khokakhchin-eke. You served us well. I swear you won't be forgotten."

"Leave me," Khokakhchin gasped. "It's the last thing I ask of you."

Hoelun took Bortai's arm; the younger woman pulled back. "Come," Hoelun said firmly. "What will Temujin think if he returns and finds you impure, forced to put up your tent outside the camp? You'd be under a ban for months."

Bortai collapsed against her, sobbing. "I promise you this,

Khokakhchin-eke," Hoelun said. "You'll be buried with great honour. A Khan will say the prayers over your grave, dear friend." She would never find so faithful a servant again. She glanced back at the old woman one last time, then went with her son's wife from the yurt.

55

THE MEN RODE at a walk, keeping the horses together. Jamukha covered his mouth and nose with the end of his scarf; even at this slow pace, the horses were kicking up dirt. Ahead of him, near the ridge bordering the steppe, more horses grazed on the dry yellow grass.

He had been out with the horses since midsummer. Two promising stallions had been separated from those to be gelded; the work had kept him from dwelling on his anda's arrogance, which had only grown since he had been raised on the felt. Temujin had acted so correctly in sending him envoys with word of his election as Khan; even after a year, the thought of that could still enrage him. Temujin would have known the news would be a spear in his side. Now Temujin rode to the camps of his followers to display his generosity, to show how little he would ask from them, but he did not need their tribute. All of them had knelt to him and offered him their swords.

Temujin had used him only to take what he wanted. Jamukha had misjudged him, had been too certain that their old ties would keep his anda tethered a while longer, that Temujin, as he often did, would hesitate before acting.

The regrets he had kept at bay tormented him again. He thought of the bloodied testicles he had cut from one horse during the gelding. That would be a suitable punishment for an enemy, to cut his manhood from him and hold it in front of his eyes before he died.

The man in the lead dropped back; Jamukha rode up to take his place. He shook the scarf from his face, breathing more easily with the dust behind him, then glanced to one side. Ogin moved closer to him; the boy smiled as he caught Jamukha's eye.

Ogin was beginning to irritate him, with his sly glances and hints for favours; he seemed to think a few joinings should earn him a reward. It had been enjoyable to go hunting with the boy, to take his pleasure with Ogin away from the encampment, but that particular fire had gone out, and he had no desire to rekindle it.

A plume of dust surrounding a tiny dark shape appeared in the distance; a man rode towards him across the parched plain. Jamukha narrowed his eyes, recognizing the rider, and wondered what Khuyhildar was doing here.

The Manggud chief slowed, passed the distant herd of horses, then continued towards Jamukha at a trot, slowing down as he came closer. The long scar on the left side of Khuyhildar's face was a white line against his brown skin; the Manggud was scowling.

"I greet you." Khuyhildar raised an arm. His horse turned and trotted at Jamukha's side. "My news is grave, friend – I sorrow at having to bring it. Many of the chiefs have gathered in your camp, and sent me to carry this news to you. Forgive me for saying this, but perhaps you should have come back sooner – you might have – "

"I left Taychar in charge. I saw no reason – "

Khuyhildar made a sign with his hand. "Maybe you should have chosen someone else. The other Noyans and I are ready to aid you in whatever revenge you seek, now that others have struck at your heart."

The Manggud was trying his patience. Too often lately, his men hesitated before telling him what he had to know. Jamukha had heard rumours that they sometimes drew lots to choose the one to bring him bad tidings. Keeping his men properly fearful of him had its drawbacks.

Jamukha turned towards Ogin, who had ridden closer to him. "Get back to your place, boy." He tightened his legs around his mount; his horse quickened its pace. Khuyhildar kept near him until they were further ahead of the others. "Speak now."

Khuyhildar said, "Your cousin has fallen, slain by an arrow."

Jamukha tensed and pulled at his reins. "How did this happen?"

"Your cousin and four comrades rode out just after the new moon. You know how he was. He'd grown impatient for a raid – so one of his friends said. They went towards the Kerulen, to the Donkeyback Steppe, and came to the camp of the Jalair chief Jochi Darmala. It was a simple matter for your kinsman to steal his horses, since Jochi Darmala's camp has only a few yurts."

The other man fell silent. Jamukha glared at him. "Go on," he said hoarsely.

"Your cousin and his comrades made camp by a spring. He must have thought he had little to fear, with so few in that Jalair camp to pursue him. He was on guard while the others slept. They awoke to see what looked like a riderless horse approaching the herd, and then Jochi Darmala suddenly swung himself up astride the horse, and before they could warn your cousin, the Jalair's arrow found his back, and the horses scattered." Khuyhildar cleared his throat. "Your men found their steeds wandering the plains later, but Jochi Darmala escaped with his own. Now your cousin lies in a wagon while his wife weeps for the husband she's lost so soon."

Jamukha sensed the words the other man was holding back. You should have restrained Taychar, you shouldn't have left him in your place, you should have known he might try something like this.

The rage would come later. He felt only numbness and shock and a hollowness inside his chest. "My kinsman will be avenged."

"We can take the Jalairs with a small force," Khuyhildar muttered.

"They're sworn to Temujin. If we strike only at their camps, Temujin would marshal his armies against us. Why strike at an arm when we can aim at the head?"

Khuyhildar's ugly face paled. "You have the right. But can you bring yourself to make war against your anda?"

"He's left me no choice." So it had come to this; he felt that he had known it would. Temujin had brought this about by leaving him, by allowing himself to be raised to a throne. Taychar, he realized, had given him an excuse to act; perhaps his death would not be in vain. "You told me you would aid me in my revenge, Khuyhildar."

"As I shall." The Manggud struck his chest. "My promise lives here. I swore to follow you, Jamukha."

"We must bury my cousin, who was as dear to me as a brother, and then I'll raise my tugh, put on my armour, and sound my drum. We'll strike at Temujin's camp."

56

JAMUKHA'S ARMY MUSTERED on the plain, its ranks swelled by the clans sworn to him. Shamans read the bones and made sacrifices before the thousands of warriors rode out, each with his string of war-horses. By the time they reached the slopes of the Alagud and Turghagud Mountains, the wings of light cavalry on the right and left had fanned out to move through the passes in smaller groups, and the scouts were far ahead of the main force. Jamukha, riding in the centre with the heavy cavalry, ordered the men carrying white flags to signal to the rest of the force to separate. The scouts had told him that Temujin was camped by the Senggur again. Jamukha's forces would converge on the camp and surround it.

They banked their fires at night to conceal them and slept on their horses. Two days after they left the mountains behind, a man rode to Jamukha with a message from his scouts. An army had been sighted; Temujin's scouts were already harrying theirs. Jamukha knew then that his anda had been warned, but his force still outnumbered what could be seen of Temujin's.

The enemy was moving towards Dalan-Galjut, the Seventy Marshes. Jamukha's generals assembled under his tugh. Temujin's forces, it seemed, were now converging.

Jamukha gave his orders. They would draw together and meet the enemy at Dalan-Galjut. When the battle began, the right wing would leave the trees bordering the Seventy Marshes and drive Temujin's army to the left. Temujin's scouts had not yet encountered much of Jamukha's right wing, and might underestimate its strength. The generals left to take up their positions; men with white flags and lanterns passed along Jamukha's orders with signals. He still had the advantage. The warning to Temujin had come too late for him to do more than prepare a defence.

They reached Dalan-Galjut at dawn, six days after leaving the mountains. Reeds and bushes dotted the marshy land; the ground glistened with autumnal frost. The earth was hard enough for the horses to find footing. In the distance, Jamukha saw the rows of the enemy's heavy cavalry, lances raised, their lacquered leather breastplates blackened with pitch. Temujin's nine-tailed tugh fluttered behind them.

Jamukha raised his arm, then dropped it. His drummer, perched on a camel, beat on the naccara; the thunder of another war-drum answered his. Jamukha's front line of heavy cavalry burst across the swamp; he let out a cry and rode after them with the second line. The light cavalry in the rear fired through the spaces between the advancing men and their arrows whistled past him.

A roar rose above the pounding of hooves and the throbbing of naccaras. Horses and riders swarmed around him. Jamukha unhorsed one rider with the hook of his lance and thrust his sword through the soldier's open mouth. A sword grazed his helmet; he slashed at a chest encased in leather armour and saw blood. A horse in front of him pitched forward, unseating one of the enemy; Jamukha's sword sliced his arm from his shoulder. His ears pounded as he fought; he would punish them all for Taychar's death, for deserting him for Temujin.

Horses slid in the blood. Arrows shrieked past him, darkening the sky, and fell on Temujin's forces. Enemy warriors tumbled from their horses as Temujin's light cavalry fired back. Above the tumult, Jamukha suddenly heard the roar of war-cries to his right; the right wing of his light cavalry had left the trees to begin its sweep.

He fought on, moving to the battle's rhythm, until he realized the other force was falling back. Men thrown from their horses were fighting on foot, cutting at the legs of enemy horses with their swords. Jamukha hooked another rider from his mount and stabbed at his neck. Temujin was getting the worst of it; his soldiers were retreating. Warriors from Jamukha's right wing moved in front of him, pushing Temujin's forces to the left; fleeing soldiers turned in their saddles to fire arrows at their pursuers.

The air was warmer, the sun higher. Jamukha shouted to the commander nearest him. A signal flag lifted; his men were driving the enemy back, trapping them between Jamukha's left wing and his right. Horsemen streamed forward; victory would be his.

Jamukha's bowmen pursued the enemy, then withdrew when a signal was passed to them. Fresher warriors took their place; Jamukha would allow Temujin a retreat, but did not intend to give him a chance to regroup.

His men carried their dead comrades from Dalan-Galjut, left the enemy bodies for the birds and jackals, and camped on a hillside far from the marsh. Jamukha slept dreamlessly near one fire, and awoke at dawn when a rider came to him. Temujin's army had disbanded, many of them riding towards the Onon. The Khan had lost many men.

Clusters of men sat by fires on the hillside; small tents had been pitched. Several men knelt over wounded comrades to suck the blood from their wounds; others were skinning dead horses. The older boys who had followed the army at a distance moved among them, tethering the horses and carrying the large kettles they had brought with them to the fires.

Jurchedei was climbing the hill. Jamukha got to his feet to greet the Urugud chief.

"We have a victory," Jurchedei said. The weary soldiers with the Urugud managed a throaty cheer. "The archers who have come back say the enemy has scattered."

"Genghis Khan." Jamukha spat, took off his studded leather helmet, and wiped his face. "We'll see how well his men serve their Khan now that he's led them to defeat. Some of his allies must be regretting the oaths they swore."

"You've shown him your strength," Jurchedei said. "Offer

288

him a chance to surrender. Those who followed him could serve you."

Jamukha said, "There can be no peace between us."

"He's your anda," the Urugud said. "Remind him of his oath. Your cousin is avenged. Take advantage of Temujin's weakness now."

"He'll have lost more supporters the next time we meet. I won't throw away a triumph later by showing him mercy now." He had won this battle; he would win the next, and leave Temujin with nothing. "How many prisoners did we take?"

"Not many. A lot of them died fighting, or forced us to kill them when they were taken. We have about eighty from the Chinos clan – their chief is one of them."

The cursed Chinos had been among the first to leave him for Temujin. "I want to see them," Jamukha said.

A boy brought them fresh horses. They mounted and rode down the slope until they came to the roped enclosure that held the prisoners. The captives sat together, hands bound; a number of soldiers had gathered there to mock them. Their armour and weapons had been taken from them. The fresh blood spotting their shirts and trousers showed that many of them were wounded.

One man looked up as Jamukha and Jurchedei dismounted; Jamukha gazed into the red-rimmed eyes of Chaghagan Uwa, the Chinos chief.

"We meet again, Chaghagan Uwa," Jamukha said. "The last time I was under your tent, you talked of our friendship, then forgot it to follow that accursed Kiyat in the night. I would hear your last words now."

"I didn't forget our friendship." The shorter man swayed, then lifted his head. "I left because it was clear that you couldn't lead us together, and Temujin saw that before you did. I never wanted to meet you in battle, but I swore an oath to my Khan, and was bound to defend him." Blood oozed from a wound on the side of his bald head; the looped braids behind his ears were covered with mud. "You brought this war about – you sent your armies against us for the sake of a horse thief."

Jamukha struck him; Chaghagan Uwa staggered, but did not fall. "You gain nothing by insulting the dead."

"I have nothing to gain anyway. You would have done better to bridle your cousin. Instead, you let him lead you into war. I obeyed my Khan, as I should. I ask only that I and these men be given an honourable death."

Jamukha glanced at Jurchedei. "Ask him for his oath," the Urugud whispered. "He was a friend. Keep them as hostages until you can – "

Shouts drowned out the rest of his words. "Give them the sword!" a man cried behind them. Jamukha raised his head. Above, on the hill, a boy was stoking the fire under a cauldron.

"An honourable death?" Jamukha said softly. "Oh no. Your death won't be honourable, and that of your men won't be easy. You deserve to die like animals for abandoning us, to become less than the beasts we cook in our pots. We kill our sheep before they're boiled, but your men will suffer that fate alive."

The Chinos chief opened his mouth; Jamukha drew his sword and swung. Chaghagan Uwa's head fell beyond the enclosure as blood spilled from his toppling body over the other prisoners. Men swarmed forward, dragging captives out. Jamukha picked up the head by one braid. Jurchedei backed away, his arms hanging at his sides.

"This is how my enemies will be punished!" Jamukha shouted. "Let those who stand against me learn what their treachery will bring!" Men streamed past Jurchedei, carrying more prisoners towards the fires; the Urugud spun around and stumbled towards his horse. Jamukha despised the man for his squeamishness. Terror would keep his men obedient, and fear of his vengeance would bring more men to him.

He strode to his horse, tied the head to his mount's tail, then leaped into the saddle. Men bellowed cheers and shook their weapons, but a few were silent as they watched him. A prisoner screamed as two men heaved him into a cauldron. Jamukha lifted his sword and rode along the hillside. The shrieks of the boiling men were a song celebrating his victory.

57

THE HAWK FLEW towards Temulun and alighted on the girl's wrist. She gave the bird a bit of meat, then secured the tether around her glove.

"You trained that one quickly," Hoelun said. Her daughter turned in her saddle and smiled; the bird fluttered its golden-brown wings.

"She's a beauty," Temulun said. "She's the best one I have." She crooned to the hawk as Guchu trotted towards them. The girl had grown quite pretty, with a small nose, sharp cheekbones, and long lashes around her greenish-gold eyes. But Hoelun still had to chide her to braid her hair more neatly, and Temulun wore only the plainest and most unadorned tunics.

She had been out with her daughter and her two adopted sons since morning, ready to enjoy a clear day without snow or a howling wind. To the east of her tents, servants were clearing away snow and feeding the sheep. Her servants and slaves had made her lazy; hands were always there to prepare her food, do her milking, shake out the blankets in her tent, even do her sewing and weaving.

Temulun sat up and shaded her eyes with her free hand. "Temujin is back," she said. Hoelun narrowed her eyes; her daughter's vision was sharper than her own. Three riders moved past the black mounds of yurts towards her circle; she recognized Temujin's favourite white charger and his dark sable coat. The second rider was Khasar, but she did not know the third.

It was unusual for her son to be in the company of so few. The Khan was almost always surrounded by his men, consulting with them, hunting or playing at war-games, going with them to examine the newest bows of his bowmakers and new arrowheads freshly hardened in salt water, drinking or reciting stories with them. This was proper for a man, especially a Khan, but she sometimes wished he would occasionally visit her tent by himself or with only his women and children, as her other sons did. He left it to Bortai and his brothers to tell her of his doings, and groups of men were always in his tent when he summoned her there.

Such thoughts should not trouble her; he was no longer a boy clinging to his mother's coat. He had not brooded long after his defeat that past autumn at Jamukha's hands, saying only, according to Bortai, that he had learned from that battle. Hoelun had been surprised when more clans, including some who had fought against her son, had asked to join Temujin for the autumn hunt, and she had wondered when he allowed them a generous share of the game. But his judgement had been sound. His new allies outnumbered the men who had fallen at Dalan-Galjut, and many had left Jamukha to join him.

Temujin had been in Jurchedei's camp for the past few days. The Urugud chief had told a tale of horror after joining her son that winter, of captives boiled alive in cauldrons; some said that Jamukha and the cruellest of his men had drunk the human broth. Such cruelty had only driven Jurchedei and the Manggud chief Khuyhildar to Temujin's side. Jamukha had lost more than he had won at the Seventy Marshes.

Her sons and their companion halted near her yurt. "It seems," Hoelun said, "that the Khan wishes to visit us. Come along, all of you."

Temulun pouted. "It'll be dark soon. Can't we – "

"A few moments only, child. I expect you to be back by the time I've welcomed your brothers and their comrade."

Temujin was riding towards her. Hoelun flicked her horse lightly with her whip and galloped across the snowy expanse. Khasar called out a greeting as she approached; the third man's face was partly hidden by the long flaps of his hat.

"Mother," Khasar shouted as she slowed, "look who has come here to join us. Our father's old friend has returned."

Temujin grinned; the man lifted his head. His moustaches had grown longer, and his face was brown and leathery, but Munglik's dark eyes were the same.

"Munglik!" Hoelun lifted a hand, too stunned to say more. Temujin laughed and beckoned her forward. Of course he would be happy, and not just because the Khongkhotat was his father's old retainer; he had won another defector from among his anda's allies.

"I greet you, Honoured Lady," Munglik said. "How is it that the years have failed to mark you?"

Hoelun smiled, then pulled the woollen scarf below her head-dress closer around her face. "This scarf hides much."

"You are too modest, Khatun. You still ride like a girl, and the face I see hasn't changed."

Foolish talk, but she could not help feeling flattered. They trotted towards the camp. "Munglik came to Jurchedei's camp," Temujin said, "and told me that he's brought his people to join us. We have much to celebrate."

About time, she thought. Munglik had waited long enough.

"I wanted to come before," Munglik said, "yet it seemed to me that my promise bound me to Jamukha, since it was Temujin who chose to leave him. But I can no longer serve such an intemperate man."

He meant that he would benefit more by being with a stronger chief. Whatever Jamukha's excesses, Munglik would have stayed with him if Temujin were not growing more powerful. He was, Hoelun thought, still the same, considering carefully what he would gain before he acted.

"I'm pleased you are here," she managed to say. His presence showed how much support Jamukha had lost. "I've thought often of your good father."

"Father served you well," Munglik responded, "as I shall now. I have many regrets, Hoelun Khatun, and one is that I couldn't risk the safety of my family and clan by coming to you sooner, but I have never forgotten my bond with your husband and my affection for his sons. Only my promise to Jamukha could have brought me to do battle with your men at the Seventy Marshes, but I cannot respect a man who deals so dishonourably with prisoners. When my son Kokochu told me of a dream in which a wolf led him to Temujin's side, I remembered my promises to Yesugei, and wept, for the omen my son saw told me where my true loyalties lie."

"Your son?" Hoelun asked.

"I have seven sons now." Munglik straightened in his saddle. "All are close in age, with only a year between one brother and the next, and Kokochu is my middle son. He's only nine, but already he begins to master the shamans' lore."

They dismounted behind her tent. Hoelun hastened around the dwelling to the entrance as a young man led the horses away. Two servants were inside; she helped the women set out broth and pieces of game.

Khasar entered, followed by the others; Temujin and Munglik whispered to each other. The Khongkhotat looked towards her and raised his brows. He might have been gazing at a young girl instead of the mother of a Khan; she was not used to such looks. The few strands of grey in her braids were hidden under her bocca, but surely he had noticed the lines around her eyes.

The men settled themselves near the bed at the back of the yurt, Temujin in the centre. Hoelun brought them food, then sat down to their left. "I'm sorry to give you so little," she said.

"We'll dine well tonight in my tent," Temujin said, "and when spring is past, we'll hold a great feast in honour of our old friend and the others who have joined us."

"See that the Jurkin chiefs have a place of honour at any celebration," Khasar muttered. "Taichu and Seche murmur that you forget some of those who made you Khan."

"Then I must see that they sit with me." Temujin frowned. "Our Jurkin kinsmen are sometimes too proud." He finished his broth and leaned back against the bed. "Mother will want to hear about all that's passed while you were parted from us."

Munglik bowed his head. "The Khatun will hear of that tonight. Now, I'd rather listen to what your beautiful mother has to say about herself."

"You're speaking to a grandmother," Hoelun said, "who has barely enough fingers to count her grandchildren." Munglik's compliments were a bit too warm. "All my sons have wives now, and Temujin alone has given me two grandsons by Bortai and a granddaughter by his wife Doghon."

"And there will be another before long," Munglik said. "The Khan tells me that Bortai Khatun will give birth again this spring. You have been blessed."

"Blessed also by two sons whom I've adopted, Guchu and Kukuchu, and Temulun has grown into a young woman." She frowned; her daughter should have been here by now. Temulun would be dawdling on the ride back, or lingering in the small yurt where they kept their saddles and her birds.

"If she's as lovely as her mother," Munglik said, "then she must outshine all the young beauties."

This praise was making her uneasy. "I hope your wife is well."

"Alas, she passed away in the late autumn. My heart aches for her, as do those of my seven sons."

Having seven sons in as many years had surely done his wife no good. "I am sorry to hear it, Munglik," she said. "I trust you'll find a new wife before long."

"I pray it will be so." He and Temujin exchanged glances. "A man grows lonely in an empty bed."

"I'm sorry to tell you also that old Khokakhchin-eke is gone," she said, anxious to change the subject. "But she lived to see my son proclaimed as Khan."

"Khasar." Temujin sat up on his cushion. "Bortai will know I'm back. Take Munglik to her tent, and tell her to boil a lamb for us. I have much to say to Mother alone."

"Bortai Khatun showed as a child that she would make a good wife." Munglik stood up, turned to Hoelun, and bowed. "If I were to count out all the days of my greatest happiness," he continued, "this day would be among them. Many Mongol clans speak of the fairness and generosity of Genghis Khan, so I knew he would deal with me honourably, but never expected such a warm welcome."

"It's a poor enough welcome for an old friend," Temujin said. "We'll join you soon." He rose; the two men embraced.

Khasar led Munglik outside; one of the servants picked up the bowls and platter. Hoelun looked at her son as he sat down again. She had him to herself for once, and he seemed in an easy mood, with a friend restored to him.

"Munglik," she murmured, "has a talent for speeches."

"He also has a talent for knowing where the game is running. Jamukha won't be happy to know he's here."

Temulun came through the doorway, followed by Guchu and Kukuchu. "Temujin!" She hung up her bow and quiver on the women's side of the entrance, then hurried to him. "You must see my hawk."

Temujin propped an elbow against a cushion. "I saw your hawk some time ago."

"You should see her now." Temulun shrugged out of her coat and threw it towards a trunk; the sash around her small waist made the slight swelling of her hips and breasts more evident. "You never visit my birds any more — I'll bet they're better hunters than yours." She sat down at Temujin's left as he nodded at his two foster brothers; the boys settled at his right, their eyes wide with awe and admiration.

"I saw Khasar outside," Temulun went on. "Who's that man with him?"

"Our old friend Munglik. The Khongkhotats are joining us."

"Good — you'll have more warriors."

"We'll feast tonight," Temujin said. "To have such an old comrade return to us is cause for celebration."

"Good." His sister flashed her white teeth. "I'm hungry enough to eat half a sheep by myself." She shook back her braids. "All the clans will join you, and then you won't have to fight — you'll have more time to hunt with me."

Temujin laughed. "There would still be the Merkits and those accursed Tatars to crush, and the Naiman Khan won't care to have me grow too strong. I'll have more battles to fight."

"You took long enough to ride back," Hoelun said to her daughter.

Temulun made a face, then plucked at her brother's sleeve. "I want to show you my hawk."

He shook off her hand. "I have something to say to you and Mother first." He paused; his eyes had the distant look that had become so familiar. "You'll be fourteen soon, Temulun."

"You actually remember!" She made another face. "The mighty Khan has so much to think of now that I thought he might have forgotten something so unimportant."

"Old enough," he said, "to think of giving up your child's clothes for the robe and head-dress of a woman. I have good news for you, sister. I've found a husband for you. You'll be betrothed soon, and married before autumn."

Temulun stiffened. "Why are you telling me this? Why isn't my suitor here with you?"

"He'll ride here soon, and offer many gifts for you, the most important of which will be a firm renewal of his oath to me.

You'll have the honour of being his chief wife, and I trust you will serve him faithfully."

Temulun bit her lip. "Who?" she whispered.

"Chohos-chaghan, chief of the Khorolas."

The girl flinched. "Never!" She jumped to her feet and spun around to face him. "You can't give me to him! He's ugly, and when he laughs, he sounds like a wild ass braying! I won't – "

Temujin said, "He's been hinting that he wants you for some time, and it's a good match. You must be wed soon anyway – you're not a child any more. How long do you think you can go on racing horses with the boys, joining them for archery practice, going off to hunt with them? What do you think they would do to you if you weren't the Khan's sister? It's a wonder I can still offer Chohos-chaghan an untouched bride."

Temulun let out a scream. "I'll never marry him!"

Kukuchu and Guchu snickered; Hoelun shot them a warning glance. "You will," Temujin said softly, "if I have to beat you and throw you into his bed myself."

The girl stamped her feet. "I won't!"

Temujin leaped up. His hand caught her in the face; she fell. Hoelun went to her quickly and dropped to her knees, shielding her daughter with her arms.

"You'll do as I say," the Khan muttered. "I need Chohos-chaghan, and I'm not as certain of him as I need to be. If he feels affronted, he may think of renewing his ties with my anda, and I can't risk that. Having you as his wife will keep him close to me."

Temulun wiped the blood from her mouth, then buried her face against Hoelun's chest. "Stop it," Hoelun said to the sobbing girl. "It's a good match. The man may not be handsome, but he seems amiable. A man is often what his wife makes of him."

"You are my sister," Temujin said. "Did you think being sister to the Khan meant only that you could play with your birds and do whatever you liked? You have the chance to serve me, to be my voice in Chohos-chaghan's tent. I expected more of you, Temulun."

"Your brother's right." In spite of her words, Hoelun sympathized with her daughter. "You won't please your husband

297

if you wail and cry and make him think you despise him. You must look for what's best in him."

Temulun pulled away from her, then clasped her brother's legs. "Please," she sobbed, "give me to anyone else, Borchu or Jelme, or Subotai when he's older. I'd rather be a minor wife to one of them than Chohos-chaghan's chief wife. My camp would be closer to yours then – I wouldn't have to go so far away."

"I have their loyalty without offering you," Temujin replied. "I must secure that of the Khorolas." He pulled her to her feet. "You misjudge Chohos-chaghan. He knows how you are, with your hunting and hawks, and yet seeks you as a wife. You'll still have your pleasures if you please him. I am Khan and the head of our clan – you must obey me." His voice rose. "If you do anything to offend the man who will be your husband, you'll lose my protection. God alone knows what will happen to you then."

Temulun's face whitened at the threat. Hoelun got up and forced herself between them. "Stop it," she said. "I won't hear such bitter words in my yurt." She drew her daughter to her. "You used to talk of how you wanted to carry your brother's tugh into battle, but you can serve him better by marrying this man. You'll have time to know your betrothed better before you're wed – use it to earn his love and respect, so that he'll listen to you later."

Temulun's head drooped. "I have no choice, do I? It doesn't matter how I feel. I'll have to smile and pretend to be happy."

"Yes," Temujin said, "for yourself and for me. Consider what I could lose if he should drift away from me, and what you might suffer. I know you'll obey me, Temulun." His hand gripped her shoulder; the girl recoiled. "Now go to your hawks, and compose yourself – I won't have Munglik see such an unhappy face. I'll visit your birds when I've finished speaking to Mother."

Temulun's tears would freeze on her face outside; Hoelun wiped them away with her sleeve. Her daughter picked up her coat and walked towards the doorway. Guchu and Kukuchu gaped at Temujin, clearly thrilled by the confrontation. "You'll say nothing of this, you two," Hoelun said firmly, "or I'll take a stick to your backs. Now go and fetch me some fuel."

The two boys scurried through the doorway after Temulun. Temujin sighed. "Temulun has my blood," he said as he sat down. "Not many would dare to speak to me in that way. I was thinking of her happiness, you know. Chohos-chaghan likes her spirit."

"Don't say your soft words to me, Temujin. That wouldn't matter if the marriage didn't benefit you. Maybe I was too free with her, but she was brave when we had to fend for ourselves, and I couldn't see the harm in letting her be a carefree child a while longer."

"You'll have to show her where her duty lies," he said. "By the time you're travelling with her wedding party to her husband's camp, she'll have forgotten she was ever unhappy about it."

The servants had settled themselves by the hearth to do some mending; Hoelun sat down next to her son. "You have more to say to me."

Temujin nodded. "I have good news for you, Mother. I've also found a husband for you."

She tensed. "So I'm another beast to be bartered."

His eyes narrowed. "You showed more wisdom when speaking to my sister."

"Temulun must be wed, but she's young — I'm too old to give a man sons."

"Women older than you bear children, but this man has several sons already. He still finds you fair, and says he wants no other wife. I thought this match would please you, Mother — it's Munglik I want you to wed."

She felt nothing. There were worse men; Munglik would not be a hard husband. She had felt a fleeting longing for him in the days after Yesugei's death, but all that had died in her long ago, and Munglik was not the man the Bahadur had been.

"I see why you want this marriage," she said in a low voice. "Munglik wasn't the most steadfast of friends in the past, but as your stepfather, he'll gain much by being loyal to you." Her son also knew that she was strong enough to keep Munglik

299

bound to him. "As you said, Munglik always knew where the game was running."

"He loves you, Mother – he says he always has."

"And that's to your advantage if we're wed. He loves what I once was, but loves the thought of marrying a Khatun even more." She bowed her head. "I must set a good example for my daughter, and show how delighted I am when he courts me."

"He'll be pleased, as will I." He rose. "I must visit Temulun's birds. She may feel happier about her wedding when she hears about Chohos-chaghan's fine falcons."

'You'll have what you want, however we feel.'

He left her. As Khan, he could not allow the pleas of a mother and sister to move him. He had to be ready to punish any who failed him; she should be grateful for his determination. Despite the tent's warmth, Hoelun felt cold. She got up and went to the hearth.

58

GURBESU KNELT, THEN prostrated herself. The three priests chanted their prayers, sprinkled holy water over the blue stone on her small altar, then offered her a gold cross. The Naiman Queen pressed her lips against it and prayed silently, thanking God and His Son for her husband's success. She had advised him not to lead his armies against the Kereits, but Inancha had not listened to her. He had believed that she thought he would fail, but that had never been her worry. She had known that Inancha Bilge, Tayang of the Naimans, would win and drive Toghril Khan from his throne, yet feared his victory would be fleeting.

Gurbesu sat back on her heels. She had summoned the shamans the day before and asked them to lift the winter storm with a spell, so that her husband could return to her more quickly; dawn had brought a clear sky. With the evil part of creation in constant struggle with the good, it was wise to have the help of as many holy men as possible. Thank you, O Lord, for giving my Tayang his victory. I pray that what I fear will never come to pass.

She made the sign of the cross, then rose. The servants of her household got to their feet; Ta-ta-tonga, the Uighur scribe who was the Keeper of the Tayang's Seal, swayed and crossed himself. Gurbesu beckoned to another scribe; he handed a small bag of gold to the priests for their prayers.

A voice called out beyond the entrance; one of the guards inside shouted back. Gurbesu turned as a young man entered, knelt to press his forehead against the embroidered carpet by the doorway, then got to his feet.

"The army has been sighted, my Queen," he said. "The Tayang's standard can be seen on the horizon."

"Thank you for telling me this," she replied. "I shall wait outside my tent, and greet the Tayang there."

The young man bowed himself out. One of the servants went to a trunk to fetch Gurbesu's favourite fur cloak. She had ordered the main camp to move here, away from the ridge of the Altai Mountains to the valley along the Kobdo River; Inancha would be pleased she had travelled there to greet him. The servant draped the cloak over her shoulders, then held out her gloves; the gold coins adorning her head-dress tinkled as she walked forward. The Tayang would expect to see her happiness, not her lingering doubts.

Lines of riders moved towards the camp along the snow-covered bank of the Kobdo. The men in the front ranks had reached the small group of birches beyond the tents as Gurbesu's servants took their places behind her. Gurbesu drew her cloak more tightly around herself. Inancha would see his queen standing in the cold to greet him, impatient to show her joy at his return.

She had been given to the Tayang three years ago, in her fifteenth year, after the death of his chief wife. Inancha rarely visited his other wives now, and had set Gurbesu above them all. She had listened to him deliberate with his generals, learned

301

what she could from his advisers, and then began to offer her advice.

That amused Inancha. Sometimes he heeded her; more often he did not. The Tayang of the Naimans had ruled his people well for years without her counsel, and could ignore her advice most of the time.

She loved him in spite of that. He honoured her, indulged her, and was kind to her. She might wish he listened to her more often, but if he had been the sort of man who was easily guided by others and uncertain of himself, she could not have loved him.

A man came around the yurt towards her, then touched his hat as he bowed. "I greet you, Queen and mother," Bai Bukha murmured. "I thought I would find you outside waiting to greet my father. I can do no less than wait with you."

"The Tayang will be pleased."

Bai Bukha stepped closer. His dark eyes gazed at her too intently. His glances made her feel naked; he would force himself on her if he could, even before his father's passing. Inancha had taken his younger son Buyrugh with him, but had left Bai Bukha behind to watch over the Naiman encampments.

Inancha Bilge deserved more promising heirs. Instead, Buyrugh went out of his way to argue with his father even over such matters as when and where to move camp. Bai Bukha obeyed the Tayang in silence, but with sullen, resentful looks; at twenty-five, he had seen few battles, and displayed the little courage he had only in hunts.

"My father will rejoice that you came here to greet him," Bai Bukha said, "even though you warned him against this campaign. You see how baseless your fears were. The Tayang will always get the better of his enemies."

"May it always be so." She crossed herself, then made a sign against evil. "I know you wanted him to fight."

"I had little to say about this venture. I merely bowed to Father's will, as I must."

She pressed her lips together. Bai Bukha had urged Erke Khara to appeal once again to Inancha; of that she was sure. Erke Khara had chafed during the years of his exile, seething with rage at his brother Toghril Khan for clinging to the Kereit throne and forcing him to flee for his life. Bai Bukha had known that Inancha was itching for a campaign, a chance to prove he was not yet an old man; the Tayang had listened to Erke Khara's pleas this time. Bai Bukha would have been only too pleased to have his father fall in battle, and to claim both Inancha's realm and his young wife before his brother Buyrugh returned.

The army was a great beast snaking along the river, where hundreds of lances glittered in the grey light. The wind had died down; the snow had drifted, revealing part of the grey stone waste that bordered the grasslands. Gurbesu's teeth chattered and she willed herself to be still.

"There was no need to ride here, Bai," she murmured. "You might have greeted the Tayang by your own tent."

"He won't ride there today, and I should let him know how I took care of things while he was gone." He leaned towards her. "How ready you are to show your devotion to him. Other young wives of old men should be as wise – an old man's more generous when he believes his wife truly loves him."

Her cheeks grew hot. She was about to retort when a cheer went up from the approaching ranks. One rider suddenly bolted from the line and galloped hard across the snow. Gurbesu's spirits lifted as she watched him; Inancha Bilge could still ride like a young man.

The horse skidded to a halt in a cloud of snow and the burly, fur-coated man swung his leg over the saddle. Gurbesu bowed low and then hurried to him. The Tayang caught her in his arms; she pressed her face against his coat.

"You didn't have to brave the cold," Inancha said.

"I would stand in a storm to greet you." Gurbesu peered up at the face she had come to love. Once, she had thought him ugly, with his broken nose and weather-worn cheeks as brown and lumpy as leather jars; familiarity had robbed him of his ugliness. "You'll warm me soon enough, my husband."

Inancha's chest heaved and he gasped for breath. The campaign, and the long ride back, had drained his strength; he should not have raced towards her in an effort to prove it had not. She clasped his hand as Bai Bukha walked towards them.

"I greet you, Father," the young man said, "and give thanks that you have returned to us."

Inancha coughed, then spat. "Give me your greetings inside."

The servants bowed. Gurbesu led her husband to the entrance and into the large, warm space of the ordu; Ta-ta-tonga and the others followed. Lanterns had been set near the throne and her bed, illuminating the tapestries that hung from the walls; a sheep boiled in the kettle over the hearth.

She stood with Inancha as he warmed himself by the fire, then helped him off with his two coats and his breastplate. Even in his long woollen robe, he was still broad, dwarfing the people around him. "Ah." The Tayang blew on his fingers, shook the melting ice from his moustaches, then tugged at his fur-lined helmet. "My other wives aren't here to greet me."

"I didn't summon them," Gurbesu said. "They will, of course, be pleased to have you visit them in the days to come." She often had to urge him to be mindful of his obligations to his other women. "There is food for you and your generals, and the Keeper of the Seal is here with three scribes to take down an account of your victory."

Ta-ta-tonga bowed. "We have already recorded the messages brought to us earlier," the Uighur said. "Erke Khara is now Khan of the Kereits, and his brother Toghril deposed. We rejoiced when we heard it, Master. If it is your will, I shall – "

Inancha waved one big hand. "My Keeper of the Seal can wait for a fuller account, and I've spent over three months with my generals – they'll ride to their own yurts and feast with their families." He shook his large body. "Toghril's son Nilkha, the one called the Senggum, is in hiding, but I doubt he'll do much to help his father. Toghril himself has fled west, towards Kara-Khitai."

"A pity you didn't capture him," Gurbesu said, "but he'll get little help from the Black Khitans."

Bai Bukha lingered near them, peering at Gurbesu across the hearth. "Father!" a voice shouted from the doorway. Buyrugh entered and strode towards them; his eyes widened as he looked at Gurbesu. "I greet you, Gurbesu-eke. I have thought of nothing but returning my father safely to his most-beloved wife.

304

I was his shield in battle, my sword his arm, and I cast many spells to protect him."

"Spells!" Bai Bukha shot his younger brother a poisonous look. "I suspect you kept well back in the ranks when you cast them."

"Not as far back as you, who go no further from your tent than a pregnant woman does to piss."

Bai Bukha's chest swelled. "Our father's shield, are you? You still stink of the shit you dropped when fear loosened your bowels."

"Silence!" Inancha roared; the servants near him backed away. "What are you doing here?"

"I came only to greet my Queen and stepmother," Buyrugh replied. His look was blatant, as hot as his brother's; Gurbesu longed to slap him.

"You've greeted her. Go help the others settle the horses." Buyrugh retreated; the big man wheeled towards his older son. "And you?"

"I was certain," Bai Bukha said, "that you would want a report of what's happened in your absence."

"I can get that from my wife and Ta-ta-tonga. I expect they had as much to do with watching over my people as you. Go to your tent. You may tell your son Guchlug that I would enjoy seeing my grandson later."

Bai Bukha left. Inancha walked towards his throne, then settled into it wearily; Gurbesu took off her cloak and laid it across his legs. "Buyrugh did show some courage," he said.

"You mean he didn't retreat."

"Come now, Gurbesu – it's enough that my sons fight each other. I won't have my wife speak against them."

She settled herself on the cushion to his left. "Bai Bukha should have gone with you, too."

"Bai's not much of a fighter. He knows it, and tries to show that he is, which only endangers any men he commands." Inancha sighed. "Better to see if he can learn to govern – with Buyrugh as his general, they might be able to rule my realm."

"It's not something you need to consider now." Gurbesu reached up and touched his hand. "May God grant you a long life."

"Heaven's given me a long one as it is."

She gazed up at him. Whenever he came back to her, she saw more grey in his sparse beard, more silver in the braids behind his ears. She could not bear to think of what would happen when he was gone. The Tayang's bravest sons were dead; all he had left were a hot-tempered boy of sixteen and a young man with little skill at war. But Inancha would not hear her speak harshly of his sons. Such talk only reminded him that she had not given him one.

Ta-ta-tonga sat down at the Tayang's right. "My master," he said, "I have recorded the orders your Queen and your son gave in your absence, under your seal. It would not take you long to look at them, or to have me read them to you if you prefer to rest your eyes." The Keeper of the Seal was being courteous; Inancha could not read a word of the Uighur script, although he sometimes pretended he could. The skills of the Uighurs who served her husband were useful, and caravans passing through the southern lands held by that people sometimes travelled north with their Uighur guides to trade with the Naimans. Inancha envied Uighur learning, which had served other Naiman rulers before him, but also wondered at a people who preferred a settled life in oases to the freer life of the steppes.

"Another time," the Tayang said. "I see what I need to know – that my people are safe. Erke Khara, in gratitude for his Khanate, sent four hundred war-horses and two hundred mares back with us."

A servant brought them wine in gold goblets; a priest came forward to bless the drink. Inancha scattered a few drops to the spirits, then drank deeply. Five girls sitting on the cushions near Gurbesu plucked lightly at their stringed instruments as another girl brought the Tayang a platter of cut meat. Inancha stabbed at the lamb as the men inside the tent sat down on cushions around the low tables.

"How my wife pleaded with me to turn aside from this campaign." Inancha smiled down at her. "You see that you had nothing to worry about."

She had known he would not miss the chance to reproach her. "I'd keep you at my side always if I could." She leaned towards him. "But I wasn't thinking only of myself. You have an ally on the Kereit throne, but I wonder how long he'll hold it. The Mongol tribes won't be happy to have a vassal of yours flanking their lands."

"The cursed Mongols!" Inancha cleared his throat. "Those evil-smelling wretches are too busy fighting among themselves to be a threat to us."

"They may unite if they see a greater threat." She glanced towards Ta-ta-tonga, knowing he shared her concerns, but the Uighur was silent.

Inancha laughed. "My dear wife – have you forgotten the story of their Khan's feast?" Gurbesu did not reply, knowing he would recite it yet again; it had become one of his favourite tales. "There they were, sitting by the Onon to feast with that dog who calls himself Genghis Khan, honouring those who had recently rallied to him, and they'd barely started to drink their kumiss when the Khan's brother and one of his cousins were at each other's throats."

The other men chuckled, even though they all knew the story well. The Tayang gulped at his wine and wiped his mouth. "My spies say that the brother called the cousin a thief, and then two old Jurkin dowagers were screaming that a minor wife had been served before they were, and soon the whole party were going at one another with churning sticks and branches torn from the trees!" He roared; the great tent filled with laughter. "Genghis Khan was in such a rage that he took the two old bitches who started it all as hostages, and the Jurkin chiefs were forced to swear peace to get them back. A fine way to celebrate their unity!"

"Indeed," Gurbesu said above the laughter, "but it wasn't the first feast that ever ended in fighting, and it seems the breach was mended." The girls near her giggled; she motioned to them to continue their playing. "I haven't heard of any ill will between the Mongol Khan and his allies in the two years since then."

"Give them time," her husband said. "With Merkit and Tatar enemies flanking them, and now a Kereit Khan who's my man, they'd have plenty to worry about even if they were united, but there's only the uneasiest of peaces among them now. You shouldn't brood so over a pack of filthy Mongols."

"I'm only thinking," she said, "that a cur arrogant enough to call himself Genghis Khan shouldn't be provoked."

"Anyone with the arrogance to choose that name will surely call down the wrath of Heaven." Inancha beckoned to a servant, who hurried forward to pour him more wine. "I need no alliances with piss-scented dogs. They'll raid one another, and be harried by their enemies, and sooner or later the Universal Khan will be warring once more with that Jajirat boy-fucker he once called his friend." The people near them laughed again; Inancha's spies were thorough. "Oh, they'll have their unity," he continued, "but it'll be under Naiman banners. When the Mongols have bled themselves in more battles, and Merkits and Tatars have picked over the bones, we'll take what's left in our talons."

Her husband believed he would live long enough to bring that about. I should have been your wife when you were young, Gurbesu thought, and given you sons that could have ruled such a realm. The Tayang would fly to Heaven before he could claim those lands, and his sons could never hold them.

She could not say so to him; that he grasped for his youth and past greatness had made her love him. Gurbesu took his hand and pressed it against her cheek.

59

TEMUJIN'S MAIN CAMP was in sight. A group of boys on ponies raced towards Hoelun. The camel pulling her cart snorted; the boys slowed, then reined in their mounts.

"Grandmother!" Ogedei shouted. Hoelun smiled and waved at him. Ogedei had his father's eyes, but they lacked the coldness she often glimpsed in Temujin's. A smaller boy sitting in front of him was tied to Ogedei's saddle.

"A fine-looking lad," one of the men riding at the side of the small convoy muttered.

"My grandson Ogedei," Hoelun said, beaming with pride. Ogedei was only four, but astride his pony, with his boy's bow and quiver hanging from his belt, he looked like a little warrior already. "And this boy riding with you – can it be –"

"Tolui," Ogedei answered. "He rides well for a two-year-old."

"He's grown much in a year." Hoelun smiled at her other grandson; Tolui's greenish eyes glared back at her fiercely from a little face as bunched up as a fist. "Now be off with your friends – you'll have time to talk to your old grandmother later."

Ogedei waved as the boys rode away. The manservant next to Hoelun prodded the camel; the cart inched forward, trailed by another with her trunks and four servants and a third that held presents and the folded panels of a yurt. Two of the guards Khasar had sent with her rode ahead towards the camp, where several men sat near two fires cleaning their weapons.

The camel was balking again. Had the chilly autumn not been so arid, Hoelun would never have travelled with the wretched animal, but it could go without water much longer than an ox. The land here was as parched and dry as the steppe everywhere, and that would bring trouble; there had already been fights over some watering holes.

The weather was colder as well; the grass had barely sprouted before turning brown and dry. Summers had once been longer; so the older people said, and it seemed to Hoelun that the days were warmer when she was young. Perhaps it was only her age that made the world seem harsher now.

After passing between the fires, Hoelun left her servants with the sentries. A man brought forward a horse, but she shook her head. Her muscles were stiff from the journey; she would walk the short distance.

People greeted her as she approached Bortai's circle, shaking their heads at the sight of the Khan's mother alone and on foot, wending her way through the pats of manure. Outside the large yurt at the north end of the camp, Bortai knelt on the ground, working a loom with two of her women; she lifted her head, then jumped to her feet.

"Hoelun-eke!" Bortai hurried towards Hoelun and embraced her. "I thought you would be here sooner."

"Blame my camel for that. Such animals have their uses, but –" She took Bortai by the shoulders and peered into her face; the younger woman's smooth skin still had the rosy glow of youth. "You look well."

"And you haven't changed, Hoelun-eke. You must have a spell that chains the years."

"I have servants and slaves," Hoelun said, "who leave me with little to do."

"Khasar sent a messenger telling us to expect you. He got here days ago."

"At the pace we were going," Hoelun said, "a child on foot could have arrived days ahead of us." She followed Bortai to the entrance and went inside. "Such trouble for this old woman. Munglik sent twenty guards with me to Khasar's camp, and no sooner had I settled myself there than I was preparing to ride here." She sat on a cushion near Bortai as a servant brought them a jug and goblets. "By the time I've begun this visit to you, I'll be getting ready to travel back to my husband, and Khachigun will expect me to stop along the way to visit him." She sipped her kumiss. "Munglik didn't want me to go, but I insisted on seeing my grandchildren before winter sets in, and with the rivers and springs as low as they've been, we'll be moving camp again by the time I return." They might be forced to move further from their usual grazing grounds.

Bortai frowned. "The shamans have tried to summon rain all summer. Some of Jamukha's allies are moving closer to our lands, and if they grow bolder, Temujin will have to act." She motioned to one of the servants, who brought them a bowl of dried curds. "He's been avoiding any battles with his anda – I think he still hopes –"

"That will have to be settled sometime."

"Yes." Bortai paused. "Toghril Khan is in our camp now."

Hoelun looked up. "I thought –"

"He arrived two days ago," Bortai continued. "The old man was wandering the Gobi for months after the Khan of Kara-

Khitai expelled him, with only a blind horse and no followers. Temujin took pity on him, sent him a message, and rode to the edge of the desert to welcome him." Her son, Hoelun thought, would not give in to pity unless he could gain from it. "I expect Nilkha will turn up when he learns his father's here, and Toghril's brother Jakha Gambu has already come out of hiding to join him." Bortai's mouth twisted. "They would have done nothing for him if Temujin hadn't brought him here."

Hoelun nodded. Nilkha, it was rumoured, had always been jealous of Temujin and the regard Toghril had for her son. "In a way," she said, "I can't blame them. Toghril Khan hasn't been much of a kinsman, what with killing two of his brothers to gain his throne. Both my son and his father might have done better when they swore their anda oaths."

"Still, we'd be safer with Toghril on the Kereit throne, foolish old man that he is. Even Jamukha would welcome his restoration – I suspect the only reason he hasn't attacked us is that he has the Naimans and their Kereit vassals to worry about."

"As do we all." Hoelun made a sign to avert bad fortune. "May the Naiman Khan ride to Heaven soon."

Bortai let out her breath. "Things would be better if women sat in kuriltais."

Hoelun laughed softly. "There would only be more talk before the men did as they liked."

Her son would make his decisions without her help. Hoelun occasionally thought that he had married her to Munglik in part to remove her from his tents, but he had stopped listening to her long before that. Everything had changed after their flight from the Merkits ten years ago, when he had rejected her advice to wait before attacking his enemies.

He would say that his judgement had proved better than hers. The campaign against the Merkits had both restored his wife and strengthened him. His defeat at Jamukha's hands, which had filled her with dread, had only made him more determined. Even the marriage he had forced on her had brought her some happiness, although it lacked the fire of her life with Yesugei.

Odd, she thought, that Munglik still saw her as the girl she had been, while her contentment was that of an old woman with little more ahead of her. Her husband would never know that when she held Munglik in her arms she still longed for Yesugei and what she had felt for him.

"Ogedei's grown," Hoelun said. "He rode out with Tolui to greet me, and Tolui looks ready for battle already."

Bortai laughed. "How he kicked inside me! I feared he'd beat his way out of me before my time. It's good that Ogedei looks after him, or he would have been in more than his share of trouble by now."

"And where are my two oldest grandsons?" Hoelun asked.

"Hunting with Temujin. I hope he can keep them from hunting each other." Bortai spread out a piece of leather and worked a hole in it with her awl. "Jochi bullies Chagadai, and then Chagadai recites the tale of Alan Ghoa's sons, which only gets Jochi angrier."

"Brothers often fight at their age." Hoelun thought of the last time she had seen them, during the midsummer feast the year before. She had beaten Chagadai herself for calling his older brother a bastard. The old rumour had never died.

"At least Ogedei and Tolui don't fight." Bortai punched another hole. "And are your foster sons thriving?"

"Kukuchu and Guchu talk of little except the time they'll be old enough to fight with Temujin. And Munglik's sons —" Hoelun fell silent. She had never admitted to her husband that she was wary of his middle son. Kokochu spent much of his time with the shamans, and some said he had learned as much as they knew. The boy seemed to see everything; she almost believed he could touch her thoughts. His six brothers were devoted to him, but perhaps they also feared him.

"Kokochu's only thirteen," she went on, "and already some say he can send out his spirit in an animal's guise. He passed through one ordeal this winter — wetting his shirt and letting it dry on his body while he sat outside in the midst of a snowstorm. He claims he never felt the cold. Now he dreams of serving his Khan with his spells."

"Temujin will be glad to hear it," Bortai murmured. "A good shaman is always useful."

He might be better off without my stepson's spells, Hoelun thought, but said nothing. She could not escape the feeling that if she spoke against the boy, he would hear her words somehow and put a curse on her. Being the stepbrother of Genghis Khan had made him even more ambitious and proud. She steadied herself. Better to have Kokochu's spells working for Temujin than against him.

"Temujin's impatient for a campaign," Bortai said. "If we don't get rain soon, we'll have to move closer to Merkit territory." Hoelun listened in silence as the young Khatun spoke of what the Khan might do. Bortai might pretend that Hoelun had something to say about such matters, but Hoelun knew otherwise.

60

GURBESU PRAYED SILENTLY as she looked towards her husband. Inancha still sat on his throne; he had not spoken since his generals and advisers had left the ordu. His sunken cheeks were dark hollows; one gnarled hand clutched his goblet. The Tayang drank much more now, needing wine and kumiss to ease his pain.

The spirit had gone out of him a year ago. She had expected him to rouse himself when the message came of a Mongol victory against the Merkits, but he had accepted the news passively. Genghis Khan had defeated the Merkit chief Toghtoga Beki and robbed him of many tents and herds, forcing Toghtoga to flee towards Lake Baikal. Some claimed that Toghril had taken most of the Merkit booty for himself, others that the Mongol Khan had given it to him, but the result was the same. The old Kereit, with more wealth and Mongol support, had the means to take back his Khanate.

Inancha had been certain that Genghis Khan would ride against Erke Khara next, and had come to himself long enough to warn his ally to strike first. But Erke Khara had done nothing, and what Gurbesu had once feared had come to pass. Toghril sat once more on the Kereit throne; the wretched Mongols were stronger than ever.

God had abandoned them. She had hoped that the birth of their first child might restore his spirit, but Inancha had rallied for only a few days before lapsing into his darker moods. Now her son lay under the ground, taken by the fever that had swept the camp that winter.

Gurbesu whispered another prayer under her breath. Every night that she lay at the Tayang's side, she slept uneasily, fearing that at any moment she would have to summon the priests and shamans. Every morning, she prayed for one more day with him before a spear ribboned in black felt stood in front of their great tent.

"My dear," she said at last, "it's late, and you must rest." She helped him up; he leaned against her as she guided him to the bed. The servants disappeared behind the curtains that hung over their side of the tent. Gurbesu tended Inancha herself, unwilling to let others see more of his weakening body. She helped him out of his clothes, but left him in his long shift and felt socks; he often shivered, despite the yurt's warmth. His bowed legs, once so muscular, were frail, knotted limbs; she covered him quickly with the blankets.

"Wine," he said.

She brought a goblet to him, held his head as he drank, then slipped off her own clothes. The darkened tent made her think of a grave; the dim glow of the hearth was a dying fire.

She crept under the blankets, careful not to disturb him. Make peace with the Mongol Khan. She had wanted to say that in front of his men. He was too proud to consider it; he could not admit that he was dying, that he needed to plan for what would happen after he was gone.

She knew what she had to say to her husband now, yet still resisted. He would hate her for reminding him of his approaching death.

"Inancha," she whispered. "Please listen, and say nothing until I've finished." She pressed against him and put her lips close to his ear. "We've had seven years together, and God grant that we have seven more, but you must think of your people now. Buyrugh and Bai Bukha can't lead in your place."

They were jackals who circled her with anticipation in their eyes. Whenever the two came to their father's tent, she knew they were disappointed not to find the spear in front of his doorway. "They'll be fighting each other instead of your enemies."

He was silent; maybe he was at last willing to listen. "There's something you can do," she continued, keeping her voice low. "Ask the Noyans to accept Guchlug as your heir, and set aside the claims of your sons. Your grandson would have Ta-ta-tonga and me to advise him until he's old enough to rule by himself."

She waited. Bai Bukha and Buyrugh would have to die if Guchlug was proclaimed; left alive, they would remain a danger. Inancha would never give the order himself, but she could do so in his place. Some of the generals said that they would sooner follow Gurbesu into battle than Bai Bukha. A whisper to them would bring death to the Tayang's sons, and even Inancha might see, however he mourned, that it was for the best.

"Inancha," she murmured, "what do you say?"

A snore escaped him; she realized he was asleep. She would have to speak to him again, when he was awake and his pain dulled by kumiss. She held him in her arms, wishing that her own life could pass into his ailing body, and prayed for one more day.

61

TEMUJIN SAID, "OUR chance has come."

Bortai glanced at the men. Temujin had been talking of the Tatars ever since Borchu and Jelme had entered the tent. He had sent for the two chiefs as soon as a scout had warned him that several Tatar clans were fleeing in their direction, forced on by an advancing Kin army. The three men were savouring this news as though it were a roasted sheep.

Temujin's eyes glowed; now he would have a chance to strike at his father's murderers.

Bortai's four sons sat on cushions, listening intently. "The Kin must have tired of their greedy Tatar friends," Jelme said. "We should help them punish the filthy tribe. The Kin would reward us for it."

Voices murmured beyond the doorway and a shadowy form entered. The light from the hearth fire illuminated Kokochu's smooth face as the young shaman approached the back of the tent; Bortai recoiled. Her husband had sent for Kokochu, but Munglik's son was always sure of the Khan's welcome.

Teb-Tenggeri, everyone called the shaman now, the All-Celestial. He had been dwelling in their camp for over a year, and many said he often climbed to Heaven to speak to Tengri. Jeren was afraid to let even his shadow touch hers.

The shaman bowed gracefully. His coat was lined with silk, his chest covered with necklaces of bright stones, his hat adorned with eagle feathers – all gifts he had received from Temujin for his spells. He sent his spirit into wolves to roam the steppe, and flew over the camps in a falcon's form; nothing could be hidden from him. Bortai stilled her thoughts, fearing the shaman might sense them.

"I greet you, Khan and brother," Teb-Tenggeri said in his musical voice. His eyes were large and dark, his hairless face as beautiful as any woman's. He did not look like his brothers, all stout young fellows with Munglik's placid gaze, and some said Munglik could not be his father. A beam of light had bred him, they whispered, reaching down from Heaven through the smoke-hole of his mother's tent to open her womb.

"Greetings, brother Teb-Tenggeri." Temujin's eyes widened; even the Khan was fearful of the shaman, who had powers others lacked. Kokochu had brought them rain when they needed it, standing beyond the camp as it fell when everyone else had run for the tents or cowered under blankets on the ground. Even Tengri's bolts could not touch him.

"I would have come sooner," Teb-Tenggeri said, "but my soul was wandering, tied to my body by only the thinnest thread, and I could not break the spell even for you."

"We've been talking of killing Tatars," Temujin said. "You'll read the bones for us at the war kuriltai.'

Teb-Tenggeri sat on a cushion between Jelme and the boys. One of Bortai's women brought him airagh, trembling slightly as she handed the horn to him. The shaman muttered a blessing, then lifted his head. "I'll read the bones," he said, "yet I already see what they will tell us. When I sent my spirit wandering, I soared above a great camp until I saw a fire below. I dropped to the ground and stood before several men, and the pale light shining from their faces told me I was among the dead. The men were drinking from the vessels that had been buried with them. One of them handed his cup to me."

The shaman swayed as he chanted. The boys covered their faces and peered at him through their fingers. "I drank from the cup," Teb-Tenggeri continued, "and tasted blood, and then the man said, 'I am Yesugei Bahadur, poisoned by my enemies when I drank from their cups, but now I sip their blood, which my son has given to me.' "

Borchu shuddered. "A powerful omen."

"And one I won't ignore." Temujin tugged at his moustache. "We'll trap the damned Tatars in a vise, between our men and the Kin army. My father's spirit, and the shades of Ambaghai and Khutula, will drink deeply of their blood." He paused. "We'll ask Toghril Khan to help us, and to claim his share of spoils. The Naiman Khan's sons are still fighting over their dead father's realm, so the Kereits needn't fear an attack from the west while they are fighting with us."

"I'll ride with you, Father," Tolui burst out.

Jelme grinned. "Only six, and he wants a taste of war."

"Jochi will come with us," Temujin said. "He's old enough to ride with the spare horses in the rear. The rest of you will stay here to guard your mother."

Jochi shot a triumphant look at Chagadai. They would all be going to war before long; Bortai felt a pang.

"I hear the weeping of Tatar women," Teb-Tenggeri said, "and see Tatar heads lying at our feet. My brother will have his victory."

Fifteen days after the army rode out to meet the Tatars, an old man galloped into Hoelun's camp with a message. The Khan's

Jurkin cousins had refused to join the campaign; now, in the absence of most of the fighting men, they had raided one camp, killing ten men.

Seche Beki and Taichu meant to break with her son at last, after years of arguing and grumbling. Temujin had been patient, and this was his reward.

Other camps had to be warned. She sent out five older boys with a message to be on guard. The Jurkin chiefs must be hoping that Temujin would fall, that they could finally take his Khanate for themselves.

Twelve days after the old man had left for his camp, one of Hoelun's servants summoned her outside. "Guchu's come back," the woman cried.

Hoelun ran from the tent. Her foster son stood by the fires beyond her circle, speaking to the older boys on guard. Two other soldiers, one of them gripping the shoulder of a boy she did not know, were with him; Guchu left them with the horses and ran towards her.

"Mother," he shouted, "we have a victory!" He threw his arms around her, crushing her against his leather breastplate. "I insisted on being the messenger to you – I wanted to be the first to tell you."

She freed herself, then reached up to caress his brown face. "We met the Tatars in the Ulja River valley," Guchu continued. "They were trapped – couldn't retreat south-east without meeting the Kin. We fought until they were pushed back to where their women waited with their carts and herds."

Hoelun led Guchu to her tent. "I trust you and Kukuchu acquitted yourselves well."

"We were with the left wing's light cavalry, under Borchu. My arrows found their mark, and Kukuchu took the head of one of their Noyans when his horse threw him."

A servant helped the young man off with his armour; he collapsed on a cushion. "The Tatar chief Megujin fled for the forest. He and his men set up a barricade of birches and pines, but Temujin wasn't going to let him escape – led the assault on the barricade himself, and not one of those Tatars lived."

The servant woman handed Guchu a jug; he sprinkled a hasty blessing, then gulped down the kumiss.

"And my other sons?" Hoelun asked.

"All uninjured, Mother, as are Munglik-echige and his sons." She chided herself silently for thinking of her sons first. "Everyone's praising Kokochu – Teb-Tenggeri – for the spells he cast. When the Tatars broke and ran, he raised a wind that swept many of them from their mounts."

"Spells would be useless without brave fighters." She quickly made a sign to avert misfortune. "There will be weeping in our camps, Guchu. In such a battle, we must have lost men."

He looked solemn for a moment, then brightened. "Many more Tatars fell, and Temujin will see that our widows and orphans get their share of loot. He took the bed of Megujin for himself – it's covered with gold and pearls."

"Stolen from a town in Khitai earlier, no doubt. The Kin general must have been pleased we came to his aid."

"The Prince Hsiang let us keep most of the booty," Guchu said, "and honoured both Temujin and the Kereit Khan with titles. Toghril is Ong-Khan now, the Prince of Khans, and Temujin is Ja'ud Khuri – the Pacifier." Hoelun's son had a greater title of his own, but perhaps the Kin thought only their titles had meaning. "As usual, Temujin isn't claiming as much as he might – he even gave away some pretty Tatar girls he took on Megujin's bed." Guchu drew his brows together. "Teb-Tenggeri has as great a share as many who fought in the front ranks, but then his spells helped us."

"There's one thing the All-Celestial didn't predict," Hoelun said, forgetting her fear of her stepson for once. "The Jurkins fell upon some of our people, and killed ten men while you were away."

Guchu paled, then sat up. "We waited six days for them in vain. Temujin was furious. We had to go on without them, but he means to pay back Seche and Taichu for disobeying him. I never thought they'd go this far."

"Well, they have. This is worse than disobedience. They must think that if they can make a Khan, they can unmake him." She took the jug from him. "A man rode here to tell me and appealed to me as the Khan's mother. I sent warnings to our people to be on guard."

"Temujin must have learned about this treachery by now. The Jurkins forgot their oaths – he won't forgive that." Guchu pulled at his short moustache. "They've been a spear in our side for years, with their slanderous talk of how Temujin claims too much. The Khan gives his men more than most would."

Her son was generous with everything, she thought, except his power; that he would keep for himself. Her joy in seeing Guchu safe was mingled with sadness. He would soon have his own tent and a wife; perhaps a Tatar girl was part of his booty.

Guchu's companions called out to him. A servant ushered them inside; the little boy she had seen earlier was with them. "I greet you, Khatun and mother of our Khan," one man said, "and would beg only the smallest part of your hospitality before we ride on."

"I almost forgot," Guchu said before she could reply. He gestured at the boy. "This boy was among the Tatar prisoners, and Temujin claimed him for you. I wanted to bring one of your prizes to you right away."

The boy looked up at her with his black eyes. His clothes were covered with dirt, but the belt around his tunic was of sable and silk, and a gold ring shone in his nose.

"You must be a Noyan's son," Hoelun said gently. "What are you called?"

"Shigi Khutukhu." He drew himself up, reminding her of how Guchu had looked when he was brought to her.

"And what has my son Guchu told you about me?"

"That you are kind, and your sons the bravest of men. That you were a mother to him when he had no one else." His throat moved as he swallowed. "I lost my mother when we ran from the Kin – my father fell when – " A tear rolled from his eye; he wiped it away.

A sudden horror of men and battles welled up inside her. Some of Yesugei's bitterest enemies had been punished, yet this boy, and countless others, had to be punished for deeds committed before they had entered life. She had stoked Temujin's hatred with her tales of his father's poisoning, stories she had told for so long that she had come to believe them herself, and this was the result.

Foolish thoughts, she told herself, weak musings unworthy of a Khan's mother.

"Honoured Lady?" Shigi Khutukhu asked. "Are you to be my mother now?"

"Yes." She took his small hand. "You'll be my son."

"Our mother," Guchu said, "would claim all the children of the world if she could."

"Yes," she whispered. "With one mother, they'd all be brothers and sisters – perhaps they'd stop fighting then."

The men laughed; it was an impossible hope. Hoelun drew the Tatar boy to her.

62

THE MIST WAS a shroud around Jamukha, the valley below hidden by a thick grey veil. As the fog lifted, the tips of evergreens seemed to drift on a pale sea. The men camped below on the mountainside were shadows huddled around a fire.

Unggur was gone. Jamukha's throat tightened as he stared at his son's grave. He had lost one son a year ago, soon after hearing about his anda's victory against the Tatars; the news of Temujin's success had mocked his grief. But this loss was harder to bear. His other son had been only a baby of a few days, but Unggur was a vigorous lad of two when the river spirits dragged him under the water. He nearly wept again, thinking of the small, drowned body his servant had carried to him. The servant had paid for his carelessness. Jamukha had severed the man's limbs from his body himself before burying him with the child.

The spirits were determined to make him suffer, to leave him childless, to lash at him with tales of his anda's triumphs. Temujin let nothing stand in his way, not even his rebellious

321

Jurkin cousins. He had swept down on Seche and Taichu immediately, taking their heads with his own sword; there had been no time for Jamukha to ride to their defence. The Jurkin clan had been disbanded, its people parcelled out among Temujin's followers.

Even then, many Jurkin warriors had willingly sworn oaths to the Khan, if the reports carried to Jamukha could be believed. The Noyan Gugun and his brothers Chilahun and Jebke had apparently made fine speeches about how only duty had compelled them to obey their Jurkin chiefs, and Temujin had forgiven them. Gugun's father Telegetu Bayan had ridden with the Jajirats before sneaking off to join Temujin; now Gugun's sons Bukha and Mukhali would serve Genghis Khan.

Jamukha's bitterness nearly overwhelmed him. Temujin's cursed mother had even claimed another foster son, a Jurkin boy called Boroghul. Temujin was surrounded by brothers, those of the flesh, the stepbrothers he had gained with his mother's marriage, and those the damned woman had adopted, while Jamukha had none.

Two riders emerged from the fog below and dismounted; one of Jamukha's men rose to greet them. They hunkered down by the fire, and then Ogin got up and walked towards the horses. The young man would ride up here and tell Jamukha it was time to leave the grave, that he had mourned for Unggur too long.

He should have struck on the last night he had spoken to Temujin, the moment his anda had refused to answer his question. Instead, his love for his friend had stayed his hand. Temujin had used that love against him. The urges of Jamukha's own body were only more weapons the spirits used to strike at him, tormenting him even now with what might have existed between him and his anda.

As long as Temujin was alive, he would steal everything that might have been Jamukha's.

"Noyan." Ogin dismounted and came towards him, leading two horses. "A messenger from the Kereit Khan waits below." Jamukha did not move. "He wants to speak to you." Jamukha was silent. "Come away from this place, my comrade."

The men might leave him if he stayed here much longer.

322

Jamukha got to his feet and gazed at his son's grave, then followed Ogin down the slope.

After Jamukha had greeted the Kereit formally, they sat down by the fire, away from the others.

"I sorrow with you," the Kereit said. "I was told at your camp that you had gone to bury a son. I've also lost two of my four sons. One rode out scouting and never returned, and another fell to a Naiman's lance."

Jamukha stared past the man. Losing sons in war, however painful, was not the same, and this man had other sons. His own had never had the chance to make their names live through their deeds.

"Why has Toghril-echige sent you?" he asked at last.

"Genghis Khan," the man replied, "wants to attack the Naimans. Naturally, he's invited the Ong-Khan to join him, since they both have reason to hate those dogs." Jamukha repressed a sneer at the sound of Toghril's Kin title; it was like the Kereit Khan to insist on using it. "Toghril Ong-Khan thought you should hear of this from him."

That was also like Toghril. Grateful as he was for Temujin's favours, he would also try not to anger Jamukha. Maybe the old man finally understood that Temujin, whatever oaths he had sworn as Toghril's vassal, would reach for even more; the Kereit Khan might need Jamukha then.

"Against which Naiman force will you ride?" he asked.

"Buyrugh's men. He won't expect that, since he keeps near the mountains – he'll think we mean to meet his brother's army on the plain."

Jamukha nodded. Temujin would take advantage of the split among the Naimans, and Bai Bukha, who had taken the title of Tayang for himself, had a larger army. It was said that the two brothers had fought over one of their father's wives. Men who would divide a realm because of a woman deserved to be crushed.

"So my anda seeks more spoils," Jamukha said, "in spite of all he has."

"You must admit there's no better time to attack the Naimans," the Kereit said, "and whatever your past differences with Genghis Khan, you'll be safer if they're beaten." He scowled as he poked at the fire. "I mean to take a hundred lives for my son's."

Jamukha tugged at his hat. There might be an opportunity for him here, some way of using this campaign for his own ends.

"I think," he said slowly, "that I may join the Ong-Khan against the Naimans. As you say, they're my enemies as well."

The messenger grinned. "Toghril Khan will be pleased to hear it, as will Genghis Khan. The hard feelings between you and your anda have troubled the Ong-Khan."

"One must forget such differences when there's more to be gained, and Temujin rides with many who once fought against him. I'll bring a thousand of my men to join Toghril-echige. Tell him this, and ask him when and where we should meet."

"I shall," the Kereit replied.

Toghril would be lulled, thinking that Jamukha was ready to forget the past. Temujin, in his arrogance, might even believe that his anda would at last make a formal declaration of peace and submit to him. He had weapons now, and would find a way to use them.

63

IN THE EARLY days of summer, before the sun parched the land, the army of Genghis Khan rode towards the Khangai range from the north-east as the Kereits approached from the south-east. The columns separated before making their way through the mountain passes; the advance troops led them to a stony waste with little forage. The men lived off their scanty rations – leather bottles of kumiss, dried curds in pouches, and meat which they put under their saddles to soften.

As they rode, Jamukha spoke to Toghril about Temujin, and how wounded he had been when his anda abandoned him.

They came to the Naiman grasslands, flat expanses dotted

with birches and poplars, and watered their horses at the lakes they passed. Buyrugh had retreated south, towards the Altai Mountains, but they saw no scouts, no sign that the Naimans had sent out men to encircle them. The army followed the trail, caught up with a camp of Naimans on the move, killed those who were too weak to travel further, took the rest prisoner, and added the Naiman herds to their train. By then, another army was following them, that of the carrion-eaters. The sky was thick with black birds, and the howls of wolves and hyenas often sounded in the night.

By day, they rode under a fierce, hot sun: by night, riders moved among the widely separated camps, issuing orders for the next day's movements. Still Buyrugh retreated, sending none of his army against them. The strategy showed his weakness. The Naiman hoped to wear them down, yet refused to risk his men; perhaps he hoped they would give up the chase, or meant to attack when they withdrew. The army spread out over more territory, alert to any sign that the enemy might turn and strike.

At night, when the men rested, Jamukha whispered to Toghril of how mercilessly Temujin had executed two of the kinsmen who had made him Khan.

The Mongols and Kereits pressed on. At the foot of the Altai ridge, near one of the mountain passes, their advance troops captured a commander of Buyrugh's rearguard. They rode through the passes, sometimes dismounting to lead their strings of horses along cliffsides. The men lived by nicking the necks of their horses and sucking the warm blood. Jagged, dark cliffs, through which evil winds howled, rose up on either side of them. Above, where glaciers untouched by the sun overhung the passes, black birds circled, waiting to feed.

They left the mountains and entered the Urungu River valley, riding past thickets of willow. The tree-lined valley throbbed with the steady, harsh tapping of woodpeckers; here, they hunted boars, and had fresh meat. A wing of Kereits forded the river, the men clinging to their horses' tails as they floated on their packs. A wing of Mongols fanned out and moved west.

Buyrugh was moving towards Lake Kizilbash, yet did not turn to fight. His pursuers held back, allowing the Naimans to think they might retreat. The advance wings of the army spread out, ready to sweep towards the Naimans from both sides. The centre of the army converged and followed the river to the reedy marshes of Lake Kizilbash.

Here, two months after their departure, amid the dry yellow hills that bordered the salt lake, the Mongols and Kereits met their Naiman foes. Buyrugh's warriors rode against them, only to be thrown back by the centre's heavy cavalry as the two wings began to enfold them. War-drums sounded; the clanging of swords, the deadly whistling of clouds of arrows, and the screams of dying men shattered the silence of the yellow hills for a day and into the night, until the Naimans pulled back. Caught between the left and right wings of their enemies, many more retreating Naimans fell. Buyrugh, his failure as a general revealed, the falseness of the omens he had read now demonstrated to him, fled from the battlefield.

By dawn, the yellow hills were covered with bodies. Some were carried away to be buried; the Naiman bodies were stripped and left there. The triumphant army sang, danced, and paraded heads on spikes; the black birds and the hyenas fed. In the midst of the celebration, Jamukha whispered to Toghril of how the Kereits had taken more casualties than the Mongols.

The army took one camp Buyrugh had abandoned, then went back along the way they had come, with exhausted mounts and prisoners in their train. At night, when they camped, the silence was broken by the wails of Naiman women and the cries of their children. They left the Altais and rode west until they reached the rapids of the Baydarik River, which flowed south from the Khangai Mountains.

Throughout their journey, they had anticipated an attack, expecting that Naimans might regroup to confront them. By the river, the officers learned from their scouts that a Naiman general was waiting upriver with his army; they would not leave Naiman territory without a fight. There, they camped, the Mongols to the south of the Kereits, resting for the battle they would soon face, and Jamukha finally saw a way to strike at his anda.

"We've fought enough," Jamukha said.

Toghril sat outside his small field tent, warming his hands

326

by a fire, his general Gurin Bahadur at his side. The light flickered over Toghril's wrinkled face, and Jamukha saw a man weary of war. Such looks usually came to a man only when he was also weary of living, but the Ong-Khan, he knew, still clung to his life.

"We have one battle left," Gurin said, "before we go home."

"I think not." Jamukha rested an arm on one knee. "Do you believe Temujin will fight with us tomorrow? His ambition is limitless – he dreams of ruling Kereits as well as Mongols."

"How can you say that?" Gurin Bahadur asked. "Didn't he restore my Khan's throne to him?"

"Do you think he did that purely out of friendship? He didn't want an ally of the Naimans to rule. He let us suffer the brunt of this battle. Now he has a way to be rid of us."

Gurin hawked and spat. "You speak lies about a good man. If his men took fewer blows than ours, that may mean only that they're better fighters."

"I speak the truth about one who abandoned me, his anda and sworn brother. He tired of me because he thought I stood in his way. I'm the sparrow who dwells in the north, whose song you hear even in winter, while Temujin is a wild goose who flies south when it feels winter's breath."

"The song I hear now," Gurin said, "sounds more like that of a jackal than a sparrow."

Jamukha would let that insult pass; Toghril was not protesting his words. "Why do you think he asked you to join him on this campaign? He hoped you would lose more men, perhaps even that you, Toghril-echige, might fall yourself. I know what he'll do now. In secret, he will send a message to the Naiman general offering peace, and we'll be the price. He'll wait until we sleep, sneak away, and leave us to the Naimans."

Toghril shook his heavy body. "It can't be so."

"It is," Jamukha replied. "Didn't he abandon me in the night, after calling me brother? Do you think he won't do the same to you, and steal what you have for himself?"

Toghril rubbed at his thin grey beard. "I can't believe it, and yet – when I think of it now, Temujin has always gained by helping me. When my son Nilkha speaks against him, I refuse

327

to listen, but now I wonder if Temujin wants me to be angry with my son, to divide us, to –"

"Don't listen to him," Gurin muttered.

"Ignore me," Jamukha said, "and you'll see what comes of it. Temujin means to rid himself of both of us. I won't stay here and become part of a Naiman's spoils. My men will light their fires to mislead Temujin, and then leave this place. I advise you to do the same."

Toghril leaned towards the fire. "But –"

"Leave," Jamukha said. "Let Temujin fall to the Naimans. Light your fires and slip away."

"You may be right," Toghril said, "and yet to leave the son of my anda –"

The old man was an archer who could not bring himself to loose his arrow. "I am going," Jamukha said.

Toghril said, "Then so must I."

"You can't do this," Gurin said.

"Will you disobey your Khan?" Jamukha asked.

The Bahadur sighed. "That I cannot do. I've said what I think, and the Ong-Khan refuses to listen. Now I must obey, whatever my doubts. Give me your orders, my Khan."

64

BORTAI HAD HOPED that she would see her husband again before autumn. Now the air was sharp and cold, the sky slate grey, and he had not returned. Temuge Odchigin, left behind to watch over the main camp, ordered them to move south along the Kerulen, then rode out with several scouts.

Temuge returned when the trees had shed their leaves, and told Bortai what he had learned in a camp by the Orkhon. The Khan, preparing to face a Naiman force near a Khangai mountain pass, had been abandoned by the Kereits and Jamukha's men. Temujin had escaped by fleeing north in a wide loop around the mountains, and was returning home unharmed.

Bortai seethed. She had expected to greet the returning army with joy, but could think only of how close Temujin had been to death, how false and weak Toghril had shown himself to be. She endured the feast celebrating the victory in silence. When Temujin came to her bed, his ardour rekindled by his long absence, she felt little of the pleasure she should have had. For some time, his visits to her had seemed only a duty and habit; now that he welcomed her as he had during the early months of their marriage, she felt little joy. His treacherous comrades had robbed her of that, too.

She waited for Temujin to speak of how he would avenge himself, but he parcelled out Naiman captives and booty while saying nothing about the war. Whenever she was about to ask him how he would punish the Ong-Khan and Jamukha, a colder look in his eyes warned her to be still.

A few days after his return, Bortai and Temujin rode out to hunt with their hawks, but did not return to the camp. Their servants set up a tent for them at the foot of a mountain; their guards left them to themselves, as though Bortai were still a new bride. Yet even when Temujin held her, cupping her face gently in his hands, her suppressed rage made her tremble. He was using her to escape the need for a decision, pretending that the refuge he had created inside this little dwelling could not be touched by anything beyond.

On the morning after they had stopped by the mountain, a messenger arrived from Temujin's camp. A Kereit envoy had come to the camp with Borchu, and begged an audience with the Khan. Bortai listened in disbelief as Temujin said that he would meet with the Kereit.

Temujin received the envoy inside the tent; Borchu left to wait outside with the other men. The Kereit held his hands out as he rattled off a formal greeting, then settled himself on a cushion at Temujin's right.

"I welcome you, Gurin Bahadur," Temujin said. Bortai sprinkled an offering, then handed the man a jug.

Gurin Bahadur downed the kumiss quickly. "You've given me a warmer welcome than I deserve."

"You fought bravely against the Naimans," Temujin murmured. "I didn't think you were a man who would run from another battle."

"It wasn't my wish to do so," Gurin replied, "but I had to obey my Khan. Jamukha filled his ears with slander, saying that you were treating with the Naiman general and would leave us at his mercy."

Temujin lifted his brows.

"I was relieved to hear that you escaped," the Kereit continued. "I told the Ong-Khan that you'd never trade our lives for such a truce, but he heard only the baying of that Jajirat." He paused. "Toghril Khan has had cause to regret his actions. The Naimans fell upon us three days after we abandoned you. Now many of our men are dead or captives, and the enemy is raiding the camps of the Ong-Khan's son. We've paid heavily for what we did."

"I grieve to hear it," Temujin said; Bortai rejoiced. "And my anda – how did he fare?"

"He separated from us and took a different route, so escaped unscathed." Gurin shook his head violently. "I'm sorry for that also. Jamukha's a jackal who whines, then offers his hindquarters to his fellows. He's –"

"He is my anda," Temujin said. "You mustn't speak of him in this way to me. The Ong-Khan's easily swayed, and my anda knows he fears betrayal. Jamukha knew what he had to say to bring the Ong-Khan to act, and maybe he only intended to lead the Naimans away from us. But if he had said that to Toghril instead, the Ong-Khan might not have been willing to take the risk."

How could he say this now? Bortai was about to speak but Temujin made a sharp motion with one hand to silence her.

Gurin rubbed at his jowls. "You have a great heart if you can believe that. Men speak truly when the talk of your nobility."

"And Toghril," Temujin whispered, "must be sorry now that he thought of betraying me instead of aiding me. As for Jamukha, whatever he intended, he'll now see that the spirits still guard me."

"Your words give me hope," the Kereit said, "that you'll listen to what the Ong-Khan told me to ask, but you would have every right to reject his request. Toghril begs you to help him now. Yesugei's son, he says, has always been loyal, and he curses himself for ever doubting you. He's a willow that bends with the wind, while you are a pine that stands tall under the Eternal Blue Sky. If you turn from him, he says, it's no more than he deserves."

Bortai could no longer control herself. "He deserves to lose everything for what he did," she said, "to die for –"

"Be silent, wife." Temujin leaned towards Gurin. "The Khatun is sometimes too zealous. Leave us now, and wait with my men. I must think about this."

Gurin rose and bowed. "I'm grateful you would even consider my Khan's plea." He bent low once more. "Whatever you decide, Toghril Ong-Khan needs me near him. I must leave you by dawn tomorrow."

"You'll have my answer before then."

The Bahadur bowed himself out. Bortai moved closer to her husband. "What is there to think about?" she asked. "Toghril deserves no help. Send that Kereit back with his braids cut off, and tell him he's lucky to keep his head."

"How fierce you are, Bortai." He smiled. "Have you forgotten that Toghril helped me to rescue you?"

"That doesn't matter now. All this time, I said nothing, because I was sure you'd see what you have to do."

"I've been waiting."

"And now you can watch Toghril suffer without lifting a hand. What are you going to do?"

He said, "I'm going to aid the Ong-Khan."

"I don't believe it! How can you –"

"Silence, Bortai. Test my patience, and my men will see how a man forces a stubborn woman to obey him."

"You killed the Jurkin chiefs for less," she muttered.

"They were of no further use to me. Toghril still is." His fingers closed around her wrist, hurting her. "What good will it do to allow Naimans to encroach on Kereit lands? I'd be risking our safety for the joy of revenge, and that I will not do." He spoke so softly that she could barely hear him, but his whispers frightened her more than shouts. "Jamukha accused me of seeking a peace with the Naimans. It wouldn't surprise me if he were considering that himself, with some Kereit lands

331

and herds to be his reward. I must show the Naimans that we're not so easily divided."

Everything in her rebelled at his words. "That creature who calls himself Ong-Khan betrayed you once – he'll do it again."

"I swore an oath to him, Bortai. It's in my interest to show him that I'm loyal, that I can forgive. I suspected he would turn to me again, and Heaven has forced this on him. If I follow Tengri's will, I cannot fail."

He was speaking of his own will, not Tengri's; perhaps he could no longer tell the difference. "I can't allow this," she said. "He and your anda will only see it as weakness, whatever you say. I'll speak to your men – they may listen to me. The Kereits meant them to be taken, and they'll want revenge as much as I do. Maybe one of them can convince you. They'll know I have only your true interests at heart."

"You are threatening to speak against my decision openly."

"I am."

He let go of her arm and slapped her, knocking her against the bed. "Toghril rode with me to save you," he said. "Don't make me regret that he did. When I held you again, did I shame you by rejecting the child you carried? My rage was great enough for me to pray the child would die, yet I put that aside for both your sake and mine."

Her eyes stung. He had never spoken of that in all the years since, but it had lain in his mind, a weapon he could wield when he needed it. Be grateful, he was saying, that I loved you. Be grateful that I could use you.

"I've given advice before," she murmured, "and you bene-fited from it. Am I now to be silent and let you do as you wish?"

"You may tell me what you think, but I'll decide what is to be done. When I do, my wife will not speak against me, or others will see her punished for it. You won't whisper to others that Toghril's faithless, or that I nurse any grudge against my anda. It's important to me that both of them believe I have forgiven them."

She could not stand against his will, and doubted that anyone could. He gazed at her coldly, the fire of the past days absent from his eyes. His warmth had been only a way to bend her to his purpose.

She said, "You must do as you see fit. I won't speak against you."

"I'm pleased to hear it." He stood up. "I think Borchu should lead a force against the Naimans on Toghril's behalf, and Mukhali and Chilahun could go with him – it's time I tested their valour. Perhaps my foster brother Boroghul can go as well. I must speak to Borchu, then give Gurin my reply. The servants will take you back to our camp."

"Temujin –"

He ducked through the entrance and was gone.

65

BOROGHUL RETURNED TO Hoelun's tent after the first snow-storm of the season, full of war stories. Shigi Khutukhu listened to his foster brother avidly. The Tatar boy had not cried for his mother since his earliest days in her camp, and Boroghul had forgotten his former Jurkin masters. Memories fled from the young as quickly as swans flew south to escape the winter; only the old had to carry their burden.

"Our brother the Khan," Boroghul was saying, "had given Borchu his favourite horse before we rode out, the grey-eared one, a rider has only to touch his mane and he flies like the wind. The Naimans were all around us, pushing to take the Senggum as hostage. A warrior bore down on Nilkha and wounded his horse in the leg. Nilkha went flying over the horse's head and hit the ground on his backside – I was sure they'd have him then."

"Did the Senggum get killed?" Shigi Khutukhu asked.

Munglik laughed. "If Toghril's son were dead," he said, "don't you think we would have heard that by now?"

"Borchu galloped to Nilkha," Boroghul continued, "and gave him Temujin's grey-eared horse. The Senggum sat on the great steed with all the grace of a supply pack." He chuckled. "He's a poor horseman, and the horse refused to move until Borchu leaped towards him and touched his mane. Off he went, neighing his war-cries so fiercely that the Naimans scattered before him. Now Nilkha is called a hero, but Temujin's horse showed more courage."

"You're a hero, too," Shigi Khutukhu murmured. "The four heroes, the arrows of the Khan – that's what the men call you and Borchu and the others."

Boroghul flushed with pride; for a moment, he seemed younger than his sixteen years. "I took my share of heads," he said, "and my comrade Mukhali showed he can lead men, but it was Borchu who won the battle. Toghril Ong-Khan gave him gold cups and a sable robe, and do you know what Borchu said? He thanked the Ong-Khan, and then said that he prayed Genghis Khan would forgive him for delaying his return to accept the gifts. That's the kind of man he is, thinking of Temujin instead of his spoils – as if Temujin would begrudge him anything."

Hoelun sniffed. "Little enough payment for what all of you did. Toghril should have given half his herds as a reward."

Munglik smiled at her indulgently. "Come now, wife – whatever Toghril may be, we're safer with the enemy gone from his lands. We'll have some peace now."

Hoelun pursed her lips. "For a time," she said.

PART SIX

Bortai said, "By the shores of the lake, there are many wild geese and swans. The master may take those birds he chooses."

66

BUYRUGH WAS THE last to arrive. "Peace," the Naiman murmured as he entered Jamukha's tent. "My men will wait outside with the others." Buyrugh spoke slowly, in the lilting accents of his people. He set down his weapons on the western side of the entrance.

"I welcome you," Jamukha said; the Naiman sat down with the other chiefs. Two servants set food and jugs near the men; Jamukha offered Buyrugh a bit of meat from his knife. Even this enemy was willing to join him now.

"I'll speak plainly," Jamukha continued. "We've all had our differences in the past, but I say again what my envoys told you. A pack of jackals preys upon our herds. To fight among ourselves will only leave more carcasses for them. It is time to rid ourselves of the scavengers."

"I came here reluctantly," Buyrugh said. "Three years ago, I suffered at your hands."

"It was Genghis Khan who chose to fight you."

"You rode with him."

"I also left him for your general to take," Jamukha said. "If he'd struck at Temujin then, we wouldn't have had to gather here."

Buyrugh scowled. "I mean to make up for that mistake. I cannot guard myself from my brother Bai Bukha with Mongols and Kereits at my back. I'll ride with you, and cast my spells on your behalf."

335

Targhutai Kiriltugh sneered. "Your spells haven't helped you much up to now."

Buyrugh glared at the Taychiut. Jamukha held up a hand. "It won't serve us to argue among ourselves."

Khudu leaned forward. "Targhutai should have taken care of Genghis Khan long ago," the Merkit said. "He could have killed the fledgeling in the nest, and my people have suffered for his failure. Now my father Toghtoga is forced to camp amid the cliffs of Baikal, and –"

Jamukha shot a glance at the Merkit. "I beg you not to speak of old grudges here. Temujin is the enemy of all of us. We must put the past aside to have any hope of defeating him." He paused. "I swore an anda oath with him, and lived to regret it. I lent him my sword and my men, and he betrayed me. I have as much to reproach myself with as any of you."

"And I bound myself to him with marriage to his sister," Chohos-chaghan muttered. "I thought I was choosing only a leader to follow in war." He grimaced, showing his yellow teeth, then rubbed at his lopsided face. "A war Khan, a Khan for the hunt – I thought that's what we would have, but my wife's brother wants more than that."

"I hope the sister pleases you more as a wife," Khudukha Beki said, "than the brother does as a Khan."

Chohos-chaghan grunted. Jamukha studied the chief of the Khorolas, wondering how much he could trust the man. Chohos-chaghan had left him before, and might desert him again.

This alliance, he knew, would be shaky. The Dorben chief had arrived with word that his people were now at peace with the Tatars, who would welcome any forays against their old enemy Temujin. Most of the Onggirats would support Jamukha but, as usual, would let others do the fighting. Khudukha Beki and his Oirats feared that Temujin might threaten their northern forests, while the Merkits and Taychiuts had many reasons to hate the Mongol Khan. Yet only a common enemy could have brought them together; they had many reasons to be suspicious of one another.

"There's no safety for any of us," Aguchu Bahadur said, "until Genghis Khan joins his ancestors." The Taychiut gnawed at his meat. "We must show that we're united in our purpose."

He glanced at Jamukha. "We should hold a kuriltai, and choose our own Khan."

Jamukha had hoped for this. "Surely," he said, "you mean only a Khan who would lead when necessary and leave you to settle your own affairs at other times."

"That's the only sort I want," Chohos-chaghan said. "It isn't the way Temujin would have it. No man leads a mingghan or a tuman in his army now until he's served in his personal guard, and the Khan has assured himself he'll obey without question."

"A Khan," Buyrugh muttered. "I suppose we must have one to lead us in this war, but which of us should it be?"

Aguchu sipped from his jug, then said, "The man who summoned us here. Who could be more suitable? He was the first to see that we had to join forces."

Jamukha looked around at the other chiefs; none of them was protesting these words. "If it is your choice," he said quietly, "and the will of Heaven that the kuriltai chooses me, then of course I would accept."

He wondered how long such a bond with these men would endure. A victory would unite them for a while, but once Temujin was defeated, each of them would be thinking of what he could gain. It did not matter; by the time the bonds frayed, he meant to be powerful enough to punish any disloyalty. He would see that they all honoured the oaths they swore to him.

67

HER BODY BURNED; her throat was parched. Bortai barely heard the chanting of the shamans. The baby had been hardly more than a bloody mass, coming from her womb too soon before the fever took her.

A hand slipped under her head; a cup rested against her lips as a bitter liquid trickled down her throat. She glimpsed the dark eyes of Teb-Tenggeri, then fell asleep to the sound of the shamans' drums.

She woke to silence. They had left her alone to die; the shamans would be outside, warning others away. Bortai opened her eyes and gazed into the faces of her sons.

"Mother," Ogedei whispered.

"You shouldn't be here," she said hoarsely.

"Don't you see?" Chagadai put his hand on her forehead. "The evil spirit's left you. Teb-Tenggeri came out earlier to tell us the fever was gone, that you were sleeping."

She slept again, and woke to the familiar sound of the servants' chatter. They brought her food and mare's milk and insisted that she rest. For three days, she was too weak to leave the tent without one of them to support her. Jochi came to tell her that the Khan had been up on Burkhan Khaldun for several days, leaving the mountain only a day ago.

Bortai waited for Temujin to come to her, but another day passed without his presence. By then, she had learned what all their camp knew. Her husband's enemies had gathered for a kuriltai; they had raised Jamukha on the felt and proclaimed him Gur-Khan, the Khan of All the People.

It was a sign. The death of the daughter she had borne a year ago, the loss of this child, the murmuring of the shamaness at her bedside telling her that there would be no more children, the loss of her husband's favour, and now the rallying of his enemies — they were all signs. The spirits, she thought, dealt with their people in much the way the Kin did, favouring one leader for a time before turning against him.

Temujin might need her now. Bortai put aside her pride and summoned one of the guards.

"Tell the Khan," she said, "that the yearning doe awaits the return of her stag. Tell him that it would give his Khatun great pleasure if he would deign to visit her tent." She sent the man away, knowing that Temujin might not come.

Only Bortai's sons and her servants ate with her that evening. She went to her bed sorry that she had sent her message. Her husband had more urgent concerns; he would be with his generals, discussing the threat that now faced them.

She was still awake when she heard voices outside. The great tent's wooden floor creaked as a servant hurried to the doorway. Bortai sat up and saw the Khan walking across the carpets towards her.

"I am happy you're well," he said, averting his eyes.

"And I'm pleased that you came to me, husband."

Temujin put a finger to his lips and glanced at the western side of the tent, where a hanging curtain hid their sleeping sons. He stripped quickly to his shift, then climbed in next to her.

"I went to the great mountain," he said at last. "I prayed for you there." He pulled the blanket over himself. "I went up alone because I didn't want my men to see me weeping for you."

"You wouldn't have lost so much," she whispered. "I can give you no more children, and you don't want my advice. I'm useless to you now."

"No, Bortai. I told myself that a wife who would have shamed me in front of my men, and urged them to disobey me, deserved to be punished." He slipped his arm around her waist. "Then, when I thought I might lose you, I raged at myself for not forgiving you long ago."

She covered his hand with hers. That admission must have cost him much.

"You're my luck, Bortai," he said. "If I lose you, I'll know that the spirits have deserted me." He was silent for a long time, then touched her cheek. "You're crying."

"There's a speck in my eye."

He wiped away her tears. "I must fight soon," he said. "I'm only waiting to see how I can do so with any hope of winning."

She drew his hand to her breast. "You were right to aid Toghril when you did, and I was wrong to protest it." He would expect her to admit that now. "You'll need the Kereits to defeat your enemies. Strike quickly, Temujin. If they're defeated, they'll scatter, and a hard enough blow could set them to fighting among themselves."

"So my men say, but I wonder —"

A sentry outside called out. Temujin sat up as Jurchedei entered the tent, hurried towards the bed, then bowed.

"Forgive me for waking you," the Urugud chief said, "but a man sworn to the Khorolas has come here, and begs to speak

339

to you. He's outside with Khasar, who brought him to us. Your enemies mean to surprise you."

Temujin was out of bed in an instant; he reached for his coat. "Send him inside." Jurchedei shouted the order and a man came through the doorway, followed by Khasar. Bortai covered herself with the blanket; Temujin sat down at her side.

The stranger bowed. "I am Khoridai," he said, "and I come in peace."

Temujin frowned. "Your chief didn't have peace in mind when he went back to my anda."

"Chohos-chaghan may already regret his oath to Jamukha." Khoridai reached under his coat and pulled out a silk scarf. "This scarf was one of your recent gifts to your sister. She sent me to tell you to flee."

Temujin's mouth twisted. "It seems her marriage wasn't so useless after all." He looked around at the others. "But I wonder how much Temulun could hide from her husband. This warning serves him. If I'm taken, he loses nothing. If I escape, he can claim he honoured his oath to me by acting as my spy."

"The Gur-Khan is marshalling his forces against you." Khoridai held out his hands. "He's to the east of you, in the Argun River valley where he was elected Khan. I had to hide from some of his men on the way here – they were travelling to him with a great yurt to raise for his victory feast. His army will advance in only a few days – you still have time to escape."

"He's moving fast," Khasar said. "You have to get away."

Temujin held up a hand. "I won't be a hare running from hunters. We'll give them the fight they want. Jurchedei, send envoys to the Ong-Khan telling him to lead his armies to me at once – Jamukha may strike at the Kereits next." The Urugud turned and hastened towards the doorway. "Khoridai, sit down. I want to hear everything you know about Jamukha's plans."

68

A SCOUT RODE to Jamukha's field tent to tell him that Genghis Khan's forces were on the move. Jamukha knew then that his anda had been warned. Yet he could still win. He had beaten Temujin in battle before, and had a greater force this time. A victory would erase the past.

Jamukha followed his light cavalry along the Argun River. Scouts reported that Kereits led by Nilkha, Jakha Gambu, and Bilge Beki were moving towards the plain around Lake Kolen; men under Daritai and Altan were also approaching that region. His own battle plan was clear. His light cavalry would fan out around the plain in a half-circle; he and his centre force would take up their positions near the mountains to the west of the steppe. When his men fell back to lure the enemy on, he would be fighting on higher ground as the two wings of archers closed around the enemy. The Kereits were likely to run when they realized the battle was lost. He would allow them a retreat before he crushed Temujin.

The later summer air was clear, the army undisturbed by Tengri's whims. As they skirted the marshes near the lake, clouds of ducks and cranes rose towards the sky, making the sound of a great wind. Left and right wings fanned out over the dusty yellow plain as the centre moved towards the mountain foothills. Flags and lanterns passed signals; Temujin's army would meet them at dawn.

Camp-fires flickered on the plain below Jamukha as his men prepared for the coming battle. He slept, his head resting against his saddle, and saw another plain. Sparks rose from the fires and became stars before winking out. A wind shrieked across the land, and in the sound of the gale, he heard the cries of dying men.

Jamukha woke. The sky was still dark, the night stars obscured by clouds. His dream was an omen; the spirits had told him what to do, and he had men who could summon them. He ordered the men around him to send for Buyrugh and Khudukha Beki.

The eastern sky was red; darkening clouds quickly doused the fire of the rising sun. In the distance, barely visible in the darkness, Temujin's nine-tailed standard was a tiny banner amid a thicket of lances. The air was growing sharply colder as the wind rose.

Jamukha did not fear the storm, which would become one of his weapons. His tools were not only swords, bows, and lances, but also the fortress of foothills, the wall of mountains behind him, and the threatening sky. There was beauty in battle, in taking many enemy lives while losing as few of his men as possible.

He waited near a small spring, watching flags dip as signals were passed. Khudukha Beki and Buyrugh rode towards him through the ranks of mounted men. "A storm gathers," Jamukha said as the two dismounted.

"Yes," Khudukha muttered. "We should order our men to hold their positions and wait until it passes. That is why you summoned us, isn't it?"

"A dream came to me," Jamukha said. "Koko Mongke Tengri is offering to aid us — that's what the spirits told me. You call yourselves shamans — I am asking you to turn this storm against Temujin." He held up his hand as the wind howled, then subsided. "It's moving towards the enemy, preparing to sweep them away."

"A wind can change," Buyrugh said. "Take my advice — draw more of the men back towards the mountains, where there's more shelter, and wait —"

"Retreat seems to be your only strategy," Jamukha said. "Can a few clouds frighten one who has the power to cast spells? They say that Temujin has a powerful shaman in his service — maybe I should have captured him to do my bidding."

The Oirat shaman-chief glowered at him; the Naiman's eyes were hard. "I have dreamed," Jamukha went on. "Tengri has promised a storm. Raise it and turn it to our advantage. Disobey me, and you'll be punished for claiming powers you do not have."

"I'll trust in my spells," Khudukha said, "not in your dreams." The Oirat and Buyrugh removed white stones from their pouches, set them on the ground, then knelt by the spring.

342

The two men chanted over the stones; the wind answered with a wail. Naccaras throbbed; the enemy was a dark wave flowing across the plain. Clouds billowed over the mountains as the wind rose. Buyrugh and Khudukha lifted their stones, spilled water over them, and called out to the spirits.

The rain came suddenly, in sheets of water as cold as ice. Jamukha could no longer see the plain; he stumbled towards his horse and mounted. The wind pushed at his back, driving him and his cavalry down the slope. The storm would drive Temujin's forces back; his own men would see that Tengri fought with them.

The wind shifted abruptly; pellets of ice stung his face. He was trapped behind curtains of ice, barely able to hear the shouts of the shadows around him through the wail of the storm. Other shadows fled towards him; Jamukha forced his horse on. His own men surged around him, panicked by the storm, blocking his way.

"Stop!" he shouted. Riders fled past him towards the mountain slopes. Unable to push forward, he turned back, riding past men and horses coated in ice. His horse climbed higher until a wall of rock blocked his way; the ice continued to fall. Ahead of him, a knot of horsemen suddenly dropped from view. Jamukha pulled at his reins, and his horse staggered at the edge of a precipice; sleet and hail pelted the bodies lying in the chasm below.

"Go back!" he cried to those behind him. "Ride for the river!" He lashed his way through the riders around him. Some turned to head back down the path, but others pressed on; the rattling of hail against stone muffled their cries. "To the river! Retreat!"

Jamukha kept moving, knowing that if he stopped for a moment, he and the horse would freeze where they stood. Let them all die, he prayed. Take them all – the enemy I fought, and those who failed me.

A cold, steady rain followed Jamukha and what was left of his army towards the Argun. His allies would be retreating to their own camps in the hope of protecting them; he would have no chance of regrouping against the enemy.

His dream had mocked him. He seemed to hear the voice of Tengri in the steady beat of the rain against his helmet: I warned you, Jamukha, and you failed to heed My warning, you failed to bow to My will.

They rode on, not stopping to rest, lest any pursuers catch up with them. By morning, the rain gave way to mist. Through the fog, Jamukha glimpsed the small dark mounds of a distant camp.

"Dorbens," a man near him muttered.

Jamukha looked back at the files of soldiers behind him. He still had the best of his men, the ones he could trust to obey him. "We won no booty from our enemies," he said. "We'll take what we need from this camp."

"They're allies," another man said.

"My allies scattered as birds do when they're startled by a hare," Jamukha said. "I owe them nothing. Pass the order – we're raiding this camp."

He took out his sword as he led them forward. He saw God's will; the spirits had cast him aside. Only blood could wash away his despair.

69

THE SURVIVING TAYCHIUT warriors fled towards their camps along the Onon, their enemies in close pursuit. There, by the river, Targhutai's son Aguchu rallied the men. They fought for a day, holding back the enemy until night fell. Their women and children, unable to escape as the battle raged around them, made camp next to the exhausted army.

She had brought this upon them. Khadagan moved past knots of men huddled around fires, searching for her husband. She had pitied a captive boy, and all of these people had paid for her pity. If she had known what would come of it, she would never have pleaded with her father to protect Temujin.

Other women crept through the camp, calling out names. A

woman wailed as she dropped to her knees by an injured man. Khadagan asked one group of men if they had seen her sons or husband, and learned more of the day's battle.

Many were dead on both sides. Several men had seen Genghis Khan's horse struck by an arrow and the Khan bleeding heavily from his neck before he retired from the fray. The warrior Chirkoadai had shot the arrows; so the men said. If the Khan was dying, his men might decide to withdraw. The soldiers fed on this hope as a starving man would gulp an onion dug from the ground.

The secret Khadagan had kept from everyone, even her husband, ate away at her. How could she hope for mercy from Temujin? He might have forgotten the girl who had guarded him while his Taychiut captors searched for him.

The camp grew quieter. The other women had either found their men or given up the search. Khadagan kept looking until a man directed her to another camp-fire. She found her husband near a makeshift pen for horses, his head against his saddle, his face drawn and sallow in the fire's light.

"Toghan." She sank down next to him and slipped her bow-case from her belt.

He gripped her arms. "I hoped you had escaped."

"We couldn't escape. The ones who tried didn't get far." She leaned back against the saddle. "Our sons — are they here?"

His sad dark eyes told her the answer before he spoke. "They were both with Uwa Sechen," he said. "He told me they were lost in the storm." Tears trickled down his sagging jowls. "It came so suddenly — the wind lashed us with ice. I saw men and horses freeze where they stood."

I deserve this, she thought; I'm being punished for what I've done. She wanted to ask Toghan if he knew anything about her father and brothers, but the weariness in his face kept her silent. He rested his head on her shoulder, and soon slept, but Khadagan was afraid to sleep. The ghosts of her sons would haunt her dreams.

Shouts roused them before dawn. Men struggled to their feet around Khadagan as a rider bore down on them. "We're lost!"

345

the man shouted. "Targhutai slipped away in the night – he and his cavalry are gone!"

People streamed towards the horse pen, tearing the ropes aside as they pushed past the wagons. Horses reared, knocking men to the ground. Toghan grabbed Khadagan's arm as arrows whistled overhead. The crowd milled around them and an arm struck her quiver, spilling her arrows. She gripped her husband's sleeve tightly as they struggled to the edge of the mob. Men rode towards them, pushing them back.

"Surrender!" an enemy soldier cried. "Resist, and you will die!"

A Taychiut leaped towards the man and pulled him from the saddle. Toghan grabbed at the horse's reins. The beast shook him off; Khadagan lost her grip.

"Toghan!" she shouted. A sword slashed past her, narrowly missing her shoulder. People ran towards the river, followed by enemy horsemen; others screamed as riders surrounded them. Khadagan darted through the crowd, looking for Toghan. Women and men raced past her on foot, the enemy just behind them. "Toghan!" she cried again. Something hard struck her head; she toppled forward.

She had fallen near a hill. Khadagan scrambled up the slope towards the obo above; in the darkness, she might be able to conceal herself amid the mounds of stones. Arrows flew by her; men rode past the hill, slashing at the people around them.

In the dim grey light, she saw the enemy herding Taychiuts towards the empty pen. "Toghan!" she screamed, heedless of her own safety. He had to be somewhere below, among the captives.

Only one man could save her husband. Temujin had told her that he would help her if she ever needed him; she prayed that he remembered that old promise.

"Temujin!" she cried. "Temujin, help me! Temujin!"

Two men reined in their horses near the hill; one lifted his head. "Who calls the name of our Khan?" he shouted back.

"Khadagan, daughter of Sorkhan-shira!" She flung her arms wide. "He'll know who I am! My husband's been captured by your men – tell Temujin that the daughter of Sorkhan-shira begs for her husband's life!"

The two disappeared into the throng. She continued to call out Temujin's name until she was hoarse, then crumpled to the ground. Knots of people were being pushed inside circles of wagons and ropes; trampled bodies littered the ground. The enemy would come for her soon. Exposed as she was on this hill, it was a wonder she had not already lost her life. The spirits of the obo were protecting her. They wanted her to see what her kindness and pity had brought to these people before she died.

The sky was growing lighter. Five men rode over bodies towards the hill. Khadagan got to her feet and held up her hands, palms out. "I am Khadagan, daughter of Sorkhan-shira!" she cried. "I beg you to let my husband Toghan live!"

A man dismounted and slowly climbed the hill; another hurried after him. She waited, expecting them to pull out their swords. "Take my life," she said, "but let Toghan live." She bowed her head.

"Khadagan." Hands gripped her by the shoulders; she forced herself to look up. He had grown tall, and his moustached face was dark with dirt and blood, but his pale eyes were Temujin's. "My men told me a woman here was shouting my name. I came as soon as they told me who you were."

"Save my husband," she murmured. "Please – I –" She leaned against him, then saw the wound in his neck, how pale he was under the coating of dirt.

"Come with me." The man with him caught his arm as they moved down the slope. "Find the Taychiut warrior called Toghan," he called out to the three men below, "and bring him to me alive."

Temujin, still weak from his wound, waited by Khadagan's side throughout the day while his men gathered prisoners and loot. A man named Jelme passed the Khan's orders on to his men; generals rode to Temujin's field tent to report to him. When no word came about Toghan, Temujin sent Jelme out to search for him.

"I owe Jelme my life," he told Khadagan as a guard laid fuel on his fire. "When that arrow caught me, he sucked the blood from my wound. He stripped off everything but his boots and crept into your camp without even a weapon, and stole kumiss for me. If he'd been caught, he planned to say that he had tried to desert us, and been robbed of all his clothes before he escaped."

"A brave man," she said.

"As you are brave, Khadagan. You saved my life long ago."

"I feared you might have forgotten." Her voice broke. "And now see what it's cost me."

He took her hand. "I'll do what I can for you. I promise you –"

Jelme was riding back to them. The man's hard face told her little. He dismounted, walked towards them, then squatted by the fire. "Temujin, I bring unhappy news."

"Say it," the Khan muttered.

"Your order came too late to save this woman's husband. His body lies with others who were executed. I said that he was to be buried with all honour –"

Khadagan let out a cry. "I brought this on him!" She tore at her robe. "May I be cursed for what I've done!" Temujin grabbed her hands; she tried to pull away, then sagged against him, too stunned to weep.

"I deserve to be cursed," Temujin said softly, "for not preventing this."

She drew her hands from his and covered her face. Tengri had touched him long ago; he had said so when he was a prisoner in her father's tent. Twenty years ago, he had promised that she would sit at his side, and the spirits had taken everything from her so that his promise could be kept.

"I promise I'll care for you, Khadagan," he continued. "I can't restore the husband you've lost, but ask me for anything else, and it will be yours – I swear it."

She lifted her head. Tears streaked his face; she had not thought he could weep. "There's one thing you can do," she said. "Show mercy to the people you've defeated here. Everything's been taken from me. Spare others my grief."

His eyes narrowed. He would refuse; he would be thinking of the men who had yoked and beaten him, of the children, now grown, who had taunted him.

"The leaders forgot their oaths to my father," he said. "They

348

abandoned me, tormented me, and joined my enemies to fight against me." He sighed. "But I made you a promise. There will be mercy, Khadagan, because it was you who asked for it."

Temujin stayed with her throughout the evening, sharing his food with her and consoling her. That night, he slept at her side, covering her with his own blanket.

Long ago, she had sometimes dreamed that Temujin might return to her. After her marriage, she had suggested to Toghan that he join the rising young Khan, but he had refused to consider it. He owed his leaders his loyalty, even when he had doubts about their wisdom. His loyalty had been ill-paid, with Targhutai abandoning them in the night. She would ask no mercy for Targhutai Kiriltugh.

At first, when she woke, she thought she was inside her own tent, then remembered. She lay under the blanket, crying soundlessly until her grief subsided.

When she sat up, Temujin was sitting near the field tent's entrance. He moved closer to her and took her hand.

"Because of me," he said, "you have nothing, but I'll always be your protector. If you wish, I'll make you my wife, and if not, you'll always have a place in my camp. My people will see that I don't forget those who helped me."

He pitied her then, and could use her to show others his nobility. He could not truly desire her. Khadagan felt a twinge of sorrow and guilt; even after all that had happened, she could still hope he might.

"You are generous," she said.

"You deserve anything I can give you. As my wife, you would be honoured, but if you can't bear to be –"

She shook her head. "I once wished for this as a girl," she whispered. "It seems my prayers were heard. I wish they could have been answered in another way, but I would be foolish to refuse you. My husband was a good man – he would have wanted me to have another to look after me."

"I am sorry, Khadagan."

"It might be kinder to send me to join him."

A voice called out his name; Temujin shouted back. Jelme entered, stooping as he came through the field tent's entrance.

"Some men have come here to surrender," he said, "and they want to speak to you. One of them says he's the father of this woman."

Khadagan started. Temujin helped her to her feet; she followed the two men outside. Sorkhan-shira, his hands bound behind him, stood with a small group of men, her brothers at his side.

"Father!" Khadagan ran to him and threw her arms around him, resting her face against his grey beard.

"Khadagan," he said. "I feared for you."

"I've lost my husband and my sons. I was afraid I'd lost you, too." She lifted her hands to cup his face. "Temujin tried to save my husband, but his order came too late." She clung to him as she wept.

"Free that man," Temujin commanded, "and his sons." Khadagan stepped back as soldiers cut at their bonds. "They gave me my freedom once – now I offer them theirs."

One guard stepped forward and gestured at a man who was still bound. "That one there shot the arrows that killed your horse and wounded you."

Khadagan recognized Chirkoadai. The Taychiut smiled slightly as he stared at the Khan. Temujin studied the man for a moment, then beckoned to Khadagan. She followed him to the fire with her father and brothers, then sat down.

"Sorkhan-shira," Temujin said, "I haven't forgotten what you and your children did for me. You daughter hasn't been harmed, and I'll do my best to make up for all she's lost."

Sorkhan-shira bent forward from the waist. "We came here to offer our swords to you. I would have followed you long ago, but I'd given my oath to the Taychiut chiefs." He sat back. "I offer you my oath now, and if Chimbai and Chilagun ever desert you, take their heads and leave their bodies for the jackals." He struck his chest. "My promise lives here."

"And I accept it." Temujin glanced at the other prisoners. "And who are these men with you?"

"Chirkoadai and a few of his comrades," Chimbai replied. "They also want to join you."

A guard pushed Chirkoadai forward. "An arrow struck me,"

350

Temujin said, "and another killed my horse. Now I am told they came from your bow."

"I admitted that to your men when I rode here." Chirkoadai's brown eyes narrowed as he grinned. "I freely admit it to you. Those arrows were mine."

Khadagan leaned towards Temujin. "I know this man," she murmured. "When I first saw you, he was the boy who was trying to keep others from tormenting you."

"Indeed." Temujin's mouth twitched. "And he nearly killed me."

"A man must defend himself and his people," the Taychiut said. "You could kill me, but then you'd have only a bit of bloodstained ground. If you let me live, I can lead armies for you. Well, what do you say?"

"What insolence," Jelme muttered.

"You're honest," Temujin said. "Somebody else would try to hide what he'd done against me, but you admit it. I won't punish a man for honesty, so I'll accept your oath." The guard with Chirkoadai freed his wrists. "I think you also deserve a new name. From now on, you will be Jebe, the Arrow, since your weapon found its mark."

The Taychiut rubbed at his wrists. "And I'll promise to aim my arrows at your enemies, not at you."

The Khan motioned to Jelme. "Give these men back their weapons, and guard this lady and her family." He stood up. "I must see to our prisoners – the wives and children of these men will be returned to them." He looked down at Khadagan. "I promised you mercy, but the chiefs and their sons must die. I can only spare the others, who were bound to follow them."

"I understand," she said. It would be the end of the Taychiuts as a clan; their followers would become Temujin's people.

A man brought a horse to the Khan. Temujin mounted and rode out, his men a shield around him. On the land below the grey sky, the prisoners were no more than another herd waiting for a new master to decide their fate. The vastness of the sky and the insignificance of those below suddenly filled her with terror. To Tengri, they were all only tiny creatures scurrying for shelter on the earth.

Her father reached for her hand. Khadagan huddled by the fire with him and her brothers, to rejoice and to mourn.

70

"THE KHAN'S ORDU," the rider nearest Khadagan announced, gesturing at the camp and at the great tent that stood in the north of Temujin's circle. They had passed several large herds on the way here. A few more victories, and Temujin's wealth might rival that of his Kereit allies.

A large yurt had been raised for her, with three smaller ones for the servants who would cook, sew, and look after the herds Temujin had allotted to her. Khadagan had expected his wives to visit her, but instead his chief wife Bortai sent a servant to her with a message. The Khatun welcomed her, grieved for what she had suffered, and would not trouble her with a visit until her sorrow was past.

Six days after her arrival, the Khan returned to his camp and invited his generals to a feast. Khadagan was summoned to the great tent with Temujin's three wives, and seated among them. The two minor wives whispered to each other, not bothering to hide their surprise that their husband had not claimed a beauty from the Taychiut spoils. Only a stern glance from Bortai silenced them.

The men talked of those who had surrendered to join Temujin. Among them had been a Bagarin and his two sons, retainers of Targhutai's who had captured the Taychiut chief. Temujin was silent as his general Borchu told the story. The three Bagarins, while on their way to submit to the Khan, had reconsidered their action, freed Targhutai, and confessed what they had done to Temujin.

"And how did they die?" the wife named Doghon asked.

Borchu Noyan laughed. "Die? Temujin rewarded them for it. They said they couldn't give up a man to whom they had sworn an oath, and the Khan praised them for doing the right thing – even made one of the young men a commander of one hundred on the spot." He laughed again. "They told us they had to put Targhutai in a cart – the old bastard's too fat to sit a horse easily. He won't last long alone."

The Khan was smiling, obviously content with his old enemy's fate. Targhutai would live for a while knowing he had lost everything; Temujin's victory was revenge enough.

Temujin did not come to Khadagan's tent until he had passed a night with each of his wives. "I've been merciful today," he said to her as they ate. "My sister's wretched husband finally showed his face. He says now that he only wanted to bridle me, not to put me under the ground, and that he's prepared to submit to me."

"And you forgave him?" she asked.

"Partly for my sister's sake, since she pleaded for him. I can also use Chohos-chaghan and his men."

When he sent the servants away, she brought him more kumiss, then retreated to the back of the yurt, grateful for the shadows. He was at her side before she could conceal herself under the blankets. He drew her shift from her, and she climbed into the bed, hoping that he would not be too disappointed; Toghan had told her that her body was still much like a girl's. A lump rose in her throat at the thought of her dead husband.

Temujin's strong hands were gentle with her, yet there was something cruel and demanding in the way he touched her and forced her to share his pleasure. He would bind her to him, compel her to forgive and love him. She shuddered under him as tears welled from her eyes.

Bortai Khatun summoned Khadagan to her tent two days later. A light snow had fallen in the night; people moved among the yurts, settling trunks in wagons and carts. They would move camp tomorrow, nearer to their winter grounds.

Khadagan passed the guards and climbed the wooden steps in front of the great tent, wondering why the Khatun wanted to see her. To assert herself, she supposed, to make it clear that, as Temujin's first wife, she expected obedience.

Bortai Khatun and her servants were in the eastern side

353

of the tent, packing clothes and pottery into trunks. Before Khadagan could utter a greeting, Bortai hurried to her and took her hands. "I welcome you, Khadagan Ujin. I'm sorry to take you from your work, but if we don't speak today, we won't get another chance soon with all that has to be done."

Khadagan bowed her head, then reached inside her coat. "Please accept this poor gift." She handed Bortai a long blue scarf.

"It's beautiful, and I thank you for it." The Khatun led her to the hearth and seated her on a cushion; a servant brought them goblets of kumiss. Bortai motioned the servant away, then sat down. "I've been wanting to speak alone to the woman whose family risked their lives to help Temujin. Without you, I would never have been a bride."

Khadagan had to smile at this; the woman still had a girl's smooth skin. "Khatun, I see what you are now. If you had even some of that beauty as a girl, your father probably could have made an army of your suitors."

Bortai flushed. "After we were wed," she said, "Temujin told me about the girl and the family who'd been kind to him. I was grateful he'd come to claim me instead of looking for her." Bortai's large brown eyes grew warmer. "He'll always honour you for what you've done, as I will. My husband has many loyal comrades, but only a few knew him as a boy and cared about him when he had nothing. You're one who did."

"He has others to love him now."

"And yet I think you do love him, maybe more truly than some others do."

"Yes." Khadagan closed her eyes for a moment; she had not expected to speak of this. "In spite of everything that's happened, I still can."

Bortai touched her sleeve. "I know what you've lost. That you can forgive my husband shows what a great spirit you have."

"You flatter me, Honoured Lady," Khadagan said. "Temujin did what he could for me, and it would have been foolish to cast his gifts aside. My lost husband was a good man, and I was happy as his wife, but Temujin won my heart long ago. Perhaps that makes it easier to forgive him."

"Our husband needs your devotion," Bortai said, "and so do I. His other wives –" She sighed. "Doghon wishes that she had him to herself, and bribes shamans to cast spells that would give her a son – she lost her first daughter and has only one other. Jeren fears him greatly, and I understand why, although I wish I did not." The Khatun paused. "I've often wished Temujin would find a wife who could also be my true friend. Temujin's good mother and the wives of his brothers aren't often in our camp, and the women of his generals see me as someone they must flatter. I have servants I can trust, but they're guarded in what they say to me."

"I see," Khadagan said. "You seek a friend who won't be thinking of what she might gain, and who has no need to fear you or to be jealous of you."

Bortai's long lashes fluttered. "Yes."

"And you think I might be such a friend. I have nothing to gain, since Temujin has given me more than I ever could have expected, and I can never have what I lost. I don't fear you, Khatun, because any suffering you might inflict on me could never be greater than the pain I've already endured. The Khan will always honour you as his chief wife, but even if that weren't so, you needn't worry that someone as plain as I could ever be your rival. I can't give him sons, so I won't be trying to secure places for them – my late husband's seed hasn't sprouted in me for years. I didn't mind that once, because I could enjoy him more easily without fearing the pain of child-birth, but that was when the sons I had still lived."

Bortai set down her goblet. "You speak freely, Khadagan."

"That is also required from a friend."

"True," Bortai murmured. "Often I have to tell Temujin what others fear to say, but there's no one to tell me when I might be wrong. With you, I'd know that, whatever you said, you'd have only our husband's interests in mind. I see what you are, Ujin. Your tent will always be in my ordu, so that I can seek your counsel."

"I'm not quite so selfless," Khadagan replied. "I know what my life with the Khan could become. He grieved for what I suffered, and owed me an old debt, but he's paid that, and regrets pass. In time, I might have been no more than a neglected minor wife, but I can remain closer to him through you, and be grateful for any scraps you give me from your platter. I think you saw that as well, Khatun." She was silent for a moment. "Of course I'll serve you both. I can do nothing else now."

71

YISUGEN AWOKE TO find her sister sitting up in her bed. Yisui's black braids were in a tangle, her face flushed with happiness.

Yisugen went to her and sat down. "Your braids need replaiting," she muttered as she combed out Yisui's long hair with her fingers; the servants had gone outside to prepare the feast. Their father was not in the great tent; Yeke Cheren had drunk heavily last night, and Yisugen had seen men carrying him to a minor wife's tent. The camp had been feasting for three days to celebrate the marriage of their chief's daughter, but Yisugen could not share their joy. She would lose her sister today.

She finished plaiting Yisui's hair, coiled the two braids behind her ears, secured them with pieces of felt, then grasped the other girl by the shoulders. In her sister's face, she saw her own long black eyes, sharp cheekbones, small flat nose, and curving mouth. Everyone said they might have been twins, although Yisui was one year older than she. The two sisters had never spent a day away from each other. Now Yisui would be taken from her.

"I don't want you to go," Yisugen burst out.

"Stop it, Yisugen," their mother said from the back of the tent. "Better to have Yisui wed now, so your father won't be distracted later when the chiefs hold their war kuriltai."

How carefree Yisugen had been a month ago, when the snow began to melt; she and Yisui had ridden out with their friends to hunt returning birds along the Khalkha River. They had returned to find Tabudai a guest in their father's tent, and the

356

young man had admitted that he had ridden to their Tatar camp to look for a wife. Warm glances had passed between him and Yisui whenever they were near each other; he had asked for her three days later.

"If Tabudai has so many herds," Yisugen said, "surely he can support two wives. Father should have said he'd have to take us both."

"What nonsense," her mother said. "He might have had second thoughts about Yisui if we'd demanded another bride-price for you. You're fifteen — a man's certain to come courting you soon." The older woman strode towards the doorway. "I'm going outside to make water, and when I come back, I want to see a smile on your face."

"You might have said something," Yisugen murmured when their mother was gone.

Yisui's arms slipped around her. "I'm sorry."

"You're not. You want to marry him."

"He might have asked for me instead of you only because I'm older. He thinks you're beautiful, too — he told me so." Yisui patted her face. "I'm lucky to have him. He'll be a chief someday, and — "

" — there's light in his eyes and fire in his face," Yisugen finished; she had heard her sister sing his praises too many times. "I hate him."

"Stop." Yisui caught her hands. "Didn't we promise each other we'd always live in the same camp?"

"You forgot that as soon as you saw Tabudai."

"I didn't," Yisui said softly. "I mean to make sure he's happy with me. When he'll give me whatever I want, I'll tell him to ask for you, before summer passes if I can."

Yisugen gaped at her sister. "But how — "

"I've been thinking of this all along. Father won't attack the Mongols before autumn, and he'll be too busy planning his war in the meantime to think of betrothing you. By then, I can convince Tabudai to ask for you. We'll be together again by next year."

"A year," Yisugen said, wondering how she could bear it.

"When I accepted him," Yisui continued, "I was thinking of you, too — I wanted us both to have a good husband." She chuckled. "I think Tabudai can handle two wives. His member is the size of a stallion's."

Yisugen was shocked. "How can you know that before you're wed?"

"I heard him say so to one of his men. He confessed that he grows so engorged at the thought of me that he can hardly sit his horse." Yisui laughed and covered her mouth.

"Men always boast about such things," Yisugen said.

"I'll soon find out if it's true."

Yisugen giggled. "Promise me you won't forget."

"I promise."

Yisugen kept near her sister as they hurried towards the horses; women fluttered around the bride. "Tabudai yearns for you," one of their cousins said to Yisui. "Make sure he doesn't catch you too soon."

"Struggle," an aunt said. "That always excites a man."

The horses had been saddled, and the women mounted and rode past the circle of tents and wagons. At some camp-fires, cauldrons simmered; at others, sheep roasted on spits. Beyond the camp, Yeke Cheren sat under a pavilion with his wives and his shamans, waiting to bless the bride and groom; a yurt guarded by some of Tabudai's men stood at a distance from the canopy.

Yisugen glanced at Yisui. Her sister's blue-edged coat and wedding robe were as white as the flowers beginning to bloom on the plain; her square head-dress was of birch bark and adorned with felt ribbons and stones. Yisui caught her eye and smiled; her light brown skin reddened as she blushed.

They rode west, towards the looming Khingan Mountains; their camp was near the birch-studded foothills. The grass was growing green; soon it would reach to a man's chest. She would be without her sister when the grass was high.

Yisugen looked to her left; Tabudai and the men in his party rode towards them from his yurt. The women lashed at their horses, keeping the bride in their midst. The men bore down on them and quickly surrounded them, whooping and shouting as they came closer. Women shrieked, reined in their horses, and blocked Tabudai as he steered his horse towards his bride.

Yisugen forced her mount to Yisui's side, then struck at Tabu-dai; he drew back and laughed, showing his white teeth.

Yisui's horse bolted from the group. Yisugen's horse reared; the others galloped after her sister, Tabudai in the lead. His horse was soon abreast of Yisui's. He leaned towards his bride; his arm caught her around the waist. In one swift movement, he pulled her on to his saddle.

The others cheered as the couple rode back towards Tabu-dai's yurt. Yisugen's eyes stung as she trotted after them. Yisui was so close to Tabudai that they looked like one rider; the bride had already forgotten her sister.

Yisugen sat near her father as the servants set down their meal. Yeke Cheren ate with a distracted air. During the five days since Yisui and her mother had left for Tabudai's camp, he had been consulting with his generals and waiting for word from his scouts. He was already planning his war. Tabudai might have to ride with the army before autumn, and then Yisui would not get a chance to talk him into paying court to her.

Maybe her father could make a truce. Yisugen thought of hinting at it, but he would never listen to talk of battle or truces from women and girls. He had given her mother the worst beating of her life that past winter, when she had suggested he seek a peace with the Mongol Khan.

Women were cowards; he said that often. They did not care which master they served, and there could be no peace with the Mongols. They had destroyed many Tatar clans with the aid of the Kin; he would have the Mongol Khan's head for that, and for his lies about Tatars poisoning his father.

They ate in silence. If Yisui had been here, she and her sister would have been chattering about the new lambs, or asking Yeke Cheren if one of their brothers might break in new horses for them. She felt her sister's absence most in the evenings. Five days, she thought despairingly, and wondered how she would endure the year of days ahead.

"You've been sullen lately," Yeke Cheren said abruptly.

Yisugen looked up. "I miss Yisui."

"She had to be married sometime."

"And I'm happy for her," she added quickly. She was wary

359

of him when darker spirits afflicted him. He brooded alone then and lashed out at anyone who came near him, and he had been drinking all evening.

"I'll have to marry you off, too. When girls your age start acting like sick calves, it's time to give them away."

"No!" she cried out. Her father's hand tightened around his jade goblet; he warned her with his eyes. "I mean, you have so much to think about now. After all, if you're going to fight a war — " His face darkened. "I meant that, when the war's over, any man who courts me would have more loot, and be able to offer you more for me."

He tugged at his greying moustache. "True." He motioned with one hand; she helped a servant clear away the platters and empty jugs.

Yisugen went to her bed on the tent's eastern side, feeling a pang of sorrow as she glanced at the spot where Yisui's bed had been. She was about to remove her robe when a sentry called out to Yeke Cheren.

A man hastened inside, went to the bed where her father sat, and bowed. "Word has come from our scouts, Cheren," the guard said. "Mongol scouts were sighted beyond Lake Kolen, and others are moving towards us from the west. The Onggirats are already moving their camps north-east."

Yeke Cheren cursed. "The damned Onggirats show their backs to their allies, then expect us to reward them for not joining our enemies. Do the Kereits ride with Temujin?"

The man shook his head. "It seems he's fighting this battle alone."

"Good. I didn't expect it this soon, but we're ready to deal with the Mongol dog." The two men crossed to the doorway. "Summon the generals — we'll meet the enemy on the steppe west of Lake Buyur."

Yisugen sank to her bed. Let it be over quickly, she prayed. Give us victory and bring me to my sister's side.

72

FOR TWO DAYS, the camp was filled with the noise of an army readying for battle. Swords were sharpened, arrows fletched, arrowheads fashioned, lances sharpened, and armour coated with pitch and then polished. Captains assembled their men, gear, and horses and, just as suddenly, the army was gone, riding west.

Ten days later, Tatar warriors were seen galloping towards Yeke Cheren's camp along the Khalkha, and the people knew from the sight of them that they were in retreat. Many were without their strings of war-horses; they fled towards the Khingan foothills, and the camp followed them. Women took what they could on carts, but many fled on horseback or on foot, abandoning their possessions and herds. The great tent of Yeke Cheren was left behind.

In the foothills, the people made barricades of tree limbs and wagons. Soldiers spoke of how the Mongols had refused to retreat, regrouping to come at them again; some claimed that Genghis Khan had ordered his men to kill any warrior who retreated. Other Tatars made their way to the foothills, men who had been captured by the Mongols and had overcome their guards to escape, and the people learned that they could expect no mercy if they surrendered. The Mongol Khan had decreed that every male Tatar would die.

A wing of the Mongol army soon appeared in the valley below. At night, their camp-fires blazed; at dawn, they struck, riding towards the barricades in waves, renewing the assault each time they were thrown back. When the first row of trees and wagons was breached by the enemy, and Yisugen saw bloodied swords slashing towards men, women, and children alike, she fled.

I am a coward, Yisugen thought. Others had fled up the forested slopes, but she had been intent on her own escape, and now she was alone, with only her bow, a few arrows, and a knife. She ran, expecting to hear men in pursuit, but the thick underbrush slowed her. When night came, she curled up against a poplar, afraid to sleep.

Her father was among those who had escaped from the Mongols, but he had been behind one of the lower barricades, in the midst of the fighting. She should have fought with him. Other women had stayed with their men. She did not deserve to be alive when so many of her people were dead.

In the morning, she looked for food. The few berries she found were not yet ripe; she dug out a root and ate that instead. She finished her skin of kumiss and knew she would soon have to find water. She did not dare to move towards the river, where the Mongols would be searching for Tatars driven there by thirst.

When the deep green light under the trees grew brighter, she heard the sound of thrashing and cracking twigs below. Slipping an arrow into her bow, she crept down the slope and came to a birch grove.

A small boy lay there, his head against a tree trunk. One look at his pale face and the bloodstain swelling over his belly told her he was dying. He opened his eyes; she knelt by him and cradled his head in her arms.

"They took everyone away," he said faintly, "the ones still alive. Then they began to measure us against the linch-pin on the wheel of one cart. They —" He gulped air. "The order was that any male taller than a linch-pin had to die."

Yisugen's throat tightened. "But only the very youngest boys would be shorter."

"I'm taller than a linch-pin — that's why I ran. Wasn't quick enough — one of them gutted me with his knife and left me for dead, but I crawled here." The child's mouth twisted. "Our men slipped their knives under their sleeves. Yeke Cheren told them to make grave pillows out of the Mongols who came for them, so many of the enemy died, too."

The boy closed his eyes. When he was dead, Yisugen searched him, but found nothing she could use. She folded his arms over his chest, whispered a prayer, then left the grove.

Her father should have made a truce. She knew at last what her mother had been trying to tell him. Wars only made spoils of women, forcing them to serve the victors; her mother had been pleading for the lives of their people.

A storm came that night. She huddled under a makeshift shelter of branches, holding out her skin to fill it with water. After the storm passed, and the forest was filled with the sounds of gentler spirits, she crept under the branches to sleep.

A dream came to her. She sat with her mother under the trees; the pale, ghostly light on the woman's face told her that her mother was dead.

"You came for me," Yisugen said.

"I have not come for you," the ghost replied. "I ask you this, daughter – why do our people weep for our dead? Why does our blood seep into the ground? Why have our yurts been desecrated and our women ravaged?"

"Because the Mongols hate us."

The ghost said, "It is also because your father, and all those who led us, failed us. There's no safety for women and children under Heaven if their men cannot defend them. No one remains among our people who can protect you – your only hope for life lies with the victors."

Yisugen said, "I would rather die."

"No, you would not. A spirit wouldn't have seized you and carried you from the barricades if you were meant to die. You must live, and seek safety however you can."

Yisugen awoke; her mother was gone. Yisui's shade had not appeared to her and that had to mean her sister was alive. If Yisui were dead, her soul would have been torn in two. Yisui had promised they would always be together; if her sister had died, her spirit would have come for her.

She stood up, knowing what she would have to do, then moved down the hill.

Flocks of black birds wheeled in the sky. Birds roosted on piles of heads; other heads had been placed on pikes. Captives, under guard, were dragging corpses away while leaving others behind. The enemy would have his own men buried and leave the Tatar bodies to rot.

Yisugen smoothed down her masses of braids. Mongols on horseback patrolled the plain of high grass, but she would gain nothing if common soldiers found her. She had to look for a Noyan who commanded many, who might keep her for himself and help her find Yisui.

She scanned the land below. To the south, near the river, several horses were tethered. A tall man strode along the bank with several men; those he passed bowed or raised their arms in a salute. He had to be one of their generals, and the tall grass would hide her until she was close to him. She crept down from the trees, crouched low in the grass, then crawled slowly towards him.

When she was closer, she halted, afraid the men might see the grass moving around her. The general took off his helmet for a moment to wipe his brow. His dark braids had a coppery tint; the metal flaps of his helmet were studded with gold. When the wind rose, she moved on, knowing the swaying grass would hide her movements, and took a deep breath. As she was about to stand, the Noyan's head whipped towards her. The bows of the men were in their hands in an instant; two of them moved in front of the general and took aim.

"Don't shoot!" Yisugen cried desperately, flinging her hands above her head. Another man came towards her, grabbed her bowcase, and dragged her forward by one arm.

"Take her knife," the general said in a soft voice. "It would be a pity to kill her."

Yisugen's hastily formed plan fled from her mind. "Kill me, then!" she shouted as a man pulled the knife from her sash. "You've killed everyone else!" She collapsed on the ground, sobbing for all she had lost.

A foot nudged her painfully in the side. "Let her weep," the general said. She cried until she felt a hand on her shoulder, then looked up to meet a pair of pale brown eyes flecked with green and gold.

"Drink this, child." The Noyan knelt and handed her a leather bottle; she gulped the kumiss. "Where were you hiding?"

"In the foothills," she managed to say.

"What brought you down?"

"I have nowhere else to go." She shoved the bottle at him and began to cry again. He slipped one arm around her, letting her rest against his breastplate. It was strange that he would be so kind when his people had shown such cruelty; perhaps he had obeyed his Khan's orders only out of duty.

He smoothed back her hair, as if she were a small child, then said, "What is your name?"

"Yisugen." She wiped her nose on her sleeve. "Daughter of Yeke Cheren."

One of the men laughed. "A beauty, and the chief's daughter, too – she'll make a nice prize for some man."

"I'm claiming this one for myself." The pale-eyed man stood up and pulled her gently to her feet. "This war is over for you, Yisugen. You'll be taken back to my tent. Mourn for your people when you're alone, but show me no more tears."

He led her towards the horses, trailed by his men. Another man rode towards them, lifting his hand as he reined in his horse.

"Your uncle has ridden to us," the rider said. "He waits by your tent, demanding to speak to you."

"Demanding?" The general's voice was still soft, but Yisugen heard the hardness in it. "He can wait."

"Your half-brother is also there, as you asked."

"Very well, Borchu." He pushed Yisugen forward. "See what crept down to us from the hills. If she pleases me, I may make a wife of her."

Yisugen's face burned as she glared at the man called Borchu; he grinned. "She looks worthy of you, Temujin."

She froze in horror. Temujin – their Khan. She looked up at him; his pale eyes danced with amusement. "You see how well you chose when you gave yourself up," he said, then lifted her to a horse.

The Khan had claimed her father's tent for his dwelling. Yisugen's mind raced as they approached the great tent. He had ridden against her people and made of them no more than the ashes of a fire. There could be no mercy in him.

Yet he also had more power to find her sister than any man here. Had her mother's spirit seen this? Could she have meant to send her into the arms of her father's most hated enemy?

Your father failed us, her mother had said; she had to seek safety wherever she could.

The Khan greeted the men waiting by the tent before climbing the wooden steps to the entrance; she followed him. Inside, harnesses, saddles, and weapons lined the tent's western wall; on the eastern side, five captive Tatar women knelt and pressed their heads to the carpets.

"Give this girl a woman's robe," the Khan said, "and something to cover her hair." He pushed Yisugen towards the women; one hurried to a trunk and pulled out a robe of blue silk. Her mother had worn that robe; a lump rose in her throat as the woman helped her into it, then put a white scarf over her head.

The Khan walked towards her father's bed and sat down. A table had been placed near it; she noticed then that the table was a plank of wood tied to the backs of two bound men on their hands and knees. The Khan's men entered and settled themselves on cushions around the table.

"Come here, Yisugen," the Khan called out. She went to him and was about to sit at his feet when he reached up and pulled her to the bed. "Next to me." She seated herself, averting her eyes from the table and the prisoners underneath. The women, their eyes wide with terror, set jugs and platters of meat on the plank; the men under it groaned softly.

"Still alive," the man named Borchu said. "We'll see how they do when we dance on their backs." The others laughed.

The Khan beckoned to a guard by the doorway. "I'll speak to my uncle and brother now."

Two men came inside, bowed from the waist, then lifted their heads. The younger one resembled the Khan, but had dark eyes; the older one scowled. The Khan was silent as he sprinkled a blessing, turning to throw a few drops towards the back of the tent. Yisugen saw then that the ongghons of her parents were gone and a carved wolf's head hung in their place.

The two men in front of them waited; the older one fingered his grey moustache as the Khan offered bits of meat to his men from his knife.

"You've forgotten your manners, nephew," the older man said at last.

366

"You forgot to obey," the Khan replied.

"My men and I took our share of blows. Now Jebe's taken all my spoils from me, and said he did so at your command. He took Altan's and Khuchar's as well. I came to you to demand them back."

"Demand?" The Khan's eyes narrowed. "No one demands anything of me. You heard my orders. Didn't I say that no one was to begin looting until the fighting was done, and that I'd see the spoils were shared equally after that? You disobeyed me, Daritai. You, Altan, and Khuchar were to give chase to the enemy instead of collecting your booty. For disobeying me, you'll have nothing."

Daritai's face whitened. "You'd treat your own uncle and your cousin so? You'll tell Altan, Khutula Khan's son, that he'll have nothing?"

"My men will know that anyone who disobeys me will be punished. For disobeying me, you'll enjoy no spoils. For daring to object to my decision, you'll no longer be privileged to attend my councils."

"You'll be sorry for this, Temujin."

"I am sorry already." He was speaking in the same soft voice; the steadiness of his tone made Yisugen shiver. "Now get out of my sight before I strip you of your rank as well."

Daritai wheeled around and strode from the ordu. The Khan gazed at the other man. "And you, Belgutei – your carelessness cost us many lives. When the Tatar prisoners heard what we intended for them, they had nothing to lose by putting up a fierce fight."

"I didn't think – "

"It was your business to think, but instead you bragged to the captives about the sentence we had passed, and many of our men died because of that. You'll also be banished from our councils – you'll keep order in the camp while we deliberate, and will enter only when the meeting is over. Go, and be grateful I've left you your head."

Belgutei left them. The men feasted and drank; occasionally a few of them leaned on the table with their elbows, making the men under it groan even more. Most of their talk was of the war, the people they had slain, the loot that was now theirs.

367

Borchu got to his feet at last. "The mares need milking," he said, "and the night guard must be posted." The other men stood up; Yisugen suddenly wanted them to stay.

"Take that table away, too," the Khan said. "I won't dance on it tonight."

"They'll be dead by morning," another man said.

"Then they'll have served us well, and have an honourable death for their reward."

The men removed the plank and dragged the prisoners away. "Leave us," the Khan said to the women; they scurried from the tent.

Yisugen sat stiffly, afraid to move. He said, "This was your father's tent, wasn't it?"

A whimper escaped her. "Yes."

"Perhaps I'll give it to you." She squeezed her eyes shut. "Don't look so unhappy, Yisugen. When you came out of hiding, what led you to me? You risked death by making your way to me – in another moment, my men's arrows would have found your heart."

She did not reply.

"I know why you came to me. You were wise enough to know that, whatever the risk, your greatest safety lay there."

"I'm not wise," she said bitterly. "I knew what your soldiers would do to me if they found me. I wanted only to find a Noyan who might take pity on me. If I had known who you were, I would have sent my arrows at you."

He chuckled. "What a child you are. Fear drove you into the foothills, and sent you back here, and now your childish pride makes you pretend you might have been braver." His hand closed around her wrist. "Had the Tatars defeated me, they would have shown no mercy to my people. This battle had to come, or there would be no peace for us. Your people welcomed my father to a feast, then sinned against the guest they were required to honour by poisoning him."

"You've had your revenge," she whispered.

"I didn't do this only for revenge. Many who once fought against me now serve me, but the hatred between your people and mine ran too deep for anything except death to end it. If I had shown mercy here, and allowed my enemies to live, that

368

hatred would have endured, and many more would have died later."

Another man would not have troubled to explain his deeds to her. She saw no pity and doubt in his eyes, only the grim contentment of a victor. "Tengri," he said, "intends that I should rule, and make an ulus in these lands."

He believed it. No one could stand against a man who saw his own will and God's as the same. She felt the talons of a hawk close around her heart.

"You may cling to your hatred and your childish resentments," he said, "or you may lay them aside. It makes no difference to me. There's pleasure enough for a man in crushing the wife or daughter of his enemy in his arms, in knowing she has to submit even as she mourns her dead."

He tore the scarf from her head, then pushed her to her feet. "Take them off," he said. She undressed quickly; he untied her tunic and pulled it from her. She scrambled into the bed, grabbing at the blanket. He was a looming shape outlined by the glow of the hearth fire behind him; he undressed slowly and climbed in with her.

Yisugen tensed, swearing silently that she would not weep. One of his arms slid under her while his hand stroked her belly; her hands flew up and pushed against his chest.

"Don't fight me," he said. He forced her legs apart; his fingers probed her cleft, circling the nub and moving closer to the opening of her sheath. He might have guessed her secret, that she sometimes lay under her blanket and toyed with herself until her pleasure sent her soul soaring; her cheeks burned with shame. She let out a moan and he continued to stroke her until her nerves felt like fire. Her hips moved, and then he was suddenly upon her, his broad body pressing her against the bed as his shaft thrust inside her. The pain made her cry out; the promise of pleasure vanished, and his hands bruised her as he claimed another victory.

Yisugen kept her eyes closed. The Khan stirred next to her. During the night, he had joined with her again, locking her hand around his member until it swelled, touching her until she quivered under him, her body as tightly strung as a bow when he finally guided himself into her.

It was easier not to think, to ignore the small voice inside her, to forget what had passed. She had pleased him, and because she had, he might grant her what she wanted most. That was all that mattered; she had to put aside the shame and sorrow she felt at responding to him. She could not help those who were dead, but might still save the living.

She rolled away from him and sat up, then covered her face.

He said, "I told you not to weep."

Yisugen forced tears from her eyes. "I'm crying because I may have lost the one I love most." She paused, trying to think of what to say next. "I have a sister named Yisui. She's a year older than I am, and all our lives, we swore we'd never be separated." Yisugen's tears were flowing freely now, her longing threatening to overwhelm her. "Yisui was married just before our men rode out to fight. Her husband may have died in the battle, but she must be alive somewhere." She shuddered. "I'd know if she weren't – we were too close for me not to feel it. Before her wedding, she promised me she'd bring her husband to take me as a second wife, so we could be together again. How can I do less for her, when there's no one to protect her?"

"I see," he said, "that you have much family feeling."

"You have the power to restore her to me," Yisugen said, "and she'd be a good wife to you. People say we look much alike, but Yisui's more beautiful than I am, and much wiser. I'd love you if she were with me again, and she would love you, too." She had to hope that Yisui's joy at their reunion would quiet any hatred she felt for the Khan.

"So you wish me to take another wife," he said. "If she's older than you, she should have a higher place than yours. Would you give up your own place to her?"

"I would." She reached for his hand. "I'd take a lower place just to have her at my side."

He pulled her down to him. "If she's like you, then I must find her. My men will look among all our prisoners, here and in other camps. If she's not found, I'll send men out to search for her. Such love between sisters touches me."

"And I beg you to spare any of my people you find during the search."

He grunted. "Very well – you may have their lives, too." His hand moved between her thighs. "Now reward me for my generosity."

73

TABUDAI AWOKE WITH a cry. Yisui held him until he stopped trembling. He was remembering the battle again, the waves of enemy horsemen who could not be thrown back.

"Steady," she whispered. He pushed her away and lay down, curling up like a child. She thought of how bravely he had ridden to war; the battle had changed him.

"I'm a coward," he said.

"You're not. The battle was lost, and you had to warn us. Men often retreat before turning to fight elsewhere." She should not have said that; Tabudai had not been thinking of finding another place to fight when he ran.

"I'm cursed," he muttered. "Admit what I am, Yisui – I can't bear to hear you repeat your lies."

"They're not lies." They had said all these words before during the days of hiding in the foothills, and her efforts to rally him only brought her beatings. He had been gentle the first time he came to her bed, brushing his lips against hers, calming her fears. Perhaps the gentleness was only a sign of his weakness.

Yisui crept out from under the branches they had used to make a hut. The sky above the forest was growing light; her belly ached with hunger. Their only food for the past days had been berries and roots, and she would have to forage further from the shelter to find any today. Their one horse was tethered by the hut; soon they would have to open a vein and drink the gelding's blood to feed themselves if Tabudai refused to hunt.

He would not let her out of his sight, as if fearing she might abandon him.

He had left her mother and his own people to fend for themselves; he had not stopped to man the barricades they had set up in the lower hills. One man who had escaped had told them of the savage assault, of Mongols riding over the bodies of their dead comrades to reach the Tatars. Her mother had made it as far as the barricades and had rallied the people as if she were a chief herself. So the man who had escaped the carnage said, before he left her and Tabudai to make his way north; he had also seen her mother die. The Mongols would not have allowed her father and brothers to live. And Yisugen —

Her sister could not be lost. Their souls were too closely linked; if Yisugen were dead, she would die, too.

The horse lifted its head and flicked its brown ears. Yisui heard only the twittering of birds. The Mongols would search this region soon; only yesterday, she had heard a distant voice call out, biting off words in the way the Mongols did.

She knelt by the shelter. "Tabudai," she said, "we must go north, to the forests. We'd have refuge there." Her husband said nothing. "I'm going to the brook to fetch water, and then we must leave this place."

He crawled out of the hut. "How brave you are," he said. "How you cling to any hope of saving your cowardly husband."

"I'm not brave. I shake with terror every time I hear a twig crack. And you're not cowardly. Some of our bravest ran from the enemy. Tabudai, you must — "

His hand caught her on the side of the head; she blinked and swayed dizzily. "I should have let them kill me. Better to be dead than shamed by my wife."

"You shame yourself," she whispered. "I have only you now, and you do nothing." She stood up and adjusted the scarf around her head. "I'll get water."

She crept down the hill, then looked back; Tabudai was following her. She moved slowly, alert to any sound, until she heard the faint trickle of the water. The brook was only a tiny stream; soon it might dry up completely.

As she bent down to fill her waterskin, a voice shouted

372

below; she froze. Someone was coming up the hill. Tabudai thrashed his way up the slope; the noise he was making would draw the enemy. She thrust the skin under her sash and hurried after him. A horse below whinnied; she tripped over her long coat and fell, then struggled to her feet and climbed towards the hut. Through the spaces between the trees, she saw Tabudai free the horse and leap to the saddle. Before she could call out to him, he was gone.

Branches clawed at her. Yisui staggered to the hut, then sank to the ground; she could not escape on foot. Rage at Tabudai rose inside her; she struggled against it. He could not have defended her by himself, and it was less likely they would kill a woman. She wondered if he had been thinking of that, or only of his own fear.

Ten horsemen emerged from the trees and trained their bows on her. "Mercy!" she cried, then pulled her scarf more closely around her face.

"You won't die," one man said. He waved an arm. "Follow the other one." Five of the men moved off through the woods; the man who had spoken dismounted, walked towards her, and pulled her to her feet. "What is your name?"

"Yisui," she whispered, "daughter of Yeke Cheren."

The Mongol threw back his head and roared. "The Khan will reward us well for finding you."

She gaped at him, stunned. "Your Khan seeks me?"

"Yes." He pushed the scarf back from her face. "Now I see why."

"Too bad," another man said. "We could have enjoyed her."

Yisui shuddered. The Khan could only want to claim a daughter of Yeke Cheren to mark his victory. She would have to endure the man who had destroyed her people.

The five Mongols took Yisui down the hill to where other horsemen waited with several Tatars, all of them women and children. One man rode ahead to tell the Khan of their capture; the rest put the prisoners on spare horses and followed, stopping to graze the animals and to make camp. They reached her father's camp in three days, and by then the other five men had caught up with them, giving up the search for Tabudai.

Yisui averted her eyes from the spiked heads near the camp, afraid she might see her father's. Her captors took her to Yeke Cheren's tent as the other prisoners were led away.

A guard greeted them in front of the great tent. "Welcome, brothers," he called out. "The Khan was pleased to hear of your find. He's hunting by the river – go there to ask for your reward, and leave the woman here."

Yisui dismounted. Another guard went up the steps and called out to those inside. Her hands trembled as she smoothed down her coat.

"Yisui!"

She looked up. Yisugen stood in the entrance, wearing the long pleated robe and high head-dress of a Noyan's wife. For a moment, Yisui imagined that she would step inside to find her mother by the hearth and her father seated near his bed. "Yisugen," she whispered, then raced up the steps and threw herself into her sister's arms.

They clung to each other, weeping with joy, unable to speak. At last Yisugen sent the other women away and led Yisui to a cushion.

"I prayed they would find you," Yisugen said. "When I was told they had, my heart nearly burst."

Yisui wiped at her face. The shock of seeing her sister faded as she understood why Yisugen was here. "I begged the Mongol Khan to search for you," Yisugen continued, "and now you're with me, just as he promised."

"You asked him to look for me?"

Yisugen nodded. "I told him I would give my own place to you, that you'd be an even better wife to him."

Yisui flinched. "I was with Tabudai."

Her sister gasped. "He's alive?"

"We escaped to the hills together. When the Mongols found me, he fled on our horse." Yisui's mouth twisted. "So now I'm to belong to our father's murderer."

"Yisui – "

"Mother died at their hands – a witness told me so. The ground has closed over many of our people."

"We're together," Yisugen said. "What else can we do except

live how we can? Those still alive may need us to plead for them. My only chance to find you rested with our enemies – that's why I gave myself up."

Yisui recoiled. "You surrendered yourself?"

Yisugen took her hand. "Mother told me to do it." She looked away. "I was hiding in the hills, and Mother's spirit came to me in a dream. She told me our men had failed us, and that I had to seek safety however I could. She sent me here – I didn't know at first, when I surrendered myself, that I had found their Khan." She took a breath. "Mother's spirit guided me to the heart of our enemy, and we can be no safer with anyone else. You're all I have left. Don't hate me because you were brought here."

"How can I hate you? I feared for you as much as you did for me. If we must belong to these people, better to be the women of their Khan than slaves to some other man." Yisui slipped her hand from her sister's. "Your plea must have touched him. I wouldn't have thought there could be any kindness in such a man."

"It isn't kindness," Yisugen murmured. "He may show kindness, but I don't know if he feels any pity or love. It amused him to bring you to me, and to claim us both. When he sees devotion, when he's pleased, he rewards those who serve him. I would never want to fail him, Yisui. If I did, one look from him would burn away my soul."

Yisui said, "And this is the man who would claim me."

"I'd rather seek the shelter of the eagle's nest than to have his shadow cover me before he strikes. He's the only shield we have now."

The Khan returned to the tent that evening with several of his men. One look at his strange, pale eyes told Yisui that her sister had spoken the truth. She shrank back as he circled her. Yisugen had given her a clean robe and head-dress, but the days in hiding could have done little for her looks.

"So you are the sister," he said, "whom my new wife begged me to find." His soft voice terrified her. His eyes were like a cat's; he was toying with her, letting her know that only he

375

could decide her fate. "She said," he went on, "that she would give up her own place to you, should I choose to keep you."

"I pray that you will." Yisui glanced at her sister, who was kneeling next to her; Yisugen's dark eyes were wide with doubt. He might give her away, part her from Yisugen, simply to show that he could.

"Yes, I'll keep you." He smiled. "My men went to some trouble to find you."

He went to the bed as she and Yisugen got to their feet. Women brought food and drink to the men; Yisui sat at the Khan's left, with Yisugen next to her. Yisugen whispered to her, pointing out each Noyan by name as the men drank and talked among themselves. Yisui thought of how her father's men had acted around him, warily, with cautious words; this Khan's men seemed at ease with him.

The men had finished their food when the one named Mukhali stood up. "I'd accept more hospitality," he said, "but you must be impatient to enjoy your new woman." The others said their farewells and left. After the women had cleared away the platters and jugs, the Khan dismissed them.

"I had my doubts," he said, "when Yisugen asked me to look for you – I didn't think I'd find another with her beauty." His handsome face wore a kindly expression, yet seemed like a mask; his eyes glittered like gemstones. "She told me you were recently wed."

"Yes," Yisui murmured. "My husband fled when your men found me."

"It was good that he did. Yisugen made me promise to spare the lives of any who were found during the search, and it would have distressed me to let him live."

Yisui forced herself to look directly at him. "We were married for so short a time that I should be able to forget him." She could not keep the bitterness out of her voice.

He smiled, apparently pleased by her answer. Yisugen rose. "Where are you going?" the Khan asked.

Yisugen looked away from him. "I only thought – "

The Khan's eyes narrowed slightly. "I'm not about to banish you from my bed. You'll stay with us."

Yisugen gasped. "While you join with my sister?"

"I can think of no better way for you to show your devotion to her. Surely it would ease things for her to have her beloved sister with us."

Yisui's cheeks burned. Yisugen's face was red; her hands fluttered. "It isn't fitting," the younger girl said.

"Are you telling me," he said softly, "that I can't satisfy two wives?"

"Oh no — I would never say that." Yisugen covered her mouth.

"Then enough of this chatter."

Yisui stood up, blushing furiously. Her sister was already shedding her clothes. Yisui slowly slipped out of her own robe as the Khan undressed, then got into the bed and pulled the blanket over herself. It would be over soon; she would try not to think about it in the meantime.

He got in next to her and drew the blanket away as Yisugen climbed in on the other side. Indecency, Yisui thought. He was only showing the power he had over both of them, that he could bring them to this. His hand cupped her breast and slid down to her belly. If she did not please him, both she and Yisugen might suffer for that. She waited, expecting him to take her at any moment, but he continued to stroke her belly and thighs, teasing her with his hand. In the shadows, she saw her sister's dark form press against him.

"Be patient," he whispered and she heard Yisugen sigh. His fingers found Yisui's cleft; her back arched as her legs fell apart. The warmth came in waves for, somehow, he had sensed what she wanted. She moaned, unable to struggle against the pleasure he was bringing to her, and drew up her knees, opening herself wider to him, not caring who he was or that her sister was near. Her hips rose to meet him as he entered; her sheath tightened around him. She cried out as the aching inside her flared; he groaned and trembled in her arms, thrusting deeply one last time before he groaned again, then withdrew.

They were still, their bodies damp with sweat. He pulled the blanket over them and stretched out on his back; in the dim light, his face seemed gentler. Her hand slid down to his member, softer now, but still large against her palm.

A hand brushed against hers as Yisugen reached for him.

Yisui drew her hand away and curled up next to him. "You see," he said, "It wasn't so shameful this way. You're much like your sister, and I know how to please her."

"Please me now," Yisugen whispered.

"Let me rest," he said. "You promised to give up your place to Yisui, and already you want her pleasure for yourself."

"And you said you could please two wives."

He was silent for a while, then sighed as he turned towards Yisugen. Yisui ran her fingers along his spine, making bumps on his flesh. The faint light from the hearth flickered over his thigh and hip; his body hid her sister's. His hand dropped towards the other girl; Yisugen's long sigh was like the sound the wind made in the pines, and then her legs rose, knees out and spread wide, toes pointed towards the hearth.

"Ah," Yisugen sighed. "Ah." Her breath was coming in short, sharp gasps. Yisui recalled how he had touched her and thought of what her sister must be feeling now. Her nipples hardened; her cleft was growing wet once more. The Khan knelt between Yisugen's thighs; the bed shook as Yisugen writhed under him. Yisui sighed; his head turned towards her. He had known, she thought; he had guessed what could bring them both to love him. Her sister moaned, locking her legs around him. Yisui closed her eyes, feeling Yisugen's pleasure inside herself.

74

THE KHAN SOON moved west to Lake Buyur, where his herds grazed the grasslands and his men hunted the ducks and cranes that summered in the marsh. The Onggirats to the north of the Khan's encampments made no move against the Mongols who had ravaged their Tatar allies, and the Khan sent no warriors against his first wife's people.

By then, Yisugen had been given her own tent, taken from another Tatar chief, and her dwelling was raised next to Yisui's.

When the sheep grew fatter, the Mongols would hold a feast to celebrate their victory; until then, the Khan was content to hunt and rest with his two new wives. The sisters had pleaded with him for their cousins and other prisoners they knew, and he had given many of them to his close comrades.

Yisui refused to dwell on the past. The times when she wanted to cover her face and weep came less often. The Tatars who had survived would be Mongols now. The children were rapidly forgetting their lost fathers and brothers; the women did the same work for their new masters as they had for the old. Tengri had willed it, and made Temujin His sword.

She was fortunate to be his woman. She had heard many stories of his earlier life, of how he had rescued his chief wife from captivity, and it was easier not to think of the husband who had abandoned her. His men talked of how he gave the greater share of any spoils to them, and she remembered that her father had always demanded more for himself. Temujin spoke often of how pleased he was with the two devoted sisters, and proved it by seeing that they lacked for nothing.

He was her only shield; Yisugen had said it. She meant to cling to that shield until all the ghosts of the past were vanquished.

Temujin stirred next to her. He had come to Yisui alone, and she had missed her sister's presence.

She leaned over him and pressed her lips against his, then drew back. "What's this?" he asked.

"Something my people do." He would not want to hear that she had learned it from Tabudai. She kissed him again, opening her mouth a little. "It's said we learned it from the people of Khitai."

"Then you should have shown me this before. I'm someone who enjoys learning new things." He pulled her down and covered her mouth with his; he was learning quickly.

She guided his hand to her cleft and moved against him. From the ashes he had made of her people, she and her sister had rescued one thing from the fire, the bond they had with each other. That he loved them both made it easier to love him; he was the thread that now bound them together. A few nights

379

ago, she had guided his member into Yisugen and held him tightly as he took his pleasure. At other times, Yisugen would kneel next to her, parting Yisui's legs for him; she remembered how her sister's hands felt against her thighs.

She knelt over him and encased him in her sheath, riding him until the waves of pleasure passed. In the darkness, she heard the movements of the slaves Temujin had allotted to her. Usually they did not enter the great tent until dawn; she remembered that the camp would be feasting today.

Yisui got up and dressed, then went to the hearth. Women knelt on the floor, folding up the tent's felt panels at the bottom so that the warm air could flow more freely. A woman at the hearth handed her a bowl of broth, which Yisui carried to the Khan. Temujin had given her Tatar slaves from distant camps, people she did not know, which made it easier not to pity them.

Temujin finished his meal, then pulled on his clothes. "There's one thing I dislike about summer," Yisui said. "The nights are too short."

He grinned as he stood up. "And if they were longer, I'd sleep even less." She slipped her arms around his waist and rested her head against his broad chest. Yisugen still feared him, but Yisui had lost her fear, sure of her hold on him.

He left the tent. The women hurried outside to join the others preparing food for the feast. Yisui followed, and found the Khan among the day guard; Borchu hastened towards them with another man.

"Jetei has ridden here from your mother's camp," Borchu said. "He tells me he has news of your son Tolui."

Yisui walked towards the men. "What news do you bring?" the Khan asked.

"Good news," Jetei replied, "although it might have been otherwise. Bortai Khatun sent Tolui to stay with his grandmother for a time, and I was one of those who rode there with the boy. A wanderer came to your mother's yurt, while she was talking with Boroghul's wife Altani. The stranger begged her for food, and Hoelun Khatun brought him inside to her hearth. Your son entered the yurt, and then this man seized him and held a knife to his throat, saying that he was Khargil-shira of the Tatars and that the boy would pay for his father's deeds."

Several guards cursed. Temujin's face was taut; Yisui saw the rage in his eyes. "Go on."

"The Tatar dragged Tolui from the yurt. Altani and the Khatun raced after him. Your mother screamed for help, and Altani grabbed the man by a braid and twisted the knife from his hand. Jelme and I were outside slaughtering a bullock, and when we heard their cries, we ran to their aid. Altani had nearly clawed the man's face to shreds by the time we killed him with our axes."

"You and Jelme will be rewarded for what you've done," Temujin said, "and Altani will have her reward as well." He paused. "I might have lost my son. The Tatars I hold here will pay for that. I showed too much mercy before. Every Tatar boy who remains with us, even the babies in their cradles, will die."

"No!" Yisui cried out. "You can't be so cruel! They don't deserve – " The Khan's eyes flickered towards her; his face paled.

"I've been too easy with my new wife. It seems she wishes to speak her last words." His soft voice cut at her like a knife. "She hasn't yet learned her place. Perhaps I should have left her body in the forest where she was found."

The men stared at her in silence. The women at the fires beyond the tent were still as they clung to the lambs they had brought there to kill for the feast. "Shall I give the order?" Borchu asked at last.

Yisui knelt and held out her hands. "I beg my husband to listen to me first."

"More pity." The Khan's lip curled. "My mother's pity for a stranger nearly cost me my son."

"It isn't pity." She struggled to find her voice. "I only – " The men near her were shaking their heads; Yisui caught her breath. "Many boys are your captives. In the years to come, they'll be your soldiers. You would lose all those future servants by killing them now. Does the hawk strike at his fledgelings?"

"Utter one more word, woman," he said softly, "and you'll become a spot of blood on the ground, and your sister will embrace you in the grave. I won't keep a wife who would

381

remind me so much of the one who displeases me so greatly now."

She heard a cry. Her sister was suddenly at her side; Yisugen knelt and threw her arms around Yisui. The Khan smiled mirthlessly as he watched them. He was enjoying this, letting them know how quickly he could crush them; she felt as though his blade was at her throat.

"The Khan must do as he wishes," Yisugen said faintly, then pressed her forehead against the ground.

"Never forget," Temujin said, "that I hold your lives in my hands." He looked around at his men. "There may be some wisdom in what this wretched creature has said. When those boys are men, I can make an army of them. Because of that, and only because it pleases me to do so, I'll let them live."

The men seemed relieved. They might have regretted the cruel command, but Yisui knew they would have carried it out. "I am grateful," she whispered.

"I'm not showing mercy for your sake. Get up, Yisui." Her legs shook as she got to her feet; he dragged her towards the tent by one arm, away from the others.

"I am sorry," Yisui said.

"Never speak to me that way in front of my men. When I've given an order, you won't protest at it." He lowered his voice. "Once I give a command, it must be obeyed without question. I'll forgive you this time, but don't test my patience again. I'll allow you only this mistake." He put his hands around her neck; she thought of how easily he could wring it. "Prepare yourself for the feast."

Shaded by a canopy, the Khan sat between Yisui and Yisugen as they feasted. His closest comrades among his generals sat in a row at his right. On Yisui's left, the Tatar women who had been given to the generals chattered among themselves as others brought them kumiss.

Yisui glanced at her sister. Yisugen's face was drawn; Yisui shuddered at how close they had both come to disaster. Yisugen was his hostage and she too would pay for any offence of Yisui's; that was the truth of their position, however he disguised it with gifts and kind words. The Khan offered her a piece of meat from the end of his knife. He had forgiven her, but his mercy seemed as cold as his blade.

Very well, she thought; I won't fail him again.

She looked towards the camp. Others had ridden there to join the feast; several men sat under a lone tree, playing stringed instruments. An easier mood had replaced the feast's earlier formality. Some men wrestled, while others stumbled from fire to fire, stopping to eat and drink by the cauldrons and spits. A group of men were walking in the Khan's direction; another trailed them, his head down. Yisui was reaching for her goblet when the man looked up.

Tabudai, she thought wildly. She caught her breath, feeling the blood drain from her face. He had seen her. Yisui's hand trembled as she grasped her goblet; she forced herself to look away.

"You're pale," Temujin said then.

"It's nothing." Her hand was shaking so much that she nearly spilled the kumiss.

"I heard you sigh, Yisui. Is anything troubling you?"

Her throat locked. His face blurred; she was afraid she might faint.

"You've seen something." He looked towards the men approaching them, then jumped to his feet. "Borchu! Mukhali!" The two Noyans leaped up and came towards him. "Someone there has frightened my Yisui. Tell every man near us to stand only with those in his own clan."

The two went off to give the order. Tabudai halted and gazed steadily at the Khan. Yisui looked at her sister; Yisugen's eyes were wide with fright. Groups of men were separating and lining up with others; Tabudai came closer, still alone.

What could have brought him here? But she knew. Tabudai had finally found his courage.

Temujin walked towards her husband and stopped a few paces from him. "You stand by yourself," the Khan said. "Where is your clan?"

"I have no clan here," Tabudai replied. "My clan no longer lives because of you." Borchu and Mukhali moved towards him, hands on their hilts.

"Who are you?" Temujin said.

"I am Tabudai, son of the Tatar chief Ghunan – it cost your men many lives to take his. I am the husband of Yisui, daughter of Yeke Cheren. I came to this camp only to see those who rode against us, and to take some of their food. Among so many, I was certain one lone soldier wouldn't be noticed." Tabudai gazed past the Khan at Yisui. "When I saw my wife, I wanted only to look upon her face again, and recall the happiness we had for so short a time. I see she's done well for herself."

He had wanted her to see him, to know that he had dared to enter the camp of his enemies. He could do nothing against the Khan now; surely Temujin would spare him.

"No," Temujin said. "I don't think you came here simply to share our feast. You came to spy and see what you could steal. You meant to lead others back here to raid us."

"I'm alone," Tabudai said, "and I'm not a spy."

"You are an enemy. I gave an order that every male Tatar taller than a linch-pin would die, and you easily exceed that height." The Khan motioned violently with one arm. "Take his head!"

Yisui clutched at her robe. The Khan glanced towards her; she did not dare to speak. Tabudai gracefully swept off his hat and knelt, stretching his neck. Borchu's sword found him first, gashing the back of his neck deeply; Mukhali's sword swept down after it. The body toppled forward slowly, spilling blood; the head dropped at the Khan's feet.

Yisugen expected her sister to scream, to weep, to run from the gathering, but Yisui sat there, her face pale but otherwise composed. She said nothing as the body and head were carried away. When Temujin sat down with them again, Yisui took the bits of meat he offered, stuffing herself until the blood from the food stained her mouth. More kumiss was poured, and Yisui drank until her face was flushed from the drink. When the Khan rose to dance with his men, Yisui clapped her hands and shrieked in a wild, high-pitched laugh.

Yisugen, numb with shock, endured the feast. The sounds of song and merriment swirled around her, whipping at her ears. She did not dare to leave until evening, when others were finally staggering towards their horses or weaving their way to the nearest yurts. By then, Yisui was so drunk that Yisugen had to help her to her feet and lead her to a row of bushes where they could relieve themselves. Yisui lowered her trousers, squatted, urinated, stood up unsteadily, then leaned forward to retch as Yisugen held her by the shoulders.

They stumbled back to Yisui's tent. Yisugen guided her to the back and settled her on the bed, then sat down next to her. "Shall I stay?" she asked. Yisui said nothing. Yisugen pressed her face against Yisui's shoulder and wept.

"Stop," Yisui said in a toneless voice. "The Khan won't want to see you crying."

"I don't care!" Yisugen coughed and wiped at her eyes. "I brought you to this. How can you ever forgive me?"

"Stop it, Yisugen. If he sees you like this, he'll punish us both."

Yisugen wrung her hands. Her sister was right. They had to put this death behind them, banish it with all the other ghosts.

She got up and paced. Yisui sat on the bed, staring at the hearth's glow. Yisugen dropped fuel on the fire, afraid to return to her own tent. The Khan might go there; she did not want to be alone with him.

She waited by the hearth until drunken shouts told her the Khan was outside. The steps creaked; he called out to the night guard, then came through the entrance.

He passed Yisugen without a glance and went to the bed. "You did well, Yisui," he said. "No pleas for mercy, no protesting at my order." He sat down. "He should have known I'd never let him leave alive."

Yisui lifted her head. "I won't mourn him," she said. "He wanted to die. He found enough courage to come here, and it must have pleased him to die bravely in front of me."

Temujin's hands balled into fists. "I'll enjoy you more now, knowing he's dead."

"He chose his death," Yisui said. "I can remember him now as a man who dared to face you."

The Khan shook her. "You're not to think of him at all."

"Of course, my husband. I must obey you."

Yisugen stood up and moved towards the doorway. "You'll

stay with us," he shouted. She went to the bed and undressed as the Khan helped her sister out of her clothes. Yisugen got into bed and curled up on the eastern side, wanting to be as far from him as possible.

She expected him to turn to Yisui. Instead, he reached for her, not bothering to caress her. He forced her legs apart and took her from the back, bruising her breasts as he gripped her. Yisugen endured him, feeling his hot breath against her ear as he gasped. When he withdrew, she turned her back to him and covered herself with the blanket.

Her sister and the Khan were silent and still. Yisugen slept, dreaming of a feast and men who stepped forward to offer their heads to the Khan and then danced, tossing their own heads above their torsos. She fled from the feast and awoke.

At first, she thought she was alone, and then the bed moved under her; she heard a wail like the sound of a woman mourning. Yisugen peered over the blanket. He was sitting on the other side of the bed, the light from the hearth flickering over the left side of his body. A small hand clutched at his shoulder, drawing blood; Yisui's knees were on either side of his hips, and as the hand clawed at him again, the wail rose, becoming a snarl. He fell back; the bed shook as Yisui, still kneeling, moved up and down on top of him, driving him into herself, clawing at him like a cat. Yisui threw back her head and shrieked, her cry as piercing as a sword.

75

"PEACE," JAMUKHA SAID.

Altan heaved his big body out of the saddle. Khuchar dismounted, then handed his reins to one of his men. Altan and Khuchar had asked to meet with Jamukha here, in the stretch of gravel-strewn desert beyond Mount Chegcher.

"Nilkha's inside," Jamukha said as he led the two chiefs towards a small yurt; five of his own men and two of Nilkha's

sat outside, honing their knives. Nilkha had been ranting earlier, lavishing curses on his father Toghril and Temujin in equal
measure. Jamukha did not have much faith in Nilkha, or in
Khuchar and Altan, but they were weapons he could use. Khutula's son and Temujin's cousin had sent an envoy to Jamukha
in secret; it had been easy to bring Nilkha to agree to meet
with them.

They entered the tent. Nilkha sat by the hearth, his hollow-
cheeked face set in a scowl. "I greet you, Senggum," Khuchar
said to him.

"Greetings," Nilkha muttered. "So now you've grown tired
of the one you made your Khan."

"We've had cause to regret that," Altan said.

"We fought with him," Khuchar said as he sat down. "We
took our losses against the Tatars and then he robbed us of
our spoils." He took the jug Nilkha handed to him. "Daritai
would have come with us, but feared alerting Temujin."

"I'm told," Jamukha said, "that Daritai is still banned from
Temujin's councils."

"Yes." Khuchar gulped down some kumiss.

"Damn Temujin," Nilkha said. "The dog dreams of displac-
ing me when Father calls him his adoptive son."

"I thought," Altan said, "that Toghril's feelings towards
Temujin were cooler. He did refuse those offers of marriage
Temujin proposed."

"Oh, I persuaded my father to refuse them." Nilkha flexed
his fingers; Jamukha saw that the Senggum was working himself
up for more ranting. "Imagine the effrontery. Betrothing his
daughter Khojin to my son Tusaga, as if his girl's such a prize,
and wanting my daughter Chagur for his son Jochi."

Altan laughed. "His so-called son."

"My daughter would deserve no less than the place of honour
in one of their tents. His would be fortunate to be left watching
the doorway."

"The girl's mother is recently dead," Khuchar said, "taken
in childbirth. The baby died, too. Trouble has come to my
cousin's household this past winter, and maybe that's an
omen." Nilkha smiled at that. "Now it's said another wife of
his is ailing."

387

"Well," Altan said, "we agreed to come here, and we're ready to act. We'll ride with you, Senggum, and with our old comrade Jamukha, but will the Ong-Khan join us?"

Nilkha fingered his moustache. "That may be difficult."

Jamukha leaned forward. "You can persuade him," he murmured. "You must. Temujin will claim the Kereit throne as soon as your father's flown to Heaven – he may not even wait that long. You can convince your father to fight. Just tell him that Genghis Khan is preparing to seize his throne."

"It may be so," Altan said. "Having his offers of a marriage and betrothal refused angered Temujin greatly. Many heard him say that those who don't yield to him deserve to be swept away."

Jamukha was sure that the Senggum would bring the old man to act. Toghril's suspicions were easily aroused, especially when his throne was at stake.

"You'll let us know," Khuchar said, "as soon as you bring him around, and you must be quick. The longer we wait, the more time Temujin has to discover our plot."

Jamukha drew up one leg. A sound defeat of Temujin would be enough; he did not want the Kereits to have too overwhelming a victory. He could benefit only if both sides were weakened; the men who might choose to desert either the Mongols or the Kereits then would have to turn to him. He would find a way to turn the battle to his advantage.

76

HOELUN WAITED OUTSIDE her tent with her husband. A rider had come to Munglik's camp that morning to tell them that Temujin would stop there for the night. Beyond her circle, Temujin and the ten men with him were passing between the two fires; with their spare horses, they had also brought other horses laden with packs. Gifts, she thought, doubting they were meant for her. Temujin usually sent others with his presents, choosing to honour his mother at a distance.

The evening wind rose; patches of snow still covered part of the pasture land. They had intended to move to spring grazing grounds soon, but a fire had scorched much of the land to the west. Many suspected it had been deliberately set by an enemy.

The Khan had his share of sorrows without that fire. The loss of two wives, an insulting refusal of his offers of marriage from the Ong-Khan and his son – Temujin was assailed even in the wake of his triumph over his worst enemies.

Temujin strode towards her, leaving the horses to his men. He seemed unmarked by his bereavements; the brown, strong-boned face under his wide-brimmed fur hat was still handsome, and he moved with the grace of a younger man.

"Greetings, Mother." He embraced her, then clasped her husband's hands. "I'm happy to see you, Munglik-echige."

"Temujin!" Shigi Khutukhu ran towards them from behind a wagon. The Khan caught his foster brother in his arms. "Are we going to war soon? When can I fight with you?"

Munglik laughed. "Temujin's only just arrived, and already you're pestering him about that."

"Be patient, brother," Temujin said. "You'll have your chance to fight."

Hoelun followed them into her large tent. By the time her son was settled in the place of honour, with Munglik at his right and Shigi Khutukhu at his feet, his men had arrived. The servants set out curds and game; Hoelun sprinkled the blessing, then went to Temujin and sat down at his left. A small beard had begun to sprout on her son's chin, but she saw no grey in it.

"I sorrowed," she said, "to hear of your recent loss." His wife Jeren had died only a month ago.

"I've mourned, but she was ailing for some time. Bortai and Khadagan now have another of my daughters to care for, but Alakha is too young to know that her mother's left us." He reached for a jug as a servant brought them a platter of meat. "Much as I've grieved, I must look to the joys ahead. Yisui carries my child, and Khojin will be betrothed after all."

Hoelun lifted her brows. "You found her another husband so soon?"

"The same husband, Mother. Nilkha sent an envoy telling me he's now ready to have his son betrothed to her, and to give his daughter to Jochi. He claims it was only the youth of his son and my daughter that kept him from giving his assent before."

"I find that very surprising," Hoelun said, "after what the Senggum told you before."

"Bortai said the same thing," Temujin said, "but Toghril must have finally seen the advantages to the match, and persuaded his son to agree. I'm riding to Nilkha's camp now – he's invited me to a feast to celebrate both betrothals."

Hoelun glanced at her husband; even the usually placid Munglik was frowning. "My son," he said, "I'm also suspicious. They disdained you, and wounded you with insults, and now they suddenly agree? I find that hard to accept."

Temujin tensed. "I want these marriages," he said softly. "They'll bind us more closely to the Kereit Khan."

"You must do as you like," Hoelun said wearily. If her son had not listened to Bortai, he was hardly likely to heed her advice. "I suppose my stepson told you the omens were favourable."

"Teb-Tenggeri has been on a mountain communing with spirits. I saw no reason to ask the bones about this, when Nilkha's only agreeing to what I wanted."

Munglik leaned forward. "Temujin," he said, "if you had consulted my son, I think he would have told you to be wary. The Senggum must know how much you wanted these marriages. What better way to lure you into a trap than to pretend to agree to them now?"

Temujin sneered. "Nilkha's a weakling. He wouldn't dare."

"He might dare," Munglik said, "if another has his ear. Temujin, I've served you faithfully ever since you were generous enough to give me your good mother as my wife. What have I ever said in your councils except that I'll obey any command you give me? Have I ever spoken against anything you were determined to do?"

"No," Temujin replied.

"They mean to trap you," Munglik continued. "I'm certain of it."

Temujin scowled. "What would you have me do?"

"Tell Nilkha you cannot come."

"And lose what I'm hoping for? What excuse do I give?"

"That it's springtime," Munglik answered, "that your horses are too thin and you need to fatten them. If the Senggum is sincere, he'll ask if he can come to your camp to celebrate the betrothals, and you'll lose nothing. If he doesn't, you'll know what he intended for you."

Temujin gazed at his men. "What do you say to this?"

Kiratai lifted his head. "That your stepfather may be wise," he said. "The Kereits have shown themselves faithless before."

Temujin ate in silence. Hoelun nodded at her husband; it had taken some courage for him to speak as he had to the Khan.

"The Ong-Khan owes his throne to me," Temujin muttered at last. "Nilkha would still be in hiding if I hadn't driven the Naimans from their lands." He rested his hands on his thighs. "Kiratai, you and Bughatai will ride to the Senggum, and tell him that I must fatten my horses. Leave at dawn, and take the gifts with you. Feast with him, but ride to me quickly if he says nothing about coming to celebrate with me. The rest of us will return to my camp." He glanced at Munglik. "If it turns out you were wrong, Munglik-echige, you'll feel my wrath."

"I knew that when I spoke," the older man said.

"That's why I believe you."

"My son once took advice," Hoelun said very softly to the Khan. "But of course you are rarely mistaken."

"Mother, if I were plagued with everyone's advice, nothing would be decided. Better that others think hard before offering me counsel."

"Yes – but don't make them too frightened to give it when it's needed." She got up to take away the platters.

The men drank for a while, then threw lots to decide who would stand guard first. Two left the tent while the others rolled out blankets. "You may have my bed, Temujin," Shigi Khutukhu said.

Temujin smiled. "Very well."

Hoelun followed her son to the boy's bed. Temujin shook off her hands as she tried to help him off with his coat. "I'm not a child," he said.

"Humour your old mother." She felt weary, as she often did at the end of the day. A slight pain caught her below the ribs as she knelt to pull off his boots; she tucked the blanket around him, ignoring his scowls. "I have a favour to ask of you, Temujin." He grunted. "I wish to ride back with you tomorrow."

"So I must delay while you pack and ready a cart."

"I need no cart. I'll go on horseback, and the ride will do me good."

"And leave me without my wife?" Munglik said from their bed. "This tent will be empty without you." It was like him to say that, instead of talking of the ewes that would be birthing soon, or the sewing that needed to be done.

"I won't be gone long." She stood up and looked down at her son. "I want to visit Bortai and my grandchildren. You might bring us together more often. Your old mother may not have many more years to enjoy their company."

Temujin poked his hand above the blanket and made the sign against misfortune. "Don't talk of such things. You're hardy." Once, he would have told her that she scarcely looked older than Bortai, but that had not been true for some time. "I'm too tired to argue with you. If your husband will let you go, I'll take you."

"She may go," Munglik muttered.

Hoelun went to the bed, took off her robe and boots, and got in next to her husband. Her arms slipped around him; he nestled against her. His love for her was an evening fire, warming her.

"First you tell me I'm to be married after all," Jochi said, "and now you say I may have to wait." Bortai frowned at her son. He had been out with the young horses, and had ridden to the ordu only that evening. He had barely greeted his grandmother before pestering Temujin about the betrothal.

"You'll be married," Temujin said, "one way or another, either to the Senggum's daughter or someone else."

"Thinking his daughter's too good for me." Jochi grabbed at the meat. "If she's ever under my tent, a few beatings will show the girl her place."

Chagadai looked at his older brother. "The Kereit agreed to betroth his daughter to the Khan's eldest son, so perhaps he meant that I – "

The Khan glowered at them and lifted a hand. Bortai drank from her goblet. Jochi was nineteen; he looked much like Chilger, with the same massive, big-boned build, small dark eyes, and a mouth that twisted as her Merkit captor's had whenever he was angry. He stared past her at Yisui and Yisugen, who were seated to the left of Khadagan. Jochi had been eyeing the sisters too intently whenever he was near them; he should have been married some time ago.

"I'll see," Temujin said, "that all my sons have wives worthy of them."

Ogedei grinned up at his father. "Then you must find me one like Mother." The Khan's face softened as he looked at his third son; Ogedei lifted his goblet and drank. At fourteen, the broad-shouldered boy drank as much as some men, but drink made him more amiable; drinking fired Jochi's temper.

Hoelun-eke murmured a few words to her son. Bortai had placed her on Temujin's left. Age had come to Hoelun suddenly; her face was weather-worn and marked with fine lines. Only her golden-brown eyes were the same.

Temujin offered meat to his wives, then to Khojin. The little girl had her father's eyes and Tolui's fierce look; there was little of her mother Doghon in her. "I don't want to get married," Khojin said.

Khadagan laughed. "You have to get married someday. Anyway, this would only be a betrothal – you wouldn't go to your husband's camp for several years."

"Your aunt Temulun used to say she didn't want to marry," Hoelun said, "and she's happy with her husband."

Khojin snuggled close to Khadagan. If the Khan's envoys to Nilkha returned without the Senggum, he would know that the Ong-Khan's son had meant to strike at him. Bortai knew that Temujin would not let that pass; he would act. She thought bitterly of how she had warned him about Toghril.

393

She got up and helped the servants clear away the platters. Alakha trotted after her; she pushed the little girl back towards Khadagan. Yisugen and Yisui rose and bowed to the Khan, then moved towards the doorway. Khadagan left with the Khan's two daughters; Tolui and Ogedei scrambled to their side of the tent to play knuckle-bone dice.

Hoelun rested her head on her son's shoulder. "You'll visit us again," Temujin murmured, "when Jochi is married."

"I'll be here to welcome his bride." Hoelun turned to her oldest grandson. "Take care you're as good a husband to her as mine has been to me." Bortai wondered if Hoelun-eke was thinking of Munglik or Yesugei. A man shouted beyond the doorway; a sentry answered him. Bortai moved towards the entrance, thinking that perhaps Kiratai and Bughatai had returned.

Jurchedei called out his name; Bortai asked him to enter. The Urugud chief came through the doorway, followed by two strangers whose clothes were caked with dirt. "I greet you, Temujin," Jurchedei said hastily. "These two herders came here from the camp of Altan's son Sheren and beg to speak to you." The two strangers knelt and pressed their heads against the carpet. "They say it's urgent, and will speak to no one else."

"Get up," Temujin said to the two men.

"Koko Mongke Tengri still watches over our Khan," the older one said breathlessly. "I am Badai, and this is Kishlik. We're servants in Sheren's camp. He swore his oath to you, so it seemed to us that our duty's to you as much as to him."

Temujin waved a hand impatiently. "Your message."

"The Kereits held a war kuriltai," Badai said. "They meant to keep it secret, but I was outside Sheren's tent when he rode in and spoke of it to his wife. I heard him say that the Senggum's trap had failed to close around his prey, but that another trap had been set. They mean to ride here by dawn, surround your camp, and take you."

Jurchedei cursed. The Khan slowly got to his feet. "My envoys must be Nilkha's prisoners — or worse. The Senggum would have put me under the ground but for Munglik-echige."

"If Sheren was at that kuriltai," Jurchedei muttered, "then

Altan must have been there, and I suspect Khuchar wasn't far away."

"The Kereits are coming for you, my Khan," Kishlik said. "I beg you to save yourself."

"Nilkha wouldn't be acting without his father's consent," Temujin said softly. "May I live to see Toghril's limbs cut from his body and his bones scattered to the four winds. Jurchedei, rouse the camp, and send riders to those near us. Every man is to be in his saddle to ride east with me — leave everything except what we need to fight."

The three men hurried from the tent. Bortai's sons were collecting their weapons. "I'll ride with you, Father," Tolui said.

"No. Stay with your mother." He gazed steadily at Bortai. "I entrust my mother, my wives, and my youngest children to you. Save yourselves however you can." He strode towards the doorway and was gone.

77

BEYOND LAKE BUYUR, near the place called the Red Willows, where stunted trees grew among the sand-strewn grasslands, the Kereits caught sight of the retreating Mongol rearguard. When night began to fall, the Mongols took up battle order, and the Kereit warriors knew the enemy had decided to fight. The sun had set when Jamukha made his way back through the lines to consult with Toghril and his generals.

What a fool the Senggum had been, with his attempt to lure Temujin into a trap; Nilkha had succeeded only in alerting his enemy. Jamukha felt as though the reins were slipping from his hands. Toghril had embarked on this campaign reluctantly, while Nilkha was so fired with rage against Temujin that he was likely to do something rash.

He dismounted near a fire; the Ong-Khan beckoned to him.

"Our enemy waits," Jamukha said. "How are we to use our forces? The men await your signals."

"I have a question for you," Toghril said. "Who, in your opinion, are Temujin's best warriors, the ones likely to inflict the most damage?"

Jamukha ground his teeth. The old man was still so hesitant that he could not decide how to order his own army. "The Uruguds and the Mangguds," he replied, and cursed their leaders silently; he had seen how they fought when Khuyhildar and Jurchedei were still with him. "They keep close together when they surround an enemy, and when they retreat, their line doesn't break. Their lances are their most deadly weapons – their boys are set to training with them as soon as they can ride, even when the lads must still be tied to their saddles."

"Then I'll put the Jirgens against them," Toghril said, "and behind them, the Tuman-Tubegens – they're the fiercest lancers and best archers we have. The Olon-Dongkhaits can follow with the royal guard, and I'll bring up the main army in the rear."

"I can think of no better plan," Jamukha murmured. "Temujin is sure to throw the Mangguds and Uruguds at us first. If we push them back and break through their line, victory will be within our grasp."

"I am thinking," the Ong-Khan said, "that perhaps you should lead the army, Younger Brother. You know more about the way they'll fight than I."

The other generals peered across the flames at Jamukha. He knew what they were thinking, that their Khan had grown so faint-hearted he was willing to give command to one who had failed against Temujin before. They would obey, but uneasily, and blame him if the battle was lost.

"I cannot accept such an honour," Jamukha said. "My sword is yours, Toghril-echige, but you and your Noyans must lead us."

The other generals looked relieved. They spoke for a while, laying out the plan of battle, but Jamukha already tasted defeat. The Ong-Khan's heart was not in this battle; only Nilkha's nagging had brought him this far. If Toghril won, his own weakness would keep him from pressing his advantage; if he lost, he would be quick to blame both his son and Jamukha for making him fight. Jamukha turned things over in his mind, trying to see what he might gain.

He left the Kereits at last and rode back to his men. Whatever the outcome, some of the Ong-Khan's men would waver in their loyalty and think of seeking a stronger leader. If Temujin's losses were heavy, some of his followers might leave him for Jamukha.

By the time he reached his headquarters, Jamukha had made his decision. He drew five of his most trusted comrades aside from the others. "The Ong-Khan will fail us," he murmured. "He asked me to tell him of Temujin's strengths, and tried to give me command of his armies. He's already lost this battle in his heart."

"What do you wish to do?" one man asked.

"If the Ong-Khan is weakened further, it will be easier for us to push him aside and use Nilkha for as long as we need to. As things are, Temujin's so outnumbered that he still might lose – unless he's given some help."

The other men frowned. "You're going to help him?" Ogin said.

"He must know I'm here – he'll have seen my tugh. Let him think I haven't forgotten our old ties. They say that Temujin is one who can forgive an old friend who helps him in times of trouble. Winning his gratitude now may give me a way to use him later."

"That may be so," another man said.

"Ogin, you'll be my messenger." Jamukha pulled the younger man closer to him. "You'll make your way secretly to Temujin's camp, and there you'll tell my anda of Toghril's limits, of how he can't even keep his own army in line. I'll give you the Ong-Khan's plan of attack to carry to him, and you will tell him to be cautious and not to fear. We'll see what use he makes of this."

Ogin nodded. "Recite the message you want me to give him."

78

KHOJIN SAT ON the hillside, gazing out at the high grass beyond the forest. Tolui and the other boys were grazing the horses below. At least two of them were always on guard, ready to call out if they saw anyone approach.

Bortai-eke had ordered everyone in their camp to scatter. Most of the people had gone north, towards the Onon, but the Khatun had led another group east, across a patch of desert, then past the salt marshes of Lake Buyur. The army's trail led towards the Khalkha; the Khatun had turned from it finally and moved north-east. Most of those who had followed Bortai were now camped by a river, to wait for any word of their soldiers and to watch for signs of pursuit. The Khatun had pressed on with Khojin's grandmother, the Khan's other wives, his youngest children, and the five boys who were their only remaining servants.

The ride had been a hard one, much of it through sparse grasslands covered by sand carried by the wind from the desert to the south. They were now in a spur of mountains that ran west from the distant Khingan range. Their first days in the foothills had given them little rest; they had found a small stream, then torn down tree limbs to make shelters. But they had milk from their mares, and the boys had brought down an antelope.

Khojin knew that she should be afraid. If her father's enemies defeated him, she and the others might have to hide for a long time. Yet she did not feel frightened. Her father would win, and then he would find them.

She thought of how he walked to his tents, tall and proud, his men swooping around him like hawks. Nothing could defeat him; he was the Khan. Whenever she thought of Koko Mongke Tengri watching over them from above, she imagined her father's eyes. He would sweep down on his enemies like one of Tengri's storms, his sword flashing as Heaven's lightning did.

She got up, moved through the forest until she came to the stream, filled Bortai-eke's wooden bucket, then climbed up the hill towards the shelters. In a hollow dug in the ground, a small fire burned, and a tripod with a pot hanging from it sat over the flames; Khadagan-eke had made the tripod from long green tree limbs lashed together.

Yisui was feeding the fire with pine needles and bits of dead wood. The others had to be out foraging, but Bortai-eke often let Yisui tend the fire, make antelope tendons into thread, and watch Alakha while the rest of them looked for food. Yisui was pregnant, although she did not look it yet, and Bortai wanted her to rest.

"Where's Alakha?" Khojin asked as she set down the bucket.

"With the others. She was getting restless. Bortai hopes to tire her out so she'll sleep later." Khojin sat down. "You mustn't be afraid," Yisui went on. "You aren't afraid, are you? Even your father didn't go out of his way to kill little girls, and I doubt his enemies would."

Yisui, Khojin thought, sounded different when she talked to her by herself. She had only been alone with her father's young wife a few times, and felt uneasy in her presence.

"I hid from your father in a forest like this," Yisui continued. She had said that before. My people once lived in these lands, she had told Khojin; your father killed all of the men. His men found me, and he made me his wife. Yisui always said such things with a strange smile and eyes as hard and black as kara stones.

"Your father killed my first husband," Yisui said.

"I know."

"He ordered his men to cut off his head in front of me and Yisugen, at a feast celebrating his victory."

"He was an enemy," Khojin said.

"Oh yes. He had to kill my people. After all, if he hadn't, he would have been trapped between them and the Kereits now, and wouldn't have lasted long."

"You sound as if you hate Father."

"You're wrong, child. I love your father. He went to so much trouble to find me and reunite me with my sister. I love him because if I allowed myself to hate him, that hatred would sear me and never touch him."

Khojin did not know what she was talking about; any woman

would be lucky to be the Khan's wife. One reason she had not cared about being betrothed was that she was certain her husband could never be as fine a man. Well, she wasn't betrothed now, and that had something to do with this war. In a way, her father was fighting for her.

"I pray that he's alive," Yisui said, "and that he finds us soon. I had to forget a great deal to love him, and being here reminds me of things I'd rather not recall."

"He'll be safe," Khojin said.

Yisui smiled her odd smile. "And if he's fallen?"

"Then my brothers will fight, and if our enemies come here, I'll shoot them and take their heads. I'll put them in piles and sing and dance around them." Khojin moved closer to the fire. "I hope he kills them all."

Yisui crawled out of the shelter she shared with her sister. Bortai helped the younger woman to her feet. "I'm sorry," Bortai said. "The child's buried near us, under a pine. I can show you the grave."

Yisui shook her head. She had not cried after losing the baby, although Yisugen had.

"I lost two children myself," Bortai went on. "You're young, Yisui — there will be others. I know that doesn't make this easier to bear, but it's true." Soon they would have to leave this place, return to the people waiting south of the mountains, and hope they had news of Temujin. From there, she could go west to an Onggirat camp, and hope her father's people would give her refuge for the winter. She did not dare to think further ahead than that.

Alakha tugged at Bortai's coat. Below, Bortai glimpsed Khojin's small form among the trees. "Bortai-eke!" the girl cried as she stumbled towards them, panting for breath. "We saw some men far away, and Tolui was going to hide the animals and come for you, and then — " Khojin gasped. "They're our men — about twenty of them."

Bortai threw dirt on the fire, then scooped up Alakha. She and Yisui followed Khojin down the hill. When they left the trees, Tolui had already ridden out to the men and was leading them towards the grazing animals. Chagadai was with the soldiers. Bortai thrust Alakha at Yisui, then ran to him.

"Mother!" Chagadai shouted. She caught the reins of his horse; he swung himself off and embraced her. "Father will be overjoyed."

She gazed up at him. "Then he's alive."

Chagadai nodded. "So are Ogedei and Jochi, and Grandfather Munglik. We rode north to hunt, and found some of our people along a river south of here. They told us you had gone north. I didn't think any of our people would hide this far east."

"Our enemies wouldn't have thought so, either. I sent most of our people towards the Onon." She clutched at her son. "Did your father – have you won?"

Chagadai frowned. "You might call it a victory. It cost us much – but I'll tell you later. Fetch the others and bring them here."

He mounted and trotted back to his men. Bortai noticed then that they had only their mounts, and no spare horses; any victory they had won must have been hard-fought. She hurried up the hill.

After Chagadai's men pitched two small tents, he gave one of them a fresh mount from among Bortai's mares and sent him off with a message for the Khan. Bortai and the other women had carried their few belongings down from the hillside; all of them settled around the fire the men had made near the tents. The mares had been milked, and two men were working a churn; three others sat on horses, keeping guard.

By then, Bortai had heard more about the battle. The Khan's army had been grazing their horses when a dust cloud in the distance warned of the enemy's approach; there had barely been time to collect the herds. By the time the sun was setting, the Kereits were near enough for both armies to make ready; the men had been arranging themselves for battle much of the night.

"A strange thing happened then," Chagadai said. "One of Jamukha's men came to Father and gave him the Kereit plan of battle. It seems his anda had doubts about the Ong-Khan's stomach for war."

Bortai pursed her lips. "Jamukha was always fickle."

"Fickle or not, he may have saved us. The Ong-Khan was going to throw his strongest forces and the bulk of his men at the Uruguds and Mangguds, so Father knew he'd have to hold the line there. Khuyhildar hurled his Mangguds at the enemy – they pushed him back. Jurchedei countercharged, and when he was thrown back, the Mangguds charged again. We finally drove them back – Jurchedei pushed them into retreat, and then the Senggum led another charge at us. It was a foolish thing to do – the Uruguds were in hot pursuit of his father's forces. If he'd sent his men sweeping towards them instead, he might have picked many of them off."

Tolui's eyes shone; Bortai knew that her youngest son was even sorrier he had not been there. "An arrow struck the Senggum in the face," Chagadai continued, "and he fell from his horse. All the Kereits surrounded him. We had small hope of breaking through that defence, and the sun was setting. Khuyhildar was wounded, and we'd lost many men, so as soon as it was dark, Father ordered a retreat. We didn't stop until the middle of the night, had no idea what our losses were. We slept on our horses, expecting another attack at any time. Near dawn, Father had some reports. Ogedei was lost, and Borchu and Boroghul – Father was frantic with grief."

"But you said – " Bortai began.

"We have Grandmother's foster son Boroghul to thank for Ogedei's life." Hoelun clasped her hands at these words. "Ogedei had an arrow wound in the neck, and Boroghul kept him on his own horse all night, sucking his wound as he made his way after us. Father wept when he saw them. By then, Borchu had reached us safely, too. He'd lost his horse and had to steal one from the Kereit pack animals." He paused. "Grandmother, prepare yourself. Uncle Khasar was captured – Borchu glimpsed him among the Kereit prisoners."

Hoelun-eke moaned; Bortai reached for her hand.

"We knew we might be pursued," Chagadai went on. "We retreated towards the Khingans. The horses, those we had left, were exhausted by then, and we were hoping only for a little time to graze them before meeting the enemy again. But still they didn't come, and then a Targhut chief rode to Father to say he had left the Kereits to join us. He also brought tales of discord in the Kereit camp. The Ong-Khan's furious with the Senggum for provoking this war, and one of the Kereit Noyans convinced Toghril to leave us for now, and gather us up later – the phrase he used was collect us like dung-cakes." Chagadai cleared his throat. "He told the Ong-Khan we were weak, that we had almost nothing left. He's not far wrong."

"And where is my oldest son now?" Hoelun asked.

"Moving west along the Khalkha. He divided the army in two – what's left of it. We have less than three thousand men. Half are hunting north of the river, and half south, and that's what has happened since I last saw you." Chagadai's face sagged. "We can call it a victory, but it feels much like defeat."

79

THEY RODE SOUTH-WEST; the men hunted along the way. In a few days, they had caught up with the Mongol rearguard. The soldiers had few spare horses, and many had no tents. When Bortai learned that Temujin was camped east of Lake Buyur, she ordered two men to ride with her and left the others with the rearguard.

It took her three days to reach him. Temujin was outside his field tent talking to Jurchedei when she arrived. The men here seemed as discouraged as those she had seen along the way; they gazed passively at the Khan's tugh as they passed his tent, as though wondering if the standard's spirit had abandoned them.

Temujin embraced her, then led her inside. "I had word from two scouts this morning," he said as they sat down. "Most of our people, those who escaped, are hiding in the mountains near the northern Onon. It seems the Kereits didn't stop to do much looting while chasing us, so it might have been worse.

403

The scouts say the enemy's withdrawn towards the Kerulen."
He swallowed. "Khuyhildar's flown to Heaven. I told him not
to hunt until he healed, but he insisted — he said he'd fought
for me, and he would hunt for me. His wounds reopened. We
buried him a few days ago."

"I am sorry," she said, seeing him struggle against his tears.

"Khasar's a prisoner, and no one has seen his family."

"Chagadai told me about Khasar."

"I can pray he's still a prisoner, that Toghril still has enough
feeling to spare a son of his anda." He let out a breath. "You
did well, Bortai — you saved those I entrusted to you."

"I didn't do well. Almost everything we had was left behind,
and the long ride made Yisui lose her child."

"You saved her and the others," he said. "I'm grateful for
that. The rest we can win again."

She leaned closer to him, feeling more heartened. His face
was thinner, his eyes sorrowful, but his soft voice still had its
edge. "Little Khojin never lost faith in you," she murmured.

He patted her hand. "Perhaps I should have listened to you
when you warned me against Toghril."

She would not have brought that up, but was pleased he
remembered it. "This wasn't the Ong-Khan's doing," she said,
"but his son's, and Jamukha must have had a hand in it."

"Yet he sent a messenger to me on the eve of battle." Temujin
sighed. "Maybe he was remembering our old ties. I regret what
has passed, and perhaps he does, too."

She did not want to talk about Jamukha. One of Temujin's
braids was loose, trailing down his back; she looped it and
secured it under his helmet.

"Bortai, I think you know what I must do now."

She tensed; he wanted her to say it, to give her assent.

"If you had fallen," she said at last, "I meant to go to my
father's people. Now I'm thinking your men and horses could
recover among the Onggirats if they'll allow us to stay here in
their lands. Those of our people still in hiding could join us
then."

"I've been thinking the same thing." He rested a hand on
her shoulder. "You know what this means."

"I know."

404

"They may reject my message, and then we'd have to fight them and take what we need."

"Yes." She had known when she married him that her first loyalty had to be to him.

Temujin shouted to Jurchedei. The Urugud stooped as he came inside, then knelt and sat back on his heels. "I have a mission for you," the Khan said. "It's time I reminded the Onggirats of my ties to them. We need to recover our strength in their lands, and if they give their oath to me, our army will have more men."

"They may not give it," Jurchedei said.

"Then we must attack." He glanced at Bortai. "They've begun to move on to some of the old Tatar grazing grounds. They may not have much stomach for war, but if they see us as weak, they may risk an attack. We'd better show them we're prepared for battle by approaching them first."

Jurchedei nodded. "I'll be your envoy, Temujin."

"Take your best men with you. You'll tell the Onggirats of my love for them, of the beautiful Bortai I found among them, of how she waited faithfully for me until I was strong enough to claim her. You'll say that her father promised me his friendship. You'll remind them that I never made war against them."

"I'll say all that."

"And as eloquently as possible," the Khan said. "If they then say to you that they've always thrived, not on their strength in war, but on the beauty of their daughters, we'll know that they'll surrender and give us their oath. But if they speak of how the falcon returns to his nest after the hunt, we'll strike."

"I'll ride to their chiefs at once," Jurchedei said.

Bortai remained in her husband's camp, with the others who had followed her during her flight. A detachment of soldiers and part of the rearguard stayed with them; the rest of the army soon rode out after Jurchedei and his men, prepared to attack if the Onggirats decided to fight. Even in its weakened state, the Khan's army could wound her people; the Onggirat men did not have their experience at war.

She was outside the field tent, helping Khadagan butcher a deer hunters had brought them, when she saw a Mongol rider galloping towards the camp. Bortai went on with her work until the man neared the fires beyond the camp; then she stood up, thrust her knife under her sash, and went inside. In a little while, she would know if there was to be war.

Bortai waited. Some of the guards by the fires who had greeted the rider would be galloping to the camp now, with word of the Onggirats' reply.

A shadow suddenly darkened the doorway. "Bortai," Khadagan said, "the men aren't rushing for their horses or gathering weapons. It must mean they haven't been ordered to get ready for battle."

She was afraid to believe it. At last she got up and went outside. A guard trotted towards her; she hurried to him. "Tell me," she said.

"Good news, Honoured Lady – the Onggirats will surrender to us. Our man said something about one of their chiefs riding here, but I was in the saddle before I could hear more."

She left him and walked back to the tent, where Khadagan was hanging strips of meat on a line between two poles. Out on the sand-strewn plain, Bortai could see the dust clouds of more riders.

"There will be peace," she said to Khadagan.

"Good," the plain-faced woman replied. "We'll have time to prepare this meat properly."

Bortai laughed. One of the distant riders was galloping towards the camp ahead of his companions, his body bent low over his horse; a memory stirred within her. She continued to watch him until he reached the fires and dismounted to greet the guards with outstretched hands. She knew that rolling gait; her hand rose to her mouth.

"What is it, Bortai?" Khadagan asked.

"Father." Bortai stepped away from the tent. "My father's come here."

She was weeping too hard to greet Dei Sechen properly. Somehow, she remembered to introduce Khadagan, then hugged the old man again. Dei's beard and moustaches were completely white, his face wrinkled and leathery, his body shrunken with age, but the arms that held her were still strong.

"Father," Bortai whispered.

"Terge and Amel summoned the other chiefs to their camp," he said, "when Temujin's envoys came there. They'd already decided to give their oath to your husband when we arrived, so of course the rest of us agreed. I told them that, as the father of Genghis Khan's first wife, I wished to go to him and offer my oath at once, so Terge and Amel sent me and Anchar as their envoys. Your brother is with Temujin now, and when I heard you were in this camp, I asked if I could go to you."

"Oh, Father," she said. "It will be wonderful to see Anchar again."

He smiled down at her. "The Khan's envoys spoke of his beautiful Bortai, but I thought that beauty had long since become only a memory. I see now it still lives."

"You flatter me, Father. This flower has faded."

"It wilts only a little, child." He bowed to Khadagan, then followed Bortai inside the tent. "Your mother is well. To see you again will give her great joy."

"And have you taken another wife during these past years?"

Dei shook his head. "I'm much too old to think of other wives now, and Shotan's too set in her ways to accept one."

Her father sat down facing the doorway; she took a bottle from the pole where it hung, then sat down next to him. "I'm sorry to have so little to give you." Bortai scattered a few drops. "We lack many things still."

"You'll grow fatter in our lands."

"Father, I told Temujin to turn to your people. He would have done so anyway, but it was easier for him to know that I agreed. He would have attacked you if the chiefs had refused his request. I knew that when I gave him my advice."

"As did we when we heard his message. I am grateful it didn't come to that." He drank, then handed her the jug. "Things aren't as they were with us, daughter. Our younger men are no longer so willing to thrive only on the beauty of our girls. They've heard many tales of the prowess of Genghis Khan. Some of them wanted to fight with the Tatars against him, to prove themselves against a worthy adversary, and we had to restrain them."

"It was good that you did," she said.

407

"And others, like your brother Anchar, talked of what they might win for themselves if they served him. I've known for some time that our more peaceful ways would soon pass, that the young men dreamed of more than raids and skirmishes. They speak of how Genghis Khan has made mighty warriors of the most commonplace herders, and generals of men who might once have been little more than horse thieves."

"He needs you now," Bortai said, "but you'll be joining him when his fortunes are at their lowest."

Dei nodded. "And if we help him win more, he'll reward us for that. The young men have also heard tales of his generosity to his followers." The old man stroked his beard. "War would have come to us eventually – our beautiful girls are no longer enough of a shield. Better to have Anchar fighting with his sister's husband than against him."

She said, "Anchar once hoped to be his general."

"Yes – Temujin showed what he was even as a boy. I knew he was destined for greater things. I didn't know then that it would mean the end of our people."

"But it isn't," Bortai said. "You've joined him, and when he's stronger – "

"No doubt he will grow stronger. Weakened as he is, he may win in time. But even that will bring an end to us as we are." Her father sighed. "Didn't he fly to you with the sun and moon when you dreamed of him? Our people will become one of his talons." His face sagged, showing his years. "We won't be Onggirats any more, but Mongols."

80

SORKHATANI GAZED OUT at the steppe. The riders were tiny black forms rippling in the heat as they galloped over the sparse yellow grass; she glimpsed the blue borders of her father's coat through the dust clouds sifting around him.

Jakha Gambu had gone to her uncle's ordu several days

ago. He had thought the campaign against the Mongols was a mistake, but had ridden off to fight. He had returned from the war with tales of how his brother Toghril had raged at the Senggum, blaming him for the men the Kereits had lost.

Jakha had gone back to the Ong-Khan's camp to do what he could to mend the breach between father and son and to assure Toghril of his loyalty. Sorkhatani's father often said it was not wise to rouse Toghril's suspicions, and the Ong-Khan had killed other brothers to assure himself of his throne.

Their servants had settled the sheep near a tent. Sorkhatani's sister Ibakha was staring at the mares tethered just outside the camp. Khasar and his son Yegu were with the men milking the mares; Ibakha's blush deepened.

"Ibakha," Sorkhatani said sharply. Her sister started, then knelt by a ewe. Ever since Khasar had been brought there, Ibakha sought any excuse to be near him, but she had been equally taken months before with an Uighur trader who had stopped at their camp.

Her sister, Sorkhatani thought, had to be the silliest girl she knew. Ibakha knew that Khasar could not marry her as long as he was a prisoner and hostage, which did not stop her from ogling him.

Milk spurted through Sorkhatani's fingers into her bucket. Perhaps she could speak to her father about Ibakha; he sometimes listened to her. His child with a woman's wisdom – that was what he called Sorkhatani. She would tell him that Ibakha was too beautiful to remain unwed much longer.

Ibakha was gazing at the men again. "Your milking," Sorkhatani muttered. Her sister giggled and resumed her work.

The red sun was low in the western sky when the two sisters finished carrying the milk inside their tent. "Father's back," Sorkhatani said as she helped her mother pour it into a kettle. Her mother was his third wife, but his favourite. Jakha Gambu would surely come to her tent if he wanted to discuss matters his other two wives should not hear; they gossiped, while Keuken Ghoa never seemed to hear anything he said.

Sorkhatani studied her mother's smooth, golden-skinned face. Keuken the Fair still looked like a beautiful girl, unmarked by age, her brown eyes untroubled by thought. It came to her that her mother had probably once been as silly as Ibakha.

"I need more fuel," Keuken said to one of her servants.

"I'll fetch it." Ibakha hastened through the doorway.

Sorkhatani set down her bucket. "My sister should be married," she said.

"I'd miss her."

"She's almost eighteen, Mother. Will you have her grow old in this tent? You should speak to Father." Her mother would not, of course; she would leave that task to Sorkhatani. "I'll help her find fuel."

She went outside. Her sister was moving towards Khasar's tent, which stood in the southern end of Jakha Gambu's circle. Other Mongol prisoners were in other parts of the camp, but her father wanted Khasar close; he was both an important hostage and an old comrade.

Ibakha leaned against a cart, obviously hoping for a glimpse of the Mongol. Sorkhatani went to her side. A few boys raced past them; Khasar's chief wife, the only one of his wives who had been captured, was outside her yurt, working at a piece of felt with another woman. Another boy trotted past them on a horse, then halted.

"Greetings, Tukhu," Ibakha said, smiling as she looked up at Khasar's youngest son. Tukhu was twelve, a year younger than Sorkhatani; he flushed and grunted a greeting. "Perhaps you and your father might come to Mass tomorrow." Ibakha fluttered her eyelids while Sorkhatani fumed in silence. Naturally her sister wanted the man she loved to attend the rite, where she would be worshipping him as much as the cross. "The priests would baptize you both."

The boy laughed. "A waste of water." He rode towards his mother's tent. Khasar was returning there, trailed by other riders and two wagons carrying sacks of milk. He had stripped to the waist; his broad brown chest gleamed with sweat.

Ibakha sighed; Sorkhatani caught her sister by the wrist. "You've seen him," she said. "Don't shame yourself by rushing over there. Anyway, now that Father's back, he's likely to come to our tent soon." Khasar often came there to drink with Jakha Gambu and to talk of old battles. He did not seem to find captivity that burdensome, but then his family was hostage to his good behaviour.

Khasar dismounted; his powerful arms bulged as he heaved a sack from one wagon. He was handsome, Sorkhatani admitted to herself; perhaps his brother the Khan was equally favoured. Once, her uncle Toghril had called Genghis Khan his adoptive son, and now the Mongol was in hiding, with Kereits in control of his old lands. Ibakha would do well to remember that; whoever her husband was to be, she would not find him among Khasar's people.

Jakha Gambu ate in Keuken Ghoa's tent that night. Sorkhatani saw how sombre he was, and his sons were equally silent. His three wives and his sons' wives chattered among themselves and hushed the children. Keuken seemed as indifferent to her husband's sullen mood as she was to his happier ones.

Jakha sent everyone away earlier than usual, dismissed the servants, then stepped outside. Sorkhatani and Ibakha helped their mother clear away the platters. Curds had formed in the milk simmering over the hearth; they had poured the whey into skins when Jakha Gambu came back inside.

"I've sent one of the guards for Khasar," he murmured to his wife. Ibakha flashed him a smile, then smoothed down her braids; Sorkhatani frowned. Maybe the men who advised the Ong-Khan had finally persuaded him to rid himself of his enemy's brother; that could account for her father's brooding.

"Call off your dogs!" a man shouted outside; Ibakha lifted her head at the sound of Khasar's voice.

"Welcome, Nokor," Jakha Gambu said as Khasar came through the entrance and bowed. Sorkhatani composed herself. If her father was inviting him inside, and calling him Nokor, his comrade in arms, he was not planning to take his head yet. Khasar muttered a greeting and walked to the back of the tent. Sorkhatani finished scooping the curds on to platters to dry; Ibakha sat down and tugged at her tunic.

Khasar seated himself at Jakha's right; Keuken Ghoa poured kumiss. "Drink deep," Jakha said. "You'll need it. Your brother sent messengers to Toghril."

Khasar nodded. "The guard told me Sukegei and Arkhai

411

were Temujin's envoys, and that my brother offered peace. He said little more than that."

"The message wasn't only for my brother, but also for some of those around him. You should hear what was said from me." Jakha Gambu gulped down more kumiss. "All the men your brother wished to address were in Toghril's camp, so that the matter could at least be settled quickly." He paused. "Arkhai and Sukegei spoke Temujin's words to Toghril first, and I'll try to capture some of your brother's eloquence. 'What have I done to you, Father and Khan?' they asked. 'Why did you force my people to flee, and scatter the smoke that rose from their yurts? Am I not the second wheel of your cart? My father restored you to your throne, and became your anda. When the Naimans put Erke Khara on your throne, I welcomed you to my camp and drove your enemies from your lands. You abandoned me once, treating me as no more than the burned meats of a sacrifice, and yet I rallied to your defence when you were attacked. Tell me what offence I've committed, so that I may put it right.' There was more to the message, but those are the essentials."

"And the Ong-Khan was unmoved?" Khasar asked.

"Oh no. Toghril cursed himself, cut one of his fingers, and let the blood drip into a birch-bark cup. He told Arkhai to carry the cup to Temujin, and said that if he ever had evil thoughts about Yesugei's son again, his own blood would surely flow."

"But I was told – "

Jakha held up a hand. "The next message was for Jamukha." He scowled. " 'You've divided me from Toghril-echige,' the envoys said. 'Once, we both drank from the Ong-Khan's cup. Now you drink from it alone, but how much longer will you drink from it?' As for Altan and Khuchar, the envoys reminded them that they had made Temujin their Khan and sworn to serve him, then asked if this was how they honoured their oath. 'Now you support the Ong-Khan my father,' they said, 'but what loyalty have you shown to me?' "

"And their replies?" Khasar asked.

"They said nothing. There was one message left to deliver, the one for Nilkha. By then, I thought Temujin might achieve his ends. My brothers regretted this war, and the messengers had reminded him of how untrustworthy Altan, Khuchar, and Jamukha are."

"Tell me the message for Nilkha," Khasar said.

"It was this. 'I became your father's son when I was clothed, while you were born to him naked. Envy caused you to break your father's heart and to drive me away. How can you bring him such grief? Is it that you want him to suffer, that even though he still lives, you wish to be Khan?' "

Khasar let out his breath. "Nilka was enraged," Jakha went on. "He ranted about how Temujin might call Toghril his father, but claimed he's also called him a blood-soaked bastard. He told the envoys that our people would graze our horses until they were fat enough for war, and that whoever won the battle would take the people of the vanquished for himself. That's the message your brother will receive." Jakha cursed under his breath. "Now Toghril and my nephew are arguing again, while those other three wretches have left for their camps. It's the end of your brother's hope for peace, but he's roused more discord here."

Khasar smiled. "Then perhaps he achieved something after all."

"I didn't want to ride against Temujin before," Jakha murmured, "and worry more about fighting him now. Toghril vacillates, and Khuchar and Altan may be having second thoughts. Our alliance may not last."

Khasar said, "And I remain your captive."

Ibakha bit her lip. Sorkhatani rose and picked up a plate of bones for their dogs. She had heard everything now; her father would have to fight, whatever his feelings.

The guards stood near the fire in front of the doorway. Sorkhatani found the three dogs behind a wagon at the back of the great tent; they snarled as she threw them the bones. She was circling the tent when she heard Khasar's voice.

"I bid you good night, Nokor and friend," Khasar was saying. Sorkhatani shrank back in the darkness. Her father and the Mongol stood alone, near the steps leading up to the doorway. "I assume you'll ride with Toghril if he's determined to fight."

"He'll fight," her father said. "Nilkha will drag him into it, as he did before."

"My fate is in your hands, Jakha Gambu. Whatever becomes of me, I can't ride with you against Temujin. My brother and I are arrows that have always rested in the same quiver."

"I understand." Jakha cleared his throat and spat. "Your family is safe with me," he murmured, "and the night guards sometimes lack vigilance."

Sorkhatani held her breath. Her father was taking a chance by letting his prisoner escape; she wondered what would come of it.

81

LAKE BALJUNA WAS nearly dry, a puddle in a sea of mud. Women moved through the marshes, stooping to pick plants or to squeeze water from the mud into jars. Bortai pressed some water into her jug, then straightened. The brackish water always tasted of clay, even when she strained it.

Teb-Tenggeri had been trying to summon rain for days; Bortai had seen him outside the camp with the other shamans, chanting as he dropped his pale jade stones into small cups of water. The herds had been driven east to graze, and the men had found watering holes there, but the water was low. Far to the north, a few birches and willows stood against the horizon; beyond them lay the wooded lands of the Tunguz. The Mongols could move no further north than this.

More of their people had joined them in the Onggirat lands, making their way to Temujin's camp with the herds and possessions they had saved during the flight from the Kereits. Temujin had led them north after his envoy Arkhai returned to tell him that the Senggum had promised war; Sukegei, after learning that his family were Kereit prisoners, had decided to go back to them. Without a promise of peace, Temujin had to retreat; the Onggirat troops were his rearguard now.

Camping circles covered the land around Lake Baljuna. Even in their precarious position, Temujin's closest comrades had remained loyal, although most of them might have found places in the Kereit ranks. The Khan had feared that his sister's husband might abandon him again, but Chohos-chaghan had led his people to Baljuna. The Khan's wives had tents now, poor and small as they were. Bortai's two oldest sons had found wives among the Onggirats, although the bride-prices were largely promises from Temujin.

Khojin and Alakha stumbled towards Bortai; the mud sucked at their boots. Khojin held up a plant in her grimy hand and Alakha clutched two wild onions to her chest.

"You did well," Bortai said. Khojin grinned; nothing could douse the girl's spirit. The child's courage made it easier for Bortai not to despair. She thought of what Arkhai had told her husband – that the Ong-Khan's allies were uncertain, that the old man lacked the spirit for fighting. The cold air bit at her face; autumn was near, the season for war. They would endure somehow, and hope Heaven favoured Temujin when the battle came.

Temujin came to Bortai's tent that evening. He was silent as they ate the plants and bit of game that were their meagre meal. At last he sent his other wives and his daughters to their tents.

Tolui and Ogedei went to the hides that served as their beds. Temujin settled himself on the narrow bed in the back of the tent and stared at the hearth. Darker spirits had claimed him once more. He had not joined with Bortai since they had moved to Lake Baljuna, and had not visited his other wives in their tents.

"We should fight," Tolui said as he stretched out.

Temujin glanced at the boy. "Be certain that we shall," he replied.

"When?"

"After the Kereits begin to move against us. I suspect they'll move east to meet the Onggirats, and then we can sweep down from the north."

Tolui said, "Maybe you should attack."

"I'd need more men for that."

"You have the Onggirats."

Temujin shook his head. "They'll fight to defend their lands, but they need more seasoning – they wouldn't do well on the attack."

Bortai heard the sound of horses' hooves outside, and then shouts from the guards; her husband reached for his sword. "Temujin!" a man cried. "Two scouts are here with Daritai Odchigin. He wishes to speak to you."

Temujin flinched. "I'll meet him outside," he shouted back, "not in my tent." He got up and went to the entrance. The boys were about to follow him when Bortai motioned them back.

"He'll kill Great-Uncle Daritai," Tolui said.

"Perhaps. Stay where you are." She went to the doorway and sat down just inside the open entrance.

Temujin was standing near a fire, his back to her. Daritai dismounted, stumbled towards the Khan, then dropped to his knees. Men stood in a half-circle around him; others had come out of the nearest tents.

"I come in peace," Daritai said, "and throw myself on your mercy."

"Then perhaps," Temujin said, "I should show you the mercy you deserve."

"He brings news of a plot against the Ong-Khan," another man said. "Your uncle and his men had to flee from the Kereits. His men are under guard a day's ride to the south, but Daritai Odchigin asked to be brought to you right away."

Bortai saw her husband's back stiffen. "Speak, Uncle," he said softly. "The Khan wishes to hear your last words."

Daritai struck his head against the ground, then sat back. "Toghril can't lead," he said. "He listens only to the last voice he hears. Jamukha finally saw this, and so did Khuchar and Altan. We held a secret council and agreed it was time to move against him. Jamukha said we could all be Khans ourselves, bowing neither to the Kereits nor to you, but I saw that removing Toghril might benefit you."

Bortai doubted that Daritai had actually been thinking of his nephew then. "We were going to surprise the Ong-Khan in his camp," Daritai continued, "but somehow he was warned, and we were forced to flee. Jamukha and the others rode west, towards Naiman country, but I decided to come to you. A man in an Onggirat camp told me you'd moved here, and your scouts met me along the way." He bowed his head. "I might have followed the others west, but now I see how unreliable they are — even Khuchar, who was like a son to me. I deserve to be punished, but maybe I can heal the wounds I inflicted by helping you now. I curse those who led me from your side, and myself for listening to them." The Odchigin took out his knife, cut his thumb, and let the blood drip. "May my blood flow if I ever betray you again."

"You would have no chance to betray me," Temujin said, "if I take your life here."

Daritai's broad shoulders sagged. "I knew that there might be no mercy for me, and yet I rode to you. Surely that shows you how deeply I regret my deeds."

"Father will kill him," Tolui whispered behind Bortai.

"You deserve death," Temujin said, "but you are my father's brother, and you've led men I need to my side. I'll let you live, Daritai, but know this — if I ever have cause to doubt you, if there's even a whisper of your possible disloyalty, if you ever speak evil words against me to others, even words uttered in drunkenness when men often don't know what they're saying, your body will feed the ravens. You must do everything you can to prove your loyalty, and pray that nothing causes me to doubt you. At the slightest mistake, your death will find you."

"You are generous, Temujin," Daritai said.

"You'll live with my sword hanging over you. Perhaps death would have been easier." Temujin waved a hand. "Take my uncle to Borchu's tent. In the morning, he and Borchu will ride to his men and lead them here to swear their oath to me."

He turned; Bortai rose and backed away from the doorway. He entered, went to the bed, and sat down. "I suppose you think," he said, "that I should have made an end of him."

Bortai said, "You need him now."

"I would have killed him," Tolui muttered.

Temujin sighed. "Son, a Khan has to know when revenge is useless, however justified. Daritai surrendered, and having his men among our troops may even make the attack you suggested possible." He pulled off his boots, then lay down. "Go to sleep."

Bortai moved to the bed. As she got in next to him, he drew her to him and covered her mouth with his. She slipped her arms around him, welcoming him.

A few days after Daritai's surrender, Heaven favoured them with rain. People cowered inside tents and under wagons, but no lightning struck near them; the lake and watering holes swelled with water.

When the storm passed, a caravan led by a trader riding a white camel stopped at the camp. Mongols surrounded the caravan, pestering the traders with questions, admiring the gold ornaments on the camels' harnesses and the camel-hair coats of the men.

The caravan's leader was called Hassan; he and his comrades Jafar and Danishmenhajib spoke the Mongol tongue. They had come north from the Ongghut lands south of the Gobi with a thousand sheep to trade for sables and pelts. The Khan was soon treating the traders as comrades, and welcomed them to his tents.

The traders talked of what was happening in other lands. The western ruler of Khwarezm had seized more of Kara-Khitai, and the Uighurs allied with Kara-Khitai were growing restive. The Ongghut ruler had doubts about how strong his Kin overlords would remain. Merchants worried that the conflict among Kereits and Mongols might disrupt their northern trade.

"What have you learned today?" Bortai asked her husband one evening when they were alone; he had spent much of the day by Hassan's tent.

"I learned more about those four boys with the traders."

Bortai had seen the boys. They had round eyes without folds, unlike any she had seen, and one had hair as red as flames. "What of them?"

"As I suspected, they're used as bedfellows."

Bortai hissed, grateful her sons were still outside. "I'd rather not hear about such things."

"If they must travel so long without their women, they have

to satisfy their needs somehow, and this way, our women are safe. It's one way of ordering such things." He gazed past her. "I'm also learning how much lies beyond these lands. Whenever I was in Toghril's camp, I dreamed of having his wealth, and yet from the traders who came there, I heard of distant rulers whose riches would shame his."

"So you wish to have more," she said. "That's natural enough."

"Having much means little if you haven't the power to hold it, and wealth tempts enemies." He paused. "We can be safe only when all who might be enemies are vanquished. God means us to be one ulus."

"So you have often said," she murmured.

"But I see it more clearly now than I did as a boy when I told you of my dream. Tengri wants me to do more than unite my people – I know it, even harried as I am by my enemies." His eyes had the distant look that told her he had forgotten she was there. "He means to make one ulus of the world."

82

KHASAR FOUND NO trace of his brother along the Onon or north of the river. He had fled hastily, the same night Jakha Gambu had spoken to him, and the moon had waned and grown fat again since then. Only his comrades Chakhurkhan and Khali-undar had escaped with him, and they had found no game among the cedars and thick undergrowth of the wild mountains beyond the Onon. Mosquitoes plagued them; their only food was blood drained from the veins of their horses, and Khasar had to chew on his leather harness to assuage his hunger. The weather turned cold; forest spirits howled through the trees.

Temujin would have gone north-east, putting distance between himself and his Kereit foes while he recovered. Khasar pressed on in that direction, and finally found a recent trail that led towards Lake Baljuna.

He was so weak by the time he sighted a few distant yurts that he had to halt while the men there rode out to him and his comrades. They were taken to a tent, fed, and given blankets; Khasar slept a dreamless sleep. When he awoke, the sun was above the tent's smoke-hole; a soldier told him that the Khan had arrived there at dawn.

"They told me you were sleeping," Temujin said as he entered the yurt. He embraced Khasar, then clasped the hands of the other two men. "I said you weren't to be awakened." He hugged Khasar again. "I feared for you."

"And I for you," Khasar said. "You couldn't have run much further without leaving the lands we know."

"The spirits will favour us again. Teb-Tenggeri brought us rain, and all those with me have sworn new oaths – we drank from the Baljuna to seal them. I have even brought some traders who stopped with their caravan to our cause."

"Good," Khasar said. "They'll be useful as spies."

The men sat down. "How did you get away?" Temujin asked.

"I was in Jakha Gambu's camp. He let me escape, and promised my wife and three sons would be safe. He doesn't want to fight, and distrusts the Ong-Khan's allies."

"With good reason," Temujin said. "Khuchar, Altan, and my anda decided to move against the Ong-Khan. Toghril found out, and his three false friends had to flee west. Daritai came here and told me of their failed plan."

Khasar cursed.

"He swore an oath to me," Temujin continued. "He knows he'll die if I ever have the slightest suspicion about him, but I need him now."

Khasar knew enough not to object. "I heard of your messages from Jakha. You would have had peace except for Nilkha."

"I hoped for peace. I didn't expect it." Temujin stroked his short beard and frowned, then turned towards Chakhurkhan and Khali-undar. "How long will it take you to get strong enough to ride?"

"We've recovered enough now," Khali-undar replied.

"Don't show your pride to me. Rest for another day – I want you sturdy enough for an important mission."

Chakhurkhan struck his chest. "We're yours, Temujin. Where do we ride?"

"Back to the Ong-Khan."

Chakhurkhan coughed. "I might have saved myself a hard ride here."

"Toghril's surprised me too often," Temujin said. "It's time I surprised him and paid him back for his faithlessness. You two will ride to his ordu, and my army will follow you south. You'll deliver a message to him, and you'll be my eyes. We'll make camp along the Kerulen, and when you return to me, you'll tell me everything you've seen in the Kereit camp. We won't be surprised this time."

"And what is your message to be?" Khali-undar asked.

"It won't be a message from me, but from Khasar." Temujin smiled. "You'll say the following. 'I've looked everywhere for my brother, and cannot find his tracks. My only shelter is the sky, my only pillow the hard ground. I long for my wife and children, who are in your hands. Give me assurances that they're safe, and I'll return to you and offer you my sword.' "

"Will the Ong-Khan believe that?" Chakhurkhan asked.

"He'll believe it," Khasar said. "He'll be grateful Temujin saved him a battle by going into hiding. Even Jakha will believe it. I told him I couldn't ride against my brother, but if Temujin's disappeared, I have no choice but to return to him." He grinned, admiring the plan, devious and treacherous as it was.

"Toghril will be lulled," Temujin said, "and then we'll close the trap and rid ourselves of that old man."

83

"I CAN HARDLY wait," Ibakha murmured. "Khasar's sure to be with us by the next full moon."

Sorkhatani peered at her sewing, barely able to hear her

sister over the wind howling outside and the chattering of the servants. Jakha Gambu, who had thought it wise to keep his distance from the Ong-Khan after Khasar's escape, had moved their camp closer to Toghril's after learning that the Mongol would return to them.

The Ong-Khan's ordu was now three days' ride away, just beyond a mountain pass. Khasar's envoys had met Toghril there, and Jakha Gambu had been summoned by the Ong-Khan just after the two messengers had departed. All was forgiven; Jakha had been careless in allowing three captives to escape, but no harm was done, since they would now swear an oath to Toghril.

Spring and summer had certainly been eventful, with a hard-won victory against the Mongols and then a plot against her uncle. Sorkhatani knew her father had been dreading war, and now he would not have to fight. Khasar would not be coming back if he held out any hope for his brother Temujin.

Not that Ibakha would be thinking of that. She had wept after Khasar's escape, as if he had betrayed her, but that was forgotten now. Sorkhatani frowned. Khasar probably would ask for her sister if Jakha Gambu dropped a few hints. He could not be completely indifferent to her beauty, and the marriage would bind him more closely to the Kereits. Sorkhatani made up her mind to speak to her father on her sister's behalf.

A few days later, Jakha Gambu's camp learned that a Mongol army had attacked the Ong-Khan. Kereit soldiers rode to them, warning them to flee, but Mongols were already at their heels. The enemy fanned out around the camping circle, cutting off escape. The terrified people, knowing a defence was futile, were herded into enclosures of wagons and ropes.

One of Sorkhatani's cousins, wounded, deprived of his weapons, and penned in near her and her sister, told of a battle that had raged for three days. The Ong-Khan, already feasting while awaiting Khasar's arrival, had been completely unprepared as the Mongols closed around his camp. The fighting was fierce, and the enemy had the advantage of surprise; many Kereits, drunk and unable to reach their horses, were forced to fight on foot. After the third day of fighting, word had spread through the Kereit ranks that Toghril and Nilkha had fled with a few men under cover of darkness; some others had managed to escape through the narrow mountain pass. By now, Sorkhatani's cousin supposed, the Kereits had been forced to surrender.

Keuken Ghoa wept, fearing for her husband. Ibakha raged, her love for Khasar now ashes. He had lied and trapped their uncle; he had never intended to return to her. Both offences seemed equally evil in her mind. Sorkhatani, frightened as she was, prayed for mercy. The Mongols were not looting, but waiting for orders before they sorted out prisoners and booty. Many among the Kereits had once fought with Genghis Khan; perhaps he would remember that.

Two days after the Mongols had taken his camp, Jakha Gambu returned with a Mongol general and more Mongol troops. As his people, still under guard, were brought before him, he announced that the Kereits had surrendered, without conditions. Genghis Khan, however, had promised not to execute men who had served their Kereit Khan faithfully, since he honoured loyalty to a sworn leader. After offering his people these scraps of hope, he led Keuken Ghoa and his two daughters to their tent, trailed by his Mongol guards.

"Temujin has agreed to meet with me," he said to his wife, "and I mean to offer him my daughters. Bringing them to him will assure him that I intend to serve him now."

Ibakha gaped at him. "You'd give us to him?" She gulped for air. "After what he and his brother did?"

Sorkhatani caught her sister's arm. "Silence," their father said. "He can enslave us and take all that we own, and I'm trying to avoid that. We'll leave today — bring only what you need for the journey."

Keuken Ghoa stared blankly at her husband. "But they'll need servants, and household goods, and all the other things brides require. We can't get all that together in a day."

Jakha scowled. "My dear wife, the Khan will decide what I own now, and I can't offer him things I may no longer possess. Pray that he finds our girls to his liking." He spun around and left the tent.

423

"I won't go!" Ibakha collapsed on the floor in a fit of weeping; Keuken Ghoa wrung her hands.

Sorkhatani knelt and grabbed her sister by the wrists. "Listen – can't you see Father's thinking of us, too? Would you rather be under the Mongol Khan's protection, or here when his men start enjoying their spoils?"

Ibakha whimpered, then wiped her nose. "However deceitful Genghis Khan was," Sorkhatani continued, "you have to admit he was clever, and we might have fared far worse. He had a lot of reasons to hate Uncle Toghril and Cousin Nilkha. Stop thinking of yourself for once, and think of our people. You won't help them if you displease the Mongol Khan, and he'll do as he likes with us anyway."

Ibakha pouted. Sorkhatani should have known that any appeal to reason could not touch her. "Think of everything he could give you," she went on. "You'd have a tent much finer than this. When he sees what a beauty you are, he'll surely want to keep you for himself."

Ibakha tilted her head. "Do you think so?"

"Really, Ibakha." Sorkhatani sighed. "Think of how others have suffered. We have to submit to the Mongols now – all we can hope for is mercy for our people. Be grateful you have the chance to win the love of their Khan."

"Your sister may be right," their mother said. Keuken's face was calm; the terror and grief of the past days had seemingly fled her childlike mind. "He's really the best husband you could have now."

"But he won't want you with a red, swollen face and tears pouring from your eyes." Sorkhatani got up and pulled Ibakha to her feet. "Father's waiting."

The outlying circles of the Ong-Khan's camp could be seen in the distance as they left the mountain pass. Sorkhatani glanced at her mother and sister. Ibakha was smiling as she leaned from her saddle to whisper to Keuken Ghoa. She was now enthralled with the prospect of becoming the Khan's wife; Khasar was quite forgotten.

The escort of Mongols riding with them led them towards the north end of the camp, skirting the tents and wagons. Burned tatters of felt flapped where other tents had once stood, and the frosty ground was trampled and marked by hooves. Mongols now watched over the Ong-Khan's herds; the people in the camp went about their tasks with bowed heads. Processions of wagons and mourners moved towards the mountains to bury the dead. Yet Sorkhatani had expected worse – heads on pikes, widows lining the trails to wail for their men.

They stopped near a large tent that had belonged to one of her uncle's Noyans, dismounted, and passed between the fires. A long line of horses was tethered to a rope next to the tent. Two young soldiers led their horses away as Jakha Gambu approached the Khan's guards.

A man climbed the steps to the entrance and shouted out her father's name. Sorkhatani was suddenly filled with dread. Ibakha's full lips were curved in a smile, her large brown eyes aglow; she was too great a fool to be fearful.

Sorkhatani kept her eyes down as she followed the others inside, then knelt on the carpeted floor, barely hearing her father's words of greeting. The tent was crowded with men, some standing and others seated. Her father and mother pressed their foreheads to the floor; she and her sister did the same.

Two booted feet moved towards them; hands reached down for Jakha Gambu and pulled him up. "I welcome you, Jakha," a soft voice said. "Whatever has passed, you're still a comrade who rode with me many times."

Sorkhatani forced herself to look up. He was taller than Khasar; she saw the strength in his arms as he embraced her father. The braids trailing below his helmet, his moustaches, and his short beard all shone like dark copper, and his eyes gleamed with gold. Khasar was only a shadow of this man, who might have been forged by God in Heaven. He wore a plain woollen robe, a tattered leather belt, and worn trousers; he had none of the jewels and ornaments she had seen on the Ong-Khan. He did not need such things; she would have known what he was even if he had been clothed in rags. He turned towards her for a moment. His pale eyes seemed to peer into her soul, and she knew why his men followed him.

When the other men had all greeted her father, the Khan sent most of them away, then led Jakha Gambu to the back of the

425

tent, seating him at his right. Keuken Ghoa was given the cushion to the left of the Khan; Ibakha and Sorkhatani sat near her. The Khan's general Borchu had remained behind, along with the Noyans Subotai, Jelme, and Jebe.

"Khasar would have been here to greet you," the Khan said, "but he is enjoying a reunion with his family. You kept them safe. He's grateful for that, as am I."

"I expected you to claim my brother's tent," Jakha said.

"I gave the tent, its servants, and everything in it to the horseherders Kishlik and Badai." The Khan served bits of meat from his knife. "I've also given them the right to claim the game they take during great hunts instead of sharing it out."

"They must have served you well."

"They did," Borchu said. "They warned Temujin when Nilkha was preparing to surprise him in the night. That allowed us to escape and fight you."

The Khan was generous, to give such a prize to common herders. Sorkhatani's hand trembled as she took meat from the Khan's knife.

"My men will secure the surrender of all the Kereit camps soon," the Khan said, "but it was never my wish to fight you, comrade. You were dutiful to your brother, and I won't punish you for that. I haven't forgotten that you once fought with me, and always meant to spare your life. Know now that I'll leave you all your herds and possessions as well. You'll remain chief of those in your encampments, but will serve me. The Kereits will no longer be a separate ulus, but part of mine, and will become members of Mongol clans."

"It's more than we deserve," Jakha Gambu said. "Toghril was my brother, but he was easily swayed and abandoned us in the end. I'll serve you now, my Khan."

Ibakha was staring at the Khan; her eyes had the same glazed look with which she had once regarded Khasar. He studied her for a moment, then smiled at Sorkhatani; her heart fluttered.

"Khasar told me of the beauty of Ibakha Beki and Sorkhatani Beki," the Khan said. "I see his eyes are still sharp." Ibakha blushed; Sorkhatani struggled to stay calm. "I'm surprised he didn't ask me if he could claim them for his spoils."

"I brought them to you," Jakha Gambu said, "in the hope you'll find them worthy. I would consider myself honoured if you took them into your ordu."

The Khan leaned forward. "Ibakha Beki," he said; Ibakha started. "Your father has spoken for you, but can you find it in your heart to become my wife willingly?"

Ibakha giggled and blushed still more; Sorkhatani heard the men chuckle. The Khan was toying with them, for there was no need to ask such a question.

"But of course." Ibakha covered her mouth and batted her long eyelashes. "I would be honoured, as any woman would – my heart would be yours."

"And you, Sorkhatani Beki?"

She met his eyes. Surely he saw how she felt; she doubted that much escaped his notice. "My father has spoken," she said, "and I know where my duty lies. I've been an obedient daughter, and pray that I would also be a worthy wife."

"But you haven't answered my question," he said. "I asked what was in your heart."

Her cheeks burned, answering his question silently. "My feelings, whatever they are, can't change my obligations," she said. "I shall do my duty to my husband, and give him no cause to complain about me."

The Khan laughed. "I see I won't have an answer from you," he said, "but then it isn't fitting for a maiden to be too open about such thoughts."

Ibakha frowned, looking bewildered. Say what you will do, Sorkhatani thought; don't torment us this way.

"Jakha Gambu," he said at last, "your daughters please me, and it will give me joy to bind your family to mine. I wish to take your beautiful Ibakha as my wife." Ibakha sighed softly. "Sorkhatani Beki also pleases me with both her beauty and her discretion. My youngest son will need a wife before long. It is my wish to betroth your younger daughter to my son Tolui – they're near the same age, and can have time to become acquainted before they're wed."

Sorkhatani kept her face still, managing not to betray the pain that lanced through her heart. "You do us great honour," her father murmured. She would be his son's chief wife, while

Ibakha would have a lower place among the Khan's wives; she supposed she should be happy about that. She knew where her duty lay; she would be a good wife to Tolui, and hoped there was something of his father in him. The Khan thought enough of her to give her to his son. You should have married me, she thought fiercely, then bowed her head.

84

IBAKHA WORKED AT a hide with a piece of bone. She had thought that, as the Khan's wife, with all her servants and slaves, she would have less to do. Yet by the time she questioned them about the sheep, the milk, food preparation, new panels for the third layer of felt she would soon have to add to her tent, and everything else, she often felt she had done their work as well as her own.

Bortai Khatun did not like to see the Khan's other wives idling. The Khan's chief wife was still handsome, in spite of her years; she had to be close to forty. Ibakha had expected to meet an old dowager, not someone who could still rival a younger woman's beauty.

Perhaps Bortai had bought a spell from the Khan's chief shaman to preserve her looks. The shaman was often with the Khan; Teb-Tenggeri, they called him. Ibakha had to fight the urge to cross herself whenever the shaman, with his hairless face and skin as smooth as a girl's, was present.

"Khadagan showed me a fine stitch for my embroidery," Yisui said. The two Tatar sisters sat on cushions, having brought their sewing to Ibakha's tent. "She uses it to sew little flowers — I'll show it to you when I learn it."

"Khadagan!" Ibakha giggled. "It's hard to believe the Khan would claim such a plain woman."

Yisugen looked up from the robe she was mending. "The Khan has never forgotten that she saved his life."

Ibakha scraped at the hide. Yisui and Yisugen had warmed

to her, perhaps because they were all close in age, but even they sometimes frowned at her the way her sister had.

"I pray our husband gets us both with child soon," Yisui said. "I would ask Teb-Tenggeri for a spell if I weren't so afraid of him."

Ibakha put down her bone and crossed herself. "My priests can say a prayer for you – you don't need the All-Celestial's spells."

Yisugen paled and made a sign against evil. "Don't say it. I saw him make rain for us at Baljuna. He rides up to Heaven on his white horse – everyone says so."

Ibakha said, "I'm not afraid of him."

Yisui and Yisugen both made signs. "He'll hear you," Yisui whispered. "He can hear at a distance, and through the ears of animals – you never know when his spirit might be near, listening." Her long black eyes grew colder. "His powers also serve our husband, and Teb-Tenggeri cherishes his rewards. You'd do well to remember that."

Ibakha hated the shaman, whose eyes always seemed to mock her silently. Her father found shamans useful, but gave a higher place to his priests. The Khan's chief shaman was like all such men, casting his spells and getting paid handsomely for them. The magic of the cross was stronger than Teb-Tenggeri's.

She would glorify herself in God's sight if she brought her husband to the true faith. Teb-Tenggeri would be banished, to practise his magic only when an evil spirit had to be driven from one who was ill or when the bones had to be read. Everyone would see how much the Khan loved her if he shared her faith.

After the great hunt, when the hides were cured and the meat dried and stored, a snowstorm raged over the Khan's camp. Ibakha helped her servants bring the sheep inside their yurts, then struggled through the falling snow to her great tent. She found the Khan there, alone for once; he stood by the hearth warming himself as her cook Ashigh watched the kettle.

Ibakha hurried to him. "You came to me," she said breathlessly, "even in this storm."

"Your tent was closest, my horse could go no further, and your cooks are the best of any here."

Ashigh grinned. "I do my best," he said. Ibakha shook the snow from herself, handed her coat to the old woman who was the only other servant present, then settled the Khan by the bed. The two servants sat near them, eating only after her husband had taken some meat.

She would not have a better chance to speak to him. She rarely had him to herself, without his other wives coming to share the meal or his Noyans drinking and singing with him, and when he was in her bed, he did not want to talk.

"There's something I wish to tell you," she said.

"Then say it," he replied.

"I wish to tell you of my faith."

The Khan lifted his brows and sighed. "Go on."

"Of course my priests could tell you more – they have more learning."

"Ibakha, tell me what you wish to say."

"Well." She plucked at her robe. "Surely you've heard something from my father or others of my people about God's Son, and how he died on a cross for our sins."

"I have, but men have other things to talk about."

"The Christ told His followers," she said, "of God's love for them, and said that if they believed in the true faith, they would have eternal life."

He shrugged. "I've heard that sages in Khitai also know the secret of immortality."

"I'm speaking of the soul," she said. "The Christ died for our sins, then rose from the dead, and promised that we would live forever in Heaven. If you believe in God's Son – "

"God has many sons," he said. "He gave my ancestor Alan Ghoa three sons, and made them the fathers of Khans."

Ibakha crossed herself, at a loss for what else to say. The chanting of the priests as they swung their golden censers always filled her with joy, and the thought of the Christ watching over her gave her happiness; she wished she could explain that to him. "It would make me happy if you shared my faith."

"Ibakha, I let you keep your priests. Believe what you like, but don't ask me to pray as you do."

"My faith is my shield against evil," she said. "In all the world, good and evil must struggle. Your shaman Teb-Tenggeri –"

Her husband made a sign. "You wouldn't need so many of his spells," Ibakha insisted, "if you – "

Something in his eyes warned her to be silent. "My step-brother has served me well with his powers," he said quietly, "and I'm not such a fool as to make an enemy of him."

The servants rose and took away the empty platters. It would have been surprising, she thought, if he had accepted her words easily, but all was not lost. He would need a prayer from her priests eventually, and then –

"Khasar and I," he said, "used to hunt marmots as boys." Ibakha blinked, wondering why he was talking of that now. "Every spring, when we heard their whistling and saw them rolling down the hillsides towards their holes, we'd set out to hunt them, and often they were all we had to eat. We would sneak up on a hole, and one of us would wave a branch while the other took aim. It amused me to see a marmot sitting by its hole, curious, transfixed by our waving branch, too stupid to notice the arrow aimed at its heart. I waited as long as I dared before making my shot, because it gave me such pleasure to watch a foolish creature doing so little to protect itself from harm."

"Men have better sport," she said, "than hunting marmots."

He gestured to her; she knelt and pulled off his boots. "Do you know why I took you as a wife?" he asked.

She looked up. "Surely because you found me pleasing."

"Because you were beautiful, but your sister is as fair. I might have given you to one of my sons and taken her as my wife, young as she is."

Ibakha felt confused. "I'm grateful you chose me."

"Yes, I chose you. Khasar told me of the beauty of Jakha Gambu's daughters. He also told me one had the look of a young eagle in her eyes, while the other seemed as flighty as a small bird. Now I'll tell you why you, rather than your sister, are my wife."

Ibakha stood up; he got to his feet and smiled down at her. "My son Tolui needs a wise woman for his first wife, one who can be to him what his mother is to me. When I saw the fire in Sorkhatani's face, I was reminded of my Bortai when she was a girl. But it didn't seem fitting to claim you both when I still have sons who must be wed, so I chose you. I have wise wives already – it doesn't matter if one is a fool."

It took her a few moments to grasp his meaning. Tears sprang to her eyes.

"Come now, Ibakha." He was still smiling. "As I said, it doesn't matter. Be as foolish as you like, but don't pretend you're wiser than you are, or chatter about things you don't understand." His hand gripped her shoulder. "Come to bed."

One night that winter, the Khan woke at Yisugen's side, crying out with such passion that she summoned the guards. His sleep had been troubled by a dream, one he could not recall, although he was certain the spirits were trying to speak to him.

The next night, he lay with Ibakha, but tossed so restlessly that she could not sleep. When he moaned and sat up abruptly, she sent for her priests.

Her husband was calmer when the three priests arrived, but scowled as they approached the bed. "I need a shaman," he shouted, "not these priests."

Ibakha flung her arms around him. "Let them pray for you," she said. "Your sleep won't be troubled again."

The priests prayed, burned incense, and made the sign of the cross over him. When they left, the Khan was sleeping soundly; Ibakha exulted.

Within a day, her servants had told others that Ibakha's priests had brought peace to the Khan. After he passed a peaceful night with Bortai and another with Khadagan, Ibakha was certain his bad dreams were banished. Several times before, the Khan had spent nights troubled by evil dreams, and only Teb-Tenggeri had been able to ease him. Some whispered that the shaman was angry at not being summoned, but Ibakha had never feared him. A few days later, when Yisui and Yisugen came to tell her they were both pregnant, she admitted that her priests had said prayers for them. Yisui wondered aloud why

432

their prayers had not yet opened Ibakha's womb, but even that could not diminish her joy.

Her rejoicing was short-lived. When the Khan came to her again, he had hardly fallen asleep before he started from the bed and shouted to the guards, ordering them to send for his chief shaman.

"But why?" Ibakha asked. "Didn't my priests help you before?"

"I want Teb-Tenggeri."

She could not argue with him. Teb-Tenggeri might fail, and then the Khan would have to summon the priests again.

The Khan's stepbrother said nothing to her when he arrived with two other shamans. Ibakha sat on the eastern side of her tent with the servants while the shamans sacrificed a lamb and boiled it in a cauldron. Teb-Tenggeri chanted, shook his bones as he danced around the bed, then offered a potion to the Khan. The other shamans beat their drums; Teb-Tenggeri hovered over the Khan, bending low several times to whisper to him.

Ibakha ached with weariness by the time the shamans were done. "My brother sleeps," Teb-Tenggeri whispered as he moved away from the bed. "A dream that rouses a man from sleep often carries a message that must be heeded." He gazed towards Ibakha with his long dark eyes. "Temujin will hear the message soon."

He left the tent. "We'll see what message my husband hears," Ibakha called out as the other two shamans were passing through the doorway. "Perhaps it will tell him to rid himself of his chief shaman." The servants gasped as she walked towards the bed; they were sure to tell others of her defiant words tomorrow. She leaned over her husband; his eyes were closed, his breathing slow and even. Ibakha took off her robe and slipped under the blankets.

"Ibakha."

She struggled to wake. Her husband sat on the bed, looking down at her. "I know what my dream was trying to tell me," he said.

She sat up and smoothed down her shift. Beyond the hearth, the tent was dark, the servants asleep. "You won't be pleased to hear it," he continued. "You weren't meant to be my wife. The spirits have ordered me to give you up."

Her throat locked. She clawed at the blankets; her voice freed itself. "You can't mean it!" she screamed. "This is Teb-Tenggeri's doing – he put a spell on you, he – "

The Khan grabbed her by both arms. Coughs and mutters reached her from the shadows. "My dreams have never lied to me," he said softly. "They've always shown me what has to be. This one says to give you up."

"You don't believe – "

"Silence." He leaned closer to her. "I'll hear no protests from you, or I'll tell others everything else my dream told me, and that can scarcely help you now."

"What could it have said?" she whispered.

"That even a Khan can be harmed by ambitious fools close to him." He called out to the guards; a soldier entered. "Who is the officer on duty tonight?" the Khan asked.

"Jurchedei."

"Tell him to come inside." The Khan stood up and pulled his coat tightly around himself. "Get dressed, Ibakha, and cover your head."

Ibakha put on her robe and a scarf, too stunned even to feel fear. The shaman had put this dream inside him. The servants were awake; she could not bear to think of what they would tell others.

Jurchedei entered and approached them. "Jurchedei," the Khan said, "you've served me faithfully." Ibakha glanced at the other man's roughened, hard face, then looked away. "You deserve any reward I can give you, and I wish to offer you a prize now. My beautiful Ibakha Beki is now yours."

The Noyan gaped at him. "Temujin!"

"I want you to know that she is above reproach, that she has been a good and faithful wife. I hoped to keep her with me, but a dream has come to me, commanding me to give her up. If I must lose her, I can think of few who deserve her more than you." The Khan lowered his voice. "Her only flaw is that she sometimes lacks sense, but you're capable of dealing with that, and her beauty will more than make up for it."

"You do me a great honour," the general said.

"She will keep her tent, and half the servants she brought with her. I must have her cook Ashigh, but the other cook's nearly as skilful – you'll feast well in your new wife's tent."

Ibakha searched her husband's face. She saw no relief in his pale eyes at being rid of her, no sorrow over losing her.

"Her descendants will be honoured," the Khan continued, "as though she were still one of my wives. Ibakha has done nothing dishonourable – I wouldn't give such a faithful friend a woman who had. I am the one who offended the spirits by keeping her." He took Ibakha's hand and thrust it into the general's. "May your joy with her be as great as mine."

The Khan walked towards the doorway and was gone. Jurchedei stared at Ibakha, clearly as shocked as she was. She tore herself from his grasp and ran to the entrance.

A man was bringing a horse to the Khan. Behind him, a few men stood around a fire, warming their hands. One of them looked up; she saw the dark eyes of Teb-Tenggeri.

"When I go to war," Tolui said, "I'll bring you a golden cup from the Tayang's tent."

Sorkhatani turned in her saddle. "Is your father planning to fight the Naimans?"

"He'll have to sooner or later. Maybe this autumn, or next year – I'll be old enough to fight then."

"Unless the Naimans make a truce," she said.

Tolui scowled, then brightened. "If he doesn't fight them, maybe we'll ride against the Merkits."

"Don't worry, Tolui. There will always be wars. You'll have many chances to show your courage."

The boys and girls who had ridden out with them were racing towards the Kereit camp across the sprouting spring grass. Tolui had beaten them all at races since coming to Jakha's ordu. He looked most like his father when he spoke of war, his round face firm and determined, his pale eyes aglow. There was fire in his face; perhaps he would grow up to be much like the man she loved.

Sorkhatani thought fleetingly of her sister, whom the Khan had given away that winter. The story was that a dream had commanded him to do so, but Sorkhatani often wondered if the Khan was secretly relieved at being rid of her. He should have married me, she thought, but knew now why he had not. She would show her love for Tolui's father by being a good wife to his son.

"I'll race you," Tolui said.

"I may beat you."

"No, you won't." His horse bolted. She galloped after him, her braids streaming behind her as the wind rose.

85

GURBESU HAD ORDERED that the head of Toghril Ong-Khan be brought to her. A silver band encircled the neck; the silver plate on which the head sat rested on a piece of white felt.

The head was on a table to the right of the Tayang's throne; Toghril's heavy-lidded eyes stared towards the hearth. Gurbesu had offered the head libations, holding her goblet to the twisted lips, and the Tayang's concubines had sung to it. The Ong-Khan had been coming to them to seek refuge, and his death was an evil omen. She hoped that his spirit would be placated by the honour shown to him.

The girls seated behind Gurbesu continued to pluck their lutes. The Tayang was muttering about the Mongols to Ta-ta-tonga. Bai Bukha had spoken of little else since hearing of Toghril's death at the hands of Naiman sentries; the guards had not believed the old man's claim to be the Ong-Khan.

There had been many such evil omens lately. A foal of the Tayang's favourite mare had been strangled in her womb and born dead. Gurbesu's third child by Bai Bukha, like the two before it, had emerged from her too soon and never drawn breath.

She had been given a poor choice after the death of Inancha Bilge. Agreeing to become Bai Bukha's wife had not kept him and his brother Buyrugh from fighting. Now the Tayang was tiring of her. Soon he might not listen to her at all.

"Damned Mongols!" Bai Bukha sank back in his throne. "Is there no limit to their Khan's ambitions?" He glanced to his right, where his generals sat. "In the sky, there are many stars, and both a sun and moon, but the Mongol would have one Khan in these lands. The Tatars are no more, the Kereits submit to him. When will it be our turn?"

"May that day never come," Jamukha said. Gurbesu had been displeased when her husband gave him refuge; she did not trust a man whose greatest talent was in shifting his alliances. Yet she had found nothing to hold against him during his time among her people. When the Tayang summoned him, Jamukha came to his ordu; otherwise, he seemed content to be left alone. His handsome face was unmarked by his tribulations, but his dark eyes had the contemplative look of an old man.

"You worry too much over Temujin," Jamukha continued. "He's spent himself in his wars, and needs time to recover. In the meantime, those under him will chafe at their bonds."

Bai Bukha scowled. "I say the time to strike is now. Do you think I called you all here only to drink with the Ong-Khan? See how low his people were brought by Genghis Khan." His eyes narrowed. "Jamukha advises us to wait. I say we must fight."

"If my father says we are to fight, then we must," Guchlug said. The young man peered past Ta-ta-tonga at the Tayang. "Our brave generals are always prepared for war." Gurbesu tensed. Her stepson longed to prove himself in battle; he would not see the risks. They might only bring the Mongols down upon themselves if they moved against them now.

"May I speak, husband and Tayang?" Gurbesu asked. Bai Bukha grunted. "Those Mongols are a barbarous, evil-smelling lot — what would we do with them even if we captured them? Their most noble and beautiful girls would be useless for any-thing except to milk our cattle and sheep, and even for that they would have to learn to wash their hands."

The generals laughed. "My wife advises me not to fight?" Bai Bukha asked.

"Leave them to their lands," she replied. "Eventually they'll fight among themselves again, and that will give you a chance to strike."

"Women know nothing of fighting," the Tayang muttered.

"You know little more, my Tayang." Khori Subechi was speaking. "A strong spear thrown by a weak arm rarely reaches its target."

Bai Bukha gripped the arms of his throne. "You insult me!"

"I speak only the truth," Khori Subechi said, "that you haven't been tested in war. But we are sworn to you, and must do as you command."

Gurbesu looked down. The generals might think her words were wise, but would obey her husband in the end. They would tell themselves that their skill as generals would make up for his lacks as a ruler.

Jamukha leaned forward. "Temujin wounded me," he said softly. "I desire nothing more than his defeat. But this isn't the time to fight. Temujin thrives on war, and those sworn to him will unite against a Naiman threat."

"Cowards," the Tayang said. "I'm surrounded by cowards. Jamukha's so fearful of his anda that he's lost his courage — perhaps he no longer wishes to replace him as the Mongol Khan."

Gurbesu lifted a hand, then let it fall. A howl outside startled her; the dogs were barking. Another omen, she thought, feeling as though wolves were circling the camp.

"I'll send an envoy to the Ongghuts," Bai Bukha continued. "They'll be wondering what designs the Mongol jackals have on them. They can be my right wing, and move north across the Gobi to strike at their camps while we advance east. The Mongols will be trapped between us."

"A good strategy," Koksegu Sabrak murmured. "That is, if the Ongghuts decide to fight."

"Will you wait until the Mongols move against us?" Bai Bukha shouted. He jumped to his feet; the firelight from the hearth flickered over the head of the Ong-Khan, making its frozen grimace look like a sneer. The Tayang cried out and pointed at the head with one trembling hand. "Even this dead man mocks me! See how he laughs! I hear him laughing now!" He seized the head and threw it to the floor.

Gurbesu gasped, horrified at the sacrilege. Three of the generals made signs against evil. The lutes of the girls were silent, the barking of the dogs louder.

Koksegu Sabrak slowly stood up. "What have you done?" he asked. "You bring the head of a dead Khan here to be honoured, and then smash it. This is an evil omen, Bai – I hear the dogs speaking of what's to come. You may be our Tayang, but your judgement's always been weak – you're more skilled at hunting and falconry than war."

"No one will mock me!" Bai Bukha shouted. "Not you, and not this dead man!" He stamped on the head; Gurbesu heard the bones crunch. "There will be no more talk that Inancha's son is only a shadow of his father. You'll take back your words, or none of you will leave this tent alive!"

"Father!" Guchlug leaped up and strode towards the Tayang. "If it's war you want, we'll give you war, but you can't bring down your prey with an empty quiver."

Bai Bukha was breathing hard. "Heaven is with me," he whispered. "I see the Mongols scattering before us."

Gurbesu got up, went to her husband, then knelt. "I beg the Tayang's permission to speak," she said. "If you are to fight, you cannot turn back. A victory will give you power over the Mongol and Kereit lands, but a defeat will be our ruin. You must hurl your soldiers at the Mongol Khan until his lines are broken. Lose, and he won't give you the chance to withdraw – he'll put an end to us."

"Your Queen speaks the truth," Jamukha said. "If Temujin defeats you in the field, he won't let you threaten him again. He'll harry you, whatever it costs him."

"Don't speak to me of defeat," the Tayang said. "Genghis Khan is weak now, and his enemies will fight with us."

Gurbesu looked towards the crushed head of the Ong-Khan and crossed herself. Her husband would not turn back now. She bowed her head, listening to the howls of the dogs outside the tent.

86

HEAVEN HAD BROUGHT him here. Jamukha stood at the Tayang's side; behind them, the Khangai massif loomed. The Naimans had advanced to the Khangai Mountains; below the Tayang, in the foothills, the army had made camp. Standards belonging to Merkits, Kereits still resisting the Mongols, and Temujin's few surviving Tatar enemies stood near several encampments.

By the time the Tayang had reached the Khangais, his scouts had told him that the Mongols were advancing towards the Orkhon. Bai Bukha had known then that the Ongghuts had decided to warn his enemy instead of fighting with him; the hope of trapping the Mongols further east was gone.

Yet the Tayang had not despaired. The Ongghuts clearly hoped an alliance with the Mongols would be useful against their Kin masters, but they would have to treat with the Naimans when the Tayang had his victory. Perhaps, Jamukha thought, he had misjudged Bai Bukha. With the Naiman ranks swelled by some of Temujin's old enemies, they still had the advantage of numbers.

The Tayang kept Jamukha at his side, so that Jamukha could tell him how the Mongols were likely to fight. He suspected that Bai Bukha also distrusted him, and wanted him near so that Jamukha would not be tempted to desert him.

Jamukha looked back at the rocky massif. On a wide ledge above a shelf of rock, a pavilion stood; Gurbesu and several of the Tayang's concubines had come there to see him fight. In spite of himself, he had a grudging admiration for the Queen. None of his own useless wives would have had such courage; it had been easy to leave them behind when he fled to the Naiman court.

He turned towards the land below. Sandhills and dunes were scattered over the yellow steppe; spring had brought little new grass to the land, and its few bushes were gnarled, twisted growths clinging to the dunes as sand sifted around them.

Always before, on the eve of battle, he had felt most alive, alert to every sight, sound, and smell. His senses were duller now; he could taste neither victory nor defeat. Once, he had anticipated battle, but now he longed only for its end. Even his hatred had become a banked fire that only occasionally flared. An invisible hand held him now, aiming him where it willed, and he was powerless to resist.

A soldier rode up the high hill to the Tayang, bringing word that the Naiman scouts had encountered the enemy's advance guard. A Mongol horse had been captured, so lean its ribs were visible. The Tayang rejoiced; his well-fed horses could easily overwhelm such played-out steeds.

Two nights later, another rider came with news of the Mongols camped on the steppe beyond Mount Nakhu. The plain there was studded with camp-fires as numerous as the stars.

The Tayang brooded when the soldier left him. "It's a ruse," Jamukha told him. "Temujin wants you to believe his men outnumber ours, and then retreat."

"A retreat would be to my advantage, not his." The Tayang looked at the other men seated near the fire. "If we pull back, their horses will get even leaner when they follow us, and then we can fall on them. If all their animals are as thin as the one we found, they won't last through the march."

"You came here to fight," Khori Subechi said, "and now you talk of retreat."

"Be silent," the Tayang said, then motioned at another man. "I'll give the orders here. Ride to my son below, and tell him to draw back."

"He won't like it," Khori Subechi muttered.

"He'll do as I say."

The man left them to carry the message to Guchlug. The others stretched out against their saddles to rest; the Tayang continued to sit by the fire.

Jamukha's thoughts were clearer now. The Tayang was showing more wisdom than he had expected, but perhaps it was already too late. His generals would see a strategic retreat only as a sign of Bai Bukha's cowardice. He had pushed them into this war, and they were determined to make their stand. If they did not retreat soon, they might not be able to later. The Mongols would force them into the mountain passes or

441

up the precipitous slopes. The Naiman generals would have to hold their ground then to have a chance at victory.

Jamukha was dozing when the rider returned. As the man came towards them, he saw that Guchlug was with him. The Tayang's son halted by the fire, then spat to the side of the flames.

"My father talks like a woman," Guchlug said. The resting soldiers stirred, then sat up. "When my men heard this messenger say you wanted us to pull back, I felt shame that your seed gave me life. I should have known you wouldn't have the spirit for war when you've hardly left your camp except to piss."

"You fool!" Bai Bukha shouted. "It's easy for you to show courage now. I wonder if you'll be as brave when death shadows you, when you see the enemy massed against you."

"My father is afraid."

"I'm telling you we can have victory if – "

"In his tent, Bai Bukha speaks brave words." Khori Subechi stood up. "Now that the battle's nearly upon us, he wants to scurry with the rabbits for cover. Inancha never showed his horses' hindquarters to his enemies."

The others were muttering; the general shook his fist. "I have never retreated," Khori Subechi went on. "Wasn't it Queen Gurbesu who said you would have to stand and fight if you took the field? We should have given her the command – she would make a better general than you."

The Tayang went for his knife; another man grabbed Bai Bukha's arm. The Tayang snarled. Khori Subechi picked up his saddle and walked away. Guchlug and the other men were still. Jamukha waited, knowing what the Tayang would have to say.

"Very well," Bai Bukha murmured. "If you say this is the time to fight, then we'll fight. All men must die, and perhaps this is the time to carry the Mongols' deaths to them. Give the order – we will attack the Mongol encampment."

The Naimans left the foothills, slipped along the Tamir River, then crossed the Orkhon River. On the other side, Naiman scouts met the Mongol advance troops, and were pushed back. Below Mount Nakhu, the Naimans took up positions in the grassy foothills. The Mongols were in sight, tiny black figures near the horizon under the darkening sky.

At dawn, the Naiman army advanced across the steppe. Bai Bukha, surrounded by his rearguard, watched from a hill below the mountain as the men rode out. Gurbesu's pavilion was a bright white spot against Mount Nakhu's black rocks.

The Tayang leaned forward in his saddle; Jamukha glanced at him, then looked below. The Mongols were moving out in close rank, as tightly together as thick grass. As he watched, the advancing light cavalry of the Naimans swept towards them. For a while, as the wing began to close, Jamukha believed that the Naimans might overcome the enemy; arrows flew as the Naiman heavy cavalry in the centre held its ground behind the archers. Bai Bukha, he thought, should now bring his rearguard forward, to be ready when the Mongols were pushed back. Then, suddenly, the Naiman archers on the left were drawing back, firing from their saddles at the Mongols pursuing them.

The Tayang rose in his stirrups. "Who are those men who harry our advance guard like wolves?" he cried out.

Jamukha saw the fear in Bai Bukha's face then, and nearly despaired. "I know those men," he heard himself say. "They are led by those Temujin calls his four dogs. Their names are Jebe and Kubilay, Jelme and Subotai, and it's said they crave human flesh on the day of battle. You can't run from them, Bai Bukha. Bring out your rearguard and force them back."

The Tayang's mouth worked. "How can I advance when we're already being pushed back?" He shouted to another man; a signal flag dipped.

The Tayang was soon retreating towards the mountain. Jamukha stayed on the hill as long as he dared; when the Mongols started to fan out around the Naiman army, he ordered his men to follow the Tayang. The Mongols spread out in the lake formation, a sea of men and horses flowing over the steppe, swallowing the Naimans trapped in the flood.

Bai Bukha was in the mountain's shadow when Jamukha caught up with him. The Naimans at the army's centre were still holding their ground, but the Mongol left and right wings swept towards the sides, just behind the forces of his anda's four dogs. From here, unable to hear the cries of wounded and fallen men, the whistling of arrows, and the clash of weapons, it seemed that the men on the battleground were engaged in only a game.

The Tayang pointed. "Who are those men," he said, "who gambol about as they fight, whose horses leap like foals at play?"

"Those," Jamukha replied, "are the Uruguds and Mangguds. They once rode with me, and they hunt their enemies without mercy, cut their throats, and seize all their weapons and clothing as part of their spoils, leaving nothing but the bodies behind. Are you brave enough to face such men?"

He had hoped this might fire the Tayang's courage. Instead, the flags signalled another retreat. Jamukha followed, not looking back until they were high on a rocky ridge above Gurbesu's pavilion. The Naimans in the rear were falling back to follow the Tayang. Gurbesu was still hidden under the white roof of her pavilion; apparently she did not intend to flee. The centre of the Mongol army was a blade stabbing through the Naiman ranks and he spotted the nine-tailed standard of his anda.

"Who leads those troops there," the Tayang shouted, "the ones who are cutting through our ranks like a sword?"

"They're led by my anda Temujin," Jamukha answered. "He swoops towards us now like a hungry falcon. Hold your ground, Bai Bukha – you must throw them back before they reach the mountain. More are behind him – those led by his brother Khasar, whose arrows can strike from great distances and skewer several men on one shaft. And there are the men under Temuge Odchigin's command. He's called the lazy one, but he's never late to battle."

The sky was darkening. The signal flags dipped once more; the Tayang and his royal guard moved up the mountain until they were hidden by the trees. Retreating Naimans fled up the slopes to Jamukha's left and right; with the enemy fanning out around them, and Temujin's troops driving through the centre, there was no other place to retreat. The wings of the Mongol army closed like pincers, steadily pushing the Naimans towards the mountain; the fallen men and horses looked like a child's discarded dolls. Through a break in the Mongol lines, some of the Merkits led by Toghtoga Beki streamed north, abandoning their allies. The Mongols would force the Naimans up the slope, then surround the mountain.

The will of Heaven was clear. Jamukha thought of the day he had danced with Temujin under the great tree, when they had sworn never to part from each other. Every weapon he had thrown at Temujin since then had been turned against him; he had only increased his anda's strength and power with each blow. The Tayang would be yet another weapon that would fail him.

He sat on his horse amid his men, not moving, not speaking as darkness came, listening to the war-cries of the living and the screams of the dying as more men fled up the slopes behind him.

"This battle is lost," Jamukha said at last. "If we are to escape, we must do so under cover of night. The enemy will have Mount Nakhu surrounded before dawn."

"So we're to flee once more," one man muttered. "And where do we run to now?"

Jamukha held up his hand. "I have failed you," he said. No one denied it. "I free you from the oaths you swore to me. If you stay to surrender, remember that Temujin has often forgiven those who were loyal to their leaders, so it's likely he'll show you mercy. There would be little for me if I fell into his hands."

His horse carried him slowly down the ridge; a few men followed him. He did not look back at the others. His mount halted; he beckoned to Ogin.

"I wish you to carry a message," Jamukha said. "When the battle ceases for the night, you'll ride to Temujin — that is, if you're willing to do this for me."

The other man struck his chest. "I am still yours to command, my Gur-Khan."

Jamukha winced at the sound of that empty title. "You'll say this. I, Jamukha, have put fear into the Tayang's heart with my words. He hides on the mountain, too frightened to face you, and my words were the arrows that wounded him. Take care, my friend, and the victory will be yours. I must leave the Naimans now. This battle is over for me."

Ogin recited the message back to him, then said, "Do you wish me to ask for a reply?"

"No reply he could give would make any difference. We'll ride for the Tangnu Mountains. Follow when you have delivered the message."

Ogin made his way down the trail. When he was gone, Jamukha led the others down the slope, refusing to think of how few of his men were following him.

During the night, the Naimans who had fled up the mountain searched for an escape. The order had been passed; they were to get away however they could, yet there was no word about making a stand elsewhere. The Naimans, deprived of direction, still reeling after the ferocity of the Mongols, could think only of flight. Their panic and despair drove them down the rocky slopes and treacherous trails. The darkness they had hoped would be their protection led many to their deaths when they fell into unseen chasms. As the Tayang came down the mountain with his guard, all that was visible below the cliffs were dark, unmoving forms stacked like logs. The way was silent; the moans and cries had ceased by then.

Gurbesu did not flee. A few of the women with her ran away with what they could carry; the others wept, but stayed. The soldiers guarding her refused to leave her even after she told them they were free to go.

Now that the battle was lost, it took little courage to face the will of God. She had done what she could for her people, and had failed them; she would share their fate.

The Mongol camp-fires flickered on the plain until dawn. By then, the Naimans who had not escaped were taking up their positions below. To her surprise, Gurbesu saw the banners and tugh of her husband and his guard. The Tayang might have found his courage, or perhaps the men with him had refused to retreat.

The Mongols attacked when the sun was just above the horizon. When Gurbesu saw the Tayang's guard pull back and mass together against the onslaught, she knew that Bai must have been wounded. The Mongols closed in around them, slashing with their swords, lifting men from their saddles with

446

lances. A cloud of arrows whistled towards the ledge where her pavilion stood, then fell on the Naimans below.

Mongol archers rode towards the trail that led up to the ridge. Several guards fell, impaled by arrows; the other Naimans answered with a volley. Gurbesu readied her bow and took aim; her arrow struck one of the enemy in the eye. A sharp pain lanced through her shoulder; an arrow jutted from her just below the blade. The other women shrieked; as the Mongols came on, climbing over the bodies of dead comrades, the screams deafened her. She sank to the ground as darkness swallowed her.

Gurbesu came to herself only long enough to know she was being carried, then fainted again. She awoke to find one of her women sucking at her wound; the arrow was gone. When the wound was cauterized with a piece of hot metal, the pain made her faint once more.

After her spirit returned to her, she saw that she was inside a small field tent. A woman, the oldest of the servants who had been with her, sat at her side, weeping.

"My Queen,' the woman said, "I thought we would lose you. You were carried here three days ago."

Gurbesu closed her eyes for a moment. "My husband," she whispered.

"But I told you before. The enemy claimed his life. Koksegu Sabrak and Khori Subechi refused to leave his side even when he was dying – they and all their men fought on until the last man was dead."

"And Guchlug?"

"I don't know, my Queen. I heard the Mongols guarding us say he had escaped. We're in the Mongol camp – those still alive among our people have surrendered, and the Mongols are hunting the ones who fled. They spared those who were left of our guard, and carried off the Tayang's other women. I – " The woman's voice broke; she was crying again.

At last Gurbesu said, "What is to become of me?"

"The Mongol Khan set a guard around you, and told me to see that you lived." The servant touched her hand. "It seems he means to claim you for himself."

A day later, Gurbesu was summoned to the Khan's tent. An escort of Mongols came for her, put her on a white horse, and rode with her through the camp. Two carts passed her, carrying bodies to the mountain for burial; defeated Naiman soldiers, confined in roped enclosures, knelt as she rode by. Her robe was soiled, the rip where the arrow had struck was still unmended, and only a scarf covered her hair; she could not look much like a queen.

Genghis Khan's standard stood in front of a large yurt to the north of the encampment. Through the doorway, she heard the murmur of voices and the sound of lutes. The guards stepped back as she went inside, followed by her servant.

She would not kneel to him. Gurbesu bowed from the waist, then raised her head. Several men sat on a platform in the back of the tent, on the western side of a wooden chair covered with felt. With a shock, she saw that Ta-ta-tonga was among them, sitting to the right of the Khan, as he had when consulting the Tayang. On the eastern side of the tent, four of the Tayang's concubines, their brown faces still bearing the pale traces of tears, plucked at their lutes.

"I greet you, Khatun of the Naimans," a soft voice said. Gurbesu forced her attention back to the Khan. He wore a breastplate, but no helmet; dark reddish braids, coiled behind his ears, hung down from under his head-band.

"Sit with me," the Khan continued. The pale eyes peering at her made her uneasy. "I've heard of the lovely Gurbesu who caused the sons of Inancha Bilge to divide their realm."

"That they fought wasn't my doing," she replied.

"I have also heard that Queen Gurbesu scorns my people."

She glanced at Ta-ta-tonga; the Uighur gazed back at her. The Keeper of the Seal, who had served two Tayangs, was already ingratiating himself with his new master; he must have told the Khan what had been said in the Naiman court.

The Khan's hands moved; he was holding the Uighur's seal. "Yet I've also been told," Genghis Khan continued, "that Queen Gurbesu advised her husband not to fight."

"That is true," she said.

"Yet you followed him to the battle."

"I hoped to inspire him," she said, "since he was determined

448

to fight. I told myself that my earlier advice might have been mistaken, that he was, after all, only fighting Mongols."

He laughed. "He should have listened to you." He motioned to her; she went to him and seated herself at his left as her servant sat with the lute-players. "Your Uighur adviser has been telling me many things, but I have more questions for him." The Khan held out the seal. "What is this for? You clung to it as though it were your master's tugh."

"It is the Tayang's seal," Ta-ta-tonga said. "When he gave his orders, they were marked with that seal."

"But how can orders be marked?" the Khan asked. "Isn't it enough for a trusted messenger to recite them?"

"Those who hear them have to know they're truly his orders. When my master required something, or gave a command, his orders were written down, and then marked with this seal. A man hearing them, and seeing this mark upon them, could have no doubt about their source. And when orders are written, one who can read will know what they are even if a messenger's memory fails him."

The Khan's eyes widened. "And you can set down my words the same way?"

"Indeed," Ta-ta-tonga replied. "The sounds of your speech and mine are much the same, and each sign stands for a sound. Together, they make words — a man can read them and hear the speaker through them. He can also record what needs to be kept and what memory can sometimes alter — the numbers of his herds, the tales of his ancestors."

The Khan stroked his short beard. "Such a thing would be useful to me. My words will live, and those who hear them can know they are truly mine." Ignorant as he might be, he had grasped that quickly. "Jochi and Chagadai!" he called out; two young men sitting among the others straightened. "You and your brothers will learn these signs from this man. I want you to know what they say and how to set them down."

The rough-hewn young men scowled, clearly dismayed. Gurbesu tried to imagine them poring over the Uighur script. The Khan glanced at her; she sensed that he knew what she was thinking.

"The Naiman army is defeated," he said. "Your ulus is no

more, and those who live will become part of mine. But what is useful to me of your ways I shall also take for myself. What this man has done for his Naiman masters, he will now do for me."

Gurbesu rested one arm against her knee. The Khan was not what she had expected, a conqueror who would only ravage what he had taken; he would not destroy all that her people had been.

The Khan withdrew from her and rested at her side. Gurbesu had expected no more than this forceful joining, the Mongol claiming his prize. Perhaps more would come later, as it had with Inancha. Bai Bukha had been no more than a body to endure in the night, one that spent itself too quickly, but this man was not like Bai.

He traced the scar on her shoulder lightly. "I was told you were wise," he said, "and this wound also shows your bravery."

"I am not wise," she murmured. "Had I been wise, I would have found a way to keep my husband from ruin. I'm not brave, either. It takes no courage to face a death one longs for."

"And do you still long for that?"

"I must accept what has to be. My first husband was a brave man and a good Tayang, but he was an old man when I became his wife. I hoped to guide his son, and find some of his father's greatness in him, but God willed otherwise. Now I must be the woman of a man who seems to have a little of Inancha's courage. Perhaps I can take some consolation in that."

He chuckled. "A stinking Mongol, fit only to be a slave in a Naiman camp. Isn't that what you said?"

"Not quite. I said that the Mongols were fit only to milk our cows and ewes, and that much only if they could be taught to clean their hands."

"And now see where you are." He was silent for a moment. "I would have spared the men who fought to the death for the Tayang. He was dying – there was no need for them to die as well."

She propped herself up on one elbow and gazed down at him. "They were loyal," she said, "whatever they thought of

450

the one they served, and they weren't the sort of men who could surrender. By dying, they showed my husband how greatly he had failed those who were better men than he was. Perhaps God intended that to be his torment."

"And for me to be yours. The beautiful Gurbesu must now be an evil-smelling Mongol's wife."

"Then it is good their Khan claimed me. The Mongol Khan might have been worthy of more than milking our cattle. We might even have given him the honour of sitting by the doorway with the servants." She drew her brows together. "You defeated only the son. You would never have won against Inancha in his prime."

He pulled her down to him. Inancha might have been like him in his youth. It was easier to think of him that way, as Inancha Bilge's heir, not her people's conqueror.

87

KHULAN WAITED BY her shelter as her father climbed the hill. Dayir Usun's long white moustaches drooped; his old face was weary and resigned. Further down the hill, the soldiers had cut down trees to build barricades. The Merkits who followed her father had fled to this forest in summer. Now the air was growing cold, and the larches would soon drop their needles. They could not hide here much longer. The enemy was certain to ride here soon, and could easily overwhelm the weakened Merkit forces.

Dayir Usun sat down by her fire, then reached over and touched her hand. Once, he had stroked her mother's hand that way. Khulan's mother had died that spring, and they had grieved for her, but in her frail state, she could never have endured the hard summer and autumn.

"What did the messenger tell you?" Khulan asked.

"Toghtoga Beki and his sons have gone west to join what's left of the Naiman army." Dayir Usun stared at the banked fire. "They'll make a stand with Guchlug if the enemy pursues them."

Khulan was silent. Her father might decide to go to them. They would have to run again, far from their own lands this time, to the Altais and the desert beyond.

"They won't add many to the Naiman forces," her father continued. "Most of Toghtoga's people surrendered, or were captured. The man said the families of Toghtoga and his sons were taken after the battle."

"Are you going to join him?" she asked.

"No." He sighed. "Khulan, I'm tired of fighting. I've had enough both of war and of Toghtoga. But surrendering to the Mongols also has its risks. Temujin will remember that I was one of those who raided his camp long ago and stole his first wife from him."

"He may be grateful to have your oath," she said, "since you'd save him the trouble of sending his men against us."

"I must offer him more than that." His heavy-lidded eyes narrowed. "Starvation hasn't harmed your looks." That was as close to a compliment as her father ever came. It had surprised him to have such a beautiful daughter when both he and his wife were so old at her birth. "It's said Temujin appreciates beauty greatly. You could be my gift to him, and perhaps he'll be moved enough by you to spare our people."

Her fingers clawed at the ground. "I can't be much of a prize," she whispered. "Our hard life has surely marked me."

"It hasn't marked you at all, child. I have little left except for you, and if I'm to go to Genghis Khan and beg for mercy, I can't go empty-handed."

"Have you told your men you mean to surrender?"

"They're telling me it may be wise to do so."

Don't do this, she wanted to say. Surrender, but don't offer me to him. It was useless to have such thoughts, but then her thoughts had always been unlike those of the people she knew. Any other girl would resign herself to this, and be grateful to avoid a worse fate.

Khulan hated war. Whenever her father had sacrificed to his tugh before leading his men into battle, she never shared the wild anticipation of others; she thought only of how many

452

would die. When her brothers sat around exchanging war stories, she imagined the widows and orphans who were weeping for those they had lost. All her life, Dayir had fought the Mongols, and it had brought him only defeat and more death. Three of her brothers had fallen, along with countless others, yet even that had not brought her father to seek peace.

Others would mock her thoughts if she revealed them. Those who fell had to be avenged; old offences had to be punished. Pity was wasted on enemies who would show little mercy to their foes.

Now, finally, her father wanted peace, and would buy it with her, as he had tried to purchase victory with his sons and men. She had prayed for an end to the fighting, never thinking she might have to be the price.

She leaned against him. "If I must go with you," she said, "then I'll go willingly." He could force her to go anyway; she would not plague him with tears and pleas. Khulan thought of all the deaths the Mongol Khan had brought to her people and to so many others. She might become the woman of a man whose greatest skill was in warfare, the thing she hated most.

Khulan and her father left the wooded hills with only five soldiers and two spare horses. A day's ride took them to land where the trees were more sparse; they camped for the night, then rode on.

Steppe covered with yellow and brown grass stretched before them. They had not gone far when they saw that some of the grass had been nibbled short; the tracks of horses ran to the east and west. Khulan longed to turn back for the safety of the forest.

When the sun was high, they spotted a group of Mongols in the distance. The men were soon galloping towards them, lances out; Dayir Usun ordered a halt, then raised his hands as the soldiers approached. "We come in peace," he shouted.

The strangers surrounded them and reined in their horses. There were ten of them; nine swiftly took out their bows, keeping their arrows trained on the group. The man nearest Dayir Usun lowered his lance. "Who are you," he asked, "and from where do you come?"

"I am Dayir Usun, chief of the Uwas-Merkits. I've come out of hiding to make my submission to Genghis Khan."

The stranger's brown eyes widened. They were large eyes, and made his strong-boned face look even more attractive. He was a young man, perhaps no more than twenty, with coppery skin and a short dark moustache. "I greet you, Dayir Usun," he said. "Our Khan will welcome your surrender."

"My people have suffered greatly, and can no longer stand against you." Dayir Usun held out his hands, palms up. "I'm ready to offer my oath to Genghis Khan, and my daughter, whom I've always treasured, as a gift to him. Her name is Khulan, and if the Khan finds her pleasing, I'll ask nothing more than that my people be spared when they submit to him."

Khulan adjusted the scarf that hid the lower part of her face as the young man glanced at her. The way he sat in his saddle made him seem tall. He smiled briefly; the smile lighted his handsome face. At a gesture from him, the other Mongols lowered their bows.

"You don't ride with much protection," he said as he turned back to Dayir. "Many of our men are roaming this region, ready to kill any Merkits they find. My name is Nayaga, and I'm a captain of one hundred. My camp is close by – you may stop there."

Dayir Usun nodded. "Perhaps when our horses have rested, you'll tell us where we can find your Khan."

Nayaga frowned. "I advise you not to travel on alone. It's your good fortune that I found you – others are impatient to taste Merkit blood. Better for you to stay with me until I can lead you safely to the Khan."

"I am grateful," Dayir Usun said.

Khulan looked away from Nayaga as they followed him. She had often hoped to see such a man among her suitors. There had been several who had tried to bargain with her father for her, all of them hard-eyed men with loud voices, heavy-set bodies, and leathery faces. None of them had possessed Nayaga's warm, open gaze, or sat as gracefully as he did when riding.

Her hands tightened on her reins. She told herself that she

454

was only happy they could wait in his camp for a time, that she would not have to go to the Mongol Khan so soon.

Nayaga's camp was ten small yurts sitting on a small rise. Some of his men were grazing the horses; others sat outside the yurts, cleaning their swords and knives. Nayaga left the Merkit warriors with a few of his men, led Dayir Usun and Khulan to one of the tents, then went off to speak to his soldiers.

The tent held several saddles; quivers and bowcases hung from the wall. A few hides covered the ground and a fire burned in a small hearth set on raised earth.

"That captain seems a good sort," Dayir muttered as he settled himself at the back of the tent. "We took more of a risk than I knew riding here, but then we didn't have much choice."

Khulan stretched her hands towards the fire. Nayaga was not as tall as he looked on his horse; she had to lift her head only a little to gaze up at him. She removed the cloth from her face, then slipped off the scarf covering her head. Under her coat, she still wore a child's short robe, but Dayir had insisted she cover her head, as a married woman would.

A voice called out to them; Nayaga came through the open entrance. Khulan turned towards him. His eyes widened, his hand froze on his bowcase, and she gazed back, unable to look away. Her face grew hot; colour rose to Nayaga's cheeks.

A pain as sharp as a thorn pierced her heart. Some of the girls she knew had talked about this feeling, the burning that felt like a fever, the pain that seemed much like an arrow striking. Nayaga had to be feeling it, too; she saw it in his flushed face and glowing eyes.

He quickly hung up his weapons. "Most of my men are out searching," he said, "but they should be back by nightfall." He went to Dayir Usun and sat down at his right. "I've sent two men south to Genghis Khan's camp, to let him know you're riding to him. When it's safe to do so, I'll take you there myself. You and your daughter may stay in this tent with your men – my soldiers and I will share the others."

Khulan seated herself at her father's left. Nayaga glanced at her; she lowered her eyes. "I regret I have only this poor field tent to offer you," the young man continued.

"We've been sheltering under the trees," Dayir replied. "This tent will suit us well enough."

Nayaga reached for a bottle hanging from the wooden frame behind him. "And I have only a little kumiss to offer."

Dayir Usun nodded. "That will also be most welcome." Nayaga sprinkled a blessing, then handed him the bottle. "I've fought against Temujin for many years, but it's said he can forgive old enemies."

"It's true," Nayaga said. "I fought against the Khan myself only three years ago."

Dayir grunted. "Indeed."

"I'm a Bagarin," Nayaga said, "and my kinsfolk were sworn to the Taychiut chiefs. My father Shirgugetu was a servant of Targhutai Kiriltugh. I served in the rearguard when we rode with Jamukha Gur-Khan against Genghis Khan."

Dayir Usun cleared his throat. "I lost a son in that campaign."

"Many lost sons when Tengri turned the storm against us. We were chased back to our camp, and there Targhutai fled and abandoned many to the enemy. It was then that I regretted the oaths we had sworn to him. We hid in the woods with him and his guard for several days, and then my father told my brother Alagh and me that it was time to think of ourselves."

Dayir passed the jug to Khulan. "So you gave yourselves up."

"Father said we should take Targhutai prisoner and bring him to Genghis Khan. He was sure we would get a great reward for him. So we seized him one night, bound him, and threw him into a wagon. When the other men tried to stop us, Father sat on Targhutai, held a knife to his throat, and said he'd make a grave pillow of him if the men came any closer."

Khulan held out the jug; Nayaga's fingers brushed hers lightly as he took it. "Targhutai begged his men not to try to rescue him," he went on. "He said that he'd known Temujin as a boy, that whatever he had done, he'd spared Temujin's life then, and that the Khan might forgive him because of that. When his men saw that Father meant to kill him, they let us go. Perhaps they had come to despise him as much as we did, after seeing him beg for his life."

"And what reward did Temujin give you?" Dayir Usun asked. "I must assume he didn't show much kindness to Targhutai, since I've heard nothing of the Taychiut since that battle."

"I'm coming to that," Nayaga said. "I had doubts about this plan of my father's, and it came to me as we rode that the Khan might not be so pleased by our deed. Whatever Targhutai was, we had sworn to serve him. I asked Father how the Khan could ever trust men who had betrayed their own chief. He and Alagh argued with me, but in the end, they saw the wisdom of my words. So we cut Targhutai's bonds, gave him a horse, and told him he was free to go. He didn't give himself up, so it seems he didn't have so much faith in Genghis Khan's mercy. We rode on and surrendered ourselves."

"Since you're alive," Dayir Usun said, "I suppose you didn't tell Temujin what you did."

Nayaga shook his head. "We had to tell him. What if men from Targhutai's guard were captured, or gave themselves up, and told the Khan we were riding there with our chief? Our only hope was to tell the truth. So Father told the Khan we were bringing Targhutai to him, but came to see that betraying our leader was unworthy, and that we had freed him."

Dayir let out his breath. "And your head's still on your shoulders?"

"He praised us, saying he had no use for men who would be false to their chief. Then, when Father admitted it was my advice he and Alagh had followed, the Khan singled me out for more praise. I was only sixteen, but he gave me a hundred men to command and said he expected great things from a young man who was so wise, so you see I did the right thing." Nayaga sipped from the bottle, then wiped his mouth. "Had we delivered Targhutai to him, I think he would have killed us and spared our chief's life."

Dayir Usun rubbed his chin. "That's quite a tale."

"It tells you what kind of man the Khan is. I've never been sorry that I gave him my oath. For traitors, he has no mercy, but he can honour honest men, and those who were once his enemies but are willing to offer him their swords."

"This eases me," Dayir Usun said. "Perhaps he'll forgive this old Merkit, and accept my daughter as his wife. She's not unpleasant to look at, and she's a good, strong girl. She's had her share of suitors, but they never offered me what she was worth, although I think a few of them were prepared to raise their price. Just as well, seeing what's happened to us."

Nayaga's throat moved as he swallowed. "I think the Khan will be pleased with your daughter," he said hoarsely. "I promise you I'll keep her safe until we can ride to him." He stood up. "I'll leave you now – perhaps you wish to rest." He left the tent quickly.

When her father and his men were asleep, Khulan went outside. Some of the Mongols were on watch outside the yurts; at the edge of the camp, Nayaga and two other men squatted by a fire. He had come to their tent that evening, and his words had been for Dayir, but she had felt him watching her.

She went around the tent and crept down to a place behind a small shrub to relieve herself, then climbed the gently sloping ground to where the horses were tethered. She could not sleep, and did not want to go back to the yurt.

Khulan sat down, rested her arms against her knees, then felt that someone was watching her. She turned; a shadowy form came towards her.

"Why do you sit here, Lady?" She recognized Nayaga's voice.

"I can't sleep," she replied.

"Forgive me for saying this, but perhaps you should cover your face, as well as your head, when you leave your tent. The night cloaks you now, but you might veil yourself in daytime."

The darkness hid his face; she thought of the warmth she had seen in his eyes before. "Is my face so displeasing to you?" she asked.

"I swore to keep you safe. I don't want any of my men tempted to behave dishonourably with you. A man can often forget himself at the sight of beauty."

He did think she was beautiful then. Her arms tightened around her legs. She should not be out here with him; her father might wake and wonder where she was. "Do you have a wife, Nayaga?"

He moved closer to her and sat down. If she stretched out

her arm, she could touch him. "I captured a woman when we fought the Tatars," he said. "She was among the most beautiful of our captives, and her beauty touched my heart, but we had sworn to offer the loveliest women to the Khan. So I brought her to him, but he put her hand in mine and told me to take her as my wife. He's the most generous of men – if one of his warriors had no coat, the Khan would give him his own. He's won much for himself, but gives as much to others."

Nayaga already had a beautiful wife; that fact pained her. Yet the Khan had given her to him; that gave her hope. "You must be missing her," she said.

"She's with child now, and that's brought her some happiness. There was little for her earlier – she was often sorrowing over those she lost, her father and young brothers, and the man to whom she'd been wed. The Khan couldn't forgive those who brought death to his father, and we'd been ordered to kill every male prisoner except for the youngest boys."

"I know what he did to the Tatars," Khulan said. "You call him generous and noble, but he showed only cruelty to them."

"They were his deadliest enemies. I didn't want to follow his order, but had to obey – if he had allowed them to live, they would have been a spear in his side. There could be no peace with them."

"There can be no peace," she said, "as long as men fight."

"Maybe the wars will end," he said, "when all the Khan's enemies have surrendered. We'd be one ulus then, and there'd be no need for fighting." He laughed softly. "That's a foolish thought. There will always be wars, and what would men be if they didn't fight? Only weak souls tending their herds, easy prey for any enemy who rode against them. How could we exist with nothing to win? Men would have no reason to live in such a world, thinking of nothing but filling their bellies and siring sons as useless as themselves."

"Perhaps they would find something else to do," she said.

"There's nothing else. It's a man's work to make war, and to be ready for it when it comes." He paused. "You're a strange one, Khulan." She tensed at the sound of her name from his lips. "A woman's work is to tend to her husband and children, to look after his tents and herds so that he's free to fight.

Without women to tend to such matters, we wouldn't be able to fight, and if we didn't fight, we'd be useless to you."

"My father's fought all my life," she said, "and it only brought us death and defeat. Now he must surrender to your Khan. Better if he had surrendered years ago."

"Without fighting at all? You want the impossible, Khulan. A man can respect an enemy who's fought bravely. One who bows to him out of cowardice can only be despised." He sighed. "And yet there's some truth to your words. I fight because I must, but I can't take the joy in war that others do. Whatever pleasure I have in my spoils, I can be grateful when the battle is over."

He was silent for a long time, then said, "Once, I wondered why the Khan gave me my command. He can see into men's hearts and know what they are – I thought he must see this weakness in me. But then I heard him tell another man, one of our fiercest fighters, a man who could endure hunger, thirst, and cold without feeling them and survive any hardship, why he wouldn't make a good commander."

"And why was that?" Khulan asked.

"He said a man who couldn't feel what his soldiers felt, who was untouched by their weaknesses and pains, wouldn't see to the needs of his men. I can hope that my weakness makes me a better commander of those under me."

She said, "I don't see it as weakness for a man not to welcome war."

"You are strange, Khulan. You draw words from me I've never spoken aloud." He stood up. "And I shouldn't be saying them to you. Go back to the tent and dream of the husband who awaits you." He strode away before she could reply.

88

KHULAN LEFT THE tent at dawn. Nayaga stood with a few of his men near the line of tethered horses. As he caught sight of her, a smile flashed across his face.

She walked towards him. As he had suggested, she had covered her face and hair. Nayaga bowed to her; Khulan gestured at the horses. "To sit in this camp," she said, "makes me restless. I'd like to go riding."

"I would have thought you'd had enough of riding for a while. Does your father – "

"He's asleep. He won't mind – he'll be grateful you didn't wake him."

Nayaga glanced at his men. "Very well, but I can't let you ride alone."

When the horses were saddled, she and Nayaga rode out together; seven men followed, keeping several lengths behind. The wind was sharp, lifting dirt from the plain. Khulan moved into a gallop; Nayaga kept pace with her. A small patch of pines stood on the northern side of a small hill to the southeast; she turned towards them, then slowed to a trot. Nayaga's men fanned out over the grass behind them.

"I'm sorry to have to keep you here," Nayaga shouted above the wind, "but it's only for your safety. I know how impatient you and your father must be to come to the end of your journey."

"I made this journey," she replied, "because I must obey my father. It was his wish to offer me to your Khan – it was never mine."

"You shouldn't say such things, Khulan. Any woman would be honoured to be among his wives."

She picked up her pace. They rode without speaking until they came to the trees. Nayaga circled the grove, then halted. Khulan dismounted and led her horse towards the pines.

"Don't go into the grove," he said. "We should keep within sight of my men."

She tied her reins around a gnarled root, then sat down. "Never fear, Nayaga. If we were quite alone, I'm sure you'd

461

never behave dishonourably towards me." She could not hold back her words. "You love your Khan too much for that. Clearly your only desire is to be rid of me as soon as possible." She wanted to hurt him then, to lash him with her words. "A man who would offer a captive he wanted for himself to his Khan can surely be trusted."

His face paled. He got down from his horse and sat a few paces from her. "Your people will have peace," he said, "when Dayir Usun offers his oath. My men and I will no longer have to hunt them down. Only last night, you were telling me how you longed for peace."

"Yes, and your Khan will be grateful you protected me — maybe he'll even reward you for that."

His mouth twisted. "It'll be reward enough to know I've done my duty."

Khulan did not speak for a few moments. "Perhaps you can tell me a little of his other wives," she said at last.

He turned towards her. "His chief wife is Bortai Khatun," he said, "who's lovely still, and wise. But of course you know of her — she was a captive of your people. Never remind the Khan of that."

"He's had his revenge," she said. "Father's had cause to regret that Merkits ever found her."

"His wife Khadagan is also said to be wise," he continued, "but she has little beauty. Yet he respects and loves her, because she helped him escape from his enemies when he was a boy. He doesn't forget such deeds — it's why so many willingly serve him. Then there are two Tatar sisters, Yisui Khatun and Yisugen Khatun, whom he took after our campaign against their people. He loves them both greatly, which is why they've both been honoured with the title of Khatun."

"And I'm sure they must love him," Khulan said, "for protecting them from the ravages of his troops."

"He also took a wife from among the Kereits, a niece of their former Khan, but when a dream came to him, commanding him to give her up, he presented her to Jurchedei, one of his bravest generals, and told him always to honour her."

"And that, I suppose, shows his generosity of spirit."

"When we defeated the Naimans this past spring," he went

on, "their Khatun Gurbesu also became his wife. She came to the battlefield to see the Naimans fight – it's said she's as brave as a man. And his most recent wife is Tugai, who was the wife of Toghtoga's son Khudu. When Toghtoga Beki and his sons fled from us, their wives and herds fell into our hands. The Khan took Tugai for himself and gave Khudu's new bride Doregene to his son Ogedei."

"A messenger told my father about Toghtoga's losses."

"And there are other women, of course, concubines among his slaves or captives to enjoy for a night or two before they're given to others."

"I'll be lost among so many," she said.

Nayaga shook his head. "You won't be lost, Khulan. You would shine among a thousand wives."

"Maybe another dream will come to him and tell him I can't be his. Perhaps – "

"Khulan!" His hands tightened into fists. "I said I'd never been sorry I swore my oath to him, but I regret it now. I – " He got to his feet. "We must ride back."

"Nayaga – "

"Now, Khulan, before I forget myself." He swung himself into his saddle. Her chest constricted; she could hardly breathe. She mounted her horse and followed him.

Nayaga left the camp later that day, riding out with a few men to hunt. By evening, he had not returned. Perhaps, Khulan thought, he would stay away until it was safe to take her to his Khan. He would not be tempted to forget his duty then.

Khulan kept near the yurt, leaving it only to collect more fuel for the fire. Dayir Usun was content to sit outside with his men and the Mongols, mending harnesses and honing weapons. It was too late for him to change his mind and give her to Nayaga instead, even if the young man were foolhardy enough to try to claim her. All these men knew that she was a gift for the Khan; only he could decide what to do with her. Dayir would think she was mad for preferring a captain of one hundred to a Khan.

That night, when the camp was quiet and Dayir Usun and his men were contentedly snoring, Khulan thought she heard

Nayaga speaking to someone outside. Perhaps a long time would pass before they could leave for the Khan's camp. This region might remain unsettled; the Khan might forget about a young woman he had never seen. It was hopeless to wish for that, to have so little concern for the rest of her people.

One of Dayir's men saddled a horse and brought it to Khulan the next morning. She told him that she would keep near the camp, and at last he went off to join her father's other soldiers.

She circled the camp at a trot. Men rode out to scout, while others were taking horses out to graze. The men who had stayed in the camp were practising their archery. She watched the arrows arch over the plain and strike the piece of wood that was the target, then turned towards the tents. Her father was outside, walking towards the edge of the camp. A hand pushed another tent flap aside; Nayaga emerged and straightened when he saw her.

She gazed at him, then lashed her horse. The animal bolted; she raced away from the camp, barely hearing Nayaga's shouts over the sound of the wind and the beating of the horse's hooves. She stood up in her stirrups and leaned forward, urging the horse on until she saw the trees ahead, then pulled at the reins.

The horse slowed to a stop. Khulan leaped from the saddle and ran under the pines, then looked back. Nayaga had followed her; he had not saddled his mount. As he neared the trees, her horse trotted out to him; he caught its reins.

"Khulan!" he shouted. "Khulan!" She ran into the grove, then threw herself to the ground. "Khulan!" His voice was louder; she heard the rustling of pine needles. "Khulan!"

"I'm here," she cried back, and glimpsed his short, broad-shouldered form among the trunks. His bowcase swayed from his belt as he halted. He stood a few paces from her, in a small patch of light; his hat shaded his eyes.

"I swore to protect you," he said harshly. "You were told not to go riding alone."

She sat up, then tore the cloth from her face. He thrust out a hand. She reached up and drew her scarf from her head.

"Khulan." His voice was a whisper. He slipped his bowcase

and quiver from his belt, then fell to his knees next to her. "Khulan." His hand smoothed back her braided hair and cupped her head as his lips found hers. She rubbed her mouth against his, surprised at how much pleasure this gave her. A wild joy filled her; there was no world beyond this grove. She opened her arms to him as his hand moved between her legs.

"Nayaga." Her hands clutched at him under his coat. His arms tightened around her; he moaned softly. "Nayaga." But suddenly he pulled away from her, jumped to his feet, then leaned against a tree, his back to her. His shoulders shook; a harsh, rasping sound came from him.

"Nayaga," she said.

"I love you," he said softly. "What I felt for my wife when I first saw her was no more than a spark, but this fire's consuming me. I can't bear it."

"I love you, Nayaga." She sat up and pressed her hands together. "Heaven covers many lands – there must be somewhere we can go. Surely we could find a place – "

"Oh yes. Some of my men would be loyal to me. We could tell the others we're riding to the Khan, then make our escape." He sighed. "It's useless, Khulan. I couldn't have you share such a life – running, having to hide. The spirits favour the Khan – I think his armies would someday ride to any place we found refuge." He turned towards her. "You and I long for peace. Genghis Khan knows there won't be peace until there's one Khan under Heaven. I can't run and wait for the day the shadow of his wing will cover me."

She said, "You're afraid of him."

"I fear him more than any man I've ever met. If I failed him, nothing would remain of me but bones for the jackals. But I love and respect him as well. It isn't the kind of love I have for you, that eats at me and gives me no peace, but I have it, and to think I might have betrayed it with you tears at me." His hand trembled as he lifted it. "I couldn't live that way, a man without honour, stealing what was meant for my Khan. I couldn't have you suffer for my weakness."

"He may not want me," she said desperately. "Maybe he'll give me to you. He gave up one wife, he let you keep your Tatar woman."

465

"When he sees you," Nayaga said, "he'll never give you to anyone else."

"You're right, Nayaga," she said bitterly. "If we ran away, he'd be losing only a girl who means nothing to him, but I don't imagine he's a man who forgives insults easily. He would be angry with my father for failing to bring him the gift he was promised, and my people would suffer for that."

Voices were calling to them; some of his men must have ridden out after him. Nayaga picked up his bowcase and quiver. Khulan covered her hair and face, then got to her feet.

She said, "I can never love him."

"Khulan – "

"Never."

His men shouted his name. He motioned to her; they left the grove.

89

KHULAN AND HER father left the camp at dawn, after one of Nayaga's messengers had ridden back to say that the way was safe and the Khan awaited their arrival. Nayaga came with them, along with twenty of his soldiers. He did not speak to Khulan when they stopped for the night in another Mongol camp, and he urged the party to quicken their pace the next day. When they spied a large herd of horses grazing on the steppe, Nayaga sent a man ahead to tell the Khan's guard that the Merkit chief would soon arrive at his ordu.

The Khan's large tent stood among several smaller ones at the encampment's north end; a long line of horses was hitched to a rope near his circle. An officer with the guard glanced at Khulan and her father as they dismounted, then frowned at Nayaga. "I hope you can bring a smile to Temujin's face," the officer said. "He's angry that Toghtoga and his sons escaped him. That tarnishes his victories somewhat." He shouted to those inside the great tent as other men led the horses away, then ushered them up the steps to the entrance.

A few men were in the back of the tent. One man sat in a felt-covered chair, his hand clutching a goblet. He wore a plain brown robe and a cloth was tied around his head, but his presence dominated the tent. His pale eyes, sharp and cold, fell on Nayaga as the young man bowed.

"I greet you, my Khan," Nayaga said; Khulan and her father knelt. "I bring you Dayir Usun of the Uwas-Merkits, since it was his wish to submit to you. I would have brought him to you sooner, but the way wasn't safe, and I wanted no harm to come to him and his daughter."

The Khan was silent. Khulan glanced to his left, where two women sat. The one nearest him was a beauty with light brown eyes and a small, flat nose; the other had dark eyes and a broad, pleasant face. On the eastern side of the tent, several women sat with lutes; their instruments were silent.

"Dayir Usun," the Khan said. His voice was soft, but Khulan heard the steel in it. "You have afflicted me for many years. Your people struck at my heart, harried me, and rode with my enemies against me."

"And you have won many victories over us," Dayir responded. "We fought you as long as we could, but we can gain nothing by fighting you now. I swore an oath to Toghtoga Beki, but am free of that now that he's fled. I'm an old man, and tired of war. Do what you wish with me, but I beg you to allow my people to come out of hiding and submit to you. They wish only for this war to end."

"I can't punish a man who kept his oath," the Khan said, "and who has come here now to give himself up."

"I see you're as noble as I've heard." Dayir Usun stood up and helped Khulan to her feet. "I have also brought you my daughter Khulan as a gift. She's the youngest of my children, and many wanted her for a wife, but I wished only the bravest and most noble of men to be her husband, or she would have been wed long ago. She's sixteen now, and strong — she does her work without complaint, and I've never known her to waste time in gossip. Many have said there is fire in her face, and I hope that you'll find her worthy. I've cherished this girl, the child of my old age, and pray that her beauty will touch your heart." Khulan heard the sorrow in his trembling voice, and knew then how much his defeat had wounded him.

The Khan gestured at her. Khulan lowered her veil, then looked towards Nayaga, unable to help herself. You shouldn't have brought me here, she thought; we might have been together, riding far from this place.

The Khan stared at her, then jumped to his feet and threw his goblet to the carpet. "Now I see why you kept her for three days," he said, still in the same soft voice. "Did you think I'd believe only that you were thinking of her safety? You wanted to enjoy her yourself. I'll make an example of you, Nayaga — I can't leave a man alive who offends me in this way."

Dayir Usun held her hand tightly, but did not protest. Nayaga's men said nothing. Khulan thought of their fleeting moment under the trees; even his men might believe the worst of him now.

"I swear it isn't so," Nayaga said. "I've never kept anything for myself that belongs to my Khan, and have accepted only what you gave to me. If I have ever done anything else, then take my life."

The Khan glared at him. "You've pronounced your own judgement with your last words," he replied. "Take this man from my sight — cut his hands and feet from him first, and then his arms, and — "

"No!" Khulan cried. The women sitting at the Khan's side widened their eyes. Guards quickly surrounded Nayaga. Khulan moved closer to the Khan and knelt before him, then compelled herself to look up at him. "Please hear me," she continued. "This man has done nothing wrong." Nayaga had said the Khan could see into men's hearts; she gazed steadily up at him. "He warned us we might be in danger if we went on alone, and thought only of bringing us to you unharmed. I beg you to let him go."

"How can I believe that, now that I've seen you for myself? I don't wonder that he kept you in his camp — it surprises me only that he brought you to me."

The men near him stood up; the guards dragged Nayaga

towards the doorway. "She speaks the truth," Nayaga called out.

Khulan stretched out her arms. "I'm still as I was when I was born," she said, "untouched by any man. My own body can show the truth of my words."

The Khan's men were backing away, as if fearing he might turn his anger against them. The beautiful woman near him raised her head. "My husband," she said, "we can find out the truth of this. Leave the girl with me and the Lady Tugai. When we've examined her – "

The Khan showed his teeth. "Leave me, all of you," he said in a louder voice. "Guard that man – if he's done nothing wrong, he has nothing to fear." Soldiers pushed Nayaga through the doorway; the other men followed them. As Khulan rose, her father looked back at her, his face taut with fear as he hastened after the men.

The Khan prowled the tent, making her think of a wolf. The lute-players were still, their hands locked around their instruments. The woman who had spoken before got up and took Khulan's hand. "Don't be afraid," she said.

"I'm not afraid," Khulan said. "I didn't lie, and neither did Nayaga."

"This will take only a moment, child. The Lady Tugai and I will try not to hurt you."

The Khan came towards them. "Step aside, Gurbesu," he muttered. "This is something I can test for myself."

"Haven't you frightened the poor girl enough? We – "

He pushed the woman away. Khulan took a step back; he threw her to the floor, then dropped to the carpet. His hands grabbed at her roughly, reaching under her robe to pull her trousers down to her knees. She closed her eyes as he fumbled at his own clothing. The weight of him pressed her against the floor; she struggled for breath. Pain lanced through her as he thrust inside her, but she did not cry out. His fingers dug into her hips; he would crush her.

It passed quickly. He shuddered and withdrew; she felt the dampness between her legs. He was fastening his trousers when she opened her eyes; his face was flushed, his pale eyes wild.

469

The woman called Gurbesu knelt next to her, but the other wife was hiding her face behind her hands.

"I see," he said, "that I wasn't deceived."

Khulan sat up and looked down at the blood on her thighs. She no longer feared him. Perhaps he had expected her to be frightened, and shamed by this act, but she felt no shame and no terror. He was the one shamed, with his suspicions and his unjust accusations; he did not deserve Nayaga's loyalty.

Gurbesu helped her up and assisted her with her clothing. "You were brave to speak to me as you did," the Khan said. "Hearing the fire in your words roused me as much as the beauty I see in your face."

She lifted her head. "It takes no courage to speak the truth."

He gazed at her for a long time, then called out to his guards as he moved back to his chair. "Are you all right?" Gurbesu whispered.

Khulan managed to nod. "Bring her to me," the Khan said. "She will sit at my side." Gurbesu led her to him and settled her on the cushion, then sat at her left with Tugai. Men entered the tent; Khulan searched the group until she found Nayaga. His arms were bound, his face tight with tension.

"I've been unjust," the Khan said. "I doubted an honest man. The blood on that carpet there shows he spoke the truth." Nayaga tensed; she saw the pain in his brown eyes. "Remove his bonds. He's a man who can be trusted, who's worthy of more responsibility."

Nayaga was silent as the men near him cut at his ropes. "Dayir Usun," the Khan continued, "I'll happily take your daughter Khulan as my wife. You did well to bring her to me, and I will honour her with all my love."

His love, Khulan thought; this Khan could know little of love. If he had, he would have seen what lay in Nayaga's heart and hers and given them some happiness. He had so many women; he could have let her go. But he cared nothing for their feelings. Nayaga had made his choice, to be loyal to his leader, and the Khan would see that he abided by that. The young man would never think of her again without imagining what had happened to her below the Khan's throne. Their love was only something else to be swept aside.

470

"You will have your own tents," the Khan was saying, "and servants from among your people. You'll have your share of my herds and any booty I take."

Khulan huddled under the blanket as he undressed. He had said all that before, while they feasted, leaning from his chair to clutch at her hands. Her father, relieved at having achieved his purpose, had drunk so much his men were forced to carry him from the tent. Nayaga had drunk nearly as much, but was able to sing and dance with the others. She had only imagined his voice was catching a little during his songs, that he seemed more frantic than joyful. Nayaga would be rewarded for his loyalty; his Khan had promised it. He would be grateful he had not thrown everything away for her sake.

"Ask what you like of me," he said. "Anything that you want will be yours."

"I have what I wanted," she said. "My people can come out of hiding. I wish for nothing more."

He came closer to the bed. "You're not afraid of me, Khulan. Many would warn you not to let your lack of fear make you careless."

"I won't be careless. I know you would punish anyone who offended you in an instant, that you'd crush me without mercy if I gave you cause, but I'm not afraid of you."

He sat down and fondled her braids. "Nayaga's a stronger man than most," he said, "if he could keep you for three days and not succumb to you."

"He couldn't betray you," she said. "He had only praise for you whenever he spoke of you. No woman could come between him and his duty to you – I doubt that anything could."

"And yet – " He stretched out next to her and circled her waist with one arm. "My desire for you is strong, Khulan. I thought I was past such feeling for any woman, but you've awakened it again."

She lay there passively as he stroked her, unmoved, feeling nothing for him. He could claim her body, but he would never have more than that. He put his lips on hers; she thought of Nayaga, holding the memory inside herself.

471

90

JAMUKHA DREW IN in his breath as the odour of roasting meat rose from the kettle. His five companions squatted by the fire. Jamukha's hunger sharpened; the argali was the best meat they had found in some time. They had followed the great-horned wild rams down a mountain slope and on to the yellow steppe before bringing this animal down.

Above him, the snowy peaks of the Tangnu Mountains seemed to float above the clouds. The larches on the lower slopes were growing green; under the pines and cedars, small currants budded in the thickets, and the honeysuckle would soon bloom.

His comrades were grim; the prospect of this meal had not raised their spirits. Jamukha was sure they would leave him soon. They had been living the lives of outcasts for months, waiting to see what he would do. He had no army to rally; few had followed him here, and only five remained. He could go north and join the reindeer people, but suspected it would not be long before Temujin rode against them. His companions would finally lose their patience and abandon him.

His joys were now small ones – seeing another sign of spring on the forested mountains, finding a pool of water, capturing an argali. His battle was over; Temujin had won. He had been no more than a way to test the one the spirits favoured.

"Rejoice, my friends," Jamukha said bitterly. "We're fortunate to have such a feast."

Ogin's face darkened. "It may be some time before we feast again."

Jamukha shook his head. "The forests are full of deer, and when our horses are fatter, we can steal more steeds. We'll – "

"This is what you've led us to," Ogin said, then glanced at the others. The men shifted their eyes from Jamukha to the younger man. "I grow weary of this life."

"You chose to follow," Jamukha said. "I freed you from your oath to me."

Jamukha's weapons lay at his side. As he rose to reach towards the pot hanging over the fire, he saw Ogin gesture to

472

the others. Before he could grab his knife, they were upon him, forcing him to the ground. He struggled briefly, then sagged against them as his hands were bound.

"What treachery is this?" he whispered.

"You'll do nothing," Ogin said as another man bound Jamukha's legs. "You'll go on this way until death finds you."

Jamukha twisted against his bonds. "You dare to raise your hands against me?"

"We don't mean to kill you," Ogin said. "You're still of some use to us alive. We'll take you to Temujin. He'll have your life, and we'll have our reward for bringing you to him."

"He won't reward you for this," Jamukha said. "I don't doubt that he'll take my life, but he won't honour you for giving me to him. Go to him, surrender and offer him your oath, but free me. It will be enough for him to know I've lost everything."

"We're finished with listening to you." Ogin kicked him in the belly; Jamukha groaned. Ogin went to the pot. Jamukha lay there as the others tore at the meat.

Jamukha was thrown across the saddle of his horse and bound to the stirrups. The men said little as they rode. Perhaps he was wrong, and his anda would reward them, savouring his victories all the more at seeing Jamukha brought so low. Perhaps the Khan would torment him before finding a way to kill him that would not violate their anda oath.

His body ached with bruises from the ride. Whenever they stopped to rest, the men gave him only enough water to keep him alive. They came to a Kereit camp, and Ogin told the men there of his prisoner. A few Kereits joined them as a guard while a messenger rode ahead to Temujin's camp.

Jamukha supposed that he would be taken to the Khan's ordu, where Temujin's wives and sons could gape at the captive, but more soldiers met them and led them in the direction of the Kentei massif. The Khan was hunting with some of his men, and would meet them there.

As they walked between the two fires outside the camp, Jamukha, weakened by the ride, struggled to keep on his feet. A circle of field tents sat on the steppe below the mountains.

They were led to the nearest tent; before the guards outside could call out a greeting, Temujin stepped through the doorway.

Jamukha, his arms still bound behind him, forced himself to raise his head. Temujin gazed at him steadily; thin lines marked the skin around his pale eyes, and his shoulders sagged under his fur coat. Jamukha waited for his anda to laugh, to order some new humiliation – a beating with sticks, a yoke around his neck.

Others left their yurts to gather around the Khan. There was old Munglik, his loyalty bought with marriage to Temujin's mother, and Jurchedei, who had once followed Jamukha. Borchu and Jelme, their faces older and browner now, were still Temujin's shadows. There was Khorchi, who had served Jamukha until a dream told him that Temujin would be the Mongol Khan. Khasar stood among the men; Jamukha looked away from him. All of them would be happy to see him die.

Ogin stepped forward. "We come in peace, O Khan."

Temujin's eyes narrowed. "You carried the words of my anda to me before. I wish to hear why you have brought him to me now."

"We can stand against you no longer," Ogin replied. "All of Jamukha's men have abandoned him. We served this man, and he led us to ruin. We wish now to offer our swords to you." He bowed; Jamukha stared at the younger man's back, imagining Ogin's insolent smile. "We beg for nothing more than to serve you, but it's said that Genghis Khan is a generous man. Perhaps the Khan whom we'll serve now will show his gratitude to us for bringing this enemy to him."

"I shall reward you as you deserve," Temujin murmured.

"We ask for nothing," Ogin said hastily, "but should you see fit to – "

"These vultures have captured a bird," Jamukha said. "Servants have lifted their hands against their master."

Ogin looked back at him, then turned towards Temujin. "We owe him nothing now," another of Jamukha's men said. "He's no more than a bandit living on what he can find. Do what you wish with him, my Khan – I'll offer you my pledge."

"They fell upon me," Jamukha said. "I told them they could

forget their oath to me if they wished to join you, but they chose to break it instead." His eyes met Temujin's. "My anda knows what such men deserve." He expected no mercy for himself; it no longer mattered what he said.

Temujin glanced at his men. "You've heard me say this before," the Khan said. "How can we trust such men? How can we have any faith in those who would betray their own leader?" He motioned with one hand. Ogin stumbled back as two soldiers seized him; others quickly surrounded his four companions. "Such men must die."

The five were dragged forward; the swords fell swiftly. Blood spurted over the ground near Jamukha. Temujin gazed at one of the severed heads, then kicked it aside.

Jamukha was about to kneel when Temujin waved an arm. "Free my anda from his bonds." A man cut at the thongs binding Jamukha's wrists. Jamukha shook himself, bewildered. Jurchedei frowned; Khasar seemed about to protest. "Jamukha and I swore a sacred oath long ago," Temujin continued. "We promised that nothing would come between us, and now my anda is with me again."

Temujin came to Jamukha and threw his arms around him. Jamukha froze, too startled to respond. "I want to talk to him alone," the Khan said. Before anyone could speak, he was guiding Jamukha inside his tent.

Temujin settled him in the back, then sat at his side. The Khan was silent for a long time. His anda, Jamukha thought, would toy with him before uttering his sentence.

"Jamukha." Temujin leaned towards him; his pale eyes glistened. "We swore an oath. Once we were like the two wheels of a cart. Even when we parted, I didn't forget my anda, and how close we once were. When I fought against you, the thought that you might die grieved me. Even when we were enemies, you sent a messenger to warn me of danger. I never wanted to fight you."

Jamukha could not speak.

"My greatest wish now," Temujin continued, "is that we might be brothers again, that you might be one of those closest to me, one to advise me of what I might forget. You were my friend when I had no one, you joined me when Merkits forced

475

me to flee from my camp. I have many Nokors now, yet none has grown as close to me as we were when we were boys. A Khan can often be a lonely man, even amid his army of comrades in arms. I can still wish for my anda to ease my loneliness."

Jamukha's heart throbbed painfully. Once, he would have rejoiced to hear these words, but too much had passed. Temujin's forgiveness seemed as cruel as any revenge.

"I swore to be your anda when we were boys." Jamukha's voice caught on the words. "We renewed our pledge under the great tree where Khutula Khan once danced, and shared one blanket between us, and then others made us doubt each other and slashed at the bond that bound us. Shame has burned my face more than the fiercest of winds, and I was ashamed to show my face to you in defeat. Now you tell me you can forgive all that."

"I have forgiven you, my brother, and also long to spare you, but I cannot."

Jamukha looked away. "Oh yes," he said. "Now that you've grown greater than Khutula and any Khan who's ever lived, now that you've made an ulus of all the tribes, I'm of no use to you. Your thoughts would be troubled by day, and your dreams by night. I would be an insect biting you under your collar, or a thorn pricking you under your shirt."

"We were brothers." Temujin clutched at his arm, then let go. "I left you because I feared you would turn against me, and you left me believing we couldn't lead our people together. We were young then, and ruled by the passions of younger men, and I tell myself it might be different now. I want my anda at my side. To know we could be friends once more would give me more joy than all I've won, yet I know it cannot be. Others would come between us again."

"I expected you to torment me when I was brought to you," Jamukha whispered, "and your forgiveness is as burdensome as any yoke."

"I don't say these words to torment you."

He still had a trace of that weakness Jamukha had glimpsed in him long ago, that hesitation, a reluctance to be as hard as a Khan had to be. Yet he would harden himself for what had to be done.

"You might have freed me, Temujin," he said. "I can fight you no more. But you won't show such weakness before your men. You want them to see you as noble and forgiving even while you punish me."

"Jamukha!" His voice was harsh.

"Your mother is wise, you have your brothers, and many brave men ride with you. I lost my parents as a child, have no brothers, and couldn't trust the men who followed me. It's clear that Tengri always favoured you."

Temujin took his hand. "I would have shared everything I have with you, had you given me your oath."

"And you would have called me brother, but I would have been only your servant. There's no place in your world for men who won't bow to you." Jamukha drew his hand from his anda's, and got to his feet. "I tire of life in the world you will rule. I ask only this of you, that I be allowed to die without having my blood shed. I also make you this promise, Temujin. When my bones have been buried, my spirit will watch over you. My ghost will remind you of what you lost to gain your triumphs. A ghost is not so easily cast aside." He chanted the words, as if uttering a curse.

Temujin stood up slowly. The lines in his face, even in the shadows, seemed deeper, his eyes duller. They left the tent together. The bodies of Jamukha's betrayers had been dragged away, but their heads still sat on the ground. The men near the tent rose; Borchu and Jelme hastened to Temujin's side.

"My anda left me, spoke against me, and fought me, but I won't believe that he ever truly sought my death." Temujin's voice shook. "He tells me he's weary of life, yet I fear to order his death – he's my anda, and I'd be cursed for taking his life."

Jamukha said, "When I first rode against you, I forgot my oath to you." He would not beg for his life now. "It can be said I deserve punishment for that."

"That is so." Temujin seemed to be forcing the words from himself. "When Jamukha's cousin Taychar stole the horses of one of our men, and the owner took them back, Jamukha forgot our anda bond and attacked me. Perhaps that's enough reason for him to die now." He lifted a hand. "Let Jamukha die as he wishes, without the spilling of his blood. We'll bury him on a high cliff with all honour, and his spirit will watch over our descendants."

Men surrounded Jamukha to lead him away. He heard a moan as Temujin sagged against Borchu and pressed his face against the other man's coat.

The air was sharp and clear. When they were outside the circle of tents, one of the men with Jamukha took a silken cord from his belt. Temujin would remember him, and mourn for him. That was the only revenge left to Jamukha now.

A hand pushed him forward. The man holding the cord stepped behind him. Jamukha was smiling as the noose tightened around his neck.

91

KOKOCHU HAD FLOWN to Heaven and returned to Earth. The voices that had murmured to him were now silent, but one presence was still near, hovering just behind him. He turned his head and thought he glimpsed a shadow. Kokochu was certain the lingering presence was a ghost, but it had not yet chosen to reveal itself to him.

Above the mountain, the vast bowl of the Eternal Sky was clear and blue; below, the snow-covered ground was nearly as blinding as Heaven's light. The yurt near the mountain was a black spot against the whiteness; the two shamans Kokochu had brought with him would be inside, waiting.

Kokochu got to this feet and moved slowly down the slope, feeling the invisible presence following him. His muscles ached; he had been locked in his trance, unable to move. Teb-Tenggeri, everyone called him, the All-Celestial; they would never know what his arts had cost him, how the spirits that lifted him to ecstasy still tore at him at other times.

His calling had come when he was a boy. The spirits had

driven him from his father's tent into a forest, and Kokochu had died there, under the trees, crying out as his body was dismembered by monstrous birds before his eyes and his spirit sent wandering among the dead. The ghosts of ancestors had shrieked at him, and then the spirit of a shaman had led him to a great tree. He had climbed the limbs to Heaven and embraced a spirit-wife before returning to his body and finding himself whole again. His father Munglik had discovered him there, and had wept as he lifted Kokochu to his horse.

Kokochu had known what his visions meant, that he would have to follow the shaman's path. The ghosts of past shamans would plague him with dreams of death and torture him with despair unless he accepted his calling. Demons would drive him into madness if he refused to bow to his fate.

Three white horses were tethered outside the yurt. The steeds were gifts from his stepbrother Temujin, part of Kokochu's reward for the omens he had read that past autumn. Kokochu had noted the fractures in the burned bones before assenting to the Khan's campaign against the Tanguts of Hsi-Hsia.

That autumn, a wing of the Mongol army had crossed the Gobi and attacked Hsi-Hsia in the south, following a route earlier raiders had used. Their horses, fattened from grazing, fed on the tufts of yellow desert grass that sprouted on the hard flat surface. In Kansu, amid the sand and desolation of the surrounding lands, they came to the oases marking the trade routes caravans travelled. There, among green willows and poplars, people who dwelled behind walls and tended fields lived along the canals that fed their towns.

The army stripped the fields of corn and millet, feasted on fat melons that had ripened on flat rocks, and seized the white camels the townsfolk possessed. Following their Khan's orders, they pressed on to the Yellow River and the city of Ning-hsia, but the Tanguts retreated behind the city's walls. Without an army riding out to meet them, the Mongols had no way to fight, and finally withdrew.

As Kokochu had predicted, the Khan had won no true victory, but that had not been the foray's purpose. The Mongols had gained booty, disrupted some of the trade on which the Tangut cities depended, and were learning that prolonged warfare against settled people would have to be conducted in a different way. They returned to their camps with captives, among them fair Tangut girls, craftsmen to use as slaves, yellow-robed men with shaven heads who spun wheels when they prayed, and herdsmen to look after their beasts. Mongol tents were filled with white camel-hair garments, jars of grain, black kara stones to be burned as fuel, delicate plates smoother and finer than stone or wood, and ornaments of jade. What they had taken made them anticipate winning even more. The Tanguts were wounded; ways could be found to bring them to their knees. A way to the richer lands of the Kin would be opened when Hsi-Hsia bowed to the Khan.

Kokochu had been given his share of the spoils, and knew that some whispered he served the Khan only for such rewards. They did not understand. The falcons, the jewels, the herds that grazed outside his camp and the girls he brought to his bed could not repay him for the torment, the trances that came upon him unbidden, the spirits that entered him and forced him to speak their words. His possessions could not give him the ecstasy of riding to Heaven, of feeling God's presence inside himself. There were shamans who did not suffer as he did, who could return from their spirit-journeys and live easily among their people, but he was not one of them; his afflictions were signs that he was destined for a harder and lonelier path.

If he could not have love, he could still ease himself with slaves; if he could not have true friendship, he would settle for the respect born of fear. Without his rewards, those who feared him would only come to scorn him; if the Khan did not honour him, others would believe that the spirits had abandoned him, and no longer truly spoke through him. Many might envy him, but none of them would have chosen his path. A man or woman marked as a shaman, having to learn spells, healing, and all the lore a shaman had to master, was one set apart. Others needed his skills, but Kokochu also sensed the resentment in their gratitude and the hatred behind their smiles. Those who knew little would always hate those who knew more; those who feared the spirits would resent a man who could summon them.

Kokochu's dreams had shown him Temujin's destiny. Tengri

480

would not have used Temujin to unite all the tribes only to sheathe that mighty weapon. The Khan knew God meant to bring more lands to the great Mongol ulus he had forged, yet there were those who might lead Temujin away from his trail. Kokochu was Temujin's shield; even those closest to the throne could not be allowed to stand in the Khan's way. The spirits would compel Temujin to follow his path, as they had forced Kokochu along his own. The Khan would rule all, and Kokochu would rule through him.

Something cold touched his face. He was about to enter the yurt when the ghost took possession of him. Kokochu fell; his arms flailed against the snow before his body stiffened, and then he suddenly knew whose spirit had entered him.

When Kokochu came to himself, he ordered his two companions to saddle the horses. They rode swiftly in the direction of Temujin's camp, slowing to a trot only when they saw a few field tents in the distance and the mottled mass of a horse herd beyond.

The ghost was still inside him, but Kokochu could subdue it now. A small band of men, the Khan among them, were riding towards the tents, a few dogs trailing them. Temujin carried a golden eagle on his wrist; his hand, covered in a gauntlet, rested against a forked stick attached to the saddle to support the great bird's weight.

The Khan called out as Kokochu approached. "Greetings, brother Teb-Tenggeri," Temujin said. "We've been hunting a pack of wolves that's preyed upon my horses. My bird and the dogs made short work of a few – they won't dine on horseflesh again."

"I must speak to you," Kokochu said. Temujin handed the eagle to the man nearest him, then dismounted. The other men were silent as Temujin led Kokochu to a tent.

"What is it?" Temujin asked when they had settled by the hearth. Kokochu gazed at his stepbrother, noting the tension in his face. This was another sign of his power, that the Khan would never turn him away or refuse to meet with him.

"I am with you again," Kokochu said, but the voice was not his own. "I speak to you now through your shaman Teb-

Tenggeri." Temujin's eyes widened as he made a sign. "You wanted me at your side, even as you ordered my death, and I haven't forgotten my promise to you."

Temujin clutched at him. "Can it be – "

"I promised to watch over you, and I am here, my anda. You longed for me to be your comrade once more, and I have come to you." Even as the ghost spoke through him, Kokochu understood why the spirit had been sent to him. Only the ghost of this man could bind the Khan even more closely to him.

"Jamukha!" Temujin cried.

Kokochu's arms slipped around the Khan as Temujin sagged against him. "I am with you again, anda Temujin, as you wished me to be."

92

HOELUN SAT WITH Bortai to the left of her son's throne. To the south of the great pavilion that shaded them, circles of yurts and wagons stretched to the horizon, and hundreds of horses were tethered near Temujin's ordu. Noyans had ridden there from all the regions her son now ruled to hear his proclamations.

Her pains had troubled her during her journey, but to see Temujin as Khan of all the tribes was worth enduring any discomfort. Kumiss had eased the dull pains in her chest and the sharper ones that sometimes lanced through her entrails; her sable coat protected her from the cold spring air. Her son had summoned his men there, near the Onon's headwaters, for a kuriltai. Hoelun thought of the day, nearly forty years ago, when she had first seen Yesugei by the river; Temujin's father had never imagined such glory for his son.

Many whispered that Teb-Tenggeri had advised the Khan to hold the kuriltai. The bones and the stars had shown the shaman that the spirits wanted Temujin confirmed again as Khan, now that all the tribes had submitted to him. All the

Noyans had gathered to raise Genghis Khan on the felt once more; Khorchi, Usun, and other shamans had presided over the horse sacrifice, but it was Teb-Tenggeri who had hoisted a tugh of nine white yak-tails and proclaimed Temujin as Khan.

Without the shaman's powers, some said, Temujin might lose Heaven's favour, and he had turned more to Munglik's son in the year since Jamukha's death. Those who wanted something from the Khan were learning that a word to the shaman could win Temujin's attention; those who feared Teb-Tenggeri were careful not to offend him.

Hoelun looked towards the throne. Temujin's sons and brothers sat to his right, and his wives to his left, but Teb-Tenggeri stood behind him, adorned in a feathered head-dress and white robes. It was said that Jamukha sometimes advised the Khan through the All-Celestial, that Temujin's anda watched over him now. She wondered if her son would ever be free of Jamukha's memory.

Temujin was listing the ninety-five men he would make heads of one thousand households each. Hoelun listened, swaying to the metre of the speech. All of the Khan's most devoted followers, including Hoelun's four adopted sons and her husband Munglik, were among the ninety-five who would command these mingghans. Her foster son Shigi Khutukhu was with the Uighur scribes seated near the pavilion, seeing that their brushes noted the Khan's words on their scrolls. Shigi Khutukhu had learned the script quickly; he could look at those strange markings and see the words in them.

Temujin fell silent. Hoelun looked up as Shigi Khutukhu stepped forward, then bowed. "My Khan and brother," the young man said, "have I served you less than any other man? Your mother raised me as her own, and called me her son. Others have served you well, but I am the one who sees that your words will live. Don't I deserve a greater reward than you have given me?"

Temujin nodded. "You are my younger brother," he said. "You will have your share of everything that is my family's, and you may break the law nine times and be pardoned. You will also be my eyes and ears — I make you the judge of all my people. You will divide them, giving a part to our mother

Hoelun Khatun, a part to us, a part to our younger brothers, and a part to our sons. You will record all your judgements and, once you have taken counsel with me and written them, no man may alter them."

Shigi Khutukhu bowed again. "I am honoured, but it is not fitting for me to take a part equal to that of your other brothers. Instead, I ask only that you reward me with a part of what you take from any earthen-walled cities."

Temujin's brows lifted as he gave his assent. Hoelun's foster son obviously anticipated greater conquests. If Temujin took cities in Hsi-Hsia and Khitai, Shigi Khutukhu's share of the booty would bring him much wealth. The Khan would grant his adoptive brother's request because it showed how much faith Shigi Khutukhu had in him.

The Khan beckoned to Munglik, who approached the throne with his other six sons and glanced at Teb-Tenggeri before he bowed. "Munglik-echige," Temujin said, "you have protected and served me for many years. You saved my life when Nilkha Senggum plotted against me and summoned me to his camp. If you had not brought me to turn back, I would have thrown myself into the fire. As your reward, you will sit near my throne, and all the generations that follow you and your sons will have my gifts."

Teb-Tenggeri lifted his head as his father settled on a cushion near the throne. His beautiful face, still beardless but with the traces of a moustache, held a triumphant look. Hoelun could almost believe that he, not the Khan, was dispensing these honours, that he meant to give his father and brothers a higher place than anyone.

The Khan had spoken to his comrades Borchu and Mukhali. Each man would command a tuman, with Borchu the general of the ten thousand of the right, and Mukhali commanding the left wing of the army. After honouring Mukhali with a princely title, the Khan summoned Jurchedei.

Khadagan turned towards her husband, narrowing her eyes as Temujin spoke of how Jurchedei had served him so well that he had been rewarded with the Khan's own wife Ibakha Beki. Jurchedei smiled; apparently the gift had pleased him.

Teb-Tenggeri had brought that about. Jurchedei might be honoured to have the beautiful Ibakha, but Khadagan knew what the servants said; the shaman had sent the Khan the dream ordering him to surrender his wife. Ibakha's banishment from the Khan's ordu was a warning to others; Teb-Tenggeri could easily rid himself of anyone else who troubled him. Khadagan stilled her thoughts. She would not be so foolish as Ibakha.

The Khan recited words of praise for his four foster brothers, with a special tribute for Boroghul. Tolui lived because Boroghul's wife Altani had defended him against a Tatar soldier; Ogedei lived because Boroghul had carried him from the battlefield. Another speech honoured the Bagarin chief Usun; that old man, a shaman himself, kept his eyes averted from Teb-Tenggeri. Even he, Khadagan knew, was wary around the younger man.

She sat up as her own father and brothers came forward. "Sorkhan-shira," the Khan said, "you cared for me when I was a prisoner in Targhutai Kiriltugh's camp. Your daughter Khadagan hid me, and your sons Chimbai and Chilagun helped me to escape. That memory lives in my heart. Ask anything of me, and I shall grant it." Khadagan's chest swelled; Temujin had kept the promises he had made so long ago.

"My son Chimbai led your army against the rebellious Merkit clans," Sorkhan-shira replied. "I wish only to camp where I choose in their former lands along the Selenga River."

"You may camp where you wish," Temujin murmured, "and your sons may come before me at any time and ask for whatever favours they like."

Sorkhan-shira bowed. Khadagan wondered if he had caught the faintly mournful tone in the Khan's voice. This should have been the most joyful day of Temujin's life, but perhaps he was thinking that this might be all he would ever gain. Much had happened since she had taken pity on a captive boy. For a moment, she allowed herself to mourn those who had fallen in the battles against him, and remembered the other husband she had lost.

Khulan gazed at Chimbai, refusing to allow bitterness to overwhelm her. Her father's gift of her had only bought peace for a time. After submitting to the Khan, many Merkits had rebelled and run off to make a final stand. Her husband had ignored her pleas for mercy, and Chimbai had been his sword against the Merkits. There was no purpose in dwelling on such thoughts; she was growing used to letting them sink below the dark, calm surface of her mind.

The Khan was a storm that came upon her, assaulting her body but leaving her soul unmoved. He spoke of his love for her and had given her the title of Khatun when their son was born. After Kulgan's birth, she had hoped she might know some peace, that her son would secure her place while Temujin found a new favourite among his women. Instead, his passion had grown, as if feeding on her indifference.

Sorkhan-shira bowed and backed away; he and his sons would camp in her people's lands now. The Khan called out Nayaga's name; Khulan composed herself as the young man bowed before him. Nayaga could have no regrets. Temujin had given him command of a thousand for his loyalty.

"When this man rode to me," Temujin said, "with his father Shirgugetu and his brother Alagh, they were bringing my old enemy Targhutai Kiriltugh to me. But Nayaga saw that a man who lays hands on his own leader commits evil, and persuaded his father and brother to let Targhutai go. He did right then, and has proved his courage and trustworthiness since in many ways. Borchu will command our right wing, and Mukhali the left – let Nayaga be a Tuman-u Noyan and take command of the centre."

Nayaga's brown eyes glowed and he bowed deeply, apparently overcome by such an honour. As he straightened, his eyes met hers; the glow in his eyes faded. Khulan looked away. He could not feel sorry, now that he had been so richly rewarded for his faithfulness. He had demonstrated his devotion by putting aside the love he once had felt.

The Khan was speaking of how he would organize his army, and of those who would serve as his guards by night and by day. Gurbesu watched as the scribes took down his words, recording them as they once had written the Tayang's.

486

Now that some Uighurs served him, perhaps the rest of that people would yield to him; the trade routes they controlled would bring more wealth to the Khan. The darker look she had seen in Temujin's eyes disappeared as he spoke of sending Subotai against the sons of Toghtoga Beki and Jebe against Guchlug. When he was rid of those enemies, the prospect of another war, a greater effort against Hsi-Hsia, would renew him. The Khan was made for wars; he would not rest with what he had won.

The child inside her stirred; perhaps she would give him a son. The Khan had saved much of what had once belonged to the Naimans. If he could not read the script that recorded his words, he understood its uses. He would reach out to take more, yet she wondered if his conquests would change him. He would have to become more than a general in order to hold what he might win, and learn how to rule those unlike himself. She glanced at his sons; in their silk robes and camel-hair coats, they looked less like Mongols.

The Khan was proclaiming his Yasa, the code of laws that would rule his people. "All the people will believe in a Supreme God," he announced, "Who alone gives life and death. All must know that we owe all to His power, and all may worship this God as they choose."

Gurbesu bowed her head. She would pray with her Christian priests while seeing that the shamans received their due; the yellow-robed monks among the Tanguts could also turn their wheels for her. All the spirits would hear her prayers, and she would not slight those Teb-Tenggeri commanded. Her heart fluttered, as it often did whenever she thought of the chief shaman. Inancha had kept a tight grip on the reins controlling his shamans and priests; she hoped Temujin could do the same.

The Yasa would forever govern all Mongols. We are all Mongols now, Yisui thought. The Khan's Yasa had forbidden anyone to be proclaimed Khan until all the Noyans had gathered for a kuriltai, although it seemed needless to say that. Temujin had taken no new title, but already many called him the Kha-Khan – the Great Khan, the Khan of Khans. No rival was left to threaten him.

"The people of our ulus will not fight among themselves," the Khan continued, "and all are forbidden to make peace with any people who have not submitted to us." Yisui glanced at her sister, and wondered how many others would suffer the Tatars' fate. Yisugen's eyes met hers, and Yisui knew her sister was remembering the dead.

"No subject of the Khan," Temujin said, "will take another Mongol as a slave." Yisui lowered her eyes; the slaves would have to be found elsewhere. She thought of the prisoners who had recently been allotted to her. It was easier to remain unmoved by the tears she sometimes glimpsed in their eyes and by the losses they had suffered, now that her own memories had faded.

"Every man must pay for his wife," Temujin said. "There will be no stealing of women among the people of our ulus, thievery that has only brought us to fight one another in the past. Our women will control what they own, trading as they see fit, for men should concern themselves with war and the hunt."

Bortai looked up at her husband. He might have been saying those words for her sake, and for Hoelun-eke's; their thefts had cost many lives. But he would not be thinking of that, only of keeping his nation united.

His voice was solemn, his face hard as he paused so that others could carry his words to the people assembled beyond the pavilion. She had hoped he would feel joy today, that his grief had left him at last. He had wept for Jamukha inside her tent, all the betrayals forgotten as he mourned the man who had once been his closest comrade. He had thrown himself into the plans for his foray against the Tanguts with a joy that seemed a kind of desperation, but he had not escaped his anda. He often went to Teb-Tenggeri to hear the voice of his old friend speak through the shaman. His anda's spirit could still be with him, gazing at him through his stepbrother's dark eyes.

Her husband fell silent. She watched Teb-Tenggeri as the shaman lifted his arms and uttered his own blessing on the Yasa. How strange, she thought, that Teb-Tenggeri so closely resembled the dead man; she had never noticed the likeness before. His handsome face had grown leaner, and his eyes had Jamukha's predatory look.

Jamukha had wanted to rule Temujin. Perhaps Teb-Tenggeri was ruled by Jamukha's old ambitions now, which might echo his own. Bortai closed her eyes as the shaman chanted. His voice throbbed against her ears, drowning out thought.

93

BORTAI PANTED FOR breath as her horse neared the camp; Khadagan's mount halted near hers. "I'm getting fat," Bortai said. "It may be good for a Khatun to be plump and show how well her husband provides for her, but the weight is a burden."

Khadagan laughed; the gyrfalcon on her wrist fluttered its wings. "You'll never be fat."

Khadagan never would, Bortai thought. Heaven might not have granted her beauty, but had given her the slenderness of youth.

Their guards waited several paces from them. Bortai adjusted her gyrfalcon's tether around her glove. She had escaped her worries for a little while, but in the camp, they would press in on her again.

The tents of the Khan's camp covered the plain on both sides of the river, which had swelled with the melting snows of late spring. Bortai drew her sable coat more tightly around her against the cold. The coat had been one of many offered to the Khan by the Oirats, and the white falcons her guards carried were also Oirat gifts. Jochi, sent out with an army by Temujin, had won the submission of both the Oirats and the Kirghiz people, and their northern forests had been added to the Khan's realm. Temujin had granted Jochi command over those people. Perhaps the rumours that Jochi was not the Khan's true son would at last die.

Temujin had achieved much since his proclamations two

489

years ago. Another foray against the Tanguts, the submission of the reindeer people and the forest tribes – the Tumats, after a brief rebellion, had also surrendered to the Khan's general Dorbei, who had cleverly sent out spies to spread false reports about his army's movements, thus taking the Tumats by surprise.

But the victories had also brought sorrow to her husband. His foster brother Boroghul was dead, killed by Tumats in an ambush. In his grief, Temujin had wanted to lead an army against the Tumats himself, but Borchu and Mukhali had dissuaded him. Bortai knew that Teb-Tenggeri had added his voice to those of the two generals. The shaman preferred to keep the Khan near his own camp and within reach of his spells.

Bortai knew what some whispered inside their tents. Teb-Tenggeri read the omens before all kuriltais. He argued with the Khan in front of others without rousing Temujin's wrath, and demanded what he liked for himself. The Khan's own mother had dared to speak openly against the shaman, and now she was ailing, which proved she had offended the spirits. Teb-Tenggeri's camp had grown nearly as great as the Khan's, and more households had gone there to serve the shaman.

Temujin must know what others were saying, yet did nothing. Bortai had carried only a few such tales to him before his glaring eyes warned her to be silent. The Khan still feared the man who spoke to him in the voices of the dead and who might hold Hoelun-eke's life in his hands.

Khadagan said, "What troubles you now?"

"I think you know." She could confide in Khadagan; most of Temujin's other wives and women were too afraid of Teb-Tenggeri even to talk of him. "Temujin must act soon." She made a sign against evil. "I told myself that Teb-Tenggeri was certain to go too far, that our husband would see he had to be put in his place. What will become of us if anything happens to Temujin?"

"You can't say such words to him," Khadagan said. Bortai sighed. Temujin recoiled from any talk of what might happen after his passing, as if he could hold death at bay by refusing to think of it. Maybe he thought Teb-Tenggeri's spells would keep him alive forever.

"He wouldn't even listen to Khasar," Bortai said. "His own brother, and Temujin let it pass." That had been the latest incident. Khasar and the shaman had been arguing. It was said that a few careless jokes of Khasar's, uttered in drunkenness, had started the fight, and Teb-Tenggeri's six brothers had beaten Khasar severely. Temujin had been in Khulan's ordu when Khasar had arrived there to demand punishment for the affront. He might have taken action against the shaman himself, but had thought it proper for the Khan to dispense justice. Instead, Temujin had sent him away with mocking words about how the mighty Khasar had allowed himself to be beaten.

Khulan, she thought, might have pleaded for Khasar; the Khan might have listened to his favourite wife. But Khulan asked him for nothing. Perhaps that was one reason Temujin still burned for her as though she were the wife of only a few days. Khulan lived as if the world could not touch her. The Merkit's beautiful face was always serene, her soft brown eyes contemplative and distant. Once Bortai had believed her to be too gentle and weak; Khulan was kind even to the lowliest of her slaves, who often took advantage of her generosity. But she held the Khan's favour, and he would not have loved a weak woman that much.

"First, it was Ibakha," Bortai said, "a silly girl who could have done nothing against the shaman, and now Khasar suffers because of a joke."

"Mockery can be a weapon," Khadagan said. "A man who laughs at Teb-Tenggeri shows that he doesn't fear him." She made a sign. "You must be careful."

Bortai glimpsed the tiny forms of distant riders to the south. One of them wore a feathered head-dress; she gritted her teeth. Teb-Tenggeri had dared to come here so soon after insulting Khasar; maybe Temujin would finally curb his insolence. She motioned to the guards, then dug her heels into her horse's flanks.

Bortai had hardly settled herself inside her tent when she heard the guards greet her husband. Temujin entered, trailed by a group of young captains; she greeted them as her women set food on the table in front of the bed. Temujin performed the blessing, then seated himself; the men sat on the cushions to his right.

Other men entered, carrying hawks for the Khan to inspect. Temujin took one bird on his wrist, peering at it in the same distantly curious way he gazed at his youngest children. He handed the hawk back, then glanced at Bortai. "My chief shaman wishes to speak to me," he said. "I mean to ask him about Khasar." She heard uncertainty in his voice; maybe he regretted his harsh words to his brother.

A guard called out beyond the doorway. Teb-Tenggeri entered, his six brothers at his back. Temujin nodded to him, but did not beckon him nearer. Bortai leaned forward; usually the Khan was quick to seat the shaman at his side.

"My brother Khasar came to me," Temujin said, "and complained about you. He told me that you and your brothers set upon him. I sent him away for disturbing my rest, and now he sulks in his tent, refusing to speak to me. The Khan would hear what you have to say."

Bortai tensed. Temujin sounded almost as though he was pleading with the shaman for an explanation.

"I came to you as soon as I could." Teb-Tenggeri took a step forward. "I knew you would want to hear my reason for acting as I did. Ever since I told my father of the dream that told us to follow you, my only wish has been to serve you, brother and Khan."

The shaman glanced around the tent. The lute-players kept their heads bowed; the servants and the captains averted their eyes. "I didn't mean to offend you by striking at Khasar," Teb-Tenggeri continued. "I was acting on your behalf."

"I had no reason to want my brother beaten."

Teb-Tenggeri's face grew solemn. "I have served you," he replied. "My dreams have told me of your greatness, the spirits I command have done your bidding. I trust my dreams, for everything they've told me has come to pass. I've flown to Heaven and seen that Tengri favours you, and yet now a darker dream has come to me."

Temujin's hands fisted. "Go on."

"The spirits spoke to me." The shaman lifted a hand. "They told me that Temujin would rule the ulus. But then another voice whispered that Khasar would rule. My dreams have always guided me, but none of my powers can tell me what may happen now. Such a dream can only mean that Khasar is plotting against you."

"I don't believe it!" Bortai cried before she could stop herself. The shaman's eyes darted towards her and the coldness of his glance locked her throat. She stared at the others desperately, then realized none of the men would speak out.

"It is so," Teb-Tenggeri said. "By mocking me, he mocks you, and shows what he thinks of us both. He wouldn't be the first brother of a Khan who wants his throne for himself."

Temujin's face was pale. "Perhaps it's true," he whispered. "Khasar came to me instead of taking his revenge on you. He must have known that if he moved against you himself, I'd discover his plans too soon. He was always ready to defend himself before — causing discord between us must be part of his plot."

Bortai's nails dug into her palms. If the shaman could make Temujin doubt Khasar, he would not shrink from striking at her or her sons. Terror filled her; if she spoke now, Teb-Tenggeri would send a spirit to silence her.

Temujin stood up. "You'll be given fresh horses to return to your camp," the Khan said. "I must ride to Khasar now, and find out exactly what his plans are." The men with the hawks were still; the other men got to their feet. Before Bortai could find her voice again, they had all left the tent.

94

HOELUN STRETCHED HER hands towards the hearth. Even near the fire, she often felt cold. A shamaness had come to her tent throughout the winter, but this spring, her pains had worsened. Those around her were aware of her suffering, even though she refused to admit to it aloud.

As long as she did not take to her bed, they might believe

the evil spirit would soon leave her. If she forced herself to go on, the others would not leave her to herself, and no spear would bar the entrance to her ordu.

Munglik would not come to her this evening. He usually spent the night in the tent of his Oirat girl, or with the Tangut woman who had been given to him. How like him it was to offer excuses for going to them, saying that he wanted Hoelun to rest, and she could sleep more easily alone. He would not admit that he did not want to share a bed with an ailing old woman.

He would not listen to her. She had begged him to warn Kokochu the All-Celestial that his arrogance might test Temujin's patience, but Munglik was fearful of his shaman son. Kokochu might have the power to heal her; the Khan would refuse to hear any words spoken against him.

A guard shouted to her from the doorway, then came inside and bowed. "Guchu and Kukuchu are here," he said, "and beg to be allowed to speak to you at once."

"My sons are always welcome." She moved towards her bed, determined not to let them see her frailty. Guchu and Kukuchu camped near Khasar's ordu now; perhaps Khasar had sent them to see how she was faring.

As she seated herself, her foster sons entered. Their broad faces were flushed; they hung up their weapons and hastened towards her. "I know what some say," she murmured, "but your old mother isn't quite so ill as they claim. Drink with me and sleep here tonight, and you may tell Khasar – "

"Khasar didn't send us," Guchu said. "We bring evil news, Hoelun-eke. We were with Khasar when Temujin arrived with his guard, shouting that Khasar was plotting against him. Khasar insisted it wasn't so, but Temujin claimed that Teb-Tenggeri learned of the plot in a dream."

Hoelun stiffened. "What are you saying?"

"Khasar's been angry with Temujin these past days," Kukuchu said, "but he would never plot against the Khan. A little while ago, Khasar confronted Teb-Tenggeri, claiming that the shaman was enticing some of Khasar's men to move to his camp. He'd been drinking, and joked that the spell Teb-Tenggeri used to lure them was bending over and parting his buttocks. The shaman and his brothers beat Khasar and drove him away. Khasar went to Temujin and demanded justice, but Temujin only dismissed him."

"Khasar's brooded ever since," Guchu added, "but when he heard Temujin was riding to him, he was sure the matter would be put right. Instead, the Khan is calling him a traitor and demanding that he confess. We managed to slip away."

Her rage had burned away her weariness. "I told my husband his son would go too far," she whispered, "but I never thought he would dare to come between Temujin and Khasar."

"The Khan might listen to your words," Guchu said. "Give us your message, and we'll carry it to him."

Hoelun stood up. "I'll go to Temujin myself."

Guchu frowned. "Mother, are you strong enough to – "

"I'll put a stop to this if it takes all my strength." She moved towards the doorway and shouted to her guards.

A man harnessed one of her white camels to a cart. Hoelun took the reins herself and drove through the night, accompanied by only a few men. Dawn was breaking as she neared Khasar's ordu. She drew up at his camping circle and climbed down, then strode towards his tent. Members of the Khan's night guard stood by the steps leading up to the doorway; Khasar's wives peered out from the tents stretching to the east.

Several guards gaped at her, then saluted. "Are my sons Temujin and Khasar inside?" she asked.

"Indeed they are, Honoured Lady," one man replied.

"Admit me."

The men stepped out of her way; she called out her name, then went inside. The tent was filled with men; they scrambled to their feet. Khasar stood at the back of the tent; his hands were bound, while his belt and hat lay on the floor. Temujin, sitting in front of Khasar's bed, shrank back as she walked towards him.

"What a disgraceful sight," she muttered. "Never were two brothers as close as you, and now you turn against Khasar with no thought of what he's done for you."

Temujin did not meet her gaze. She went to Khasar, untied his wrists, then stooped to pick up his belt and hat. Temujin did not speak; no one reached out to stop her. She pressed the belt and hat into Khasar's hands. His face was bruised, and blood trickled from one side of his mouth.

"I did nothing wrong, Mother," Khasar said. "I am falsely accused."

"I know."

"Yet Temujin refuses to believe me."

She glared at the Khan. The men glanced from her to him. Temujin's face was drawn. She thought of how he must have passed the night, shaming his brother and himself with his baseless suspicions, refusing to see the truth.

Hoelun sat down before the bed, opened her coat, then ripped her robe aside. "Look at these breasts!" she shouted. "Look at the breasts that fed you!" A few of the men covered their faces. "Look at the mother who gave you both life! Khasar couldn't have done anything against you, and yet you would strike at your own flesh!"

Temujin leaned back, his face pale. "I'll tell you this," Hoelun continued, lifting her sagging breasts in her hands. "Temujin could suck the milk from one breast, and Khachigun and Temuge could barely empty one between them, but Khasar could drain both of milk and ease my aching so that I could rest. Temujin, who is so wise, got his wisdom from my milk, and Khasar his skill with the bow. How often that bow has served his brother. His arrows brought your enemies to surrender, but now that you've killed those who fought against you, you wish to be rid of him!"

Temujin seemed about to speak. She shook her head at him and closed her coat. "All speak of how fair Temujin is in his judgements," she said, "how he rewards those who are loyal, and yet now he tears at his own brother, the archer whose arrows struck fear into the hearts of his enemies. He's thrust a knife through his old mother's heart, and brought misery to her old age."

Hoelun lifted her head. Temujin got up and paced in front of the bed. "Go on," she said. "Ignore the truth, threaten your brother, drive your old mother from this tent. See how much honour that brings to your name." If he tried to harm Khasar, she would cling to her younger son until the Khan's men dragged her away. She would curse Temujin as long as she had breath to say the words.

"I've done nothing wrong," Khasar said.

"You shouldn't have to say it," Hoelun said. "The man some call the Great Khan should have seen it for himself."

The men were still. The Khan paced in the shadows; Hoelun kept her eyes on him. At last Temujin moved towards her, his shoulders sagging. He helped her up with one arm and she knew that she had won.

"Any man would fear the anger of such a mother," he said. "I'm ashamed of what I've done. Khasar is free, and I'm sorry for disturbing his rest." He let go of her, refusing to gaze into her eyes. "I'll leave you now." His men quickly gathered around him; they left the tent.

"Sorry for disturbing your rest." Hoelun clutched Khasar to her. "He should have gone on his knees to beg your forgiveness."

"Temujin would never have been brought to this by himself," Khasar said.

"I know. That makes no difference."

"A spell is on him," Khasar said. "He must believe he can't keep his throne without his shaman."

"He may not keep it with him." Hoelun leaned against her son, suddenly weary.

Temujin's shame did not last. Within days of Hoelun's return to her ordu, the Khan stripped Khasar of most of the households he commanded, leaving him with only a thousand.

It was Guchu who brought this news to Hoelun. She sent him away, telling him to watch over Khasar, and wondered where Teb-Tenggeri would strike next. Khasar was free, but weakened; one of his Noyans had fled to the west, according to Guchu. The shaman would collect more followers when people saw that the Khan would not confront him even for his brother's sake. Teb-Tenggeri would separate Temujin from anyone who might challenge his influence.

She had one hope left, faint as it was. Munglik had been in the camp of his sons during the past days, perhaps because he feared she might turn her wrath on him. She summoned a guard and ordered him to ride to her husband.

Hoelun greeted Munglik in front of her tent. She had adorned herself in her favourite blue robe, painted her face, and lacquered the braids under her head-dress with sap. Munglik approached her with a worried look on his creased face, then smiled as she took his hands.

"You look well, wife," he said.

"Spring has renewed me." She led him inside, seated him on the bed, then beckoned to her servants. "I have missed you, my husband."

Munglik had brought only a few men with him. They ate the lamb Hoelun's cook had prepared; she smiled and laughed while they told stories and sang songs. The men were soon too drunk to notice how little she had eaten, how much she had to drink to dull her pain.

Her husband's face was placid when the other men stumbled from the tent. Hoelun sent her servants away; as Munglik stood up to take off his robe, she reached for his hand. "Before we sleep," she said, "I have something to say."

His brow wrinkled; he sat down next to her. "This is about Khasar, isn't it?" he said. "Everyone knows what you said inside his tent. A mother should love her sons, but you can't know what he might have been plotting."

"This isn't about Khasar, and sometimes a father's love can be as blind as a mother's."

Munglik tugged at his grey beard. "I see."

"Hear me out, Munglik. I'm not thinking just of my own sons now, but of yours. Think of how quickly Temujin might turn against your son if he goes too far."

"You're wrong, Hoelun. Temujin knows what he owes to Kokochu."

"Temujin owes what he has to his sword, and to those of his brothers and generals. The All-Celestial did no more than put his blessing upon it."

Munglik made a sign. "Be careful what you say."

"I'll say what I please. I've lost what fear I had of Teb-Tenggeri. You're his father — it's up to you to tell him what

498

others fear to say. Tell him to lift whatever spell he's cast on Temujin before that spell is turned against him. Tell him to restrain himself — if you can bridle him, your other sons can easily be curbed."

"I can't say that to him, Hoelun."

"Then maybe it's time you gave him one of the beatings you should have given him long ago."

Munglik thrust out an arm. "You may not fear him, but I do. He would put a curse on us both if he — "

"His own father?" she said harshly. "His father's wife? You can believe that, and still not have the courage to face him? What kind of man are you?"

"Hoelun — "

"But I know what sort of man you are." The words forced themselves from her throat. "You may be afraid of him, but you're also thinking of what you might win for yourself through him. I see what you were all along. When we were outcasts, you pitied us, but did little for us. When Temujin parted from his anda, you stayed with Jamukha, and only came to us when you saw my son would be stronger. Temujin wanted us wed, and I made the best of that — I knew he had to secure your loyalty. You haven't been a bad husband, and your advice saved Temujin's life, but you were always one who held his finger to the wind before acting. Now you think you'll gain more by appeasing Teb-Tenggeri."

He grabbed her arm. "Be silent."

"I curse your son, Munglik. If you won't hold him back, may you have my curse as well. I spit at your feet, I turn my face from you."

His face twisted. She saw the struggle in his eyes, and thought he might relent.

"Call back your words," he muttered, "and I'll forgive you. It will be as though they were never spoken."

"The bow has loosed its arrow," she said. "I can't call it back. Only you can keep it from finding your son's heart."

He got up and strode from the tent. The evil spirit's claw tore at her again; she sank back against the bed.

499

95

Bortai heard the soft sound of footsteps; Temujin was coming to bed. He had been brooding by the hearth for much of the night. She reached for him as he slipped under the blanket.

"Bortai," he said, "there's so much I don't know. My words live in what Ta-ta-tonga sets down, and yet I can't read his markings. The people of towns and cities can make paths for water and force it to do their bidding, while we must roam our lands in search of it. Teb-Tenggeri can trace and call up the spirits, while I must struggle to hear them on Burkhan Khaldun. I thought men grew wiser with age, but instead I see how little I know."

"You grasp what a Khan must know," she said.

"But there is more I can't grasp."

He joined with her, but she sensed his thoughts were elsewhere. She held him until he was asleep. The shaman had raised such doubts in his mind; she knew what Teb-Tenggeri must have said. Listen to me, and you will keep your throne; only I can summon the spirits that will aid you.

She was dozing when she heard shouts outside, and recognized Temuge's voice. Temujin's youngest brother was demanding to see him.

Temuge burst through the entrance, came towards them, and knelt at the foot of the bed. "I demand justice of my brother the Khan," Temuge said in a choked voice.

Temujin sat up slowly. "Some from your own camp went to join Teb-Tenggeri," the Odchigin continued, "and you didn't stop them. Now some of my men have done the same. I sent my comrade Sokhur to the shaman to ask that he return my followers, and he and his brothers beat Sokhur and sent him back to me with his saddle tied to his back. How can I endure such insults?"

Temujin reached for his robe and pulled it around his shoulders. "Go on."

"I didn't come to you then," Temuge said. "After what happened to Khasar, I saw I'd have to settle this myself. I went to Teb-Tenggeri. His brothers set upon me and forced me to kneel to the shaman before driving me away without the men I sought." He opened his coat and shirt, then thrust his bruised face towards them. "See the marks those Khongkhotats left on my body! What will you do about that? Must Khasar and I believe that our brother cares for us no longer?"

Bortai sat up and drew the blanket over her chest. "How can you allow this?" she asked.

"Khasar served you well," Temuge said, "and you treated our brother poorly for his loyalty. I did nothing more than demand what was mine. What will you do for us, Temujin?"

The Khan was silent. "Don't you see what they're doing?" Bortai cried. "While you're still alive, they dare to raise their hands against your brothers." Tears trickled down her face; she refused to hold them back. "When your fine, strong body crumbles into dust, what will become of us?"

Temujin shuddered and made the sign against evil. "Yes, I'll speak of that," she went on. "Your people are grass in the wind – who will rule them when you're gone? Do you think men who would strike at your brothers will ever allow my sons to rule?"

He looked towards her. He would order her to be silent; she would not obey him, not this time. "Whatever powers he has," she said, "it's you who made yourself Khan. Will you lose what you've won? Let the shaman go on affronting you, and your great ulus will slip through your fingers. Move against the All-Celestial and test the powers he claims to have."

"My anda speaks to me through him," Temujin said. "He has become the comrade I longed for and lost."

"Give it up, Temujin." Bortai clutched at the blanket. "The shaman is only using your grief and your regrets against you. Let him go on dividing you from those who love you most, and you risk everything. He tests you by shaming your brothers – do yo think he'll hold back from striking at our sons next?"

"His knowledge – " Temujin began.

"He uses it only for himself. If you treat Temuge as you did Khasar, I promise you that all will know what I think of such injustice. Teb-Tenggeri will have to deal with me then – maybe that will bring you to see what he is."

The Odchigin looked from her to his brother. "Your wife is wise," Temuge said. "I beg you not to ignore her advice." He got up and went to the hearth. Temujin stared past Bortai; she saw the despair in his eyes.

"Once, my dreams were clear," he said at last. "Now I only glimpse them through a mist. Once, the spirits spoke to me, and now they're often silent. Only the shaman can ease the doubts that torment me — I can still hear the spirits through him. I can speak to Jamukha, and know he has forgiven me. Do you see what you're asking of me? If I strike at Teb-Tenggeri, and his powers are what they seem, he'll turn them against me. But if I succeed in punishing him, it will show that the spirits have abandoned him, and I'll have to wonder if he ever truly commanded them." He paused. "If I lose my shaman, I'll lose my anda again."

"You are the Khan," Bortai whispered, "the great tree that shelters us all. You must think of the living — your people and your sons."

"Yes, I must, and bring myself to believe that my shaman only clouded my thoughts with his spells. You've given me good counsel, Bortai, but I'll suffer for acting on it." He stood up. "Temuge."

The Odchigin turned towards him. "You may settle your dispute with my chief shaman," the Khan continued. "I shall summon the Khongkhotats to my side, and you may do as you like with Teb-Tenggeri. It wouldn't be fitting for me to raise my own hand against him."

Temuge struck his broad chest with a fist. "I'll meet with him," he said, "and make certain I have strong men at my back."

"Don't speak to me of what you'll do. If Teb-Tenggeri learns of your intentions, he may turn his spells against you. If he doesn't, I'll know his powers have failed him at last."

"He won't be suspicious," Bortai said. "He's too filled with pride to think anything could harm him."

Temujin shot her a glance, then gestured at the Odchigin. "Go!"

Temuge left the tent. The Khan sat down, his back to her. "I'll meet with the Khongkhotats here," he muttered.

"I'll be at your side," she said.

"It would be better if you weren't. There may be danger."

"Then I'll face it with you." She would not let him give in to his fears.

"You told me to leave Jamukha," he said. "You were right to do so, but that parting caused me much pain. You warned me that Toghril would prove false, and I ignored you only to find that you were right about that. Now you tell me I must rid myself of Teb-Tenggeri. Must I forever distrust those around me?"

"Your brothers love you," she said, "as do your generals, and so do I. You have no need of false friends."

"And I must think of what I have to win. God means me to be the greatest of Khans, to rule all the lands under the sun's path, and my ulus is Tengri's weapon. It seems I must find all my joys in my destiny, in taking what Heaven offers to me."

He got up and went to the entrance to summon the guard.

Bortai kept her face still as the shaman and his six brothers entered, followed by Munglik. Teb-Tenggeri seemed calm as he and the others hung up their bows and quivers on the western side of the doorway, even after he caught sight of Temuge sitting at Temujin's right. Twenty members of the day guard were inside the tent; the three muscular men Temuge had brought were beyond the entrance.

The shaman murmured a greeting. Temujin said, "My brother Temuge Odchigin has complained to me about you."

Teb-Tenggeri frowned. "He has no reason to complain," he said in his musical voice. "Some of his men chose to join me. Does it matter if they serve me or the Odchigin, as long as they serve their Khan? If he's such a poor leader that he cannot hold them, then surely they should have the right to choose another. I suspect they came to me only because the Odchigin may harbour ambitions much like his brother Khasar's."

Temujin nodded at Temuge. The Odchigin jumped to his feet, bounded towards the shaman, and seized the collar of his white coat. "We'll settle this," Temuge shouted. "You forced me to kneel to you – we'll see who's stronger now!" Teb-Tenggeri thrust his arms up; Temuge wrestled him to the floor.

The shaman's feathered hat fell to the carpet and Munglik stooped to grab it. Teb-Tenggeri kicked with one leg, catching Temuge in the knee, then leaped to his feet. His dark eyes glittered as he looked towards Temujin; the faces of his brothers were pale with shock.

"Settle this outside my tent," Temujin called out. "You may prove who's stronger there."

Temuge dragged the struggling shaman outside. "What's this?" Munglik asked as he came towards the throne.

"Temuge has been insulted," Temujin said softly. "Your son has overstepped his bounds."

Munglik's face sagged; his sons eyed the Khan's guard. Bortai heard the shouts outside, and then a sudden silence. Temuge, his chest heaving, stumbled back through the doorway. "That shaman isn't much of a fighter." Temuge gasped and showed his teeth. "He fell, pretended he couldn't move, and now he won't get up. His limits are clear."

Munglik lifted his hands and groaned. "What have you done?" The old man covered his face; a harsh sob came from him. His other sons were moving towards Bortai and Temujin, hands on their knives. Temujin leaped up and pulled Bortai to her feet, then lashed out with one arm as one of the brothers lunged towards him.

"Stand back!" the Khan shouted. The guards quickly massed around him and Bortai; others poured through the entrance. Soldiers surrounded the Khongkhotats as other men guided Temujin and Bortai outside.

"They dared to lay hands on the Khan," one man said; another cursed. Temujin, his arm still holding Bortai tightly, pushed his way towards Temuge. Other guards, swords out, were ringed around the men who had ridden there with Munglik and his sons.

Temujin stopped in front of his brother. "So you have settled your dispute," the Khan said.

"See for yourself." Temuge grinned mirthlessly and led them to the wagons near the great tent. The three burly men who had come there with the Odchigin stood next to one wagon; the shaman's body, twisted at the waist, lay at their feet. Bortai caught a glimpse of Teb-Tenggeri's glassy eyes and made a sign against evil.

"His back is broken," Temuge said. "No blood was shed. As I told you, he wasn't much of an opponent."

Temujin gazed at the body; his mouth worked. "Rise," he said in a voice so low that Bortai could hardly hear him. "Rise." She pulled at his arm, but he looked down at her with dead eyes, as if his own spirit had left him.

Munglik and his sons were being led to them. Temujin let go of Bortai and held up his hand.

"Your son's powers have left him," the Khan said as Munglik was pushed towards him. "The spirits have withdrawn from him. Because you couldn't control your sons, Munglik-echige, one of them is dead. You deserve to be punished for not restraining him, for allowing him to trouble the peace of my ordu and my kin, for letting him mislead me with his spells."

"I've been punished," Munglik whispered. "My son's been taken from me."

"You're at fault," Temujin said, "but so am I, because I didn't fight the spell he wove around me, because I wanted to believe – " He shook himself. "I promised you that you would be honoured, and can't go back on my word now, or no one will believe any oath I might swear. I can't kill you, and make my own mother a widow – your death would serve no purpose, and your ambitions are now at an end. You and your sons are free to go, but take care that you trouble me no more. You may think about what you might have gained if you had been truly loyal to me."

The Khan turned to the guards nearest him. "Place a tent around the shaman's body. Close the flap and the smoke-hole, and see that it's guarded for three days. The shaman was a man of power – I want to be certain his spirit has left him before he's laid to rest." The shaman still bound him, Bortai thought. Temujin would rather see him rise from the dead, even if that meant his own death, than to know that the voices that had once spoken through Teb-Tenggeri might forever be silent.

Munglik bowed his head as his other sons led him away. "Usun will be my chief shaman," Temujin said tonelessly. "He's both wise and too old to have many ambitions." He pulled his coat close around him. "Bring me a horse – I won't remain so close to evil spirits." He walked away without looking back at Bortai.

Hoelun had not wanted her daughter here, but Temulun had insisted on coming, with three shamans in her train. The shamans had chanted and sacrificed a sheep. Temulun, it seemed, was determined to pretend that the evil spirit clinging to her mother could be dispelled.

Now she sat by Hoelun's bed, babbling of the white falcons that were her husband's share of the Oirat tribute. Her pale eyes, so like Yesugei's, shone as she talked of her favourite birds; one would have thought the falcons were her children. Temulun had said little about her sons.

The servants moved quietly around the tent, sweeping the carpeted floor of dirt and insects. Go, Hoelun thought; she did not want Temulun near if she suddenly failed.

Hoelun closed her eyes. When she opened them, one of the servant women was whispering to Temulun. "I've heard that rumour," Temulun said; her handsome face filled with scorn. "It's only foolish talk." She looked down at Hoelun. "If Munglik-echige has anything to do with spreading those stories, maybe you should warn him to stop."

Hoelun sighed. Temujin had broken her husband; Munglik could do nothing against the Khan now.

Temulun looked up at the servant. "What must have happened," she went on, "is that my brother's guards took the shaman's body away and buried it in secret. The shaman didn't rise from the dead on the third day, and his body didn't float out through the smoke-hole."

"But they say the entrance was still closed, and that the smoke-hole was opened from the inside."

"Perhaps the Khan shouldn't have buried the body secretly," another woman said. "If people had seen it – "

"I don't have to see it," Temulun said, "to know the story's false. Those who feared the chief shaman may be willing to spread it, but it only makes others admire Temujin all the more for being stronger than a man with such powers. Anyway,

Temujin has declared that it was Tengri who took the body, that it's a sign Heaven no longer loved the shaman and wouldn't allow him a burial, so my brother's found a use for such talk."

The servants made signs; talk of death and burial was inappropriate around an ailing woman's bed. Temulun waved the women away, then leaned towards Hoelun. "When you're well, Mother, you'll have to come to see my birds."

"Temulun, your birds will have to hunt without me, and you should be with your sons, not here. Will you carry evil spirits back to them? You've done what you could for me – it's time you were on your way."

Temulun lifted her mother's hand to her cheek; Hoelun felt her daughter's tears against her palm. "Mother."

"I love you, daughter. Now let me rest."

Temulun wept. Hoelun closed her eyes and drifted; when she opened them once more, her daughter was gone, but someone else stood near the bed. She squinted and saw Munglik's shadowed face.

"I've lost a son," he said. "I can't lose my wife." His body was as stooped as a much older man's, bowed by grief. "I should have listened to you. My remaining sons have lost their courage, and what will I do without you?"

She lacked the power to answer him. "I loved you when I first saw you so long ago," he said. "I know I was never the man the Bahadur was, but you gave me some strength. What will I be without it?"

She managed to lift her hand. Munglik clutched it in his, set it down, and smoothed her blanket over her.

At last he left the tent. She heard nothing but the wail of the wind outside, and realized her servants were gone. She knew then that a spear stood in front of the tent, warning everyone that death was inside.

Hoelun slept. When she woke, her pain had lessened, but perhaps she had only grown used to the talons of the evil spirit that still clutched at her. A man was with her, gazing at her with Yesugei's eyes; her husband had come to fetch her.

"Your name will live, Yesugei," she said softly. "Temujin has surpassed all your hopes for him. Thousands know that our greatest Khan came from your seed."

"Mother," the man said.

"Temujin," she gasped. "You risk a curse by being here."

"Then I'll risk it. I can't let you go without seeing you one last time. I've begged Khasar's forgiveness and restored all his herds and households to him. I've cursed myself for bringing you sorrow."

"I feel no sorrow now," she said. "I lived to see you make a nation. Leave me to my rest, Temujin. My life is completed, and you are the Khan."

"And with everything I win, something else is taken from me. I can't – "

"We must all die alone. Your father awaits me – go."

He whispered a prayer, and was gone. A shadow fluttered on the western wall of the tent, the form of a man. Hoelun slowly raised her head, heedless of the pain tearing at her.

"Yesugei," she whispered, and fell back. Her soul rose from her body and flew to him.

PART SEVEN

Temujin said, "The greatest joy for a man is to bring death to his enemies, to herd them before him, to hear the weeping of those who loved them, to mount their horses, to hold their wives and daughters in his arms."

96

HER WOMEN WERE weeping. Ch'i-kuo looked around the nearly empty room. Her favourite ivory incense burner, her oil lamps, and her scrolls of silk and paper had been taken away and put on the backs of the mules that would carry her belongings from the city. Her jewels and robes of silk, linen, damask, brocade, and fur had also been packed for her departure.

Ch'i-kuo clapped her hands sharply. "Go," she whispered. "I wish some time alone before I leave."

The women bowed themselves out of the room. A film of the yellow dust spring always brought covered part of the floor. Ch'i-kuo knelt on the carpet of ivory strips and gazed at the painted screen that stood before the window. Even in the midst of a crowd, she had always lived at court as though a screen stood between her and those around her.

She held her mind still, making it as blank as a scroll before she set her brush to it, and the first of the images she wanted to recall came to her.

A man holding a brush sat at a low lacquer table. He wore a robe of fine white linen, fastened on the left with a jewelled clasp; a long black braid hung down his back. He had been the Emperor Ching during his life, and known as Ma-ta-ko to his own people, but the name that came to her now was Chang-tsung, the name by which he would forever be known.

509

This was how she saw her father, clothed in the garments of his Jurchen people while practising the calligraphic art of the Han, although she had no clear memory of ever seeing the Emperor Chang-tsung alone. As the Emperor Shih-tsung had done before him, he had encouraged the practice of his own people's customs, followed before they had left their forested lands in the north to rule the Han. Their own language would be spoken, their people forbidden to wear the clothing of the Han, and those who did not kowtow in the accepted manner at court risked a beating with willow sticks. Yet Chang-tsung had also conversed in the Han tongue, studied their writings, and gathered their scholars around him; the Jurchen nobles had often violated his edicts.

Another image came to her, of Chang-tsung astride a white horse, in pursuit of a deer. A man who could not hunt would be unable to fight; the Emperor had demanded that his meng-an and mou-k'e, the officials who guarded his realm, pass a test in archery. Yet he himself had hunted only in the land around Chung Tu, never in the wilderness of the Jurchen homeland.

Chang-tsung had ascended to the throne after the death of his grandfather Shih-tsung. He had come to the throne as a Jurchen ruler, but had also seen himself as the heir of the Han. Only the protests of his ministers had kept Chang-tsung from making his favourite Han slave his Empress, a place that had always belonged to a Jurchen wife.

In the Year of the Tiger, when Ch'i-kuo was six, one of her father's concubines, briefly a favourite, had taught her how to paint. The lady had suggested that Ch'i-kuo might benefit from studying with a master, but such a prospect hardly seemed likely. Ch'i-kuo was the child of a minor Han concubine who had died without giving the Emperor a son, and she showed every sign of being as sickly as her mother.

But in that same year, the southern Emperor of the Sung rashly attacked the Kin realm, only to be defeated. Ch'i-kuo's father had received the head of Han T'o-chou, the Sung prime minister who had provoked the war, and guarantees of peace and tribute. A minor master of painting and calligraphy had appeared in Ch'i-kuo's apartments shortly after the victory celebration to instruct her. Perhaps the Emperor had been in a generous mood when his concubine appealed to him.

She thought of a day when she had seen her father at a distance, surrounded by his eunuchs and advisers, in the park that bordered his summer palace. It was the last time she had seen him. Two years after his victory, the Emperor of the Kin, successor to the Kings of Gold who had destroyed the Khitan dynasty of Liao, had joined his ancestors.

The image of a bamboo stalk was before her. Ch'i-kuo's favourite place in the summer palace's park had been near the shore of its lake, where bamboo stalks grew. The summer palace of Chung Tu was almost as large as the imperial palace at the city's centre, and nearly a city itself, with its thousands of ministers, courtiers, eunuchs, visiting nobles, imperial guards, and legions of servants and slaves. Carts arrived daily with food and other necessities for the court; traders in turbans, white head-dresses, or the small caps of the Han often stayed within the palace walls.

Ladies of the court often passed Ch'i-kuo, ignoring the solemn girl who sat by the lake with her slaves. The Jurchen ladies strolled by in their silk gowns, each with a slave carrying a parasol or canopy to shield her from the sun. Many of the Han ladies had tiny lotus feet, which made their hips sway as they minced along in their birdlike gait. The ladies with lotus feet did not often walk; they were usually conveyed in litters over the arched bridges and along the park's tree-lined paths.

The Jurchen ladies were golden-skinned, with a rosy glow in their cheeks; the Han were delicate creatures with skin as pale as fine parchment. Ch'i-kuo looked much like the Han, having taken after her mother, but was grateful her own feet had never been bound. She had grown stronger since her father's death, and often walked through the park with a few of her sisters and her slaves.

Her sisters and the other court ladies talked of love affairs and palace intrigues. Occasionally they touched on matters outside the palace walls. The Ongghuts outside the Great Wall still refused to send tribute; the Tanguts of Hsi-Hsia had finally submitted to the northern barbarian king, and were now raiding the Kin provinces bordering Hsi-Hsia. The Emperor did not seem concerned. The Tanguts were too weak to be successful against Kin armies, and the barbarians north of the desert would resume fighting among themselves.

Ch'i-kuo, while she painted, had learned how to render the essential lines and strokes, to be undistracted by what was unnecessary. In the conversations she heard, there were also essentials to be grasped, however obscured they might be by much of the chatter. She saw that many viewed Yung-chi, who had become the Emperor Wei, as weak and indecisive, and that those nearest him preferred him that way. He left his meng-an and mou-k'e to collect their revenues, and did not demand that they hone their skills at hunting and fighting. That much of his military strength now rested on Khitan generals and soldiers did not seem to disturb him.

In the Year of the Sheep, the talk of the court ladies took on a slightly more worried tone. The northern barbarians had taken several outposts; the army sent to meet them had been defeated. Some murmured that the Emperor had been ready to flee from Chung Tu, until his advisers convinced him to stay.

Ch'i-kuo was powerless to influence such events, and had other concerns. At thirteen, she worried that the Emperor might give her in marriage to a man far from the court, a distant official whose favour he needed. She meant to avoid such a fate.

She had begun to present a few of her paintings to the Emperor. A slave presented the scrolls to the Emperor's slaves and returned with grudging words of praise for the work. When a minor minister came to her apartments with a request for a new painting for the first time, Ch'i-kuo rejoiced. If the Emperor admired the paintings, he might want to keep the painter near him. The gossip of the ladies, which she nurtured, would paint a picture for him of a girl too fragile to survive away from the court.

The brushstrokes of her paintings took on more sureness. She painted pictures of ladies playing a game with tiles, a group of courtiers in the wide courtyard, musicians plucking at their lutes, the mulberry trees outside her windows. She wanted to preserve these images of the imperial palace, and the summer palace in the north of the city she loved even more, if the court were forced to abandon them.

Ch'i-kuo remembered a tall young man, a courtier who had spoken to her briefly in the imperial garden. Not many people lingered there in late winter, but Ch'i-kuo welcomed the sharp clear air and the sight of bare tree limbs only beginning to sprout leaves. Her slaves were with her, although they had protested that their mistress would grow ill from the cold.

She halted along the path, expecting the young man to go on his way after his ceremonial greeting; instead, he lingered. His name was Ye-lu Ch'u-ts'ai, and he was a son of Ye-lu Lu, a Khitan descended from the former Khitan royal house, but his family had served the Kin since the reign of Shih-tsung. Ye-lu Ch'u-ts'ai was already winning renown as a scholar, despite his youth; he had passed his chin-shih examination, and served the Emperor at court. That he had won such honours was unusual for a Khitan, most of whom preferred the army; Jur-chen scholars with only a shaky grasp of the classics were often granted chin-shih degrees over more learned Khitan or Han men.

"I wish to tell you, Highness," the young man murmured, "of how much I admire one of your bamboo paintings. It was of a single stalk, and the strokes were both delicate and sure."

"Your praise honours me," she replied. "I know of your father's writings, and of your own recent accomplishments. That such a scholar could take pleasure in my pitiful efforts is a joy to me."

"There was another painting I also admired," he said, "in the apartments of the Chief Astronomer, of a tree shaded by the roof of a palace wall." Ch'i-kuo nodded; the Emperor sometimes favoured courtiers with the gift of one of her scrolls. "I felt that the wall might suddenly vanish, leaving the tree to stand alone. But a painter's soul is more clearly revealed in the bamboo art, and there I found both delicacy and power."

"I thank you for your words," she said.

Ye-lu Ch'u-ts'ai bowed, drew his fur collar more closely around his neck, and left her.

She might have forgotten the young man, but that day in the garden now seemed one of the last peaceful ones she had known. Later that spring, another Khitan, the prince Ye-lu Liu-ko, revolted against the Emperor and declared himself Liao Wang, King of his people, before joining the barbarian invaders. The enemy began to move along the roads and passes that led to Chung Tu.

The face of a young Han woman rose before her. The woman was a slave, given to Ch'i-kuo several months after the traitor Ye-lu Liu-ko had deserted to the enemy. The slave's head was bowed; her half-closed eyes were crescents, her ivory cheeks suffused with a peach-coloured glow.

The woman's name was Mu-tan. She had not been born a slave; a Jurchen meng-an who had desired her noble family's land had gathered enough false evidence to have her father executed and his family sold into slavery. Like most of the palace slaves, Mu-tan had a network of trusted fellow slaves who could be relied upon for information. Through them, she often learned of events in the court and beyond the palace walls before they became the subject of talk among the ladies.

Ch'i-kuo found herself more dependent on what her slaves could tell her, since the court ladies were more guarded in their talk. Mu-tan brought her tales of famine, of peasants, with failing crops and land ravaged by the barbarians, streaming to Chung Tu's twelve gates to beg for food. The carts entering the city with provisions now came from K'ai-feng and the other cities along the Yellow River in the south. Mu-tan told her of towns that had burned for days and of roads littered with the bones of the dead. Ch'i-kuo thought of such stories whenever she was summoned to one of the Emperor's banquet halls, where the court still feasted on food brought there from the south.

The Emperor sent an army, under the command of his generals Wan-yen Kang and Chu-hu Kao-ch'i, to engage the enemy that summer. Through Mu-tan, Ch'i-kuo learned that a general pardon had been given to all prisoners in Chung Tu, Hsi Ching, and Liaotung, in order to add them to the army's ranks. The Emperor's desperation was even more evident when he sent for Ke-shih-lieh Chih-chung, a general who had already suffered disgrace after his defeat by barbarian forces. Against the advice of most of his ministers, the Emperor pardoned Chih-chung and made him Vice-Commander of the Kin armies.

Ch'i-kuo remembered gazing at a black autumn sky above the imperial palace. The stars were hidden by clouds, and then the blackness was suddenly alive with the bright sparks and glittering streams of trees of fire and flaming flowers as thunder crashed. Chih-chung, once Vice-Commander, now Regent of the Empire, had ordered the display.

That autumn, word had come to the Emperor that the army led by the generals Kao-ch'i and Kang had suffered a crushing defeat. It was said that the barbarian King himself had led the assault against the centre, while two wings of the enemy had descended on the fleeing army's rear and flanks. The Emperor's rage mounted when he was told that Chih-chung, ordered to stay within the city's walls to protect it, had left Chung Tu with his men to hunt. Suspicious, fearing that his Vice-Commander might be prepared to join the enemy, the Emperor Wei sent a messenger to strip him of command.

News of the Emperor's anger raced through the palace. According to Mu-tan, some in the court were preparing to leave the city. Ch'i-kuo never learned whether any of those courtiers had escaped. A few days after the Emperor had sent his messenger to Chih-chung, the Vice-Commander entered Chung Tu and surrounded the palace with his men.

Screams echoed through the courtyard; the halls outside Ch'i-kuo's door were filled with the clashing of weapons and the shouts of triumphant or dying soldiers. She waited inside her rooms, her women huddled around her, until the sounds died. Before she could rise from her chair, three soldiers pushed through the door, swords in hand.

She saw immediately that they were not palace guards. "How dare you enter my apartments." Her voice shook as she spoke; fear of these red-faced, violent men nearly overwhelmed her. "You stand before a daughter of the Emperor Chang-tsung."

The soldiers drew back. One said, "We mean you no harm."

"And you will not harm those with me. If you lay a hand on them, the Emperor will have your heads."

"The Son of Heaven will do nothing without the consent of our Commander. The city belongs to him now."

Her courage nearly failed her, but she compelled herself to keep her eyes on him. The men stared at her for a while, then bowed and retreated from the room.

She waited with her women, afraid to leave the rooms. That evening, a soldier came to tell Ch'i-kuo her presence was requested at a banquet. Her women dressed her in a green robe trimmed with gold brocade, then led her into the hallway.

The gold-encrusted corridor was filled with soldiers posted by each door. More were stationed along the open passageways that connected the palace wings and before the entrance to the largest banquet hall. On the dais where the Emperor usually sat, Chih-chung presided, surrounded by ladies with painted white faces. The Emperor was nowhere to be seen.

Thousands of courtiers sat at the long tables and feasted as a minister announced that Chih-chung had proclaimed himself Regent. The women seated with him were the most famous courtesans of the city, commanded to be present. The courtiers gulped hot soup and devoured their food without showing any of their usual restraint. When the wine was served, and flowers of silk, as was customary, were presented to the guests, many laughed loudly before twisting the flowers into their hair. Formality was forgotten as the babble of voices drowned out the sombre music of the lute-players.

Ch'i-kuo ate little as one minister after another toasted the Regent; their bows and speeches seemed a mockery of ceremony. The court was beyond shame, and all too aware of the soldiers inside the palace walls. Perhaps they thought Chih-chung could save them from the Mongol invaders. Maybe they were simply celebrating while they still could.

Chih-chung did not dismiss them until well into the night. By then, he was quite drunk, his head resting on the shoulder of one of the white-faced courtesans. Fewer soldiers were in the halls and passageways when Ch'i-kuo returned to her rooms. Her women stood by the antechamber's window watching the display of fireworks over the courtyard.

"Bring me my inks and a paper scroll," Ch'i-kuo said as she sat down at the low table where she usually painted. Two women brought her the tools; another set oil lamps on the table to give her more light. She waved the women away and began to rub her inks on moistened flat stones.

The picture came to her in an instant. Her brushes moved across the paper in firm, sure strokes. The man seated in the Emperor's chair had one hand clutching a goblet and the other in the disordered hair of a white-faced woman. A soldier stood to one side, his shield raised, a sword in his hand, his head turned slightly towards the seated man.

Ch'i-kuo set down her brush and stretched her arms, feeling the ache in her shoulders. A faint light glowed beyond the window; most of the women were asleep on couches and cushions, but Mu-tan was awake, and Ch'i-kuo motioned to her.

The young woman rose, came to her, and knelt by the table. "He is not the Emperor," Mu-tan said as she gazed at the painting, "and the woman looks much like a common harlot. As for the soldier, I can't tell if he is protecting them or about to turn on them."

"The man is the Regent Chih-chung. The woman is the sort of guest he should have summoned to the banquet instead of those he did, and the soldier – "

Mu-tan gasped. "What if he saw this? If it were found – "

"Then we must see that it isn't," Ch'i-kuo said, "and if it is, does it matter? We are lost, but I am grateful for my art – it will live in me for a little while before the end."

Ridding herself of the illusions that still gripped many in the court had freed her to see more clearly. Painting without fear of what she might reveal about herself and her own thoughts, as any true master had to do, brought more strength to her art. Her earlier paintings, she saw now, had been, for all their skill, largely the work of a girl anxious to please. The best of them – the bamboos, the painting of the tree the Khitan Ye-lu Ch'u-ts'ai had admired – had been done when her mind was free of such worries. Whether she escaped the storm that threatened her city, with only her paintings to remind her of what was lost, or was caught up in it, no longer mattered.

Hearing that Chih-chung had executed Wan-yen Kang had not surprised her. Kang had been one of those commanders defeated by the Mongol armies and was a possible rival of

Chih-chung's. The news that he had also had the Emperor Wei murdered left her indifferent. Only the advice of the ministers, she knew, had kept the Regent from claiming the throne himself. Within a few days of taking the palace, Chih-chung summoned Wan-yen Hsun, a half-brother of Ch'i-kuo's father, to the capital to become Emperor.

The Regent's disdain for the new Emperor was evident. Ch'i-kuo had painted a scene of the court, the Emperor Hsun sagging against his throne while Chih-chung, who always remained seated in the Emperor's presence, addressed the court himself. The painting would have offended both men, showing as it did an Emperor too uncertain to demand proper respect and a general drunk with his power.

Two months after declaring himself Regent, Chih-chung rode out to meet a Mongol force north of the city. He returned to Chung Tu claiming victory, then sent Chu-hu Kao-ch'i against the enemy, threatening Kao-ch'i with death if he did not drive the enemy back. It was clear by then that Chih-chung's victory had been costly, and that only desperation could have brought him to turn to Kao-ch'i, who had been in disgrace after his earlier defeat.

Kao-ch'i was overwhelmed by the Mongols, but the sentence of death Chih-chung had promised him if he failed was carried instead to the Regent. Before word of the rout could reach the capital, Kao-ch'i returned to the city, surprised Chih-chung in his residence, and beheaded him as he tried to escape. Emperor Hsun forgot the man who had put him on the throne, pardoned Kao-ch'i, and made him Vice-Commander.

Ch'i-kuo listened to such reports, and wondered what the enemy, who surely had spies among the traders in Chung Tu, was making of these accounts. The lines and strokes in her paintings of the court grew thinner, and her colours more translucent, as if the figures in them were hardly more than shadows.

She remembered the first time she had painted one of the Emperor's hawks. The effort had been a childish one, with little sense of the bird's swiftness as it struck at its prey.

Ch'i-kuo thought then of her last months in the imperial palace, when she was often in the quarters of ministers and

518

their wives, or in offices where scribes and scholars laboured over scrolls of documents. Sometimes she brought her inks and brushes; at other times, she simply studied the subjects she hoped to paint. She had given paintings to a few ministers, and they were soon easy enough in her presence to ignore the minor princess who cared for nothing except her art.

She had been in the office of a minor minister of war when two officers came to report to him. The two had fought against the Mongols, and had much to tell.

"The enemy is most dangerous in retreat," one officer said. The minister nodded, clearly aware of that fact. "He withdraws, and lures soldiers to pursue him, then turns back to strike. It's said that this is how they succeeded in getting inside the Great Wall, and I can well believe it, although some claim they also used bribes."

"They are mastering the art of siege," the second soldier said, "thanks to the traitors who have joined them. The enemy forces his captives to man catapults and build siege towers, and pushes them to the front when a city is stormed."

"They move more swiftly than I thought possible," the first officer said. "Armies separated by thousands of li advance as one, so swift are the riders who move between them carrying their generals' commands. I spoke to people who had managed to escape from one town and went east to another, only to find, when they reached their destination, that the Mongols they had fled were attacking that place, too."

The game had not escaped her father's hawks. Ch'i-kuo had not painted a hawk later that day, or the minor minister and the officers, but a hare, ears back, legs poised to flee.

Ch'i-kuo had a vision of Chung Tu as a bird hovering overhead might see the city. Her father had ordered artisans to construct a scale model of the capital in one of his halls, where only the imperial family and the most favoured courtiers were allowed to view it. Tiny walls with brick battlements and twelve small gates had surrounded the miniature city; nine hundred towers lined three moats made of blue gems.

She had marvelled at the curved ruby-studded eaves of the miniature summer palace and the delicately carved trees that lined the ivory paths of its park. Outside the model city's four sides stood four forts, each a town in itself, surrounded by towers and moats. She had learned that the craftsmen had even reproduced the underground tunnels that led from the main city to these forts, although no viewer could see them.

At the beginning of the Year of the Dog, the Emperor Hsun sent an envoy to the enemy requesting peace. By then, the town of Cho Chou had fallen to the Mongols, and three more generals had deserted with their forces to the enemy. The Emperor's plea for peace was refused; the capital prepared for a siege.

During her sixteen years of life, Ch'i-kuo had moved through the streets beyond the palaces only in a carriage or litter. Shortly after the new year, at the Emperor's command, she and the rest of the royal house left the imperial palace for Chung Tu's northern fort. The city's wealthiest citizens had been ordered to the eastern fort, officials and their families to the southern one, and minor relatives of the royal house to the western. The forts, with their soldiers, granaries, arsenals, and defences, could hold out even if the city's high walls were breached; so the Emperor hoped.

A wide, straight street beyond the palace's vast courtyard was cleared for their passage, but Ch'i-kuo caught glimpses of frightened faces behind the lines of soldiers. Carts loaded with food and hay brought in from the countryside, and others filled with tiles and stones to hurl down at the enemy from the battlements, stood on either side of the road. Snow sifted down from the grey sky; by the time they reached the tunnel that led to the fort, the city was hidden behind a white veil.

Inside the mansion allotted to the imperial family, Ch'i-kuo and her slaves were given three small rooms. The soldiers at the walls might hold back the enemy; the Mongols might settle for what they had already won. Ch'i-kuo did not dare to hope.

The Mongols attacked Chung Tu twice that winter. The first time, they forced their way into part of the city, but were driven back when a street was set on fire by Chung Tu's defenders. When the enemy made a second attempt to storm the main city, soldiers from the four forts repelled them. Yet Emperor Hsun could take little comfort from these successes. Most of the enemy forces had moved south. The few who were able to escape them and carry word to the capital told of the ravaged great plain along the Yellow River and of towns, expecting attack from the north, being surprised by Mongols sweeping up from the south.

The court now expected a prolonged siege. Fewer dishes were served at the royal banquets; Ch'i-kuo bathed less frequently with the small amount of heated water her women brought to her. By spring, the court knew of the Emperor's losses; the rapidly moving enemy had taken most of the plain to the south. Yet the Mongols seemed weary of battle. When a Mongol envoy entered Chung Tu to propose peace, Emperor Hsun refused the offer. To everyone's surprise, the envoy returned and offered peace once more.

In the more restricted confines of the fort, news travelled quickly, and Ch'i-kuo heard nearly as much about the negotiations as if she had been present at them. The Mongol King had sent a Tangut called A-la-chien, a man fluent in the northern Han tongue, as his chief envoy. His speech, stripped of elaborate phrases, had been to the point.

"All your provinces north of the Yellow River are in my possession," the Tangut had said, "while you have only Chung Tu. God has brought you to this, but Heaven may turn against me if I press you further. I am willing to withdraw, but my generals counsel war. What will you give me to appease them?"

That question, with its implicit admission that the enemy was not prepared for a prolonged assault, divided the Emperor's advisers. One faction, led by Kao-ch'i, urged rejection of the demand. But Wan-yen Fu-hsing, commander of the troops in the main city, led a faction pressing for peace. The troops inside Chung Tu had families in outlying districts. If they were defeated in battle now, they would abandon the city; if they won, they would want to return home, leaving Chung Tu nearly defenceless.

It came down to that — not the strength or weakness of the enemy, but the loyalty of their own troops. Ch'i-kuo, hearing of these deliberations, had little doubt about the Emperor's decision. Hsun would appease the Mongols to gain time to strengthen his defences. She was not surprised to learn that Fu-hsing had gone with A-la-chien to the Mongol camp to discuss terms.

By late spring, Fu-hsing and the Tangut had returned to Chung Tu. There would be a truce; the enemy's demands would be granted.

The last time she was brought before the Emperor, Ch'i-kuo saw how much the weakness around Hsun's mouth resembled that of his predecessor Wei-shao Wang. Emperor Hsun had spent much of that day summoning imperial princesses to the large room he was using as an audience hall; even then, with a truce at hand, he still clung to the security of his northern fort. The spring wind outside had died at last, but the yellow dust that always choked the city during this season had sifted inside through cracks and doorways, settling on carpets and even in a fold of the Emperor's robe. He glanced at Ch'i-kuo for only a moment before dismissing her.

She was in her room painting when a minor official came to her door. Her slaves knelt around her as Mu-tan ushered the man and his two attendants inside. The official went through his bows and murmured his ceremonial greeting. She waited, sensing what he would tell her, yet refusing to believe it.

"Our Mongol brother," the official was saying, "has said he will accept a tribute of gold and silk. We shall grant him ten thousand liang of gold and ten thousand bolts of fine silk. He has said he wants horses, and he will be given three thousand of our finest steeds. He has said he wants five hundred skilled boys and five hundred beautiful girls to serve his people, and they shall be granted to him. He has said a royal bride will appease his wrath when he leaves our city. Honour is yours, Imperial Highness – the Son of Heaven has decreed that, of all the royal princesses, you are most worthy to be wife to the Mongol King."

Her women were still. She was, Ch'i-kuo realized, the most suitable choice Hsun could have made. The Mongol would not know that she was one of the least of the imperial line, a woman whose rumoured frailty might bring her an early death. How clever of the Emperor to have found a use for her, and to insult the enemy under the guise of granting his request.

"So I am to be the partridge," she said, "delivered to the tiger's claws."

"The Emperor has granted you three days in which to prepare

yourself. You will of course be given everything you need for your comfort – the Son of Heaven will select many of your gifts himself."

Ch'i-kuo gazed at her painting; a few more strokes would complete it. The Emperor Hsun sat in a garden, looking on as a few members of the royal guard practised with their bows. One man's bow was lowered, as though he had just taken his shot. An arrow jutted from the ground, having fallen short of the target; other arrows were embedded in the grass near it. Her brush moved over the paper. The official stood in silence as she waited for the ink to dry. She did not ask him to sit, or tell her women to bring him tea.

At last she looked up. "I must obey," she said. "As much as I shall mourn my exile, I am honoured that the Son of Heaven finds me worthy of a place at his brother monarch's side. If Chung Tu is saved, I shall hold its memory in my heart and be grateful my beloved city survives. Should it fall, I will not have to witness its end."

The official's face paled. "We shall have a truce."

"Let us hope it endures." She rolled up the paper scroll, stood up, and handed it to the man. "This is the last picture I shall paint in my own land. Please give it to the Emperor, so that he will remember me."

The man bowed himself out of the room as he murmured more phrases. Ch'i-kuo sank to the floor. Mu-tan held her as she wept against the young woman's shoulder.

"Highness," a voice said. Ch'i-kuo looked around, caught now in the present. Mu-tan came towards her from the door. "Lady, they are waiting for you."

Ch'i-kuo rose. Hsun, she had been told, had scowled at her last painting, cursed, and stamped on it with his foot. She had achieved her purpose; he would remember her. Mu-tan took her arm and guided her from the room.

97

CH'I-KUO STARED AHEAD at the broad road that led away from Chung Tu. She would not look back at the distant city, where soldiers would be standing in the slots of the crenellated battlements, gazing down at the tribute sent outside Chung Tu's walls, the wagons of silk and gold, the horses carrying the thousand boys and girls who would now serve the Mongols in return for this bartered peace.

A carriage had carried her and her women to a gate, where Commander Fu-hsing's soldiers had brought horses to them. The Commander and some of his troops had been ordered to accompany the retinue as far as the Chu-yung pass north-west of the city. Mongol troops on horseback lined the sides of the road, their hooked lances held upright; another force of barbarians led the procession.

All of them were thickset, heavy-boned men like those who had met Fu-hsing's soldiers at the city gate. Their slits of eyes peered out from brown, wind-burned faces; their stench, even at a distance, nearly overwhelmed her. Many wore brightly coloured silk tunics under their gleaming black breastplates. Some wore the metal helmets of Kin soldiers, with plated sides hanging to their chins; others had wide-brimmed hats with flaps. Their heads were so close to their broad shoulders that they seemed to have no necks.

She had expected a bestial herd. Yet the men at the sides of the road sat proudly in their saddles, while those leading the way rode in straight, unbroken rows.

In the distance, a river wound through brown fields. Blackened hulls of boats rested along its banks; herds of horses grazed on what millet remained. A small mound marked a place where a narrower, rutted road led away from the main thoroughfare, and when she was closer, she saw that the mound was built of severed heads.

Ch'i-kuo saw many more hills of heads during the day's journey. Small settlements and dwellings lay in ruins, surrounded by wagons, tents, and an occasional siege tower. Prisoners moved among the tents, their backs bent under the weight

of the sacks they carried; others, bound together and impri-
soned in yokes, pulled wagons. Near the ruins of many houses,
limbs had been torn from mulberry trees whose fruit had once
nourished silkworms. Wherever she turned, she saw destruction
– hills of freshly turned earth that might have been mass graves,
levelled towns, trampled fields, and horses grazing amid it all.

By evening, they arrived at the largest camp she had yet seen.
Ch'i-kuo and her women were separated from the procession
and led to a great tent. A young woman with the porcelain
complexion and slender build of a Han waited by the doorway;
she bowed low as Ch'i-kuo approached.

"I welcome you, Imperial Highness," the woman said in the
Han tongue. "The Great Khan of the Mongols has sent me
here to serve you. I am called Lien." She beckoned to a group
of boys; they moved towards the carts that held Ch'i-kuo's
belongings. "Perhaps you wish to rest after your journey."

The woman led her and her slaves inside. An older woman
was tending a fire that smouldered in a round metal enclosure.
Carpets and mats of bamboo covered the floor. A carved bed
sat at the back of the tent, with cushions heaped around it.
Two large chests stood on one side of the tent; the three women
standing near them knelt.

Ch'i-kuo, aching from the ride, sat gingerly on the bed as
two boys carried the first of her trunks inside. The young
woman was still standing. She was clearly Han, but her coiled
black hair was covered by a scarf, a wide sash marked her
waist, and under her gold-trimmed blue robe, she wore woollen
Mongol trousers tucked into boots.

"Please be seated," Ch'i-kuo said. The woman bowed, then
sat on a cushion. "I had expected to be led before His Majesty
when I arrived."

"The Great Khan and Emperor of the Mongols is most anxious to be in your presence, but there is a form to such things.
Surely you did not expect the Great Khan to pull you from
your horse and drag you to his tent."

Ch'i-kuo flushed; that was exactly what she had expected.
"The general who travelled here with you," the woman continued, "will go with the Khan's envoys to his ordu. After
he has presented himself and begged the Khan to accept the

Emperor's gifts, the Great Khan will most graciously accept them, if it is his wish to do so."

Ch'i-kuo's hands fluttered. "Is there any doubt of that?"

"Have no fear, Imperial Highness. When his men tell him of the beautiful Lady who awaits him, he will be even more impatient to hold you in his arms."

Ch'i-kuo shuddered. "When the Khan has accepted his tribute," Lien went on, "his brother Shigi Khutukhu, who is one of his most important ministers, will see that gifts are given to those most deserving of them after the Khan has received his share. Then a feast will be held to celebrate your marriage."

"Have you been among his people long?" Ch'i-kuo asked.

"Nearly two years."

"I sorrow for you."

"There's no need for sorrow, Royal Lady. My parents sold me as a child to a brothel. When my city fell, it was my good fortune to be among those women offered to the Khan himself. If I must be a man's receptacle, surely it is better for him to be a ruler, and he has kept me with him even after tiring of many others. I was among those he took with him when he returned to his own lands, and when he began this campaign I was among those he commanded to follow the army. I am grateful he still finds me pleasing, since I've given him no son. He might have put me among the slaves to be killed before he returns to his home."

Ch'i-kuo lifted a hand to her mouth. "He enslaves them only to kill them?"

"He keeps those he needs, the ones skilled in crafts, the strongest, the women who please him and his men the most. The others would only die crossing the desert. I have no craft except for the arts of the bedchamber, and a Mongol is more versed in battle than such arts, but in a brothel where traders seek rest, one hears many languages, and I was quicker than most at learning them. I have mastered the Mongol tongue, and the Khan finds me a useful servant."

"Then you are to be my interpreter."

"It is the Khan's wish that I teach you his tongue."

She had heard the Mongols speak in their grating language during her journey. The tongue was filled with unfamiliar sounds and seemed as rough as the men who spoke it. "I know the Jurchen tongue and the Han," Ch'i-kuo murmured. "Perhaps it will not be so difficult for me to master a third."

"I shall do my best to be a good teacher." Lien lifted her head as the women opened one trunk and took out scrolls. "Have you brought paintings with you, Mistress?"

"I've brought paper and silk on which to paint."

"I didn't know that princesses were taught such arts."

"Most are not," Ch'i-kuo replied, "but I showed a small gift in childhood, and my father the Emperor humoured me by having me instructed."

"Paintings from the hand of a wife may please the Khan."

"I can't imagine that he would be interested in such things."

"I beg you not to judge him too quickly, Highness."

Ch'i-kuo studied the young woman. Lien might call herself Ch'i-kuo's servant, but she also served the Khan, and could either ease matters for her master's new wife or make them more difficult. "You must guide me, Lien," she said at last. "I have no wish to displease the man I am to wed."

"It is my greatest hope that you do not. Lady, may I speak plainly? You may find what I say illuminating."

Ch'i-kuo nodded. "When the Mongols took me prisoner," Lien continued, "I saw only beasts in animal skins, creatures who could do no more than rob, kill, and destroy. Perhaps that is all they were once, but the ruler who calls himself Genghis Khan is making something more of them. I have served the Khan, and he is a man of two natures, Lady. One is as honed as his sword, hard and sharp and prepared to strike. The other searches and longs to encompass the world. In a weaker man, two such natures might have been at war, but in him, each feeds the other. The sword clears his way, and the other part of him reaches out for what is there."

"I am surprised that you can find anything to admire in a people who have caused you to suffer."

"What have I suffered, Lady?" Lien said. "Once, the most I could have hoped for was that a wealthy merchant might have bought me for a concubine. Instead, I have become the woman of an Emperor and the servant of an Emperor's daughter."

527

"Perhaps you can advise me on how to behave with my new husband."

Lien turned her perfect oval face towards her. "You are not the first princess who has been given to the Khan. The Princess Chakha, daughter of the King of Hsi-Hsia, was offered to him when the Tanguts surrendered. I glimpsed her in the ordu of the Khan. She had, so I was told, once been a beauty, but I saw only a thin-faced woman with dead, staring eyes." She paused. "It was said that when the Lady Chakha was first taken to the Khan's tent, she could only weep for her palace in Ninghsia. Whenever the Khan went to her, she greeted him with tears in her eyes. Even after many months, her tears still flowed freely."

Ch'i-kuo said, "She must have displeased the Khan greatly."

"You are mistaken, Lady. She pleased him very much. It's said that he went to her tent often, and in time her weeping stopped. Now there are no more tears from the Lady Chakha, and there is also no laughter, no contentment, no peace. She is paid the honour owed a Lady who has given the Khan sons, but she dwells in his camp as a ghost. It is the way of the Mongols, Lady – to take what they can use and destroy what they cannot. Chakha fed only that part of the Khan's nature."

Ch'i-kuo swallowed. "Then I shall not weep."

Lien rose gracefully to her feet. "Perhaps you wish some refreshment, my Lady. I shall have some tea prepared."

The Mongol Khan sent for Ch'i-kuo two days after her arrival. Lien had told her that, with this campaign concluded, Genghis Khan was impatient to begin the journey to his own lands.

Her woman bathed her with warm, damp cloths, dressed her in silk trousers and a red robe trimmed with gold brocade, and set jewelled combs shaped like butterfly wings in her upswept hair. With Lien and Mu-tan to attend her, she was led outside, where soldiers waited with horses. Commander Fu-hsing stood with his officers, all of them wearing their plated metal armour; the Tangut A-la-chien had brought a detachment of Mongols.

With a line of Kin soldiers to their left, and Mongols on their right, Ch'i-kuo and the two women rode along the edge of the camp. Prisoners near the tents were simmering food in cauldrons, unloading wagons, mending harnesses, and collecting dried dung. She could not tell which people might have belonged to a rich merchant's household, a peasant's, or a meng-an's entourage; they were all slaves now.

Lien, when speaking of the Khan, had gently implied that the Kin had brought this storm upon themselves. Hsi-Hsia had submitted to the Mongols, as had the Ongghuts; the Golden Emperor of the Kin might have acknowledged the Mongol Khan as his brother. Instead, the Kin had supported a faction of Ongghuts who had overthrown their leader three years earlier. The Khan's own daughter Alakha, wife of the Ongghut prince's oldest son, had lost her husband and been forced to flee to a Mongol camp with the surviving members of the Ongghut royal family. It had all been for nothing. The Ongghuts had gone back to the Mongols within the year, preferring the Khan's Ongghut allies to the commander the Kin had placed over them.

It had also been wise of the Khan to support the Khitan revolt. The Liao Wang himself had turned to the Mongols, and Genghis Khan had sent Shigi Khutukhu and Anchar Noyan, brother of the Khan's first wife, as his envoys to secure a Khitan oath of loyalty. The Khitans might never have revolted if Jurchen settlers were not encroaching on their homelands bordering the Khingan range. One could hardly have expected the Khan not to take advantage of the situation. Lien had painted a portrait of a reasonable man pushed into war, a picture quite different from the one Ch'i-kuo had formed at court.

The Khan's tent was at the north end of the camp, but a pavilion had been raised in the field beyond it. Horses were tied to ropes outside the pavilion; Mongols crowded the space between it and the camp, moving in an awkward, rolling gait on their bowed legs. Outside the pavilion, rows of Mongols stood at attention, hands on their sword hilts.

Ch'i-kuo could dimly see the Khan under the pavilion. His face was shadowed, and a jewelled cap covered his head. He had adorned himself in a short silk tunic and embroidered robe, and sat in a chair on a raised platform. She had expected that, a barbarian clothed in looted finery.

She dismounted; Fu-hsing and A-la-Chien led her forward. Carpets were strewn over the ground under the pavilion. At the Khan's right, Mongol men sat on cushions around low tables; several Han women sat in the space to his left.

Fu-hsing began his speech as the shadow of the pavilion covered them; A-la-Chien quickly translated it into the Khan's tongue. Lien had told her what to expect. There would be speeches, and a welcome from the Khan to his bride, followed by the blessings of the Mongol shamans, a sacrifice, and a banquet likely to go on for the rest of the day.

Ch'i-kuo knelt, pressed her head against the carpet, then looked up. She saw the Khan more clearly now. He had the same massive build as the others, and thick coiled braids behind his ears; his long moustaches and the dark beard covering his chin had a reddish tint. He was leaning towards a man seated near him, and then his head turned towards her.

She had not expected to see such eyes. His had the folds of his people and hers, but they were pale eyes, more green and yellow than brown. A demon's eyes, she thought, eyes from which nothing could be hidden, terrifying eyes she might see in her worst dreams.

"The Khan welcomes his bride," A-la-Chien was saying in the Han tongue, "whose beauty shines forth as does the light of the moon."

Lien had not told her the truth. Whatever excuses this man had found for his deeds, his eyes showed what he truly was, a weapon aimed at the world. Only surrender could turn that weapon aside.

Ch'i-kuo sat at the Khan's side, enduring the feast. Slaves moved from table to table, and among those seated on the ground beyond the pavilion, carrying dishes and goblets. The Mongols did not use eating sticks with their food, preferring to pass it around on knives or to grab at it with their hands. The food itself was largely strips of partly cooked meat dipped in salted water or soybean sauce, and the soy did not mask the scent of the dung over which the meat had been cooked. Perhaps the barbarians had killed most of the skilled cooks as well.

The men were soon drunk; they shouted their guttural songs over the gentle music of the flute-players seated near the pavilion. When they danced, they leaped on to the tables, crushing pale porcelain dishes and goblets under their feet. Their fermented, sour-tasting milky beverage was as repulsive as the rest of their food, but they guzzled it and the wines brought to them, often with a goblet in each hand.

The Khan's eyes narrowed, and she knew he was aware of her disdain. He spoke then, the first words he had addressed directly to her. She bowed her head as he finished, then glanced at Lien.

"My Lord says," Lien murmured, "that a man must savour what is given to him to eat and drink, and enjoy it to the full. To do otherwise is an insult to his host."

"He does not have to excuse this behaviour to me."

Lien shook her head. "The Great Khan has no need to make excuses to anyone. He is telling you that his men are behaving properly, and that you are not."

She would have to live among these people. "Lien," Ch'i-kuo said slowly, "you must tell His Majesty that I learned my manners at court, where the Emperor picks daintily at sumptuous dishes and sips only the smallest part of the wine in his goblet while his people starve and his soldiers fall before Mongol warriors. It is clear that the Great Khan's manners are better than mine."

The Khan smiled as Lien translated, then offered Ch'i-kuo a piece of meat from his knife. She took it, chewed it quickly, and drained her goblet of wine in one gulp.

The raucous feast was still going on at sunset. Mongols led horses to the pavilion; the Khan lifted Ch'i-kuo to his white steed, then mounted behind her. Men shouted and lifted their cups. The arm around her waist felt as heavy as iron.

Before her departure from Chung Tu, the Emperor had sent a book to her with his presents, one printed on leaves of paper bound together with thick gold threads. The book, which contained several woodcut illustrations, was a suitable gift for a bride, since its subject was the bedchamber's arts. Now the Emperor's parting gift seemed meant to pay her back for her last painting. Hsun would know what the Mongols were, and how unlikely it was that their Khan would follow such a book's prescriptions.

Another large tent had been erected to the east of the Khan's; silk curtains fluttered at its sides. The guards who were posted around the tent saluted, striking their black breastplates with their fists, as the Khan dismounted and lifted Ch'i-kuo from the saddle.

He led her inside; Mu-tan and Lien followed them. Her possessions had been moved to this tent; her slaves knelt near the bed at the back.

"I shall tell our master," Lien said, "that your women will prepare you for bed before they go to their own tent."

"Their tent?" Ch'i-kuo asked.

"The small tent nearest this one. Should they be needed later, a slave will summon them."

"But surely – " She had assumed her women would stay with her. "Do not say this to the Khan, but I fear being alone with him."

"My Lady, I don't intend to leave you alone." Lien lifted her brows. "The Khan may need me to convey his words to you."

She could not imagine that he would have much to say. He watched them with his pale demon's eyes as two of her women helped him off with his robe. He glanced around the tent as they were led to the bed, then sniffed at the ivory incense burner on one table. Lien murmured a few words to him. He lifted his cap from his head before one of the women could reach for it; the top of his head was shaved, with a tuft of hair left over his forehead. His gaze fell to the bed and the book lying on the silk coverlet.

One of her women must have put it there; Ch'i-kuo longed to thrust it out of sight. The Khan scowled at the book, then picked it up as he muttered to Lien.

"The Khan," she said, "is asking what this is."

"It is a book about the Clouds and the Rain," Ch'i-kuo replied, "but I am certain that the Khan, who has brought the joy that banishes a thousand sorrows to so many wives, will have no need of it."

One of the women untied the belt around his tunic. He waved

her away and sat down on the bed, squinting in the soft light of the lamps. His broad hands turned the pages until he came to an illustration; he held up the book as he spoke.

"The Khan is asking what this is," Lien said.

The other women giggled softly. Ch'i-kuo's cheeks burned; the picture showed a naked man, his legs looped around a kneeling woman as they joined. "That," Ch'i-kuo said, "is called The Hovering Butterflies."

He pawed through the book to another illustration. "And this?" Lien asked with a smile.

"Mandarin Ducks."

"And this one?"

Ch'i-kuo forced herself to glance at the picture. "Frolicking Wild Horses."

"He says that one looks more familiar."

The Khan shook his head and pointed to another picture of a man licking the cleft between a woman's legs. Ch'i-kuo's throat tightened. "That one is called The River of the Yin Nourishes the Yang."

"He is surprised that people actually do such things."

Ch'i-kuo stared past the young woman. "Then he has learned few such arts from you."

Lien laughed. "I have explained to him that a man gains most from the act when it is prolonged, so that his precious yang can be properly augmented by the woman's yin, but he told me any man who indulged in such acts to excess would surely grow weaker rather than stronger. As I told you, the Mongols have little use for the arts of the Jade Chamber." She laughed again. "But as I have also told you, the Khan is a man of two natures, and he's capable of giving much pleasure to those willing to accept it. Your cinnabar gate will happily open to his vigorous peak."

Ch'i-kuo doubted that very much. The Khan set the book on a table. Her women undressed them; she kept her eyes averted from him, feeling his gaze. Mu-tan combed out her hair, then helped her into the bed. Ch'i-kuo closed her eyes as he stretched out next to her. The coverlet floated over her and settled against her.

When she opened her eyes, her women were gone, and Lien

was kneeling at the side of the bed. Ch'i-kuo lay there, afraid to move. He reached for her and then lifted a long lock of her hair to his face as he whispered his strange words.

Lien said, "The Khan is saying that you are beautiful, Lady." He drew the coverlet from her, cupped one small breast in his hand, then murmured more words. "Now he is telling you that the sight of your jade mound delights him."

Hearing the Khan's words from Lien's lips was not making matters any easier, but the young woman was silent after that, and the Khan was soon past any need for speech. He touched his lips to hers; she managed not to recoil. His hands roamed over her and came to rest between her legs.

To feel his roughened hands trying to bring dew to her lotus petals was worse than if he had simply thrust himself into her. She supposed that she should caress his jade stalk, but could not bring herself to do so. He reeked of sweat and the meat he had eaten; the weight of him threatened to squeeze the breath from her. As he thrust inside her, she tensed against the pain; he gasped, shuddered, and then withdrew.

Lien rose and covered them. "There's no need for me to stay longer." She bowed, murmured some words to the Khan in his language, then left the tent. Perhaps she had told the Khan that his bride was too overcome by her pleasure to display her joy properly.

He lay at her side and cupped her face between his hands; his eyes searched her. She thought of what Lien had said about his Tangut wife. She would not allow herself to become such a creature, wailing for what was lost.

I'll be your wife, she thought, and live among your people, and give you no cause to wound me, but I won't forget what I saw of your work beyond this camp.

His lip curled, as though he sensed her thoughts; he drew her to him.

98

THE PLACE NAMED Yu-erh-lo, near the lake the Mongols called Dolon Nor, was flat yellow grassland empty of trees, with patches of drifting sand. This was Ongghut country, where the Khan would graze his animals until autumn, when the desert leading north to his homeland could be more easily crossed. The water of Dolon Nor was brackish, and the flocks of birds that rose from the lake made the deafening sound of a whirlwind with their wings, but Ch'i-kuo welcomed the wildness.

They had left the ravaged towns outside the dragon's spine of the Great Wall behind. She had not wept while passing through the Mouth of the Wall, or at the sight of the messages other exiles had scrawled on the arching stone gate. The barbarians had slaughtered the slaves they could no longer use and abandoned the bodies. She preferred not to be near the raven-infested graveyard the Mongols had made of her land.

Ch'i-kuo gazed at the picture she was painting, then added one last stroke. During the last two months, those in the Khan's encampment had grown used to the strange sight of the Kin princess seated under a canopy outside her tent, screens at her sides to protect her from the wind as she dabbed at a scroll of silk or paper with her brushes. Even in this wild land, she had little more to do than she had in the palaces of Chung Tu. Slaves and servants tended the herds the Khan had allotted to her, and took care of her tent and belongings. Lien remained at her side to guide her through her new life.

Ch'i-kuo looked up; the Lady Tugai, with two of her servants, was walking towards her from a cart. Tugai was the most important of the four Mongol wives the Khan had brought with him on this campaign; she had warm brown eyes and a body nearly as thick as a young Mongol man's. The other three wives were pretty, sturdy girls with broad faces and red cheeks. They had remained in Ongghut territory with other Mongol women and a rearguard, and had rejoined the Khan during the journey to Yu-erh-lo.

Ch'i-kuo and Lien got to their feet. "I greet you, Elder Sister,"

Ch'i-kuo murmured. She had learned more of the Mongol tongue, although Lien often had to prompt her.

"I greet you, Noble Lady," Tugai said. Her high square head-dress made the squat Mongol woman seem tall.

"It would give me pleasure – " Ch'i-kuo hesitated; Lien whispered a phrase to her in Mongol. "It would afford me a great deal of pleasure if my Elder Sister would partake of my humble hospitality."

"I would be most pleased," Tugai Ujin replied. She sat down at Ch'i-kuo's table, shifting her bulky form as her women settled near her. Lien hurried around the tent, returning with Mu-tan, who carried a silver tray with a porcelain pot and teacups. Tugai had learned to like tea, and Ch'i-kuo was grate-ful for that; she still choked on the fermented mare's milk the other lady offered to her in her tent.

They sipped their tea. Tugai craned her short neck, obviously trying to look at the painting. Ch'i-kuo had given the other woman a painting of a swan nesting in the salt marsh around the lake, and had also sent such gifts to the other wives. The women took a childish pleasure in the pictures quite unlike the cooler appreciation offered by the courtiers in the imperial palace.

"It is a poor effort," Ch'i-kuo said as she pushed the painting towards Tugai. The picture showed a burned wall and a patch of ground covered with bones.

Tugai's smile broadened. "It's a fine picture, Ujin. That skull looks like a child's, and I can tell that bone there was part of a leg. And those ribs – you are very clever, Noble Lady."

"I am grateful for your praise, Elder Sister."

Tugai let out her breath. "Perhaps when we are home, you'll make pictures of our land."

"I look forward to the sight of your beautiful country," Ch'i-kuo murmured.

"Summer will soon be past," Tugai said. "The Khan will tend to matters at home before returning here." Ch'i-kuo raised a brow. But of course he would return, to ravage what was left, to destroy whatever the survivors had managed to rebuild. "I suppose he'll leave me behind then, and bring another wife, although he scarcely needs us with so many beauties to choose from among your people."

"Our women are but lilies compared to the rich beauty of a Mongol lady," Ch'i-kuo said courteously; the heavy-boned Tugai looked powerful enough to ride with the Khan into battle. "Your bloom is that of the peony, which we call the king of flowers." She offered this compliment in the Han language; Lien translated it. "I am certain none of our young swans will find more favour with him than do you."

"Oh, but I've never been his favourite. That honour still belongs to Khulan Khatun, even after all these years. Now there's a woman with the beauty of fire in her face – you'd find her a fitting subject for a picture. I was with the Khan when she was brought to him, and his desire for her was so great that he threw her to the floor and took her there and then."

Ch'i-kuo frowned at the thought of such rough affections. Tugai went on to speak of the Khan's oldest sons, who had accompanied him on this campaign. Ch'i-kuo had seen them; the three younger ones resembled their father, while the oldest was a hulking brute with small dark eyes. His name was Jochi, and it was said that he quarrelled often with his brother Chagadai. The two younger sons, Ogedei and Tolui, had drunk so heavily at a recent banquet that their men had needed to carry them from the tent; this was apparently a common occurrence.

"And there is another with the title of the Khan's fifth son," Tugai continued, "Barchukh, the Idukh Khut of the Uighurs."

"How did he earn such a great distinction, Elder Sister?"

"His people came to hate the Kara-Khitans, who demanded much tribute from them. Barchukh decided he preferred Temujin to the Kara-Khitan Gur-Khan as a master, and proved it by driving off some of the Khan's Merkit enemies who had fled to the Uighur lands. When Barchukh came to our camp to swear his oath, the Khan was so moved that he declared he would always regard the Idukh Khut as his fifth son and brother of his four oldest sons."

"Indeed," Ch'i-kuo murmured. "Perhaps the Great Khan was pleased that the Uighur saved him the trouble of subduing his people by force."

"Oh, our husband made a fine speech about that, saying that

Barchukh hadn't caused the Khan's men to suffer or his geldings to sweat, and deserved to be honoured for that. Of course, many Uighurs had already found favour with the Khan, as scribes who set down his words. They are nearly as clever as your people."

Ch'i-kuo gazed into the other woman's guileless brown eyes. Tugai had clearly not meant to insult her; to a Mongol, even an Uighur would seem civilized. Tugai chattered then of her own sons, a little boy who could already ride a horse without having to be tied to it, and an older one who could unerringly hit his target with an arrow.

"They long to win glory in battle," Tugai said. "One's nearly old enough to tend the horses of the rearguard, and my younger takes such pleasure in seeing the tribute and slaves brought in."

"I am sure they will both be mighty warriors," Ch'i-kuo said. "With the blood of the Khan in their veins, they could hardly be otherwise."

"You speak our tongue quite well, Noble Lady, considering how little time you've spent with us. You will soon be a Mongol yourself."

Ch'i-kuo winced at this high praise. "You honour me greatly, Ujin."

The Khan came to Ch'i-kuo that night. She had bathed earlier in a little heated water before donning a robe of blue silk; his nose wrinkled at the smell of her perfume.

"You've washed yourself again?" he asked.

"A month has passed since I last bathed," she said. "I am accustomed to washing more often."

"Water's too precious to waste, and you risk offending the water spirits if you wash in a running stream. My Yasa decrees death for such an offence."

"So Lien has told me," Ch'i-kuo said, "and that bathing during a storm will surely draw lightning to one's tent. But perhaps the spirits of your land will forgive my using a few drops of water to make my body more fragrant for my husband."

"A woman doesn't have to smell like a flower."

"Neither does she have to carry the odour of a horse."

He sat down on the bed. It had grown easier for her to speak to him in this way. Lien had told her that he despised timidity, although he would also take offence at any insult.

Two of her recent paintings sat on a table near the bed, and he picked one up as she settled herself next to him. Two of her women stood near to fan them; Mu-tan approached with a jug.

"What is this one called?" he asked.

It was the painting she had shown to Tugai. "It is called The Great Khan Leaves His Mark Upon the Land."

He scowled, then grabbed for the other. In this one, a Mongol soldier stood near a mound of severed heads; she had painted the heads of women and children. "And this?"

"The Mighty Mongol Is Triumphant Over His Enemies."

He threw the scroll on the table. "If you must make pictures, do horses and birds, or tents and wagons. You could do pictures like the ones in your book."

"I must paint what I see, my husband."

He said, "I see nothing like that here."

"I must paint what I see inside myself. Often my hand seems to find the image and begins its strokes even before I see it clearly. Once the first brushstroke is made, I am committed to it."

"You're painting what you think of these things, and not just what you see."

She said, "I shall not paint them if you don't wish – "

"Paint what pictures you please. If they displease me enough – " He tore the second painting in two, then reached for the jug Mu-tan held.

He drank in silence. The Khan had not been with her often that summer, with his duties to his other wives and his share of the slaves to divert him. He had travelled to the main camp of the Ongghuts, where his daughter Alakha dwelled; the Ongghut chiefs were sworn to him, but it was said that the Khan's daughter ruled through them. The rest of the time, he hunted or consulted with his generals in their ordus.

At last he waved the women away. Lien was about to follow the others to the doorway; he summoned her back. "You'll stay," he said.

"If it's your wish," Lien said, "but the Lady knows enough of your speech for you not to require my words."

"It isn't your words I want."

Ch'i-kuo felt no embarrassment at having the other woman join them; to know that Lien was near eased her. The Khan had brought her little pleasure before, but she could gaze at Lien's oval face as he caressed her, and when he entered her, it was Lien who guided him. She shuddered under him; he might think he had brought her this joy, but it was Lien who filled her thoughts.

The Khan held his court in Ch'i-kuo's tent the next day. She sat at his left; his general Mukhali was at his right. She had learned more about some of the generals seated near Mukhali. The Khan had given the one called Jebe his name when that man had sworn an oath to him after fighting against him. Borchu had formed a bond with her husband when they were both boys, apparently after helping the Khan retrieve some stolen horses. Mongol friendships, it seemed, were sealed with such exploits – shared battles and raids, missions of vengeance to settle old feuds.

Lien sat behind her, in case she needed her interpreter, while Tugai and the Khan's other wives were at her left. The men drank wine, but the Khan contented himself with kumiss. He did not approve of too much wine-drinking. Ch'i-kuo wondered if he would make a law against it, but thought not; his sons Ogedei and Tolui would be the first to object. Their goblets had been filled several times while the Khan murmured to Mukhali, and Ogedei had already staggered outside to vomit and relieve himself.

As Ogedei stumbled back inside, another man entered behind him, covered with yellow dust, as if he had ridden many li. He strode up to the Khan, inclining his head only a little, and Ch'i-kuo knew that he had to be one of her husband's most trusted comrades. For all the awe he inspired, Genghis Khan often dispensed with ceremony in a way unthinkable for an Emperor.

The man rapidly recited a greeting, then said, "I bring news you should hear, Temujin."

"Sit down, Samukha, and tell it to me."

"I thought I should come myself instead of sending a messenger. It won't please you." Samukha sat on a cushion near Mukhali and accepted a cup from a slave. "The King of Gold has abandoned Chung Tu."

Ch'i-kuo's hand tightened around her goblet as the man continued. She grasped enough of his hastily spoken words to understand what he was saying. The Emperor Hsun had left Chung Tu almost immediately after the Mongol army's departure, and had gone to the city of K'ai-feng, abandoning the lands north of the Yellow River to make a stand there.

"We had a truce," the Khan said when Samukha was finished. "He promised peace. I told him I would leave, and now he shows he distrusts my word. He'll be bolder in resisting me from K'ai-feng." He spoke calmly, but Ch'i-kuo saw the rage in his eyes. "I would have left him his capital once he surrendered it to me and took his oath. Now I'll leave him with nothing."

"There is some good news amid the bad," Samukha said. "Many of the Khitans in his own royal guard deserted him during his flight, and have joined our brother the Liao Wang."

Mukhali's moustache twitched as he watched the Khan. The generals wanted this war, Ch'i-kuo thought. They all wanted to fight; they would still have been trying to take Chung Tu if the Khan had not ordered them to withdraw.

"The King of Gold has only shown how much he fears us," Tolui said. "He knows we can take Chung Tu."

Samukha glanced at the young man. "Taking it won't be easy," he said. "Twice we entered, and twice we were thrown back. They'll surely hurl their thunderclap bombs at us from the walls, and panic our horses with those terrible sounds. I wonder how we can scale such high walls, and we still lack experience in laying siege."

Tolui sneered. "Nothing is impossible for a Mongol."

The Khan lifted a hand. "We won't have to storm the city," he said. "Those inside are weaker than they were. They won't find much to feed them in the regions we've sacked, and the loss of their Emperor will dampen their spirits. We can starve them into surrender."

"They're likely to send to their northern homeland for food," Mukhali said.

"Unless we strike there first." The Khan leaned back in his chair. "Autumn will be upon us soon. By then, the scouts I'll send out will have prepared our way." He moved his hands. "Two wings can strike east, across the Khingans. Another force will move south to surround Chung Tu."

Mukhali was speaking to the Khan, muttering of war councils to be held and the need for reinforcements. Ch'i-kuo drained her goblet; a slave refilled it.

"You are grieving, Lady," Lien whispered in the Han tongue. "May the wine ease your sorrow."

"I do not grieve," Ch'i-kuo said in Mongol. The Khan looked away from Mukhali. "The city will fall to my husband. I rejoice that he has removed me from danger by holding out his hand to me." She lifted her cup and drank.

99

CH'I-KUO LAY IN her bed. Above the howl of the spring wind, she could still hear the drunken shouts of Mongol soldiers cheering the fall of Chung Tu. The Khan himself had danced that night when the news was brought to him.

He had not returned to his homelands that past autumn, and had kept her with him. That winter, he had sent two wings of his army, one commanded by his brother Khasar and the other by Mukhali, against the Jurchen homeland; Samukha had gone south to attack Chung Tu. The Khan had followed at a distance, moving slowly south to make his camp near the Tu-shih K'ou River.

By then, she had believed that the capital might hold out after all. The Khan, perhaps fearing that, had sent A-la-Chien to K'ai-feng to offer peace to the Emperor, but Hsun, in spite of the thousands of refugees who had fled south, had turned the Tangut envoy away. Emperor Hsun had tried, too late, to send food to the besieged capital, only to have Mongol troops capture the supplies. The people of Chung Tu had grown desperate; the Khan would wait.

He did not have to wait long. Spring was barely upon them, and Chung Tu had surrendered. The Mongols, who could have stormed it only at great cost, had starved it into submission.

Lien stirred next to her. "It surprises me," Lien murmured, "that the Khan doesn't wish to go to Chung Tu."

"He has his triumph," Ch'i-kuo said. "Inspecting the city himself would add only a few drops to his cup of joy." He had sent his chief judge Shigi Khutukhu there instead to take charge of the plunder.

She covered her belly with one hand. The child inside her did not yet show. She was likely to be in the Khan's homeland before their child was born. There was little to keep him here now; part of his army would remain behind to pillage what was left and to strike at any resistance.

The Sung Emperor would feel safe, with what was left of the Kin lands lying between him and the Mongols. She wondered how long it would be before the Khan's thoughts turned to the south.

Lien sighed, and Ch'i-kuo moved her hand over the other woman's abdomen. Lien's belly was rounder; she would also give the Khan a child. Perhaps the love they shared between themselves had opened their gates to his seed. A man at court would not have been jealous of what passed between two of his women when they were deprived of his attentions, but the Khan had been displeased to find out that they took such delight with each other. He might have forbidden it had Ch'i-kuo not explained that such practices would not harm them and would only make them more desirous of his mighty peak. Their pregnancies seemed to prove the truth of her words, and he had learned a little from the pictures in her book. As he often said, he was willing to learn new things.

He did not have to know that having Lien's love made it possible for her to endure him, that without it, she could have taken no joy with him. They had created a little world of their own, in which he was only an occasional intruder. She pressed

543

her lips to Lien's, and ran her hands over the slender body so like her own.

The Khan was examining a few of his treasures. Ch'i-kuo watched as one man handed him a cup; the Khan held it at arm's length as he admired the porcelain. He took as much delight in fine goblets and delicately crafted and painted pottery as in the gold heaped in the carts outside his ordu.

He had also asked that some of the more notable prisoners be sent on to him, but those men waited outside while the Khan toasted Samukha and his commanders and listened as Shigi Khutukhu listed what he had won.

"I would see the prisoners now," the Khan said when his chief judge fell silent.

"You said you wanted the most important," Shigi Khutukhu said. "Among the prisoners taken at the palace, these seem the most worthy. I asked who among them held the highest positions, and certain men were pointed out to me. Then I asked which men were the wisest, and others were led to me. Those are the ones I brought to you."

Ch'i-kuo looked down as the prisoners were led inside, afraid she would see men she knew. "That tall one there looks impressive," the Khan said.

"He was found by a cart near the palace grounds, ministering to some of the injured. The men who discovered him thought there must be treasure in the cart, from the way he clung to it, but they found only scrolls." Shigi Khutukhu cleared his throat. "I ordered my men to bring the cart with him – there might be useful writing in the scrolls. If not, they can feed our fires."

"Ask him what the scrolls say."

Another man translated the Khan's question. "The scrolls tell of the stars," a man replied in the Han tongue. Ch'i-kuo had heard that voice before; she raised her head.

Ye-lu Ch'u-ts'ai, the Khitan who had praised her paintings, was speaking. His silk robe was as spotted and worn as those of the men with him, and his face was thin and drawn, but he stood erect and gazed steadily at the Khan. "They are astronomical charts," the Khitan continued. "The Han have studied the stars for countless years, and have made many records of their positions. Such observations not only show us the skies as they were in the past, but can also tell us what may come. I can, for instance, look at them and calculate when next a dragon will attempt to swallow the sun. I can know when certain of the tailed stars, Heaven's Banners, will return to warn of troubled times."

The men near the Khan made strange signs with their hands and fingers as this was translated; the Khan frowned. "Our shamans know the stars," he said, "but I do not know if even they can tell us that. Can this man read what the stars foretell?"

"I have some knowledge of heavenly omens," Ye-lu Ch'u-ts'ai replied. "The Emperor has great need of such lore, which is why only men who have the court's permission may study the stars. The Son of Heaven must know when the auguries are right for conceiving an heir, or if an omen foretells disaster."

The Khan leaned forward. "Then why did he not see the fate in store for his capital?"

"We saw evil omens," the Khitan said when this was translated. "But knowledge is useless if the one who seeks it refuses to make use of it. The Emperor listened to others, not his astronomers, and in the end, events showed him what he refused to see in the stars."

"This man is a Khitan," Shigi Khutukhu murmured, "and claims descent from the royal house of Liao."

The Khan smiled. "Then tell him this. The House of Liao and the House of Kin were enemies. Once his people ruled, and the Kin took their realm from them. I am his avenger. Surely he should rejoice that he no longer has to serve his enemy."

The Khitan raised his brows as this was translated. "I cannot lie to you, Majesty," he said. "My grandfather, my father, and I have always served the Emperor of the Kin. From the time I was born, I was taught to serve my sovereign. To betray one's king only creates disorder. While my Emperor dwelled in his palace, my duty was to him, and when he left us, my duty was to his city."

These were not words to say to the Khan. Surely the scholar knew that he risked the Khan's anger.

"You speak truly," the Khan said. Ch'i-kuo concealed her

surprise. "A man who would betray his master is of no use to me. Tell him this – his King has fled, and he is in my hands now. I would have him serve me with his knowledge."

Ye-lu Ch'u-ts'ai was silent for a long time. His eyes met Ch'i-kuo's for a moment; she thought she glimpsed despair.

"I shall serve you willingly, Majesty," he said at last. "I can say that because your words show me you are wise, and that is part of the truth, but not all of it. Serving you is also the only way I can serve my people now."

The Khan laughed. "He's honest," he said. "This Khitan will do better serving me than he did serving the Kin."

Ch'i-kuo lowered her eyes as another scholar was brought forward. Of course the Khitan would serve the Khan, if only to save his own life.

Ch'i-kuo sent for the Khitan scholar two days later. She greeted him in her tent, surrounded by her women, with two Mongol guards posted inside the entrance.

Ye-lu Ch'u-ts'ai murmured a greeting. The women ushered him to a cushion; Mu-tan stood behind him with a fan as two others brought him tea.

"Do you still paint, Highness?" he said. "I ask because I see that you are keeping your hands supple."

She curled her fingers around the jade ball she used for that purpose. "I have done a few pictures. They are not the same as the ones I used to paint."

"I am certain they are most pleasing to the eye. To be in your presence again is most welcome, Highness."

"I asked my husband if I might speak to you." She tossed the ball lightly, then caught it. "He has most graciously allowed us to meet." She rolled the jade ball against her palms. "It pleases him to allow us to talk together of what is lost, of what he took from us. Let us speak frankly, Wise Scholar. Whatever we were before, I am now a wife of the Mongol Khan and you are well on your way to earning his respect. I didn't look back when I left our city, but I shall tell you what I often paint now. I paint the bone-filled fields I saw, and the hills of heads, and the despairing captives who know they are going to die. Such subjects present their own challenges to the artist." She shook her head slightly. "I asked you here, Learned Brother, because I wish to hear of what the Khan's armies brought upon Chung Tu."

"It is a sorrowful tale, Highness."

"I did not expect it to be otherwise."

"By winter, we were starving," he said. "In the city, there were rumours of people eating the dead. Soon, it was said that many weren't waiting for others to die before feeding on them. Towards the end, Wan-yen Fu-hsing pleaded with Mo-jan Chin-chung to open the gates and challenge the Mongols in battle – we couldn't go on as we were. They quarrelled so violently that we feared their men might war among themselves. Chin-chung fled to K'ai-feng, and Fu-hsing killed himself in his despair. It's said that he wrote a fine poem before he died, accusing Chin-chung of treason." He paused. "Chin-chung had promised to take the princesses left in Chung Tu with him, but abandoned them instead. They also killed themselves rather than be taken by the Mongols."

Ch'i-kuo closed her eyes for a moment. The other women wept softly.

"The gates were opened," Ch'u-ts'ai continued. "The officers surrendered to General Ming-an, who had deserted us for the Mongols. The enemy soldiers slew so many in the city that the bodies clogged the streets – even a rat couldn't have found a path through them. They looted, and ravaged anyone in their way, and set fire to the buildings, for some were still trying to resist them. There is a story that the Mongols set fire to the tails of cats and dogs and the feathers of birds before turning them loose to burn the city."

The Khitan took a breath. "Many were dying of starvation or disease, and more would have lost their lives even without the fire. Perhaps the Mongols wanted to cleanse the city with fire. Perhaps they were simply in a rage after besieging it for so long. Chung Tu is a blackened ruin, Lady. The Imperial Palace burned for nearly a month, and is no more."

She thought of the paintings she had left behind, now only ashes. Perhaps it was fitting that they had not survived the life they had recorded.

"I saved what I could," Ch'u-ts'ai murmured. "I used what herbs I had to ease the ill before the Mongols found me."

She said, "Now I know why the Khan refused to ride to the city. He has what he wanted from it. Grass will grow amid Chung Tu's ashes, and someday his horses may graze there. That is his vision of the world, Honoured Scholar and Adviser to the Khan. We shall see him turn everything under Heaven into a pasture for his herds."

"Perhaps that is what he sees now, and yet he has ordered his men to guard my books and to see that I have everything I need. I can help our people only by serving him."

"You speak of our people," Ch'i-kuo said, "but surely you mean only your Khitans. The Khan will gladly reward them for assisting in the destruction."

He said, "I was speaking of your people, and mine, and the Han as well – perhaps even the Mongols among whom we must live. It may be that I can bring the Mongol Khan to see that he can gain more by preserving what he wins."

"You say that even after seeing what he brought to our city? Accept what he is, Honoured Adviser, and live in his world. To hope for anything else is futile."

"I see a man who reaches out for what lies beyond him. Am I to respond to that by building a wall between his world and mine? That would be an easier life for me, to accept his world while holding myself apart from it, or to see it as an illusion that will soon pass, but I cannot live that way." He paused. "I have obligations to others. That is why I served the Emperor, and why I must now serve the Khan. I think you see this, whatever you say. It may be why you paint the pictures you do."

"You are mistaken. It's simply that I am often unable to paint anything else. Once, such pictures angered my husband, and now he's indifferent to them. The Khan tires of his new toys quickly."

"Yet he doesn't forbid you to paint them."

"He prefers to know what those around him are thinking. He enjoys seeing my thoughts, desolate as they often are." She waved a hand. "You may leave me, Adviser to Genghis Khan. Our master may have need of you."

548

The Khan sat on Ch'i-kuo's bed. He had stripped to the waist against the heat. They would go north soon, to wait out the summer in cooler lands before crossing the desert.

He was gazing at a painting she had done a few days after speaking to the Khitan. It showed a burned wall, with a tree in front of it; a misty rain was falling from a grey sky.

"What is this picture?" he asked.

"There was such a wall in the palace," she said, "and a tree much like that one."

"Your picture lies," he said. "My men told me that not even that much remains of the palace, and the tree would have burned as well. Your paintings are deceitful, wife. You show none of the joy of war."

"I am only a woman, and blind to such joys."

"Only a woman, but I had thought you weren't a fool. Every man I kill gives me a little more space for my tents, a bit more land for my herds, a longer future for my people. A man's work is war, and I take joy in my work, as any man must if he is to do it well. I won't mourn the dead. What were they before I came? People who dug at the ground and put walls around themselves."

Ch'i-kuo sat at his feet. "Yet you have found some of those people to be of value."

"A craftsman who can make a fine sword or a goblet, or a man learned in the lore of the stars – that's of use. But I saw many of the people of your cities, and they made nothing except children as useless as themselves." He sighed. "Your pictures of death grow tiresome, wife."

"The one you hold is the last such picture I shall paint."

"I am pleased to hear it." He glanced up at Lien, who was standing behind him with a fan. "The Princess speaks my tongue well now, and has little need of you. Perhaps I should put you among those of my women who haven't yet learned it."

Ch'i-kuo stiffened. Lien lowered her eyes as she continued to fan him. "If that is your wish," she said softly.

"You wouldn't be unhappy at losing your cherished royal playfellow?" he asked.

"It is you I could not bear to lose, my Lord," Lien replied.

549

"Do what you like with me as long as I am still yours." She lifted her head.

"It's good you're with child. Otherwise, I would have given you to Mukhali — he admits to admiring your beauty when he's drunk."

Lien's eyes glistened. "I could not bear being sent from your ordu, my Khan."

Lien had spoken the truth, Ch'i-kuo realized; their moments together were only a diversion to Lien. The Khan had hurt her, as he had intended, and shown her how easily he could destroy her refuge by depriving her of Lien. It did not matter. The woman's reply to him, her admission that it was he whom she loved, had destroyed it already.

The Khan set down the painting, then picked up another. His eyes widened. "You have painted me upon my throne!"

"Yes," Ch'i-kuo murmured.

"But who are these others in the picture?"

"The woman by the mulberry tree is watching a silkworm weave its cocoon, the man by the wagon has brought in a harvest of grain, and the boy is gathering grapes."

"How obvious you are, wife. I see so easily what you're trying to say — I hear it from my Khitan adviser, of how I might gain more by ruling cities instead of razing them. It's a better subject for a painting, but it doesn't show the skill of the others. You paint me as though you're uncertain of what you see."

"I know." Hope had blurred her vision; to hope that she could touch what Ye-lu Ch'u-ts'ai believed was inside him had only made her brushstrokes more tentative. She prayed that the ruler was there, the man who could do more than destroy. If he were not, her hand would falter; the scrolls would be as empty of hope as the world he might create.

100

To the west of the encampment, black cliffs jutted towards the sky. Between the mountains and the flat yellow grassland were a few barren hills. A white canopy trimmed with gold had been raised on the south-east slope of one hill; the Kin princess sat in its shade with several of her women.

Gurbesu's horse slowed to a trot as she neared the three wagons at the bottom of the hill. The Kin woman had left her tent at dawn to come here. One of the boys watching the princess's wagons reached for Gurbesu's reins as she dismounted. Gurbesu's son was about to follow her; she motioned to him to remain with the horses, then climbed the small slope.

The princess sat behind a low table, a brush in her hand; small flat stones and coloured sticks lay by her scroll. A blue silk scarf covered her glossy black hair. Lien was with her, as always, and Mu-tan stood behind them with a large painted fan. They were so small and delicate, these women; they fluttered through the camp like birds.

Gurbesu bowed. "I greet you, Honoured Ladies." The princess murmured a greeting; Gurbesu settled on a small cushion near her. The other women were sitting to the left of the table, murmuring in their strange musical tongue at the two little boys who were the sons of the princess and Lien.

"I see you are making another picture," Gurbesu said.

"It is almost done." Ch'i-kuo set down her brush. The picture was of a bamboo stalk, with painted lettering beside it. The woman painted them often; they all looked the same, feathery strokes surrounded by emptiness.

"You are skilled, Ujin," Gurbesu said.

"Perhaps I shall paint some horses next, or the Khan hunting with his hawks. Our husband prefers such pictures." Ch'i-kuo squinted slightly as she turned towards Gurbesu; labouring at her art had to be making her short-sighted.

"Our husband's armies," Gurbesu said, "have defeated another old enemy."

"So I was told." The Princess's fine-boned face was still. "I heard that a messenger carried the news to you immediately after leaving the tent of Bortai Khatun."

"The Khan knew I would be interested in the outcome."

"How is that, Lady?"

"The enemy defeated by Jebe and our ally Barchukh," Gurbesu said, "was Guchlug, the son of my former husband Bai Bukha. He fled to Kara-Khitai some years ago, after the Khan triumphed over my husband's armies."

Ch'i-kuo's lovely dark eyes were expressionless. She had dwelled here long enough to know of Gurbesu's past; her apparent ignorance of the lives of those around her had to be a mask. But perhaps not. The invisible wall around the woman seemed as high and thick as the one that bordered her old land. They were all barbarians to her – Naimans, the Muslim traders that came to the camp, even the Uighur scribes.

"Do you mourn for this man, Lady?" the Kin woman asked.

"No. He fled from the battlefield and abandoned us to the Mongols. When he took refuge in Kara-Khitai, their Gur-Khan welcomed him and gave him his own daughter in marriage, but my former stepson Guchlug wasn't content with that, and seized the throne of Kara-Khitai for himself."

Ch'i-kuo picked up her brush and added another stroke to her bamboo. "It seems he has the distinction of having lost two lands to the Khan."

"Guchlug was foolish," Gurbesu said. "He became a follower of the Buddha when he wed the Gur-Khan's daughter, and his new faith turned him against his Muslim subjects. By the time Jebe and Barchukh rode there, the people of Kara-Khitai were ready to welcome them as saviours. That's why our victory was so swift, Honoured Lady. It's said the people there rejoiced when Guchlug's head was carried through the streets of their towns."

Ch'i-kuo lifted her head. "That our husband has a victory pleases me," she said. "I shall tell him, when he honours me again with his presence, that I heard this story from you. That will save him the trouble of recounting his army's exploits to me himself."

The woman cared about nothing, as long as she had her scrolls and paints. Perhaps that was why the Khan was losing interest in her; there were certainly enough other women to beguile him.

Gurbesu gazed towards the camp. The Orkhon River was a thin blue ribbon near the horizon; the tents of the Khan's four favourite wives sat to the east of the great tent where his standard stood. Each tent was at the head of a circle of smaller tents that housed minor wives, concubines, servants, and slaves, and there were other minor wives in other camps.

She wondered if Temujin would remember how many wives he had, or how many children, without his Uighur scribes to keep a record. More women arrived, captured or given as tribute, each year, to be turned over to one of the households each of the four Khatuns supervised. Each woman remained a concubine unless a son was born to her, when she was raised to the status of minor wife and given her own tent and slaves. The fortunate ones were kept in the Khan's main camp, while the less favoured raised their yurts in other regions and watched over the flocks and herds assigned to them. Most were his bedfellows for only a night or two, and none had become a favourite. That honour still belonged to Bortai, the two Tatar sisters, and especially to the still beautiful Khulan.

Gurbesu's tent belonged to Bortai's circle, as did Ch'i-kuo's. She was grateful for that. If she was never to be a favourite again, she preferred being here to living in an outlying camp, where other minor wives did their work, loaded wagons with the shares of wool, milk, hides, and meat owed to the four Khatuns, and waited in their tents hoping that the Khan might stop with them for a night.

Gurbesu glanced at Ch'i-kuo, who was still studying her painting. "As it happens," Gurbesu said slowly, "I didn't come here to speak of battles. There's something else I must say. Please believe that I have only your welfare at heart."

Ch'i-kuo raised her thin brows. "What do you wish to tell me?"

"Perhaps I should say it out of earshot of your women, Ujin. This concerns you and the Lady Lien."

The princess waved a hand. "I have no secrets from Mu-tan, and the others cannot understand this tongue."

"Perhaps they understand more than you know," Gurbesu

553

said. "I've heard rumours of things you might wish to keep secret, which means Bortai Khatun is likely to hear of them before long. She would be most offended, and the Khan would surely punish you if he knew. I do not want discord under his tents."

Ch'i-kuo and Lien exchanged glances. "We have done nothing to offend either the Khan or the Khatun," the princess replied.

The woman was making what she had to say even more difficult. "We are virtuous women," Gurbesu said. "That should be evident to you, since you've lived among us for almost three years. I beg you both to consider the wisdom of behaving virtuously yourselves."

Ch'i-kuo was smiling, but her dark eyes were blank. "I don't know what you mean, dear Sister."

"I'm speaking of what you and the Lady Lien do together." Gurbesu flushed. "You often keep her in your tent at night, and not because you have need of another servant." She took a breath. "You lie with each other – that's what is said. Maybe you thought your secret was safe, but – "

Ch'i-kuo threw back her head and laughed; Lien giggled behind her hand. "That?" the princess said. "But why should that remain a secret?"

Gurbesu swallowed. "If the Khan knew, he would kill you both."

"I think not." Ch'i-kuo's lips parted, showing her small white teeth. "There is nothing the Khan likes better than to see Lien's dainty fingers parting the petals of my lotus, or to watch as Mu-tan tastes of the dew on its folds. You are easily shocked, Lady. I haven't noticed that Mongol women are modest in their talk of the bedchamber, and the Khan has been known to enjoy more than one woman at a time in his bed."

"I'm not speaking of your doings with him, but of what you do alone."

"And how can that offend him?" Ch'i-kuo asked. "What we do results in no bastard, and our sweet yearnings are satisfied when we're deprived of his attentions. This only ensures that we remain faithful to him, and when he's fatigued, he takes pleasure in watching our frolics. Still, I am grateful you spoke of this to me. The Khan would only laugh at your accusations, but I would not want the Khatun Bortai angry with me. That honourable Lady isn't as open to different ways as is our husband, so we shall be more discreet in the future."

Gurbesu could not speak.

"I hope you won't speak of this to others, Lady," Ch'i-kuo continued. "It would only bring more discord to the Khan's household than you intend. Others among the Khan's wives sometimes seek such solace. They wouldn't look kindly on you for bringing this to the Khatun's attention, and perhaps that great and wise Lady is aware of our deeds and simply chooses to ignore them. You might do well to ease your loneliness in such ways. The Khan visits your tent less often than he visits mine."

Gurbesu stood up, longing to be away from these women. "But of course that's why you spoke to us," Ch'i-kuo said, "not to warn us, or to prevent trouble, but because you envy us our small pleasures. You would have us all pining for our mighty stag, with no solace, as you do. Carry your tales to the Khatun, if you wish. Others will whisper the true reason for your telling them."

Gurbesu made the sign against evil as she walked down the hill. The trilling laughter of the women under the canopy was a lash stinging her. She did not know what disturbed her more — that the women sought such pleasures or that Temujin enjoyed viewing them.

The Khan wanted to conquer the world. That world would bring its evils to his people.

101

SORKHATANI LIFTED HULEGU from his cradle. Tolui sat by the bed with their two older sons, speaking of what he had seen in Khitai.

"Their soldiers wear shirts of raw silk under their armour,"

Tolui was saying to the boys. "If an arrow goes through the armour, it doesn't pierce the shirt. A man can pull it out and go on fighting."

Mongke, his oldest son, nodded. Khubilai, who was only three, toyed with an arrow his father had given him. "But here's something even more useful." Tolui held up a thread from which a flat piece of iron shaped like a fish dangled. "This is a south-pointing fish. A man can float it on a small bowl of water and, when the bow's shielded from wind, the head of the fish will always point south. Rubbing the metal against a magic stone gives the fish its power. A commander can know where to move his troops, even under an overcast night sky in land he doesn't know."

Sorkhatani had rarely heard Tolui speak of the treasures he had seen in Khitai, or the ways of the craftsmen who made them. Her husband talked of what he had learned about war. He reddened with pleasure when he spoke of catapults that could hurl stones over a wall, or of vessels called cannons that made a sound like thunder as balls flew from them. His father the Khan might value his Khitan scholars; Tolui sought out those who knew the secret of the explosive powder that fuelled the cannons, or how to erect a siege engine.

Sorkhatani rocked Hulegu gently as she suckled him. She had given the Khan three grandsons, and saw more of Temujin in Mongke's thoughtful eyes and Khubilai's curious ones than she did of Tolui.

A slave refilled Tolui's cup. She had to speak to him before drink dulled his senses. The Khan rarely let drink get the better of him, but Tolui could match even his brother Ogedei cup for cup. Ogedei grew more placid with drinking; Tolui bellowed songs and danced, staggering around his father's tent, restless for another war.

"While I'm hunting with Toguchar," Tolui said, "you two may practise archery with your aunt Khojin – you'll learn something about how to shoot from her."

Sorkhatani tied Hulegu to his cradle. Khojin did not wait in her tent when her husband Toguchar fought, but rode into battle at his side. Some called her Toguchar's Hawk; she loved battle as much as the general and her brother Tolui did.

"Our sons should also know other things," Sorkhatani said. "I would like the scribe Tolochu to teach Mongke the Uighur script, and Khubilai will soon be old enough to learn it."

Tolui scowled. "It will ruin their eyes," he said.

"I'll see they don't strain their eyes."

"I struggled with those markings for years, and still mistake one word for another. What good will it do them?"

"They'll have to help rule the lands you and your brothers win for them. Such learning may make them better advisers to the one who follows your father to the throne."

Tolui shook his head and made a sign to avert misfortune. With all the death he had seen, he was as wary of such talk as Temujin-echige. The Khan, Sorkhatani thought, thinks he will live forever. She could almost imagine that was possible, that Heaven itself would preserve the greatest of Khans.

"They can't rule without fighting." Tolui draped one muscular arm over Mongke. "Listen, boys, and remember this. Any man who hasn't surrendered to us, or sworn an oath to the Khan, is our enemy. I've seen more of the world than you have, and countless numbers of people live under Heaven. No matter how many lands we win, there may be others beyond them still, and until those in them bow to us, we must regard them as enemies. The Yasa commands it."

"Yes, Father," Mongke said.

"Fear and swiftness are your weapons as much as the arrow and the sword. Move fast enough, and your speed will give every man under your command the strength of ten – the enemy will no sooner halt his retreat to regroup than you'll have struck at his rear. Terror in the heart of your enemy can win you a battle even before you march against him."

"When are you going back to war?" Mongke asked.

"Soon, I hope," Tolui said, his pale eyes brightening. "When your grandfather has a treaty with the western Khan, we'll launch a final sweep against the Kin. Mukhali's army will have softened them up by then."

Mongke tugged at his father's sleeve. "But why does Grandfather want a treaty?"

"Because a wise man never leaves a potential enemy at his back."

Sorkhatani picked up her sewing. The Khan had sent an envoy to the western land of Khwarezm. The envoy, a trader named Mahmoud Yalavach from the Khwarezmian city of Bukhara, was a suitable choice to deal with the Shah Muhammad who ruled that land. The Khan wanted trade with Khwarezm, but wanted a promise of peace even more. With Kara-Khitai part of the Mongol ulus, the Khan's domain now bordered the Shah's; the Mongols had to be certain that the vast Khwarezmian army would not encroach on their territory when the flower of their army moved east. In the meantime, the Mongol caravan that was following the Khan's envoy would trade and gather more information about the western lands. Temujin-echige might want peace, but would also be prepared for war.

The Khan still had much to conquer, and her sons might have to rule people unlike themselves. They would need to know more than the arts of war.

"May I summon the scribe Tolochu?" Sorkhatani asked.

"You may do as you like, Sorkhatani." Tolui grinned at her, then took out his knuckle-bone dice. "Let's see if you two can beat me. There's a game called chess I'm learning from a trader, with pieces on a board. I'll have to teach it to you — it's like war." He sprawled on the carpet with his sons. With his broad, ruddy face and sparse moustache, he looked little older than a boy himself.

Sorkhatani wondered how suited Tolui would be to his future duties. As the Khan's youngest son by Bortai, he was the Prince of the Hearth and would have to look after the homelands when a new Khan was chosen. He would be a war-horse champing at the bit, yearning for battles in far lands, longing to be the sword of the one who was Khan.

She did not know who that Khan would be. Temujin shunned any talk of his dying, and the Noyans might not have his wishes to guide them when the time for a choice came. If the kuriltai turned to either of his older sons, the one who was passed over might even take up arms against his brother. How could Jochi be Khan, with people still whispering that he was not his father's son? How could Chagadai rule, who thought of his father's Yasa as something that could never be bent, even in the interests of justice? Neither of them would ever bow to the other. If the two contended over the throne, Temujin's ulus might not outlive him.

102

BORTAI GLANCED AT her husband. He had been pacing by the hearth all evening. Apparently he planned to spend the night here. Once, he had come to her with fire inside him. Now, he came to her tent to rest, to have a night of unbroken sleep.

He was troubled, and she did not know why. His envoy Mahmoud Yalavach had returned only a day ago to tell him that the Shah Muhammad would welcome trade and had no designs on territory the Mongols held.

"Temujin," she said at last, "one would think the western Khan had rejected your offer."

"Perhaps he wished to do so." He stopped pacing and turned towards her. "Mahmoud spoke to me alone after he told me the words of the Shah. I'm not sure Muhammad really wants peace."

"But he sent envoys to you even before you left Khitai. He spoke of peace then."

"I thought he feared our armies," he said, "and wanted to avoid a battle. But I've learned more about him since then. His father and then he made an ulus in the west while I was uniting our people, and maybe he thinks Heaven will favour him." He tugged at his beard. "His forces are greater than ours. If I lead my armies to Khitai, there would be little to stop him from attacking in the west."

He glanced at the two slaves sleeping by the doorway, then came towards her and sat down on the bed. "Mahmoud delivered my message," he said, "and then the Shah took him aside. Mahmoud repeated my words, that I would honour the Shah as I do my own sons, and that peace would be to the advantage of both of us. The Shah was angry that I called him my son,

and said I was an infidel who demeaned him with such words."
He let out his breath. "He then appealed to Mahmoud, as a
man of Bukhara, to return here as his spy."

"And what did Mahmoud Yalavach say to that?" Bortai
asked.

"He accepted a bribe from the Shah – he would have gained
nothing by rousing Muhammad's suspicions. He told the Shah
that I had taken many of the Kin cities, but that my armies
weren't as strong as Khwarezm's. That seemed to placate
Muhammad, and he renewed his offer of peace."

"Then I don't see why you're worried. When your caravan
arrives, he'll see what he can gain with peace." The caravan
was carrying gold, silver, and silk from Khitai, furs from the
north, and the camel-hair coats of the Tanguts – a taste of
what trade supervised by the Mongols would bring to Khwarezm. "He'll have more than he could win through war."

"But I don't yet have what I want from him."

Temujin, she thought, would see it that way. Become my
son; that was his message to the Shah. Keep what you have,
as long as you acknowledge that I am your superior, that I am
meant to rule over all. Temujin would never accept peace with
a ruler who saw himself as the Khan's equal.

"Swallow your pride," she said, "and accept whatever peace
he offers. You have a war to fight in Khitai. My sons are itching
to fight there again, and at least that would keep Chagadai and
Jochi from fighting each other."

"I have forbidden them to fight."

"That hasn't made them love each other. They restrain themselves only because they fear you." He could settle matters by
choosing an heir, but she could not say that to him. Perhaps
his refusal to face his own mortality was what gave him his
strength.

A few days after Mahmoud's return, a camel-driver who had
been with the Mongol caravan rode into the Khan's camp
and was hastily brought before Temujin. At the Khwarezmian
border town of Otrar, the trade goods had been seized by the
town's governor Inalchik, and all those travelling with the

560

caravan slaughtered. Only the camel-driver had managed to escape.

Somehow, the Khan conquered his anger, but Bortai knew how deeply this news had wounded him when he left for Burkhan Khaldun. He often prayed on the mountain when he was most unsure of himself, when the will of Heaven seemed hidden. Her unease grew when she learned that Temujin had sent two Mongol envoys and a Muslim named Ibn-Kafraj Boghra to the Shah, demanding that he surrender Inalchik to the Mongols for punishment. If Muhammad gave the man up, there could still be peace, but Bortai remembered what her husband had said about the Shah. Muhammad might see Temujin's offer as a sign of weakness; the Shah might be willing to risk war.

When the northern winds began to howl, the Khan moved his main camp towards the former Naiman lands, and Bortai realized that he was preparing for war in the west. The men set out on their great hunt that autumn, and people murmured that the Khan had killed the game driven to him with unusual ferocity, slaughtering animals until the carcasses were heaped as high as hills.

Not long after the hunt, the two Mongol envoys returned, with heads shorn of their braids and word that the Shah had put Ibn-Kafraj Boghra to death. Bortai did not have to ask what Temujin had said when faced with this affront. An envoy had been killed, and two others shamed; there could be only one response to this crime. The final assault on Khitai would have to wait until the Shah paid for his deed.

103

YISUI TOOK UP her sewing as her sister sat down. "You haven't asked about your children since I entered your tent," Yisugen said.

"I assume they're well," Yisui murmured. "You would have

sent word if they weren't, and they're only a short ride away, hardly the far end of the earth."

"They should be here with you," Yisugen said. "You are a poor mother, Yisui."

"Then it's fortunate you're such a good one." Temujin would come to her tent soon. Yisui would tell him, as she often did whenever they were absent, that she missed them but hated to keep them apart from Yisugen's children, to whom they were so close. He probably suspected that she did not yearn for their company, but he seemed content to leave them in her sister's care.

She looked up at Yisugen's long dark eyes and high-boned face, still so much like her own. Some of the newer concubines often mistook one sister for the other, but the bond between them had frayed just a little. Yisugen's duties to her household took much of her time, as did Yisui's to her own, and they did not see each other as often.

Even after seventeen years with their husband, she felt her bond with Yisugen most when they shared him. They were one soul then, feeling each other's joy.

"You might spend a little more time with your oldest," Yisugen said, "before he goes away."

"He'll stay in the rear at his age – he'll be safe enough." Temujin was sending her oldest son, and Yisugen's, to fight with Mukhali in Khitai. It was useless to fret over one's children. Her sons would ride away to fight, and her daughters would leave her ordu when they married. "I'm worrying more about what may happen here if Temujin doesn't return from Khwarezm."

Yisugen made a sign. "Don't say it." She glanced towards Yisui's slaves, as if fearing they might be listening. Two of the girls were skimming curds from the kettle while the other three laid down carpets they had beaten clean. None of these Han slaves could hear, and they were unable to speak of what they saw. It was clever of the Han to make them that way, to put hot pincers into their ears to deafen them and to cut away the power of speech. Yisui had seen their usefulness immediately, and had asked the Khan to give them to her. Now some of the other wives wanted such slaves for themselves.

"My dear sister," Yisui said, "I pray that our husband will

562

live for a thousand years, but consider what may happen if he doesn't. He says nothing about which of his sons should succeed him. Jochi will have his supporters, and so will Chagadai. Neither of them will ever bow to the other, and our fate will be in the hands of the one who becomes Khan. He might not decide to keep us both as wives, especially if he wants to use us to reward men who supported him. We could easily end up far from each other, in different camps."

Yisugen lifted a hand to her mouth. "I can't bear to think of it."

"We had better think of it, and do what we can to prevent it. Temujin must decide on an heir before he goes to war."

"He won't listen. Even Borchu and Jelme wouldn't dare to bring it up, especially now."

That was true. The Khan had more to worry about than a war with Khwarezm, now that his Tangut minions had refused to send a force to fight with him. If you cannot fight alone, their envoy had said, then why are you Khan? The reply had enraged Temujin, but he could not punish the Tanguts for their insolence without abandoning his plans. Perhaps the people of Hsi-Hsia suspected he would not return from Khwarezm, that the Khan would not live long enough to punish them.

Yisui said, "I'll speak to our husband about this."

Yisugen leaned towards her. "You can't."

"I have no choice." Her needle pricked her, drawing blood. Yisui raised her finger to her mouth. She thought of the time she had confronted him before his men, how close she had been to death. She remembered how he had looked at her, almost daring her to protest, when her first husband's head had rolled across the ground. She would have to face him again, and in front of others, hoping that some of them found the courage to echo her words.

Yisui lifted her cup. The Khan had decided to hold a banquet in honour of Mukhali, who would soon return to Khitai, where the Liao Wang's Khitans would aid the Mongols against the Kin. This was the last easy moment Temujin was likely to enjoy before he said his prayers, made his sacrifices, and had his shamans and his Khitan adviser read the bones. His spies and scouts were already at work in Khwarezm.

The court had dined on platters of lamb and drunk the strongest wines, those left outside in bottles so that the pure spirits would separate from the frozen water. Lute-players had entertained them, and Han slaves had danced and juggled for them, but Yisui had seen more cheer at funeral banquets. Mukhali's war stories had barely roused the Khan from his sullen silence. The laughter of Borchu and Jelme was forced, while Ogedei and Tolui were drinking even more than usual.

Temujin had summoned his four Khatuns to the feast. Yisui sipped her wine. Perhaps someone else would speak first; she had watched the others glance from the Khan to his sons, as if waiting to ask him the same question. Temujin might listen to Ogedei or Tolui; he had always shown more affection to them than to his other sons. Khulan might have said the words without offending him, but the Merkit wore her usual calm and distant expression. Subotai or Jebe would soon start reciting old stories, and then there would be no chance to speak. The Khan leaned towards Mukhali from his throne; Yisui took a breath.

"May I speak, my husband?" she asked.

He turned towards her. "You may."

"The Khan will cross lofty mountains and wide rivers," she said. "Those who have offended him will be drowned in blood, and the weeping of their wives and daughters will be a song to his ears." She could stop there, and say no more. He was smiling, but his eyes had narrowed.

"Yet every man," she continued, "even the greatest of men, is mortal."

The murmurs died; the lute-players lapsed into silence. Yisui could not turn back now. "I can hardly bear to speak of this," she said, "but if the great tree falls, what will happen to the birds nesting in its limbs? Where will they fly if there's no one to lead them? You have four noble and brave sons, but which of them will be your heir? This question isn't mine alone, but that of all your subjects. We beg to know your will."

His eyes were like stones. He would punish her for speaking of his death, for casting such a shadow over the coming campaign.

"I don't welcome these words," he said softly.

The blood drained from her face. He would not punish her here, but would let her wait, fearing what he might do.

"But you have spoken bravely, Yisui," he went on. "My brothers, my sons, even Borchu and Mukhali haven't dared to ask me this."

Yisui swayed dizzily. She would be spared.

"My Yasa decrees that a kuriltai must choose the next Khan," Temujin said, "but my Noyans should know my will." Jochi and Chagadai watched him intently. "You are my oldest son, Jochi. What do you have to say?"

Jochi opened his mouth; Chagadai suddenly jumped to his feet. "Why are you turning to him?"

"Father asked me to speak!" Jochi shouted.

"What's Jochi?" Chagadai bellowed. "Only a bastard you found in Merkit lands. He doesn't deserve the throne!"

Bortai's large brown eyes filled with shock and rage. Jochi leaped up and grabbed Chagadai by the collar. "You have no right to call me a bastard!" Jochi shouted. "You're no better than I am – I challenge you now! Show me you're a better archer, and I'll cut off my own thumb! If you can pin me in wrestling, I won't rise from the ground!"

Chagadai sneered. "How well you fight with words. You're no braver than the piss-scented jackal who sired you, who ran from Father's armies – "

Jochi's fist caught him on the jaw. Chagadai fell across a table, scattering dishes, then rolled to his feet. His hands were around Jochi's throat as Mukhali bounded towards him and seized his arms. Borchu climbed on to another table and launched himself at Jochi, knocking the big man to the floor. The Khan's two sons bellowed curses as the generals struggled to restrain them. Yisui watched as the four wrestled amid shattered plates and spilled food.

"Stop!" Mukhali shouted; his arms were locked around Chagadai. "Chagadai, you've always upheld the law. Does it tell you to fight with your brother?"

"Does the law say a bastard should rule?"

Jochi hissed. Borchu gripped Jochi's big shoulders tightly. "Listen to me!" Borchu cried. "I rode with your father when we were boys, when all the tribes fought one another and there was no safety anywhere. Jochi, will you bring those times back? Chagadai, will you demean the mother who gave you life?"

Jochi stopped struggling. Chagadai glared at him, his lips drawn back from his teeth. Bortai's face was pale as she gazed up at her husband; Temujin was silent. He would punish his sons, Yisui thought, and then her for bringing this about.

"Your father shed blood for us," Borchu continued, "and fought for us, even when he had no pillow but his arm and nothing to drink except his own spittle. And your mother stayed at his side, and gave you food when her own belly was empty. Didn't you and Jochi come from the same womb? How can you insult the noble woman who gave birth to you?"

Temujin lifted his hand; everyone turned towards him. "Chagadai," he said softly, "Jochi is my oldest son, and I forbid you to say otherwise."

Chagadai's lip curled. "He is my brother – I'll admit that much, but no more."

Jochi got up and started towards him; Borchu held him back. "This is a fine display of brotherly feeling," Mukhali shouted as he grabbed one of Chagadai's braids. "I've seen more love among jackals fighting over a rotting carcass."

"Silence," Temujin said then. "It seems I have to tell you again what you should know. A shaft of arrows tied together can't be broken. An arrow by itself is easily bent. If you ever raise your hands against each other again, you will lose your strength." He was still speaking softly, but his voice filled the great tent. "When I was alone and friendless, and had only my brothers at my side, one of them stole from me, fought with me, and claimed my place for his own. Jackals soon gnawed his bones."

Chagadai tensed; Jochi's big body trembled. Yisui knew the Khan meant it, that he would kill even his own sons if they threatened the unity of his ulus. A man who would not shrink from that could easily crush a wife whose question had brought such violence to his court.

Chagadai glanced at his older brother, then drew himself up. "We are your oldest sons," Chagadai said, grimacing as he spoke. "It's clear now that the Noyans couldn't choose either of us. I couldn't offer my vow to him, and he'll never offer his to me, but we are bound to serve our father the Khan and whoever follows him." He looked towards Ogedei and Tolui. "Ogedei is your third son. Let us agree on him."

"Is this also your wish, Jochi?" Temujin asked.

Jochi hung his head. "My younger brother has spoken for me. If I can't be Khan, at least I won't have to bow to him." He shuddered as he gazed towards the throne. "I meant to say that I'll serve Ogedei willingly."

"You'll both offer your oaths to him?" the Khan said. The two brothers nodded. "Take care that you don't forget them. I am going to give you both the people who once served Altan and Khuchar. When you look at them, I want you to remember what happened to their chiefs when they forgot their oaths to me." He leaned back against his throne. "The earth is vast. Your pastures will be wide, and your camps far apart – you'll have no need to fight among yourselves. Honour Ogedei as the Great Khan, and you may rule the lands I'll win for you."

Chagadai and Jochi stumbled back to their cushions. The Khan's face softened as he gazed at Ogedei. Yisui could rest more easily; the soft-hearted Ogedei would see that she and Yisugen were not parted if the Khan fell in Khwarezm.

"Well, Ogedei," Temujin said, "your brothers want you as Khan, and I find myself in agreement with them. What do you have to say for yourself?"

Ogedei straightened. His strong face and pale eyes were much like his father's, but his smile was quicker, his eyes gentler. "What can I say?" He lifted his cup, spilling a few drops of wine. "Can I refuse to obey my father? I'll do the best I can. If my sons and grandsons grow so lazy that their arrows can't hit the broadside of an elk, then another of your descendants can succeed them." A few men chuckled. "I've got nothing more to say."

"Then it's my wish that the Noyans choose you." The Khan paused. "Tolui, you'll speak now."

"I'll stay by Ogedei," Tolui said in his loud, boyish voice. "I'll be the whip that reminds him of what he forgets. I'll fight at his side in every battle."

"Very well," Temujin muttered. "All of you will remember

what's been said today." He glanced at Yisui; he was still watching her when the others resumed their feasting.

"Ogedei was always your favourite," Bortai said as she thrust a garment into a chest. "You might have made your choice right after Yisui spoke." She picked up a robe. "She was brave to say what she did."

"Her concern for herself fed her courage," Temujin said from the bed. "Yisui is a bit too quick to anticipate my end – I must pay her back for that sometime." He propped a cushion under his head. "My advisers have told me of wise men in Khitai who know the secret of prolonging life. I plan to summon one such sage. Let us hope a long time passes before my son follows me to the throne."

Bortai reached for another robe. "Put that aside," he said, "and come to bed."

She closed the trunk and walked towards him. "I'm angry with you, Temujin." She said it softly, so that the slaves sleeping by the doorway would not hear. "You could have kept Jochi and Chagadai from fighting by making your decree earlier. You let Chagadai shame me, to say openly what others only whisper. You might have said you wanted Ogedei on the throne. You wanted that all along. I saw that when you agreed to it so quickly."

"It was better for Chagadai to say it." He folded his arms across his chest. "I knew he'd object when I turned to Jochi. I couldn't choose Chagadai without showing that what people whisper about Jochi is the truth, and to choose either of them would only have divided my ulus. But now it's settled, and it was Chagadai who offered to give up his claim, and Jochi agreed with him." He squinted up at her. "I knew that they might also settle the argument with a fight, and Jochi's burly enough to have broken Chagadai's back. He would have had to die for killing one of my sons. That would have settled it, too."

"How wise you are, Temujin," Bortai said. "I wonder how your people could manage without you."

"Perhaps they won't have to if that sage of Khitai yields his secrets to me, but Ogedei will do well enough. He's well liked by the men and has his wife Doregene to advise him – she's ambitious enough for herself to see that he holds the throne. And Tolui will protect his brother from any who try to take advantage of Ogedei's kindliness."

He thought he would outlive them all; that was why he had forgiven Yisui for her question. But the mighty oak would fall in time, however many nations sat under its leafy limbs.

"I'll tell Temuge and Khasar to consult you often while I'm away," he said, "and to listen to your advice."

"They would do well enough without it."

"They'll do better with it. Are you hoping I'll take you with me on this campaign?"

"I have no such hopes." She took off her robe and let it fall to the floor. "I'm content to be as far from this war as possible." She turned away to remove her head-dress, grateful for the dim light. A loose grey braid fell over her chest; her long tunic hid her sagging breasts and the belly and hips marked by thin white lines. "I'd rather you stayed here, and let your generals fight for you, but you aren't yet an old man who could be happy sitting by the fire and telling stories." She finished undressing and climbed into bed, pulling the blanket to her chin. "You're looking forward to this war."

"I did everything I could to avoid it."

"I know the truth. You held back only to see what the spirits willed. Now you're forced to fight this war, and will have to wait before you ride against the Kin, but you don't truly regret that. Wars against new enemies renew your life."

He said, "A man savours life more when all his enemies are dead."

"Of course. Once you had so many against you that I didn't know how you could survive. Now I don't think you could live without enemies to fight."

His arm slipped around her. "You sound like an old woman, Bortai."

She sighed. "I am an old woman."

104

KULGAN'S HORSE STREAKED ahead of hers. Khulan brushed her whip against her horse's neck as her son raced towards the riverbank. The boy skidded to a halt; his white gelding reared.

Khulan slowed to a trot and rode towards him. The horses danced under them as she reached out to touch her son's cheek; he shied away from her.

They turned away from the river. Riders were moving towards the camp, the Khan among them. On the flat grassland beyond Khulan's camping circle, two teams of boys flailed at an animal carcass with poles. The carcass flew from one pole and landed several paces from the battling boys; they raced after it. Kulgan had wanted to spend the day with them, even though he had been away grazing the horses for nearly a month.

She thought of how he had trailed after her when he was small, how he had beamed at her when he brought her fuel. The slaves would treat him to bits of freshly baked bread made of wheat from Khitai; their affection for the boy had mirrored her own. The women were wary of him now, with his loud demands and threats of beatings for disobedience. He spent more time with his half-brothers and friends, away from her.

Kulgan reached up to adjust his head-band. He was short for his age, and would never be as tall as his father, but many said he was one of the most handsome of the Khan's sons. His cheekbones were sharp, his skin a golden brown; two thick black braids hung down from under his scarf. He had large amber eyes and broad shoulders; he often bragged that he could beat bigger boys at wrestling.

The Khan and the men with him had halted to watch the boys at their game. Temujin had not let her know he was coming to her ordu. Usually she was told that he would be with her; at other times, he simply appeared, occasionally when she was already asleep. In her bed, they did the things he had learned from some of his women. Khulan knew that he would enjoy having her resist him, so she did them without complaint.

Sometimes he hurt her, speaking of his love for her even as she cried out from the pain.

She had told herself that he would tire of a wife who could neither respond to him nor give him the pleasure of overpowering her. It had not turned out that way.

"Father must have come to say farewell," Kulgan said. "Everyone says he may be fighting in Khwarezm for years. I wonder – "

The Khan skirted the boys and rode towards them, leaving his men behind. Kulgan set off at a gallop; Khulan followed more slowly. Temujin stopped under a lone tree, and Kulgan reined in at his father's side. Their two white horses, both sired by the Khan's favourite stallion, circled each other; Temujin had given one to Kulgan a few months ago.

The two dismounted and sat down under the tree as Khulan approached. Temujin draped an arm over the boy's shoulders; her son's eyes were wide with awe.

"Are you better with the bow?" Temujin said to Kulgan.

"I shoot well enough."

"My sons should be the best archers. You might be a better one if you spent more time practising instead of at your mother's side."

Kulgan's cheeks reddened. "I was out herding until yesterday. I only went riding with Mother because she asked."

Once, he had gazed at Khulan with that wide-eyed admiration; such looks were only for his father now. "I'll leave you to talk," she said. "I should see to the cooking, so that you and your men are well fed this evening."

"You have servants and slaves for that," Temujin said. "You do enough of their work as it is. Sit with us."

She dismounted and sat next to her son. "You're thirteen, Kulgan," the Khan said.

"Nearly fourteen."

"I want you to come with me to Khwarezm." Kulgan gaped at his father. "You'll help herd the spare horses," Temujin continued. "You'll have a taste of war."

Kulgan grinned. "I'll show you how well I can fight."

Khulan lowered her eyes. She had known this day would come, but he did not have to look so happy at leaving her, at going off to kill and fight. He might be a man by the time she saw him again, hardened by battle. She had wanted to believe it could be otherwise, but those hopes were nearly gone. She had seen the Khitan scholars, who preferred their scrolls to weapons, and had thought her son might become such a man. If she could have kept him from war a little longer –

She touched Kulgan's arm; he shook off her hand. "You had better prepare yourself," Temujin said, "by practising your archery. Ride to my men and show them what you can do. I want to hear them praise your aim by supper time."

"I'll do well." Kulgan jumped up and hurried to his horse. "I promise I won't miss the target once!" he shouted as he rode away.

Temujin rested his back against the tree. "He'll keep that vow," he said. "He has a strong spirit. Even his mother's reins haven't overly tamed him."

"He's your son, Temujin." He would follow the Khan anywhere, as all the men would, as Nayaga did.

He drew away her scarf and cupped her face in his hands. "My beautiful Khulan." Whenever she sat next to him at court, he would reach for her hand or draw her closer to him. The men sang songs and recited poems about the Khan and his beloved Khulan, and of how her love for him was as great as his for her. How could it not be, since he was the greatest of men?

"I'll miss Kulgan," she said.

"You won't miss him. I won't be deprived of my favourite wife during a war that may be long. You'll come with me, Khulan." He smiled at her, but there was a trace of malice in his eyes. "What do you say? Aren't you pleased?"

"I've always obeyed you," she said. "I have never asked you for anything."

"When have you needed to ask? Your tents are filled with riches I won for you, and you couldn't count your herds. I've given you much, and it's no more to you than a clod of dirt. Perhaps it's time you saw the effort that pays for your comfort more closely."

"Please – "

He gripped her chin tightly. "I want your household with

me, and you as my chief wife in Khwarezm, and you scorn the honour. This courtship has gone on too long, Khulan. I love you more than I've loved any woman, yet there's no fire in you for me. I no longer care how I rouse it, whether it's love or hate that fuels it. You'll come with me, and you will never be far from my side. You'll see your son become a warrior."

He knew how much she would hate that. She should have known that he would not leave her behind, to do what she could to comfort the captives whose tears and suffering brought him such joy. He would force her into the midst of deeds she had heard about largely at a distance. He would have his victory over her by breaking her indifference to him.

He would enjoy watching her cry, having her plead with him. "If it's your will," she said, "then I must go."

105

THE HORSEMEN WERE locusts on the land. They breathed fire and drank blood; so said the peasants who had streamed through Bukhara's gates. The refugees had taken shelter in the rabat, the suburb and pleasure gardens that bordered the main city, with the invaders at their heels. Now the enemy was surrounding Bukhara itself.

Zulaika, hidden by a trellis, peered through the vines and listened as the men with her father talked. "The enemy's army is great," one man was saying, "but their numbers are swelled by their captives, who are driven to the front to take the first blows."

Only a short time ago, word had reached them of the fall of Otrar. The border city had been besieged for months. Her father had believed it would stand, but it had been taken, and its governor Inalchik, according to rumour, was executed by having molten silver poured into his eyes and ears. Now the barbarians had come to Bukhara.

"A man told me that Sighnagh was taken," another man said. "Can this be the same army that rode there?"

"They must have divided their forces," one of Zulaika's brothers muttered. "That could make it easier to push them back. The Shah, may he be blessed, has divided his as well, to protect the cities."

"He might have done better," a wine merchant said, "to have thrown them all against the savages at the start."

"We can withstand a siege," her father said. "The garrison in the citadel will protect us, God willing."

The slaves sitting with Zulaika were silent. The garden was peaceful, untouched by whatever was happening outside. The turbaned men visiting her father Karim lolled on their cushions near the marble fountain, looking much as they always had. Her father seemed more concerned about the trade he might lose during a prolonged siege than with the battle itself. If God willed it, the horsemen would tire of the siege and content themselves with ravaging the countryside.

The men murmured among themselves, and then her two brothers and the other guests made their farewells. Usually they stayed longer, until the shadows lengthened under the trees and the evening call to prayer was heard from the Friday mosque. They seemed anxious to return to their homes, to assure themselves that all was well there.

"Buy what food you can," her father Karim was saying. "The price is already higher than it was a day ago." She knew then that he was more fearful than he seemed.

Outside the seven-gated wall surrounding the shahristan, the centre of Bukhara, and the twelve-gated wall enclosing the rabat lay the citadel, with its many towers and a wall nearly a mile around. The enemy attacked the citadel for three days, hurling stones from catapults and storming its walls. The thousands of Turkish mercenaries inside withstood the assault.

Then, after the third day, most of the garrison fled from the citadel under cover of night, perhaps to make a stand elsewhere with other troops, perhaps out of fear.

Zulaika's brother Aziz carried this news to her father, but his slaves had heard it earlier, in the streets. Karim was preparing to leave the house when the two men arrived.

"A few hundred are still in the citadel," Aziz said.

"We can't fight with so few," Karim replied. "The enemy will storm the shahristan itself, and we won't be able to hold them back. It's said the enemy spares those who surrender."

Her brother pulled at his beard. "A surrender to such men may cost us too much."

"A battle with so few to defend us will cost even more," her father said. "I go now to meet with the imams and others to see if we can buy ourselves some mercy."

One of the slave girls behind the trellis moaned. Zulaika twisted her fingers around the vines.

Karim returned to the house only to sleep. By morning, he left with the delegation that would offer the jewel of Bukhara to the enemy.

Karim did not come back in the evening. The servants of the household whispered of the terms of surrender and the horsemen who would enter the city tomorrow. Zulaika slept uneasily, wondering what they would demand.

She awoke to silence. Usually, from her bedroom, she could hear the sounds of the women and boys going about their morning work. She dressed hastily and went from room to room, finding no one. The garden was empty; even her father's new concubine and the boy who sometimes shared his bed had vanished.

In her thirteen years of life, she had never left this house alone. While her mother was alive, Zulaika had accompanied her to the bazaar, and since her death, had gone there with a boy and a female slave, as carefully veiled as herself. Even alone, she might be safer in the street now. She could hear the sounds of crowds beyond the gate. Enemy soldiers might come to the house to loot it, to dig for whatever gold her father had buried.

Zulaika veiled her face, covered herself in a long black chador, then went to the gate. She had barely closed it when she was caught in the press of bodies thronging the street and carried forward. They moved past houses and gardens towards

575

the shops that stood near the Friday mosque. A shout rose from the crowd; over the veiled and turbaned heads, she glimpsed a row of raised lances.

The throng suddenly parted. She heard screams and was forced to one side of the street as people pushed around her. Horsemen trotted down the stony street; their faces had dark, narrow eyes, skin as brown as leather, flat noses, and long thin moustaches that drooped from their upper lips. Their bodies were so thickset that they seemed deformed; there was nothing human in them.

She wanted to run back to her house, but the people around her pushed forward until she was within sight of the mosque's golden domes. Other horsemen were looting the shops, throwing carpets, copper pots, and other goods into the street. More horsemen rode towards the mosque from the gate of Ibrahim. A man at the head of these riders shouted words in his outlandish speech at the mullahs outside the mosque.

"The Great Khan asks," a man near the enemy said, "if this is the palace of the Shah Muhammad."

"It is not," a mullah replied. "It is a holy place, the House of God."

"There is no grazing for our horses in the countryside. The Khan orders that they be fed."

Zulaika watched in horror as the horsemen rode through the mosque's entrance. Some of the veiled women near her tried to get away, only to be herded towards the mosque's wall. She struggled to stay on her feet, afraid she might be trampled if she fell. Barbarians spilled into the mosque; horsemen lashed at the crowd. Zulaika was pushed towards the entrance and stumbled through it with the others.

The courtyard was filled with men and horses. Helmeted warriors grabbed at women, tearing away their veils and chadors. Zulaika ducked as a brown hand grabbed at her. Men in the white turbans of imams wailed as jewelled cases were heaped with grain and put before the horses. Scrolls were scattered across the tiles. God would punish them for this, for desecrating the mosque and casting the Holy Korans to the ground. Turbaned scholars were being forced to carry grain to the horses while others bore jars of wine to the barbarians.

A hand clutched at her chador and ripped the garment from her. Zulaika caught at her veil, lost it, and pushed past knots of people until she was near the pulpit. The man who had led the horsemen there climbed the steps to the lectern, followed by two other men, then turned to face the mob in the courtyard. He lifted an arm; the noise faded until she heard only choked sobs and the whinnies of the horses.

The man began to speak in his harsh tongue. With his broad shoulders and bowed legs, he was like the other creatures, but his eyes were the greenish-yellow ones of a cat. Another barbarian stood near him, along with a bearded man who might have been one of her own people, although he wore a breastplate and helmet like the enemy's.

The pale-eyed man was silent; the thick-bearded man spoke then. "The Great Khan speaks these words to you," he called out, "and to all of Bukhara, which has now opened its gates to him. You are a people that has committed great sins, and the greatest among you have sinned the most. Look at me, and know what I am. I am God's punishment for your sins, and the proof of this is that I have been sent against you. You have no defence against the power of God."

It had to be true, Zulaika thought wildly; God had abandoned them. She was suddenly pushed towards the steps. A hand grabbed her by the wrist, dragging her up to the pulpit; she shrieked as a yellow-eyed face loomed over her. The courtyard rang with the songs of barbarians and the screams of women. The man threw her down and pushed her robes up to her hips. The weight of him crushed her against the tiled platform as pain tore at her insides. An evil spirit had claimed her; there was no one to protect her. Her soul had entered the dark realm of punishment.

The Scourge of God and his minions celebrated until the sun was high above the courtyard. The learned men of Bukhara brought more wine to the barbarians and set grain before the horses in cases that had once held the scrolls of the Koran. The singing girls of the city were forced to dance before the Great Khan's soldiers hurled themselves upon them. Zulaika sat at the Khan's feet; whenever she moved, his hand caught her by the hair and jerked her back. He had forced her twice, and her clothes were spotted with blood. Now he laughed and drank, apparently content to watch the debauches of his men.

Her shame should have killed her. She wondered dimly if her father and brothers were in the courtyard, witnesses to her wretchedness. A foot caught her in the side; the Khan was on his feet, striding towards the steps where a horse was brought to him; he mounted and rode through the milling crowd.

The horsemen were leaving the mosque. Zulaika was shoved down the steps as the crowd was pushed towards the arch of the entrance. She followed the mob passively. It no longer mattered what became of her; she was only another soul condemned to suffer for the sins of her people.

Near the gate of Ibrahim, the Khan ordered all the wealthy men of Bukhara to yield their possessions to him, and then the people of the city were commanded to leave it with nothing but the clothes they wore. They were herded through the gate and past the canals that fed the gardens of the rabat, until they came to the plain. Dust had darkened the sun, making the plain seem red as blood. Those who left the city spent the night on the plain, surrounded by their captors.

The soldiers left in the citadel held out behind their high wall. By morning, smoke and flames rose from the high ground where the central city stood. The resistance of those still brave enough to fight, to hide behind walls and then attack the looting savages, had only condemned Bukhara. Catapults hurled stones at the walls until only mounds of brick and earth were left. Men and boys – merchants and scholars, imams and slaves – were driven towards the citadel and forced to fill in the moats, where the bodies of those who fell soon clogged the waterways. Flaming pots flew over the wall at the citadel's defenders; after five days, the citadel fell. The heads of the defenders were heaped in front of the levelled wall. Bukhara was a smoking ruin, its canals flowing blood.

Zulaika waited with the crowds of captives and watched her city die. Barbarians moved among them, taking some prisoners off to be slaughtered and others to their tents. Scraps of food were thrown to the captives and they scrambled for jugs of water while the soldiers laughed. Women wailed as their children were torn from them; girls screamed as they were dragged off by groups of soldiers.

She did not know what had happened to her father and brothers. They might have been among the men tortured into confessing where they had hidden their wealth; they might have hidden in the shahristan only to be consumed by fire; they might have met their deaths in the citadel's moats. Better, she told herself, if they were dead, so that they would never know of the devils who used her, then threw her back into the midst of other ravaged women and girls. Better if their suffering was at an end.

Several days after the Wind of God's Wrath had swept through the gates of Bukhara, the horde took down their tents, gathered up their plunder, and moved east along the Zerafshan River towards Samarkand, driving their captives before them. The old, the injured, the dying, and the weak were left behind, those whom they did not want or who would be useless in besieging Samarkand. The green land that once marked the flourishing oasis was grazed nearly bare; the canals leading to the city, with no one to tend their locks, were drying up. The horde had cut down trees to build siege towers, and their horses had trampled the flower gardens. The ruins of Bukhara smouldered; only the stone walls of its public buildings, a few minarets, and scarred domes stripped of their gold showed where the city had once stood.

Zulaika was one of those left behind. Vultures picked at the bodies strewn across the plain; others perched on hills of heads. A child, a girl already nearly blind from years of labour as a carpetmaker's slave, her small body ravaged by barbarians, crawled to Zulaika's side and died in her arms.

After covering the girl's body with sand, Zulaika sat by the river, ignoring the survivors who passed her. Some were walking back to the city, although they would find little there. A few stopped near her, told her they were going to seek shelter in an outlying village, and begged her to come with them. She refused to answer and stared past them until they moved on.

For three days, she wandered along the river, her only food

bits of rotting melon in the devastated gardens. She slept on the river-bank wrapped in a chador taken from a woman's body. Death would come for her soon: with nothing to eat, the cold night winds chilling her, and drifting sand threatening to bury her by morning, there was almost no life left in her.

When the fire of the sun flamed in the east, she saw a dark mass moving across the land. Zulaika propped herself against a tree stump, but was too weak to stand. She gazed north-east at the apparition, waiting for it to vanish; instead, the mass grew until she could see wagons and camels, horses and other beasts, and riders carrying the standards of the invaders.

One of them might take pity, and end her suffering with his sword. As the horde came closer, she saw large tents on wagons hovering above the dust. The sky darkened; she fell into a black pit, hearing the shrieks of other condemned souls before the silence swallowed her.

She opened her eyes. She had to be dead, but felt dirt under the palms of her hands and water against her lips. Several creatures stood around her with square, elongated heads; devils had come for her. An arm was around her, holding her up; she stared into a woman's face.

The woman whispered a few words. Zulaika shook her head, then saw that the other creatures were also women, with high square head-dresses decorated with feathers; their small dark eyes peered at her from above white veils. Two men with them held bows, their arrows trained on her.

The woman holding her spoke sharply to the others; the men lowered their bows. Leave me, Zulaika tried to say, but the words did not come. The stranger's large brown eyes searched her face.

A young man wearing a turban was suddenly pushed towards her; the woman murmured to him. He nodded, then knelt as Zulaika drew the edge of her chador across her face.

"The Khatun says you will be safe now," he said. "Do you understand? You'll be carried to her cart. When the animals have been watered, you will come with us."

Let me die, she thought as arms reached for her.

106

THE TRADERS FROM Khwarezm had often spoken of the beauty of their land. As Khulan followed in the wake of Temujin's army, she saw little of that beauty. A few walls and monuments of skulls were all that remained in some towns and villages; their only inhabitants now were black birds. Sand drifted over the yellowing grass that bordered drying channels; the desert would reclaim this land.

Khulan's wagons followed a trail of bodies. Occasionally she saw people who had survived. Sometimes they hid among the ruins; more often they stood and watched her pass, seemingly waiting to die.

A few towns still stood, those that had surrendered without any resistance, but even there, the fields were ravaged. Temujin had spared Samarkand, but a mound of heads stood outside the burned walls of its citadel. Those in the citadel's garrison had been the first to surrender, but the Khan did not trust Turkish mercenaries who fought for the Shah's gold; he had executed them all. Samarkand had been looted, and thousands of its craftsmen were captives, following the Mongol army or making the long journey to the Khan's homeland, but the city had survived.

Khulan's wagons held copper vases and cups taken from Bukhara, along with the carpets that city had produced. Her trunks were filled with brightly coloured silks and cottons, silvery fabrics, and jars of wine and oil looted from Samarkand. Grain from the cities fed her animals; round fruits called melons, with succulent flesh inside a hard rind, fed her. Khwarezmian slaves helped tend her herds, prepare her meals, and care for her possessions. She did not want any of this booty, but the slaves might have been killed if she had not accepted them. So she told herself, while feeling that Temujin had won a victory over her by forcing her to take her share of plunder.

"You will never be far from my side." Her husband had kept that promise.

In some of the places where people still lived, Khulan had left what she could for them – a trunk of clothing, a cow, baskets of grain. Kulgan mocked her for that, echoing his father when he told her that she was only prolonging their futile struggle for life. Her small acts of mercy ended when her son rode back with other young men to one wretched village to reclaim what she had left and to have some sport with the people there.

After that, Khulan turned to bringing some of the survivors with her. One of the first was a young girl she had found outside the ruins of Bukhara, a starved creature with round dark eyes. The other women called her The Mute, since she never spoke, but Khulan knew that she had a voice; she had heard her choked sobs in the night, and her sharp cries when she started from sleep. Temujin had let her keep The Mute; he enjoyed seeing the girl's lovely face grow ashen and her eyes widen with terror whenever he was inside Khulan's tent.

He had not been so kind to others she found. One girl was thrown to some of his men for their amusement. Another was given to Kulgan; she remembered the sound of the girl's weeping as her son dragged her to his tent. She never knew what her husband would decree for those she tried to save, and The Mute's sad eyes told Khulan that her mercy had brought the girl no peace. She no longer searched the oases and deserts for people to rescue.

After Samarkand's surrender, the Khan made camp south of the city, where green grassland shaded by trees offered grazing for the horses. By autumn, when Temujin's wing of the army moved on to Termez, the land was grazed clean. The people of Termez had made the mistake of holding out; the town was taken and levelled, its people led out to be killed. Temujin gave Khulan pearls from Termez, taken, so he claimed, from the belly of an old woman. Some of Termez's people, it was rumoured, had swallowed their jewels; the Khan had ordered his men to slit open the bellies of the dead.

Even with his victories, the slightest setback could rouse Temujin's wrath. He laughed and sang with his men when they celebrated, but brooded after they left his side. The Shah still eluded him, and Khulan had thought that was the cause of his black moods and his savagery. Shah Muhammad had fled from his capital of Urgenj towards Balkh, then south-west to Khoras-

582

san, Jebe and Subotai at his heels. She had assumed that tales of arguments between Chagadai and Jochi also troubled him, even that her husband longed for his homeland.

Yet none of this was enough to account for the emptiness she often saw in his eyes. His dark mood lifted only when he rode out to rejoin his forces; his only joy now was in war.

She had glimpsed this void in him before, the last time he had come back from Khitai. He had stared at his loot – the painted cups, delicate jade carvings, the scrolls for his Khitan advisers that he could not read himself – with a bewildered, haunted expression. The void inside Temujin seemed to increase the more he won; he toyed with his spoils as if uncertain of what to do with them. Khulan did not know what caused the hollowness in his soul, but realized at last that he wanted his enemies to share his emptiness.

Understanding that made her pity him, while a part of her felt it was just for him to suffer. He would scorn her pity, although he might also be pleased that she felt even that much for him. She was no longer indifferent to him.

107

"THAT REPORT WAS true." Borchu sat down and wiped the dust from his face. "Urgenj still stands. The men were thrown back when we last tried to storm the walls. Over two thousand died on the bridge, and more in the streets."

Temujin glowered at him. "You didn't have to ride here to tell me that."

"Your two oldest sons bear much of the blame."

"I didn't need to hear that, either."

The mute girl from Bukhara set a jar of wine near Temujin, then scurried to the darkest part of the tent. Khulan knew the girl understood more of the Mongol tongue; she followed the orders Khulan gave her, but remained silent. Her despairing face spoke, saying that every visit of the Khan's tormented her.

583

He might demand that she share his bed, or give her to Kulgan; Khulan had heard the screams of girls from her son's tent and the silence that often seemed worse than the screaming. The Khan might leave her behind when they moved on. So far, he had done nothing, but the girl always had to fear that he would.

"Your sons asked me to come to you," Borchu said, "and I knew only you could settle this. Jochi won't speak to Chagadai, and Chagadai wants to take command. The spirit of the men isn't being helped by their dispute. Chagadai says Jochi's disobeying you by refusing to do what's necessary to take Urgenj. Jochi wants to save all he can, since the city is in the lands you promised to him."

Temujin shook his head. "Then you'll say this to both of them. They are to follow Ogedei's orders, and you'll tell Ogedei that Urgenj is to be taken even if he has to burn it to the ground."

Borchu nodded, finished his wine, then stood up. "Ogedei won't fail you."

"I know." The Khan looked up at his old friend. "Stay a while, Borchu. My wife can hear of how you helped me to steal my horses back."

"The Khatun's heard the tale many times before, and each time, our arrows find more of the thieves." The lines deepened around Borchu's eyes. "I should start back, Temujin. The discipline of the men gets worse every day. They'll be heartened by your order."

The Khan nodded. "A safe ride to you, Nokor."

Borchu left the tent. The winter wind howled, shaking the tent's walls. Temujin stared towards the side of the tent where The Mute sat with two other slaves; the girl's hands fluttered to her throat. He gazed at her for a long time, and then his mouth grew slack; he had tired of that amusement.

"Send them away," Temujin said. Khulan dismissed the slaves as her husband prepared for bed. "My sons." He stretched out and covered himself with the blanket. "Tolui is the greatest of warriors, but if all the world submitted to us, he wouldn't know what to do with himself. Ogedei has the talent to rule, but also has a talent for enjoying what he wins. He'll be a good Khan if he doesn't drink himself into an early grave. Chagadai thinks of my Yasa as a whip to beat men with rather than as reins to guide their actions, and Jochi hates me for not giving him the throne he thinks he deserves. Those are my heirs, Khulan. I could have done much worse, but I might have done better – not that you care about any of that." He sighed. "I must hope that the sage from Khitai brings me the elixir of life, and then perhaps – "

She stripped to her shift, then sat down on the bed to comb out her braids with her fingers. Ever since his campaigns in Khitai, he liked seeing her hair loose around her shoulders and back, the way the women of that land wore theirs in his bed.

"Your son hasn't caused me to worry," he said. "I'm going to make Kulgan a captain of one hundred when we move against Balkh. The boy did well at Termez. There he was, with over a hundred he had captured, and he ordered them all to tie one another's hands so he would have less trouble executing them. One man tried to escape, but when Kulgan took his head, the rest were cowed. He dispatched them all by himself."

She had heard the story from Kulgan. Most of the men had such stories, of prisoners who might have run away kneeling to offer their necks to the sword.

"You should look happier, Khulan. Our son has done better than I expected."

Her heart throbbed painfully as she lay down next to him. He reached for her and buried his face in her hair.

A shriek awoke her. Khulan sat up, clutching at the blanket. A guard shouted, but the wind drowned out his words.

"I'll speak to my father!" That was Khojin's voice. Feet drummed against the steps leading up to the tent's platform, and as Temujin lifted his head, his daughter burst into the tent.

Khojin wore a leather breastplate and a helmet, as she did even when she stayed in the rear with the other women. Toguchar's Hawk had remained in the Khan's camp while her husband followed Jebe and Subutai through to Khorassan. The Khan had given the order; a skirmish was one thing, but having his daughter in the forefront of a siege was another. Khojin dropped her bowcase to the left of the doorway, then stumbled towards the bed; her wild, handsome face was streaked with tears.

"What are you doing here?" Temujin asked.

"My husband has fallen!" Khojin cried. "An arrow took his life at Nishapur!" She threw herself across the bed and sobbed. Khulan huddled against a cushion; the Khan gripped Khojin's shoulder.

"I am sorry," Temujin said at last. "He was one of my best generals."

"I was his luck!" Khojin wailed as she sat back on her heels. "I was his shield in battle, the hawk that caught his enemies in her talons, and I wasn't there to protect him! Now the army has withdrawn, and that cursed town still stands!"

Temujin took her hand. "It will fall," he muttered. "Tolui will avenge your husband. Dry your tears, daughter. We'll hold a feast for him, and I'll make the sacrifices myself, and then you must think of your children."

Khojin pressed her face against his chest; he held her until her weeping subsided. "What do you want?" he asked. "I can order Tolui to give you the greatest share of what's taken from Nishapur when it falls. Or, if you wish, you may begin the long journey home. Maybe the sight of our land will ease your sorrow."

Khojin looked up. "I don't want Nishapur's riches, and my husband would despise me for leaving before he's avenged."

"Then what is it you want?" her father asked.

Khojin said, "I want the city." Her lips drew back from her teeth. "I want nothing to live where my husband fell."

"That won't bring him back," Khulan said. They turned to look at her with their yellowish eyes, the same cold emptiness in them both.

"The Khan my father will say what he wants," Khojin whispered. "A weak woman who indulges in pity won't decide this for him. Your pity would vanish fast enough if your son met his – "

"You've said enough, Khojin," the Khan said.

"It's your doing that I wasn't with him," his daughter replied. "He would have taken me along, but I wouldn't have him risk punishment for disobeying you. All my life, what I wanted most was to fight for you — for you, Father, not just for my husband. You tethered his hawk, and now he's gone."

Temujin said, "You should have been my son."

Khojin's eyes glittered with a fierce joy before tears filled them once again. "This is my decree," he continued. "You may follow Tolui, but you're not to interfere with his decisions. You'll keep to the rear — I don't wish my grandchildren to lose both their parents. But you will decide Nishapur's fate. Tolui will be told that."

Khojin kissed his hands as she wept. "That's all I ask."

"Leave us, child. We'll hold a feast for your husband's spirit tomorrow."

Khojin left them. Khulan was about to lie down when Temujin's hand clamped down on her arm. "Speak to me, wife," he muttered. "I know what you're thinking. Tell me why those souls in Nishapur shouldn't be dispatched to serve my daughter's husband."

"The city may surrender," she said, "if the people believe they'll be spared. That would cost you less than taking it. Some of your men would be lost in a siege."

"They'll do as Tolui commands. His men know he won't be careless with their lives, or risk them needlessly."

"But some will be lost. Enough have died already."

"They will do their duty." His fingers dug into her. "I hear nothing but pity in your voice. Your pity's useless — it only makes those you pity suffer more." He drew in his breath. "I think I might be at peace if the world were empty of people, if they no longer scarred the land with their cities and their walls."

"How heartless you are, Temujin."

"Heartless? Do you think our enemies would have left us in peace? Had we been weaker, they would have taken our lands and put us behind their walls." He paused. "The Khitan Ch'u-ts'ai tells me a ruler can win more by sparing the cities and allowing their people to labour for him. Mahmoud Yalavach and his son speak of levies and taxes, and Barchukh talks of all that the caravans can bring to us, but there's a danger in that. If we ever forget what we are, and find such ways more pleasing than our own, we'll lose everything we've taken.

587

There's much to learn from the conquered, and yet we might be safer if we destroyed them."

He was silent for a moment, then said, "I wouldn't want everyone to die. I would sorrow at the loss of my comrades, my sons, my beautiful Khulan." His fingers were a vise. "I was sent against Hsi-Hsia and Khitai, and saw that it wasn't enough to take what we needed, that Tengri meant me to rule there. I thought that the Shah Muhammad would submit to me, but I deceived myself. I allowed myself to be tempted by thoughts of peace, and that was foolish. Heaven wants me to live until I've won the world – it must be – "

His throat moved as he swallowed. His eyes moved restlessly; she saw a pain and desperation that shocked her. Perhaps, in spite of himself, he longed to turn back.

His eyes cleared. He pushed her against the cushion and crushed her mouth under his.

108

WHEN KHOJIN SAW a strip of green on the horizon, she knew that she was near Merv. The green land was an affront to the desert that surrounded it. The barren land through which she had ridden, with its black rocks, pale salt-flats, and sand so fine it ran through her fingers like water, was strangely comforting, a bleak landscape that mirrored her grief. Now she saw life.

She rode at the head of the procession with the men, trailed by her slaves and wagons. As she neared the fertile land of these oases, she noticed that the fields had been grazed nearly bare; deep ruts scarred the land and trees had been reduced to stumps. Beyond the blackened heaps and mud walls, a small Mongol force was camped.

A rider galloped to her and told her that Merv had surrendered several days ago. He rode at her side, speaking of how the people had been ordered to come out from behind the city's walls. Tolui, seated on a gilded throne looted from the city, had waited on the plain as the captives were led before him. The soldiers of Merv had died first, and then the people, divided among Tolui's men for execution. The man's dark brown face glowed with good humour as he mimicked the piteous cries of the doomed.

The hills she had seen at a distance turned out to be heaps of heads. There seemed to be thousands in each pile, each hill crowned by perching black birds. Tolui's army had moved on to the south-west.

The rider told Khojin of green fields and gardens, of a great mosque with a blue dome where a sultan had been buried, of shops filled with silks, cottons, copper pots, and woven fabrics. All she saw were ruined walls, piles of bricks, a long row of mounds over an underground channel of water, and a large dome blackened by fire. Sand had drifted over the pale green fields and ruined gardens; the man said that the underground canals were drying up. Tolui's army had destroyed the dam on the nearby river.

Khojin's spirits lifted at the sight of the destruction. Her brother's methods during his campaigns were familiar to her — savage punishment for even a show of resistance in the beginning, so that those he met later would be weakened by terror. Tolui would punish Toguchar's killers.

Scattered bodies marked the way to Nishapur. She urged the procession on, stopping only to sleep or when the sun grew red and winds raised the desert sands. She caught up with Tolui's rear forces at the edge of an oasis. Two of his men rode with her to Tolui's tent.

She passed horseherders and cavalry, camp-fires and tents, siege engineers from Khitai and wounded men being tended by comrades, until she caught sight of her brother's standard. In the distance, ballistas, hundreds of catapults, and siege towers stood around the walls of Nishapur. The plain between Tolui's camp and the city was a sea of men, many of them captives driven towards the city's moats and the ladders that had been thrown against the earthen walls. The dark sea rippled, then grew calm, as if waiting for a wind to move it.

Tolui was outside his tent, surrounded by men. She dismounted as he came towards her. "I've been waiting for you," he said grimly. "Nishapur has offered to submit – a delegation came to me this morning. They'll let us take what we want if we spare their lives and let the city stand. I told them they would have my answer soon."

Khojin gazed at him silently.

"Father said it was for you to decide," Tolui went on. "I can lead my men into Nishapur to claim our tribute, or I can send them against the walls."

Khojin's hand darted towards her knife; she lifted it above her head. "There can be no mercy for them," she called out. "Order the attack."

Tolui smiled. "Khojin, I've dishonoured you in my thoughts." His soft voice sounded much like their father's. "I believed you might shrink from punishing them in the end. May I be cursed if I ever doubt you again. Nishapur will be yours."

He spun around and shouted his commands.

Stones hurled from catapults battered the walls of Nishapur. The defenders answered with volleys of spears, arrows, and bricks from the walls and towers. During the night, the besiegers hurled flaming pots of naphtha over the walls and pushed prisoners forward to fill the moats. By morning, the moats were clogged with rocks, fallen trees, dirt, and bodies, and several breaches had been opened in the walls. Men carrying ladders swarmed over the filled moats and climbed through the breaches to open the gates. Soldiers fell; others took their places.

When Khojin, surrounded by soldiers, entered the city, her brother's men had been fighting inside for two days, taking Nishapur street by street. The defenders had fought hard, clearly knowing what was in store for them after Tolui rejected their surrender. They would pay for their resistance, for taking her husband's life.

Tolui was waiting for her in a large square near one gate, next to a platform on which his golden throne sat. He took her by the hand and led her to the throne. "The city is yours," he said. She barely heard his words over the screams and the roars of triumph echoing through the nearby streets.

Men fanned out around her, riding under the arches that bordered the square. Plumes of smoke rose above the roofs; Khojin gripped the arms of the throne as people were dragged before her. A baby dangled from the end of a curved lance, then fell at her feet, its blood spurting over her boots. A man's knife sliced at the throat of a red-haired woman; her body, nearly stripped of clothing, crumpled to the ground. A group of turbaned men wailed as swords slashed through them, streaking their garments with red. Soldiers hurled themselves upon shrieking women, pushed up their robes, and took them, one after another, until the women lay still and silent. Dogs and cats were spitted on spears and thrown against roofs and walls. Knots of people were herded into the square, forced to tie one another's wrists together, and then beheaded.

The man whose arrow had found Toguchar might be among them. Khojin prayed that he was, that he had seen his wife violated and his children gutted by swords, that he had suffered before meeting his own death.

The slaughter was still going on at nightfall. Tolui moved among the men, shouting orders. Torches were brought into the square, now filled with heaps of bodies and the stink of blood and rotting flesh. Khojin did not sleep, but remained on the throne, ignoring the aches of her body, listening to the useless pleas for mercy that sounded in the streets.

Towards dawn, when the distant screams were fainter, she slept, her head against the back of the throne, her hand in Tolui's. She awoke to see soldiers clearing bodies from the square, severing the heads before they cast the torsos aside. Tolui would make certain that no one escaped by lying down among the dead, as it was rumoured some had done at Merv.

The men laughed as they arranged the heads in the square. One mountain was made up of men's heads, another of women's, the third of children's. Khojin gazed at thousands of eyes, at faces frozen in horror or contorted in grisly grins, at cheeks streaked with the pale marks of tears. Toguchar would have many to serve him in the next world.

Khojin rose unsteadily to her feet; Tolui got up and took her arm. She leaned against him as the stiff muscles in her legs cramped. The men were still clearing the streets and dragging out those who had hidden in houses; one group was herded through an arch and forced to stand against a wall as men took aim with their bows. A little boy's scream was cut short as an arrow entered his mouth; the archers roared their praise for this feat of marksmanship.

"This will go on for some time," Tolui said. "Do you wish to leave the city?"

"No," Khojin said.

"The bodies will clog the streets soon."

"When they do, you'll bring the ones still alive outside. We'll cover the land with them — nothing will live here again."

Tolui bowed, took out his sword, and moved towards some of the men holding captives. Khojin sat down again; a man brought her a jug of wine. She suddenly recalled Khulan's words, that all of this could not bring her husband back. She hated the Khatun for saying it; the words were cords squeezing her heart, bringing her pain and despair instead of the joy she should have felt.

She shook off the thought. When Nishapur was a graveyard, she would have peace.

109

CH'I-KUO HAD SUMMONED Ch'ang-ch'un to her tent. The Taoist master had been in Bortai's camp for two days, sent on from Temuge Odchigin's camp in the Khalkha River valley. The Odchigin, knowing that the Khan wanted Ch'ang-ch'un to travel in comfort, had given him an escort and nearly a hundred oxen and cattle. The Khan might respect this Taoist greatly, but was demanding an arduous journey of him. The monk had been summoned to an audience with the Emperor Shih-tsung over thirty years ago, and he had not been a young man then.

"Liu Wen claims that the monk is nearly three hundred years old," Lien murmured. Ch'i-kuo did not believe it, but the Khan did. Liu Wen had told him that Ch'ang-ch'un was said to be the wisest man in Khitai, that the Taoist would surely have an elixir, and Genghis Khan was only too willing to believe that.

She expected nothing from this monk herself, but was curious to see a man reputed to be so wise. After his arrival, she had sent him sour milk, curds, millet, warm clothing, and silver for himself and his followers; the Tangut princess Chakha had done the same. The lamas who surrounded Chakha had brought the Khan's Tangut wife little solace; perhaps this Taoist would. Chakha's soul was a desert thirsting for rain. This world had failed Chakha; she had turned her thoughts to the next.

A guard announced the visitors. Two men entered, followed by a third, all of them clothed in the woollen robes Ch'i-kuo had given them; the midsummer heat could quickly change to cold. The men pressed their hands together, but did not kneel. The third man raised his head and gazed at her.

She knew this man had to be Ch'ang-ch'un. His dark eyes were clear and untroubled; the pale gold skin above his thin white beard glowed with health. She thought of how the Khan's eyes seemed to pierce men's souls, seeing what was hidden there, and how cold they often grew, as though he despised what he glimpsed. This monk had such a look, but his eyes were kind and forgiving. All the speeches she had prepared fled from her mind; she was suddenly uncertain of herself.

The man at the monk's right murmured a formal greeting. His name was Yin Chih-ping, his companion's Chao Chin-ku, and they had been disciples of their master for many years.

"I am pleased you were willing to honour us with your presence," Ch'i-kuo said when Yin Chih-ping was finished. She motioned to some cushions; the three monks seated themselves, but took none of the tea and food her women set before them. The Master, Chao Chin-ku explained, took no tea or meat; the dish of millet he had eaten that morning would be enough. The Master was grateful for her gifts.

"I have longed to see you ever since I heard you were travelling here," Ch'i-kuo said. "When I was young, I was told of the wise man whom my great-grandfather summoned to his court. It's said that your wisdom gave him solace in the last year of his life."

Ch'ang-ch'un nodded. She knew then that he saw her true

thoughts – that he had not succeeded in prolonging the Emperor Shih-tsung's life, that he was only another man who pretended to knowledge he did not have.

She flushed and looked down. "You honour my husband the Khan by undertaking this journey at last," she murmured.

"I could not refuse such a summons," Ch'ang-ch'un said. His voice was gentle, but not weak; he did not sound like a man who would have obeyed out of fear.

"Yet you waited before starting on your journey."

"There were disciples to see before I left," he said, "and festivals to attend. After that, Liu Wen, the honourable servant of the great Mongol Emperor, asked me to travel with the girls he was collecting for his master, but of course I had to refuse. Such company would not have been fitting."

"I am surprised that the Khan was not more insistent."

"He has been most gracious, Highness, and has told me not to tire myself too much on my way to him. His servant A-la-chien, who travels with me now, led me to the camp of the Prince Temuge, and from here I will go to the ordu of the Khan's honourable servant Chinkai. I'm told that many crafts-men from our land dwell in that camp."

"There are ladies there, too," she said, "taken from the palace when Chung Tu surrendered. They'll surely wish to see you." She could not keep the bitterness from her voice.

"I see what you suspect, Imperial Lady," the old man said. "You think I am an old man who travels to the Mongol Emperor out of fear, or that I am a crafty one who seeks some advantage. I am neither of those things."

His frankness stunned her. She could not deceive him; her carefully prepared phrases would be useless.

"It's true that a refusal would have gained nothing for the followers of the Way," Ch'ang-ch'un continued, "and that I may win some favour for us. Our land has suffered at the hands of the Prince Mukhali's soldiers, and many have learned to fear that prince and his master. But I do not fear the great Genghis Khan. When I delayed my journey, he assented to my requests. Had I told the men he sent to me that I would have to wait until he could travel to me, he would have agreed to that, too."

"Forgive me, Wise and Learned Master," Ch'i-kuo said, "but

594

you are wrong. He won't tolerate disobedience. You have seen what his armies did, and he gave those commands."

"Soldiers are much the same, whatever commanders they follow. The Khitans swept down on us, and then their iron was overcome by the golden Kin. Now the Emperor of Gold retreats from the Mongols. It may be the turn of the Mongols to rule us, and if their Emperor wishes to hear of the Way, then there must be nobility in him." He pressed the tips of his long fingers together. "I have seen that his people help one another in their camps, share what they have with those in need, and keep the promises they make. In their own way, they may be closer to Man's earlier natural state."

So that was what he saw. The Mongols, knowing that the Khan wanted him well treated, would go out of their way to please him. He was only passing through these lands. He would not have to endure years of howling winds and sudden ice storms under the vast sky that revealed how indifferent Heaven was to their fate. He would not have to spend the rest of his life trembling before the emptiness beyond the camps. That was what she painted now – the wide blue sky, a steppe of yellow grass bowing to the wind, a lone tree with twisted limbs, a tent near a hillside, a herd of horses grazing under a mountain of black granite. She could no longer envision what lay beyond this land.

"My husband the Khan," she said, "is a curious man. He has surrounded himself with learned men and wants them to yield their wisdom to him as the cities have their treasures. But it isn't only wisdom he wants from you, Adept Master. He wants an elixir that can prolong his life."

Ch'ang-ch'un smiled. "But I have no such elixir."

"You are called an alchemist, Master."

"There is much knowledge to be gained in such study, but not the secret of prolonging life. My alchemy is of the soul. I can only guide the Emperor to nurture the heavenly elements in himself and to check those that are closer to Earth. He must rid himself of desire in order to allow this transmutation – only then can he prolong his life."

Ch'i-kuo's mouth twisted. "He will be most disappointed to hear that."

"I must tell him what is true," the monk said. "Perhaps when he puts such desires aside, he will be ready to hear of the Tao."

She leaned forward. "I will tell you what others have told me," she said. "Once, a shaman served the Khan. This man knew many powerful spells, but when the Khan had no further use for him, he allowed the Prince Temuge to break his back. I pray that you won't suffer such a fate."

"I do not fear death. Change comes to all things, and death is only another change. From decay, life grows, and the soul becomes a flame rising to Heaven." The old man stroked his beard. "You say that this shaman was destroyed. That tells me that the man's magic may not have been so great as some believed, and perhaps also that the Mongol Emperor is not easily deceived. All the more reason to speak the truth to him. If he is to rule us, then I must speak to what is best in him. Do you not do so, Honourable Lady?"

Ch'i-kuo did not reply.

"But I see you do not," he said. "Highness, you cannot know peace unless you see the world as it is, and stop measuring it by your own needs, desires, and disappointments. You cannot see men as they are until you know that something of the nobler element lies inside them all. You must become like water, which feeds the ground over which it flows and takes the shape of the container into which it is poured."

"I am that now," she said.

"Then why do you have no peace? Perhaps instead of accepting the bright flame that lies inside others, you've allowed what is base in them to corrupt you."

"I can't let you speak to me in that way, Master."

"Then perhaps you will allow me to leave your side." Ch'ang-ch'un stood up. "I thank you again for the generous gifts you sent to me and my followers. I shall look forward to my audience with the Emperor."

She gazed after him as he left. Lien had told her years ago that the Khan was a man with two natures. It had been easier to forget that, to see only the cruelty and nothing else, to have some of the pleasure of her own small cruelties and look for little else in the world. The Master's way was harder.

The flame had died in her; Ch'ang-ch'un had seen that.

596

Perhaps it was too late for him to rouse whatever noble spirit might lie inside her husband, as it was too late for her, yet he would try, and remain untouched by what was base.

Ch'i-kuo waved a hand at Mu-tan. "Bring us some wine."

"You aren't going to paint?" Lien asked.

"Not today. It's so much more pleasant to drink and imagine the lovely pictures I might render." It had been for many days now. Ch'i-kuo flexed the fingers that had grown less supple, then reached for her cup.

110

FIVE SOLDIERS MET Khulan and her guards. Above them, in niches carved in the cliffs, monstrous carved figures many times a man's height, their lips frozen in gentle smiles on granite faces worn away by the wind, stared out at the nearby ruins of a high citadel.

Chagadai's son Mutugen had fallen here, one of the soldiers told her; her own son was badly wounded. The Khan had decreed that she stay with Kulgan.

Most of the army had moved on, but Khulan saw Temujin's work in the valley. The citadel's high rocky walls were blackened by fire and riven by breaches; heads covered the rocks below. Colourful shards of pottery glittered among the rocks, and in the river valley, vast charred stretches marked what was left of the town of Bamiyan. The fields were rutted, trampled, and grazed bare; black birds perched atop countless hills of heads.

A cold wind fluttered the scarf over her face. The peaks of the Snowy Mountains loomed above the valley. The mountains were covered with ice even in summer; winds howled through the high stony passes, and dragons were said to live in the cliffs, ready to hurl rocks at those passing below. Temujin might have left her in the base camp south of Balkh, but had promised she would never be far from his side, and he would not forget that promise, whatever the risks of the journey. She would sit with him, as she had at Balkh during the last day of the slaughter, masking the pity and despair that would only drive him to greater cruelty.

The men riding with her were silent as they passed stumps of willows and poplars and mounds of severed heads. The streams running from the river were clogged with bodies, masses of twisted limbs and gashed bellies; the sickly odour of rotting flesh filled the air.

"The Khan ordered us to take no prisoners and no plunder," one man said at last. "He commanded that every living thing – people, babies still in their mothers' wombs, birds, even the dogs and cats – be killed. We took nothing from Bamiyan, and the Khan has decreed that nothing will live here again. These people paid for the death of the Khan's grandson, and for wounding your own son, Lady."

Her son might be hovering between life and death. Khulan searched the distant field tents in the south of the valley, expecting to see a black-ribboned spear near one of them. The Khan had punished his enemies. If Kulgan died, she could have her revenge only on the father who had so eagerly led him to war.

Khulan was taken to the tent where her son lay. She lifted his blanket and saw deep scars on his thighs and along his ribs; a makeshift splint was around his right calf. He would live, but his scars would mark him.

She nursed him for two days, sleeping at his side. By the third day, he had recovered enough to hold the jug she handed to him. The kumiss wetted his thin moustache; she wiped his mouth with her sleeve, as she had when he was a child.

"Mother," he said.

"If I had lost you – " She could not say it; even wishing for her husband's death was treason.

"I'll limp," he said, "but a man doesn't have to walk far, and as long as I can mount a horse – " He gave a choked laugh. "Better my leg than my sword arm, and my hands can still use a bow."

"You're not going to fight for some time."

He finished the kumiss and handed her the jug. "Chagadai

got here in time for the executions," Kulgan said. "I'd been carried from the field, but Suke told me about it later. Father ordered the men not to tell Chagadai his son was lost, and then he questioned Chagadai, saying he had doubts about how obedient he was. Maybe Father was thinking about Urgenj."

"Perhaps," she said quietly. With Ogedei in command, Temujin's three oldest sons had finally taken that city last spring, but had divided the plunder without offering a share to the Khan. Ogedei had wanted to ease the hard feelings between his brothers by giving them most of the loot, but his act had enraged her husband. Only the pleas of Temujin's generals had saved the three from punishment. Since then, Jochi had remained in the regions around Urgenj, claiming they needed to be secured.

"Anyway," Kulgan continued, "Chagadai said he would rather die than disobey Father. Father asked him if he'd keep that promise, and Chagadai swore that Father could kill him if he ever broke it. Father told him then that his son had fallen, and forbade him to show any grief. Suke said Chagadai kept his promise – he didn't weep until he was out of Father's sight."

It was like the Khan to test a man, even a son, at such a time. She wondered when he might demand a show of loyalty from Jochi, still sulking in the north, securing a realm in place of the throne his father had refused to give him.

Khulan touched the braids coiled behind her son's ears; he pushed her arm away. "I have to heal," he said. "There's more fighting to do."

Khulan returned to the base camp in autumn; the Khan reached it in early winter. Word had come earlier about his successes in the south, where the Shah's son Jalal-ed-din had mounted a fierce resistance. The Khan himself had ridden to the aid of Shigi Khutukhu after his foster brother's defeat, and had managed to push Jalal-ed-din across the Indus.

Some of the men sang a song about the encounter. The Shah's son had leaped with his horse from a high cliff into the river. The Khan, admiring this display of courage, had let him escape and had praised his example. The song did not mention that only Jalal-ed-din was granted such mercy. The enemy soldiers trying to follow him across the river had been slaughtered, his sons taken prisoner and killed.

Three nights after his return, the Khan came to Khulan's tent. None of the guard had alerted her; she awoke to see him looming over her bed, her slaves cowering in the shadows.

He shrugged out of his coat. "You haven't thanked me," he said.

"For what?" Khulan asked.

He grabbed one of her braids, yanking her head up. "For allowing you to stay with our son, and to bring him back here. For letting you see the revenge I took for that and for my grandson's death." He let go. "It will make a good song – the beautiful Khulan riding to her eaglet, finding him safe, rejoicing that those who wounded him are dead. That will have to be part of the song, that you laughed when you found Kulgan alive and the enemies of your beloved husband destroyed."

She said, "I wept for them."

"Yes, you would have wept for them, and raged at me." He stared down at her. "If our son had died, what did you plan for me? A cup of poison, or a knife in my side as I slept?"

"I never – "

"You would never have had a chance to strike at me, and it would have grieved me to have you executed for trying. But it gives me joy to know that even my gentle Khulan can hate." He tore the blanket away, then threw himself across her.

The reeds by the rivers that flowed south from Balkh were hard and sturdy, strong enough to be used as sticks or as wedges under mired wagon wheels. Khulan and her women had been gathering reeds for most of the afternoon, cutting at them with knives. They had moved to the grasslands south of Balkh to graze their animals; the rivers ran clear, and the trees scattered over the land were growing green.

Life had renewed itself here, and even in the ruined city to the north. Wagons from Balkh arrived bringing melons, dried fruit, grain, and a strange fruit with seeds called a pomegranate. Slave boys set nets in the water or fished with rods from the banks.

As Khulan rode towards her tent, she saw the Khan and

Kulgan sitting by one wagon, making spears from the hard bamboo stalks that grew along the river. The two were often together. The young man hunted with his father, sat with Ogedei and Tolui during councils in the Khan's great tent, and rode with Temujin's entourage of guards.

Several men sat with the two, Nayaga among them. Khulan thought of the young man who had told her that he could not take the joy in war that others did. Nayaga had his share of victories, his monuments of skulls. Perhaps he had learned to love war.

She dismounted; the slaves with her lifted bundles of reeds from their horses and set them under the wagons. The guards by her tent drew themselves up as she climbed the steps to the entrance. The four women inside were preparing meat as the Khwarezmians did, spearing the pieces of lamb on skewers to be broiled over the fire. The guards would have to be fed, and her husband usually had several of his men dine with him.

But when Temujin and her son entered, they were alone. This would be an evening for the Khan to flatter Kulgan with his full attention.

Kulgan limped over the carpets behind his father. He would always drag his damaged leg, but no longer used a walking-stick. He stood by the fire with Temujin, warmed his hands, then glanced around the tent. Zulaika grew paler as Kulgan's eyes met hers. The girl they had once called The Mute spoke now, but not often, and when Kulgan looked at her, she kept a fearful silence.

The two went to the back of the tent and sat down on cushions near a low table. Khulan brought them kumiss, then settled at her husband's left as he sprinkled the blessing.

"I thought I would have more to feed," Khulan said.

"The men went to the horses," Temujin said. "More of the mares are giving milk. Nayaga was impatient to ride back to his tent – he's still besotted with a girl he found outside Kabul." He rested his hands on his knees as the slaves set melons in front of them.

Khulan cut at a melon with her knife. That winter, the Khan had finally learned that the Shah Muhammad had died on an island in the Caspian Sea, abandoned by all his followers, hounded there by Jebe and Subotai. Some said he had taken his own life, others that he had died of despair and weariness. The Khan had nearly won Khwarezm, and Tolui was wiping out the last pockets of resistance in the south with the thoroughness he had shown in taking Khorassan. The greatest of generals, the men called him in their songs, perhaps even the equal of his father. Never had so many died at the hands of one man.

"I think I shall order prayers to be said for me in the mosques," Temujin said. "Now that these people have no Shah, they must regard me as their lawful ruler and protector."

Kulgan laughed. "There aren't so many left in these lands to pray for us."

"A year from now, they'll have bred more of themselves. People, like herds of deer, should be thinned out from time to time, or they would become as numerous as insects." The Khan swatted at a fly. "Here's another thing to remember, son – take what the cities can give, but don't be tempted by their ways. We must live as we always have, and set those who understand cities over them to govern them."

Khulan sipped her kumiss. Apparently the talk this evening would be advice on governing. She wondered how much Temujin really understood about the men who advised him, his Khitans and Muslims with their wisdom and their books. He spoke as if he had learned many things from them, but his thoughts quickly turned to what he knew best. He might wonder at what Ye-lu Ch'u-ts'ai told him of the movements of the stars, but he would be thinking of the lands under Heaven that he still might claim – Khitai, and perhaps even the land of Manzi that the Sung ruled. Subotai and Jebe were also riding far to the north-west at his orders, to see how the lands there might be taken.

The slaves set out skewers of meat; Temujin and Kulgan gulped the food down. "The Muslims share some beliefs with us," the Khan mumbled, his mouth full. "They honour the warrior, as we do. They worship Tengri, even though they call Him by another name." He wiped his hands on his silk tunic, then reached for his goblet. "But a man shouldn't think too much of the next world." He paused. "You fight well, Kulgan.

Your men obey you without question. I plan to give you a thousand to command."

"Father!" Kulgan's amber eyes glowed. "You honour me."

They looked much alike, her husband and her son; Kulgan's smaller body had his father's bearing. How foolish she had been to hope Kulgan might be a man like Ye-lu Ch'u-ts'ai, or that his injuries might turn his thoughts from war. Temujin had seen what their son was more truly than she had.

111

"IF THERE IS such an elixir," Ye-lu Ch'u-ts'ai said to the Khan, "then this man may know the secret. But even if he does not, there will still be much he can tell us."

Khulan glanced up from where she sat among the women. The Khitan was the only one of her husband's advisers who had shown doubts about the sage's reputed powers. Temujin had laughed off his misgivings. He would have the secret; it was Heaven's will.

The Khan had summoned close comrades and his favourite women to his great tent to welcome the sage. Ch'ang-ch'un had finally arrived at his camp, led south through the Iron Gate pass by Borchu and his men. The monk had been travelling for over a year, and had passed the winter in Samarkand. The Khan, who had waited this long to summon him, had demanded to see him immediately.

Liu Wen entered, followed by Borchu and the general Chin-kai. Liu Wen made a speech, murmuring of the wise Ch'ang-ch'un who had travelled so far to offer his wisdom, then fell silent as an old man came through the doorway, followed by several younger men. Their plain woollen robes might have been those of simple shepherds. The younger men bowed from the waist; the old one pressed his hands together, then gazed directly at the Khan as he spoke.

"The Master says," Liu Wen translated, "that he is honoured to be in your presence."

"He honours me by coming here." Temujin leaned forward, searching the old man with his eyes. "Other rulers have summoned him, and he did not go to them, yet he has travelled a great distance to be with me. I am flattered."

Ch'ang-ch'un murmured to Liu Wen. His voice was low, and gentler than the Khan's, but Khulan sensed the same strength in it. "That I came at Your Majesty's bidding," Liu Wen said in Mongol, "was simply the will of Heaven."

"I beg you to be seated," the Khan replied, then clapped his hands. Women and boys entered, carrying platters of meat and jugs of drink. Everyone was soon grabbing for the food and wine except the monks. Liu Wen explained that Ch'ang-ch'un and his disciples took no meat or strong drink; the Khan quickly ordered that they be given rice.

"The Master lives an ascetic life," Liu Wen continued as he sat down near the sage. "He eats little, and also doesn't often indulge in welcoming the dark demon of sleep."

Temujin laughed. "We'll all sleep soon enough – some of us, at any rate." He had not looked away from the monk seated before him. "It is said that you have an elixir that can prolong life. Have you brought it to me?"

Liu Wen leaned towards Ch'ang-ch'un. The others all watched the monk; Khulan looked up at the Khan. "The Master says this," she heard Liu Wen say. "I can protect life. I have no elixir that can prolong it, nor do I think such an elixir exists, but this I do know: long life can be found only by working with Nature, not in opposing it. Perhaps we will find the secret someday."

Temujin was very still. Khulan had expected to see disappointment or rage, but not the terror that filled his eyes, as if he had heard his own death sentence – and for the second time, after hoping to escape the first that belonged to all men. The fearful look vanished in an instant; she looked at the sage and knew he had seen it, too. The old man's eyes warmed; there was pity in them for the Khan's despair.

"You are honest, Wise Master," Temujin said softly. "I must respect you for that."

"I can offer Your Majesty some advice," Liu Wen interpreted. "Abstain from strong drink, and eat only enough to nourish yourself. Sleep alone for a month, and Your Majesty's spirit will be greatly revived. A good night's sleep can do more for a man than a hundred days of swallowing medicines. But such advice, however sound, is commonplace. I travelled here to speak to you of the Way."

The Khan sank back against his throne. The men glanced at one another uneasily. "I would hear of the Way," Temujin said.

"Heaven and Earth, the moon and sun, the stars, all demons and spirits, all men and animals, and even the blades of grass, grow out of Tao." Liu Wen's voice took on some of the quiet power of the monk's as he translated. "The Tao is the Way. I do not mean the way of people, but the Way of the world, the order of Nature and the universe. Only by yielding to it, instead of forcing one's illusions upon it, can a man reach understanding. A man must embrace the universe, seek to know its workings, and to see the unity that is Tao. Do not seek for the beginnings of things, or to follow all changes to their end. Do not demand a purpose of things as they are. The universe is eternal, and was no more made for us than for the locusts that swarm over the earth."

"I have seen the world for what it is," Temujin said. "Yet I had hoped there was more . . . " His voice trailed off.

The monk spoke again in his gentle voice. Whatever he was saying could give the Khan little solace. Men lived and died, and the world endured; that was not what Temujin wanted to hear.

"When Tao produced Heaven and Earth," Liu Wen translated, "Man was born from both. Man shone with radiance, but in time his body grew more earthen and his holy light dimmed. He came to desire, and his appetites wasted his spirit. You must nurture the spirit in yourself, that which can rise to Heaven. You have become the greatest conqueror the world has yet seen. Become the greatest ruler, and your memory will live on Earth as long as your spirit does in Heaven."

Temujin was silent for a long time. He would send the monk away, Khulan thought, perhaps even drive him from the camp.

"We'll feast," Temujin said, "and two tents will be raised for you. I must hear more from you when you have rested."

Pride, Khulan thought. Having brought the sage so far, Temujin could not admit that the journey had been for nothing.

Temujin sent his guests away after the feast, but kept Khulan and Ye-lu Ch'u-ts'ai with him. "You are disappointed, my Khan," the Khitan said.

"You had your doubts."

"I had also hoped, but never doubted the Master's wisdom. It pleases me that you are willing to learn from him still. What he tells you may help you be a wise ruler. Your battles are nearly won here – it is time to build."

"An empire won on horseback," Temujin said, "cannot be ruled on horseback. So you have often told me." He sighed. "I wonder if I'll live long enough to rule it."

"You have vigour still," Ch'u-ts'ai said, "more than most men in their fifties, and much of life ahead."

"You may go, my friend," the Khan said.

The Khitan left them. Khulan waited for her husband to dismiss her.

"The last time I prayed on Burkhan Khaldun," he said at last, "the mountain was silent. That silence terrified me. I couldn't tell what Heaven willed for me. I haven't heard the spirits since then, and in this land, my dreams sometimes – "

He sagged against his gilded chair. "I've felt myself swallowed by the earth, trapped in my body, with no place for my soul to fly. I have seen nothingness. It came to me that a man's soul may die with his body, that there's nothing beyond this life. This monk was my only hope to escape that fate."

"I didn't understand everything he told us," she said, "but he spoke of the spirit that lives inside all men."

His mouth twisted. "And he said that the world wasn't made for us, as if what we do is no more than what a herd of horses does when they seek new pastures, or a flock of birds when they fly south. He talks of a spirit inside us, but I haven't sensed it for some time."

He stood up, swayed, and sat down heavily; his lined brown face sagged with weariness. "Once, Tengri spoke to me. I heard what the spirits whispered clearly in my dreams. The ghosts of my ancestors were as real to me as if they still walked the earth. Once I heard them speak to me through the shaman Teb-Tenggeri, and even when I allowed Temuge to decide his fate, I still hoped Teb-Tenggeri might summon his magic, even if it meant my own death, because it would have shown me that what he claimed was true." He drank from his goblet, then let it fall from his hand. "When I saw his broken body, I knew that the dead had always been silent, that he had possessed no way of reaching them, that perhaps there were no ghosts to speak to us. Since then, I've known little peace. I pray and hear no answer. I grab at joy and see it flee from me. I think of the grave, and tremble."

Something in her exulted at his despair. "You have such visions," she said, "and yet you sent countless people to their deaths. All I could hope for was that the spirits of the dead would know some happiness at last, and now you say that you don't believe that and think they are no more."

"We are few," he said, "and our enemies numerous. We could defeat them only by making them too fearful to resist. But I must admit that I took more joy in their deaths than I might have. To think that they might be nothing, that only a void awaited them – I could be happy believing that."

"You thought they would become nothing," she said, "but that you might live. I didn't think such evil could be inside one man. If I believed that was all that awaited us, I would have wanted joy for all people while they still lived."

"Then you're a fool, Khulan. If there's nothing beyond, it doesn't matter what we do here."

"It matters," she whispered. "You won't have your elixir now. You'll have to fear the death you brought to so many others. Perhaps that's a fitting punishment."

"How you hate me," he said.

"I don't hate you. I pity you. You'll fear death for the rest of your life, and all anyone will remember of you is how much death you brought to the world."

"Get out of my sight," he said. She expected him to strike her, but his limbs seemed bound to his chair. "Never come before me unless you're ready to say your last words. I won't look upon your face again."

"I don't fear death, Temujin."

"Then fear what I'll make of your life if you ever defy me. Fear the suffering I'll inflict on those you love before you die."

The Khan always kept his promises. She stood up and crept from the great tent.

The Khan moved his camp to the foothills of the Snowy Mountains to escape the summer heat. Whenever Khulan glimpsed him in the distance, she turned away and covered her face, knowing what would happen if he saw her. She kept inside her own tent when he visited Kulgan's; at least her son had not lost his favour.

Ch'ang-ch'un and his disciples had come there with the Khan, who had set aside an auspicious day to hear the monk's teachings. Khulan often thought of that gentle old man, and the solace his words might bring her, but did not dare to approach his tents or summon him to hers. Her husband would hear of it, and forbid the sage to speak to her. Temujin would hear of the Way, and she would never know more about it. That was part of her punishment, too.

Before the Khan could meet again with Ch'ang-ch'un, word came of rebellion in the south. The Tao was forgotten; the camp was filled with the tumult of men preparing for battle. The Khan would ride with his army to crush the rebellion, to send more people to the death he feared.

She did not go with the other women to see the army off; her son did not say farewell to her. Ch'ang-ch'un, it was rumoured, had asked that he be left behind; the Khan had given the monk permission to return to Samarkand. Two days after the army's departure, the old sage left the camp. She would have no chance to speak to him in the Khan's absence.

Khulan still had her guards, her servants and slaves, her herds and wagons of booty. Temujin would not dishonour her publicly; that would only show his bad judgement in having made her a favourite. She would always be his Khatun, living on his plunder, viewed by others as the beloved wife who inspired him to his bloody triumphs. That was also part of her punishment.

112

IN AUTUMN, AFTER the Khan defeated the last of his enemies in the south, his people broke camp. They skirted ruined Balkh, crossed the Amu Darya River over a pontoon bridge, and camped south of Samarkand. Occupying troops, along with the Khitans and Muslims who were to govern the conquered lands, would remain behind, but most of the Mongols would return to their homeland.

Delegations and wagons of provisions arrived from Samarkand. Jars of red wines, newly picked almonds, melons packed in ice brought from the mountains near the city, silks, and jewels were conveyed to Khulan's tent. To the north of the camp, a pavilion was raised, where the Khan would at last have his delayed audience with the Taoist sage.

The autumn weather, clear and dry, was still holding when the monks arrived, accompanied by A-li-hsien, the Khitan governor of Samarkand who would act as interpreter. The Khan sent nearly everyone from his pavilion when Ch'ang-ch'un was ready to preach to him. Only three of Temujin's men – A-li-hsien, Liu Wen, and Chinkai – would have the privilege of hearing the monk's teachings this time.

The old man had failed to bring the Khan eternal life, yet Temujin grasped at his teachings. People murmured of the changes that had come to Genghis Khan. When he was not with the monk, he consulted with advisers and received envoys; his only recreation was an occasional foray with his hawks. He kept away from the tents of his women, and Khulan remembered that Ch'ang-ch'un had advised him to sleep alone.

The Khan, some said, had grown more contemplative. Khulan suspected that he was only more desperate, still hoping that he might cheat death after all.

"You are with child," Khulan said; she knew the signs.

Zulaika looked up from her sewing. "I have known it for some time, Lady."

Kulgan had taken the girl to his tent nearly two months ago. She had gone passively, without protest, so Khulan had said nothing. Zulaika was only a slave, and Khulan lacked the power to defy her son now. The girl had been with him for three nights; he had tired of her quickly, as he did of all his bedfellows.

"I am pleased," Khulan said. The other slaves gazed at Zulaika with narrowed eyes, clearly wondering what favours the girl might win for herself. "You'll give my son his first child." Khulan thought of when she had first known that Kulgan was growing inside her. The child would console her; that was what she had believed. There would be someone she could love fully, who would return that love to her. "The greatest happiness a woman can have is a child," she murmured, but her words sounded hollow even to herself.

The girl said nothing. The other slaves shook their heads; any of them would have been exulting, ready to claim any privilege a woman carrying a grandchild of the Khan deserved.

"I'll see that you're cared for," Khulan continued. "We are bound by the Yasa, and it imposes certain obligations. My son will have another wife to give him heirs, but you should have a second wife's place. You'll have a share of Kulgan's herds, and slaves to serve you. You'll have your own tent."

"Forgive me, Lady, but I would rather remain with you."

"There is an order to these things. You must dwell in my son's ordu if you are to be his wife."

The girl bowed her head. "Yes, Lady."

Khulan was at a loss. This was what her kindness had brought; the girl preferred being her slave to becoming Kulgan's wife. "Perhaps," she said at last, "you may stay with me until your time's nearly upon you. I'll tell my son you will go to his tents after that."

"I am grateful." Zulaika's dark eyes glistened as she bent over her sewing.

They broke camp and moved to the east of Samarkand. Ch'ang-

610

ch'un and his disciples were allowed to move back to their former resting place inside the city, and several of the Khan's retinue took up residence there, but Temujin remained outside the walls; what he wanted from Samarkand could be brought to him. The pavilion where he met with his men and listened to Ch'ang-ch'un's discourses had been raised to the north of the circles of wagons and tents.

In the west, Khulan could see the domes and minarets of the city. Samarkand sat on the bank of the Zerafshan River, which the people here called the Bringer of Gold. Often, when the sun was high, golden lights glistened in the water as it flowed west from the mountains towards the plain on which Samarkand stood. The city on the horizon beckoned to her. Once, she might have gone to her husband and asked if she could stay in the palace that overlooked the city from a high hill, and he would have granted her wish. Those of her slaves who were taken from Samarkand had told her of the canals that carried water along its streets, and of terraces that overlooked gardens and orchards. She might have gone to the markets teeming with traders from Khitai, the Uighur oases, and the west. She longed for the city, as unreachable for her as a desert mirage.

Perhaps it was better not to enter it. Inside its walls, she would also see the marks of her husband's work – empty houses whose residents were dead, faces made thin by the recent famine, eyes filled with sorrow and hatred.

The clear autumn sky soon turned grey. A misty rain fell, sifting down lightly from the sky. The city faded in the mist, then vanished behind the veil of rain, lost to her.

Ye-lu Ch'u-ts'ai, after returning from Samarkand, had been in the Khan's camp for three days before Khulan sent a servant to ask if she might speak to him. The Khitan had said that he would receive her.

This afternoon's rain was heavier and colder, threatening to become snow. Khulan was apprehensive as she climbed down from her cart and approached the Khitan's tent. When the Khan learned of this visit, he might order his adviser to avoid her. A guard at the doorway called out her name; she entered, followed by the two slaves she had brought with her.

Beyond the hearth fire, the back of the large yurt was bright with light; oil lamps covered the low table where the scholar sat. Scrolls and bound books from Khitai sat on shelves, along with jars of herbs. She saw no colourful tapestries, golden cups, or treasure looted from the cities, and no retinue of slaves hovering around the Khan's most trusted adviser. Except for a boy pouring tea into cups, the Khitan was alone.

He looked up as Khulan's women knelt by the hearth. "I greet you, Honoured Lady," he murmured, then set his brush next to his scroll.

"I greet you, Wise Chancellor, and am grateful you are willing to see me." She sat on a cushion to his left; the boy set out a cup and a plate of almonds. "I have heard you spent much time with the learned men of Samarkand."

"Indeed I have. Their astronomers as wise as those I knew at court."

Khulan sipped her tea. Unlike her husband's other advisers, Ch'u-ts'ai had always addressed her with warmth in his voice. "My husband," she said, "has been much interested in knowledge lately."

"He has been trying to follow a few of the Master's prescriptions. He drinks less often, but as your people say, a man cannot stand on one leg, so he hasn't given it up entirely. He spends his nights alone, and surely that is the Master's doing, or he would have honoured you, Gracious Khatun, with his presence." His handsome face was pensive; she was suddenly sure he suspected the truth. "I have been setting down one of the Master's discourses, as the Khan requested."

"The Master is a wise man," she said.

"A wise man," the Khitan said, "and one willing to display virtue. He's given much of what the Khan gave him to the most wretched people of the city. The Master has also presented a few of his poems to me. I believe he expects me to render a few verses to the rhymes of his own. I hope my efforts don't disappoint him. Even the wisest men sometimes lack the gift for poetry."

Ch'u-ts'ai was too subtle for her. She could not tell if he was disparaging his own skill at that art, or Ch'ang-ch'un's. "I would have enjoyed hearing the Master again," she said, "although I don't have the learning to understand all he might say."

"Many wise men haven't understood all that the Taoist Masters say and write. Some say that their alchemists have powerful magic, others that such alchemy can only show the workings of Nature, and still others that it is the alchemy of souls rather than matter that concerns them." He stroked the short dark beard that covered his chin. "The confusion you may feel is common among others."

Such words, from another man, would be only flattery, but this Khitan was not given to flattering anyone. He was not speaking to her now as a Khatun, or even as a woman, but as another questioning soul.

A strange joy, unlike any she had ever felt, filled her; she felt removed from herself, yet at peace. A vision came to her of a world filled with such men, ones who would share their learning freely across the barriers that separated them now, and then it faded, another mirage, another city swallowed by mists.

"I have come to you, Learned Brother," she said, "because I have something to ask of you. As you may know, another grandchild to the Khan will be born this spring – my son's first child."

The Khitan nodded. "The Khan is always happy to see more additions to his numerous progeny."

"I wish to ask you to find a teacher for this child, if he is a boy, one who could teach him the Uighur script and maybe yours as well. I know you can be trusted to find a wise man."

"Is this also the wish of your son?" he asked.

"I haven't spoken to him. He isn't drawn to such learning, but I can't see why he would object."

"I am certain the Khan wouldn't object, either."

"I'd rather not ask him myself," she said. "He has so many children and grandchildren – he can hardly be bothered with all their doings. Perhaps, when the time comes, you might suggest it."

His eyes widened; he understood. He had seen that she could not ask Temujin herself. "Yes, Honourable Lady," he murmured. "When the boy is old enough, and if he has the makings of a scholar, I may suggest it. But I must wait until then. The

Taoist Master would tell you that it's useless to force things to perform functions unsuited to them. The Khan's four heirs, for all their greatness as warriors, have only learned to scorn the knowledge that was forced on them."

"For all their greatness," she said, "I can hope that my grandson is a different sort of man. I would wish he might be more like you, Wise Councillor. I've sometimes wondered why a man such as you entered my husband's service, one who seems more at ease with quiet pursuits than with war."

Ch'u-ts'ai laughed softly. "If I had not, my bones would lie in my land now, and my people are cousins to yours – we are not unacquainted with war."

"You don't glory in it."

"Some of us do not. We learned that from the Han, to fight and yet weep at what war brings."

She said, "All my husband knows is war."

"Yet he must rule now, and a ruler needs more than force, even though it is one of his tools." He sipped his tea. "When I was brought before the Khan," he continued, "I saw that he honoured men of learning, even if he does not – forgive me for saying this – comprehend much of their lore. His nature made him a conqueror, and he could not go against it, but his nature isn't only that of a warrior. He is also a man who longs for the answers to things. Isn't that why he sent for the Master?"

"He sent for him," she said, "because he wanted to live forever."

"And isn't such a wish a longing for answers, for the time to find them? The Master can't give him that, but if the Khan learns no more than to nurture his conquests, rather than pillaging them, that will be enough. If there were no men around him who could touch the thirst for wisdom in him, his warrior's nature would have overpowered the rest."

"I've always hated war." She should not saying that, but the Khitan had somehow opened the dam inside her. "I am the wife of the greatest of warriors, yet I can long for a world without war." She steadied herself. The two slaves she had brought knew only a little of her tongue, and the Khitan's boy seemed as uncomprehending as they, but she had said too much already.

"This is not the world you dream about," Ch'u-ts'ai said gently. "We must live in this one as it is. It gains a man nothing to turn away from war when he's surrounded by those who embrace it. That would truly be going against the nature of things."

He gazed past her. "Perhaps if the Khan had lived in ancient times, when men knew nothing of war, he would have served his nature in seizing at questions, making spears of them to thrust at the universe, but he doesn't live in such a world. You wish that things were otherwise, Lady, and suffer because you can't change them. I accept them as they are, and do what I can with what I am given. I tell myself that many here, and others in Khitai, may live and preserve some of what they have built because I have the ear of the Great Khan. The Master himself tells us that there's peace in acceptance." His hands trembled; he set his cup down. Whatever he said, he had not found that peace; she glimpsed the torment in his dark eyes before they cleared.

"I can't accept it," she said. "I can do nothing about it, but I can never accept it."

"When a storm comes," he said, "a man must run to his tent or cover himself. To stand and rail at the storm for being what it is would only bring a bolt from Heaven. Storms pass, Honoured Lady." He leaned towards her. "I think you didn't come here only to ask for a teacher for your grandchild. Perhaps you also wanted some wisdom from me, and I have little to give you."

"You are mistaken, Learned Councillor. You are wise, and I am foolish." Khulan stood up. "Your wisdom is wasted on one so ignorant, a woman who can only wish for the impossible and mourn for what men do."

113

WHEN THE SNOW stopped falling, and the wet ground was turning green, the Khan prepared to leave the region near Samarkand. Wagons and carts were lashed together; horses, cattle, and sheep were gathered by herders. The Khan and Tolui rode at the head of the army, followed by the women and their carts, then the herds. The ox-drawn platforms carrying the great tents trailed the herds with a mounted rearguard and thousands of slaves on foot.

Khulan rode in one of the lead wagons, with a slave to hold her camel's reins. Ahead of her, rows of mounted men and strings of horses stretched to the horizon; tughs and banners fluttered above clouds of sand and dust.

They soon came to a village, where orchards of almond and apricot trees, fed by a canal, were in bloom. Khulan heard a high, piercing wail before she saw the crowd of women and children at the side of the road. The women's heads were covered by long, gauzy scarves of purple or black; some lifted their arms to Heaven as they wailed while others knelt and pressed their heads to the ground. The women had belonged to the Shah Muhammad's household; the Khan had ordered them brought there, to lament their lost empire before they joined the other prisoners. They screamed out their despair as the procession wound past them, crying out for the land they would never see again.

The progress of the Mongols was slow and halting. In the evening, the animals were grazed and milked, camp-fires were built, and the people slept inside wagons and field tents. Khulan often dreamed of the homeland she had left nearly four years ago, the land that was at peace because the Khan had carried war elsewhere. Three days after the beginning of their journey, a fierce storm forced them to halt; when it passed, the ground was covered by the bodies of sheep, cattle, and people frozen by the cold and ice. Men and women lit fires to thaw carcasses and butcher them, saving what meat they could. The bodies of soldiers who would never see their homeland again were covered with stones, but the bodies of dead slaves were abandoned.

They came to the Syr Darya River and forded it on bridges of boats lashed to each bank, then moved on until they came to a valley bordering the great plateau. Here, along a smaller river, they would rest. The Khan's pavilion was raised once more, and riders were sent to fetch Ch'ang-ch'un from Samarkand.

Khulan gazed at the pavilion to the north. Except for the men guarding it, there was little sign of activity. The Khan was out hunting. When he was not holding court, listening to Ch'ang-ch'un, or greeting messengers and envoys, the Khan hunted, despite the monk's disapproval. It was rumoured that the Master was impatient to leave for Khitai, but Temujin still held him, urging him to stay until the weather was better for travel, then to wait until Chagadai and Ogedei arrived there from Bukhara with their men.

Khulan's great tent and wagons still stood to the east of his, but her husband's pretence deceived few now. She had fallen from favour. His other women said that openly, although not to her face. He went to their tents, as he had before, but not to Khulan's. She knew the women said such things, so she snapped at them as they tended the sheep, butchered game, worked on embroidered flaps for their doorways, and did their weaving.

Tents and wagons covered the valley, stretching as far as the mountain foothills to the east and south along the river-banks. The city of tents would have to move on soon to new pastures before the ewes lambed and the horses dropped their foals. Perhaps her husband would finally let Ch'ang-ch'un and his followers depart. The Khan had been waiting for Jochi to join him, but his oldest son had sent a carefully phrased message, according to Kulgan, saying that he would remain in the lands to the north of Khwarezm, the pastures his father had promised him, and hold them for the Khan. Temujin might have ordered him to return, but seemed resigned to leaving Jochi where he was.

A cloud of dust to the east caught her eye; men were riding towards the camp. Her husband was among the distant riders; she could not let him see her. Khulan turned, walked past the women working their looms, and climbed the steps to her entrance.

Kulgan came to her tent that evening. Khulan had come to dread his visits. He was usually with comrades who drank heavily while bellowing their most gruesome war stories.

Kulgan was alone this time. He pinched Zulaika on the cheeks until she whimpered, then moved towards the couch where Khulan sat. One of the slaves brought him some wine and cooked game; he picked at his food in silence.

"Your father didn't hunt for long today," Khulan said.

He glanced at her with a wide-eyed, fearful look she had not seen for years. She touched his cheek; he covered her hand with his, then gently pushed her away.

"Father had a warning today," Kulgan said. "That's what the Master called it."

"A warning?"

"When we were hunting in the foothills," he said, "Father wounded a boar. He rode after it, and we followed, and then Father's horse threw him. Before he could get up, the boar charged him, then suddenly halted." He swallowed. "If it hadn't, we couldn't have reached Father in time to keep him from being gored. We brought him another horse, and the boar was still standing there when we rode away."

Kulgan gulped down some wine. "Heaven stopped the animal," he continued. "That's what the Master said when Father told him about it. He said it was a warning, that to Heaven all life's precious, that it would be as wrong for Father to take the boar's life as for the boar to take his. He advised him not to hunt, now that he's grown older."

"He might as well tell the Khan not to breathe," Khulan murmured, "or to stop making war."

"Father called it good advice. He explained to the Master that we hunt as children, and can't easily put such habits aside, but said he'd try to follow his counsel." He touched her hand. "Mother, when I saw him there, helpless for that moment, I was terrified. I've never been so frightened before, even when I was wounded and thought I might die myself. I can't imagine the world without him."

"You mustn't fear for your father. Sometimes I think that, whatever happens, he'll outlive all of us in the end."

"Why don't you go to him?" he said. "What did you do to offend him? You were his favourite – he'd forgive you if – "

"I can't go to him," she said, "and you are never to ask why."

He finished his food, then said, "I want Zulaika to leave your tent before my child is born."

Khulan did not look at the girl, knowing she would see only despair in Zulaika's eyes. "She'll be with you by then," she said.

114

A MONTH AFTER Heaven had saved the Khan from death, the Taoist monk and his followers said their farewells. Khulan gazed at the Khan's pavilion from behind a wagon as Temujin embraced the old man and horses were brought to the Master and his disciples. A-la-chien would guide them to Khitai, and many of the Khan's officers would ride with the monks as far as the foothills.

Two days after the sage's departure, the people took down their yurts; teams of oxen were harnessed to the platforms holding the great tents. Tolui and Ogedei rode on ahead with their men; the Khan, who had refrained from hunting since his encounter with the boar, would hunt along the way.

That evening, when they stopped to rest, Khulan saw how pale Zulaika was and made her lie down in her own covered cart. Her sleep was disturbed by the girl's stifled moans; by morning, Zulaika's face was beaded with sweat. Khulan lifted the girl's blanket and saw a red stain spreading over the crotch of her woollen trousers.

She climbed out of the cart, sent one of her guards for a shaman, then beckoned to nine of her servants. "You'll stay with me," she said. "The others will go on." Khulan said the words firmly, hiding her fears.

The women drew up wagons in a half-circle and raised a tent. The men riding past on horseback and the women and children in their carts glanced towards the yurt and the shaman sacrificing a sheep in front of it, but did not stop. If the spirit afflicting the girl inside proved too strong for the shaman, it was better to be far from the evil.

The shaman cut out the sheep's heart, carried it inside the tent, and set it on the small altar that held some of Khulan's ongghons. Zulaika was screaming by the time the sheep was butchered and cooked; two of the women held her down as the shaman fed the tail to her.

The girl drifted into a trance. Khulan sat with her while the shaman chanted and beat his drum. He leaped and circled the hearth; his shadow fluttered on the walls of the tent. By dawn, Zulaika was bleeding again. The shaman shook his head, then sent everyone outside.

The guards, their horses tethered, sat around a fire just beyond the wagons. Khulan's women gathered fuel and made another fire. Khulan glanced back at the tent as the shaman came outside; he took a spear from one wagon, wrapped a piece of felt around it, and stabbed it into the ground.

She hurried to him. The shaman thrust out an arm. "You can't go inside," he said. "I've done all I can. An evil spirit is upon her, and she does nothing to fight it."

She went back to the fire. More riders passed, following the great tents; clouds of dirt billowed around them. They would see the spear, and know what it meant. Khulan called out to one of her guards and told him to ride to Kulgan.

The shaman stood by the tent, chanting. Towards evening, he went inside. The girl might live, Khulan told herself; the child could survive. Others had given birth before their time, and their babies had lived. The shaman emerged from the doorway clutching a small, wrapped bundle. She got to her feet and held out her arms.

"Your grandson, Lady," he said. "He came out with the cord around his neck, robbing him of breath. He – "

620

Khulan cried out; the other women wailed. "He must be buried," the old man went on. "There's no hope for the girl. Put her outside the tent and leave this accursed place."

"No," Khulan said.

"Lady – "

"No."

They buried the baby under a mound of rocks, then spent the night outside, huddled around the fires. In the morning, the shaman went into the tent. Khulan got up to follow him; he blocked the entrance before she could go inside.

He said, "Her soul has left her."

Khulan shrieked. The women ran to her. She tore herself from them, took out her knife, and slashed at her arms. Her grief was mingled with rage; Zulaika had struck back at her in the only way she could, by robbing her of her grandson, the boy who might have mastered the wisdom Khulan longed for, who might have shared some of that knowledge with her.

She stumbled around the tent, weeping and slashing at herself until a woman took the knife from her. She sank to the ground and sat there listlessly as the shaman bandaged her bleeding arms.

Someone was riding towards them. The figures of the riders were blurred by her tears; they had dismounted and handed their reins to her men before she recognized her son.

The shaman went to Kulgan, then led him to her. "She didn't want to live," Khulan said hoarsely, her throat raw. You brought her to this, she wanted to say; you made her long for death.

"Mother, was it – " He reached for her; she recoiled, then got to her feet. Kulgan looked towards the stones that marked the grave. "Was it a son?"

She nodded. He tensed, then said, "Don't mourn too much, Mother. I'll have other sons." He gripped her shoulders. "When you knew she was failing, you should have left her. Now the wagons and the tent and everything here will have to be purified."

She pulled free and flew at him, clawing him with her nails, slapping him hard across the face. He took the blows without flinching, then pinned her arms to her sides.

"Stop it," he said. "We must bury my son's mother now."

She pressed her face against his coat and wept.

They buried the girl next to her son so that her spirit would be near when he needed her. The tent was set over the grave; the two would have a dwelling in the next world.

When the wagons were purified, they followed the trail north. Kulgan and his comrades rode ahead of Khulan's guards and were soon out of sight. They would be anxious to rejoin the others, to put this death behind them.

Khulan stopped before the sun had set, and slept alone in one cart. In the morning, she ignored the worried looks on the faces of her guards and told them she did not wish to travel that day. The others set up shelters of hides and sticks to shade them from the hot sun and slept under them the following night. Khulan thought of when she had first found Zulaika. It came to her that the girl had been dead since then, that she had left her soul with the dead in her city.

They moved on at dawn. The trail now led east, towards more mountainous land. When they stopped to rest their oxen and horses, Khulan saw how the others drew aside to whisper about her. They would be saying that an evil spirit had entered her, that only a madwoman would mourn for a slave so deeply.

The next morning, after they had harnessed the oxen to the carts, two riders appeared over the crest of a distant hill. Khulan watched them approach, saw who they were, then climbed into her cart and crawled under the covering.

Her guards shouted greetings to the Khan and Kulgan. She huddled in the darkness, listening as her husband answered them. The cart shook slightly as someone climbed aboard.

Temujin peered in at her, swung his legs over the seat, and crept to her side. "All this fuss over a slave," he muttered.

"She carried your grandson." Khulan covered her face with her scarf. "You're breaking your word, husband. You decreed that you would never look upon my face again."

He pulled the scarf from her. "I no longer see the face of my Khulan. Look more closely at yourself in one of the mirrors I gave you. Even here, in the shadows, I see what you've become. Age is setting its mark on you – the face I loved didn't have those hollow cheeks."

"You shouldn't have come here," she said.

"I told my men to wait up ahead. I wanted to spare them the presence of a woman driven mad by evil spirits. I have more to grieve for now than a girl and a grandson who never drew breath. A message reached me from Khitai only a short time ago, just before I rode out to look for you. My greatest general has fallen, the man who would have helped me take all of Khitai. Mukhali has flown to Heaven."

Khulan whispered, "You mustn't say his name so soon after – "

"I'll say it – I'll see that it lives. What can it matter to him now if I say it again and again?" He put a hand over his eyes. His grief would be deeper than that of other men; he did not believe that he would ever meet his old comrade in the next world. "He won so much for me, yet I'm told his last words were an apology, that he regretted not being able to take K'ai-feng for me."

"I am sorry," she said.

"If the Master were with me, maybe he could have eased my grief. Sometimes, when he spoke, I felt I could look beyond this world, but he's gone, and the voice I once heard grows fainter." He sighed. "I can even wonder if he spoke the truth, or only misled me. He accepted few gifts when he left me, only horses and cotton clothing, but I gave him something more precious than that. I told him that the Taoist Masters in Khitai wouldn't be taxed, and set my seal on the proclamation. Perhaps the old man wanted that all along when he agreed to travel to me."

Temujin doubted Ch'ang-ch'un already; he would never be free of his doubts. "I saw the Master only once," she said softly, "but I know he's worthy of such a favour."

"Let us hope so. The wise Ch'u-ts'ai didn't object, but warned me that the Master's followers might take unfair advantage of the privilege. As he says, I must rule lands where people believe many different things, and it won't serve me to have one group turn on another. I may be a better ruler if I believe in none of their teachings."

He was silent for a while before he spoke again. "There is disorder in your tents, Khulan. The women mutter that you've lost my favour, even that I may cast you aside. Soon, the bolder ones may refuse to obey you, and that will make trouble for me. Things can't go on this way. You have a duty to supervise your household, and I refuse to be distracted by such matters. You will sit at my side, and we'll pretend things are as they were."

"Very well," she replied, knowing she had no choice.

"It shouldn't be hard for you. It was always a pretence for you anyway, and I'm free of your spell at last. Perhaps when you understand what you've lost, you'll come to regret that." He got up and made his way to the front of the cart.

115

"HOLD ON," SORKHATANI said as her youngest son settled behind her on her saddle. Arigh Boke hooked his fingers around her blue sash. Children and young women were streaming from the camp on horseback to greet the returning army.

Mongke mounted his horse; Sorkhatani trotted after her oldest son. Tolui had been pleased to learn she had come to the western edge of the former Naiman lands to wait for him.

She rode past the lines of wagons that surrounded Doregene's great tent and the smaller ones of her servants. Ogedei's chief wife had also decided not to wait for her husband in Karakorum. Doregene would have preferred to stay in the great camp along the Orkhon, but clearly wanted to appear as devoted as Sorkhatani.

A slave girl called Fatima stood near one of Doregene's wagons. Doregene and the girl had been inseparable ever since Fatima arrived from Khwarezm. Perhaps there was no harm in a wife's amusing herself with such a girl while her husband was away, although such pleasures had never appealed to Sorkhatani. The girl lifted her head and gazed directly at her; one would have thought she was a Khatun rather than a slave.

Beyond the camp, yellow grasslands, with hills of drifting dunes, stretched along the banks of the Black Irtysh River. Above clouds of sand, a wall of horsemen carrying lances, standards, and banners advanced across the plain. Riders galloped towards the returning army, shouting the names of fathers, husbands, and brothers.

Sorkhatani reined in her horse and waited with Mongke by a dune. Several riders had come to the camp three days ago, saying that the Khan would soon be among them. Khubilai and Hulegu had ridden out the next morning to meet their father. Arigh Boke clutched at her; Tolui had never seen his youngest son. She glanced at Mongke, who had the strong-boned, broad face of his father. He would soon be old enough to ride to war with Tolui.

"I see Father's tugh," Mongke said, "and the Khan's."

She lashed her horse lightly; her mount quickly moved into a gallop. When she saw the men clearly, she drew on her reins, then raised her hand. Khubilai and Hulegu broke away from the army and galloped towards her on their grey geldings, their father just behind them. Tolui's moustaches were longer, his body broader under his padded silk coat. He shouted to Mongke, then halted a few paces from Sorkhatani.

She dismounted, then reached for her youngest son. "I greet you, husband," she said. "This is Arigh Boke, the son you left inside me before you went away."

Tolui leaped from his horse and embraced the boy. Arigh Boke squirmed in his arms. Tolui laughed; he still had his wide, boyish grin. She had expected a more solemn man, one marked by the hardships of the long campaign. Perhaps he was a bit sorry to be back. He had left Khwarezm nearly a year ago, and had not hastened from his father's side to her.

She approached him warily; he caught her in his arms. "Sorkhatani," he murmured. "You haven't changed — what magic do you have?"

She warmed with pleasure at his words. "Magic from

625

Khitai," she replied, "a lotion the women of that land use to protect their faces from the sun and wind."

He chuckled. "My honest Sorkhatani. My other women don't admit their secrets, but pretend only God gave them beauty." He hugged her again. "Have you missed me?"

She nodded; she had missed him, but in a placid, distant way. He would be content to stay at her side for only a little while, until he rode out to his next war.

Their other sons gathered around them. "We hunted on our way to Father," Khubilai said. "I killed a hare, and Hulegu took a small stag."

"We told Grandfather it was the first game we'd taken alone," Hulegu said. "He anointed our fingers with fat himself, and said the blessing for us."

Tolui beamed at his sons. "Hulegu's more skilled with the bow than Khubilai," Mongke said, "but Khubilai reads the Uighur script better than either of us."

More men rode towards them. A tall man with coiled, greying braids hanging below his hat was in their midst; Sorkhatani tensed as she recognized the Khan. The dark, reddish hairs of his thin beard were mingled with grey, the copper turning to silver.

Sorkhatani bowed. Tolui grabbed Arigh Boke and lifted him high. "Here's a grandson you haven't seen," he shouted.

The Khan halted; a smile flickered across his face. The lines around his pale eyes were deeply etched, his lids heavier, his face more leathery. Sorkhatani had not thought he could age so much in a few years. What would become of them without him?

The Khan's weary eyes met hers. "Your husband did well, daughter," he murmured. "Some would tell you that he's the greatest of generals, a man against whom no enemy can stand."

"He's your son, Temujin-echige," she said. "He could be no less."

"I rejoice that he's returned safely to you." The Khan rode away, his men a shield around him.

People sat around fires and wandered from tent to tent. Children and slaves darted through the spaces between yurts

626

and wagons, fetching food and drink. Tomorrow, the Khan would preside over a more formal banquet, when Khulan Khatun and the rest of his entourage reached this camp.

The Khan moved from fire to fire, a wall of men around him. Sorkhatani watched as he stopped by one family, accepted a cup from the men while the women and children gaped at him, and then walked on. He had to be tired from his travels, yet he had ridden throughout the camp to greet his people.

Mongke and Khubilai were showing off at wrestling for their father. Mongke suddenly flipped the younger boy on to his back, nearly throwing him into a platter of meat. "Good for you, Mongke," Tolui bellowed. "Maybe if your brother spent less time reading, he could beat you." He belched; he had been drinking heavily all afternoon. "I'll have to see if you boys can beat me at chess."

He was already looking forward to the next wars. Sorkhatani had expected him to dwell on his exploits in Khwarezm, but instead he was anticipating future battles. The Tanguts were becoming more troublesome; the Khan would have to deal with them. Tolui had also spoken to the boys about the lands Jebe and Subotai had found far to the west on their long ride. Beyond the rugged plateaus of Persia and the mountains of the Caucasus lay forests and green steppes, grazing lands richer than their own. The people there, according to Tolui, were divided, tribe against tribe, nomad against city-dweller, ripe for conquest. He had laughed while telling of how Subotai and Jebe had used one tribe, the Kipchaks, against the mountain peoples there. The two generals had made allies of the Kipchaks by promising them loot, then had turned on the Kipchaks after the battles in the mountains were won. It was the sort of tactical treachery that appealed to Tolui.

"Father," Mongke said, "will we go hunting together soon?"

Tolui grunted. "Maybe. I doubt the hunting will be as good as we had this past winter. Your uncle Jochi had herds of game driven from his grounds towards ours, and there were so many wild asses among them that every man claimed three of four for himself after Father took his share."

"Why didn't Uncle Jochi come back with you?" Hulegu asked. Tolui scowled; Khubilai shot Hulegu a warning look.

"Jochi wants to stay in the grazing lands Father allotted to him," Tolui muttered, "and keep them secure. So he claims in his messages. Your grandfather prefers to leave him there, because his camps will be useful as a base when we strike further west – at least that's what Father says." He cleared his throat and spat to one side. "But the fact is that the bastard's still bitter about being passed over for Ogedei. I think he dreams of setting up his own Khanate apart from Father's. If he does, Father will crush him." He stabbed the air with his knife.

Sorkhatani shook her head. Tolui would not have dared to say that had he been sober.

"You insult your brother," she said, "and set a poor example for your sons. Jochi fought for the Khan, and was granted those lands – you shouldn't speak of him in that way."

"My wise Sorkhatani," Tolui said. "I take back my words. Maybe it's better for Jochi to stay where he is – he may be more loyal at a distance." He got to his feet and staggered past the wagons towards the back of the tent. Arigh Boke crawled to his mother's side; the other three boys were suddenly on their feet.

"I greet you, Sorkhatani Beki," the Khan said.

He was alone. She stood up, pulled her youngest son to his feet, and bowed. "I welcome you, Khan and Father. I would be greatly honoured to have you dine with us."

"The wives of Chagadai and Ogedei filled me to bursting outside their tents, but I'll share a drink with you." He looked around. "My son must be relieving himself of his wine. At an ordinary meal, he drinks what most would at a festival, and at a feast, he and Ogedei drink more than any ten men."

"Drink eases my husband," Sorkhatani replied. "Much as he's missed his sons and his homeland, he's a soldier, and grows restless apart from battle."

"Don't make excuses for him." They seated themselves by the fire; a woman brought a jug of kumiss to Sorkhatani. She sprinkled a blessing, made the sign of the cross over the jug, and handed it to the Khan. "The Muslims say their laws forbid them strong drink," he continued, "and that made me think Tolui should practise that faith. But such laws don't keep those

men from their wine any more than Ogedei's promise to Chagadai restrains him."

Sorkhatani lifted a brow. "What promise was that?"

"Last autumn, we were feasting after a hunt. Chagadai grew
so angry with Ogedei's excesses that he made him promise to
take no more than a goblet of wine a day, and Ogedei was
drunk enough to swear such an oath. He's kept the promise,
in his fashion." The Khan's mouth twitched. "Ogedei had a
craftsman make a goblet so large that he can barely lift it."

Tolui stumbled towards them and sat down by his father; a
woman quickly brought him more wine. Night was coming,
and the wind was colder. Around other fires, people danced;
the wailing of flutes and the sighs of fiddles drowned out the
baying of the dogs. Those passing by were not stopping at
Sorkhatani's fire to drink and talk now; they glanced at their
Khan respectfully, then moved into the shadows.

"I have a question for my grandsons," the Khan said. "I wish
to see what they've learned. All the laws of my Yasa must be
kept, but which do you think is the most important?"

"That no Mongol shall take another Mongol as a slave,"
Mongke answered, "since that keeps us from fighting among
ourselves."

Hulegu shook his head. "Maybe that every man must obey
his commander without fail," he said, "since an officer has to
count on his men."

Arigh Boke frowned; at four and a half years of age, he was
still memorizing the Yasa. "Never make peace – " The little
boy scratched his head. "It's forbidden to make peace with
anyone who hasn't submitted to us."

"That," Tolui muttered, "would be my answer."

"And you, Khubilai?" the Khan asked. "What do you say?"

Khubilai lifted his head. "All the laws must be kept," he said,
"but I think that for a Khan, the most important is to respect
and honour the learned and just, and to despise the evil and
unjust."

His grandfather nodded. "And that would have been my
answer. But I'll tell you this, lad – that's often the most difficult
part of the Yasa to obey. The unjust can disguise themselves

629

in the cloak of virtue, and the just and wise can be tainted by the words of evil men."

A few boys lurked beyond the fire, apparently waiting for a chance to approach the Khan's grandsons. Tolui suddenly toppled to one side. The Khan leaned over him, shook him, then got up and hauled Tolui to his feet. "I'll take him inside," the Khan muttered.

"That isn't necessary, Temujin-echige," Sorkhatani said. "I've put him to bed before." The Khan was already leading Tolui towards the steps, supporting him with one arm.

"You may stay out here with your friends," she said to her sons, then followed the men into the tent. The women inside knelt as the Khan dragged Tolui past the hearth and towards the back. He lowered his son to the bed, put Tolui's hat on a table, then pulled off his son's coat and boots.

Sorkhatani sent the women outside. Tolui snored softly; the Khan covered him with a blanket. "It won't be much of a reunion for you, daughter," Temujin said.

"I'm content to have him with me."

He came to the hearth and stretched his roughened hands over the fire. "We've won much," he said, "my sons and I. They and their sons and grandsons will wear the finest damasks of Khwarezm and silks of Khitai, eat the most delicious of meats, mount the strongest horses, and claim the most beautiful of women, but they'll forget the one who led them to all of that."

"You will never be forgotten, Father and Khan," she said. His words were unlike him; he was speaking of his own death. "God will see that you are remembered."

"God is as indifferent to us as we are to the insects." Sorkhatani crossed herself. "But you're a Christian," he continued, "and believe that God loves men."

"He must love you, to have given you so much."

He turned towards her. "You've been a good wife to my son, and your boys show me you've been a good mother. They all have the makings of Khans."

She bowed her head. "I don't deserve such praise."

"I've said my third son will follow me," he said, "but Ogedei himself declared that if his descendants proved unworthy, others would have to succeed them. I know you'll always obey my wishes, Sorkhatani. A time may come when one of your sons will have to hold my ulus, and you'll be wise enough to know if my people need him. You won't be disloyal to my spirit if you encourage his ambitions."

"May that day never come," she whispered.

He sighed, then touched her face lightly. Despite the fire's warmth, his fingers were cold. "How like my Bortai you are," he said. "When I saw you by the fire with your four sons, I was reminded of our early years, when all I have now was only a dream."

Tolui moaned; she looked towards the bed. When she turned back, the Khan was walking towards the doorway, his back bowed, as if he carried an invisible burden.

116

BORTAI HANDED HER hawk to a guard. Another man took Khasar's hawk as he held out his arm. Bortai ached from the riding; she was getting too old for such pursuits, but had wanted some time outside Karakorum.

Thousands of tents now stretched from the banks of the Orkhon to the mountains that bordered the valley. Merchants with camel trains came to Karakorum from the oases to the south-west, bringing goods from Khitai and Khwarezm; envoys with petitions for the Khan were sent there from Temuge's camp in the east. News travelled swiftly through her husband's realm, carried by riders who had only to show an official seal at the posts where they stopped in order to be given food, rest, and a fresh mount.

Bortai had never seen a true city, but the vast encampment of Karakorum seemed much like one. The smoke of thousands of fires often hung over the tents until the strong winds dispersed it. The noise of men and women bartering with merchants, of craftsmen beating metal into tools, goblets, plates, and small sculptures, and of smiths hammering at their forges, could even drown out the sound of the wind. The lowliest soldiers had the wealth of Bahadurs, and captains owned as much as Khans had in the past. Yet she felt that the spirits that had once roamed this valley had fled from the river and steppe to the mountains and forests beyond.

Ogedei's wife Doregene had often told her that the Great Khan should have a great city, since all the world would send ambassadors to pay homage to him. Bortai sensed that the younger woman was thinking of Ogedei and not Temujin whenever she spoke of her ambitions for Karakorum. Doregene dreamed of palaces, perhaps even of walls.

Khasar squinted at her from his horse. His once-sharp vision was not as keen; he could still spot a mouse at a distance, but often narrowed his eyes to peer at anything near him. "We should ride back," he said. Bortai's guards and the young women who had ridden out with them were already trotting towards the encampment. "That messenger from your brother will be waiting to speak to you."

Anchar's envoy would have a personal message for her, as well as a report that would have to be passed along to Temujin. Her brother was with the army in Khitai, defending territory Mukhali had taken from encroachments by the Sung, while the King of Gold continued to resist in K'ai-feng.

Bortai sighed; she did not want to return to the bustle of Karakorum just yet. There would be others wanting to see her – merchants seeking permission to trade, reports from Temuge with requests for advice, a commander with more beautiful girls selected as tribute for the Khan. Temujin, still camped in the west near the Altai Mountains, was not rushing to her side.

"Temujin should come back soon," she said. "He's left too much in the hands of women for too long." She was not the only woman tending to the Khan's affairs. The Lady Yao-li Shih, the widow of their Khitan ally the Liao Wang, had ruled her husband's northern domain for the past three years in the absence of the Liao Wang's oldest son, who had gone west with Temujin. The Khan's daughter Alakha was still holding the territory of their Ongghut allies. Both women had the respect of their subjects, but it was time the heirs of those lands assumed their responsibilities.

"Don't fret over my brother," Khasar said. "He can handle things where he is as easily as he could anywhere else."

That was true enough. Their greatest worry in the Khan's absence had been the Tanguts, who had been bold enough to encourage a few subject tribes to attempt a raid on the borders of the Mongol homeland. They had clearly believed the armies left there could not put up much resistance, but Temujin, directing the campaign from his camp in the west, had ordered a counter-attack. The Tangut raid had failed, and a new king on the throne of Hsi-Hsia had sued for peace and promised to send Genghis Khan a son as a hostage. The Tangut envoys had met with Khasar on their way to Temujin's camp; her husband, for now, had an uneasy peace with the Tanguts he had sworn to punish.

"He should make more haste," Bortai murmured. "The Khan's wives yearn for him. Khadagan Ujin is weaker, the Lady Gurbesu grows old waiting for him, and his Kin princess and her ladies drown their loneliness in drink. Yisui and Yisugen have children unborn when he left who long for a glimpse of their father."

Khasar's grey moustache twitched; the wrinkles in his brown face deepened as he grinned. "Why, Bortai – I might almost think you're jealous of the beauties he's acquired during his absence."

"There are many wild geese and swans in the lake. The master may take those birds he chooses." Perhaps Temujin did not want to return to an old woman, one who would only remind him of his lost youth.

"I heard talk in the market-place," Khadagan said. "A man was saying that the Khan's forgotten us, that he prefers to while away his days hunting with his comrades and enjoying his spoils. A merchant whispered to one of my women that the Tanguts begged for peace only to gain time to plot more treachery."

Bortai had her own doubts about the Tanguts. Vassals who had refused to send her husband troops for his war in the west could not easily be trusted. But such matters were not for her to decide.

"It's foolish talk," Khadagan continued, "and hardly worth repeating. Still, I hear such talk more often." The other woman glanced at Bortai's slaves, but the women were murmuring among themselves as they worked their hides. "Bortai, if you summoned Temujin, he would come."

"Perhaps." She would have to swallow her pride to do it; the Khan, like Khasar, might assume she had grown jealous. "Winter is almost upon us — spring would be soon enough."

"For him to return," Khadagan said, "but perhaps not for the message. I think you should summon him now — send a message before we move to our winter grounds. He'll know you won't expect him to travel here in winter, so he'll wait until spring. That way, it won't look as though he's hurrying back because he fears your wrath."

Bortai smiled. "Sometimes I think you're much wiser than I am." She patted Khadagan's hand. "Temujin has given me much, but I value you more than anything he's brought to me. When he took you as a wife, he gave me a true friend."

Khadagan's wrinkled face softened. "You've been a good friend to me, Bortai, and that was more than I expected in the beginning." They often spoke that way lately, reminiscing about the past and assuring each other of their friendship, as if sensing that they might have little more time to do so.

Khadagan slowly rose to her feet. Bortai picked up the other woman's walking-stick and handed it to her. "I'm going to take your advice," Bortai said. "Please tell the men outside that I wish to see the captain of the night guard."

"I shall." Khadagan's head-dress bobbed as she nodded. "Good night." She hobbled towards the entrance and went outside.

The captain entered the great tent a few moments later. "I have a mission for you," Bortai said after he had greeted her. "Tomorrow, I want you to carry a message from me to the Great Khan."

"I am ready to deliver it."

"One of the scribes will give you a tablet with a seal, and this is my message. The great eagle makes his nest at the top of a high tree, but while he lingers in other lands, other birds may come to prey upon his fledgelings."

The young man repeated the message, then said, "Some may worry, Most Honourable Lady, but surely they can't believe our Khan has forgotten us."

"There are always a few with doubts and faint hearts. They'll be reassured when they know I've sent him this message. You may also tell the Khan that I pine for him, but that he may return at his pleasure."

The captain bowed. "I'll ride at dawn."

Temujin would see more in her words than concern for his realm and a longing for his presence. Fly back to me, rest at my side, grow old with me and do not leave your people again. He would hear that in her message, and would not welcome it.

117

SHOUTS AWOKE HER. Bortai sat up, her mind still fuzzy with sleep. The night rang with voices. Genghis Khan had returned; Temujin was among them once more.

Her slaves were awake, moving through the shadows. Bortai beckoned to one woman, who quickly brought her a robe as a man called out from the doorway.

"You may enter," Bortai said.

A guard came inside. "The Khan has ridden here," he said. "He's passing between the fires, Most Honourable Khatun, and begs permission to – "

"Of course my husband may come here."

The guard vanished. A woman helped her on with her boots; another brought her a small bowl of water. Bortai dipped her fingers into the water, dabbed at her face, then smoothed down her braids.

"I shall fetch a mirror, Honoured Lady," one slave said.

"I need no mirror." She was suddenly furious with Temujin.

There would be no time to paint her face, to hide the ravages of age.

A woman looped her braids, oiled them with sap, then secured Bortai's favourite plumed head-dress on her head. She had slept in a tunic and trousers against the cold; a slave adjusted her robe and tied a sash around her waist.

"My husband will need refreshment," she said. "You'll serve the kumiss in my porcelain goblets."

"And some wine also?" a young girl asked.

"The Khan disapproves of too much wine-drinking. I doubt that he – " Bortai steadied herself; he might have changed during the six years he had been gone. "You may set some out," she said at last. No time to prepare a feast, or to clothe herself in richer garments – she cursed under her breath. The messenger he had sent had told her he would be near Karakorum five days from now.

She went outside, trailed by two of the women, and descended the steps. The lines of guards around the great tent and her wagons stood at attention; rows of lighted torches made the space around them as bright as day. Others had gathered outside their yurts. A cheer went up, flowing towards her like a wave.

"The Khan! The Khan!" Others took up the cheer. "Temujin! Temujin!" Some knelt; others lifted their arms. Dogs howled above the cries.

A group of men walked towards her from the row of tethered horses outside her circle. She saw him then, in the midst of the men. She had expected him to be with Borchu or Subotai, but the men with him were young, hardly more than boys. Bortai gritted her teeth. He would have laughed while gathering the young men for a swift ride to Karakorum, acting as if he were still a boy himself.

Temujin passed a few men who were holding torches. The braids under his hat were greyer, the skin around his eyes more wrinkled. Her anger faded. He still moved gracefully in his bowlegged gait, but his body was heavier, his back not quite as straight. As he looked at her, a smile flashed across his face; for a moment, she saw the boy he had been.

636

He halted a few paces from her. Bortai bowed from the waist; the cheering died.

"I greet you and welcome you, my Khan and husband," she said. "To have the eagle fly to us so unexpectedly gives us great joy."

"It isn't so unexpected," he said. "Didn't I say that I'd be among you soon?" The young men around him grinned and chuckled."It's true that my cherished Khatun was told I would arrive somewhat later, but my impatience increased the nearer I came to her ordu. Riding here as I have has also shown me that my people haven't grown lax in their duties. The herdsmen I passed were on guard, and the sentries challenged me. They would have hastened here to alert you had I not forbidden it. Now I see that the guards here have kept their breastplates polished and their weapons honed, and stand before me as proudly as they did when I left. My wife has rushed from her bed to greet me, and my people have broken their sleep to welcome me. Had I come when I was expected, I would have deprived myself of such pleasures."

The young men laughed. Bortai smiled in spite of herself, remembering other times when he had hurried back to her.

"I rejoice to see you, husband and Khan," she said. "I am only sorry that I could not greet you with the feast you deserve."

"There will be time for feasting." He came to her and took her hands. "When we feast, I'll sit on my throne and observe the formalities. Tonight, I'm only a husband who seeks the welcome of the wife he's greatly missed, if she will deign to let me enter her tent."

She shook her head at him. "Of course you may enter."

Temujin turned to his companions. "Those of you who have families here may ride to them now. The night guard will see to food and shelter for the others." He released Bortai's hands and climbed the steps; she followed him into the tent.

They were alone, except for the slaves. The Khan went to the bed and sat down; jugs of kumiss and wine, along with white porcelain goblets, stood on a table near him. A woman went to him and set down a plate of dried meat.

"I beg your forgiveness for this meagre hospitality," Bortai said. "If you wish to forgo sleep a while longer, I'll have a lamb killed for you."

"This is enough," he said. "Sit with me, wife, and tell these others to return to their beds."

She murmured to the women; they retired to the eastern side of the tent. Bortai settled herself on a cushion by the bed. "What a reunion," she muttered. "You might have arrived in a more dignified manner. When I first heard the shouts, I almost thought an enemy was upon us."

"Now you sound more like the Bortai I remember." He sprinkled a blessing, drank, then handed her a goblet. "You mustn't chide me for responding to your message."

"And you replied by saying you'd return at your pleasure. After waiting all winter and much of the spring, another few days wouldn't have mattered."

"The more I thought about it, the more I disliked the prospect of greeting you with the harness of protocol restraining me."

"You act like a boy." She looked up at him; his hand rested on her shoulder for a moment.

"I have missed you, Bortai." In the shadows of the tent, he looked younger. She could still imagine him as he had been, and perhaps that was how he saw her.

"You look well," she said. "I see that Khulan's cared for you properly. I look forward to seeing her again – I hope she's more talkative than she was. I'm told her son and his Uighur bride have already given you another grandson, and – "

"Let's not speak of Khulan." His pale eyes stared at the hearth; that flame had apparently died. There was sorrow in his voice, and a deep weariness she had not heard in him before. He could not be so troubled over a woman, even Khulan. The war must have marked him; the deaths of comrades would have left their scars.

His eyes focused on her. "What a message you sent," he continued. "One might think that my realm was threatened on all sides."

"I didn't say that it was threatened, only that it might be." She poured more kumiss. "Well. I suppose you know that the Lady Yao-li Shih is travelling to meet you with a petition."

"So I've been told."

"I've sent word that she's to be sheltered in our camp along the Tula, since we'll be moving there soon. I think she's going to ask you to send the Liao Wang's oldest son to rule the Khitans. She's led her people well since losing her husband, and deserves your respect, especially after taking the trouble to travel to you herself. I'm told young Ye-lu Hsieh-she showed valour in your service."

"He's a good lad," Temujin said. "I'd hoped to keep him at my side a while longer."

"He will be of more use to you in his father's land, and the Lady Yao can advise him. You could send your brother Belgutei with him as commander of his troops."

"You've obviously thought about what I should do."

"Alakha's served you well also, and I see no reason to deprive the Ongghuts of her guidance. I suggest you wed her to young Po-yao-ho, and allow them to rule there together. I've been told he also fought bravely in the west, and marriage to one of your daughters will both honour him and make those lands even more secure for us. Alakha's loved by the Ongghuts, and Temuge has informed me that she's accepted Po-yao-ho's Christian faith, which should please that young man."

"Bortai, I'm hardly inside your tent before you're telling me what to do."

She sniffed. "These matters must be settled, and it's time the heirs to those lands took their thrones. If they have even a portion of the wisdom your daughter and the Lady Yao have shown, they'll be good rulers." She sipped her kumiss. "I'm only advising you, Temujin. You must decide what to do."

"You've done well, Bortai. I couldn't have left my homelands in the care of anyone wiser." She warmed at his praise. "I've missed my old grazing grounds," he went on. "Maybe I'll hear the spirits once more when I ride to Burkhan Khaldun."

He had been away too long; how could he doubt that they would speak to him? She gazed at his gnarled hands. The sage from Khitai had not brought him youth and long life, but she had not expected that he would. All the magic in the world could not save men from death; his spirit would find youth only in the next world.

She was truly an old woman if she could think such thoughts.

A young person gained no solace from contemplating the final rest that awaited them all.

She said, "The spirits told me the truth in my dream."

"Your dream?"

"The one I had before I met you, when a gyrfalcon brought me the moon and sun."

"Ah – the dream you shared with your father."

"You have brought me the sun and moon, Temujin." The ghosts of her parents seemed near, as they always did whenever she thought of her early life.

"I must sleep, Bortai. Long rides tire me more than they used to." He took off his coat and hat; she pulled off his boots. More wars surely lay ahead, but his sons and generals could wage them while he directed them from the homeland. As he drew her to him, she prayed that he would know some peace at last.

PART EIGHT

Subotai said, "The waters are dried up, the most beautiful gem is shattered. Yesterday, O my Khan, you soared over your people like a falcon. Today, you have fallen from the sky . . ."

118

THE CAMP ALONG the Tula was the largest Checheg had ever seen; she would be lost amid so many camping circles. She had ridden past herds of horses and cattle for days; near the camp, the flocks of sheep looked like great clouds that had come to rest on the yellow grassland.

Beyond the eastern edge of the camp, sentries waited by two fires. The encampment rippled in the heat; the mountains bordering the valley on the north were a brown and black wall dotted with green. One of the men riding with Checheg and the other girls galloped ahead to greet the sentries.

Chosen, Checheg thought, chosen for the Khan. Every year, her Onggirat people sent such a tribute to Genghis Khan, as did all the tribes and clans of the ulus. Nine Onggirat girls had been selected this year, and she was among them when the Khan's soldiers came to claim the tribute. Her father was both chief and shaman in their small camp; a dream had told him that his daughter would be the woman of a great man. No man was greater than Genghis Khan.

Artai reined in her horse near Checheg's. "The Khan has so many women already," the other girl murmured. "He only accepts us because it would be insulting to refuse us."

"But he decreed that the most beautiful girls be given to him," Checheg whispered back.

"He could hardly take back that decree now. People might wonder if he's still able to join with a woman if he did."

Checheg shook her head at Artai; the soldiers might hear her. Better to be the Great Khan's woman, even among so many others, than to be the wife of a young soldier or chief.

Yet the sight of the camp dampened her spirits a little. There would be so many girls here, Merkits, Kereits, and Naimans, girls from Khitai, girls from northern forests, western lands, and the oases to the south. The Khan was not even in this camp now, having gone north to the mountain of Burkhan Khaldun. He was, rumour had it, still grieving for his old comrade Jebe Noyan, who had recently died. Others spoke of a campaign against Hsi-Hsia. The Khan had been camped by the Tula only since the beginning of summer, but some said he might ride with his army against the Tanguts. It might be some time before the Khan favoured her.

Checheg drew herself up. The spirits had spoken to her father; they would show her the way to the Khan's side.

After the girls and their escorts had passed between the fires, they were guided to a circle of tents at the northern end of the camp. In the evening light, Checheg could see a row of great tents, each of them surrounded by smaller tents and hundreds of wagons. The small yurts were black, the large tents golden in the dusky light. A tugh of nine yak-tails, the Khan's standard, fluttered in front of the largest tent.

An old woman greeted them, told them her name was Kerulu, then led them to one of the yurts. Small wooden beds with felt cushions stood on the tent's eastern side; the girls set down their packs near them. Kerulu peered at each girl closely while asking her name. When they had finished a meal of curds and kumiss, and gone outside to relieve themselves, the old woman sent them to their beds.

Checheg slept deeply, tired from the journey. When she awoke, old Kerulu was sitting by the hearth. Her wrinkled face sagged with weariness; Checheg suspected that she had been watching over the girls during the night.

"Take off your shifts," Kerulu said as two other women entered the yurt. The girls giggled and blushed as the women checked their teeth, sniffed at their breath, prodded them, and poked fingers between their legs to confirm that they were maidens. "Your breath is sour," the old woman said to one girl. "This one here tosses in her sleep, and the one next to her is a bit too tall, while this little one doesn't seem as strong as the others." She scowled at the girl standing next to Checheg. "And you, dear child, have a very faint snore."

The women murmured among themselves as the girls pulled on their clothes. When they were dressed, the five Kerulu had singled out were told to pick up their packs; the other two women led them outside.

"Where are they going?" Artai asked.

"They'll be taken to other camps," Kerulu replied, "and be given to men the Great Khan esteems. Lovely as they are, only the most perfect girls are kept here. You are fortunate, young ones. Many girls await the Khan's summons in other camps while they tend the flocks and herds of minor wives. Many are never sent to one of the Khatuns to serve in her household. You will have the honour of living in the ordu of Bortai Khatun, and you have just passed your first test."

Checheg supposed that the second test might be how they conducted themselves during the morning meal. She was careful to sit in a respectful posture, one knee raised, the other folded under her, and sipped her broth, trying not to seem either too gluttonous or too dainty of appetite.

They had rinsed out their cups when a guard called out beyond the door; Khadagan Ujin, one of the Khan's minor wives, wished to enter. Checheg longed to go outside and urinate, but said nothing; a weak bladder would surely be a mark against her.

Khadagan Ujin's plumed head-dress was so tall that she had to stoop to pass through the entrance. The girls knelt as Kerulu bowed. The Ujin carried a walking-stick, and the body under her pleated cotton robe was slender for an old woman, but her narrow face could never have been beautiful.

"I greet you, Ujin," Kerulu said. "Five of the Onggirat maidens were found lacking, but these four are all they should be. Their bodies are well formed, their teeth strong, their braids thick, their breath sweet when they wake, and they won't disturb the Great Khan's sleep with any restlessness."

Khadagan Ujin turned towards them. "Honour is yours, young maidens," she said. "You will perform what tasks you are given, and Kerulu-eke will dwell with you. If you're fortunate, you may soon be summoned to wait upon Bortai Khatun in her tent. If you're very fortunate, you may catch the eye of the Khan, and please him enough for him to give you to one of his sons or Noyans. And if you have the greatest luck any woman can have, the Khan may take you to his bed."

The Ujin frowned. "I'm sure that you're virtuous girls," she continued, "but this must be said. Don't dream of enticing some young man who catches your fancy. The Khan is very jealous of his possessions."

Checheg could not restrain a sigh. Khadagan glanced at her. "Is there something you wish to say?"

"Only this, Honoured Lady," Checheg replied. "I don't know how a girl who's been given to the greatest of all men could ever dream of love with a lesser one."

"Don't raise your hopes too high, child." The Ujin's small eyes were gentle. "You're the most favoured of maidens, but the Khan has many flocks. Those whom the Khan favours are often only the bedfellows of a night, and others kept their maidenheads for some time before their master honoured them with his love."

Checheg refused to be discouraged. Bortai Khatun was an Onggirat. Perhaps the Khan was fated to fall in love with another Onggirat maiden. The spirits had spoken to her father; she would surely be singled out.

119

BORTAI GLANCED AT her husband. He was still sitting in front of the bed, as he had been since the departure of his guests. The Khan had said little during the evening meal, and had ignored the Onggirat girls she had summoned there to wait on them.

He was angry; she saw that in his eyes. Perhaps that was better than being in the grip of the darker spirit that had haunted him since Jebe's death. Jebe had gone suddenly, collapsing outside the tent of one of his wives. The man Temujin had called his Arrow had flown far to the west, only to fall to earth here.

Bortai had not believed a man could mourn so deeply; even Subotai, who had grown close to Jebe during their long ride west, had not grieved as much. "You don't understand," Temujin had said to her after returning from Burkhan Khaldun. "Jebe is no more." The agony in his voice had frightened her; Bortai had feared he might give up his own spirit.

Now he stewed in a silent rage, gulping kumiss and staring at the hearth. There would be war, but she had expected that. The Tangut King had promised Temujin a hostage and a truce, but no hostage had arrived and none would be sent. The Khan's envoy had returned from Hsi-Hsia with that message, and Temujin had also learned that the Tanguts were treating with the King of Gold, trying to secure the aid of the Kin armies. Before he could finally crush the Kin, he would have to strike at the Tanguts, and quickly.

He had sworn to avenge himself on Hsi-Hsia, and the time of vengeance had arrived. The spirits had brought this about, so that her husband would be forced to keep his promise.

"There must be a war kuriltai," he said at last, "and before the great hunt."

"Of course," Bortai said. "I suppose you always knew this war would come."

"I knew. I couldn't have trusted the Tanguts again even if their King had kept his promise. They'll pay."

"Your generals are invincible," she said. "They'll bring you the head of the Tangut King."

He turned to her as she sat down next to him. "I mean to take it myself. I've decided to lead my men against Hsi-Hsia. Chagadai will stay with you, and you will advise him."

Bortai stiffened. "Temujin, I beg you not to go."

His eyes narrowed. "And have my enemies call me a coward?"

"No man can call you that. You've shown your courage. Your generals and your sons can fight for you now."

"I never expected to hear such advice from you, Bortai. Would you have me behave like a feeble old man?"

You are an old man, she thought. She could not say that, or tell him how much she feared for him. "Let others fight for you, Temujin. Surely you've earned some rest."

"I'll rest soon enough. I'll see the Tanguts punished first."

He was admitting that death awaited even him, yet he was rushing to meet it. "I beg you," she whispered. "I waited long years for you – my sixtieth year will soon be upon me. How many years can we have left? Haven't I earned –"

The cold rage in his eyes silenced her. "I forbid you," he said in his soft voice, "to say any more about this matter. Chagadai will guard the homeland with the aid of Temuge and Khasar. If you've grown so feeble that you can't give them good counsel, then stay out of their way."

"Temujin!"

He stood up. "When I came back to you," he said, "it didn't matter that the hair once as black as a raven's wing had became as pale as the swan's. I could look past that wrinkled brown face and still see my beautiful Bortai. But you no longer sound like the woman I loved. Wait for death if you must, but wait for it alone. I won't wait for it in fear with you."

He strode to the entrance and disappeared into the night.

The Khan stirred next to her. Yisui pressed closer to him as the wind howled outside. The winter storm had nearly ripped the door from the tent when he entered, his hat and coat gleaming with ice. Ever since the great hunt, he had come to her ordu often. He was still a young man in her bed; she could arouse him as she had, and delight him with her cries. Her three youngest children, as usual, were staying in her sister's tent, and her Han deaf-mutes could not hear what passed between her and her husband.

"Get me something to drink," Temujin said.

The slaves were sleeping; she would have to kick one awake

646

to fetch the kumiss, so it was easier to get it herself. She hurried to where the jugs hung from horns set in the tent's wooden framework, took one down, then hastened back to the bed, sprinkling the blessing before she slipped under the blankets.

"I know you enjoy seeing me naked," she said, "but in such weather, you might leave me my shift."

He laughed as he propped one elbow against a pillow. "You are refreshing, Yisui."

"Refreshing?"

"Because you think only of yourself, and care nothing for anyone else. A cat has more feeling for her young, and you love me chiefly for what I've given you, but I find such selfishness and practicality amusing. Others mouth noble sentiments and assure me of their devotion. With you, everything is so much clearer."

He was mocking her, as he did so often lately. "But I care greatly for you, and for my sister." She paused. "And I've always loved my children, whatever you say." She had not heard from the oldest two in some time. Perhaps she should send gifts and a motherly message to them.

"Don't lie, Yisui — it spoils your charm." He lifted the jug and drank. "I don't doubt that you can summon up some feeling for Yisugen, but that's only because you see yourself in her, and because she relieves you of caring for your own children."

"You wound me, husband." She pulled the blankets up to her chin. "Haven't I shown my love for you?"

"Your love for me is that of a crow grateful for the sparkling stones it hoards in its nest, or that of a tiger in heat, who forgets her mate easily once they have joined. Don't look so hurt — I had my share in making you what you are. I can count on your loyalty, because you care so much for yourself, and know your interests and mine are the same."

She peered up at his shadowed face. She disliked this part of him, the part that was bitter and resigned.

He said, "I find you so refreshing, in fact, that I don't want to be parted from you. I'm going to take you with me when we ride against Hsi-Hsia."

She had not expected this; he could not mean it. "I'm honoured," she said slowly, "that you want me as your companion, but – " Her teeth dug into her lower lip. "Yisugen, as you know, is somewhat more frail than she used to be. Oh, she's quite strong enough for her duties here, but I fear she may find the rigours of a campaign hard to endure."

"I said nothing about Yisugen. She'll stay behind and look after your children and her own. I'm sure you won't miss your young ones too greatly, since they're often under her tent as it is."

She sat up. "Yisugen and I swore we'd never be separated."

"That was a promise you made to each other," he said. "It doesn't bind me."

"I assumed – you always let us think – "

"Are you telling me you won't go?"

"I must obey you, Temujin. I only ask that you not take me from – "

"You're selfish enough to use her as an excuse." He swallowed more kumiss. "I want one of my four cherished Khatuns with me. Khulan grew tiresome when we went west, and Bortai must stay here to advise Chagadai. Yisugen is, as you say, somewhat weaker than she was. That leaves you, Yisui, and your protest surprises me. You have your faults, but I never thought cowardice was one of them."

"Give me a bow and a lance," she said, "and I'll ride into the fray at your side. It's only that to be parted from my sister – "

"Spare me any touching speeches. You claim to love your sister, so I offer you this choice. Yisugen may stay behind, or she may travel with us. You may decide whether your love for Yisugen demands that she be at your side, or that you leave her."

Tears streamed from her eyes. "Whatever I choose, both Yisugen and I will suffer."

"I'm leaving your sister's fate to you. I'm curious to see what you'll decide."

"You know what I must do," she said harshly. "I can only show my love for my sister by parting from her now, by breaking the promise I made."

"Cover yourself, wife. We can't have you falling ill." She stretched out under the blankets; he set down his jug and slipped his arm around her waist. "I was wrong about you, Yisui. You're a little less selfish than I thought. Your sister will be sorry to lose you, but her life will be little different in your absence. Maybe she won't miss you too much."

"Stop it," she said.

"You'll have time to say your farewells. I know you'll serve me well, if only so we can return to Yisugen more quickly."

"Yes," she said.

120

THE WIND BIT at Yisui. Along the banks of the Onghin River, the short grass was just beginning to turn green. The rows of wagons had halted by the river; camels and oxen, freed of their yokes, grazed. The Khan was hunting in the wooded slopes to the north, where musk deer and wild asses roamed.

The sky was still light, but Yisui and those with her would camp here tonight. Girls had built fires near the covered wagons; boys took up positions as guards with the men. If the hunting party did not return that evening, they would move south at dawn and wait for the hunters to rejoin them.

They had left the camp along the Tula a month ago. Here, the Onghin was thick with ice and women warmed water near the fires before letting the animals drink it. Temujin had not waited until early spring to send out his scouts; they had clothed themselves in heavy sheepskin coats and covered their horses in felt blankets before riding south to the borders of Hsi-Hsia. Their reports were encouraging. The Tanguts, it seemed, did not expect an attack so soon, and were also counting on the forces stationed in their cities and towns. The Mongols would move towards the Etzingol River, graze their animals there, then strike at Hsi-Hsia in the west.

Yisui looked upriver at the rows and circles of wagons and tents that stood on the sand-strewn, rocky ground beyond the thin grass. The other women had been uneasy during the journey. A rumour had swept the Khan's camp before the army's departure, of a shaman dreaming that a star had fallen to earth and that a shadow had darkened the sun. Yisui had ignored the stories. Ye-lu Ch'u-ts'ai had read the bones for the Khan, and had predicted victory.

She had been more troubled by Bortai's visit to her tent. Bortai had made Yisui swear that she would be the Khan's shadow if any harm came to him. "Stay at his side," Bortai had whispered, while admitting how much she feared for Temujin. To see Bortai consumed by doubt seemed another evil omen.

A tiny cloud of sand moved towards an outlying circle of wagons. Yisui watched as the rider pulled up and two boys rushed to him. One of the boys suddenly bolted towards another horse, saddled it, and began to gallop in her direction.

Her mouth grew dry when she caught sight of the boy's face. His lips were chewed raw, his eyes wide with terror. "The Great Khan!" he shouted when he was near. "He fell from his horse – he's badly hurt!"

Yisui turned away and shouted to her servants.

By the time Yisui and her women had pitched a yurt, tying a second layer of felts over the first against the cold, the hunters were back. Borchu was leading Temujin's horse; Subotai sat behind the Khan, holding him up. Temujin groaned as Subotai dismounted, helped him down, and led him to the tent. Yisui hurried inside after Borchu, followed by the shaman she had summoned.

The two generals laid the Khan on a bed of cushions. "Temujin's horse threw him," Borchu said. "The damned steed reared when some of the men were driving the game towards us. He's been complaining of pain ever since."

Yisui beckoned to the shaman. The old man knelt by the Khan, poking at him under his coat until Temujin pushed him away. "Let me be!"

"At least one rib is broken," the shaman said, "and you may have other injuries, my Khan. You should be bound up, and then a sheep must be brought here so that you – "

"Bind me up," Temujin muttered, "but spare me a sheep's

fat tail. I'd only choke on it." He moaned as Subotai propped him up and removed his coat and hat; the shaman bound his midriff with a length of silk. The Khan's face gleamed with sweat, and his breath came in short, sharp gasps. "Leave me – let me rest." His voice was faint.

"Go," Yisui whispered to the shaman. "Sacrifice a sheep, and bring the tail to me." The old man scurried outside. Temujin would recover, she told herself; to doubt that was akin to believing the sun would not rise at dawn.

The Khan closed his eyes; a rasping sound came from his throat. "Shall we stay with him?" Subotai asked.

"Let him sleep," Yisui said. "I'll watch over him. Come back in the morning, and we'll see how he's faring then."

The two men got up. "The Master from Khitai warned him not to hunt," Borchu said.

"My husband will recover." Yisui walked with them towards the entrance. "The mightiest of men can hardly be felled by a skittish horse."

She sat with him throughout the night. She covered his fevered body with blankets, wiped his face, and lifted his head to give him mare's milk. The shaman returned with a sheep's tail; she tore off bits of fat and put them between her husband's lips.

He could not die. She huddled near him, listening to his laboured breathing as the shaman chanted outside. She had feared him, and the mingled rage and joy she felt when they joined was as close to hate as it was to love, but he was the centre of her world and that of his people.

At dawn, she went outside. Borchu and Subotai had come back, but they were not alone. Men crouched around fires; the shaman had been joined by others, all of them beating drums and crying to the spirits. Ogedei squatted next to the general Tolun Cherbi; Tolui stood with Mongke and Khubilai, the sons he had brought with him to look after his horses. The guards around the tent drew back as Yisui walked towards the men.

"Take heart, brave warriors," she said. "You'll see no spear before this tent."

"The Khan is better?" Subotai asked.

"He's feverish. He was still for most of the night. He's no worse."

Tolun Cherbi got to his feet and peered at her with his small bloodshot eyes. "We must speak to him," he said.

"I'll see if he's awake."

When she went back inside, Temujin lifted his head. "Who's out there?" he asked.

"Ogedei and Tolui. Several of your generals."

"Help me sit up," he said.

"Temujin – "

"Help me up, Yisui."

She knelt next to him, raised him into a sitting position, and propped cushions against his back. His jaw tightened as he clenched his teeth; his face was sallow and beaded with sweat. "I'll see them now."

She went to the entrance and rolled up the flap. Borchu and Subotai entered, followed by Tolun Cherbi and the Khan's two sons. Others gathered by the doorway of the small yurt.

"I'll hear what you have to say," Temujin said as Yisui sat down at his side.

"I think I can speak for all of us," Tolun Cherbi said. "My Khan, we should turn back. The Tanguts have walled towns and camps that don't move. They won't pick up their houses and go elsewhere. We can return to your camp on the Tula, wait until you recover, and when we come back, the Tanguts will still be there."

"And do the rest of you agree?" the Khan asked.

"Tolun Cherbi speaks for me," Tolui said. "You know me, Father – I'd never turn aside from war without a good reason."

"I spoke with my son Guyuk before coming to your tent," Ogedei said. "He says that the Tanguts can't stand against our might, whether we fight them now or later."

Temujin looked towards the entrance, but the men peering inside were silent. "Now hear the words of your Khan. The King of Hsi-Hsia will soon know we're riding to him. If we withdraw now, he'll say it was fear that drove us back. I swore they'd be punished. They sent me no soldiers when I requested them, and have been a spear in my side ever since. Must I wait even longer to have my revenge?"

652

Subotai leaned forward. "Le Te Wang wasn't ruling Hsi-Hsia when we went to war in the west. It's true that he's insulted you, and refused to send the hostage you demanded, but it was his father who wouldn't send us troops. This King may turn aside from war if he's offered the opportunity, and you'd have time to regain your strength." The general smiled. "Le Te Wang is likely to give us an excuse to war against him later."

"Very well." Temujin frowned. "I'll give him one last chance. Subotai, find the most trustworthy man among your Tangut officers, and tell him to take this message to the King." He paused. "You swore to be my right hand, yet sent no army when I rode west. I took no vengeance then, but now I demand your surrender. You will submit to me and send a hostage from among your sons, along with the tribute I am owed, or God alone knows what will happen to you."

Subotai nodded. "It will be done, Temujin."

A few days after the envoy's departure, the army moved south along the Onghin. In spite of his injuries, the Khan refused to be conveyed in a wagon, and rode with his men. The soldiers were heartened at seeing he was not so weak as they feared; the women no longer whispered of evil omens. Only Yisui heard his groans at night, his feverish mutterings as he sought sleep.

The Khan's envoy returned three days after they had stopped to pitch their tents once more. Although Temujin was resting, he insisted that Yisui prop him up so that he could greet the man properly. Borchu and Subotai came with the messenger to the Khan's tent, their faces grim, and Yisui's last lingering hopes vanished.

"Give me your report," Temujin said.

"I delivered your message, my Khan," the Tangut envoy said. "The King wavered. I heard him murmur that it was his father Li Tsun-hsiang who was responsible for offending you, but in the end, his minister Asha Gambu spoke for him."

"And what did he say?" the Khan asked.

The messenger took a breath. "He said this. If the one called Genghis Khan wants to fight, tell him to come and test his strength. If he wants treasure, tell him he can try to wrest it from our mighty cities of Ling Chou and Ning-hsia." The man swallowed. "I think I was fortunate to return here with my head."

Temujin's face was pale. "After that kind of challenge, we can't withdraw. I'll march on Hsi-Hsia if it means my death! I swear it by Koko Mongke Tengri!"

"No man can call back such an oath." Subotai's hand shook as he gulped down his kumiss.

"They've been strengthening their defences," Temujin muttered, "but their forces are scattered among their cities and towns. We'll strike at Etzina, as we planned. Once it's taken, the river to the south will lie open to us." He took a shallow breath. "We must strike hard and fast. We move tomorrow."

The men finished their kumiss, then stood up. "Your men will be ready," Subotai said.

When they were gone, Yisui crept closer to her husband. "You may have need of me," she said. "I can think of no safer place to be than at your side while you direct this war." She touched his face lightly. "I wish you'd turn back, and let the others go on without you, but I also see that your men will fight harder if you remain with them. Let them see your pain – let them know that even your suffering can't dull your courage. They'll do anything to preserve their Khan's life, as would I. What would become of us without you?"

He sighed hoarsely. "Why, Yisui – I might almost believe you've come to love me."

It had nothing to do with love. She could not see him as a man like other men. For Heaven to take him from the world would be as if the sun were to vanish from the sky, or the moon were no longer there to light the night.

She said, "I swore an oath that I would be your shadow until you return to your old camping grounds, that I would stay at your side if any harm came to you."

"Then I'll allow you to keep your oath." He lifted a brow. "Perhaps the thought of hearing songs praising the bravery and devotion of Yisui Khatun also appeals to you."

She would keep her promise. He did not have to know that

Bortai, who had feared she might never see him again, had brought her to make the pledge.

121

THE MONGOLS CROSSED the desert, driving south towards the Etzingol River, and even the desert spirits seemed to tremble before the Khan. The sudden storms that reddened the sky and blotted out the sun, forcing people to cling to their animals and cower next to wagons, lashed at them for only a short time before lifting. The winds that ceaselessly swept across the desolate plain died a little as the army passed. The voices that whispered in the desert, spirits that might lure unwary travellers from their path, instead seemed to beckon them on their way; the funnels of sand spirits swirled in the distance without touching their train. During the cold nights, the sky was black silk, the stars bright lanterns unveiled by clouds, the silence so intense that even a distant whisper could be overheard.

They pressed on, heedless of the lakes that shimmered on the horizon, illusions sent by desert spirits to tempt them. When at last they caught sight of a true lake, it took them three days to reach it. Beyond the sand and swampland around the lake, the ramparts of a city could be seen, looming over siege towers, catapults, and the dark mass of the army.

The city was burning. Subotai and his advance forces had assaulted Etzina, battering its walls with rocks; flames arched over the ramparts and fell. Temujin watched the destruction from his horse, gazing over the gravel-strewn land and the massed army at the dying city, and Yisui saw the pain leave his eyes. Etzina was a fire that would warm him, and restore his strength to him.

Yisui had sworn to be his shadow, so when the gates opened, and the people came out to surrender, she stayed with the Khan as his men ordered the Tibetan defenders of Etzina to bind themselves, and then beheaded them. There was rhythm and order to the executions; the enemy officers and soldiers knelt, the swords slashed down, the bodies were stripped and cast aside. Hills of heads rose around the Mongol soldiers; their coats, tunics, and armour were spattered with blood.

The enemy soldiers had known what their fate would be. But others were also led before Temujin, women clutching the hands of children, boys and girls too terrified to weep, old men in yellow robes, babies who wailed as they were torn from the arms of their mothers.

Yisui knew Temujin would demand their deaths; he had sworn to wipe the Tanguts from the earth. Their King had brought this upon them as surely as her father had led his Tatar people to their doom. Odd, she thought, that she should remember that. She had believed it behind her, forgotten, a cruel fate she had been powerless to prevent.

It came to her that Temujin knew he was dying, that he would not survive this war. This slaughter was not just the Khan ridding himself of enemies, but a funeral offering. This was what Heaven willed for her, to serve her husband in his last war. She had been plucked from the ashes of her own people. Now she would hear their forgotten cries once more in the throats of dying Tanguts.

The fields around Etzina provided fodder for their horses, and the cattle of the Tanguts were added to their train. Along the banks of the Etzingol, the wutung trees were growing green, narrow leaves sprouting on their lower branches, while the broad-leafed branches above made high arches overhead. In the dark green light of the arched alleyways created by the trees, the spongy growths covering their trunks glistened like tears.

The Mongols came to stretches of sand, where tamarisks were half-buried by the mounds. The army wound its way among the maze of tall hills and tangled branches until they came to willows and tended fields. Ahead lay grazing lands and the sweet waters of the widening river; behind, the Mongols left a trail of burned towns, ravaged fields, and monuments of heads.

When the animals were fatter, and they had reached a fork

in the river, the army divided into three. Subotai crossed the Etzingol and drove east towards Kan Chou; another wing moved west towards the city of Su Chou. By the time the Khan and the centre of the army came to the stretch of land called Kansu, the Etzingol was a torrent filled with loosened boulders and rocks, its whirlpools and currents too treacherous to ford.

The Khan's army had skirted the wall to the north of Kansu; its ramparts and watchtowers were useless to the enemy now. The ruts of the trade routes that scarred the yellow land were empty of caravans and the fields outside the levelled towns of the oases were sown with bodies and bones. Horses grazed under rows of poplars and willows; the advance forces had begun their work here.

The heat of the summer was upon them; wind raised the sands of Kansu and darkened the sky. The high snow-covered peaks of the Nan Shan Mountains beckoned in the south, a refuge where the Khan could make his headquarters. He moved on, and as he moved, his soldiers cut down bands of fugitives trying to escape.

Above black granite escarpments and yellow cliffs of loess, the Khan found shelter in a wide mountain meadow. Tents rose along the sides of a rapid stream; the animals grazed on clover and grass dotted with blue flowers.

The Khan no longer wore a silk bandage around his middle, but Yisui saw him grimace when he moved and heard his moans at night. She was always at his side. Men came often to his tent to inform the Khan of the war's progress, and Temujin insisted on hearing all the reports.

Listening to messages, making changes in tactics, and deciding on the signals to be passed along to the armies took most of Temujin's waking moments. His pains troubled him too much to allow him the diversion of a hunt; he summoned none of his women and ignored the Tangut girls he might have claimed. Only Yisui knew that he no longer held her in his arms; that pleasure had been taken from him, too.

She urged him to rest, to let the cooler air revive him, but he was driven by this war. His oath had set him on this course; the arrow had flown from his bow and would impale itself in

657

his enemy's heart. His men were to do as they liked with the Tanguts, destroy every wall that hid them, level every house where they might find shelter. If his spirit was to fly from him, he would not let the Tanguts survive him.

With her women, Yisui tended the yurt, cooked, gathered dung and dry tamarisk branches for fuel, butchered game, and cleaned hides. Even as she nursed her husband, she pitied the Tanguts. Temujin's men would rejoice at the chance to do as they liked with their victims; only the Khan could hold them back. She prayed for swift victories, even knowing the suffering they would bring, because the triumphs might soften Temujin's heart.

But news of victories only hardened the Khan's resolve. Su Chou fell that summer, all its people slain for refusing to surrender. Kan Chou was taken by the general Chaghan, who settled for killing only the officers who had urged the town to resist. Temujin allowed that act of mercy because word had come to him of the death of the Tangut King; Le Te Wang's brother Li Hsien had succeeded him to the throne.

Temujin might have sent envoys to the new King demanding surrender, but did not. Early that autumn, when the meadow was grazed bare, he and those with him left the mountains.

The gorges and canyons gave way to a band of burning desert. To the east of the sands lay the Yellow River, which flowed past the earthen battlements of a wall; its defenders had fallen or fled. The advance force moved along the river's fertile bank, laying waste to the tiny villages in their path. The wind coated the invaders with sand and soil until they were as yellow as the loess, a golden army moving towards the heart of Hsi-Hsia.

The western trade routes now lay in the Mongols' hands, cutting off the cities on the Yellow River. Ying-li was the first large town in the path of the invaders. The Tanguts there, knowing that surrender would only leave the cities of Ling Chou and Ning-hsia open to attack, held out against the assaults of siege engines and the waves of men storming the walls until winter came and snow swirled around the battlements.

When Ying-li finally fell, the Tanguts sent a great army to

meet the Mongols in the field and to strike at the Mongol force
besieging Ling Chou. The Khan, after learning of this from his
scouts, ordered a retreat to the west of the Alashan Mountains.
The Tangut army followed, meeting no resistance in the mountain passes. The Mongols lured them on, fell upon them in the
desert beyond the mountains, and crushed the army of Hsi-
Hsia. The Khan was rewarded with the head of Asha Gambu,
taken during the slaughter.

The irrigation canals around Ling Chou were frozen over
when the Mongols renewed their siege, and the river that had
blocked their approach before now aided them, for they could
cross its solid surface. Ling Chou was doomed, yet surrendered
only after most of its defenders were dead and the Mongols
were pouring through its gates.

Part of the army moved north to surround the Tangut capital
of Ning-hsia; the Khan himself moved west to take the town
of Yen-chuan Chou. There, from his headquarters overlooking
the town, Temujin, with Yisui at his side, watched as distant
plumes of smoke rose towards the grey winter sky.

Winter had weakened the Khan. His fever flared again after
the fall of Yen-chuan Chou; Yisui summoned a guard and told
him to fetch Ye-lu Ch'u-ts'ai.

The sky was still light, but the camp was quieter than it had
been for days. She no longer heard the cries of the survivors
who had been dragged there, to be raped and butchered or
crushed under planks by dancing men. Most of the Mongol
women had been left behind near Ying-li; they had been spared
those sights and sounds. Yisui, sworn to be the Khan's shadow,
had endured them.

He was a dying man, whose pain fuelled his rage; that was
how she explained it to herself. It was he who had ordered the
extermination of the Tanguts, but his generals sought even
more destruction. For days now, they had sent petitions to
the Khan complaining of poor forage during the campaign,
suggesting that the Uighurs who dwelled in Tangut towns, the
Han who tilled the land, and the other subject peoples be killed
as well. Such men were useless as soldiers, and the land could
become pasture.

Yisui had even more reason to preserve her husband's life. Only Temujin could give the commands that would keep his men from such a course. How strange it was to have such pity for people she did not know. She had thought she had overcome such weaknesses long ago.

She went inside the yurt. Temujin was sitting up on his bed of cushions, but his breathing sounded laboured. "I've sent for your Khitan chancellor," she said. "His medicines may ease you more than a shaman's spells."

"He's returned to this camp?"

"You know he has," she said. "He arrived several days ago, and sent one of his men to ask if he might come to you. You've forgotten." His fever might have blotted out the memory, but she doubted it. He knew what Ch'u-ts'ai was likely to say about his generals' demands for pasture; perhaps that was why he had not summoned the Khitan.

If Ch'u-ts'ai pleaded for mercy, the Khan might listen. She would let the Khitan tell Temujin what she could not.

Ye-lu Ch'u-ts'ai arrived with two young men. "I welcome you, friend and brother," Temujin muttered. "My wife thinks you may be able to relieve my suffering."

The Khitan glanced at Yisui with his large dark eyes. Temujin would have given him a far greater share of plunder, yet Ch'u-ts'ai was content with the writings, herbs, and odd devices he had salvaged from conquered cities – a piece of glass that turned a ray of light into bands of colour, a bronze magic mirror through which light could pass and cast a pattern on a wall, a metal needle that pointed south when attached to a cork floating in a bowl of water. He had often made her feel uneasy with herself, as if all she possessed were nothing to him.

"I am sorry I could not come before," Ch'u-ts'ai said. "I had to tend many of our soldiers at Ling Chou when disease broke out among the ranks."

"So I was told."

"And when you didn't summon me, I hoped you were resting, which is often the best cure for ailments. I've been most anxious to speak to you, my Khan."

Temujin grunted. "As everyone is."

"I've brought you ma-hwang," the Khitan said, "to ease your breathing. I made the mortar from the twigs myself, and mixed it with lime." One of the young men handed a small pouch to Temujin. The chancellor was silent as the Khan chewed on the remedy, then continued, "I've seen an omen in the heavens. I also know what your generals wish to do in these lands."

Temujin scowled. "What does one have to do with the other?"

"Heaven, Great Khan, has revealed what you must decide."

"I know what to do. I said those people are to die. They're useless to us."

"How can you say they're useless? Leave them to their labours, and they would yield much for your troops. You'd gain more that way than by turning the land into pasture."

"My wishes are known," Temujin said, "and the demands of my generals are in accord with them."

"And Heaven itself protests them." The Khitan leaned forward. "Great Conqueror, I've watched the skies, and seen the five planets drawing closer to one another. They are now in conjunction. When the sun sets, look to the south-west, and you'll see them, a beacon warning you against such a decree."

"My shamans see the same stars." Temujin wiped his mouth. "They say the Five Wanderers have come together to hail my triumphs."

"They hail you, my Khan, but they also warn you. I've read the writings of men who have seen such signs in the past, and they are always a warning to turn aside from slaughter and cruel deeds." He had said what Yisui hoped he would say, and this omen gave his words more power.

"I haven't known for some time what Heaven wills," Temujin said softly. "My shamans tell me of omens, but I no longer know if they're speaking of the will of the spirits or only saying what they think I wish to hear."

"I have always told you what I know to be true," the Khitan said. "When you march against the Kin, your men will need supplies. The peasants here can pay you for their land, and the merchants can offer tariffs on their goods. The taxes you might collect would give you silver, silk, and grain, all of which you

661

can use. To wipe these people from the earth will give you only a few poor pastures."

"I'll admit something to you, Learned Brother," Temujin murmured. "In the lands I took, I found many wise men. Some have served me well, but often I wonder if I can truly rule them." His voice was slurred, but his breathing easier; the ma-hwang was having an effect. "And if I ignore your advice?"

"It isn't mine alone, but that of the stars. I would mourn to see you reject this warning."

"Whether I do or not, my end will be the same." Temujin turned his head towards Yisui. "Wife, what do you say? I would hear your thoughts."

She shrugged, trying to show no pity. "If you allow more of those wretches to live, I'll have more slaves. It's also wise to obey the signs of Heaven, is it not?"

"It's wise to know good sense when one hears it," he said, "however unwelcome. Very well, my Khitan brother – I'll tell my generals to limit their killing to the troops who oppose us, and to restrain their men from pillaging. You'll draw up plans for getting what we require from these people. All my chief officers in this camp will be summoned to hear my decree."

Yisui heard resignation and despair in his soft voice. It came to her that his rage at his approaching death was past, that he was accepting it now. His anger had kept death at bay; his desire for revenge had preserved his life. Now he was thinking of what would come after he was gone. The Tanguts would be granted some mercy, but Temujin's death would find him sooner.

To save Ning-hsia, the Tangut King sent the rest of his field forces against the Mongols. Once again, the Mongols retreated behind the Alashans, fell upon the army, and defeated the enemy. The siege of Ning-hsia resumed, while Ogedei and Subotai rode south to the Wei River to take the valley and move against the Kin. The Khan went west to secure Kansu and to take the few towns that remained.

Some whispered that the Khan, with his final triumph near-ing, would quickly regain his strength. Others looked at the aged, stooped figure amid his guards, and feared this victory would be his last.

Yisui bought prayers from the shamans, welcomed officers to Temujin's tent, and rallied those who cast worried looks at the Khan. When he was among his men, listening to reports of their successes, she could almost believe that the evil spirit might leave him. But at night, when they were alone, she listened to his whispers as he slept, and wondered what dreams the spirits were sending to him. The shadows inside the tent seemed an army of ghosts. A morning might soon come when he would not rise from his bed, when those ghosts would finally claim him.

122

TEMUJIN OPENED HIS eyes. An invisible falcon clawed at his chest, gripping his heart in its talons. He could not recall how it felt to be whole, without the pain.

The sky above the smoke-hole was light. Yisui and her women were outside the doorway, murmuring softly as they worked at their sewing. He remembered that they had moved his headquarters to the Ling-pan-shan Mountains days ago to escape the summer heat of the lowlands. He had lain in a cart during the journey, but had managed to ride to his great pavilion to greet Subotai and to meet with his officers. The kumiss he had drunk during the meeting had robbed him of any memory of what was said. The potions of Ye-lu Ch'u-ts'ai, the spells of the shamans, and Yisui's solicitude no longer helped him. Only drink could ease his pain, and never for long.

Subotai, he recalled then, had brought him a gift of five thousand horses and a report of victories in the Wei River valley. Ogedei was advancing along the river, pushing closer to K'ai-feng; the Kin Emperor had sent two delegations that spring to plead for peace. Other envoys were in this camp now,

663

begging for an audience with him. Temujin wondered if he would have the strength to leave his bed and meet with them.

His mind was as clouded as an old man's vision. Once, every report brought to him, every signal passed along by flags and lanterns, had added more images to those he held in his mind. He had seen the movements of his troops as a bird might – a wave of men thrusting against a city's walls, another force feigning retreat, tiny horsemen wheeling in their saddles to shoot volleys of arrows at an enemy as another wing of cavalry swept down on the foe from hills.

But he had also seen what no bird could see, the moves an enemy might make, and how they could be countered. His scouts gave him a picture of the lands in which he had to fight, and his spies a grasp of an enemy's weaknesses. He had held his conquests inside himself before his armies seized them.

Yet he could not see this war clearly now. When he centred his thoughts on one engagement, the rest of his army's movements eluded him. He had always seen any war in its entirety, as a pattern of pitched battles, sieges, tactical retreats, divisions separating to engage the enemy in different places, then coming together again. He remembered that Ning-hsia had been under siege all spring, that his general Chaghan had not yet negotiated that city's surrender; but then the positions of his forces along the Yellow River and the Wei, and near the oases of Kansu, vanished from his mind. Ning-hsia was suddenly the whole of the war, all that his clouded thoughts could grasp.

The city would have to submit soon. Illness and starvation inside its walls were doing as much damage as his troops.

He did not care for siege warfare, but if an enemy refused to meet him in the field, he had no other way to take its cities. There were ways to shorten a siege – a city by a river, with dams and canals, could be flooded, a walled city set on fire by burning arrows shot over the walls, or afflicted with illness when diseased bodies were hurled from catapults into the streets. He took some satisfaction in having mastered the art of the siege, in knowing that so many of his enemies had mistakenly trusted in their walls.

His enemies had possessed weapons he did not have, and he had seen that he would have to change his way of waging war to counter them. Volleys from enemy crossbows could fell a wall of advancing men, flame-throwers on ramparts could repel invaders with streams of fire, and bombs of metal fragments hurled from walls could deafen, maim, and panic the soldiers below. He had learned that the men who made such weapons were as essential to him as fearless and disciplined troops, and that their tools changed the nature of war.

His mind was wandering. He heard no music in his tent, then recalled that he had ordered the musicians to leave. The sound of their lutes had lulled him; he thought of sending for the girls, but was too weak even to call out to Yisui.

The invisible talons clutched at him once more. He would have to force himself to rise, to go to his pavilion and hold court, listen to couriers and envoys, and watch those around him pretending that his illness would pass.

A horse was brought to Temujin. His pain increased as he rode to the pavilion, then dismounted; men pressed around him as he entered. His throne sat on a platform at the back of the open tent, surrounded by cushions. The claws dug inside him as he made his way across the carpets.

The pretence began again. His Uighur and Khitan scribes lifted their brushes; food and drink were carried to the men seated at his right and to the women sitting with Yisui at his left. Pain raced up his arm as he served bits of meat to the men nearest him. His insides burned; the fire he had felt there ever since his horse had thrown him sometimes blazed and occasionally subsided, but never left him entirely. He lifted his goblet, and the talons tightened around his heart.

He gulped down the kumiss; more was poured for him. By the time the Kin envoys were led before him, the drink fogged his mind, so that he could barely comprehend the speeches Ch'u-ts'ai was translating. The struggle to appear in control, to show these ambassadors the strong man the pretence required, left him unable to concentrate on their words.

"The tribute you demanded has been brought," the Khitan was saying. "These servants of His Majesty the Emperor humbly beg his brother the Great Khan to accept their silver and silk, their horses and slaves, and the lustrous pearls that will adorn him and his favourites, in return for peace in their land."

Temujin came to himself. He gazed at the two envoys, then turned to his men. "Have you not heard my orders?" he asked. "Is there anyone among you who would dare to disobey my commands? I made a decree when the five planets were conjoined, forbidding excessive slaughter and plundering, and this decree still stands. I command that you make this known to all, so that all shall know the will of Genghis Khan. I have spoken."

Ye-lu Ch'u-ts'ai translated these words as Temujin sank back against the throne. His statement bound him to little, but the King of Gold would take it as a promise of peace. The forces commanded by Ogedei and Tolui would encounter a less prepared enemy later.

He would not ride with his sons, or direct those battles. He was not likely ever to know their final outcome. That was the hardest thing to see inside himself, a vision that only increased his torment – the world as it would be when he no longer lived in it.

Yisui stirred next to him. She was always near, and every night found her under his blanket. Part of the pretence required that he lie with a woman. Since the woman was always Yisui, who was too proud to let even a slave know that her beauty no longer stirred him, the pretence was maintained.

She called herself his shadow, and seemed a shadow of herself. The hardness in her voice was gone; he sensed the pity in her for his enemies. She would not dare to pity him.

How she had angered him, when she was bold enough to speak openly of his end and the need to choose an heir. It had embittered him to know that she was looking beyond his death. Now he was dying, and she shrank from that as though it meant her own demise.

How he had feared death once. Even now, everything in him rebelled at the prospect, but there was nothing to save him – no generals to hold it back, no guards to shield him, no shamans who could drive it away, no elixir, and no God. He had retreated from death, as he might from an enemy; soon he would have to turn and meet it.

Heaven had spoken to him once. Tengri's voice had been as clear as those of the people around him, and his dreams had shown him Heaven's will. What he had won surely proved that God had guided him, yet the more he seized, the larger the world he could not grasp seemed to grow. The voices of the spirits had grown fainter, until he could no longer hear them. Sometimes it seemed that he had possessed the world more truly as a boy, when his dream had carried his soul to a mountaintop and shown him a vast camp stretching to all horizons, than he did now, with all the lands and tribute he had won.

He was a boy again, sitting in Dei Sechen's tent, telling Bortai and Anchar of his dream. He did not know how he would find his way to that mountain summit, but had refused to doubt that he would. Heaven had tested him, forging him into the sword that would unite all who lived under the Eternal Blue Sky. He had learned his first important lesson after his father's death – that everyone who did not submit to him was a potential enemy, that there was no safety for him until all those enemies bowed to him or were destroyed. He might never have learned that without being an outcast.

"Temujin," Hoelun said. He heard her voice calling to him more often lately. Of all the women he had known, only his mother and Bortai had ever frightened him, because he had known they truly loved him. Their advice had often been sound, but he had resented the power they had over him.

"Bortai," he whispered. His first important battle was fought for her, but accepting Jochi as his son was part of the price of winning her back. He had always suspected that the son of Bortai's captor might eventually become his foe. When Ning-hsia was taken, and the Kin thoroughly cowed, he would punish Jochi for his affronts, for refusing to come to his camp, for imagining that he could grow strong enough to challenge him.

But Jochi was dead. He had forgotten that, as he had so much in recent months. A courier had brought the news to him that spring; he had presided over a feast in Jochi's memory and sent a message to his heir Batu. With Jochi gone, a grave threat to the unity of his ulus was removed, but the loss of Bortai's oldest son also made his own death seem closer.

Too many were gone — Mukhali, faithful Jebe, the often faithless Daritai, his stepfather Munglik, whose soul had quickly followed Hoelun's, generals and loyal followers, sons and grandsons he had barely known, and Jamukha. He could still grieve for his anda, but to become what Jamukha had wanted him to be would have meant turning away from his destiny, to become no more than one chief among many. His people would have gone on with their old feuds and struggles, and never known greatness. Jamukha had been another of Heaven's tests. So he had believed, and now Heaven was silent.

The warmth of the tent was oppressive; he wondered if his fever was returning. His passion for Khulan had been another fever, but winning her love would only have weakened him. She would have softened his heart then with her pity for his enemies; he had understood that when his fever for her broke. To love any woman too intensely meant giving her power she could not be allowed to have. To bring women to feel what they called love ensured their loyalty, but to share that love deeply was folly. Love alone would not have shown him how to rescue Bortai. Even as he had raged at her loss, a part of him had seen how he could use her capture for his own ends.

Bortai would watch over his people until the kuriltai approved his successor, but what then? Would his descendants remember the story of Alan Ghoa's sons, and take their ancestor's advice to heart? Would they remain bound together, or, when they had won the world and vanquished their enemies, contend among themselves?

His aim had been so certain once. His conquests would go on, and if he did not live to see them to their end, his sons and grandsons would continue them. They would go on living as their people always had, but with the wealth the conquered lands would yield to them. The least of them would be the equal of past chiefs; the best of the peoples under Heaven would have the world kneel to them. They would remember the one who had led them to greatness.

So he had believed, before his doubts deepened. If his descendants learned the ways of the conquered in order to rule them more wisely, they might fall victim to all the weaknesses of settled people, and become prey for stronger men. Yet if they kept their own customs, and remained honed for war, they were likely to fight among themselves when they had no more lands to win.

The world was not made for Man; the Taoist Master had told him that. If this were true, all his efforts had been no more than those of a stallion leading a herd to better pastures. His people might have only a brief moment of glory, as had the Khitans, the Kin, and the Khwarezmians before them.

His old dreams mocked him now. The world might shrug off the yoke of his ulus in time, and then his people would have nothing but the memory of what they had been. Perhaps they would lose even that memory. All his work would be for nothing, his name forgotten, his empire lost.

The tent was filled with men. Temujin had kept to his bed ever since his headquarters had been moved to the foothills overlooking the Yellow River, but his generals still sought audiences with him. He received them in this great tent now, instead of under a pavilion open to the summer air; the effort of moving from his bed had grown too great. Yet as long as no spear stood outside his doorway, the men would go on pretending that their Khan would recover.

The Han further upriver had a device for grinding grain, a watermill much like a boat. Its paddlewheels, powered by the river's currents, rotated ceaselessly, turning the millstones that ground the grain. As long as the current flowed, the wheels rotated, and the stones continued their work. His army was much like one of those watermills. He had set his forces turning, and they would go on with this war until the current in him subsided.

"The envoy waits outside your camp." That was Tolun Cherbi's voice. Yisui had propped cushions behind Temujin, but he lacked the energy to lift his head and look at the general. "He has been told that he won't have the honour of an audience, that the Great Khan has shown him enough courtesy by allowing him to wait while I bring you his message. Li Hsien will surrender his capital of Ning-hsia. The city's running out of food, and many are dead of fever. The envoy asks only that you give his sovereign a month to gather his gifts. His Majesty will bring the tribute to you himself."

"I'll grant him that month," Temujin said.

"Li Hsien also begs you to spare those left in Ning-hsia after he submits." Chaghan was speaking now. "He knows that you swore to wipe his people from the earth, but also that the stars warned you against such actions."

"This is my order," Temujin said. "When our army enters that city, they'll take what they want and do as they please with the people. The mercy I've shown to others will not be extended to the defenders of Ning-hsia." He had another decree to make, in case he did not live long enough to give the command later. "Tolun Cherbi, I give you this task. You'll ride to Ning-hsia, keep close to the Tangut King, and convey him and the tribute here. When I've accepted it, and he's bowed to me, you'll take his life and those of his sons." He paused. "You'll spare his Queen. I'm told she's beautiful."

"She is," Chaghan said with a laugh.

"Then I shall claim her. She will be brought to me when her husband is dead." More pretence, he thought, but his men would expect it of him.

The wheel would go on turning; he was powerless to stop it. The Tangut King would be crushed by the stones Temujin had set in motion, and the Kin brought to surrender after that. He would have his revenge, but somehow the old hatreds had vanished; it was only that he could not stop the mill.

He closed his eyes. When he opened them again, the men were gone. Yisui leaned over him, a goblet in her hand.

"The King may have to die," she said, "but surely you could spare his children and the people of his city. I would enjoy having princes to serve us, and those left alive in Ning-hsia can't threaten you now." There was pity in her voice. He felt disappointed in her, and in himself; he had failed after all to crush that weakness in her.

"I've given the order," he said. "I won't call it back to give you the pleasure of owning more Tangut lives, when I can have the greater pleasure of knowing they won't outlive me. Few pleasures are left for me now."

"You'll live forever, Temujin. Couldn't you let them live to labour for you?"

"Be silent, Yisui. I showed mercy once when you begged it of me, and you are violating the agreement we made then."

He closed his eyes. The pleasure he had spoken of would be fleeting, a flame fluttering for an instant before it was extinguished.

Ye-lu Ch'u-ts'ai, who was so wise, had never truly understood him; Temujin had always known that. The Khitan could not share his world of doubts, or even comprehend it. Whatever torment Ch'u-ts'ai had felt after seeing his world die, he had accepted the one Temujin had made. To bring order to this world, to keep it regulated and in harmony, to act correctly — those were the tasks of a man. He would say that Temujin's nature was that of a ruler, and that he had fulfilled that nature. Man affected Heaven, according to the Khitan, no more than Heaven affected Man. To think that a voice from Heaven might speak to a man would strike Ch'u-ts'ai and his learned comrades as madness; they did not seek a purpose outside the world they were given. But the Khitan had never been an abandoned boy alone on a mountain, hearing the voices of spirits in the wind, seeking for something beyond himself to harden him and guide him.

In the midst of his pain, as the claws gripped his heart, Temujin pondered the void that might lie beyond death. Was the Eternal Sky only a vault empty of God, or had Tengri simply fallen silent? Perhaps it was easier to believe that Heaven had never truly spoken to him than to fear that the spirits had withdrawn from him.

His doubts had finally freed him from the fears his shaman Teb-Tenggeri had used to control him, but had also shown him a bleak world without purpose. The more he gained, the more futile his efforts seemed. His end would still be the same — the extinction that his Buddhist subjects saw as a soul's highest goal, but without any Heavenly Presence to swallow that soul.

He recoiled from that prospect, clinging to the old memories that seemed so much clearer than more recent ones. Perhaps the spirits were silent now only because he had carried out his purpose. Yet part of him still resisted that notion, and whispered that he was only a dying man who would grasp at any consolation.

He gazed up at the smoke-hole. Yisui was outside, speaking to the guards, but her voice seemed distant. A light suddenly filled the smoke-hole, as though the sun had drawn close to the earth; forms fluttered in the beam of light.

The ghosts took shape around him. He could not make out who many of them were, but his father and mother were among them, their shining faces those he remembered from his boyhood. Jebe was there, his bowcase and quiver hanging from his belt, and Mukhali, clothed in the silks of Khitai. Jamukha lifted his head; his dark eyes peered into Temujin's soul. At the sight of his anda, the talons squeezed his heart.

Had the spirits sent these ghosts? No, he told himself; they were only the fevered imaginings of an ailing, desperate man. Already, they were fading; the bright light dimmed. Above the smoke-hole, he saw only a patch of blue sky.

What purpose was there in his deeds? His descendants would surround themselves with treasure, for a while. They would rule until stronger men surpassed them or the settled lands swallowed them.

An old man's face hovered over him; Temujin recognized the sage Ch'ang-ch'un. The monk's lips moved, but Temujin could not hear him. The Taoist had given him some practical advice, suggestions for helping the people of Khitai while they recovered from war's devastation and grew accustomed to Mongol rule. Knowledgeable men were needed to administer those lands if the Khan was to have the greatest benefit from them. His advice had echoed Ch'u-ts'ai's, but Temujin had seen the dangers in this course. His successors would grow more dependent on such men, but his people could remain Mongols only by leaving such tasks to them.

"Consider the body of a man," Ch'ang-ch'un said. "What is its ruler? It has one hundred parts; which do you prefer? Are some servants, and others masters, or does each part become now ruler, now servant, at different times? Can it be that they are simply a whole that grows and changes, that follows the way of Nature, with no need of a ruler?"

The Taoist sage was repeating words he had said before. Temujin had barely understood them then, had even wondered if the Master was questioning the rightness of his rule. Now they hinted at an answer to his questions.

He knew so little. Once, he had believed old men were wise. Now he was an old man, and wondered how many other old men had simply cloaked their ignorance in pretended wisdom.

Before he could question the monk further, the face disappeared.

Temujin remained inside his tent when the Tangut King arrived with his tribute. Li Hsien was forced to kneel outside and make his speeches by the entrance as a procession of guards displayed the tribute to the Khan. The tent was soon filled with golden Buddhas, strings of pearls on silver trays, and gleaming cups and bowls. The men spoke of other gifts – a great tent of silk, camels and horses in the hundreds, handsome boys and beautiful girls clothed in fine camel-hair coats.

Temujin allowed the King to come to his tent for three days, but refused to admit him. On the third day, Temujin gave a sign to Tolun Cherbi. The cries of the dying monarch and his kin eased his pain; when the King's head was carried to him on a silver plate, he felt that the evil spirit wringing his heart might leave him.

In the morning, his pain worsened. He drifted into an uneasy sleep, and woke to find Yisui hovering over him.

"Your men are here for the feast," she said. He struggled to sit up as she smoothed down his robe; one of her slaves knelt to help him on with his boots. Men streamed into the tent, followed by slaves with jugs and platters of food. A woman in a red silk robe and a high golden head-dress was led through the doorway with her attendants; he had forgotten that he meant to claim the Tangut Queen.

"Your new wife greets you," Tolun Cherbi shouted. "She is called Gorbeljin Ghoa, and you see she merits her name. The King of Hsi-Hsia and his kindred are no more, his city is ours, and his Queen yours, my Khan."

The red-robed woman looked up. Her skin had a soft golden hue, with no traces of tears on her cheeks. Her long eyes were as black as Yisui's, her form as graceful and delicate as that of a Han woman as she bowed.

Gorbeljin came towards him, bowed again, then seated herself at his side. The men roared with laughter. "She can't wait to fulfil her duties!" one shouted. Yisui leaned towards the Queen, her face pale, her eyes wide with pity. Temujin smiled as he grabbed at the goblet a slave was handing to him.

Temujin woke. His head swam, but his pain had lessened. He recalled that he had risen from his bed as the men danced. He had managed to stagger outside to relieve himself; someone had helped him back inside. Perhaps the death of his Tangut enemy would restore him. It had been cowardly of him to fear, to doubt, to think the evil spirit would take him.

He was alone with Gorbeljin. Someone had taken off his clothes and boots, and laid his blanket over him. His comrades and the Queen's women were gone; Yisui would not be his shadow tonight. The hearth fire was burning low, but he glimpsed the Queen's face in the shadows. She had removed her head-dress; her hair was a mass of dark plaits. Her head turned towards him, and he looked into eyes as black and cold as a snake's. He tried to rise from the bed; the invisible falcon, protesting, gripped his heart.

"I am your death," Gorbeljin said, and the claws around his heart dug deeper. He had heard her words in his own tongue, yet her lips did not move. Her high cheekbones were flushed; beads of sweat gleamed like jewels on her forehead.

Cold fingers brushed against his hand. "I am your death," Gorbeljin said again. Her lips were pressed together even as her voice surrounded him; he was trapped in a spell, one he could not escape.

She stood up. The robe fell from her shoulders; her body was a slender stalk silhouetted by the light. She came towards him, lifted the blanket, and crept into the bed.

The pain inside him flared. Even as he struggled against her, he felt himself grow stiff. Her nails clawed at him, raising welts on his arms. He grabbed her wrists, and his heart felt as though it would burst. Her legs were a vise around his hips as she drew him into herself.

674

He struck her hard, knocking her from the bed, then fell back against the pillows. She scrambled to her feet and leaned over him.

"Get away from me," he said. A soft sound came from her; she was laughing. She crept towards the hearth and brought her hands together, then rocked from the waist. He tried to call out, but his voice died in his throat. She moved to the bed and knelt at its foot, near the plate that held the head of Li Hsien. He heard a small, choked gasp, and knew that she was weeping.

He tried to rise; the falcon tore at him. An eddy caught him, sweeping him into a black pool, and he surrendered to it, fleeing his pain.

When he came to himself, he felt the emptiness of the tent. He struggled to sit up, his arms throbbing with pain. Gorbeljin's golden head-dress sat on a chest near the bed; the woman was gone.

Temujin stumbled from the bed, grabbing at his clothes. He was pulling on his boots, heedless of the pain, when one of the night guard called out. He staggered to the entrance; the officer on duty rushed towards him. Other men were running towards the line of tethered horses beyond the wagons.

"The Queen," Temujin gasped.

"I am to blame." The officer struck his chest. "I saw the lady come out and go behind the tent – I thought only – " The man shook himself. "When she didn't return, I ordered a search."

"Bring me a horse."

"My Khan – "

"Get the horse!" he shouted. The officer barked an order; a boy was soon running to him with a bay gelding. Temujin grabbed the reins and heaved himself into the saddle. His insides flamed; his heart was a fist contracting inside him.

His tent, and the smaller yurts near it, stood at the north end of the camp. The sky was overcast, the land beyond the torchlit camp dark. Riders fanned out, and leaned from their saddles, searching the ground for tracks. Temujin rode north with one search party. The woman could not have gone far on foot. He would punish her for trying to escape him, for casting her evil spell.

The moon sailed from behind a cloud. A gem glittered in a patch of short grass. The silver light revealed the faint marks of footprints in this softer, wetter ground. She would suffer for this; he would break whatever spirit remained in her. He would live long enough to conquer her completely, and see that she lived the rest of her life in fear of him.

The moon hid from him, and when the bright orb shone once more, he saw her standing on a distant hill overlooking the river. Her red robe seemed black in the moonlight, her braids a mass of snakes along her back.

He lashed at his horse and galloped ahead of the others. Gorbeljin turned towards him, her eyes black slits in her white face. As he bore down on her, she spun around and leaped from the hill. He raced up the slope; his horse reared, nearly throwing him.

The woman was caught in the rapids below. The silvery water swept over her, then lifted her up, carrying her as easily as it would a leaf. The river swirled around her, swallowing the small dark form and spewing her up again until he could no longer see her.

The men behind him were shouting. Blood pounded in his ears; his heart constricted. The talons tore at him; he cried out as he pressed his face against the horse's mane.

I am your death, she had said, and he sensed the death inside himself.

After the body of the Tangut Queen was found, caught in reeds along the river-bank, they moved camp to the cooler foothills overlooking the Wei River. By the time Temujin was carried to his tent, his body burned with fever.

The men around him could no longer pretend he would recover; the Khan's tent had been raised beyond the fires outside the camp, with no tents near it. Only Yisui remained to care for him; the other women were sent away.

A dream came to him during the night, in which he saw his people following a horse without a rider. Before dawn, he summoned Khasar's son Yesungge and told him to fetch Ogedei and Tolui. When he heard the drums of the shamans outside, he knew that a spear ribboned in felt stood outside the tent.

676

He had to reach beyond death through his sons. He would offer them his counsel, but that last task might be no more than an empty gesture, a grasping at a future he could not control.

His sons took three days to reach him. Yellow soil sifted down from their silk tunics as they entered the tent and settled themselves near him. Yisui's hands shook as she offered them goblets, and tears streamed from her eyes. Temujin disliked her weeping, which she no longer bothered to conceal, but felt a bitter joy at knowing how deeply she would mourn him.

"Father," Tolui said. "I didn't believe what Yesungge told me until I saw the spear. I can't believe it even now."

Temujin shivered under his blanket. The fever came in waves, but had abated for the moment. He had to speak while his mind was clear, before the fever burned in him again.

"Listen to me," Temujin said. Ogedei's moustache twitched as his mouth worked; Tolui gripped his goblet tightly. "My end is near, and you must hear my last words."

Ogedei made a sign against evil. "Don't say it, Father."

"Listen while I can still speak. I've conquered so much for you that it would take you a year to ride through the lands I rule. Now you must keep what we hold and extend its boundaries. I'll tell you – "

The pain gripped him. Yisui held out a goblet; he turned his head away from her. "I've left much unfinished, but I can tell you how to defeat the Kin. The best troops of the King of Gold are in the fortress of Tung-kuan, and can't be taken there. To the south, mountains protect them, and the Yellow River flows to the north. Here is what you must do."

His pain eased as he thought of the strategy he had hoped to use himself. "The King of Gold," he continued, "will trust his men to guard the pass at Tung-kuan. You must ask the Sung for passage through their territory. Because the Kin are their enemies, they'll agree. From the south, advance on K'ai-feng. The King of Gold will then have to call the forces at Tung-kuan to his side. The long march will tire them, and you can defeat them easily."

"It will be done, Father," Tolui said. "I swear it."

"And when the Kin are crushed, there will be no buffer between our lands and those of the Sung." Temujin took a breath. "Remain united, act together against your enemies, and reward your loyal followers. You know what I've often said about how a man should conduct himself."

"I know," Ogedei said in a choked voice. "In your daily life, be as joyous as a young calf or a frolicking fawn, but in battle be like the hawk. When you feast, behave like a colt, but in war fly at the enemy like a falcon. By day, be as alert as the wolf, and by night as cautious as the raven."

Ogedei covered his eyes; Tolui's shoulders shook. "Save your tears for when I am gone," Temujin whispered. "I've said that Ogedei will be my successor, and your brother Chagadai will respect that choice — see that he makes no trouble. Heed the counsel of your mother, who will watch over my homeland until the kuriltai is held. Remember — "

He gasped for air. "Ogedei, you'll take those women you want from among my lesser wives and concubines, and give the rest to whomever you choose. You will, however, allow my four Khatuns to remain faithful to me. Since they have been mine, there's no need to wed them to others." They would remain his while they mourned him.

"I swear — " Ogedei coughed. Tolui lifted Temujin's hand and pressed it to his cheek.

"Tolui," Temujin murmured, "you are my Odchigin, the Prince of the Hearth. See that our homeland is protected and preserved. Many of our people will be tempted by the ways of the lands you conquer — see that they don't forget — "

He could tell them no more. The world would be theirs, and if those who succeeded them lost it, their ancient homeland would be their only refuge.

"And now you must leave me, my sons. I long for my old grazing grounds — see that I'm led there to rest on the slope of the great mountain that protected me. Hide my death from all until I'm brought home."

"Farewell, Father," Ogedei said.

"Farewell." His face burned; the bird tightened its grip. They would have to do what they could with his legacy. His work was done, but to what end?

678

Temujin said, "Go from this tent."

Yisui clutched at his hand. "I cannot."

"Leave me, Yisui." The scribes had taken down his last commands, the lands and possessions that would go to each of his sons and brothers, but he realized then that he had neglected one loyal follower. "Give the Tangut King's tent and all his tribute to Tolun Cherbi. He warned me to postpone this war, so it's fitting for him to have it."

"Yes, Temujin."

"See that I'm avenged by the deaths of all in Ning-hsia. You'll tell my generals that order still stands. Swear it to me." A rushing sound filled his ears, drowning out her voice and the chants of the shamans beyond the doorway. He could not hear her answer, but she would obey; she would fear his ghost too much to do otherwise.

"Go," he said. He heard her wail as she passed through the doorway, and felt eased when she was gone. He could issue no commands to death. It was useless to struggle against that which would finally relieve him of his pain, yet part of him still resisted.

Give me an answer, he thought; tell me now what my purpose was.

"Do not ask after the beginnings of things, or inquire about their ultimate ends." Ch'ang-ch'un was speaking. There was something else the sage had told him, something that might yield an answer. He had strained for understanding when the Master spoke to him, imagining that he could seize the Taoist's knowledge and make it his own, and that had been a mistake. Ch'ang-ch'un had told him that the way to wisdom lay in accepting the world as it was, in knowing its workings, not in forcing one's will upon it. His will could bring him nothing now.

The rushing sound came to him again. Ch'ang-ch'un had spoken of becoming like water, yielding to the shape of the container that held it, reflecting all of Nature in its surface. It seemed to Temujin then that he was floating on a vast river that flowed through all the world. He closed his eyes and drifted along its currents.

He saw a city of Khitai; through the open gate of its

679

crenellated wall, he glimpsed the curling eaves of houses and the towers of pagodas. Tiny scows crowded with people and larger duck-shaped craft with sails bobbed on the water. In the distance, the Great Wall snaked across the land. How useless that Wall had been at repelling invaders; it had only made the people behind it believe that it could shield them from the outside.

The river carried him past yellow lands and loess cliffs, past earthen-walled cities fed by canals, and rows of green willows and poplars that marked an oasis. The waterway wound through a desert of sand and then flowed past a stretch of black Gobi, a wide expanse of rock without sand or dust. He passed a patch of steppe dotted with tents, then a forest thick with pines and larches. He came to a town with golden-domed mosques and slender minarets adorned with coloured tiles; near the hills outside the town, a trail of dust marked a caravan's passage.

The river swept him on. People made their way down to its banks, and soon it seemed that all the world had come to watch him pass. People with pale skins and dark ones, some with the sturdy frames of Mongols and others with the slighter bodies of the Han, gazed at him as he drifted on the waters. Yellow-haired people lifted their arms, and black-haired people knelt by the reedy shore. He saw black eyes and brown ones, yellow eyes with drooping folds and the round, fierce blue eyes of outlanders.

His descendants might lose the world, but would leave their mark upon it. While they held it, the caravans would move between its easternmost regions to distant lands in the west. His realm would link the east and the west for a time, connecting lands long divided and unknown to one another, and something new would grow from them. The seed of his people would be scattered. Even if they were driven back to their homeland and forgot what they had once been, they would leave their mark on the people of far lands. His realm was a crucible and the iron race forged there would transform the world.

The river bore him on to unknown lands hidden by a thick grey mist. He could not see what lay ahead, but understood now that a mighty force bound the world. He had thought of it as God, but whatever it was, it underlay all things and united them in a whole. He knew at last that its purpose would always remain unknown, but that it was the nature of men to seek to understand this force even as they were driven by it. Nature would give them the means to know its ways; they would have the power to become more than they were, to live forever as he had hoped to do, or to destroy themselves.

What he had done was part of this process, and others had to make of it what they would. When all the peoples of the earth were one ulus, they would be free to find another purpose. Heaven had offered him an answer, but how cruel to let him glimpse it only now, with no one near him to share the vision. He listened, straining to hear the sound of a voice, but he was alone on the endless river, with an empty desert stretching before him.

The desert deepened into purple, then vanished. The river swept him on into the unknown.

123

THE BODIES OF men and camels lay near a watering hole. Yisui averted her eyes from the corpses. She had seen other bodies along the cortège's route, those of travellers unlucky enough to cross the path the Khan was taking on his last journey. Merchants with caravans, families moving between towns, and herdsmen at oases had all fallen to the swords of grieving soldiers. Her husband's death would remain a secret until he reached the homeland.

He was gone, yet the sun still beat down upon them; at night, the stars shone as brightly as before. It seemed impossible that they could, that Heaven's glory had not dimmed after his passing.

The man driving Yisui's cart prodded the camel with the end of his whip. Ahead, lines of men on horseback moved slowly among the dunes of Kansu. The land shifted around them, a sea of sandy waves swept by the wind. Subotai was just behind the advance guard, leading the bier with Ogedei and Tolui. More troops followed the procession, along with the women, children, herds, and those slaves fit enough to survive the journey.

The bier dwarfed the carts around it. Its wooden wheels were each as tall as a man, its platform so wide that twenty camels were needed to pull it. Trunks filled with treasure sat on the platform, and a white canopy on golden poles fluttered above it. Under the canopy, on a bed heaped with cushions, the Great Khan was being borne home.

Yisui glanced up at the body and repressed a tremor of fear. The Khan was propped up by felt cushions, his helmet on his head. Under his breastplate, he wore a blue silk robe; one hand clutched a sword, the other a silver goblet, and his bowcase and quiver lay at his side. His skin, dried by the desert air, was drawn so tightly over his face that she could see the bones beneath it. She imagined him suddenly downing his drink, then shaking his sword as he shouted commands, shrugging off death as he had every misfortune. His eyes would open, and find her.

He would wait for her. She had hardly believed he was gone, not when the shaman left his tent to cry out that he had flown to Heaven, not even when two shamanesses had led her between the fires. She would always feel him near her, waiting to clutch her to him once more.

His death had spared him the knowledge that his old friend Borchu had fallen in a skirmish against the Kin only a few days before. The two, so close in life, would be companions forever.

The Khan had also not learned of the command she had given in his name. She had told his generals that the survivors in Ning-hsia were to be spared, that Temujin had decreed it before sending her from his side. For an instant, she had felt a thrill at defying him, at knowing he was powerless to prevent her act of mercy. She had seen relief in the eyes of the men; weary of carnage, they were willing to obey. There had been enough death; Heaven had ordered the Khan to show mercy, and she was only obeying Heaven's will.

But she had not obeyed Temujin. After it was too late to call back her words, she had seen what lay before her. She would fear her own end for the rest of her life. Death would come for her, and the Khan would be at Death's side; his spirit would punish her for her defiance. Her ghost would flee from him, racing across the steppe in the body of a wolf, hiding in the darkness of a northern forest in a leopard's form, trembling at the sounds of the hunter pursuing her. She would never escape him.

The waters are dried up, she thought; the most beautiful gem is shattered. Subotai had said the words after the funeral feast. "Yesterday, O my Khan, you soared over your people like a falcon. Today, as a young horse after a run, you have stumbled, O my Khan." The general had slashed at his face; the guttural wails of the men had nearly drowned out his speech. "How can it be, O my Khan, that after sixty short years, Heaven has taken you from us?" Subotai had thrown himself against one of the great wheels, as if wanting the bier to crush him.

Yisui brushed sand from her face. Her sleeves fell back, showing the scars on her arms. She had slashed herself so deeply with her knife during the mourning that a shaman had been summoned to tend her wounds. If the Khan's spirit saw her grief, perhaps he would forgive her.

An axle creaked; the giant bier shuddered to a halt. The drivers on the platform lashed at the camels; two men jumped down to look at the wheels. The dunes in the distance became a moving pattern of light and shadow as the wind rose.

Yisui's driver drew his reins taut. Subotai shouted to the men around him; soldiers leaped from their steeds to secure the horses against the rising wind. Others surrounded the bier and dug at the sand around its wheels. Tolui trotted towards the bier, followed by Khubilai and Mongke. Yisui heard voices in the wind, the spirits of the desert calling to the Khan. If the sky darkened and the spirits sent a storm against them, the shamans might not be able to turn it back.

Subotai dismounted and approached the bier. He knelt, pressed his forehead against the ground, then looked up to where the Khan sat under the canopy.

"O my Khan," the general shouted above the wind, "do you wish to depart from your people? Will you abandon us now?

683

The country where you were born, your noble and wise Bortai Khatun, your empire, your Yasa, your people in the tens of thousands – all await you, O my Khan."

Subotai's grief had given him eloquence. He lifted his arms, pleading with the spirit of the one he had served so loyally, and the wind seemed to retreat from him. "Your beloved wives," he continued, "your great tent, your just realm, the spirits of the comrades who loved you – all await you, O my Khan. Because this country is fair, because the Tanguts are now yours, do you wish to remain behind with the ghost of their beautiful Queen and abandon us, O my Khan?"

Yisui drew her scarf across her face. Some said that the dead Queen had cast a spell on the Khan. The men wanted to believe that only powerful magic could have taken his mighty spirit from them.

"We can no longer protect your life!" Subotai flung his arms wide. The wind died suddenly; men pried at the bier's wheels with poles. "I beg you to let us take the jade jewel of your body home to the noble Bortai Khatun and your people!"

The camels bellowed; the bier lurched forward. Subotai stumbled to his feet as a man brought his horse to him. Yisui huddled against the seat of her cart. Even the desert spirits could not hold the Khan. His spirit would remain with his people, and with her.

She thought of Yisugen, as she had not for some time. Once, she had yearned to be with her sister again, but felt no longing now. Her love for Yisugen had been the only deep feeling she had allowed herself, before pity for the Tanguts pierced her armour. The frayed bond with her sister had finally unravelled, and the great tree that had sheltered them both was gone. Better, she thought, if Yisugen had forgotten her instead of begging the Khan to find her. Yisugen had wanted her safe, but could not protect her against the ghost that would always haunt her.

124

IN AUTUMN, WHEN ice was forming on the Kerulen, a herds-man rode to Bortai's ordu to tell her that a wing of the Khan's army bearing his standard had been sighted a few days' ride to the south. She questioned the man, found he knew little more, then sent him away.

No courier had come to her with a message from Temujin. Perhaps he meant to surprise her again. She had heard reports of his victories, and had expected him to press on with his war against the Kin. Now, without warning, the army was returning.

The dread Bortai had felt when he left her gripped her once more. The night before, she had dreamed that she was alone in a dark pine forest. Temujin had called out to her, shouting as he had when she was fleeing with the Merkits in the night. She had run through the forest crying out to him, awakening before she could find him.

"Bortai, Bortai!" His voice was in the wind that whistled past her tent. She went to the doorway, almost expecting to see him outside. The sky was growing dark; snow had dusted the ground lightly. Dogs barked as women herded sheep towards the yurts. The soldiers stationed at her tent leaned against wagons, waiting for the night guard to relieve them; children scurried by with baskets of dung. The camp along the Kerulen was filled with the noise of people and animals prepar-ing for night.

He needs me, she thought. Temujin might be injured or ill; if so, he would have crossed the Gobi in secret before his enemies could learn he was stricken. She refused to think of other reasons for secrecy.

She descended the steps and beckoned to a captain of the guard. "A dream has come to me," she said. "The spirits have told me to travel to my husband, and welcome him home. Send a rider to Chagadai's tent, to tell my son that I wish him to accompany me. Bring ten of your best men with you when we leave at dawn."

"Yes, Honoured Lady."

She climbed the steps. Khadagan stood in the entrance; Bortai caught her hand. "Don't leave me," Bortai whispered, suddenly filled with foreboding.

Bortai left the camp with Khadagan in an ox-drawn cart. Except for two wagons carrying a few servants, provisions, and the panels of a yurt, she brought no other retinue. Chadagai was waiting for her outside her camping circle; he scowled as the men with him greeted her guards.

People had gathered at the edges of the camp to watch her pass. Chagadai rode at the side of her cart, glowering at her in silence. He would be thinking that travelling this way was not dignified, that she should have brought her great tent, more servants and slaves, more guards, more splendour. She gazed at the tents along the river and the animals grazing beyond the wagons; she would not see the last of the great camp before sunset. The cloudless blue sky promised a fine day. Had harm come to Temujin, surely Heaven would have darkened, and sent a harsh wind filled with the voices of grieving spirits.

Chagadai leaned towards her from his saddle. "Mother, it isn't fitting."

"Don't scold me, Chagadai."

"You might have brought a driver, at least."

"I could handle five oxen in harness when you were still sucking at my breast," she said. "I can manage one beast. Bringing more with us would only slow our pace."

"Rushing to him this way." Her son shook his head. "It was in my mind to forbid you to go, but it would hardly be suitable to argue openly on the eve of Father's return. You're stubborn enough to have gone anyway, and then —"

"Chagadai." She drew on the reins, then stared at him until he looked away. "I'll hear no more of this from you. You can be as unyielding as a stone. Have some consideration for your old mother, who may have need of you."

They followed the Kerulen south for three days. On the fourth, they stopped in the flat yellow land that bordered the desert. At dawn, Bortai left her tent and gazed towards the distant rocky massif that loomed in the south. A mass of milling dark shapes was moving towards her across the land; a wide platform with a broad white canopy seemed to float above the dust clouds raised by the procession's movements.

Her eyesight had grown less keen. She squinted, and thought she saw her husband's standard among the men's banners. Under the canopy, she glimpsed a seated man.

The others gathered near her. Chagadai was the first to cry out. "Father!" One of his men caught him in his arms. "Father!"

"The great eagle flies no more!" another soldier shouted. "The mighty Khan has fallen!"

Khadagan shrieked, tore at her head-dress, and clawed her face with her nails. The men grabbed at one another, filling the air with lamentations. Bortai continued to stare at the massed forms moving against the veil of dust, willing them to be a mirage, one that would disappear from view. The platform was a bier, but the man sitting under the canopy, wearing Temujin's gold-studded helmet, clutching a sword with bony fingers, could not be her husband.

A man with the Khan's broad-shouldered body was riding ahead of the procession. But the bier did not vanish, and then she saw that the man galloping towards her was Ogedei.

"He has left us," a guard near her said. "What will become of us now?"

Bortai leaned against a cart. Her heart went on beating; she was dimly surprised that it could. The others would be wondering why she showed no grief, how she could stand there so calmly when the centre of her life was gone, but if she gave in to her grief now, she would never stop weeping.

At last she went to Chagadai and took his hands. "Your father called to me in my dream," she said, "and the spirits sent me to him. We must guide him back to his people."

Rows of soldiers stood on either side of the bier; the camels pulling it had been led away. Two fires burned in front of the bier, and nine shamans sat there, beating their drums as Ogedei led Bortai and Khadagan to the platform.

Khadagan leaned heavily against Bortai as they knelt; Chagadai was sobbing behind them. Bortai looked up at the wasted, bony body under the canopy. That husk, with its thin grey beard and withered face, was not her husband; his spirit still lived in his sons, in all his people. He had made them what they were, and would watch over them. Then she remembered that she would never feel his arms around her, or look into his pale eyes again, and her sorrow nearly overwhelmed her.

A shadow fell across her; she looked up as Yisui bowed, then knelt next to her. The other Khatun's black eyes darted restlessly, and her lips were bitten raw.

"I was his shadow." Yisui clutched at Bortai's sleeve. "I didn't leave his side, dear Lady, not until his death was nearly upon him and he ordered me from his tent."

"Did he say anything to you towards the end?" Bortai whispered. Were there, she thought, any words for me?

"Sometimes he muttered words I couldn't understand," Yisui said, and Bortai wished she had been there to capture them. "His will was clear at the end. Your two youngest sons came to him, and the scribes were able to record his decrees."

"I know." Ogedei had managed to tell her that much. The Khan had been failing throughout the campaign, but his men were so used to obeying him that they could not have refused his orders even to save his life.

"I was his shadow," Yisui said, "I kept my promise to you."

Bortai rose, then helped the other two widows to their feet. She longed for the release of tears, but grief had dried the spring within her.

Ogedei would send couriers to every camp and city in the Khan's realm. Noyans and chiefs would stream to the great camp along the Kerulen to pay their last respects. The Khan's body would rest outside her ordu and the tents of the other Khatuns while they held their feasts; his spirit would hear the songs and praise of his people. Even when he was laid to rest, her work would not be done, for she would have to watch over his ulus until Ogedei was proclaimed Khan.

But she had done her duty before, looking after his people until he returned to her. This would not be so different. She had only to wait a short time before her ageing body failed and they were together once more, never to be parted again.

The silence woke Yisugen. She had thought the wailing might never stop, but the camp was still.

The Khan's bier had been brought to Bortai's circle of tents and then to Yisui's ordu. Noyans and soldiers, sons and daughters of the Khan's minor wives, and chiefs from camps between the Altais and the Khingans had come here to say their farewells. Some climbed upon the bier to toast the Khan, pour drink into his cup, sing favourite songs, and cry out their grief. Had their tears fallen into the Kerulen, the river would have swelled to its springtime height, but they had mourned for over a month now, and their tears flowed less freely. The mourners in her tent that evening had even managed weak smiles as they told their cherished tales of their Khan.

Yisugen had not seen Bortai weep, but the Khatun's tormented eyes revealed her suffering. At times, she thought that Bortai longed for the grave herself, but the Khan's first wife had never failed him, and would not do so now. Bortai kept near Ogedei at the feasts, and was at his side during audiences with the Noyans. Ogedei would be Khan because his father had decreed it, but also because Bortai's counsel had shown him ways to give the Noyans confidence in him.

Yisugen slipped from her bed, pulled on her boots, then covered herself in a sable coat. Her three youngest children slept on; her oldest son, too drunk to ride back to his own tent, stirred on his cushions. She crept past the sleeping slaves at the entrance and descended the steps, motioning to the guards to be silent as they saluted her.

The bier sat in a wide space in front of her tent; a few men huddled around the fires near the platform. The canopy was silvered by the moonlight; the Khan's body, heaped with furs, was hidden in the darkness.

She approached the bier, pulled her coat tightly around her, and knelt on the thin layer of crusty snow. Her mother's ghost had sent her to him, and her plea had brought her sister to his side. She had escaped death by joining her life and Yisui's to his, and the years had freed her of the dreams that once troubled her, of small boys dying at the hands of his men and of headless bodies kneeling before the Khan. She had saved her sister, and having Yisui near had helped her conquer her fear of the man

689

to whom they were bound. She had lived her life honouring her old oath to her sister, trying to forget the carnage that had reunited them.

The Khan was gone, and she and Yisui would not be parted, yet it seemed that he had taken her sister's spirit with him. Yisui stared at the other mourners with empty eyes as they feasted, drank, sang, and wept; she left her tent only to attend sacrifices to the Khan's spirit, or to present herself at another funeral feast. Yisugen had expected her sister to turn to her for comfort, but Yisui did not seek her out, and had told her nothing of their husband's final days. Yisui shivered and made signs against evil whenever she passed the bier; she had surrounded herself with shamans and the children she had always ignored before. She lived amid chants and spells, appeasing the spirits and warding off whatever unseen evil she feared.

Yisugen looked up at the Khan. If Yisui's despair deepened, she would lie with him before long. The Khan had won a victory over them both; his death had severed their bond. She covered her face, torn by her loss.

Khulan's son was the last mourner to leave her tent. Kulgan embraced her at the entrance, then tottered awkwardly down the steps to Nayaga, nursing his bad leg. The two men threw their arms around each other and mumbled drunken laments.

Khulan watched them from the doorway. She had mimicked the grief of others, wailing as she circled the bier, cutting at her arms with her knife, but the cuts were barely more than scratches. Her tears flowed more easily when she thought of the lives the dead man had taken, the victims who had suffered so much at his hands.

A boy brought Nayaga a torch. The general and Kulgan weaved their way towards the horses. The wind rose, lifting the snow until they were hidden by a white veil. The Khan had decreed that she would have no other husband, but her love for Nayaga had long been a desert, and his for Temujin ruled him even now.

Two men climbed on to the bier, one holding a torch as the other tightened the ropes binding the canopy to the poles. The light flickered over the face of the corpse; the cold had preserved the body, but the skin was drawn tight, giving the dead man a grisly grin. The snow was falling more heavily, and soon she could no longer see the bier.

The guards below looked up at her, then crouched by their fires. Khulan let the flap fall behind her, ignoring the cold, and gazed in the Khan's direction.

I am free of you now, she thought, and wondered how he had met the death he feared, whether he had reached out to the spirits or cowered in terror of oblivion.

She understood why his people mourned him so deeply. His iron will had welded them together and demanded their obedience, and in return, he had kept his promises to them. They would follow the path he had set for them for a time, perhaps for several generations, but would lose their way without him.

Temujin had once believed Heaven guided him. He had looked so much towards Heaven that he had forgotten Etugen, the Earth. Heaven assaulted the land with storms and ice, tore at it and lashed at it, but flowers and grass always returned to the steppe. He would be remembered as another of the storms that had come upon the earth and darkened it for a while before the clouds were swept away.

She was free of him and his spirit. His ghost would not haunt a woman who could think of him only with a cold and distant pity. There would be no place in the stories people told of him for a man whose fears, as much as his courage, had made him a conqueror.

She considered what lay ahead. After he was made Khan, Ogedei intended to make his main camp at Karakorum, in the lands once ruled by the Kereit Khans. Travellers would come there from distant lands to honour the new Khan, and among them would surely be wise men and learned ones, scholars as wise as Ye-lu Ch'u-ts'ai and the Taoist sage. She would summon them to her tent, learn from them, and hear of the truths that would endure when Temujin's conquests were only a memory.

Khulan turned away from the bier, lifted the flap, and moved towards the warmth and light.

125

CHECHEG YAWNED AS she sat up and pushed her blanket aside. Two months of serving the Khatuns and Noyans at the funeral feasts had wearied her, and there had been her other work to do as well. The mourning would be over soon, the Khan buried before the worst of the winter weather set in.

Her sorrow over his passing was heartfelt. After over two years in Bortai's ordu, she remained untouched. Yet in the midst of her sorrow, her hopes had begun to flower again. Ogedei would be Khan. He had been too grief-stricken to notice her when she filled his cup, but his sorrow would pass. Her father had said she would belong to a great man; maybe he had meant Ogedei.

The lambs by the doorway bleated. Old Kerulu peered into the kettle that hung over the hearth. The other three girls grumbled as they left the warmth of their beds. Checheg smoothed down her braids. She had slept in her woollen shift and trousers, but shivered as she pulled on her felt boots; the yurt had grown cold, in spite of the fire. She moved towards the hearth, then took a cup of broth from Kerulu-eke.

"I've known many sorrows," the old woman muttered as the girls settled around the hearth, "but this is surely the greatest, knowing that the mightiest of conquerors has completed his life."

A man's voice shouted a greeting outside, and Kerulu went to the entrance. Checheg wondered if the shamans had come to claim more sheep for the sacrifices they would make during the Great Khan's journey to his final resting place. Slaves had already been chosen to accompany the Khan; such a great ruler would need many to serve his spirit.

Kerulu stepped back as five soldiers in sheepskin coats, with the blue sashes of the Khan's guard around their waists, entered and set down a large trunk. "I greet you," one man said, as the girls rose to their feet. "I have come here to speak the words of Ogedei, son of the greatest of men. Ogedei has decreed that thirty of the most beautiful maidens in this ordu be given a great honour, and these four shall be among them."

"I hope they are worthy," Kerulu said. Checheg narrowed her eyes; surely it was not fitting for the heir to gather maidens he desired before his father was buried.

"These maidens," the man continued, "will garb themselves in the finery we have brought. When we take the greatest of warriors to his final resting place, they will accompany us. The Khan's son has decreed that they shall be made bedfellows and companions of the Great Khan, and shall serve him in the next world."

Checheg's lungs constricted. Artai screamed, rushed forward, and threw herself at the soldier's feet.

"I beg you!" Artai cried. "Beat me, send me far away, give me to the lowest of men, but not this!" She clung to his ankle. "Take me to the Great Khan's son – let me speak to him – "

The man kicked her aside. Kerulu reached for the girl and pulled her to her feet. "Kerulu-eke!" Artai pawed at the old woman. "Help me!"

"There is nothing I can do." Kerulu shook her; tears trickled from the old woman's small reddened eyes. "Don't disgrace yourself."

Checheg's heart hammered against her chest. The other girls wailed. They had to obey, and might at least be brave. Her father had spoken truly, she thought with despair; his prophecy would be fulfilled.

The cortège left the camp on a cold, grey morning, and people lined the route to watch the procession pass. A shamaness on a white horse rode in front of the ox-drawn bier, leading a stallion by the reins; shamans in animal masks and hats adorned with eagle feathers sat on the platform beating their drums. Rows of soldiers rode at the sides of the wagons carrying the Khatuns, the Khan's sons and their chief wives, and their servants. More wagons followed with the treasures, slaves, and maidens that would lie in the grave, and behind them came more men with the cattle, horses, and sheep to be sacrificed to the Khan's spirit.

The people along the route shrieked and tore at their clothes as the procession moved slowly over the bare, brown land. Checheg did not weep and said nothing to the man driving the cart that bore her and the other three Onggirat girls. She had not lost her courage yet, not when the girls were clothed in silk robes and camel-hair coats, not even when they were led to the cart. Their families would be honoured for having their daughters chosen, and would have the rank of those who had given the Great Khan wives. She and her companions could not serve the Khan well in the next life if they showed cowardice in this one, and they would die honourably, without their blood being shed.

She had spoken this way to Artai, and the words had eased the other girl's fears a little. Being chosen was a tribute to their beauty; the other maidens – Merkits and Naimans, Kereits and Khitans, Uighurs, Tanguts, and round-eyed girls from the west – were among the most beautiful in the camp. Ogedei would honour his father with nothing less.

Checheg's thoughts were still until the camp was far behind them, the lines of mourners more sparse, the herds only distant forms grazing near the slopes that bordered the valley, and then the terror came upon her. She had felt it before, and now it locked her so tightly in its grip that she could hardly breathe.

The wind wailed, the carts creaked as they moved, the horses whinnied, and bowcases rattled against the sheathed swords of the men. Checheg's heart throbbed to the distant beat of the shamans' drums. She would lie in the ground, and the earth would close over her. She would never see spring return, taste the first kumiss of the season, laugh with her friends over a bit of gossip, hear Kerulu-eke praise her for her embroidery, milk another ewe, or nurse a small lamb. All the chores she had done sullenly were tasks she would welcome now. She would never be a wife, with her own tent and herds; she would never have a child.

They might be spared. That futile hope taunted her. Ogedei was said to be kind; he might be moved to spare them, and bury only their ongghons with his father. The shamans might receive a sign that the Great Khan wanted no maidens buried with him, that the girls should live and breed more warriors to fight for his heir.

Useless wishes, she thought, ones that would only make her

694

end harder to endure. Better to prepare herself for death instead of clutching at her hopes.

The greyness of the morning was gone. Checheg lifted her eyes to the clear blue sky. Heaven was boundless and pitiless, and the Great Khan was Heaven's Son.

Tengri sent no ice storms to trouble the Khan's procession, and held back the frightful winds that could carry men from their saddles. The stars shone with a brilliance Checheg had never noticed before; at dawn, the sight of the massif in the north filled her with awe. It was strange that she had never seen how beautiful the land was, even now, with the dry, bitter air promising a harsh winter. She no longer feared the openness of the steppe, the wide expanses that had often made her feel exposed and helpless, or the dark forests where spirits could lead someone astray. The valleys between the hills were precious refuges, as comforting as a warm tent; the spirits of the river slept under a covering of ice.

Each dawn, the shamans sacrificed sheep to the Khan's spirit, and Checheg's lungs filled with the odour of burning flesh. When the Khatuns gathered the other women to burn bones and to pray, Checheg sat among the girls who looked most in need of comfort. While she murmured to them, her own fears were distant. Only when waking, when she recalled where she was bound as if hearing of it for the first time, would the terror seize her before it was dispelled.

They had been travelling for six days when they came to the swampy land at the base of Burkhan Khaldun. Men had ridden ahead to cut paths through the underbrush and to dig a grave on the forested slope above. The swampland had hardened in the cold, making passage for the bier and carts easier. Amid the foothills below the massif, the mourners raised their tents and prepared to say their farewells.

The Khan was to be buried on the northern side of the great mountain, where the trees were thicker than on the southern slopes and would grow more quickly over the grave. Two pits were dug, one for the Khan and the other for the animals to be left with him. From the slope, the Khan would look towards the Onon River in the north-east, where he had spent so much of his boyhood.

The shamans circled the wide, deep pits nine times, striking their drums as they chanted. The Khan's sons, brothers, and generals moved around the pits next, and many of the men said their prayers in choked voices; Temuge Odchigin and Khasar Noyan clung to each other as they wept. The women circled the grave last, their high head-dresses trembling as they threw back their heads to cry out their sorrow. Smoke rose from fires near the grave, filling the air with the smell of burning meat, and Checheg thought she saw spirits dancing in the smoke, hovering near to feed on the sacrifices. Shamans swayed by the fires, their hands and white fur coats splashed with blood; the heads and hides of four horses hung from poles at the sides of the grave.

On the day the shamans had set for the Khan's burial, Checheg and the other girls were led to the tents of the Khatuns. The Khan's four favourite wives were inside one large yurt with the chief wives of the Khan's brothers and sons; shamanesses in birch-bark head-dresses adorned with hawk feathers sat behind them.

"I greet you," Bortai Khatun said to the girls. "It is my wish that you, who will have the honour of joining my husband, share this feast with us."

Checheg peered at the Khatun's shadowed face. The folds of Bortai's lids drooped over her eyes; her gnarled hands trembled. Checheg glanced at the girls nearest her, then bowed.

"We greet you, Wise and Noble Khatun and Honoured Ladies," Checheg murmured; the others were leaving it to her to speak. "Unworthy as we are to be among those our Khan loved so much, we are honoured to be summoned into your presence."

The girls seated themselves in a half-circle on the felt carpets in front of the ladies. Platters of meat and goblets of kumiss were brought to them, and the air soon grew close. Checheg's cheeks flamed as the kumiss warmed her. Most of the girls took little of the horsemeat, but gulped at the drink and held up their cups as the servants near them poured more.

"I would not have chosen this fate for you," Bortai said,

696

"and sorrow to see ones so young complete their lives, and yet I could wish to be among you."

She meant it, Checheg realized. Had the Khan commanded it, Bortai Khatun would have gone to his grave with joy in her heart.

Checheg lowered her eyes and glanced at the other ladies. Yisui Khatun stared past the girls, as if she saw something beyond the hearth fire, while her sister Yisugen leaned towards her. Their faces were still much alike, but Yisugen's eyes darted restlessly, while Yisui's seemed blind to everything around her. Khulan Khatun's lovely brown eyes glistened with tears as she looked at the youngest girls, and for a moment, Checheg thought she might plead for them. Ogedei's wife Doregene lifted her cup; her large dark eyes were cold. Only Sorkhatani Beki, with her haunted eyes and trembling mouth, seemed to be mourning as deeply as Bortai.

"You'll ease my husband's spirit," Bortai said, slurring her words; her cup had already been filled several times. "I must tell you this – the Khan was not like other men."

"He was the greatest of men, Honoured Lady," Artai said; Checheg touched her friend's hand lightly.

"I meant," Bortai continued, "that he was a man who welcomed the love of women as much as he desired their bodies."

Khulan Khatun lifted her head. The Khan, Checheg knew, had loved her more than any of his women. A light had come to Khulan's face since the Khan's death, restoring the beauty he had cherished.

"I say this, young maidens," Bortai went on, "so that you won't be afraid when your spirits join with his." The Khatun covered her face, then grabbed at the arm of a servant, who quickly poured more kumiss into Bortai's goblet.

The shamanesses moaned softly; Doregene dabbed daintily at her eyes. "I was his shadow." This voice was low and hoarse, the sound of an old woman speaking, yet the beautiful Yisui had said the words. "I stayed with him until he sent me from his tent. He told me once that if I ever disobeyed him, nothing would be left of me but a spot of blood on the ground." Yisugen Khatun clutched at her sister's hand.

"I hear his voice still," Bortai said. "When I thought I would

697

never see him again, he came for me and rescued me." Checeg's head swam from the drink and the heat inside the tent. This would make it easier, she thought; she would be feeling very little by the time she was led away. Bortai went on murmuring disjointedly of the past, of the times the Khan had triumphed and the times she had feared all was lost.

You had your life, a voice whispered inside Checeg. You had your husband, your sons and grandchildren, your joys and your sorrows, and I'll never know any of those things.

"You will lie with my husband," Bortai Khatun was saying, "as my son has commanded. I can't change his decree, but when I burn an offering to the Khan's spirit, lambs will be sacrificed for you. Love my husband as I have, but also be friends to one another. A man's love binds a woman and protects her, but it's the friendship of women that nourishes her when her husband is absent from her tent."

Checeg would watch over the other girls in the next world as she had tried to do during this journey. The next world was much like this one; all her people believed it, so it had to be true. The Khan would hunt with his comrades as he had here, and they would tend his tents and herds with the others who would serve him. Fixing her thoughts on the next world could almost make her wish this life were already past.

The shamans came for the girls at dusk. Checeg swayed as she got to her feet. Bortai rose, then clasped Checeg to herself.

"You are brave," Bortai murmured. "My husband will be pleased with you." The Khatun released her, then embraced each of the other girls. A young Khwarezmian whimpered, and one of the Khitan girls was crying, but they all followed the shamans from the tent without protest.

They climbed towards the grave. Torches flickered around the open pit; as Checeg approached, she saw that the Khan's body had been placed in the centre of the grave. He was seated before a table, a cup of kumiss in one hand, and plates of meat had been set around him. The Khan had been given a grave pillow; the legs of a slave who lay dead beneath him protruded from the furs that covered him.

Men climbed down the sides of the pit to set trunks and

698

golden images near the body. Others set the curving wicker poles of a small tent around the Khan and tied felt panels to them. The Khatuns and the other ladies circled the open grave, tore bracelets from their wrists, and threw them into the pit. Drumbeats sounded as the shamans began their chant.

Checheg's head was clearing in the cold. The people pressing in around the grave were as thick as the trees that had once stood here. Mourners covered the slopes, and their torches seemed as numerous as the stars above.

"My father and Khan!" Ogedei moved towards the shamans, Chagadai and Tolui at his right. "I cannot bring life to you, but I shall be the shield that protects your great ulus. I shall be the arrow in the heart of your enemy, the scourge of any who dare to defy us, the sword that will increase the empire you gave us." He halted by the grave and flung his arms wide. "I cannot give you back this life, but you will have all you desire in the next. You will live forever, O Father and Khan, and all the world will bow to your descendants – I swear it to you."

The shamans turned towards Checheg. The moment had come, and she would be the first. Her ears pounded to the beat of the drums as she walked forward; a shaman tightened a silken cord between his hands as she came to the edge of the pit. She would show the others there was nothing to fear.

The shaman lifted the cord, and then he was suddenly behind her, looping it around her neck. She thought of how the body had looked before the tent hid it, the grinning face with jawbone jutting through the skin, the claw clutching its cup. She would lie with that corpse, with cold earth heaped over her. The vision of the world beyond had vanished; there was only the grave, the odour of blood and burned flesh, the darkness of the pit below her. Checheg's hands rose to her neck, catching at the cord, and as she struggled, she knew that she had failed, that the others would see only her terror and not her courage. The cord bit into her neck, and the red sea sweeping towards her in the darkness turned black.

126

THE OBO STOOD on a grassy hill below the northern slope of Burkhan Khaldun, a short ride from where Jelme and his Uriangkhais were camped. Seven piles of stones had been placed at the top of the hill; a spear jutted from the mound of stones in the centre of the row. Once, the obo had honoured the spirit of this hill, but the Uriangkhai shamans had come to believe that they could feel the Khan's presence there.

Sorkhatani's horse slowed as she neared the hill. She had travelled to the Uriangkhai camp to make sacrifices to the Khan's spirit. She had brought her youngest son, a few servants, her shamans, and her Christian priests. Jelme had been surprised to see her at this time, while he was preparing to ride to the kuriltai, but her guards carried a tablet with Ogedei's seal, and he had welcomed her.

A square latticework of wood, its sticks adorned with felt streamers and shreds of cloth, stood just below the shrine. A shamaness in a coat made from the hides of snow leopards was kneeling in front of the latticework; her tethered horse grazed at the bottom of the hill.

Sorkhatani and Arigh Boke dismounted, took the small packs that held their offerings from their saddles, then handed the reins of their horses to the two boys who had ridden there with them. Sorkhatani looked up at the obo, bowed deeply three times, and began to climb the hill.

The grass was high, reaching to her knees; the spring flowers were fading. The shamaness had hollowed out a spot for a fire; a sheep's shoulder-bone burned in the flames as she chanted. Sorkhatani bowed three more times, knelt by the wooden lattice, and took out a piece of meat, a jug, and a bowl. She whispered a prayer, poured out the kumiss, sprinkled a few drops on the ground, then pushed the meat and bowl under the sticks of wood as her son tied streamers of silk to the lattice.

The shamaness turned towards them. She was hardly more than a girl, but her dark eyes had the sly, watchful look of an old woman. "I greet you, Beki," the shamaness said.

"I greet you, Idughan," Sorkhatani replied. Arigh Boke finished tying the last bit of cloth; she sat with her son in silence as the shamaness peered at the shoulder-bone.

"Ogedei will be Khan," the shamaness said at last.

"No one doubts it," Sorkhatani said.

"Ogedei Kha-Khan – the Great Khan. That is how he will be proclaimed, yet it's said some among the Noyans might have chosen another, despite his father's wishes."

"It isn't so." Sorkhatani sat back on her heels. "Ogedei is a wise man. He felt that the Noyans needed time to feel confident in their choice before he held the kuriltai." Doregene had sown doubts in her husband's mind, imagining that some of the men were looking to Tolui as a possible successor. Sorkhatani had never spoken of the Khan's words to her, of how he had said Tolui's sons might one day have to rule, but Doregene was capable of seeing rivals even where there were none. Doregene resented the fact that Ogedei often consulted with Tolui, who was fiercely loyal to his brother, because she knew that Sorkha-tani advised Tolui.

When Ogedei was finally raised on the felt, as he would be this summer, perhaps Doregene, her ambition fulfilled, would learn the wisdom of cultivating those who would serve her husband best. If Ogedei preferred Sorkhatani's counsel and his brother's to that of his wife and her beloved slave Fatima, that was Doregene's doing. She had tried to surround Temujin's heir with her own favourites, and that, as much as anything, had spread doubts about Ogedei. Doregene had gone so far as to speak against Ye-lu Ch'u-ts'ai when Ogedei asked the Khitan to continue as his chancellor; the woman was too avaricious to understand a man who was selfless.

Ogedei, fortunately, was as stubborn as he was placid. He indulged his chief wife, heaped treasures upon her, and largely ignored her advice. The Noyans no longer had to worry that, with Bortai Khatun failing, he might rely more on people his wife favoured. There would be no disputes during the kuriltai, and no talk of other candidates.

Sorkhatani had come here to placate the Khan's spirit with sacrifices and prayers, to tell him that his will would at last be done, but she would return to Ogedei's camp with Jelme before the kuriltai. She sighed and lifted her eyes to the obo. She should have been thinking of the spirits in this place, not these other matters.

"It grows harder to hear the spirits," the shamaness said. "They spoke to us more clearly once – so the old ones say."

Arigh Boke was fidgeting. "Go and watch the horses with the boys," Sorkhatani said to her son. "I'll come down in a little while." The boy got up, bowed three times towards the shrine, then hurried down the hill.

She looked to her left, at the distant slope where the Khan was buried. In the year and a half since then, tiny saplings had sprouted over the site, and the yurt raised over the grave was little more than tatters. The Uriangkhais camped below would guard the slope until the forest claimed the site and the trees covered all traces of the grave. The Great Khan's rest would not be disturbed.

Sorkhatani's eyes stung. She could weep for him even now.

"Ogedei will make a good Khan," the shamaness said, "but I wonder if his son Guyuk will be the equal of his ancestors."

"Ogedei is far from settling on a successor," Sorkhatani murmured.

"Guyuk is his oldest by his chief wife. There would be no reason to turn to another, unless – "

Sorkhatani looked away from the woman's sharp eyes; the shamaness saw too much. They all have the makings of Khans; Temujin had said it himself about her sons. Khans they would be, but they would serve the Kha-Khan unless Heaven willed otherwise. She would not push them to a higher place, but would see that they were prepared for it if the ulus should need one of them. Temujin had charged her with this; he had envisioned a time when one of her sons might have to rule. She would not fail the man she had loved.

A bird fluttered above the tattered yurt on the mountainside. It rose, opened its wide wings, and glided in Sorkhatani's direction.

"An eagle," the shamaness said softly. "I see them often above the Great Khan's resting place." The eagle soared towards the obo. "They usually avoid this hill."

Sorkhatani was still. The black-feathered bird circled them in a wide arc and dropped to the obo, alighting on a stone next to the spear. She looked into its golden eyes and sensed the presence of a powerful spirit. Only one had ever filled her with such awe; somehow she had drawn his spirit to her.

The shamaness made a sign acknowledging the spirit and passed her hands before Sorkhatani's face. The eagle spread its wings, gazed up at the vast blue sky, then sprang from the obo and climbed the wind.